DE CINERIBUS

FROM THE ASHES

THOMAS VACCARO

Book 1 of the De Cineribus series

Copyright © 2018 by Thomas Vaccaro

This edition published in 2021

Library of Congress Control Number: 2021914298

The right of Thomas Vaccaro to be identified as the author of this work has been asserted by him in accordance with the Copyright, Designs, and Patents Act 1988.

www.unicornofwar.com

Cover design by *Damonza*.

ISBN 978-1-7352895-0-2 (ebook)

ISBN 978-1-7352895-1-9 (paperback)

ISBN 978-1-7352895-2-6 (hardback)

DEDICATION

To my friends Gillian, Cynzi, Chris, Emily, Madison, Dan, Eva, Savannah, Danni, Thomas (Al), Maxwell, Blake, and Hammy. You all believed in me when I couldn't believe in myself, and taught me just how strong I am.
I wish you all happiness.

To my family, who was there to pick me up whenever I was down and love me for the hot mess I am. Even in the months I would go radio silent while busy making videos or writing, your love has remained unconditional.
If I ever need to hide a body, clear your pantries. Please.

To the Union of War, my viewers on YouTube, who proved to me that my voice does indeed matter. The people who gave me a platform to begin with. You guys are a huge reason this was even possible. I hope I don't let you down.

To the Patrons, past and present, who've pledged their support for my content. You guys enabled this book, along with my ability to not starve to death.
I am eternally grateful to you all.

To Jenna Moreci, whose vulgar writing tips helped many more writers survive the shit show that is writing a book, and proved it's possible to beat the odds. Wish you, Cliff, Buttercup, and Peter the Penguin the best.

To Arnold, a.k.a. Murder of Birds, for believing in me when I was just starting out on YouTube and giving me that initial push out the gate. I wouldn't be where I am right now without your faith, and I'm forever grateful. Wish you and Cal the best.

To Monty Oum, whose views on the human spirit inspired countless people to hold on and tell the stories hidden in their hearts. Rest in peace.
Keep moving forward, forever and always.

And to Lisa, the strongest woman I've ever met who would MAKE an afterlife just to kick my ass. I know if I gave up on writing, you'd definitely come back to haunt me, and I'd deserve it. I wish you were here for this, and not just all my future books, but the rest of whatever life has to offer Zach and I. So many days I wanted to give up, where I felt hopeless, unloved, and alone, and I would picture you there, by my side, telling me to keep going.
I love you, Mom. Rest in peace.

CONTENT WARNING

The following novel contains:

- Profuse swearing and strong language
- Bullying
- Mentions of health issues, hospitalization, and life support
- Mentions of mental illness and medication:
    - Shaming of mental health problems
- Mentions and discussions of the Holocaust
- Graphic violence:
    - Blood
    - Drowning and near-drowning
    - Gun violence
    - Immolation (burning a person alive)
    - Murder
    - Severe injury to characters and life-changing injuries leading to disabilities
    - Stabbing
    - Violence to children
- Mentions of human experimentation
- Death:
    - Character deaths
    - Death and possibility of death of a loved one
    - Mentions and descriptions of corpses and reanimated dead
    - Themes of death and mortality
- Themes of mental and emotional abuse:
    - Emotional and mental parental toxicity and abuse
- Themes of prejudice and discrimination:
    - Biphobia and bi erasure within the LGBT+ community
    - Classism
    - Institutional and systemic racism
    - Racist microaggressions
    - Xenophobia
- Themes and descriptions of police/authoritarian violence & brutality:
    - Threat of police violence
    - Police racism
    - Police attacking protestors
    - Police murder
- Acts of terror

If any of these are potentially triggering for you, please proceed with caution. Otherwise, please enjoy.

TABLE OF CONTENTS

Chapter One

A Single, Misshapen Spark

THE SCORCH.

Not a soul born on this scarred earth could forget how those thirteen days forever changed the world. On Christmas Eve, 2052, families settled into bed excited for the holidays. The one time of year you'd have a good reason not to dwell on the world's woes, and pray that maybe next year would be better. Parents quietly laying gifts beneath the branches of the Christmas tree, only for impatient children to sneak out of their rooms, hoping for a quick glimpse of their presents before sunrise. All of them burned alive in their sleep. Roasted like pigs on a spit.

Over the course of two weeks, tens of thousands of innocents were slaughtered by Jason Reavey: a power-crazed, red-eyed sorcerer flying across the midwestern United States on the back of his crimson dragon Ira. Even almost sixty years later, no one knew why he did it. But to many, the answer was too obvious to need proof—he wanted to eradicate humanity.

Felix had heard this tale from his father countless times during his childhood. And though every time Frank would hammer home that these sorcerers, the magi, were dangerous, and that they'd sold their souls for dark forces humans were never meant to wield, Felix could never shake the idea that perhaps they were human, too. Were magi truly wicked?

Rain, punctuated by hail, battered the gutters outside. A clap of thunder shook the small, dark bedroom as Felix desperately rolled onto one side, then

the other. Already 2 a.m. In just a few hours, he'd have to be up for school. After begging his parents to let him attend public school, the last thing he wanted was to give his father any reason to pull him out this late in the year. Felix rolled again, staring through the darkness at his outstretched palm. He clenched his fist, cursing himself, but stopped himself before he spiraled. Slowly, he opened his hand, then with a snap of his fingers, pink sparks flickered before dying out.

Am I wicked?

A shrill screech ended his rest. He panted, scanning the shadows. A pair of amber eyes peered, unblinking. Vibrant red, white, and azure feathers, along with a gleaming golden beak twisted into a sneer, surfaced from the black. The bird sat atop his desk, as if waiting for him to awaken.

Felix, shaking, reached out. "H-Hello?"

The bird squawked, taking off and flying 'round the ceiling. The storm, the elysian thunder refusing to go unheard, covered the thuds of toys, books, and family photos as they fell from the shelves. Too concerned about the racket to care for the bird's origin, Felix forced open the window, blinded by a flash of lightning. He staggered as the freezing rain and piercing wind pelted his skin. Wings flapped as the bird took off into the night.

"Couldn't sleep?"

The hairs on Felix's arms stood on end. This disembodied voice, gravelly with a slight whistle, carried through the squall. As though the wind itself were whispering into his ears. Even so, there wasn't a soul in sight. Nothing but the silhouettes of trees, branches breaking and falling in the rain. One tree towered above the rest. A red maple, tall and once bearing scarlet leaves. His father had tried to cultivate it in Felix's youth, only to lose interest and abandon the maple a couple years in, leaving it to wither and die. Gnarled branches warped into mangled claws, reaching down as if to strangle the house below. It often served as fuel for Felix's nightmares.

He reached for the window frame and pulled, only for it to jam. Another flash illuminated the tree line. As his gaze returned to the dead maple's trunk, his heart stopped.

A silhouetted figure, some tall, hunched humanoid, stood before the tree. Though its appearance was obscured by both the dark of night and the ire of the storm, Felix's instinct screamed for him to slam the window shut and hide.

But he didn't. His feet remained cemented, his gaze fixed on the now-approaching drifter.

"I'll take that as a no."

Felix leapt into bed, pulling the covers over his head. He trembled as the gusts grew louder. Cold dread permeated the room. Fear and apprehension weighed down on him, sinking their fangs into every nerve in his body, refusing to let up as they gnashed his composure.

"¿Mijo? Are you okay?"

Lydia's voice broke through the chaos, silencing Felix's fear the moment the window slammed shut. She rushed to his bedside, curls of her dark-auburn hair hanging over her aqua-blue eyes. Wrinkles lined her face, spread across her dark-brown skin like the tiny ripples of a lake after a pebble was tossed in. "Another nightmare?" she asked.

"Y-Yeah…" Felix's voice, like his mettle, was brittle. "Sorry, Mom."

"You don't need to apologize." She gave a long look at the window. Though the curtain was closed, and his mother was here to calm and protect him, Felix's stomach welled with anxiety. He couldn't shake the feeling that something—or someone—was watching them, observing them from afar, even now. And he was certain his mother felt it as well.

"Lydia!" Felix flinched at his father's bellow from down the hall. "What's going on in there?!"

"Nothing, Frank! Everything's fine!" Lydia turned back to Felix and kissed him on the forehead. "Get some sleep, honey." Her voice, however quiet, was equal parts sweet and strong through her Mexican accent. "Te quiero, mi cielito."

Felix, not knowing a lick of Spanish, didn't understand what his mother had said, but was too embarrassed to ask. Once she left, Felix wrapped himself in his blankets. He tried his best to tune out the howls of the wind. But at the back of his mind, that strange figure refused to be forgotten.

"Why did magi let the Holocaust happen?"

Hurricane Gillian raged outside, thunder rattling the classroom desks beneath the flickering overhead lights. The students remained quiet through

Ms. Wallis' footfalls as she paced through the aisles. She stood tall, her posture unnaturally straight, shoulders raised. Her gray-green tweed jacket seemed to blacken the room around her, as did her dark-gray hair and pasty, wrinkled white skin. At points, Felix could've sworn his social studies teacher's stare fell squarely on him.

"It's a simple question," Wallis said, her voice strident with a slight whistle as distressing as that of an oncoming steam train. Unafraid to leave you behind if you couldn't make it in time, and unapologetic if it was your misfortune to fall upon the tracks. "If sorcerers have existed as long as humans, why would they allow these atrocities and tragedies to happen?" Her eyebrows furrowed as another thunderclap followed. Felix, avoiding eye contact and gripping his arms tight, kept his eyes on the clock. *Just a few more minutes*, he kept telling himself.

From the back corner of the room, Felix could see the rest of the class wasn't invested in the lecture, but none were on edge like him. To the contrary, Carson and his goons Billy and Buck, all decked out in camouflage jackets and jeans, constantly turned to one another, chuckling amongst themselves. Felix couldn't make out most of their jokes, but it didn't take a genius to know they weren't kind towards magi. Carson seemed especially callous, contrasting with his soft, rounded features. His freckles faded each time his pale cheeks reddened from laughter. His sandy-blonde hair had been buzzed to a thin layer over his scalp, and Felix wondered what he would've looked like had he let it grow out.

Felix's sight wandered towards the window. As the lightning flashed, a silhouette flew past the glass. His blood chilled as he jumped from his seat, the metal legs scraping across the tiled floor.

"Felix?"

Now everyone's eyes fell on him, and the scorn of Carson's group left a sickness in his gut. The room went silent save for the slight whirring of the lights and the weak roars of dying thunder.

"Well?" Wallis dragged out the syllable. "What do you think?"

Cold sweat trickled down Felix's forehead. "I, uh… well…" He gulped. "It seems like an unfair question. I mean, didn't the U.S. sit out World War II until after Pearl Harbor?" To him, his response was a fair one. He may not have agreed with the reasoning, but at the very least, it meant the magi weren't held to a different standard.

4

Wallis' frown suggested otherwise. "The U.S. did not get involved to avoid wrapping ourselves up in the problems of other countries, especially after the First World War. Once it came to our soil, we had no choice but to step in."

"R-Right." Felix hung his head, covering his reddening face as he fell back into his seat. He wished he could take back his question. Or better yet, disappear altogether.

"What's the difference then?"

A dark-skinned girl with short brown-black hair crossed her arms. Her bright-pink hoodie seemed to glow in the dreary gray classroom, and even behind her thick glasses, she challenged Wallis' infamous grimace with an unwavering poise. "What makes the Medeian Empire not getting involved with the human world any different?"

"Cuz they're walking nukes," Carson mumbled. His buddies snickered along with him.

"Because, Rosie…" Wallis' voice boomed. "With their power, they could've prevented every tragedy the world's ever known. Instead, they decided to—"

"Avoid wrapping themselves up in other countries' problems?"

You could've cut the tension in the room with a butter knife. Some students looked away, while others murmured. And all the while, the girl in pink—or rather, Rosie—sat there, answering Wallis' cold stare with a triumphant grin. Felix could only dream of mimicking her defiance without immediately crumpling into the fetal position. Wallis folded her hands behind her back as the end-of-period bell rang. "Class dismissed," she croaked.

Ready to thank God himself, Felix threw his backpack over his shoulder, only to drop it as Carson bumped into him on his way out. Papers, notebooks, and pens flew out, and Felix scrambled to gather them.

"Nice sketch."

Rosie stood over him, holding one of Felix's stick figure drawings. a person, if you could call it that, holding a star wand. Instinctively, Felix tried to play off the fact he'd leapt back in shock. He gave a nervous laugh, waving his hand dismissively. "I-It's nothing!"

She raised an eyebrow. "You okay?" Quickly glancing over at Wallis, whose gaze was currently fixed on her computer screen, Rosie knelt and held Felix's head. A strange noise, like the jingling of wind chimes in a slight summer breeze, rang as the pain subsided. A pale-yellow light hung just out of sight. For a moment, Rosie's brown irises briefly shimmered violet.

"A-Are you—"

"Rosie?!" Wallis bellowed from across the room. "I'd like to have a word with you."

Rosie rolled her eyes. "One sec," she said to the teacher.

"Now!"

Standing back up, she helped Felix to his feet and handed back his sketch. "Nice meeting you, Felix," she whispered.

"F-Felix?"

"Your name, genius."

"O-Oh. Right." Felix wanted to stay by Rosie's side, but let his fear pull him out into the hallway. Perhaps it would've been best to forget it all. He'd go enjoy lunch, finish the rest of the day, and then head home without causing any more problems. He hadn't eaten so much as a measly sandwich since morning, yet his stirring anxiety didn't encourage him to satiate his appetite.

Like usual, he planted himself in the far corner of the cafeteria. The only table not crammed from bench to bench with students, albeit still marked by odd stains, gum wads, and obscene graffiti. He looked forward to scarfing down the turkey sandwich and apple slices his mother had packed for him, but both physically and emotionally exhausted, he decided that could wait. He rested his head within his folded arms, ready to sleep through the next 40 minutes.

"Not much rest?"

Felix's head jerked up. The cafeteria, just moments before lively with chatter, now lay silent, the tables all empty. A thick mist hung in the air, chilling his skin. Heavy layers of rime coated the floors and walls. Against his better judgment, he followed the whispers into the hall, his footsteps the only sound echoing down the corridor. Not a single sign of life to be seen. Yet even so, something was watching him.

A cold hand touched his back.

He sprinted. Invisible strings sewn from wall to wall snapped, one by one, flickering silver light glistening with each successive snap. Felix burst through the entrance. The storm outside had stopped, but all the trees around the school appeared dead. A deafening silence hung in the air. Somehow, the lack of chaos was more unsettling, especially once his focus shifted to the rest of the devastation. Bodies lay about the parking lot, lifeless husks whose eyes had all been gouged out into empty pits. What had done this to all these people? To the world?

Felix was so overwhelmed by what he'd seen, it took all his strength to dare look upwards. A black sun hung in the crimson sky, golden threads weaved over the horizon. His surroundings perfectly matched his father's description of Judgment Day.

"Not a nice view, is it?"

The figure from the previous night. Felix knew this was it—or rather, *him*. A cloak, earthy red like dried blood, hung from his shoulders, draping down to his feet. Beneath the hood, a golden mask veiled his face. Its ornate details were obscured by the fabric. A flower, its wilting scarlet petals twirling out into azure tips, reposed over his heart. Of those seven petals, five were especially worn. One seemed on the verge of wilting away into nothing.

"No need to fret. I'm here to help."

Felix froze. Again, he couldn't bring himself to run. The words died on his tongue as he tried to shout. "S-Stay away from me!"

"I'm afraid I can't. My message must be delivered today."

"Then… then wait 'til I'm asleep! Wait until I'm home! I don't care, just leave me alone now!"

The man's chuckling sent a shiver down Felix's spine. "That's all I needed to hear."

Instantly, Felix questioned why he'd conceded any ground to this… thing. Who even was this? Had he caused all of this destruction, or was he simply the herald of what was to come?

The man pulled a dreamcatcher from his cloak. A spider the size of his fist, its body cyan and legs golden, sat in the center of the strings. Beady red eyes fell on Felix. White fangs twitched as it waited for the right moment to lunge. Felix turned on his heel, only to be caught in the silver threads of the spider's web. More spiders, crawling down the walls of the school, circled him. He closed his watering eyes, struggling to break free.

"You alright?"

As Felix awakened, he found a pale, freckled boy with messy, curly red hair seated across from him. There was something oddly familiar about his air. A warm presence, glinting through the occasional flicker of his hair, like a candle glowing bright within a dark, cold room. Felix peeled his face off the table, rubbing the numbness from his cheek. "I-I'm fine." His voice was hoarse, cracking from his dry throat.

The boy let out a jokester's chuckle. Before Felix could inquire, the boy reached into his backpack and threw a red marble notebook onto the table. "You dropped this by the way."

Felix swiped it. Though it read "Math" on the cover, he'd turned this notebook into his makeshift sketchbook. Doodles of dragons, fairies, and other fantastical creatures covered the pages, all drawn when he was sure no one was looking. Right in the middle of the book, where he'd hoped no one would bother checking, were sketches of himself as a powerful wizard, complete with a starry robe and crescent wand.

He flipped through as quickly as possible. While ensuring the drawings hadn't somehow been tampered with, he kept the book barely open for fear of anyone around glimpsing its contents. He let out a heavy sigh of relief. "I'm such an idiot," he grumbled. He forced a smile for the boy. "Thank you."

The boy shrugged. "Happens to the best of us. You're an artist?"

Felix blushed. "N-No, I…" He usually did his best to restrain his imagination, lest he put enough on the page to give someone ammunition to use against him. This journal was the one place he could let his creativity fly free. Even his own mother, the person he trusted most, didn't know what lay hidden within the book's pages. If his father ever discovered what was inside…

"So you don't have…?" The redheaded boy pointed to his bright-pink wristband.

"No. That's a… what's it called?"

"Wearable." The band projected a faint blue light, forming a screen filled with scribbles and notes, most of which were stick figures and indecipherable script, some of which didn't even seem to be written in English. "Most people don't use them though. Never found them convenient enough to fully replace pen and paper. But it's definitely some *Back to the Future* shit."

Felix raised an eyebrow.

"You're kidding. You've never seen it?"

Felix rubbed his neck, averting his gaze. "I… haven't seen much." He'd never dared seeking out anything his father would disapprove of. No violent movies, and definitely no movies to do with magic. Whenever his schoolmates discussed a new film or show, he'd often read through their Wikipedia pages for the synopses, but only using the school computers. No TV or internet to be had back home.

"We'll have to change that." The boy simpered, revealing braces over his misaligned teeth. "Not enough people appreciate the classics." He held out his hand. "I'm Alec, by the way."

Felix tried to keep himself from smiling, but couldn't help it as he slowly took Alec's hand. He bowed his head slightly. "Felix." He squinted. "You... seem familiar."

"We both go to Saint Oriona's."

"Really?"

Alec shrugged. "Sometimes. My dad's Catholic, but my mom's Jewish. At least, culturally. They wanted me to learn about both their cultures and decide what I believe for myself."

"They... let you choose?" Felix would've felt a twinge of envy if the thought wasn't alien enough to confuse him. Still, he struggled to remember the boy. "But I... I've never seen you." While Felix hardly spoke to anyone his parents didn't pressure him into addressing, like the priests or religion teachers, he was able to recognize the faces of the other kids. Especially the ones who acted more like little devils.

"I like to stay in the background. Bit of an observer."

"... O-Okay."

The boy certainly fit the strange description. Despite the seemingly callous jokes the boy made on a whim, he felt like what Lydia called an "old soul." Someone who was wise beyond their earthly years. Who watched those around him, observing with great care, and always keeping their hand close to their chest.

"So..." Alec leaned forward. "Red or blue?"

"Uh..."

"Simple question: red? Or blue?"

Felix took a moment to ponder. *I've heard this somewhere before.* "Well, red's my favorite color. So... red?"

"Good choice," Alec said.

Felix wasn't so sure, though his uncertainty waned as his eyes wandered over to Rosie, who'd just gotten her food. *She's in the same lunch period as me? Am I just that oblivious?*

"Hmm?" Alec looked back. "Oh. Her. What about her, exactly?"

"She stood up for me back in class. So… I'm gonna invite her over." Felix moved to stand, but stopped as he heard an all-too-familiar voice.

"Hey, wait up!"

Carson ran to catch up with Rosie, who'd been walking away as quickly as she could. Billy and Buck blocked her path. Billy's tall and lean frame made him appear sickly, as did his gaunt, narrow face and buzzed blonde hair to match Carson. Buck appeared more amicable thanks to his short, pudgy stature, betrayed by his ugly sneer, gap tooth, and oily brown hair.

"Yeah, you." Carson moved to spin her around, only for Rosie to turn and shoot him dagger eyes. "You one of them wizards?"

"The term is magus," Rosie said.

"Whatever." Carson scoffed, practically breaking into a laugh. "You sure seem to care about 'em a lot."

"It's called empathy."

"Hmph." Carson gestured to Buck, who grabbed Rosie's tray. She fought to pull it back, only for her pizza, lunchmeat, and chocolate milk to spill all over the ground. Carson burst into laughter. "Go on!" he said. "Use a spell to clean it up!"

"Maybe she's lost her wand," Billy said.

"Or she's too stupid to know how to use it," Buck said. All three boys howled like jackals as the kids around either laughed along with them or kept their mouths shut. The only lunch aide in the room, a thin, pasty old man sitting at a desk by the entrance, glanced up, only to look back down when Carson stared directly at him.

"Why isn't anyone helping her?" Felix asked.

"Carson's dad is the sheriff," Alec said. "No teacher would dare touch him or his infamous 'Camo Crew.'" He tilted his head. "How do you not know any of this?"

"I try not to get involved with this stuff, okay?" Felix stopped, realizing what he'd just said. He hadn't talked back to anyone in his entire life for fear of rocking the boat. But now, he'd be more than happy to do so if it meant taking Carson down with him.

"Whoa, whoa, please tell me you're not getting any crazy ideas."

"We can't just let this happen! This isn't fair!"

Alec stared down at his food. "Life isn't fair."

Carson's smirk disgusted Felix. His blood boiled, and ready to pick a fight, he pushed himself up. "Time to change that. You going to help?"

"Not my battle. But I'll be cheering you on." Alec winked.

With that, Felix marched around the table. He made a conscious effort to stand tall and strengthen his stride as he approached the Camo Crew. Even if he couldn't put up much of a fight, he'd know he tried. But that courage began to die as Carson directed his attention towards Felix, contempt falling across Carson's face. "If it isn't the mute himself?" Carson asked.

It took all of Felix's willpower not to so much as flinch. He stared Carson right in the eyes, puffing out his chest. "Leave her alone."

"Hey," Rosie whispered. "I've got this."

"I won't just sit by and let this happen." *I've stood on the sidelines long enough.* Felix knew he'd probably get his ass kicked, but that didn't for a moment erase his yearning to smack that sick, smarmy look off Carson's ugly face.

"And just what're you gonna do, runt?" Carson asked.

Felix readied a rebuttal, only for his confidence to crumble as reason crashed through with a single, overdue question: *What AM I gonna do?*

Giving him no time to think, Carson punched Felix right in the gut. Felix fell to his knees. Reeling in pain, he held his aching stomach as his eyes shut tight. Laughter pierced his ears from all around, only to come to a sudden stop as a brief yell, coupled with a collective shout, gripped the cafeteria, followed by a sharp whimper. There Carson knelt, holding his groin tightly and rocking back and forth. Billy and Buck's mouths hung wide open. And all the while, Rosie stood there whistling, kicking the tips of her purple sneakers against the tiled floor.

"So," Rosie said, folding her hands behind her back. "You're gonna leave us alone now. Right?" Carson, through his tears, nodded. Rosie popped her shoulders, she walked over to Felix and held out her hand. "You wanna get outta the lunchmeat now?"

Only now did Felix realize his knees were steeped in Rosie's spilled food, smearing his sweatpants. Normally he'd have cursed himself out of embarrassment and shame. But after such an ordeal, he savored the silliness.

Rosie held out her hand. "Thanks for trying," she said. "I—"

Carson lunged at Rosie. Felix pushed her out of the way, taking the hit himself as he was tackled, not that Carson seemed to care. A punch square in the eye knocked Felix back onto the floor. Grabbing Felix's shirt, Carson swung down his fist. Felix grabbed it and struggled to hold it back. Though the adrenaline running through his blood kept him from fully processing the sting in his eye, his vision blurred all around Carson. His arms burned from holding back the attack. *Have to resist.*

His mind went back to the previous night. To the embers he'd created with just a snap of his fingers. He held Carson's fist tight and dug in his fingers.

Spark!

A small purple-pink flame leapt from his fingers and ran down Carson's sleeve. Carson screamed, releasing Felix and flailing as he tried to extinguish the fire. He'd jumped back, pushing himself away, panting and looking at Felix in a strange mixture of terror and hatred.

"Y-You…" Carson stammered. "You're…"

"I-I…" Felix held his hand to keep it from shaking, only for both his arms to tremble. "I didn't mean to—"

Another flame, this one a bright orange, sparked above them. The entire cafeteria gasped in terror as the smoke alarms and sprinklers went off, though the roar of the blaze had dulled Felix's hearing. Students screamed as they ran past the aide trying to herd them like cattle. Rosie rushed to Felix's side, kneeling and holding his shoulder. "Are you okay? Did you do that?"

The sting under Felix's left eye made him wince. With the fight over, the pain had no qualms announcing itself. Sweeping aside his hair, he held the bruise, wondering how bad it must've looked. He shivered. That same feeling of being watched crept over him. "I-I… what just—"

He had no time to even process what just happened, as a security guard dragged them down to the principal's office. As Alec handed Felix his things, he mouthed, "Good choice," which only served to confuse Felix more as to what choice he'd even made.

Their shoes squeaked, each one making Felix cringe with doubt. The main office was freezing, and Felix's ice-cold sweatshirt and pants made him long for the hot, muggy air of the cafeteria. Sadly, he regretted not taking the beating from Carson. It would've been better than the risk of hurting someone with his curse, or revealing the secret he'd tried to bury.

But that fire on the ceiling that set off the sprinklers. Was that Felix's fire, or *his*?

He twitched as that same pale-yellow light peered into the corner of his vision. Rosie held her hand over Felix's cheek, her palm glowing and emanating the same wind chime sound from earlier. "Relax," she said. The light and sound faded, as did the aching. "There. All better."

Felix pressed his fingers under his eye. No pain. "Thanks."

"What's your name again? Sorry, I suck at names."

He paused, stuttering.

"You have a name, right? Cuz if not, that's child abuse."

Felix flinched at the term, but telling himself to relax, composed himself. "Felix," he said. "My name's Felix."

"Right, right, Felix! Fits your feisty personality."

"Um… thanks?" Felix said curiously. "How about you, huh? Rosie seems kinda flowery for how you act."

"Even the prettiest rose needs thorns." Rosie flipped her hair. "Nice pun, by the way."

"Pun? Oh. R-Right." Felix laughed, though stopped as one of the secretaries shushed him, frowning at him and Rosie. He slunk back into his usual slouch, twiddling his thumbs. "So are you… a magus?"

Rosie hushed him. Felix hunched over, lowering himself further into shame. "Not around other people," she whispered.

"S-Sorry. It's just…" Slowly, Felix craned his neck to look at Rosie. "Your eyes."

She sat back. "What about them?" Her voice grew serious.

"Aren't they usually weirdly colored? Your eyes are…"

"Brown. Just brown." Rosie nudged him. "Just like yours are gray."

Felix had heard the rumors and speculation, but knew nothing about actual sorcerers. Whenever he was able to go looking for information online, there was little to find, aside from news stories about the latest Truthseer riots and killings by magi. All he'd gathered beside their ability to perform magic was their unusual eye colors. Though his eyes, as Rosie had pointed out, were only extraordinary in how dull and lifeless they were in their grayness. Even Rosie's brown eyes seemed to glimmer beneath the surface.

He held his arm. "Right…"

"Rosie, what did you get yourself into this time?" A tall pale man with black hair and a goatee walked in. His yellow buttoned sweater vest and beige sleeves, along with his sandy-brown khakis, almost glowed against the cold, sterile blues of the office. He tapped his black dress shoes, awaiting an answer.

Rosie sat up, her aura immediately brightening. "Hey, Dad!"

"What happened?" he asked.

"Guy was a jerk to me and my new friend here," she said. Felix flinched as Rosie threw her arm around him. "I set him straight."

"You…" Her dad rubbed his temple. "What do you think your father would say if he heard that?"

"Father"? But aren't you…?

"I think Pop would be proud!"

Felix felt ashamed of how long it took for him to put two and two together. Thankfully, his mother had been there to provide him with the knowledge his father tried to shelter him from. "Some people like boys," Lydia told him. "Some like girls. Some like both, and some like neither. And sometimes, people born one way realize they were meant to be the other way, or that they don't really fit into either. But no matter what, we're all people. And no matter who you turn out to be, I'll always be your mother, loving you unconditionally."

Though Felix was sure to keep any mentions of how he felt quiet, his mother's words had assuaged any fears he might've otherwise had when he realized he not only imagined holding hands with some of the girls in his classes, but the boys as well.

Rosie's father looked at Felix. "Is this true?"

Felix shrunk. "M-More or less. Some guys were picking on her. I tried to help, and…" He couldn't think of what else to say, and so, he silenced himself.

"I guess I should thank you then." Rosie's father gave a warm, if slightly disapproving smile. "But please be more careful. You seem like a nice boy, so no more fighting. Okay?"

Felix nodded.

"Mr. O'Brien." A woman in a dark-gray suit with the dullest of auras approached, eyeing Rosie's father from head to toe with judgment.

"*Giordano*-O'Brien," he corrected.

"Yes," she droned. "A word with you and… your daughter?"

Rosie jumped up, looking ready to challenge the woman to a fistfight then and there. But instead, she winked at Felix, said, "Wish us luck," and followed her father into the principal's office. Felix swung his legs and stared at the clock every few seconds. His parents had to have been called too. It was only a matter of time until his father flew into the office in a rage, ready to get right in Felix's face and scream—

"Felix!" Lydia hugged him tight.

As startled and suffocated as he felt, Felix felt at ease in his mother's embrace. "H-Hi, Mom."

"Are you alright?" She checked his arms. "Any bruises? Pain? Anything?"

"N-No. I'm fine."

Lydia took a sigh of relief. "Good." She had the uncanny ability of sensing whenever Felix was upset. But instead of forcing his troubles out of him, they both remained quiet, Felix relaxing as his mother held him close. Rosie grumbled as she left about her suspension. She was flustered as to why Carson and his pals got off scot-free, to which her father simply said her brother would explain when they got home. She waved Felix goodbye and said she'd see him again before leaving with her father, after which Lydia and Felix were called in.

Felix did his best to tune everything out, save for moments they asked for his account. He'd heard bits and pieces though: Sheriff Boyce not being a fan of Felix after this encounter; the alleged witnessing of magic; the consequences of a magus using a spell in public, let alone being unregistered with the government in the first place. Supposedly there'd be an investigation into the family's history to double check whether Felix was one, but he wasn't sure what to think of that. He didn't even fully know what the word meant. Nothing besides it making him a threat. A menace.

A monster.

After the meeting, Lydia led Felix outside. She assured him there was no mention of the magical fire to Frank. Even so, Felix ran through the story he'd tell his father, nor could he help the terrible thought of what might happen if his father were to discover the truth.

The downpour thankfully seemed to let up as the two ran outside. Yet as if on cue, the torrent returned to its full force as Frank's old black pickup truck swung around the corner up to the curb. Hesitantly, Felix climbed inside, resting his head against the window as country-rock music rattled the glass and seat. He prayed, unsure of to whom, that he wouldn't pick up too much of his parents' conversation, and that his father would forget the incident and leave him be.

"I never should've let you go to public school."

Felix's palms grew clammy at his father's voice—quiet, solemn, and foreboding. He kept his eyes shut tight. So long as he didn't talk, if he didn't rock the boat, he would be okay. He would survive.

"Frank." Lydia's voice, normally cooled and collected, cracked. "I'm sure this won't happen again. Felix is a good kid, he didn't mean to—"

"It wouldn't have happened at all if it weren't for those other kids." Frank's voice boomed over both the rain and his music. "At home we can keep our own in sight."

Felix squinted, tears seeping out despite his best efforts.

"What happened, Felix?"

Pretend you're asleep. Pretend you're asleep.

"Felix!"

He twitched at the righteous anger in his father's voice. Unable to avoid confrontation, Felix opened his eyes and mulled over every word. "There were some kids… making fun of this girl. I thought—"

"I told you to stay out of other people's business." Frank didn't bother looking back, or glancing at Felix through the rearview mirror. His eyes remained on the road. With each turn, he jerked the steering wheel, his knuckles white.

"R-Right," Felix choked out. "Sorry, Father." He closed his eyes again. Relishing in the momentary respite, he focused on the whirring of the tires and the pitter-patter of rainfall.

"What were they saying?"

"O-Oh." Felix played out each eventuality in his head as quickly as he could manage. "T-They… uh… I—"

"Speak up."

Felix straightened his back. "They were making fun of her for… for saying… magi didn't deserve the blame for—"

Frank slammed on the breaks. The seatbelt dug into Felix's neck as he was thrown forward, then back, crashing against the back seat. The red traffic light ahead glowed through the soaked windshield, spilling crimson onto everything inside. All was silent save for the pounding rain, and the honking of the car just behind them forced to brake at the last second.

"Was she a magus?"

Felix gulped. "… N-No. She wasn't."

Frank sighed. "This is exactly why I didn't want him there." His sternness waned, weakening into a more brittle, concerned tone. Felix eased as the tension dissipated. But as Lydia reached out to hold Frank's shoulder, he swiped it away, and Felix's apprehension snapped right back into place. "Felix," Frank said, his voice again growing severe. "I thought I told you—"

"Magi are dangerous. But I—"

"DON'T…"

Felix shriveled up at his father's yell. The car again fell into silence, the rain swirling with the deafening despair.

Frank took a breath. "Talk… over me." His voice, though softer, was still stern.

After a long pause, Felix finally felt safe speaking. "S-Sorry…"

The rest of the ride home was silent as death. Rainwater and wet leaves flooded the ranch-style house's gutters from the storm, and the front garden, its weeds and grass advertising the neglect it had long faced, looked even more of a mess than usual. Mud and soil seeped out onto the stone walkway. Felix's love for the soothing sound of rain had now been ripped away, perverted into a metronome of anxiety. After stamping his muddy sneakers on the torn and discolored "Welcome home" mat, he followed his parents inside.

"Aeris!"

Felix flinched again at his father's bellow, while his sister Aeris dashed into the living room. The way her chestnut-brown hair had been tied back into a ponytail seemed almost painful to Felix. Then again, everything about her put him off, from her constant chipperness to the blinding sheen of her rose-gold dress. It made her light olive skin appear ghostly. She always said she "dressed to impress, especially to make up for Felix looking like a bum." All this would made ironic by the fact she was actually older by two years. Yet she was more than happy to suck up to their father, including her disdain for Felix not wanting to be homeschooled this year. Her toothy grin glinted more than her blue rosary beads, her blue butterfly barrette, and her sparkling crystal-blue eyes.

"Hi, Daddy!"

Frank knelt before her. "Could you get my book on magi, sweetie? The red-and-gold one?"

Smiling, Aeris rushed back in with the book shortly. Everyone gathered in the living room. While Frank and Lydia sat on the old green-brown couch at an arm's length apart, Felix and Aeris seated themselves on the white carpeted floor before the coffee table. Felix dug his fingers into the carpet as Aeris clapped. "Are you gonna read us another story?" Her sweet, high-pitched voice grated Felix's ears.

"Not today," Frank said. "I wanna tell you both about the Scorch."

A chill ran down Felix's spine.

"Again?" Aeris whined, not an ounce of fear in her voice. "But why?"

"Because you both need to remember why magi are a threat," Frank said. "You both love Christmas, right? Waking up to presents under the tree? Maybe sneaking in during the night to get a peek?"

Aeris happily obliged, and not wanting to cause any further upset, Felix went along.

"Well, imagine you go to open your presents, and in an instant, every part of your body is in excruciating pain. Everything is up in flames, and our whole family is burned to a crisp."

Felix shuddered at the thought. The unimaginable searing pain that would be coursing through his body, razing every hair, melting every organ from the inside out. For a disturbingly ironic moment, he found some comfort in the fact his display of disgust seemed to convince his father that he'd gotten the message.

Frank carried on with the story. Though he'd repeated this lecture word for word many times over the years, the wounds they imprinted upon Felix were fresh as they'd ever been. His father leaned forward, staring into his eyes as though scanning for any hint of dissent. Looking for any sign that his son wasn't his own.

"Do you know who would do that, Felix?"

Felix tried so hard not to shake. He couldn't bring himself to even think of the word. "I-I... I—"

"A sorcerer. A... 'magus.'"

He... Felix couldn't be that. He wasn't that. He'd never hurt anyone. Not unless they tried to hurt someone innocent, or that he cared about. But then again, what happened today with Carson... Felix didn't want to hurt him, yet he nearly burned his arm. Did this mean he'd end up just like Jason? If he was a magus too, was bloodshed inevitable?

"What a monster." Aeris' eyes were filled with as much scorn as Frank's. "Those poor kids, and their parents."

Frank lay back into the couch, looking at the ceiling. "It was a long time ago, before your mother and I were even born. But that pain, the scars… they never healed." He leaned forward, giving a look far more comparable to Rosie's father's. "And that's why I want to keep you both safe." That kindness quickly regressed into bitterness as his gaze drifted away. "From those monsters."

Felix stared at the carpet. He told himself not to tremble, not to give away any suspicions about himself. But despite his best efforts, he was screaming on the inside, resisting the urge to cry. How odd, he thought. How odd that he felt too frightened to cry in the arms of those who brought him into this frightening world.

"Do you understand?" Frank asked.

Slowly, Felix raised his head, looking into his father's dull blue eyes. In this moment, his round face and dirty-blonde hair, swept into a combover, made him seem like a completely different man. A gentleness Felix had seen so rarely, he couldn't even remember the last time he'd seen this side of his father.

Felix's mind was still in shambles, his lungs hardly able to take in air. "Y-Yes."

To both Felix's comfort and heartbreak, his father smiled. "Good," Frank said. "Now, I'd like you to read through some of this book tonight before bed. To help you understand better."

"A-Alright…" Felix took the tome, clutching it against his chest. His stomach growled. Only now did he realize he'd never gotten the chance to enjoy his lunch. "So, um… can we have dinner?" He tried to feign eagerness, hiding the panging of his hunger. "Maybe… pizza?"

"I think you've had enough junk food." Frank walked over, turning Felix around and grabbing his belly through his shirt. "Looking a little fat."

"… O-Okay." Fighting against his shock, Felix rushed into his bedroom, shut the door behind him, and sank against it onto the floor. Tears fell down his cheeks in the darkness. His backpack with his uneaten lunch was still in the truck, but even now he didn't want it. Pinching his belly fat made wish he could tear it off. His dark-olive skin, naturally greasy, was often used by others to make him view himself as innately disgusting, as was his dark-brown hair constantly hanging in his face, far darker and curlier than that of his sister's.

Perhaps his father was right. After all, that was the only correct train of thought in this house.

Once he was sure he'd be left alone, Felix leapt into bed. He skimmed through the book's passages, barely even registering the prose as his hunger moaned, begging for a measly morsel. Hours passed. Finally, ready to shut his strained eyes and end this terrible day, he put the book on the bedside table, lay back, and listened to the pitter-patter of rain.

The door opened. "Felix?"

He sat up. "Mom?"

Lydia shushed him as she quietly closed the door. "I brought you something." She spoke barely beyond a whisper, but Felix nearly shouted as she handed him a box of cookies. "I know it's not pizza, but…"

Felix jumped to hug her. "Thanks, Mom!" He stopped himself in terror at how loud he might've been. Frustrated with himself, he sat on his bed, and Lydia sat beside him.

"How're you doing?" she asked.

"Well… I've gotten pretty far in my Bible readings. I'm pretty sure Judas and Jesus are—"

"No, not that book." She took his hands, meeting his gaze. "How are *you?*"

"Oh. Um…" Felix looked away, shrugging. "O-Okay, I guess." He pulled his hands away. He stared out the window as a flash of lightning caught his attention. Collecting himself, and believing his mother deserved the truth, he forced out the words. "What Father said about… magi. I… I don't think they're all bad."

Lydia held Felix close. "Neither do I. But… you know your father." She pulled back a bit, looking off at the wall and sighing. "He's… very set in his beliefs."

Even if I'm… "But…" He cursed himself for even daring to think the words. "I think… I think I might be…"

Lydia's hold tightened. "You can talk to me. It's just us."

As much as his mother's embrace comforted him, Felix couldn't bring himself to so much as consider the idea, let alone vocalize it and risk making it real. But it was only a matter of time until the truth surfaced, even if he didn't know what the truth looked like. His mind wandered back to the cafeteria. To that fire. To the man in the mask.

Lydia held Felix's chin. "I promise I won't be mad."

"In that fight at school…" His eyes grew misty. "I made fire. From my hands."

She looked away.

"Mom… you know it too. I'm—"

"Don't worry about it, mijo." Lydia kissed his forehead. "Get some rest. Okay?"

Felix couldn't press the issue further. Even if he wanted the answer, the sadness in his mother's eyes told him to drop the subject. But he knew the truth deep down. A truth which would soon be thrust into the open.

The door creaked as Lydia opened it. "Te quiero, mi cielito. Más que el mundo. Sé fiel a ti mismo, porque no perteneces a nadie más que a ti mismo."

"Um, Mom? What does that mean?"

She held him close. "I love you more than the world. Be true to yourself, because you don't belong to anyone but yourself."

Felix had always found it endearing when his mother spoke Spanish to him, even if he couldn't understand it. And though he hadn't seen his grandfather Lionel in years, and could hardly remember him, he'd heard of the hardships he endured to give Lydia a better life here in America. The least Felix could do was show interest in the culture they'd come from. To help show them that rather than leaving it behind, they could instead bring it here to their new home. "Could you… teach me some Spanish?"

"Of course," Lydia said. "Starting tomorrow."

Felix tucked himself into bed as his mother left. He tossed and turned, unable to silence the gnawing fears at the back of his mind. The storm gave him something else to focus on. A clap of thunder shook his bed, rocking him as if he were wrapped like a newborn in its cradle. The darkness lulled him as his body, ever tense, fell into sleep.

"Wake up."

Dragged from his dreams, Felix rubbed his eyes. He jumped and covered his mouth as a pair of amber eyes stared from across the room. That same bird with red, yellow, and azure feathers, its beak twisted once more into a sneer, watched. Felix reached towards the bird, determined to catch it this time, only for it to sting his ears with a harsh squawk and fly 'round in circles. *Not again!*

He considered opening the window, but as the image of the masked man before the dead maple tree flashed in his mind, he instead thrust open the door to the hallway. He fumbled after the bird. It vanished, and as Felix stumbled into the living room, he stopped dead in his tracks. A dark figure loomed by the burning fireplace, staring at the pictures atop the mantel. Slowly, it turned.

"What are you doing up?"

"U-Uh… sorry, Father. I… couldn't sleep."

Frank groaned. "C'mon." With his face turned away, Felix couldn't make out whether his father's tone was kind, or frustrated. Frank sat on the couch. He gestured Felix to sit beside him, and tentatively, Felix complied. "Have you read through the book?" Frank asked.

Felix nodded.

"Use your words."

"Y-Yes." The firewood crackled, just as the tension in the air dissolved Felix's nerves. "Can I ask? Why are you… afraid of magi?"

The silence that followed was the most nauseating moment in Felix's young life. His fear was exacerbated as his father let out a deep, albeit quiet chuckle. "You still don't get it?" he asked.

"N-No." Felix sincerely wanted an answer. All his life, he'd never had the courage to simply ask why his father believed these things. Until now. "Did something happen?"

Shadows fell over Frank's face, his profile half illuminated. "I'm not afraid of them."

Thunder rumbled in the distance.

"I hate them."

Felix gulped. All the warmth in the room slipped away as a cold dread swept over his spirit.

"The reason you've never met your grandparents," Frank said. "My parents. They were taken. I lost them to magic. It was a long time ago, but…"

"… What happened?" Felix asked.

Frank remained silent. The shadows cast from the fire grew darker, an oppressive gloom falling over the room. The light dimmed. His eyes became totally eclipsed.

I'm sorry.

"How tragic."

Felix's leg rammed into the coffee table as he and his father jumped. The pain numbed as the figure, standing over in the kitchen, came into view. Its hood ran down to a flowing cloak, weaving in and out of the inky blackness, as if threaded from the shadows themselves. A pair of faintly glistening white orbs peered through the darkness. Only now were the mask's finer details revealed by the firelight. Red and gold, like one worn at a masquerade ball, covering his entire head. A sharp, glassy black beak protruded from the mouth, while an ornate arm, wing-shaped, fell across his left-eye slit.

That same phoenix, having vanished mere moments before, now perched itself atop the figure's shoulder, cooing as he petted it. "Good girl, Cinder. You got his attention."

Felix trembled. He wanted to scream, but the shock left his throat dry.

"No need to worry, young Felix." The figure's voice was that of an old man, gravelly and deep. "I'm here to help." He glided across the floor, almost slithering. "You're the whole reason I'm here, after all. The one who opened the door." From his cloak, he revealed Felix's sketchbook, flipping through the pages for Frank to see. Every drawing Felix had hoped his father would never so much as glimpse, there, all on display. Felix couldn't see his father's response. But at this moment, that was the least of his concerns.

"Don't worry," the man said. "After tonight, there won't be any secrets left to hide." He tossed the sketchbook into the fireplace. It fell open to a sketch Felix had drawn of himself as a magus, wand and all, and he teared up as the page was slowly chomped away by the flames.

M-Mom… Mom.

The man reached out his hand.

"MOM!"

The door to Felix's parents' room swung open. Lydia rushed into the living room, pulling Felix back. Frank, meanwhile, ducked back into their room, returning with his handgun. His eyes quivered as he muttered something indecipherable.

The masked man snickered. "This got complicated."

On impulse, Felix reached his hand out to the fireplace. He envisioned himself sending the coals right at the intruder's mask. The reddish glow turned bright blue, and sparks flew about, only to fall and catch onto the floor and couch. The phoenix screeched, sending forth its fiery breath. Orange flames spread 'til the entire room was ablaze with their dance.

Felix covered his eyes instinctively. The heat was enough to take off his eyebrows, but quickly dissipated. He parted his hands to witness what was happening, and nearly leapt back at the sight before him: Lydia holding back the flames with a wall of water.

"M-Mom?!"

"Not now, honey!" She waved her hand, and a stream of water flicked across the room, dousing some of the flames. Yet even so, the fire raged on.

A high-pitched voice screamed from Aeris' room. "Mom?! Dad?!"

"Aeris!" Without hesitation, Frank rushed through the fire, only for part of the ceiling to fall and pin him to the ground. His gun clattered to the floor. A single shot flew into the fire, rupturing Felix's eardrums, but not before Aeris' scream followed. Adrenaline coursing through him, Felix tried to lift the planks off his father. Frank shouted, his face beading with sweat, though all Felix could hear was an incessant ringing.

Embers jumped onto the pile, and Frank's screams broke through. Felix threw out his hands and shouted. "STOP!" The fire stilled, slowly turning indigo and receding until the charred wood was free of the blaze. Felix fell to his knees as his muscles burned.

Frank broke free, his skin covered in dirt and soot. He glanced at Felix. The distortion from the blaze made it impossible to glean his expression. As Aeris screamed again, he dashed through the fire and carried her out through the front door.

"Mom?" Felix looked back, finding his mother facing off against the masked man. She attempted to ensnare him with a whirlpool. The man dodged, releasing a vortex of flames. The force sent Lydia flying back onto the ground, knocking her out cold as the man and his bird disappeared into the blaze. Felix ran to her, trying to shake her awake. "Mom! Mom, please! Please wake up!"

Heavy thuds were followed by the sound of a cocking gun. Frank towered over them, his face warped in hatred. Embers bounced back through his scathing eyes. He held the gun tight, his finger on the trigger, the barrel pointed directly at Felix.

Memories flooded through his mind. Every white lie he'd made up to appease his father, and trying to keep track of them all when questioned. The fear of what Frank would do if he'd found his sketchbook, or if he'd discovered Felix's crushes on boys. Every single chiding and lecture he'd received in all twelve of his years on Earth, and how every time, Felix told himself it was so he could reach paradise with his parents forever. That the cruelty was his father's way of showing he cared.

Despite overflowing with sheer terror, Felix slowly stood, looking past the gun and right into his father's eyes.

He conjured up every memory of going down to the beach with his family. Building sandcastles with his father. Going crabbing all the way out in New Captree State Park. Frank's concern when Felix had broken his leg after trying to climb that damned maple tree, showing true affection instead of yelling like Felix was used to. He prayed that with each happy memory, he'd dispel a bad one, and it would be enough to break through the hatred and reach his father's heart.

"I... I love you."

Frank's grimace faded. He turned away, the flames casting shadows over his form. He spun. With a sharp pain to the back of Felix's head, not from a bullet, but from the blunt end of the gun, his vision blurred, the red and orange mixing into the black.

"Wake up, little one."

The gravelly voice, as well as a thunderous roar, shattered the silence. Distant shouts and sirens followed. Felix, his head pounding, forced himself up, clutching the soil and wet grass. The storm raged on overhead, yet there was no rainfall. Tall trees surrounded the clearing, their leaves not so much as rustling, all still despite the howling gales. "W-Where...?" He looked around. "Mom?" He called out. The memories began to return, and freezing up, his voice was reduced to a croak. "F-Father...?"

With an unyielding force, the memories crashed through at full force. His father, staring right through him, eyes filled with hate. The barrel of the gun, leading to a pitch-black void.

"Your father is gone."

Felix jumped. There was no sign of anyone, yet the masked man's voice carried all around. "Left you for dead," it continued. "If it wasn't for me, you'd have—"

25

"Shut up!" Felix tensed up. "Y-You... you did this!"

"Believe what you will."

From the trees fell a book. At first, Felix thought it might've been one of his father's books, but upon closer inspection, he found it to be his sketchbook. Tattered and burned black, small chunks of the fabric and paper falling off and dissolving in his hands like dying sparks. He sank further into despair, shedding a few tears "Where's my family?!"

"Your mother and sister are fine." The man was still invisible, yet his voice seemed to change direction every few seconds. "And as I said, your father—"

"My father would never!" Felix's voice cracked. "He loves us! He loves me!"

"You call holding a gun to your face love?"

A flash of lightning bathed the clearing in a pure white light. "Who... are you?"

"A friend." The man dropped from the branches. He glided into the small meadow, his maroon cloak covering the faint gleam of his golden mask. "A friend who simply wanted to help."

Felix stepped back, though he couldn't run. His eyes were stuck on where the man's eyes ought to have been. "Y-You're no friend of mine!" Felix yelled.

"In due time, you'll understand. Trust that our paths will cross again." He approached. Felix tried to run, but his feet wouldn't budge, as though they'd sunken into the dirt. "Until that day," the man said. "Hold onto that anger. That passion. On that day, we will make this world bow to us. And 'til that day, if I were you, I would keep one question in mind: What does the name Dragora mean to you?"

Dragora?

With the flap of his cloak, the rain and wind returned as he vanished into the storm. Felix fell into the mud. He tried to piece together the man's message, but as the blaring of the sirens grew louder, his mind tore itself from his stupor. He rushed towards the source of the commotion, then stopped as he exited the woods. His house was completely up in flames. Police and firefighters blocked off the scene, yet even through the downpour, the fire raged on.

"Felix!" Lydia, rushing up, hugged her son tight. Her cheek was bruised and coated with soot. "¡Gracias a Dios que estás bien!" She checked him over for bruises along his arms and legs, then held his face. "Where have you been?"

Felix couldn't answer. He hadn't fully processed what he'd just been through, not even noticing as a third firetruck raced onto the scene to join the effort to extinguish the blaze. Putting the matter aside, his mother guided him over to the sidewalk across the street, where Aeris sat drenched, trying in vain to shield herself with a thin blanket. She stared at the road, eyes vacant. Gauze had been wrapped around her upper right arm, red.

Felix held his mother's hand tighter. "Mom? What you did back in the house. With the water. Are... are you a...?"

She didn't respond. Instead, she hung her head.

"Get back!" The firefighters ran, scurrying to get clear of the inferno. With a deafening crash, the house collapsed in on itself, smoke rising into the clouds. A terrible screech followed. Giant golden wings broke free from the rubble, and that same firebird, now larger than even the house, stood tall. It met Felix's gaze before flapping its wings, pushing back the authorities with a powerful gust as it took off into the sky.

The sight left Felix in shock. As he looked upon the damage while the firefighters put out what was left of the blaze, and one of the officers yelled at the others to send the "magus ops" after the phoenix, he wasn't fully sure how he should feel. He shed no tears, nor was he upset. Yet... something dark was festering within him. Something bitter.

A policeman, displaying a golden star badge, approached Felix's family. The glimmer inspired an uneasiness in his mind. Sheriff Hannity Boyce, who seemed to catch onto who Felix was rather quickly before electing to ignore him. Like Frank, Hannity's brown hair had been swept into a combover, although far more crudely. His swamp-green eyes appeared murkier than his mud-brown uniform, which sagged around his stocky build.

"Ma'am," Hannity said in his booming voice. "Surely you know that keeping any kind of magical creatures is a felony."

"You can't seriously think that thing was a pet?!" Lydia said.

"If it wasn't, then where did it come from?"

"I don't know."

"Mhm." He gestured for his fellow officers to come over. "Ma'am, I'm afraid we're going to have to take you all in for questioning."

Felix expected Lydia to argue back. Instead, she quietly resigned while the other officers joked about "keeping a pet that lights your house on fire." A massive crowd had gathered, looking on as the rain put out the few cinders remaining on the structure's carcass. Some onlookers tossed slurs and insults, while others tossed stones. The message was clear all the same. Filled with distress, Felix returned to the look of hatred in his father's eyes. To his finger ready to pull the trigger. To the bullet, waiting to be fired.

Lightning danced through the sky, crackling along with the thunder. Pressing his head up against the police car window, Felix imagined himself commanding the storm, mastering his powers and showing the world just how terrifying he could be if given the chance. He'd never believed in fate. But if he was truly a magus, perhaps this was meant to happen, and he was meant to be freed from his father's zealous grip. Perhaps this was destined.

Passion seized him as he scowled at the angry crowd. A burning desire to spite every last person like the officers, like Carson, or like his father. To show them all what he could do, and what fools they were to mistreat him and those who shared his gift. *They* were the ones with power. *They* were the ones with magic. And it was time *they* were the ones to be feared.

Felix shut his eyes, earnestly recalling his father's teaching one last time. *"Wizards are a threat,"* Frank would say. *"Monsters."*

They want a force of destruction?

There Frank stood, in his mind's eye, ready to pull the trigger.

He imagined himself, ready to let his magic loose.

I'll give 'em one.

Chapter Two

Burnout

BLOOD burned across the emerald grass.
There, gathered in the conservatory garden of Central Park, men and women huddled, trying to shield each other from the onslaught of rubber bullets and tear gas. From all sides, police, armed head to toe in black riot gear, corralled their targets. Those furthest out were thrown to the ground, then pepper-sprayed, beaten with batons, or both.

Then, a light.

One of the protesters ran, wand in hand, and threw a fireball directly at one of the officer's faces. Others followed, protecting those who couldn't cast spells. Shields of light held back bullets. Vines sprouted from nowhere, seizing the officers' weapons, and blocking their paths as they charged at the unarmed.

"We see the truth!" one voice shouted, its source indistinguishable. "We see past your lies!"

But in a massive tide of water, all were swept off their feet. New officers, donning themselves in gear lined with brightly colored gems and glowing batons, swarmed the protesters. Meek fireballs were overwhelmed by an infernal barrage. Barriers were broken, and one by one, protesters displaying magic were detained, thrown into vans just outside the park, and driven away en masse. Those who couldn't were simply beaten further, the lucky ones crawling away unnoticed, red trailing behind them.

One boy, a thin, pale young man with sandy-blonde hair, ran for his life, along with his cameraman. Both had their escape route cut off by a torrent of flames, the camera being shattered by a massive chunk of ice.

"I'm press!" the blonde boy screamed, his voice cracking. "I'm press!"

The officer, their face obscured, looked down. Their chestplate read: "M.S.O.U."

"I don't care."

The officer's wand glowed blue, and the boy's vision blurred in an icy swirl.

Felix shot up from bed. His palms were cold, his fingers grown numb, as though he'd been frozen alive. Another nightmare. A nightmare far too vivid to be mere dread at the state of the world, picked up from the horrifying videos spreading across social media.

He yawned. His forehead ached, feeling like he'd somehow lost sleep. Turning onto his side with his blanket wrapped around him, he looked forward to falling back into slumber, hoping this time his mind wouldn't project itself into the world's horrors yet again.

"Sleeping late again?"

A bright light engulfed the room, and instinctively, Felix curled up. Reluctantly, he emerged from his makeshift fortress. The hideous yellow bedroom light exposed clothes, socks, and a garbage can overflowing with crumpled up sketches and fast-food bags tossed about the floor. The old pale-blue carpet was coated in a thin layer of dust, revealing it hadn't been vacuumed in weeks. The desk, bedside tables, and especially shelves were in an even worse state, crowded with childhood knickknacks.

But the worst sight of all? Aeris, leaning in the doorway and shaking her head. Her straightened hair, as always, was tied back into a ponytail with a snow-white scrunchy, matching her white summer dress. Silver teardrop-shaped earrings sparkled in the room's darkness, seeming to radiate light. "C'mon. We're going driving."

Felix groaned. "What time is it?"

"Noon thirty," she said, mocking his raspy, slurring voice.

Putting two and two together, Felix grabbed his phone: 12:25 p.m. "Fuck! I've got work in 5."

"Your own fault." She smirked. "Which is why I'm here to help. I suppose. You're lucky I'm so generous."

Felix hissed. Aeris simply rolled her eyes and left, and once she was out of sight, Felix spun in his cocoon and rolled onto the floor, groaning once more. Even after all these years, Aeris hadn't changed a bit. As much as he didn't want to take her uncharacteristic offer, Felix's usual bus commute would've taken too long, and Lydia was currently out with his stepfather Ian and half-sister Tracey. His frustration nearly made him miss high school.

Shedding his apathy, and with no time to shower, Felix threw on his clothes: a black buttoned-up shirt with an obnoxiously bright-red tie, coupled with black pants and sneakers. How a fast-food joint could "serve with a smile" while mandating such a morose uniform for its employees was beyond anyone's understanding. That is, of course, until you remember the shit these employees have seen in mismanagement, terrifyingly irate customers, and appallingly low wages and working conditions, upon which the world makes perfect sense again.

Felix flinched at the blare of Aeris' car horn as he ran outside into the apartment parking lot. The cherry red exterior popped, gleaming obnoxiously bright in the sunlight. Silver shimmered in the star-shaped wheels, as did the dove emblem on the front grill. Frank's old cross necklace hung from the rear-view mirror, and as it dangled, the sunlight bounced off and stung Felix's eyes. At the very least, Felix appreciated the new car smell.

Aeris sat in the passenger seat. "That's funny," Felix said. "Is your car so shitty, it can't drive itself?"

"Driving yourself is fun. Not that people nowadays would know." She didn't even bother looking up from her phone. The only time she buried herself in her phone was when she wanted to ignore her mother, her stepfather, her little half-sister, and most often, Felix.

"Whatever," Felix said. *Hope this rust bucket's got good insurance.* He nudged himself into the driver's seat. As much as he hated to admit it, he did appreciate the fact this car wasn't cluttered with old papers and empty bottles—better than the mess Rosie always left her car in. "Keys, please," he said.

"Catch." Aeris tossed them nonchalantly, and Felix dropped them, shame gripping him instantly. "Oh, give me those." Aeris swiped the keys, holding up a gilded one. "Remember it. Now, foot on the brake."

Felix complied.

"The other pedal."

But he forgot the breaks were usually on the left. "Me lleva," he muttered.

Aeris jammed the key into the ignition and turned on the engine. "Now put it in reverse."

Following her instructions, Felix pulled out of the spot and drove onto the main road. He'd always had a fear of driving, so much so he'd only just recently gotten his learner's permit. Cars gave him very little in the way of feeling in control. To him, he wasn't safe unless he was keeping maximum distance between himself and any other drivers, even while being the only moving car in a parking lot. He understood the necessity of being able to drive despite self-driving cars being the norm, but this understanding hardly quelled his resentment. The best he could do now was take deep breaths, focus on only the road, and pray nothing might set off his anxiety.

"So what do you wanna do with your life?" Aeris asked.

God, crash this car and end my life, please. Not peeling his eyes off the road ahead for even a second, Felix eased back. "Don't know yet?"

Aeris shrugged. "Fair. But have you thought it over?"

Felix's hands were already coating the wheel with sweat. "Can't I just take a year off from school? Maybe I need a break. Time to think things over?"

"I'm just saying, college isn't nearly as tough as you think."

"I know." Felix's graduation had been the week before, and though he was glad to be free from that high school hellscape, he still had no idea what to do once it was all over. He'd killed his dream of going to Dragora a long time ago. Not only was it ludicrously expensive, but he'd been reluctant to even attempt practicing magic after… the incident.

Lydia had somehow dodged the magus registration system her entire life. But after that night, both she and Felix had to be cataloged. "For reference," the authorities said, along with a hefty fine and a warning as subtle as a dragon's roar for dodging registration for so long. There wasn't a day that went by where Felix hadn't cursed his existence for what happened. The fear of somehow getting into trouble again was ever pervasive in the back of his mind, especially when everyone at school steered clear of the "demon kid."

It was almost enough to make him forget his curiosity as to who the masked man was, and where he was now, along with the question of whether he was still hanging around somewhere, waiting, watching from afar. Almost.

Felix had to wonder, in spite of whatever potential he might've shown, how far he'd fallen out of favor with the rogue since that night.

"Look out!"

Felix swerved out of the way as a truck, honking its deafening horn, flew by, nearly swiping Felix's side of the car cleaning off.

"Pull over!" Aeris screamed. "Pull over!"

"Okay, okay!" Once on the side of the road, Felix rested his head on the steering wheel trying to compose himself. Aeris hyperventilated and gripped her seatbelt. Felix's fear and shock dissipated as he mentally apologized to his sister over and over, unable to voice his sentiment without crippling under the shame. Finally, he mustered his courage. "Are you okay?"

"Do I look okay?!" Instinctively, Aeris clutched her right arm, where a faint scar ran from where the bullet had grazed her skin. The bullet from their father's gun as it fell to the floor, the night of the fire.

"I-I'm sorry, I—"

"I just had this refurbished. It's a 2045 Mustang! Do you know how much I had to save up to get this car, let alone get it back into shape?!"

"I said I was sor—"

"Move. I'm driving."

"O-Okay," Felix mumbled. They switched seats, and Aeris drove them the rest of the way to the shopping center, while Felix sat in guilt-ridden silence.

Aeris pulled up to the curb. "I am never driving with you again."

"Look, I'm sorry, I—"

"You know, maybe if you weren't up all night feeling sorry for yourself, you wouldn't be so skitzy and unaware."

Felix paused. "E-Excuse me?"

"You heard me." Aeris didn't even look his way. "Let me guess. You were up all night staring at the website for that magic school you wanted to go to? How about you get your head out of the clouds and join the rest of us in reality?"

Felix clutched the side of the seat. "I don't need a reminder of *your* version of reality, ogro."

Aeris glared. "What did I tell you about—"

"¿Tu apodo? ¡Oh, pero amo tu apodo, ogro!"

She groaned. "Just, get out! Your Spanish is awful, by the way."

"Okay!" He played up the stereotypical Spanish accent as he undid his seatbelt. *How dare you say things that are entirely true, ogro!* "But you know what? Thanks for the ride." He resisted any true insults and swear words entering his mind as he tried to keep his cool. In an attempt to look down on his taller sister, he straightened his back as he hopped onto the curb. He slammed the door shut, and after huffing and puffing, Aeris took off. The anger faded, replaced by a general sense of discontent. *Some things never change, I guess.*

At this point, Felix wasn't even concerned with getting to work on time. He was already 15 minutes late, and wasn't likely to stop fuming for a couple hours at the least. He headed for the Sandwich Shack, an all-around hell on Earth—or rather, a low-budget hell. Hell proper would've thoroughly cooked the food. (Not that there was any real cooking involved) Even so, it was one of the few places that still hired "low-skilled labor," let alone magi, instead of relying on automation. With all of his measly universal income going straight to his savings every month, and with his parents wanting him to get some real-world experience, he had no other choice.

The place was empty. Not a single customer at any of the retro gray tables or red leather booths. The TV in the corner, however, was loud enough to make it sound like they were hosting a party. It had been tuned into CUSN, also known as the most vanilla news network to ever exist. Grimy water dirtied the black-and-white tiled floor, while the garish yellow wet floor sign sat on the opposite side of the room.

Behind the front counter was just one person: Rosie's older brother Marcus, the only coworker Felix felt comfortable chatting with—minus the butterflies fluttering about his stomach, of course. Marcus' black dreadlocks cascaded into a basket-woven ponytail, and his biceps peeked out from his T-shirt. His rich-brown eyes beckoned Felix's gaze, officially christening him as one of the gays. Felix looking away, though, confirmed him as an awkward bisexual disaster.

"H-Hey, Marcus," Felix said, trying to hide his nervousness. *Fuck. I didn't sign up for this.* "Didn't know you were working today." *Or that you looked really good in an ugly yellow smock and blue cap.*

"Yeah." Marcus' smooth voice glided across Felix's ears like a summer breeze. "Uh, where's your smock and cap, though?"

Fuck. And not the good kind. Felix groaned. "Crap. I forgot them in the rush."

Marcus shrugged. "I think there's extras in the back."

"You don't have to—"

Before Felix could finish, Marcus left.

Why must he be my knight in shining armor when we both know it's a ship that shall never sail? So inconsiderate. Once he clocked himself in, Felix leaned on the counter and stared blankly at the TV. President Kendra Brooks stood at her podium, giving answers to reporters at a press conference, all as she faced a thousand clicks and flashes of cameras. Her beige suit complemented her dark skin, deep-brown eyes, and black afro. The States' first black female president in all its history, running for her second term that November.

The news then cut to the standard political analysis, featuring news anchor Jane Whyte. Felix crafted a tragic backstory for her given the vacancy in her stare and the dryness of her voice. In his imagination, she'd spent her whole life wanting to become a journalist, much to her parents' vocal dismay. She dreamt of spending her days searching for the truth, fighting corruption and injustice everywhere. Yet here she was on a shitty news station making quarters, reciting lines from a teleprompter with her higher-ups yelling at her through her earpiece, and hoping one of the stage lights would fall and end her misery mid-broadcast. *Same here, Jane. Same here.*

"Back." Marcus held the smock and cap. "Gimme your head."

Felix blushed. "Huh?"

"Your head."

"R-Right." *You filthy child. Qué sucia.* Felix lowered his head, craning it so he wouldn't be looking at Marcus as he placed the smock over his neck. Getting lost in Marcus' eyes would've definitely resulted in a blush or two… or twelve.

"Turn please," Marcus said.

"I-I got it!" Felix struggled to tie the back ribbons. He threaded the knot, and Marcus put the cap on his head. "Thanks."

"Welcome." Marcus grinned. "Nice ass, though."

After a few moments of silence, they laughed. Minutes must've gone by before Felix noticed there was still no sign of life anywhere. "Has it been this slow all day?" Felix asked.

"Yep. Not that I'm complaining. Anyway, you're going to Suffolk next year, right?"

Felix looked away, holding his chin. "That's the plan…"

"Cool. Maybe we'll see each other there before I transfer."

"Sounds nice." Rosie was headed to Suffolk Community College this year herself. Like her big brother, she wanted to finish all her general studies before transferring elsewhere. Presumably she'd be majoring in political science and history. As much as she tended to distance herself from her identity as a magus, she still wanted to do her part to try and change things, even if she wouldn't see the fruits of her labor within her own lifetime. Felix envied her optimism and strength. Rosie insisted that he wasn't obligated to join the fight, especially after all he'd been through.

I suppose one-and-a-half-friends are better than none. Even if the half-friend is way outta my league, romantically and academically.

"You okay, bro?" Marcus asked.

Felix tensed. "Y-Yeah." *Every time he says "bro," I die a little inside.*

Marcus patted him on the back. "Relax. You're a smart kid. You've got a bright future."

Does my plan to hide in a cave far, far away from civilization count? As much as Felix appreciated the faith of his friends and family, he could never share that faith in himself. When he looked in the mirror, all he saw was a lost child. A child with no real path forward. Nothing but a shell of anger and exhaustion, one fueling the other in a never-ending, but ever-worsening cycle.

"You've proposed a draft requiring all able magi to serve in the Magus Special Ops Unit, Mr. Schmitt." Whyte was now interviewing Bernard Anthony Schmitt: presidential candidate, supposed successful businessman, and incarnation of everything wrong with humanity. "Why do you say this?" she asked. "And why would this make you appealing to voters as the Republican nominee?"

"Yes," Schmitt said, nodding his fat head aggressively, his slicked black hair bobbing as it glistened with an overabundance of Schmitt-brand hair gel. "We have a whole military of brave, ordinary Americans for a reason. To defend our home. It's time we ask these wizards to do the same. Show a little gratitude to humanity. Someone's gotta purge this bloated, corrupt system, and I'm the guy to do it." He looked into the camera, right through the screen, as though he might spit in the viewer's face. "Unlike Brooks."

Marcus cringed in utter disgust. "I can't stand that guy. How is he winning? He's a buffoon!"

"One look at history will answer that," Felix said.

Marcus held his forehead. "Fuck."

Hey, that's my line.

Jokes aside, Marcus was right. Felix certainly wasn't a fan of Brooks. Far from it. Totally willing to overlook human rights violations to remain allies with the New Ottoman Empire. Broken promises to end military interventions in South America, Asia, and Africa. And lots and lots of campaign contributions convincing her of a more "center of the political aisle" approach. Still, one could still say the country was marginally less on fire under her watch, and a second term wasn't likely to trigger the next near apocalypse.

But Schmitt? Not only did he pander to people's fears and prejudices, but he also knew how to push their buttons in just the right way to win their trust and screw them over later. The ultimate conman. As much as Felix wanted to ignore the current political shit show the country had become in recent years, common sense told him he'd better keep on his guard if there was a massive part of the country that wanted people like him gone. Magi didn't get the luxury of being apolitical. And Felix knew he'd rather die than be conscripted into the MSOU.

"Just think about it!" Schmitt rambled on, his voice blaring through the speakers. "How much safer we'd be if these wizards bothered helping us! Magicians, Janet! Magicians!"

Whyte frowned. "Jane."

"Yes, Janette! Magicians! Reading fortunes, riding on brooms, pulling rabbits outta hats! If they pulled out a fix to our problems, I'd love it. But they haven't. They've pulled out dragons and monsters terrorizing our cities! They've ignored horrific human tragedies for centuries! They're profiting off our pain and it's not right for the ordinary folks! It's time they changed their tune."

Felix grit his teeth. *"Ordinary folks."* If he heard that term one more time, as though he weren't struggling to get by just like everyone else, if not more, then surely he'd have lost his mind. If only he could do all those things people thought magi could. Fly at will, or throw giant fireballs and tornadoes everywhere without breaking a sweat. Then he'd personally take the time to pay Mr. Schmitt a visit to set the record straight.

But he was used to setting his anger aside. This was the man the Camo Crew flocked to in search of a guide from the abyss. A good number of humans had the decency to acknowledge how grateful they should've been to magi for bailing them out of a disaster they'd created for themselves; for the barrier systems they'd helped shape to keep out the worst effects of climate change and the magical creatures roaming the planet. But sadly, not enough.

Schmitt himself served as the perfect lightning rod for people's insecurities: someone who could rally together those who felt left behind; the ones dying for someone to blame for all the devastation across the globe in the last few decades.

And what could've made for a better target than magi?

Just as Felix could've sworn the idiocy levels couldn't peak any higher, the front doors swung wide open, and Camo Captain Carson himself and his parents, all dressed in black from head to toe, entered. Bags wrinkled beneath their bloodshot eyes. Carson's mother dabbed her cheeks with a pink handkerchief, sniffling. Her pale skin appeared red from her fluster, her black fedora with a marigold flower barely containing her draping grayish-blonde hair.

"I got this." Marcus' voice had never felt so reassuring.

Felix nearly swooned. *My knight in shining armor.*

"Marcus!" Though their boss Helen hadn't made her presence known all day, likely sitting comfortably in her back office, she'd apparently decided to summon Marcus with her gravelly bellow at the worst possible moment. "I need you to refill the 3D printer resources!"

But we've had hardly any customers. Did she make herself food with the printers? Okay honestly, can't fault her for that. I should've done that, cuz I am starving.

"Never mind then," Marcus said. "All yours." He disappeared into the back kitchen, and Carson's father, the ever-menacing sheriff Hannity Boyce, approached the counter.

And now my knight has abandoned me. Wonderful. "Welcome to the Sandwich Shack," Felix said. "Where whatever you say is law." *And whatever we say is grounds for being fired without severance!* "How may I help you?"

Hannity looked over the menu. "Number seven," he droned. "Delilah?"

Delilah blew her nose. "Same as you, dear."

"Carson?"

Carson stared dead at Felix. "Five."

Hannity snickered in his raucous voice. "You heard it. All large."

Felix punched in the orders. "To stay or to go?" *Please go. Go far, far away.*

"Stay."

Fuck. Begrudgingly, Felix rang up the price. "That'll be $42.35."

Hannity growled. "Unbelievable."

"Running us into the ground, Hannity." Delilah's voice was brittle, her pink nose now bordering on red. "Killing us."

As much as Felix agreed that the slop this place had on offer wasn't worth the price, his pride refused to concede even an inch of ground. "I mean, if the employees could, we'd definitely lower the prices. But we gotta make a living somehow, so—"

"Can it," Hannity said. "You're pushing buttons all day. Want decent money, get a real job and quit complaining."

Felix nearly cracked his jaw trying to keep the facade from turning into a murderous gaze. He authorized the transfer, but before he could hand them the receipt, the Boyce Clan had already seated themselves at the corner table. *Now stay there. Please.*

Marcus returned, almost as if he were the Lord of Terrible Timing. "So what'd they want?"

Felix handed Marcus the receipt. "Two sevens and a five. Large." *The knife, I mean.*

Nodding, Marcus headed back into the kitchen. The food printers would spit out the meal in a matter of minutes, but they were so old and worn out, Felix expected them to give out at any moment. He couldn't help but agree with Hannity. If their job was only to take orders and tell the printer to do all the work, why not just hand that position off to robots? If you were gonna go out of your way to brand yourself as "the last bastion of a human's culinary touch," why not go all out and let them cook on grills and stovetops? They sure as hell weren't a retro or high-end restaurant, but it'd be less mind-numbing than this strange middleman position.

Felix redirected his attention back to the TV. Pope-Emperor Janus Angelov had recently delivered a speech from Vatican City, which was being replayed all over. The old man's white gown and cap definitely did not complement his ungodly pale skin. An odd choice, given Felix was used to seeing pictures of Angelov's predecessors dressed like the most pompous hybrid of a priest and a king imaginable, complete with gold crowns, a thousand rings, and a useless ornamental scepter that could double as a bat. Yet something about the way Angelov carried himself brought an unexpected comfort, like that of a doting grandparent who'd have a stroke at the slightest swear. A comfort which grew as he adjusted his tiny reading glasses.

"My beloved brothers and sisters," Angelov said with a slight Russian accent. His hoarse voice croaked between syllables. "While it's true our world has changed, we mustn't forget our mission to bring salvation to all of God's children. To bring His grace to a world in desperate need of it. And while these sorcerers who walk the Earth may possess forces wicked in nature, we cannot win them over to our side of the pearly gates through brute force and shame. Rather, we must work to better our own temperaments and give them an honest chance to hear our words and reflect."

Huh. That was… not what I expected. Beats championing live executions of heretics, I guess. But Felix couldn't shake the fact this man's creed brought back painful memories.

"What a fuckin' joke." Hannity slammed the table, sending a shock down Felix's back. "Talk to them?! They're monsters."

"Right, dear." Delilah rubbed her nose. "No cooperating with such vile creatures. They just deceive us by looking and acting human." There was a slight trembling in her voice as she clutched her handkerchief.

While his parents talked, Carson silently stared Felix down. Felix jumped, looking off into the parking lot, pondering whether to attempt an escape. They'd left each other alone since that day, but Felix could always feel Carson's hatred whenever they passed each other in the halls. That resentful look that quietly said, "What I wouldn't give for the existence of you, and everyone like you, to end."

The Boyces switched the TV over to the local news. Commentators described how a recent Truthseer demonstration in the city turned violent, resulting in a clash between radical protesters (human and magus activists), and members of the MSOU. The body count was unknown, but the footage of armed soldiers encasing protestors in ice and even burning some of them alive was disturbing enough. Felix's gaze was glued to the screen as one officer approached a young journalist, extending his wand before the footage cut away.

"Hey there, Francis." Carson leaned on the counter. His appearance had hardly changed very little since he was young. Same buzzed sandy-blonde hair, same blue eyes, and same boorish fleer.

Felix backed up a bit. "It's Felix."

"Felicia."

Very funny. "Do you want another—"

"You weren't at graduation." Carson grimaced. "Why?"

Felix had asked himself the same over and over. His mother and stepfather were rather disappointed in not attending the ceremony, missing the chance to take graduation pictures. But Felix felt there would be no happiness there. Surrounded by students with bright futures, far brighter than his, and only one real friend he wouldn't even be able to sit beside beneath the hot June sun. Yet now, he'd have taken the blistering heat of a thousand summer suns over dealing with Carson. Felix shrugged. "Wasn't interested."

"I bet you wish you were one of those kill-happy Ops Unit goons, huh?" Carson asked, squinting. "Yeah. I know what you are. A wizard."

Felix balled his fists. "The term is magus."

"Same damn thing. A monster by any other name is still a monster. You blew up your house, for God's sake. My dad was there. He knows what you are, and so do I. I wonder whether you'd join those Truthseer terrorists, or that magical task force that loves to rough people up." Carson hunched over the counter, getting in Felix's face as much as he could. "I mean, either would help you get payback on me, right?"

"… You need to get a grip."

Carson's face reddened as his voice grew angrier. "Do I?! My cousin's a journalist. He goes into these protests all the time to write about them. And sure, we may not have agreed with him, we may have fought, but he didn't deserve what those wizards did to him! He…" Delilah grieffully glanced at Carson, while that same ire beamed from Hannity's eyes towards Felix.

"Carson?" Felix asked. After an ashamedly long pause, it clicked. *Shit.* "C-Carson…" He immediately regretted every mental jab and passive-aggressive rebuttal he'd uttered. "I… I'm so sor—"

"I don't need your pity!" Carson slammed the counter. "Only apology I need is from your freak parents for making you." He hung his head. Before Felix could get a word in, Carson gave a sick chuckle coated in a twisted sense of dark humor. "At least you had the decency to kill one of 'em for me."

"I didn't…" Felix searched for the right response, but his need to end the altercation took the driver's seat, especially as a righteous fury took hold. "Forget it. I'm not dealing with this. I'm sorry. What happened to you and your family was horrible. But whatever you want from me, I can't give it to you."

"Okay. Maybe you didn't kill your dad." Carson leaned in further. "Maybe your mom did."

Felix clenched his fists, knuckles whitening.

"Or maybe he realized Mommy was a monster and came to his senses."

"Shut. Up." Felix's blood boiled. As hard as he tried to hold back his rage, a fire lit inside him, filling his entire body with indignation. Sparks could've flown from how hard he ground his teeth.

"Can you blame him? After fucking her created such a hideous, monstrous—"

Felix grabbed Carson's shirt. "SHUT UP."

The sprinklers went off. Felix released his grip as Marcus ran from the kitchen, shouting. Smoke poured out from behind him. "The printers! Fire!"

"The fuck?!" Hannity knocked his chair over as he grabbed Delilah and rushed out the door. Giving Felix one last glare, Carson followed his parents outside. He didn't need to say anything else for Felix to get the message.

Marcus grabbed Felix's wrist, pulling him out into the parking lot. They were all dripping from head to toe. Felix was silent, still processing what had even happened. "I don't get it," Marcus mumbled. "I just checked the printers, and they were fine. Then all of a sudden, this fire bursts up outta nowhere."

Felix, slightly shaking, stared at his hands. All he could ever manage were a few pink sparks from his fingertips. The one time he wielded true flames, they were blue. "Marcus, what color was the fire?"

"Red. What else would it be?"

Those red-orange flames in the cafeteria that day. The ones that mysteriously appeared over him and Carson, manifesting from nothing. The ones that consumed his childhood home and reduced it to ashes. *No. Could it have been... him?*

"YOU." Carson, his face completely red, grabbed Felix's tie. "You tried to fucking kill me!"

Marcus jumped between them, pushing Carson away. "Back off!" He glanced back. "You okay, Felix?" Felix couldn't bring himself to answer.

Helen ran out, her uniform soaked. "What's going on?"

Hannity pushed past Carson, flashing his badge. "Your employee clearly started this fire after trying to hurt my son." A vein bulged from his neck. "He's a magus." He dragged out the syllables with every ounce of vehemence he could muster.

Delilah, makeup running down her face, hugged Carson. She stroked his hair and cupped his cheek. "Are you okay, honey?" Carson simply pushed her away.

Helen leaned against a nearby van. "Yes, Sheriff. Felix is a magus. But do you have any proof he wanted—"

"The more proof do you need?" Carson asked. "His spells can make fire. He's a freak, and he—"

With a single glower, Hannity hushed his son, then continued. "Ma'am, this is the same delinquent whose house 'inexplicably' burned down just a few years ago. It may not be on his criminal record, but what law-abiding citizen has a history with the law starting at age 12, let alone one so horrid?"

"You can't be serious!" Marcus gripped Felix's shoulder. "Felix is a good kid! He'd never—"

"Stay outta this, kid. You wouldn't wanna get involved with their kind."

Felix sighed. *My "kind."* As disgusted as he was, Felix silently begged Marcus to remain silent. The last thing he wanted was to drag his friend into his problems. Besides, he knew exactly how this would play out. He didn't even have a criminal record, but to Sheriff Boyce, his being a magus was enough to merit one.

"I'm calling in my squad now." Hannity reached for his radio, returning his attention to Felix. "It's high time you learned a lesson in respecting order, kid."

"It was my fault," Marcus said.

Felix was taken aback. Everyone stared at Marcus, yet he looked undaunted, head held high, meeting Hannity's gaze. "I didn't check the printers, and I accidentally caused the fire. Felix wasn't even in the kitchen. Besides, he'd never do something like this."

"If this is true," Helen said. "I'm afraid I'll have to let you go, Marcus. It's too much to smooth over. I'm sorry." Unexpectedly, Helen assured Marcus that he wouldn't be held liable for the damages. She'd take the heat with her district managers, a courtesy which Felix imagined probably wouldn't have been so generously extended towards him. Marcus handed over his cap and smock. "You too, Felix."

"What?!" Marcus and Felix asked in unison.

She kept her attention on Marcus, talking right past Felix. "I'm afraid having him here will only lead to more trouble. It's just business."

Fed up with everything, Felix handed over the smock and cap, simply content that the worst was behind him. Helen rushed back over to the fire trucks by the restaurant. Unfortunately, Carson didn't seem as satisfied as he marched towards Felix, and instinctively, Felix shrunk in stature. Marcus jumped in again, towering over Carson. "Move along."

Begrudgingly, the Boyces left, though Carson didn't once let up his scowl at Felix as his family got in his father's truck and left.

I'm sorry.

Marcus insisted on taking Felix home. Felix was hesitant, but quickly complied. Though Marcus made it clear he didn't blame Felix for what happened, Felix still blamed himself, and he certainly was not looking forward to explaining how he'd just lost his job and nearly made the news again to his mother and stepfather. Once they were in the car, he just stared out the window.

"Quit it."

Felix glanced over at Marcus. "Huh?"

"The self-pity thing," Marcus said. "That dude said awful shit. If someone said that about my dads, let alone Rosie, I'd go apeshit."

"But…" Felix stuttered. "You shouldn't have to take the fall for me."

"It was neither of our faults. And you shouldn't be blamed for some freak accident. Besides, it's just a job. I can find another one."

Felix slouched in his seat. He'd hoped a summer job would help take his mind off things, even if it proved tedious. Help him pretend he was being productive and making strides, in-between him and Rosie going camping, or heading to the beach between shifts. Lying on the sand, listening to the waves. The thought alone brought some comfort. "Can you take me down to the beach instead?" Felix asked.

Marcus raised an eyebrow. "Yeah, sure. You want me to—"

"No, I'll be fine. Just need to clear my head for a while."

"Whatever you say." Marcus readjusted their destination.

Felix pressed his head against the glass. He wondered what the rest of his graduating class were up to now. All enjoying their last summer at home before heading off to college, all while Felix enjoyed a future of squabbling in failure.

The New Horizon Beach parking lot was completely devoid of life, save for some seagulls fighting over food wrappers by an overflowing trash can. "You sure you don't want company?" Marcus asked. "Or someone to talk to? Rosie's at work 'til later tonight, but I'm sure she'd come down if I told her what's up."

"I appreciate it," Felix said. "But I'd rather not bother her when she's busy. Besides, I need some time alone to think things over." He crossed his arms, shivering at the faint chill in the air.

"Okay." Marcus leaned against the car. "I'll wait here for you."

"N-No. You don't have to, I can walk home later."

"With people like that kid at the shop on the prowl?" Marcus shook his head. "Hell no. I'll stay here as long as you need. *And* I'll be checking on you now and then just to make sure you're safe."

Felix tried to conceal his blush. "Thanks."

"No problem."

Goddamn knights.

The beach, like the parking lot, was empty. Ocean waves beat against the shoreline. Felix sat back on the sand and closed his eyes, the sound of rolling tides soothing his nerves, and the taste of sea salt from the breeze dancing on his tongue. Even the occasional squawks of seagulls helped him relax. How wonderful it would be if the magical levees and barriers around Long Island, designed to keep out both severe storms and rogue magical creatures, randomly failed. Only long enough for some monster to slither up from the depths and devour him. Then he wouldn't have to worry about his future anymore, and his end would come while he was, for once, at peace.

He'd never been to this beach specifically with his family, but his parents adored the sea... Lydia and Frank. Frank insisted on getting them a boat when Felix was little, and taking him and Aeris out fishing and crabbing. They'd even camped along the beach at one point, cooking crabs over the fire, while Frank and Lydia recalled fond memories of how they'd met.

Part of Felix wished they never had.

To think this all used to be part of the island. But not anymore. Once, long before Felix was even a thought, this place was still above water. Towns,

45

shops, and homes, filled with ordinary people living in peace. Until the Revelation. Magical creatures across the world suddenly went on a rampage, exposing the existence of magi and, immediately after the Scorch, the Medeian Empire.

Soon enough, the sea swallowed up Fire Island, Jones Beach, and a good chunk of the Hamptons. Anything not completely engulfed quickly became the new home to sea dragons, sylphs, and other wild beasts. How far past the horizon did the north shore used to stretch? How many lives between here and there were lost?

Felix curled up. Clouds gathered, covering the sky, turning it and the ocean a dark, murky gray. Over all these years, his desire to attend Dragora and compete in the Ancient Dragons' Tournament had been chiseled away, day by day, until it had completely collapsed in on itself. The place of his dreams. A castle he knew only in his imagination, where he could become all he'd ever wanted to be. So far out of his reach now. He tucked his head into his arms, clutched his knees, and cried for what felt like an eternity.

So long as none of them see me cry.

A peculiar squawk startled him. A shriek far shriller and more aggressive than those of the seagulls, and much closer. It almost sounded… human. Felix wiped away his tears. There, sitting before him, was a bird. Red and gold feathers shone in the sunset, contrasting with azure tips. A sealed maroon envelope, upon which shimmered a golden crest, hung from its beak. Felix reached out, only for the bird to drop the envelope and bite his finger. He shouted in pain. As the bird took off, he squinted. *Was that a…? No. It couldn't be. Could it?*

Slowly, Felix picked up the envelope. The seal was the crest of the Medeian Empire: a golden phoenix spreading its red-and-blue tipped wings. Behind it bloomed a white flower, its seven petals twirling outwards to peach-colored tips. He ripped it open. At the bottom of the enclosed document was the signature of Headmistress Ramidha Hakim of the Dragora Institute of Magic. Felix's heart nearly jumped out of his chest.

No. Fucking. Way.

Chapter Three

Rekindled

BREATHE. *Just breathe.*

Felix looked out the train window, though now all there was to behold was a constant darkness, broken by the occasional blur of light. It was at least a far less grating sight than all the gaudy ads plastered across the train car's screens. He held his arm, doing his best to dispel his anxiety. All across the country, young magi were heading out to MSOU centers, most of the time making out-of-state trips, for exams to apply for the new grant program to attend Dragora in the fall. To prove they were indeed worth the effort.

But Felix wasn't so sure he was.

And even then, everyone else had received that same letter from Headmistress Hakim through the mail. Yet he was given the information by a phoenix? Was it that same phoenix from all those years ago? The one that accompanied… no. No, he couldn't let that even be a possibility in his already anxious mind.

Rosie, sitting beside Felix, held his shoulder. "You okay?"

He nodded.

"You sure?"

He shook his head. As he suspected, his lousy attempt to diffuse the tension had failed. His stomach had been in knots for weeks ever since he'd gotten the letter. No amount of time could've prepared him. Today he'd have to use every ounce of strength he had to prove himself worthy of his dream, and if he succeeded, he would soon begin his journey to become all his father feared.

"You'll do fine," Rosie said. "Everyone here is rooting for us. For you."

She gestured to their families. Lydia and Ian sat across the aisle, Lydia napping on Ian's shoulder while he scrolled through his phone. Bringing Tracey into the city would've proven a massive challenge. And without the funds to afford proper daycare, the family counted their lucky stars that Grandma Alicia was free to watch her for the day. Rosie's dads Bennie and David, meanwhile, sat across from Felix's parents.

And all the while, Felix kept trying to avoid so much as glancing at Marcus, seated directly in front of him. Thankfully, Marcus' eyes were shut as he tapped the wall in rhythm to the music blasting from his headphones. Felix found a tad of humor in Aeris being unable to keep her eyes from occasionally drifting up from her book towards Marcus, nor trying to inch away from him. If the one struggle they ever shared was pretending they weren't head over heels for the same guy, so be it. Even if it did spark a bit of jealousy for Felix.

Felix hugged Rosie tight. "Thanks."

"It's what I do. That, and provide commentary."

"Mhm." Felix stopped himself once he took note of Rosie's still-brown irises. "Oh, what about your…?" He gestured to his eyes.

Rosie leaned back. "I'd, uh…" She glanced at the other passengers. As though despite their faces being absorbed by their phones, they were all listening. "I'd rather leave my contacts in, until we get there."

Her concern was fair. Felix hadn't ever actually seen Rosie's natural eye color, as she was too afraid of what might've happened if she removed her colored contacts. She might've been a registered magus, but only the school staff would know about that. As confident as she appeared, Rosie was utterly terrified to think of what might happen should everyone, especially people like the Camo Crew, be able to tell what she was through the color of her eyes. Ever since the day they met, her boldness seemed to regress into timidity.

Felix looked back out into the darkness. "Alright."

The maglev train had remained completely silent the whole trip, rendering the journey so quick, Felix didn't even feel secure dozing off for a while. This was his first time aboard the Long Island Railroad, and he was hoping that seeing the city for the first time might help downplay his anxiety. But even then, he kept flashing back to the coverage of all the Truthseer protests. Heading right into the heart of the MSOU's headquarters didn't promise comfort.

The train zoomed through the tunnel, into the underground beneath Manhattan, but Felix didn't even feel a slight descent. What might it have looked like if the tunnels were see-through instead of solid rock? Being able to view the city from below the waves of the East River, along with all the marine life swimming around, would've been a great sight to behold.

Once the train pulled into Penn Station, Felix, unable to help himself, made his way for the exit. Unfortunately, his escape attempt resulted in him being pushed over the gap by other passengers, right into the shoulder of the person ahead. "S-Sorry!"

The girl simply glared at him. Her faded blonde hair draped over her milky pale face, her contemptuous stare shooting right through Felix, beyond petty annoyance. Yet it wasn't at all like Carson's glare, rife with emotion and hatred. No. This was resentment. The look of bitterness born of depravity, and the drive in your eyes to do whatever it took to claw your way out. It was the look Felix saw in the mirror whenever he hit his lowest point, envisioning what he'd do to Frank with all the power he'd accumulate after attending Dragora.

Without a word, the girl walked off. But somehow, Felix knew he'd be seeing more of her soon enough. *What a great omen.*

Trying to revive his optimism, Felix elected to focus on the sights. Unfortunately, Penn Station wasn't nearly as grand as he'd hoped, signaled by a rat the size of his fist scurrying about as he climbed the steps. The obnoxious lights of coffee shops and fast-food joints clashed harshly against the dim overhead lights, beneath which sat a man in a tattered black coat with tired eyes. Empty pizza boxes and garbage bags overflowing with bottles and cans surrounded him. As he asked passersby for change, everyone simply averted their gaze and kept up a brisk pace, including, much to his dismay, Felix. He raced to both keep up with his family through the underground labyrinth, and outrun his guilt.

He certainly wasn't a fan of how crowded the city streets were. How could anyone drive through these cramped roads without so much as nicking another vehicle, or even a pedestrian? With Manhattan flooded, all the buildings' foundations were below water level. The streets rested above, all shielded through hard light levees: small energy barriers reinforced by magic. Even then, the water wasn't a particularly lovely sight to behold. Gray, murky, and like a thick soup, with any sign of life replaced by crumpled soda cans and food wrappings.

Blinding neon jumbotrons hung from every building, either playing advertisements or, interestingly, calls for magi to join the MSOU. The state knew there'd be plenty of magi in the city today. And surprising exactly no one, they'd made no effort in hiding their attempts at recruiting what they saw solely as potential tools of war.

Those disappointments faded the moment he caught a glimpse of his test's location: the MSOU office. The ground the UN Headquarters once stood upon was now entirely underwater, the East River being held back only by a hard light barrier, much larger than the street levees. There, built right on top of the river, jutting out from the streets, stood the building. Four or five stories tall, and as gray as the rest of the city. But the radiant white light emanating from the roof, extending out into glowing veins running down the edifice and feeding into the barriers, was refreshing enough to lift Felix's spirits just a tad. Ordinary people likely paid no mind to whatever maintained these magical levees, but Felix knew. For a moment, he held a distinct sense of pride by proxy, courtesy of his fellow magi.

But then, the memory of what he'd seen on TV—the atrocity he'd witnessed through his vision—snatched that pride from his clutches and ground it into dust. This was the headquarters of the "task force" trained specifically to serve as the government's lapdogs. To terrorize dissenters into silence and submission, be they human or magus. A mangled vision of the kind of sorcerer Felix envisioned himself becoming, warped into a mindless weapon for those in power. He didn't think the despair could get any more profound.

Until he heard the chants.

Gathered all around the building was a large crowd armed with signs reading "Demons in our midst," "Support our troops, not freaks," "Stop the Next Scorch," and all the such. Their cries, laced with cruel insults and inhumane threats, exacerbated Felix's anxiety. The protesters had targeted a Greyhound bus. Nearly all of its now exiting passengers ranged from young adults to even those in their early 60s, all with purple and gray bloodshot eyes. The exams were specifically meant for magi fresh out of high school or at the grad level, but perhaps that's just how desperate these older folks were to beg their way out of this hellhole. A small security team of MSOU officers herded them through the crowd and into the building.

Felix stepped back, unsure whether to fear what the angry crowd might do to him, or to curse them for the pride they took in their bigotry.

Lydia held his hand tight. "We're here for you no matter what." She looked into his eyes. "This is *your* day. Forget everything else."

Felix, grateful for his mother's wisdom, did his best to march forward. As he and Rosie's families were guided inside, tuning out the crowd's words seemed impossible. "Freaks!" "Murderers!" "Monsters!" The hatred, though rooted in laughable zealousness, was overwhelming. It was as if he'd been pulled back to that fateful day. Back to the hate in his father's eyes. Even once he was safely inside, the now muffled roars and insults still rang his ears.

No. I won't let them make me feel small. Felix's fury subsided as he glanced at Rosie, who looked at the floor and held her wrist. "You okay?" he asked.

Rosie nervously smiled, said, "Never been better!", then returned to her grimace.

Felix scowled back at the crowd. *Just you all wait.* Though his anger seemed a decent motivator, it was probably best to clear his mind for what was to come. Especially in a place like this. He turned to his parents. "Rosie and I are gonna go check in."

"We can go with you," Ian said. He adjusted his glasses, making sure they were perfectly in place, just as his blue buttoned-up shirt and tan slacks. The yellowish overhead lights made the freckles of his dark skin almost vanish, while his buzz cut and stubble contrasted with his concerned frown. "If you—"

"No. We've got it."

Ian nodded. "If you say so."

Lydia kissed Felix on the cheek. "Creemos en ti, mi cielito."

"Gracias," Felix said. "Te quiero, Mami."

Lydia and Ian headed over to the guest area with Rosie's parents. Aeris, eyes glued to her phone, followed behind. *Thanks, sis.*

"What's up with her?" Marcus asked. "She's usually so nice."

Not when it's about me. Felix waved his hand dismissively. "Let's just go, Rosie."

Marcus hugged Felix and Rosie tight. "Best of luck, kiddos!" He walked off, shooting finger guns with Rosie. Felix blushed, turning away to hide his embarrassment, only to have it immediately replaced with self-doubt as he glimpsed the long line of examinees. After checking in with the reception desk for the exam, they were given identification numbers and sent to wait with the others. The queue seemed like a conga line of misery, winding around the dark, narrow corridor, everyone in it either made to stand or sit against the wall.

"Nerves getting to you?" Rosie asked.

"What do you think?" Felix whispered, furrowing his brow. "Sorry. I just… this is my only shot. I can't afford to screw this up." *It's not like I have anything else planned.* All these magi, young and old, had to fight their way through that same crowd outside. They'd all made their way here to try and get into Dragora and make something of themselves. *What makes me any different?*

"You know what this all reminds me of?"

Felix was caught off guard as Rosie held his shoulder.

"When I was eight," she said. "A couple years of living with my dads, they were nervous about taking me to Pride. They weren't sure whether Marcus and I were gonna be safe at something bigots were likely to interrupt. I'll admit, I was scared too. But it turned out to be one of the most fun experiences of my life. Being there, seeing how proud my dads were to be together, and to be there with us… it made me proud too."

Felix nearly teared up at the story. "That's really sweet."

"Plus, having to keep track of Pop's bi flag became a tradition." Rosie rolled her eyes. "Good lord, I love him, but he's more absent-minded than you."

Felix raised an eyebrow. "A bit backhanded, but I'll take it."

Eventually, after everyone turned in their phones (*If there's a God, only They know why*), the examinees were guided upstairs into a small waiting room. Rosie snatched a chair beside a plastic ficus, which Felix was forced to stand by once the other seats filled up in seconds. Swatting away the fake leaves proved his most difficult task yet. There had to have been nearly a hundred people crammed into a space clearly designed for less than a third of that count. He could've sworn he'd seen some of the people here before, and then it hit—the protesters who'd been carted off on the news.

Felix envied Rosie's nonchalance as she kicked her feet, while he wished he had his phone to listen to music. *Breathe. Just breathe.*

"You good?" Rosie asked. "You wanna vent?"

Felix exhaled. "No," he whispered. *That'll make it real.* He hunched over, his back tensing. "How're you not nervous?"

Rosie shrugged. "Guess I'm just not that invested."

Yet you'll probably pass, and I'll fail, like I fail at everything. He glanced around the room, wondering just how many of them would even be admitted to Dragora, if any. He closed his eyes, refocusing himself. *I can do this. I've got Rosie with me. So long as nothing else throws me off my game…*

"Hey, Felix! Smile!"

Oh God no.

Before Felix could cover his face, a flash blinded him, making him jump like a gazelle being chased by a wild manticore. The one holding the vintage Polaroid camera (*Why can't he just use a phone?*) was a tall young man with shining red hair and freckles. "Alec," Felix said through the most half-hearted smile he could muster. "What a surprise." *I'd be happier if I wasn't ready to vomit at any moment. Not from you, but from… everything else!*

Alec's aura hadn't changed one bit over the years, even after his straightened teeth nixed his need for braces. "Long time no see," he said. "How're things?"

"Fine. Just fine." Felix didn't want to be rude. Alec had graduated a couple years before Felix and Rosie, yet while they weren't ever that close, he always made for good company. Minus when he was snapping unexpected photos of Felix dreading his existence. "What exactly are you…?"

"I'm doing an editorial on today's exam for the local paper." Alec paused, registering Felix's air of anxiety. "Uh, I can leave out any photos including you, if it bothers you."

Felix took a sigh of relief. "It'd be appreciated." Alec had grown more sincere over the years. There was a light in his eyes that had grown brighter since the day they'd met, and warmer. That comfort, however, turned to panic at the memory of Carson's cousin. The freezing sensation as his vision went an icy blue, numbness consuming his body. "Uh… y-you're careful when you're out reporting, right?"

"If you're worried about me," Alec said. "Don't be. I know how to handle myself." He flexed his scrawny, nonexistent bicep. "I've had my brushes with death before. Not the least of which being my ex-boyfriend." He shivered before laughing.

"Oh? I didn't know you liked guys."

"And girls, and everyone else." Alec shrugged. "I'm pan. Not that it helps when assholes come in all genders." After a moment, he and Felix both snickered. Rosie simply gave her usual devious smirk, but Felix elected to ignore it. Before he could say anything else, Felix caught a glimpse of something that instantly revived his anxiety: the girl from Penn Station. Gray eyes glaring at him, contemptuous as ever.

Alec glanced over his shoulder. "Oof. She seems nice."

Felix rolled his eyes. *It was just an accident. Sheesh.*

"Attention examinees." The detached female voice boomed through the loudspeakers. "Please proceed to the first exam room."

Jumping from her seat, Rosie nudged Felix. "Here we go!"

"Right," Felix said. *I can do this.* "Dios, dame fuerzas," he muttered to himself.

"¡Buena suerte!" Alec playfully slapped Felix's shoulder, not letting up his obnoxiously goofy grin for even a second. "No es que lo necesites."

Felix raised an eyebrow. "You speak Spanish?"

"Un poco," Alec said. "Pero non bien."

Wow. We really gotta catch up. Felix followed Rosie and the others, not looking back. Whatever was in store for him, he'd need all the luck he could get.

The exam room was roughly the size of the Alderwood gymnasium, which somehow invoked even more isolation and lifelessness. No windows. No natural light. Not even the barest amount of decor to suggest this was indeed a place other people inhabited. Nope. Nothing but cream-colored walls, a marble floor so polished you could slip on it like it was ice, and a harsh chill from the air conditioning being on full blast. Truly, there was no escaping the horrors of the education system. The examinees were ordered into their seats by their numbers, and silently, Felix prayed for mercy.

The proctor—a pale old man in a black suit—stood at the front of the room, his voice echoing as he gave instructions. Before the test began, they'd have to provide the Magus Relations Department with basic information, and permission for them to do God knows what with said information. Several staffers handed out papers, Scantrons, and pens. One such paper struck terror into Felix.

"I hereby agree," it read. "That should I be rejected from the grant program initiative, I consent to attending the International Academy for Magi United, seeing education there through graduation, and then serving at least ten years in the U.S. Magus Special Ops Unit."

Oh, fuck this. He wanted to stand up, tear the paper in half, and tell everyone in the building to go fuck themselves. But if he did... what realistically awaited him afterwards? This was his only true shot at reaching Dragora. If he left, he'd be guaranteed no way forward. Some examinees protested the waver, and upon refusing, were escorted out by fully armed MSOU guards. Did he really want to join them?

Mustering his courage, he gave his signature at the very bottom.

I hope I don't regret this.

Then came the actual questions. Despite the proctor's instructions not to go ahead, Felix's impetuousness got the better of him, only for the universe to punch him in the teeth for his impatience: "What are the element and alignment of your prime pact?"

What in the actual fuck?

"Prime pact," the proctor said, "refers to the elemental pact you were born with. Water, fire, earth, or wind. Your alignment is either light or dark."

Oh. Okay then. "I... don't... know." There. Resisting the urge to scribble in his snarky comment, he bubbled in "Unknown." His ability to laugh away his anxiety faded as he approached the last few questions:

"Why would you like to attend Dragora?" "Would you consider joining the MSOU of your own volition upon graduating Dragora?" "Would you consider relocating to the Medeian Empire as a full citizen upon graduation?"

The first two questions were easy to answer. This was all Felix wanted, and he'd rather have dinner with Frank than become a glorified killing machine. But... what would follow graduation? That question about the MSOU reminded him that here in the States, that was practically all he could do. Yet the idea that an entirely different life could possibly be awaiting him overseas felt even crazier.

After everyone had finished, test booklets were passed out for the written portion of the exam. One hour, forty questions. Should've been easy enough, Felix thought. Until he opened the booklet, of course, and immediately longed for the sweet release of death:

"Approximately how old is the Medeian Empire?

"A. 500 years old.

"B. 750 years old.

"C. 1,000 years old.

"D. 1,500 years old.

"E. 2,000 years old."

How about "F. I don't fuckin' know"?

He nearly let out a groan, but preferring not to cause a scene and broadcast his despair, he kept quiet. *Okay, okay. Let's just skip this question and come back to it later. Next up…*

"What is the major text of Medeism?"

COME THE FUCK ON—*Oh wait, no, "The Book of Medeis" sounds legit. Ha! One down… 39 to go.* The cheerful attitude dissipated once he'd seen two-and-a-half minutes had already passed. *Welp, becoming a military deserter is looking real appealing right now.* At one point he had to wipe away the sweat collecting on his forehead, crack his back as it ached from hunching over the desk, and rapidly blink as his eyes stung from reading the same text over and over. He knew the answers to almost none of the questions, though one of his own stuck out in his mind: *Why am I even here?*

At last, the hour was up. Felix was ready to accept his failure, go home, and cry until he was hauled into conscription. But it wasn't over yet—far from it.

"Would all examinees please follow the proctor to the second exam room."

Fuuuuuuuck.

Rosie rammed into Felix's shoulder. "How'd you do?"

"I want the floor to fall out from under me."

"C'mon! I'm sure it wasn't that—"

"Just give me some space, please." Felix rushed ahead. He didn't want to push Rosie away, but in that moment, all he wanted was for today to end. Whatever could keep his fragile composure intact, he'd take it.

The next exam room was upstairs, far larger, and thankfully equipped with massive windows providing a view of the city and East River below. Unfortunately, there were no desks here. Just dark-blue mats rolled across the floor. If only this part of the test was outside along the river. Some fresh air, along with the sound of bustling life and running water, might've helped assuage his doubts.

This portion of the exam was a "test of basic magical skills," designed to see firsthand the prime elements and alignments of each examinee, and measure their spellcasting endurance. Granted, Felix still had no idea what the hell alignments had to do with this, but at the very least he thought the ease with which a chaotic neutral joke came to mind was a good sign.

Felix's inspector was a woman. Tall, pale, and lean, with golden eyes to match her short blonde hair. He gave his name, and as he bounced on the balls of his feet, she scribbled on her tablet. "Do you know any spells?" she asked.

"Uh… no. But—"

"Just 'no' is fine."

Right. Felix mentally kicked himself.

"Hold out your hand and focus. Repeat after me: Protection of Tides."

Felix closed his eyes, held out his hands, and cleared his mind (as best he could manage). "Protection of Tides." He felt no change in his body. He sneaked a look to find… nothing. Unsurprising.

She scribbled. "Frost Lance."

He closed his eyes and focused again. "Frost Lance." Still, embarrassingly, nothing.

They went on, but Felix couldn't pull off a single spell, each failure dashing his hopes even further than the last. No matter how much strain he put on his muscles, he couldn't even make a measly puff of air. They came to the last spell:

"Fireball!"

A puff of smoke pulsed from his palm. Excited, he tried again, and purple sparks flew from his fingertips. With one last effort, a small indigo flame kindled in his hand, and Felix laughed with joy.

"Nice effort. Though I didn't peg you for a dark alignment."

Felix raised an eyebrow. *So is that basically chaotic neutral, or...?*

"Now, try to make the fire as big as you can, and we'll see how long you can make it last."

He bobbed his head, ignoring the urge to make a crappy sex joke. The fire returned, and Felix stretched his wrist, trying to strengthen the flame. He envisioned his palm as a stovetop, his wrist the dial to light the fire. His arm ached. After only thirty seconds, the fire weakened, his hand shaking, and not even a minute later, the flame died out. Felix found himself panting and covered in sweat.

"A little below average for a cobalt, but still impressive for someone with no background knowledge of magic."

Wow. That still kinda hurts my ego, but thank you!

The inspector let him be until everyone else finished. Comparing himself to others was obviously a bad move, but as Rosie held out her healing spell for what must've been a few minutes by that point, the envy crept back in.

Sighing, Felix fell back onto the mat. He closed his eyes, trying to catch his breath, only to have his respite interrupted as a pair of dagger eyes seared into him. Gray eyes. He jerked up. Before he could say a word, the girl just walked away again, not even so much as glancing back. *What is her problem? Jesus.*

Once everyone had finished, the examinees were moved to the far sides of the room, their eyes all on the proctor circling the center, hands folded behind his back. "Now we move onto the final portion: one-on-one sparring."

I. Want. To. Die.

Each pair would be randomized into several matches: five pairs fighting at a time using standard-issue mythril armor to protect themselves and amplify their powers to a degree. Felix simply sank back against the wall, clasping his hands, begging for mercy.

"Hey," Rosie whispered. "It'll be fine. Just... let your inner raging bitch take control."

He frowned.

"Being your cheerleader is the worst job. Ever." As the proctor called out the first round of pairs, one including Rosie, she winked before heading out. "Wish me luck! Imma kick some ass!"

I'm the one who'll need the luck. Yet even through his shaky nerves, a dopey smile cracked through. *But you got this, Rosie.*

"I'd just give it up if I were you." That same blonde, gray-eyed girl, her voice dry and emotionless, towered beside Felix. She fixed her gaze on the fights. "You don't seem cut out for this."

Felix didn't respond.

"I mean, so long as you turn off your brain and just follow orders, being a lapdog doesn't seem like it'd be too bad."

Felix kept telling himself he belonged here. Rosie carried on in her fight, healing between attacks. If she could handle this, and she believed in herself, then why couldn't he?

"I mean—"

"I'm not interested," Felix snapped back. "Okay?"

The girl glowered, but now, Felix was more than happy to return the favor. Even more so as the next round's pairs were announced: Tilda Schneider, and Felix Brasher. The gray-eyed girl peeled herself off the wall and marched into the fray.

Oh shit. Oh shit, let's do this.

Felix followed, his anxiety now mingling with righteous anger. They donned their protective armor—black foam helmet, vest, and gauntlets; Felix's lined with small red crystals, and Tilda's with yellow—as a barrier went up around them. *Okay, relax. I can do this. Just focus on the match, and—*

"Begin!" the proctor yelled.

Tilda rushed in swinging. Felix ducked, then jabbed. She dodged. In a swift motion, she tossed seeds from her pocket. "Bramble Network!" The seeds sprouted, vines growing forth, tangling around Felix's legs.

He stopped. Before he could balance himself, Tilda knocked him to the ground. Had it not been for his helmet, he'd have cracked his skull.

"Wanna give up now?" she asked.

Felix's grip tightened as his fury bubbled over. "Fireball!" Blue sparks tore through the vines. He jumped. Lungs burning, he swung at Tilda, but missed.

She punched him in the gut. Felix stumbled back, his body aching. Tilda went in for the finishing blow. No way in hell was anyone taking this away from him. Not when he'd survived for this long. He screamed at the top of his lungs, and everything vanished in a swirl of flames. For a split second, the masked man's silhouette came into view, his small phoenix perched upon his shoulder. As the fire extinguished, Felix fell. The barrier around them dissolved.

Was... was that...?

"You little..." Tilda grabbed Felix by the shirt collar. "Were you trying to kill me?!"

"That's enough!" An officer pulled Tilda back. "He cheated!" she yelled. "Somehow, he cheated!" Her face became red with rage, her glower growing more severe. "Cobalts don't have that kind of raw power! I worked my ass off training and studying for this! Not to get hauled off into the military!"

The proctor swept the seed shell remnants in his palm, along with ashes of the charred vines. "Your quick thinking is commendable, Ms. Schneider. But your attitude could use some work."

Felix took some of that time to rest. He had no idea how he released that amount of fire on his own. Yet it had to have been his. It was blue, and the masked man's flames were always orange or red. But that was the furthest thing from his mind at the moment. He couldn't shake the fear that came with knowing Tilda was staring him down, and the guilt of potentially sentencing them both to conscription.

Once all the matches were finished and results recorded, everyone was dismissed, told that they'd receive news on whether they'd be receiving grants in the coming weeks. Hoping to try to make amends, Felix approached Tilda. "H-Hey. You were really—"

She left.

Goddammit.

Rosie slapped him on the back. "Nice job, buddy! That was awesome! Legit looked like a spell pulled from those Dragora tournaments you never shut up about!"

Felix held his neck. "T-Thanks." The Ancient Dragons' Tournament. He'd kept himself from thinking about it for so long. An ancient tradition in the Medeian Empire, where not only Dragora students, but renowned magical athletes would compete until one was crowned the reigning champion of sorcerers: the Dragon Skinner. The tournament was only held once every seven years, the last time being the summer following Frank's disappearance. If Felix hoped of being able to compete at all within his own lifetime, when he knew for sure that being in the Medeian Empire was feasible, it would have to be at the end of his first year of Dragora.

"God," Rosie said, rolling her eyes. "Even when you kick ass, you're still a downer. I'm sure you did fine. Maybe some pizza will cheer you up?"

"Sure." *I can eat away the failure before they drag me away.*

Upon reuniting with his parents, Felix was greeted with a hug from both of them and assurances that he did his best. Aeris, unsurprisingly, remained silent, even refusing to eat at the pizzeria afterwards.

Weeks passed. Nothing, from either Dragora, or the state. At that point, it seemed guaranteed Felix had been rejected, and like any job he'd applied for, they hadn't even bothered telling him outright. That was until the end of July, when an email popped up in his inbox from the Magus Relations Department.

He sat there, staring at the thing and too terrified to click it. Finally, spurred by Rosie's barrage of texts about how she got in, he opened it:

"Congratulations, Felix Brasher! You've been approved for the new grant program…"

Felix didn't need to finish reading. His jaw dropped. He leapt from his chair and shouted, running up and down the stairs yelling, "I GOT IN. I FUCKING GOT IN!" A celebratory dinner of soul food, courtesy of Ian's cooking skills, was enjoyed by all. All except Aeris, of course, who simply went out for seafood without so much as a word to Felix. But even his sister's bitterness couldn't kill Felix's joy. He had done it. He was finally going to the school of his dreams. Now, he had the opportunity to become a truly powerful sorcerer. And for once, he wished Frank was still here, just so Felix could see the look on his face.

That was until he woke up in the middle of the night to the sound of something sizzling, and the rank smell of smoke.

He'd left the window open to let in a cool breeze, and sitting on the windowsill was the phoenix. A note was clamped tightly within its beak. Before Felix could process the sight, the firebird flew off into the violet sky through a hole in the screen, slightly singed and letting off faint fumes.

His stomach dropped out as dread, singing its somber tune, paralyzed his body. Once the shock wore off, he unfolded the note left behind. A cold disquiet crept into his soul.

"You've done well. The power you've sought for so long awaits within Dragora Castle. Our paths will cross again. P.S. The beach is far lovelier at night, especially at sunset."

Felix peeked out the window, staring into the dark and expecting to see that golden mask staring back. But nothing. Nothing but the chirps of crickets and whispers of the wind. He shut his window, lowered the blinds, and rolled back into bed beneath the covers. He shut his eyes tight, silently praying that his fears were wrong.

The black skies and gray-green seas seemed to stretch on forever, merging at the horizon as lightning illuminated the crashing waves far below. Vagus' barrier kept him and Cinder perfectly safe and dry as they flew over the ocean. Yet even so, part of his conscience imagined how quaint a quiet burial at sea would've been. Pulled into the dark depths by the undertow, lost to the tides forever. Forgotten. It already matched the melancholic monotony of his day-to-day life.

From the water emerged eleven black obelisks: eight formed in a circle around three larger central towers. Even with the gibbous moon mostly obscured by the inky-black clouds, the stones glistened with an unnatural light. Cinder perched herself atop the largest stone and, once Vagus dismounted, bathed herself in golden flames, assuming her small form and resting on Vagus' shoulder. "Good girl." He petted beneath her beak as she cooed.

Vagus knelt, placing his palm firmly on the white rock. A purple glyph appeared beneath him. The outer stones glowed, each pair a different color: red, blue, orange, and green. The innermost stones shook, and a whirlpool formed as the central tower submerged beneath the waves. Cinder flinched, though Vagus stroked her wing and shushed her. "It's alright, girl. Steady."

An air bubble materialized around them as the water rushed in. Schools of fish swam past the dome, almost as if observing Vagus from the outside. *The world truly is a giant, unfiltered fishbowl.* Darkness enveloped him as the tower fell beneath the seabed, barely broken shortly thereafter by the dim torches glinting along the walls of the green stone chamber. The platform reached the floor, clicking into place with a deafening boom. Eleven dragons, etched with painstaking detail into the ground, spiraled outwards from beneath Vagus' feet. The art hadn't so much as smudged despite its age.

No taste. A waste of talent.

"Lord Vagus." A young figure, his face obscured by a simple black hood, knelt before Vagus. "The high council has been expecting you." His brittle voice tapered off as he spoke.

"Of course they are. Why else would I be here?" Vagus rolled his eyes, knowing his garb kept him from having to hide his expressions. One of the few things he could keep secret within these accursed walls, and he cherished that.

"Y-Yes. Forgive me, sir!" The young man stood. "Allow me to escort you—"

"I know the way." Vagus strode past, but as his pity caught him, he stopped just before he left the room. This child couldn't have been any older than 18. So much younger than even he was when he entered the fold, docile and lost. If only Vagus could tell this young fool, wherever he came from, whomever he came from, to run as far from this place as possible.

But they could never outrun Her.

"S-Sir…?"

Vagus glimpsed back. "Clean the torches. It's dreadfully gloomy in here."

"Y-Yes, sir!"

The halls stretched on and on, splitting off into different directions every ten steps or so. They wound around and around, spanning countless miles beneath the surface, cutting through coral reefs and trenches. Yet the beauty of the sea was only in Vagus' mind. The tunnels blocked off any visibility beyond the dark, narrow corridors, not a trace of life to be found down here. The eerie silence and coldness even permeated Vagus' cloak, enough to make him shiver. Cinder twitched, to the point even Vagus was unable to calm her, and he shortly found himself sharing that sentiment once he reached the doors to the council room.

This should be fun.

Vagus had always found the council's tastes obnoxiously pompous. The circular chamber's walls were crafted from obsidian reinforced through yellow earth mythril and archaic, needlessly complex glyphs. From the outside, all any divers would see was an empty crater. But from the inside, you could see all the creatures of the depths swimming past, along with the elegant columns of coral the council had spent decades forcing their followers to construct and cultivate for them.

In the center of the room, bottoming out the sloped white marble floor, was a small pool of white crystal. Six white pillars rose around the pool, with a gap to make room for an empty throne of lustrous blue-black stone. Massive bat wings and tentacles jutted out from either side of the chair, and at the top shone a menacing pair of gleaming orange eyes. Even with no one in the room, you felt them watching you. Assessing your worth. Scathing, unrelenting, and patiently awaiting the day they'd finally pass their judgment.

No sign of the "Supreme One" today, it seems.

Cupping his hands, Vagus took Cinder off his shoulder and kissed her on the forehead. "This will be over soon." He set her on the floor, then hesitantly stepped into the pool. A wave of golden light washed over him as his old heart skipped a beat. Any hope of self-defense was eroded the moment his boot touched the water, rendering any and all attempts at spellcasting null and void. Pushing himself, he made his way to the center of the pool. He reached into his bag, pulled out a pink seashell ocarina, worn and slightly chipped from decades' worth of decay.

He played the notes of the summoning song. Glyphs appeared all around the dome and spun as the music echoed across the chamber. Golden wisps in the form of crows flew around, their wings flapping in rhythm with the song. Murders huddled above each of the pillars until they formed six golden figures of blinding light—four male, two female—all looking down on Vagus from the comfort of their anonymity.

"About time." The Welsh accent of the airy male voice, emanating from one of the spires, grated Vagus' nerves. But he didn't dare grit his teeth, even behind the mask. "If I had to wait any longer, my garden would've died of neglect."

Vagus bit his tongue. "Apologies, Your Eminences. But the task is complete. The second candidate will be attending Dragora for the upcoming school year."

"Yes." This voice, female and sickeningly honeyed, rang in Vagus' ears. "Young Mr. Brasher will be on his way soon! How time flies."

One of the male figures, incredibly stern, crossed his arms. "I still fail to see why this child is so significant to us."

"As do I." This voice, also male, but much older and with a heavy Middle Eastern accent, followed immediately. "I resent being left in the dark."

"Be careful whose bad side you get on." The other female figure, her voice hoarse, slouched. "When Salvation has chosen you, it's wise not to spurn Her."

"We must trust Her," a new, relatively younger male voice said. His apparition frantically glanced at his fellow consuls. "Even if we reside on the other side of the world."

Vagus, forcing himself to speak, couldn't contain his curiosity. "Your Eminences, if I may inquire, where is Her Beatitude?"

The Welsh voice scoffed. "Got some gall, I'll give you that. She's still recovering from the latest ritual. But rest assured She'll be hearing of your fashionably late entrance."

Vagus nearly choked up from a deep, guttural fear.

"Now, now, Rhosyn," the sweet voice resounded. "Vagus is our most accomplished and devoted quaesitor. And need I remind you he's helped us locate nearly all our current calathi?"

The calathi: unlucky children considered prodigious enough by the council to serve towards their ultimate mission. Nearly all of them had already been selected, though whether they'd been contacted and either tempted to join their ranks or forcibly recruited was kept beyond Vagus' knowledge.

"Exactly," Rhosyn said. "'Nearly.' Still short on the last pyro, if your memory's failin' you, you old coot. How do we know either of those brats will cut it? Especially considering one of them is…" Vagus didn't need to see Rhosyn's eyes to feel his contemptuous glare.

"This is why we have faith, brother." Her voice turned darkly sweet, almost mockingly so. "In any case, Vagus, you are to keep your eye on our darling Felix once he arrives at Dragora. However you decide which candidate will become our final calathus, please… be gentle. It pays to keep backups, after all."

"Of course." Vagus bowed. "I have faith in Felix. He will not let us down."

"For your sake," Rhosyn said. "Let's hope so."

For my sake indeed.

Chapter Four

Across the Sea

WITH the news that he and Rosie had been approved for the grant program to attend Dragora that fall, Felix could hardly contain his excitement. Yet even so, the "What ifs" festered at the back of his mind, building into a powerful sense of impending doom.

Especially if the masked man had anything to do with this after all.

Still, Rosie insisted they celebrate. So now Felix and his family were getting ready for a small party at her place. While Felix was thankful it wasn't a huge house party, he wasn't too keen on his stepfather and even Aeris badgering him on dressing formally for the occasion. "Do I need to wear this death trap?" Felix asked, his neck chafing as Aeris adjusted the crimson tie.

"Not my orders." Aeris didn't look too happy either. "Blame Ian." She took a step back. Her hair was tied back into a downward ponytail, with her front bangs curled. Her black dress and matching heels made for the perfect attire—for a funeral. And in the coffin: all the fucks she did not give about Felix getting into Dragora (or for Felix in general).

Felix loosened his tie, taking in as much air as he could. "I don't get it. It's not some fancy dinner, it's Rosie's house. That's about as far from formal as you can get." He looked in the hall mirror. Nothing more than a clueless child stared back, silently screaming, "Save me!"

"I think you look like a gentleman." Lydia entered the room. Her dark-blue dress contrasted with her shimmering lapis beaded necklace, while her hair was tied into a bun. She gave Felix a kiss on the forehead.

"Yeah. Qué distinguido." *Qué payasa.*

Ian laughed. "Sarcasm won't make this go any quicker." His thin frame lent itself to his tuxedo, making his limbs appear bone-thin. Despite his frailness, his bright smile, kind brown eyes, and dark skin made his presence warm and sincere, as he'd been since first entering Felix's family's life. He worked as a social studies teacher at Alderwood High School. Funnily enough, both Aeris and Felix had his classes for both their senior years. Felix felt awkward calling him "Dad," but he was certainly more of a father than… Frank.

Tracey, Felix's little half-sister, held onto Ian's pinky. The little rascal broke free, spinning in her sparkling blue gown with white trims and kicking off one of her white sandals. Her coiled black hair was tied into pigtails. Thankfully, her blue scrunchies managed to keep her hair in order.

"Really?" Felix asked, hand on hip. "I thought sarcasm was a powerful magic all its own."

"Hilarious," Ian said. "Welcome to the adult world." He gave Felix a tight hug, to which Tracey joined in.

Felix cracked a smile, kneeling to reach Tracey's height. "Aren't you the most refined young lady here this evening?"

She simply stared at him, tilting her head.

Aeris scoffed. "Did you whisk her costume outta thin air?"

Felix ignored her comment. He'd actually taken Tracey's princess outfit from last Halloween and made a few touches here and there, primarily thanks to Rosie's help and some cheap craft supplies he'd ordered online. Tracey couldn't fully communicate her excitement given her speech impediment, a symptom of her moderate to severe autism, yet Felix could tell she absolutely loved the gift. He just hoped she wouldn't react too badly to him being away for so long once he left. Gods knew Aeris wasn't going to pay her any mind.

Ian gestured everyone outside, locking arms with Lydia once she grabbed her purse and strolling with her out to his purple SUV. Summer fireflies flew on the cool night breeze, lighting up the evening sky. The scene felt like it'd been ripped right out of a romance flick. Simply replace the romance, of course, with food, booze, and inappropriate jokes, coupled with the attire of a questionably affluent middle-class family (which they very much were not), and you had yourself the makings for a good time. Once Felix settled Tracey down and locked her into her booster seat, Ian punched in the directions, and they took off down the road.

Felix sat in the back window seat, resting his elbow against the ledge. Within just a few weeks, he and his best friend would be on a light to the Medeian Empire, and a new chapter would begin in his life. It was too good to be true. Everything felt so surreal, Felix kept pinching his arm expecting to be jolted awake. Though Aeris seemed able to break through his dazes with ease.

"Dude. Exit. The vehicle."

Felix struggled for a few painful seconds before she climbed past him. He did his best to ignore his sister just as she ignored him, helping Tracey out of the car and following his family inside.

Rosie's parents most definitely did not share Ian and Lydia's financial worries. David was a lawyer, evident not only in his articulate, matter-of-fact way of speaking, but also his incredibly dry sense of humor. Bennie, though, was David's polar opposite. Fun-loving, admittedly childish, and most definitely loud. Then again being a streamer, that came with the territory. But together, they'd brought in enough money to buy themselves a two-story house complete with a full garden, pond, and bird bath in the front, a garage, and a massive backyard. The kind of picket fence life Felix at points wished he'd gotten a chance to enjoy, even when he and Rosie would poke fun at the idea.

The Giordano-O'Brien household rang with the sounds of laughter and the smell of a gourmet Italian banquet. Marcus sat on the couch playing some sports game on his console, while Rosie was up on the windowsill with, as usual, her nose deep in a book. Bennie and his mother Marisa drank champagne in the dining room, laughing their asses off at incomprehensible jokes and old stories, with some Italian words and phrases tossed into the mix, while David and his father-in-law Roberto prepared the food in the kitchen.

And not one of them is formally dressed. Point: Felix.

"Evening." David wore his signature pink apron and floral-printed oven mitts. He smirked as his eyes fell upon Felix's family, snickering. "Aren't you all dressed for success? First course is almost done: spaghetti with choice of vodka, marinara, or Alfredo sauce."

Alfredo sauce. Felix could already taste the pasta. *Bless*.

"You missed antipasto, but there's still some Italian bread left on the table."

Roberto's grayed hair was cut short, though with the world's shortest ponytail poking out. His sagging fair skin was offset by a bright-red buttoned shirt. "Assuming those two over there haven't eaten it all yet!"

"Hey!" Bennie cackled like a giddy hyena. His blonde hair, much like his father's, was tied back with a tiny ponytail. He shared his father's paleness, along with his portliness, though with a few freckles. "I get hungry when I'm drunk!" The drink sloshed in his wine glass.

Marisa frowned, the dimples of her light olive skin fading away. Her curly black hair, along with her bangs hanging over her red glasses, was halfway to gray. She knocked Bennie right on the back of the head. "No talkin' back to your father!"

"Ow, alright!" Bennie yelled. "Sheesh, Ma!" David laughed at his husband's comeuppance, much to Bennie's chagrin. "Hey, what're you laughing at?"

"You," David said. "You big idiot."

Bennie trudged over and threw his arm around David, slurring, "Be respectful of the drunkards!" David replied with a kiss on Bennie's cheek, to which Bennie grinned from ear to ear. "See? Was that so hard now?"

"Yes."

Bennie groaned. "*You* are why I need all this alcohol."

The witty banter, the stupid comments, the authentic connection. Felix envied all of it. It was everything he could've dreamt of in a partner, regardless of gender.

"Come over her, piccolo mago!" Marisa raced over and pinched Felix's cheeks, then before he could brace himself, gave him a tight bear hug, "You've grown so much! So proud of you!"

Rosie, still over in her little introvert bubble, glanced up. "Please don't kill him, Nonna. I'll need him intact if I want someone to complain to."

"Oops!" Marisa released him. "Scusa, dearie!"

Felix cracked his back. As much as he found the openly affectionate attitude of the Giordano family endearing, he'd never been able to quite get used to it. "I-It's fine."

"So where are Lionel and Alicia?" Marisa asked.

"Running a bit late," Lydia replied. Felix didn't keep in touch with his grandparents, but they were elated when they heard the news. Lionel, Lydia's father, had flown all the way up from the Orlando Keys just to congratulate Felix in person. Felix hadn't seen him in years. Not since Lydia and Ian's wedding.

"So," Marisa slurred, turning her attention to Lydia and Ian. "You two up for drinks?"

"Can't," Ian said. "My blood sugar's fine, but I'm designated emergency driver."

"More for me then!" Lydia laughed as she followed Marisa into the kitchen.

Ian swooned. "God, I love that woman."

Aeris approached, rocking back and forth, hands folded behind her back. "So, Ian. Can I…?"

"Nope. You're 20, not 21."

Aeris grimaced, situating herself on the couch a couple feet from Marcus, who took no acknowledgment of her presence. Ian, meanwhile, lent David and Roberto a hand in the kitchen, while Tracey followed to watch.

Felix, crouching past the TV as not to obstruct Marcus' view (while psychically demanding his attention), sat on the other side of the couch, next to Rosie. "Salutations, fellow socially inept person."

"Ciao," Rosie said, eyes still buried in her book.

"Any traumatizing character deaths so far?"

"Nonfiction." The cover read, "*Dragora: An In-Depth History of the Sorcerers' Rituals and Agenda,* by Ottavio Acerbi." The name rubbed Felix the wrong way.

"Why're you reading that guy's books?" he asked.

"It's one of the few sources of information I can get on the place," Rosie said. "Aside from their ugly-ass website." She glanced over at Marcus. "Hey, bro." Marcus kept playing, his eyes glued to the TV. "Marcus!"

Startled, he paused the game. "Huh? O-Oh. What's up?"

Rosie shook her head. "You're just going to ignore a young lady in need of a dialogue? Some gentleman." Marcus' expression was blank, to which Rosie pointed at Aeris, who blushed.

"Oh…" Marcus scratched his head. "Uh… hi, Aeris." He nearly blushed in turn. "You uh… wanna play?" He held out the controller.

"N-No thanks," Aeris said. "I'm good." Nodding, Marcus resumed his game, both he and Aeris wide-eyed and awkwardly silent.

As much as Felix wanted to laugh at Aeris' stiffness, he also pitied the both of them. *Maybe I dodged a bullet with Marcus after all.* Roberto called them in for dinner, to which Rosie dropped her book and sprung over the couch. Felix, following her lead, plopped some pasta shells bathed in Alfredo sauce onto his platter, grabbing some soda before returning to the couch. "What'd you get?" he asked Rosie.

"Gnocchi. You need to expand your culinary horizons."

"You got beer, didn't you?"

"No…" She took a sip, relishing in the sophisticated taste, and letting out the most satisfied of sighs. "White wine."

The front door slammed, and in the entrance stood a tall, lean man with short dark-brown hair and a mustache. For a man supposedly well into his seventies, the lack of any wrinkles across his tanned skin gave him a youthful glow. His aqua-blue eyes, matching Lydia's, glimmered. Lionel looked almost exactly the same as Felix had remembered him. Beside him stood Felix's stepgrandmother Alicia, a dark-skinned woman with gray curly hair beneath a shimmering purple flower hat, which seemed an odd choice to go along with her indigo floral shirt and skirt.

"You made it!" Lydia ran up to them, and they met her with open arms. "You're late, Papi." She kissed Lionel on the cheek.

"Only because I had to wait for this one to get herself together while picking her up."

Called it.

"Good to see you, Mr. Elutus." Ian reached out to shake Lionel's hand, only for Lionel to grab him and pull him into a tight hug.

"How many times do I have to tell you? It's just Lionel!" He laughed as Ian squirmed.

Alicia huffed. "No hello to the woman who taught you manners?"

Ian wriggled out, sighing. "Good to see you, Mother."

"You too honey." They hugged. Grandma Alicia was always a little too uptight for Felix's liking, but she meant well. "Felix!" She dashed over and nearly crushed Felix's spine in her smothering embrace.

"H-Hello, Grandmother," he choked out.

"I'm proud of you, sugar!" She took a seat on the couch, forcing Rosie to readjust herself. Rosie said nothing. She merely gave a powerful death glare, not that Alicia noticed.

"Thanks." Felix nervously chuckled. "I mean, it's not much, so—"

"Are you kidding?! It's *everything!*" Alicia's voice must've raised an octave. "Just don't forget the little folks when you're out there, slaying dragons and riding on brooms." She never really understood what a magus was. Terms like wizard or sorcerer were more of an occupation of magi rather than a name for their kind, at least to Felix's understanding, yet Alicia used them all interchangeably. Still, it was leagues better than her wanting to burn Felix alive like the Boyces. Alicia genuinely tried to connect with Felix and show her love and affection, even if it made her ignorance all the more apparent.

Lionel playfully punched Felix's arm. "We're all proud of you, Papito. You're gonna do great things."

"T-Thanks, Abuelito," Felix said. "I admit, it's kinda exciting."

"Kinda? You're going across the sea to a whole other country, and not for a single damn penny! I'd have killed for that at your age."

"It's like going to Hogwarts," Alicia added, clapping her hands. "I know you're the bookish type!" By which she meant nerd, because Felix hardly read anything—least of all the works of a historic author who themselves indulged in a tad of ye ol' bigotry.

Lionel rolled his eyes, then focused on Felix. "This is a once-in-a-lifetime opportunity. To really, truly find yourself. You can't put a price on that." He reached into his coat pocket, revealing a turquoise beaded necklace. From the chain hung a teardrop-shaped pendant. The aqua-blue stone shimmered, almost obscuring a small crack running through it. "This was your abuelita's. Since she died, I've carried it with me every day. It keeps her spirit with me. And now…" He placed the necklace around Felix's neck. "She will be there to guide and protect you."

Felix had never met his abuela Ava. Even Lydia hadn't, given Ava passed while she was so young. They'd both heard stories about her through Lionel; how the two of them fought tooth and nail to bring Lydia here to America, to give her a chance at a better life. As headstrong as Lionel was, he was nothing compared to Ava, whose golden heart gave her the courage to yell "¡Que te folle un pez!" at an MSOU border agent in Matamoros before dumping his entire squadron into the Rio Grande. Lionel had many qualms with Frank, the least of all him being a Protestant. But no way in hell Ava would've tolerated his nonsense.

"… Thank you."

"Promise me that you'll make the most of it," Lionel said.

Felix was a bit taken aback. He'd been so fixated on his spite all this time, he hadn't given much thought as to what else could've awaited him at Dragora. The sights to see, the people to meet, and maybe even a girlfriend or boyfriend. He had no concrete idea of what he'd do upon graduation, but he had four whole years to figure that out. No need to rush.

"I promise.," Felix said.

"Good. Now, if you'll excuse me, the food's calling." Lionel headed into the kitchen, followed by Alicia once she gave Felix one last peck on the cheek. Felix held his face, his mind returning to his grandfather's words.

I promise.

Felix lay in bed, scrolling through his phone in a desperate attempt to escape his insomnia, as well as his boredom. His room was still a mess of tossed clothes and slanted anime posters, the red walls now rendered purple from the absence of light. He knew he'd have to pack all his belongings sooner rather than later and just get it over with. His procrastination was not born of a lack of motivation, but rather his continued disbelief this was really happening.

He'd been texting Rosie earlier. Not about Dragora, but just exchanging endless memes as usual, only for her to sadly doze off not too long after midnight (*Weakling.*), leaving Felix in search of something else to keep him company. He mulled over the party's events, returning to Lionel's advice.

At long last, his tongue parched, Felix dragged himself downstairs into the kitchen, cursing his bed, door, and all the wooden floorboards as they creaked. Once at the bottom of the staircase, he squinted until his eyes adjusted to the darkness. The kitchenette, dining room table, and sofa solidified from hazy mirages into black silhouettes. He crept towards the fridge, placed his plastic water bottle beneath the slot, and activated the switch, to which the fridge responded by gargling like a dying virtual pet.

"Look who's still up."

A chill ran down Felix's spine. Every hair on his body stood on end. He held the bottle as if it were a sword, ready to bludgeon the unholy demon back into the infernal pit from whence it came. Lydia, in her blue nightgown, stood right before the bottle, looking ready to burst into laughter. "I knew you were a night owl," she said as she pushed the bottle away. "But I never took you for an attempted murderer."

Felix put the bottle on the counter. "Sorry I woke you up, Mami."

"I was already up." She kissed him on the cheek. Felix, realizing he'd just spilled all his water, grabbed some paper towels and got to cleaning. "You stressed?" Lydia asked.

"Just a bit."

"Then paint me a picture." Lydia waved her hand halfway through Felix's cleaning. "Don't worry about that. Ándale. Hablemos." Complying, Felix sat at the round wooden table, at whose center sat a stack of bills. The grandfather clock next to the TV ticked as the pendulum inside swung back and forth. "So," she said. "What's on your mind?"

Felix clasped his hands. He wasn't sure what to say, as he couldn't pin where his hesitation was stemming from. Of course there was the masked man, but Felix didn't want to raise alarms if it wasn't necessary, especially if it meant losing his only chance of going to Dragora. Or worse, worrying his mother. "I don't know," he said. "I'm excited. But… what if I'm not good enough?"

Lydia leaned in. "Is this about your father?"

The question stunned Felix. "What? No, Ian's a good guy. He didn't—"

"No. I meant Frank."

His father's words came back with a reckoning, along with the roaring flames, and the phoenix's squelch. After Frank's disappearance, Felix couldn't care less whatever had happened to him. They'd sometimes pass the charred remnants of their old house, which lay vacant since their departure, rumored by the town to be the "cursed pyromancer house." To Aeris, it held memories of a bright childhood lost in a horrific blaze. But to Felix, its ashes were the leftover scraps of his old cage. He clenched his fists beneath the table. His eyes fell downward. "What's he got to do with anything?"

Lydia held Felix's shoulder. "Mira, I know you've wanted to go to Dragora for so long. And I am proud of you for never letting go of that. Pero… you can't live your whole life driven by spite."

Felix searched for a response.

"Do you remember what I told you that night? Before…?"

"I… think so. 'Be true to yourself,' or something like that? I, uh… actually haven't learned how to say that one in Spanish. I mean, I can try, but it'll probably sound like I've got a golf ball stuck in my throat. Would make it more dramatic, I guess."

"Mijo…" Lydia's tone cut through Felix's deflection. "You can't hold onto this forever. I want you to be happy."

Felix held his forehead and hunched forward. Tears rolled down his face; the same tears that rolled down 12-year-old Felix's cheeks every night after that day. The day he cemented his resolve. *No. That fucker will not make me cry again.* He sniffled before dabbing away the drops with a napkin. "I'd be happy forgetting he ever existed." He looked into his mother's eyes. "I promise, he's as irrelevant to my life as I'm sure he wishes I was to his."

Lydia teared up. "Te quiero, mi cielito."

"Yo también te quiero, Mami." He got up and hugged her tight. Through it all, the twelve years under Frank's roof, and the last six in the aftermath of it burning down, his mother was his biggest reason to keep moving forward. Even more so than his hatred. He wanted so desperately for her to be happy, and she finally was with Ian. And moreover, he wanted to make her proud, and now, at long last, he had the chance to do so.

"Don't mind me." Ian stood in the kitchenette in his pajamas, holding a glass of water while spreading peanut butter over some apple slices. The mess Felix had left behind had seemingly been tidied up in an instant. "Just getting some late-night snacks. And yes, dear, before you ask, I checked my blood sugar."

Felix broke into a laugh. *This is why my stepdad and I are practically best friends. We are the same person.* "Way to kill the moment, Ian."

"Now, now," Lydia chimed in. "Only I have the right to degrade him."

And now my mother has beaten me at my own game of being the snarkiest person in the room. Well played, Mami. Well played.

75

"Thankfully the food doesn't judge me," Ian said while chewing. "Want some, Felix?"

"Nah." Felix waved his hand. "I'm gonna try to get some shut-eye." He headed upstairs, chiding himself for not appreciating his mom and stepdad until he was so close to leaving them for an entire school year. Almost. As he leapt back into bed, making himself comfortable, he made his decision. No longer would the negativity of whatever he faced control him. He was about to go on the adventure of a lifetime with one of his favorite people in the world, and nothing in the world could've ruined that.

Welcome to Dragora

GOD, I wish I could fly there.

  The thought had crossed Felix's mind countless times during the eight hours he'd spent crammed into the small airplane chair. He would've appreciated the window seat if the sun hadn't blinded him, though while the sea of clouds wasn't the most captivating of sights to behold, he preferred it to any kind of prolonged eye contact with other people in the aisle.

Even the thought of the plane being attacked by rogue familiars during the journey, while always a legitimate threat, felt exhilarating. Especially if it meant getting to see the MSOU in action. That'd be a welcome spectacle as opposed to agents hiding somewhere on the plane amongst the human passengers, or just committing old-fashioned murder. The most exciting part of the flight was the turbulence as the plane passed through the barriers while leaving Long Island and entering the Medeian Empire.

Rosie was knocked out with a book in her lap. Thankfully she didn't snore, but the guy on the far right was a different story. His snoring, coupled with the cries of children—*God help the parents*—rang through Felix's headphones even at max volume.

Felix spent the past hour reading up on his classes. Most were mandatory for first years: History of the Medeian Empire 1 and 2; Intro to Magical

Technology; The Roots of Medeism. The only electives he'd managed to squeeze in were two fashion courses, apparently taught by famous international designers Dezirae and Videl Labelle. His magical technology professor, one Gennadi Pasternak-Ivanov, had his own blog dedicated to, of all things, conspiracy theories.

Joy.

A blip startled him. Aeris texted, "Don't die by jet lag." (*It's something, I guess.*) Lydia hadn't sent anything, though Ian texted him three basic requests: "1. Don't do drugs. 2. Don't have sex. 3. If you *do* have sex, use protection."

Thanks, Dad. Felix still had issues in calling Ian his father off the cuff, but he did appreciate him. Even before Felix's plane took off, Lydia had cried her eyes out, and thankfully Ian knew by that point to bring extra tissues. He fit right into the family dynamic.

Yet even with all the good things that had come along in the last six years, Felix still couldn't erase the memories of his first twelve years of life. Scars that would never fully heal. And now, closer than ever to the school of his dreams, he wandered back to the masked drifter's words:

"What does the name Dragora mean to you?"

Felix closed his eyes. *It's where I can become all I'm meant to be. Where I can become the sorcerer I've always wanted to be.*

"The power you've sought for so long awaits within Dragora Castle."

Tell me. Felix envisioned the masked man seated right beside him. *Who are you? How do you know me? And what do you want?*

"You'll find out soon enough."

Felix nearly jumped out of his seat. The voice echoed in his head, as real and audible as though the man really was there, standing mere inches from his ear.

"Attention passengers. We'll be arriving at the Enchanted Dawn Airport in a few minutes. Thank you for flying with us, and welcome to the Medeian Empire."

A hand brushed past Felix's face. Rosie yawned and stretched, and Felix pushed her arm away. "Morning, sunshine," he said.

"Is it morning?" Rosie cracked her back. "I can't tell."

"Yep. Our day's just begun."

"Wonderful." She cracked her knuckles. "So tired."

Felix raised an eyebrow. "You slept through the whole fight."

"Exactly. Life's so unfair."

"Whatever." Felix stared out the window, ready for whatever awaited him on the ground. *We're finally here.* The plane descended through the clouds, and a strange hybrid of a bustling metropolis and an ancient capital came into view. Skyscrapers clashed against old stone buildings. The mixed emotions over the hodgepodge, however, vanished as Felix's eyes wandered towards the cliff beyond the city limits. Atop the peak sat a shining golden castle. Statues of dragons adorned the towers and rooftops, and magnificently vibrant gardens filled the massive courtyards. Here he was at long last: the Dragora Institute of Magic.

If only he was here. Felix sat back in his seat, unable to help himself from savoring the thought of how much Frank would've hated to be here. To see Felix here, thriving. *What I wouldn't give to laugh in that fucker's face.* The spite festering in Felix died down as he turned to Rosie. He tilted his head, puzzled by the fact her eyes were still disguised as brown, but elected to leave it be.

He was simply grateful to be here, and that his best friend would be right by his side. Rosie specifically made it her mission to get Felix ready for a fresh start with a new wardrobe. Felix usually tended towards darker colors and baggier clothes. But now he found himself wearing a well-fitting pink T-shirt with burgundy jeans, which boosted his confidence a bit. As it turned out, clothes really did hold the power to bolster your ego, as did his grandmother's necklace. The crystal pulsed between his fingers. With its beautiful blue shine, it served as a charm for Felix's composure.

Rosie, meanwhile, wasted absolutely no time in upgrading her style. A black-and-gray plaid buttoned-up T-shirt and salmon pleated skirt, complete with pink heels she had no problem running in (or threatening her enemies with). She even gave her hair light-brown highlights and braided it into cornrows.

In all honesty, Felix loved the experience. Rarely did he ever treat himself to anything, especially clothes. So the fact he had this great opportunity, along with his insane interest in fashion, really did help him feel he was truly ready for a new beginning.

Upon landing, they shoved their way off the plane to fetch their belongings. The conveyor belt inched like a snail. Once it came 'round, Felix grabbed his suitcase, and Rosie snatched her cat-themed rolling case. The plush ears and whiskers were bent from the trip. "And you say *I'm* immature?" Felix asked.

"Cats are perfect. Besides, it means a lot to me. Reminds me of home." Rosie waved her hand. "Not to mention it's super practical. No hassle in trying to find it."

"Except in mixing it up with a little kid's case," Felix said. "Make sure there's no diapers in there, alright?"

Rosie furrowed her brows. "How dare…" She unzipped her bag, looked inside, and closed it. "Okay, we're all good."

"'Scuse me." The voice caught Felix off guard. A tall man greeted him as he spun around. His black hair, crudely tied into a ponytail reaching down to his waist, swept over his dark-bronze skin. Bangs slightly obscured his golden eyes. His goatee caught Felix's gaze, as did his toned biceps peeking out from his black muscle shirt over loose gray sweatpants. "I think you might've…" He held up a suitcase identical to Felix's.

Collecting himself as quickly as he could, Felix examined his case: a hot pink name tag read "Argent de la Mort." He could feel Rosie's devious smirk without even having to turn around to see it. "O-Oh! Sorry about that! Guess I was in a rush. I'm just grateful to be off the plane, you know? Ready to go out there and see the city! Starting the first year at Dragora strong!" He cut himself off so abruptly, he practically knocked the wind out of his own lungs. All he could do was chastise himself for droning on and on like this in front of… whoever seemingly nice hot guy was.

Argent. His name is Argent. I just read his name tag. FUCKING DAMMIT, SELF.

"No worries. I'd have done the same if I hadn't checked." They exchanged suitcases, and Felix was sure to avoid any hand-to-hand contact, so much so Rosie wouldn't stop snickering. "Nice doll by the way." Argent pulled out a small plushy of a girl with snow-white hair, icy-blue eyes, and a flowing white dress.

Felix gasped, snatching the figure.

"Feisty, are we?"

Felix's cheeks were red hot, and Argent's strange mixture of Scottish and Middle Eastern accents added to the intimidation (and most certainly the infatuation). He tossed the plushy into his suitcase.

"Relax," Argent said. "I don't judge." His smile instantly melted away Felix's anxiety. "Nerd out to your heart's content."

"O-Okay," Felix said. "Hey, are you going to Dragora too?" He paused. *Self, what the fuck are you doing? Why would you ask that? You are such an idiot, I swear!*

"Yep. My second year."

Felix jittered in a mix of stress and excitement. "Cool, us too!"

Argent raised an eyebrow. "I… I know. You said that."

In the eons Felix felt paralyzed by shame trying to formulate a response, Rosie threw her arm around him. "Yep. First years, and remarkably unproud to hail from the States!"

Please don't tell me you're hitting on a guy we just met. Wait, am I doing that? Fuck.

"Ah, I see." Argent stroked his goatee. "You got freebies, right?"

"Y-Yeah." Felix could barely breathe. "We got lucky. I personally don't think it's fair, but you know." *Then why would you be here, you dolt? Great. Now I'm a freeloader, a hypocrite, AND an idiot!*

"I don't see it that way. I think it's great more people get to come here. Even more if it pisses off the stuck-up rich kids."

"Good." Rosie held out her hand. "We won't have any problems then."

Argent left her hanging. "Not with me." He turned his attention back to Felix. "But you probably wanna keep it under wraps around certain people. 'Specially Gottschalk."

"Goat chalk?" Felix asked.

Argent snickered. "Gottschalk," he enunciated as slowly and obnoxiously as possible (which nearly made Felix swoon). "Medeism professor. She's a real bitch." He looked around. "But you didn't hear it from me," he whispered loudly.

Felix and Rosie nodded.

"Might I ask from whom I've been given the honor of a luggage mix-up?"

Felix stuttered.

"He's Felix, I'm Rosie," she cut in. "Nice to meetcha." She held out her hand again, this time waiting for a fist bump.

"Argent." Again, he left Rosie hanging. "You need help getting to the school?"

"No," Felix said. *SELF!*

"Sure!" Rosie said, nearly jumping. "Why not?"

"Then it's settled," Argent said. "Let's go."

I don't know whether to be grateful to Rosie or curse her name. Wait, what am I even doing? What do I want? Why am I here— oh shit, they are walking away. Felix rushed to catch up, all the while trying to keep himself from outright running. "Though we have to stop by the post office and grab our wands." *Apparently they're too "dangerous" to be allowed on flights. I mean, yeah, they are, but it's inconvenient so fuck all y'all.*

"No problem," Argent said. "We can use the streetcar."

"The what now?"

Argent led them outside, and Felix was in awe of the city of Cendrillion's beauty. Far more beautiful than Manhattan, without the streets suspended above the water and all the advertisements constantly shoved in your face. And surprisingly, all of it was built on the modern grid layout of most American cities. Thankfully, the lack of a need for hard light levees meant there was much more room to walk. There weren't even any cars. People simply walked or cycled, whether on the sidewalks or through the roads. The only comparable vehicle moving through was a red-and-gold streetcar reading "Della Luce."

"This is so cool!" Rosie looked around like a wide-eyed child on a sugar high.

Up close, the city felt far more charming than Felix had ever anticipated, and far more welcoming than anything back home. "There are actual stores here, too!" he said. Restaurants, supermarkets, and even a massive library were dotted about the street, and through the storefront windows were actual clerks behind the registers. No sign of automation anywhere. "You think they'd have the textbooks in the library?"

"You waited 'til the last minute to get your books, didn't you?" Rosie asked.

"No. But I *was* tempted to sell my kidneys to buy them." Felix's parents already had to pay for a plane ticket and a cheap wand, along with sending the wand to a completely different country on another continent. He couldn't bring himself to ask them for any more than that. And even beyond that, he wanted to ensure he kept all his savings untouched for emergencies. He'd planned on sharing books with Rosie or any classmates willing to help. The embarrassment, though, still hit him like a truck.

"Unfortunately if you're on a budget," Argent said. "You're outta luck. Nearly all the school's textbooks are sold outta the Spring of Light bookshop, and they charge a fortune. Special wee little deal from what I hear, given the Della Luces—or as I like to call 'em, the Lightheads—own nearly everything here. Case in point..." He gestured to the streetcar. "I had to buy a season pass just to use it whenever I need. Avoid the hassle with another hassle."

Felix let out a heavy sigh. "Great." *Even here, money still fucking sucks.*

"What do you need?"

"It's for History of the Medeian Empire. I forget the author's name, but it's supposed to be an autobiography."

"By Veronique?" Argent asked.

"Y-Yeah, that's it." Felix held his chin. "Does she have a last name, or...?"

"It's a pen name," Rosie said.

"Oh." *Felix, you dimwit.*

"I'll get you a copy," Argent said. "Hate giving those assholes my money, but I hate people getting screwed over by them more. And you'll need a copy of the Book of Medeis too."

"O-Okay." Felix's guilt swelled. "You don't have to—"

"Don't be so uptight." Argent waved his hand. "My way of educating the youth. And anything else you need, just say the word."

"A-Alright. Thanks." Felix had always hated asking for things, but in this circumstance, he couldn't really argue. Putting it out of mind, he followed Argent and Rosie to the post office for their wands. Rosie's was a shining silver right out of a fairy tale, while Felix's was a low-grade ugly brown, the cheapest they could find online. Not like buying a wand in the U.S. was easy in the first place. They only managed to bypass all the rigorous licensing crap because Felix was attending Dragora. *If only it was an assault rifle. Then I'd have it in my hands no question.*

Argent cringed at Felix's wand. "You sure you don't want a better—"

"It's fine," Felix said. "It'll do the job."

"Alright. To the bookshop!" Argent took off.

Rosie nudged Felix, smiling. "You know, I'm pretty sure he—"

Felix rushed out. *No. No, no, no. I am here to learn. Fuck emotions.*

The words "SPRING OF LIGHT" almost glowed in the sunlight above the bookshop's recessed entrance. Once inside, they headed up the spiral staircase to the second floor. The place was surprisingly quiet for the afternoon. Though Felix didn't know how much drakons were worth in comparison to dollars, the book couldn't have been cheap given Argent's constant looks of "Yikes" at the price stickers along the shelves.

"What trash." A boy over by the window held a purple-and-silver book. The cover read, *A True Reflection: The Dark Underbelly of Medeian Society*, by the one and only Veronique. The boy was about Felix's height, with slicked hair so blonde it looked bleached, which matched his beige trench coat. Beneath the coat was a dark-red sweater vest, tan slacks, and black dress shoes. His eyes looked glassy: silvery white irises with a faint hint of peach, easier to notice thanks to the scorn in his stare. "How could we possibly carry this slander?"

Oh god. Is there no escaping the stuck-up rich white kids, even in a land of magic?

Argent marched up to him. "Can't handle the truth, Lighthead?'

The boy glowered. "As much as you can't handle minding your own business." His attention drifted to Felix and Rosie. "I'm assuming you're both attending Dragora as well? It'd do you well not to fraternize with lowlives such as this one." He pushed past them, mumbling, "I pray to Seraphina you heed my advice." He carried himself as if he was royalty. His eyes were bottomless, like a spiral leading down to a white void.

Rosie crossed her arms. "Blowhard."

"Who was that?" Felix asked.

"Lucas," Argent said. "One of the Della Luce kids."

"As in… the people who own…?" Felix pointed up.

"Yes." Argent cracked a gin. "They own the ceiling. Nothing else."

I'd find that funny if I wasn't so on edge. "So I'm guessing he gets discounts on all his stuff?"

"Or puts it on Mum and Dad's tab." Argent shrugged, grabbing copies of the books Felix needed and handing them over. "You alright?"

"Yeah. Just thinking." Felix grimaced at the books, weighing down on both his arms and his conscience. "Are you sure about this? I can—"

"Don't stress it." Argent headed downstairs.

Rosie held Felix's shoulder. "What's up?" she whispered. "Are you sure you're—"

"It's nothing." Felix followed Argent. He still couldn't bring himself to look at the register or listen to the cashier state the price, keeping his eyes on the books even as Argent announced they were good to go.

"Is he always like this?" Argent asked.

Rosie looked on with concern. "Kinda, yeah."

Argent sighed, holding his forehead. "In any case, the coaches should still be running up to the school."

Felix's guilt faded as confusion took hold. "Coaches? How old fashioned is this place?"

Argent snickered. "The Lightheads make a killing in transportation 'round here: streetcars, ferries, *and* the coaches to and from Dragora. Since the castle's a decent hike from here, their coach service is the only practical way to get back and forth to save on time without killing your feet. It's no pumpkin-turned-carriage, but the path has a nice view over the cliffside."

"Oh." *Might as well look for the silver lining.* "That sounds pretty cool."

"And the spark returns to his eyes!" Argent playfully hit Felix's shoulder. "Good to see you're no longer comatose." They made their way to Della Luce Coach Services, a rather small yellow building where, on the inside, students stood in a line through several zigzagging barriers waiting to purchase carriage tickets. All that before going to *another* line towards the back leading outside. And unsurprisingly, everyone was complaining about the wait times and ticket prices. Some grabbed papers from the newsstand. Papers which read, "Lightspring News," and it took Felix all of one guess to figure out which established family published the empire's news.

"You weren't kidding," Rosie said. "Is this really the only way to get there?"

"No," Argent said. "Not unless you feel like dying on an hour-long uphill hike. Trust me, I've tried, and I've got the scars from the blisters to prove it."

Felix twiddled his thumbs, the guilt returning. "You... gonna cover this too?"

Argent scoffed. "How selfish of you to assume." Again, he played up his accent.

Felix hung his head.

"Wow. You really can't take a joke." Argent held up his card. "As if I'd let my two new minions exhaust themselves on that hellish trek."

"I'd like a promotion." Rosie held her hip. "And a raise."

"Tell it to the union." Argent paid for the tickets, and after a solid 20 minutes of waiting, the misfit trio's carriage pulled into the dirt lot outside. Its silver wheels spun, carrying its azure body with golden trims. At the front, pulling at the conductor's behest, strode a white horse with light-blue fins. Argent opened the door and bowed. "Ladies first."

Rosie climbed inside. Felix tried not to blush as Argent held his hand out, giving a gentleman's bow. "Really?" Giving into Argent's courting, Felix coyly took his palm. He lost his footing for a second, then rushed inside, hoping Argent hadn't noticed. He sat beside Rosie, and Argent sat across.

The horse neighed and pulled the coach uphill, past trees and bushes, along with another coach headed back down. Felix could see what Argent meant as he glimpsed other students taking the uphill hike to the castle. Each one of them looked exhausted, and hardly kept pace with the coaches. In the valley past the cliffside was a vast forest with a flowing river. Trolls, ogres, and orcs (Oh my!) roamed the basin, while multicolored sprites flew above the forest. Mermaids swam through the river. And off in the distance, high above the mountain crest, flew great dragons, whose beastly roars carried all the way to the coach.

Felix tensed up. "That's the magical creature reserve, right? Home to all types of familiars? I had no idea it was so—"

"Amazing?" Argent asked.

"Terrifying."

Argent crossed his legs. "Better get used to it. You'll be headed down there for one of your beast hunting classes."

Rosie sat up, her eyes sparkling. "Do we get to tame dragons?"

"Um... no. Not first-years."

She fell back and pouted. "Dammit."

"But..." Argent waved his finger. "You *will* be making some wisps of your very own."

"Wisps?" Felix asked. "Are they like familiars?"

"Eh..." Argent shook his hand to and fro. "Familiars are a hassle to create. And once they take form and turn sentient, they're basically living things of their own. Way too much for first years to be trying. Don't want any loose dragons shagging and leaving stray whelps everywhere."

"I mean, that I understand. But... what's a wisp then?"

"They're like…" Argent stroked his goatee yet again. "Temporary familiars. Kinda like spirits in the shape of a familiar that you can make on the fly."

Instantly, it clicked, and Felix's face lit up. "They're summons!"

"Uh… I guess?".

Gods, I'm such a fucking nerd. But maybe he found it cute. Felix scratched his head. "But it sounds way better than dying in the reserve."

"Pretty sure the administration agrees," Argent said. "Lord knows they don't wanna get sued for getting a kid burned alive. Again."

Felix's blood chilled. "A-Again?"

"I kid, I kid." Argent struggled to contain his laughter. "I had a whole story planned out, but oh well."

"Okay then," Felix said. "So what's that horse-looking thing up front?"

"A kelpie."

"I've heard about those," Rosie said. "They're these weird-ass water horses. But that one doesn't look like the ones in the legends. Usually they're darker with mangled hair and tentacles, and they love to drown people for fun. Stuff of nightmares, it's great."

"Ironically," Argent said. "That one pulling our carriage is only nice-looking cuz it was inbred."

Felix and Rosie went silent.

"You've heard of purebred dogs, right? Same with these guys. They can't swim for shit. Fins are completely useless. The rich folks here absolutely love seeing what new breeds of familiars they can cook up."

Felix cringed. "That's—"

"Horrifying?"

"Yes. Horrifying."

"Is there a magical equivalent of P.E.T.A.?" Rosie asked. "Without the mismanagement?"

Felix's eyes drifted to Rosie's. "Oh yeah, Rosie. Do you feel comfortable…?" He gestured to his eyes, while Rosie simply held her arm. "I-It's okay," Felix said. "You don't have to if—"

"It's fine." She held her phone like a makeshift compact, removing her colored contacts before replacing them with normal prescription lenses. Her irises glimmered in their true violet radiance. Felix was taken aback. This was the first time he'd ever seen the eyes of his friend—his best friend. She raised her head. "I—"

"I get it," Argent said. "People suck."

"You deal with that kinda stuff where you're from?"

"Yeah. It's not as bad in Britain as it is in the States. Much more… subtle. Unfortunately, idiots know no borders."

Rosie hung her head. "I just don't wanna cause a problem."

"You're not the one to blame—humans are." The anger in his eyes unnerved Felix, especially when Argent turned to him. "What about you, Felix?"

"Well…" Felix didn't want to lie, but he also didn't want to spout off his history to every person he'd just met. This was his chance at a clean sleight. Why let the sorrows of the past weigh down on him now? "No. Not really."

Argent shrugged. "Makes sense. You pass for human."

"Yeah." Felix slouched. "My magic isn't the best, so—"

"Oh no, I meant your eyes."

Felix looked up. "Huh?"

The coach jerked up to a stop as the kelpie neighed. Argent led them as they climbed out, though Felix took a moment to process Argent's words.

"Tip for the coachman?" A short, gray-eyed man held his hand out to Felix, tapping his boot in the dirt. "A man's gotta make a living. One cobalt to another."

"Cobalt?" Felix asked.

"I got this." Argent handed the man a tattered bill.

"Thank you, good sir," the man said. "Welcome to Dragora."

Students walked through the courtyard, up the stairs and ramps, past great golden columns supporting the roof. Daylight broke through the lobby's stained-glass windows, the tiled dragons iridescent in the sun. After double-checking with security over their registration, students were directed by staff members through an open set of double doors, and Felix, Rosie, and Argent followed and seated themselves at the very back. The auditorium was packed to the brim. Row after row was rife with the chatter of anxious students, some of whom had to sit in the aisles. Dragora clearly wasn't used to housing so many pupils from outside the empire.

"WHAT'S THIS FOR, ANYWAY?" Felix had to shout over all the noise to be heard. And still, he could barely hear his own voice.

"JUST A GENERAL 'WELCOME' THING," Argent yelled back.

"GOOD. FOR A SECOND, I THOUGHT WE'D HAVE TO SIT THROUGH SOME LONG LECTURE. THEN WE'D BE FUCKED."

The entire room went dead silent just before Felix's final word, whose echo rang across the hall. A woman in a lavender suit stood at the podium. Her glare sent Felix sliding back, begging for whatever cruel god ruled over him to show mercy and smite him right then and there.

The woman's stern posture and gaze assured Felix so long as he kept quiet, he'd be fine. Her suit, freshly pressed, was accented by a white flower, whose seven peach-colored petals swirled out. Her darkly tanned skin was slightly wrinkled, almost as if giving the impression she was constantly fatigued in spite of how she carried herself. And her black hair, beginning to gray at the roots, flowed down into a ponytail reaching the center of her back.

Then, in a heartbeat, her frown turned into a warm smile. "Glad to see you're all eager to begin the year." Some students laughed. "I'd like to welcome incoming students to our prestigious institution. I'm Headmistress Ramidha Hakim, and I hope you find your time here to be educational, productive, and above all, transformative." She went on addressing policy and guidelines: no entering the magical creature reserve and other restricted areas without authorization, no "illicit substances" in the dormitories, and no "frat parties" (despite Dragora having no fraternities, nor sororities).

Professors rotated between speeches, including some Felix had read up on. None of them stood out, as they all gave the standard pleasantries and poorly timed jokes that made approximately two students laugh in a room of hundreds. The highlight, ironically, came from the one professor Argent had warned Felix and Rosie about: Gottschalk of the Goat Chalk.

She sauntered onto the stage like a queen. Her silvery, semi-transparent sleeves reached down to her wrists, decorated with rose-gold flower and vine patterns, coupled with her long, ruffled white dress flowing down to her white heels. Her corn-yellow hair was braided like a golden crown, shining beneath the stage light. Likewise, her milky-white skin was rendered ghostly pale. But most arresting were her eyes—irises piercing Felix's mettle like icicles. The severity of her aura alone gave the impression she was the personification of a blizzard. Delicate and fragile at first glance, like freshly fallen snow. But once you were unlucky enough to piss her off, you'd see through the storm's eyes just how unrelenting, unforgiving, and cold she truly was.

I'm gonna fuckin' hate her class, aren't I?

"I'm Professor Isolda Barnas-Gottschalk." The syllables sounded like musical notes. The notes of not a symphony, but a requiem. "I'd like to extend an olive branch to those who join us thanks to our beloved headmistress' recent grant program. She fought tooth and nail to hammer out this deal with the Brooks administration, and she believes you will all thrive here in the… 'magus' homeland." She looked disgusted with herself. "Even though it's clear our school's infrastructure may not be designed for it."

She gave a patronizing simper. The room grew colder. Some students even snickered and booed. Beyond that, not so much as a whisper of confusion. The whole room felt suffocated, as though a glacier was sitting before them all, ready to sink them at the slightest provocation.

"I know not all of us agree, not even amongst the faculty. However, what's done is done. The best we can do is continue the proud traditions we've kindled for centuries. I urge all of you to carry yourselves honorably in our school's great name." The crowd applauded as she walked offstage, albeit hesitantly. Even Felix clapped, afraid that if he didn't, he'd be found frozen alive in his sleep.

After a brief conclusion from the headmistress, she dismissed the students to situate themselves before classes started in a few days, advising them "not to stay up too late having too much fun." She winked, and as hokey as it was, it was a welcome change to Gottschalk's Ice Queen routine.

A horde of students poured through the aisles towards the exits. Argent suggested they wait, but Rosie retaliated with a loud "FUCK THAT" and pushed her way through the stampede. Eventually, Felix and Argent followed her into the lobby, where she awaited with her arms crossed and foot tapping. "You guys have no hustle."

"No," Felix said. "We just don't like bulldozing our way everywhere."

Rosie shook her head. "So Argent, you know your way around here?"

"Want a tour?" Argent asked.

"Obviously!" Felix yelled, cutting off Rosie. Whatever anxiety held him back from showing his excitement quelled itself as his voice rose in pitch. "I wanna see every nook and cranny of this place. Secret corridors, ancient libraries. Oh, and that observatory I've heard so much about!"

Argent held his hip. "You might be setting the bar a little high."

"Whatever." Rosie yawned, waving her hand. "But can we save this all for another day? I'm beat. Jet lag is hell."

Argent shrugged, looking unbothered. "What about you, Felix?"

Felix held his chin, mirroring Argent stroking his goatee. He'd spent so long staring at low-res image galleries of the school, and now, he was finally here, holding the reins. "Oooh, how about the hall of illusions?"

Argent raised an eyebrow. "The Chamber of Kagami? Don't expect to go in there unless you've got a divination class or something. And even then, only in large groups with a professor."

Rosie laughed. "Did you cook up another story about a kid who died in there?"

"Nah," Argent said. "Just dangerous for novices. Illusion magic's nothing to sneeze at."

"Fair enough."

"Oh, plus the demon haunting it."

Rosie's face drained of color.

Argent's grin spread from ear to ear. "Afraid of ghosts?"

"She won't even look at a Ouija board," Felix said. Her reaction nearly made him bust a gut. Since they'd known each other, Rosie had sworn up and down her house was haunted. Something about a kid who died on train tracks a few miles out. Why would this child have decided to haunt a house completely unrelated to his death? No one knew. But as far as Rosie was concerned, one unexplained knock on the wall was enough to exorcise the specter with a pitcher of holy water.

"No!" Rosie pouted. "It's all parlor tricks and placebo effects."

"Then it's settled," Argent said. "We're getting one."

Rosie's eyes nearly popped out of her skull. "Do you *want* to die?!"

Felix scoffed. "I thought you said—"

"Shut up!"

Argent clapped. "Anyway, we should get you both settled into your dorms. What houses are you in?"

"House Ley," Rosie said.

"Pyre," Felix said.

"A child of nature and a pyro," Argent said. "Huh."

"I can handle myself," Rosie said. "You two enjoy your tour. Imma go snore." She yawned even louder this time, giving Felix an obnoxious wink as she headed off. She switched her cat rolling case into a backpack and strutted down the corridor. Her voice echoed across the lobby: "Don't do anything illegal!"

Felix turned to Argent. "So, House Pyre then?"

Argent stared at the ceiling, thinking to himself. "Actually..." If Felix had a dollar for every time Argent stroked his goatee while pondering, he'd be able to buy a dozen oxygen tanks with all the air he used up swooning over it. "I know the perfect stop before we hit your dorm!"

Felix felt comfortable around Argent thus far, so he felt no hesitation in brandishing his usual arsenal of dark humor he shared with Rosie. "Does it involve me waking up in a tub of ice with one or both my kidneys gone?"

"Ha-ha. Funny. Trust me." Argent held his thumb to his chest. "I've got friends in moderately high places."

"Encouraging." Felix followed Argent outside into the inner quad. A stone path cut through a grassy field, surrounded by red stone walls. In the center of the court stood a large fountain of four kelpies (the nice-looking inbred ones, of course). Topiaries decorated the gardens, complemented by stone columns and birdbaths. "So Argent, which house are you in?"

"Sican. You know what that means, right?"

"I'm not an idiot," Felix tensed up. "Sorry."

"What's up with you apologizing all the time?" Argent asked.

"I mean, I was—"

"No more a dick than me. Yet you swing from saint to smartass at the drop of a hat."

Felix shrugged. "Just how I am." He hoped this wouldn't upset Argent any further. "Anyway, I'm pretty sure I've pieced together the houses. Pyre is fire, Sican's water, Ley is Earth, and Zephyr's wind. You get put in the element you're born with."

"And lemme guess. Your prime pact's with Seraphina?"

"Uh... prime pact?" Felix recalled the term from the exam, but no one ever sat him down and fully explained what it meant. Particularly, the term alignment.

"You don't know who the hell Seraphina is, do you?"

"Nope."

"Did your parents never talk to you about this?" Argent asked.

"My dad is…" Felix slowed his breaths. "Human. And my mom doesn't like talking about magic."

"Makes sense. A lot of magi decide to keep their mouths shut. Rather forget about magic and blend in with the humans. I'd never be able to myself, but that's life." Argent's words struck a chord with Felix. Whenever magic was brought up, Lydia went quiet. Deathly quiet. She'd usually sleep away the pain, and even after she met Ian, the scars remained, as did the silence. The last thing Felix wanted to do was tear open old wounds. His mother's happiness was far too important to risk. "You seem to lose yourself in thought," Argent said. "A lot."

Felix furrowed his brow. "What makes you—"

A metal clang rang through his bones. Without even realizing it, he'd strayed right into one of the lampposts, and now his aching head was paying the price. He stepped back and let the pain sit with him.

"Are you alright?" a female voice asked. "Let me help!" Light filtered through Felix's closed eyelids. As he opened them, a girl with brown skin, wavy black hair tied into a short ponytail with a purple butterfly barrette, and metallic-gray eyes came into view. Her giant black glasses clashed with her small nose. She sat him down on the bench.

Felix held his head. Just like when Rosie healed him all those years ago, the pain faded. "Did you heal me?" he asked.

The girl blushed. "Y-Yes. I mean, it was the least I could do." She was almost as docile as Felix was as a kid, and it seemed rather endearing. Her air of innocence was accentuated by her bright-purple blouse and pastel-pink poodle skirt. In her hair was a large pink bow.

"Thanks," Felix said.

"I'm Argent." He plodded over to them. "This is Felix. We appreciate the help." Despite his words, his lips rested in a thorough grimace.

The girl's hands trembled. Argent didn't seem too intent on scaring her as much as slightly unsettling her. But by the way she carried herself, a deer could've given her a heart attack. "Can I ask your name?" Felix inquired.

"I-I'm Zahra," she said. "Nice to meet you."

"You too." Felix smiled twice as much to make up for Argent. Zahra was kind of cute, looking like she couldn't hurt a fly. "Are you a first-year?"

"Y-Yes!" Zahra stuttered, looking around nervously. "I mean, I've been here before, but never attended. I mean, I am from here. But not *here* here. The Medeian Empire, but not Cendrillion. Well, my parents live here during the school year, but otherwise we live over on Zephyr Isle." She scratched her head. "And I don't really know anyone, and my mother says I'm too shy for my own good, but…" She let out a deep sigh.

Felix empathized with her feeling out of place. "No worries! You've got a couple friends right here. Right, Argent?"

Argent rolled his eyes, but gave into Felix's frown. "Sure."

"Thank you." Zahra checked her phone (complete with a purple, pink, and blue polka-dotted case). "Oh! I should be going now! Maybe I'll see you both around sometime?"

"I'd like that," Felix said.

Smiling widely, Zahra ran off.

Argent groaned. "She's a real talker."

"She hasn't let me walk face-first into a pole yet." Felix gave a devious grin. "Solid ten points, minimum."

"Whatever. We're nearly there."

"*There* there?" *Oh, now I see why Rosie has so much fun messing with me.*

"Funny," Argent said. "You'll see." As they walked, Felix checked his necklace, just to make sure it was intact, or the crack hadn't worsened. "Jeez, you want me to buy a new one for you? That atrocity looks ready to crumble into dust at any second."

Felix held the necklace tighter, then loosened his grip, worried he'd crush it just as Argent suggested. He'd normally have made a quip about this kind of offhanded comment. Or, in less malicious conversations, simply explain why the item was so dear to him. But instead, he simply shriveled up, then continued.

Argent guided Felix over towards an old man seated on a bench. His saggy pale skin seemed thinly coated with dirt, as did his pale-blonde beard. An old, slightly worn gray cap barely concealed the thinning hair over his balding scalp. His lumberjack flannel shirt, dark-green overalls, and muddy brown boots clashed against the garden's serenity. As they approached, a scar came into view. It ran all the way from beside the old man's left eye down to the right corner of his lips.

Felix was certain this old man had five ticks on his body count, minimum. "Who's the creepy old dude?" he whispered to Argent.

"Relax," Argent whispered back. "That's Ol' Samuel Baisley, the groundskeeper. Basically like a janitor, except grumpier and he never cleans anything." Clearing his throat as loudly as possible, Argent waved. "Hey there, Samuel!"

"What do you want, Argent?" Samuel's voice croaked every other syllable. "Can't you see I'm busy?" He tossed a handful of crumbs onto the grass. A squirrel ran up, but didn't eat the food Samuel offered. Samuel held out his palm, filled with crumbs, but whether he was smiling was impossible to tell beneath his beard. The squirrel smelled the gift, only to knock them out of Samuel's hand with one smack of its tail before scampering away. Samuel leaned back against the bench, sighing. "Fuckin' dick squirrel."

Argent snickered. "So—"

Samuel pointed at Argent. "I ain't hidin' no bodies."

"Chill, Samuel. I just need into the Chamber of Kagami."

Felix's jaw dropped. "You were serious?"

"What do you take me for, a liar?" Argent asked. "Don't tell me you're afraid of ghosts too."

"N-No! Of course not." One of the few shreds of information Felix could gather was that this place, the Chamber of Kagami, was often used by high-level sorcerers to channel spirits or master illusory magic. In Felix's mind, the sooner he could get acquainted with the chamber and exposed to those kinds of spells, the better. Even if the thought was beyond intimidating.

"You oughta be afraid, boy." Samuel stood, cracking his back with an unsettling snap. "Kagami don't play nice with folks who spurn her name."

"Say what now?" Felix asked.

"Oh, never mind the old coot," Argent said. "Ol' Samuel here just loves his superstitions."

"'Specially when he's right about 'em," Samuel said. "But knowin' Argent, you kids won't leave me alone 'til I let the spirits off you, so let's get this over with."

They followed Samuel inside, climbing five flights of spiral staircase—which made Felix long for death as he hauled his suitcase up the steps (and also cursed Samuel for his weird fear of the elevator's they'd installed within the castle)—and heading down a long dark corridor lined with torches. A

95

corridor that looked like it'd been ripped straight out of an old Dracula movie. Shadows danced in the flickering torchlight, wrapping the hall in a breathing darkness.

An uneasiness stirred in Felix. "Are you sure about this, Argent? Is this safe?"

"Of course. If anything goes wrong, Samuel's right here to get you out." Samuel scratched his back. "Don't need more lawsuits."

More?!

"And it's Groundskeeper Baisley to you youngins. Gotta hold onto what little prestige I got." He grumbled about his "pompous little brother."

"Yeah, yeah." Argent waved dismissively, turning to Felix. "The chamber's designed to respond to your instincts. Reads your mind like a nosy bugger. So whatever you do, keep calm. I know that's hard for a pyro, especially given your…"

"Ambition?" Felix fluttered his eyelashes. "Drive? Passion?"

"Smartassery."

They reached a pair of massive doors at the hall's end. Upon the dark-blue stone was carved an eastern dragon, its tail coiled the silhouette of a woman with hair flowing all the way down her back, turned away from those approaching. Samuel took out a set of what had to be a dozen keys, holding up a copper one with the face matching that of the dragon on the door etched into it. He turned the lock. Thunder boomed all around as the doors opened wide, revealing a pitch-black interior pouring out a faint mist.

Felix backed up. "Oh. Hell. No."

Argent grabbed Felix's shoulder. "You got this. Besides, we're right here."

Felix gulped. But not wanting to embarrass himself, especially in front of Argent, he nodded.

Samuel examined the doors. An eerie sense of foreboding surrounded him, and if something scared this guy, then there really was a reason to be afraid of whatever awaited inside the chamber. "One cobalt to another," Samuel said. "I wouldn't be doin' this." His eyes were dark gray, like the conductor's, and like Zahra's. "Forget it, you'll be fine. Just go before you say or do somethin' that makes me change my mind."

Opting not to ask, Felix marched into the darkness. A cold wind rushed over his body. The dread was so strong, his instincts told him to double back.

But it was too late. The entrance had vanished, lost to the darkness. He now stood, directionless, within the void.

"Felix?"

The voice, soothingly maternal, faintly echoed across the space. A mirror appeared in the distance. Despite the lack of a reflection unnerving him, Felix reached out to touch the pane, only to pull back as his fingertips froze upon contact with the glass. Despair flooded his soul. Hopelessness, as pervasive as the darkness. The only other feeling he had was that someone, or something, was watching him, staring him down. Yet no one was there.

"Felix."

The voice resounded. Lydia appeared in the mirror, a tear on her cheek shining through the glass. Felix reached out, wanting nothing more than to hug her, but the second his finger tapped the glass, it cracked. The cracks spread. With a deafening crash, the mirror shattered. The force sent Felix falling back, plunging him into the abyss as the mirror's shards spiraled around him. Then, with the audible snap of fingers, the glass went up in a blazing vortex.

Felix hit the ground. The slam sent pain shooting through his body. His muscles burned, his legs and chest aching. He curled to cover his face as he gasped for air.

"Burn!" The deep voice let out a bellowing cackle. "Burn, you little freak!"

A figure with cold, scathing eyes emerged from the orange fire: Frank. The fire lunged forth, lifting Felix up in a pillar of raging flames. The inferno reached deep into his core. Every part of his body felt like it was being reduced to cinders. Searing pain was everywhere, unrelenting. And through it all, Frank's laugh cut through the roaring flames.

No. Felix would've cried had the fire not evaporated his tears. *You won't win. You will not win.*

He opened his eyes, and a spark ignited within him. A deep-blue flame grew within the orange. In a flash of firelight, the column disintegrated, sending Felix falling with a thud. His hand still burned. And yet this flame was blue, and it didn't hurt. It didn't feel like fire. It felt like power.

As a new fury took hold, Felix yelled as he leapt forth, extending his arm like a wolf's claw. He knocked Frank to the ground, encapsulating his body with the azure blaze. The fire intensified as Felix yelled again. As he heaved, he stood over the burning body, and when the flames cleared, Frank's body shriveled. But it didn't look like Frank anymore. It somehow became... smaller.

Then, looking closer, he found his body was no longer Frank's—it was Felix himself. Or rather, his twelve-year-old self. The smoldered child's eyes shot open, bloodshot. Felix screamed in horror, and a pair of hands grasped his shoulders. He fell back, finding himself inexplicably back in the hall. Samuel shut the doors. Argent knelt next to Felix, keeping his head from cracking on the floor. "Are you okay?" Argent asked.

Felix panted. "Never. Make me do that. Again." Argent helped him to his feet. "Nothing's broken." No bruises, no burn marks. Nothing. He was perfectly fine. Physically, at least.

"What'd you see?" Argent asked.

"I..." The memories were difficult to gather, almost as if when Felix sought them out, they scurried away from the light. "I saw fire. A lot of fire. And..." The corpse flashed in his mind, enough to make him feel queasy. "That's it."

Argent sighed in relief. "I'm just glad you're okay. I shouldn't have—"

"Glad to see you give a shit. Even if it's not that much." As petty as Felix wanted to be, he couldn't keep up the front. He chose to go in there; taking it out on Argent didn't feel right. "Sorry. But uh... I really wanna go to my dorm. Get some rest."

Hesitantly, Argent bobbed his head in agreement. "You got it."

After what felt like hours, they finally made their way to House Pyre. The large red door was covered in golden flames. At the center was the Crest of Pyre—blue and orange flames swirling around each other, similar to the yin-yang symbol.

Inside was a circular room, at whose center stood a statue of two dragons entangling each other and spitting fire into the air. This was one of the castle towers, and so the dorms were all built in the outermost ring, surrounding the common area. Suspended walkways separated each level of dorms, and three sets of spiral staircases connected them at both ends and the middle. Thankfully, both ends also featured freestanding elevators (which Samuel probably feared more than squirrels). The tower's ceiling was a skylight, from which dangled a golden chandelier with blood-red jewels, each one shimmering like a candle. Felix would've been more impressed had his visions in the chamber not left him so groggy.

"Afternoon." A young woman approached. Her black uniform with the Crest of Pyre sewn into it, along with her hands tucked behind her back, gave her the air of a military officer, or perhaps even a general. That attitude clashed with her light red hair, which cascaded into gold further down her long ponytail. It wasn't clear which color was dyed, or both. Her eyes were like Lucas and Gottschalk's: pearly irises, though hers had a warm red tint that appeared less... inhuman. "I'm Ornella Fontana, prefect of House Pyre. Welcome." She glared at Argent. "You do not belong here."

"Why my dear and respected Nella'rela," Argent said. "I'm simply showing this little rascal his way. I'll be out as soon as—"

"Your assistance isn't required. I'll show him to his quarters." Ornella's eyes narrowed. "I suggest you hurry to your proper place, Mr. de la Mort."

"Fine, fine." Argent winked at Felix. "See ya, Felix. Play nice with Ms. Nella'rela here."

"You. May. Go."

Argent folded his hands behind his head and whistled as he left, giving Felix one last over-the-top wink.

Ornella sighed, the tension escaping her body as she eased up. Felix somehow felt for her. She seemed uptight, but also incredibly stressed. Something heavy weighed down on her mind, and Ornella appeared to do everything in her power to hide it and remain in control. He knew that tendency well.

Felix gave her his name, after which she guided him up five flights (*WANT. TO. DIE.*) and seven doors down. The dorm was about two or three times the size of Felix's bedroom back home, and nowhere near the size he expected from the common area. There were no spells for manipulating physical space or creating pocket dimensions, as much as Felix wished, so more likely this was simply the result of airtight blueprinting.

A rich maroon wood paneling covered the floor, with a loft at the far end fit for two queen-sized beds. Beneath the loft were bookshelves with two writing desks fit with lamps, which Felix could only assume were powered by magic, given they had no wires or cords. A couch and two love seats sat over a red carpet, all right in front of, as improbable as it seemed, a fireplace along the wall. The chimneys all around had to be connected, and the smoke could simply be guided up and out from the top of the tower using wind glyphs. Felix had read up enough on those to have a basic understanding that if magi needed to mimic technology, glyphs were the way to go.

But what really caught Felix's attention was his roommate, sitting on the couch and nose deep in a book: Lucas della Luce, the boy from the bookshop.

"Lucas," Ornella said. "Meet your roommate."

Lucas tossed his book onto the coffee table. "Finally. I was admittedly hoping I'd end up getting the dorm all to myself."

"I suggest you not complain. Unless you'd like me to notify your sister and aunt."

Lucas sighed, returning to his apathy. "Who might this be?"

Ornella turned to Felix. "Go on. Introduce yourself."

"R-Right." Felix held out his hand, silently praying Lucas wouldn't recognize him. "Nice to meet you! My name's Felix." Lucas simply ignored the gesture.

"I remember you from the bookshop."

Fuck me, am I right?

Lucas examined Felix, looking on as if he were pitying a stray cat, contemplating whether to give it scraps. "I hope you heeded my advice about staying with the right crowds."

"I…" *Might as well make the most of it.* Calling upon all of his terrible experiences, Felix forced a smile. "Certainly appreciated it."

Lucas simpered. "Lucas della Luce. A pleasure."

Ornella put away her tablet. "Lucas, see that Mr. Brasher meets the expectations of our house. I expect nothing less from you." She closed the door behind her.

"Would you like assistance unpacking?" Lucas asked.

"No," Felix said. "Thanks, but I'll be fine."

"Very well." Lucas returned to his book, kicking his feet up on the coffee table. Felix stood still, trying to get a feel for Lucas' personality. He didn't seem to be the friendliest person, but he wasn't terribly arrogant like Argent made him out to be. "Can I help you with something?" Lucas didn't even glance up, and Felix stepped back.

"S-Sorry! I…" Felix searched for the right words, doing his best not to turn his roommate into his new mortal enemy. The last thing he needed was a goddamn nemesis. "Your family owns that bookshop in the city, right?"

Lucas hesitantly nodded. "And the coaches. And the streetcars. The ferries, the papers, and the news channels. And yes, before you ask, even the kelpies." He shivered. "Dreadful practices."

"So… why were you there? Do you… get discounts?"

"Contrary to what your friend Argent might tell you…" Lucas shut the book. "No one gets handouts here. I work there part-time. I don't mind the labor; I find it quite rewarding, if tedious at times." He looked into the fireplace. "I just wish it weren't because of my parents that I held the position."

"Oh, uh… okay then." Abandoning his line of questioning, Felix climbed up to the loft, somehow managing not to fall and die while carrying his suitcase (only to realize there was a small lift on the side of the room he could've used). He put his clothes in the wardrobe on his side. The nicer looking bed had already been claimed, and was in complete disarray.

"Perhaps rooming with a cobalt won't be as bad as I thought," Lucas mumbled.

Not even gonna ask. Felix jumped into bed. His eyes wandered to the window behind him, sunlight fading, the sky now a light orange. It was now late afternoon, though it felt like the dead of night. *Damn jet lag.* He closed his eyes and rested his head on the pillow. Try as he might to relax, the image of his younger self's charred remains had burned itself into his memory. Eventually, he drifted to sleep, his true first day having yet to begin.

"Sleep well."

Chapter Six

Eyes Don't Lie

THE YOUNG BOY'S FACE was charred like coal, covered in ash. His eyes opened—bloodshot. His dry, raspy gasps gave way to a shrill banshee scream.

Felix flung out of bed in a cold sweat, panting heavily. That image from the Chamber of Kagami had been rearing its ugly half-burned-half-decayed face every night since. He was almost thankful when a new, far less impending doom took hold. *Fuck, I've got classes today.* Lucas' bed was empty, and the clock read 7:55 a.m. *Thanks, buddy. Appreciate the wake-up call. Whoever invented 8 a.m. classes should be burned alive.*

He tossed on his uniform: a pale-gold button up t-shirt, coupled with black dress pants and dark-brown leather shoes. The red cardigan overtop bore the Crest of Pyre. He nearly tripped as he grasped the doorknob, hesitated, then chastised himself for his assuredly bad memory, rushing back for his notebook, textbooks, and wand. Cradling them in his arms as best he could, he ran. His unkempt hair bounced. A fierce growl erupted from his stomach, but he shushed it. *No time for breakfast when your life's a mess! Sometimes starvation is a necessary part of getting your shit together!*

It was in fact not. Breaks are vital, kids. Don't be Felix, unless you wanna wind up… well…

Felix raced to the first floor, repeating the room number in his head. *114. 114.* He threw open the classroom door and, using his belongings as a shield between himself and the floor, fell forward with a resounding thud. He flailed trying to gather his things, only to drop them yet again as the sound of an old man clearing his throat caught him off guard. The shame engulfed him once more as the class snickered.

The man, Professor Gennadi Pasternak-Ivanov, sat in his wheelchair, chuckling. His stocky build matched the general pear shape of his body, stretching his light-blue buttoned-up shirt. The shadow under his black cap slightly obscured his thin glasses and lilac eyes. His gray, untamed beard, so long it reached halfway down his belly, looked like it hadn't been shaved in who knows how long. Then again, from what Felix had gathered from Ivanov's conspiracy theory blog, it was likely he thought barbers would collect tiny blood droplets for some secret vampire cabal.

"I hope you're not expecting extra credit for that entrance." Ivanov's croaky voice, through his thick Russian accent, nearly cracked through his chortles. His cheeks were so red, he looked on the verge of howling with laughter. "Though it *was* hilarious."

Only the first day, and already Felix was cast the role of the stereotypical problem student he'd hoped he could've avoided. He rushed to collect his items and stood. "S-Sorry, sir."

"Damn right you are! Now take your seat."

Felix complied, sitting in the only open seat in the front row. The whole room seemed to be rife with contradictions. Instead of desks, there were metal benches lined with stools in place of ordinary chairs, above which hung work lights and garish green goggles. Towards the back of the room were large industrial sinks and cabinets. Precisely what you wouldn't expect from an ancient castle for magicians, but exactly what you'd anticipate for a class all about technology. It was enough to give Felix war flashbacks to workshop classes from middle school.

"Nice entrance," whispered the girl on Felix's left. Her bright-golden eyes stood out amongst her pale white skin with faint freckles, her black glasses, and her short chestnut-brown hair. Her uniform bore the Crest of Pyre. She gave a crafty grin through her English accent. "Really, a great first impression!"

"Maybe if *someone* was kind enough to wake me up…" He leaned around to shoot dagger eyes at Lucas, who simply ignored him. They'd had no issues in getting along thus far. To the contrary, Lucas seemed mildly happy about having most of their classes together. But this put a sour taste in Felix's mouth immediately. The only solidarity he could find was in how exhausted the boy beside Lucas appeared to be, bags under his golden eyes, his curly brown hair clearly unbrushed and his skin as pale as a ghost. The boy's head fell, tucked into folded arms. *I'd kill for even an extra bit of sleep right now. How I envy thee. And also a Long Island bagel with a truck load of cream cheese, my God.*

"That's enough," Ivanov said, mumbling offhandedly in Russian. "You're all adults, and I expect you'd like to be treated like adults. I also expect you to get that you're all stuck on this miserable rock together. So you might as well make the best of it and not act like jackasses."

The girl snickered. As much as Felix wanted to call her out, he couldn't help but agree with Ivanov's sentiment.

"I'll bet you've all heard of me," Ivanov continued. "The crackpot who spends way too much time wondering whether jet fuel could melt steel towers instead of talking about curriculum." Felix anticipated some kind of message behind the conspiracy theories. Perhaps a unifying theme of skepticism, or thinking for yourself.

But nope. Just Ivanov rambling on and on about his mind's maniacal machinations, including some mention of a secret society. Eventually he got himself back on track, discussing the broader impacts of magic on modern technology: vehicles running on mythril rather than solar or wind; electric systems relying on glyphs rather than circuits and wires; jet fuel not being able to melt steel nearly as well as advanced fire magic. (Some first impressions do turn out to hold water.) But through his entire lecture, not once did his jovial demeanor let up.

"Now everyone take out your wands, and take 'em apart!"

What the fuck?

Despite his apprehension, Felix, along with the rest of the class, did as Ivanov instructed. *Please dear God let this wand stay intact.* The process was easier than expected, not because of the wand's ergonomic design, but rather its frankly poor construction. Parts chipped off even with his gentle approach. Metal plates surrounded the wand's base, and inside was a small clear red orb.

"That little glass ball," Ivanov said. "Is the wand's core. While most wands have a normal core, like this young man's here…" Felix flinched as Ivanov pointed at him, nearly dropping the orb as he expected to be humiliated for doing something wrong. "Higher-end wands are custom-built. When you cast a spell, you're taking that potential energy and channeling it through your body. The core makes it easier, acting like a catalyst. Custom cores, like Mr. della Luce's…"

Lucas held up his core. The ball gleamed, shining through its deep crimson. An orange insignia, some serpentine creature, appeared in a flash before vanishing.

"Are specialized for your element and power source, be it light or dark. Of course, you can use magic without a wand, but since most people like not dying from exhaustion, I personally don't recommend it. The cores themselves are crafted from mythril, a special material with magical properties, and a magus' most vital tool. The wand uses Hyper Spell Casting Language, or HSCL, to cast spells quickly. The stronger the spell, the more complicated the 'code' will be. So while you *can* use spells on instinct without a thought no problem, more complex spells, and definitely glyphs or oaths, will require thorough HSCL knowledge. There are additional languages stemming from Base HSCL for different elements, hence why you can't cast a fire spell the same way you'd cast a water spell."

Felix raised an eyebrow. *Coding? For magic?* Thankfully this "thorough knowledge" wasn't mandatory, because Felix dreaded the thought of needing complicated algorithms in order to spellcast. Or, God forbid, math. But if it was necessary to advance through the ranks and become a full-fledged sorcerer, Felix was ready to haul ass and get it done… in his second year, of course. Honestly, it seemed all the fun stuff—creating new spells, glyphs, and familiars—were saved for the later years anyhow.

Ivanov went on about having been a "spell engineer," but once he'd seen that most of the class had checked out by that point, he checked his watch "You know what, forget it. Class is over. Hope you all learned something, if you cared enough to stay awake." Though most of the students left immediately, the sleeping boy beside Lucas drooled heavily. A truly revolting sight.

"Ugh." Lucas shook the boy. "Ulrich? Ulrich, wake up already!"

The boy raised his head. "Huh? What? Did the apocalypse finally come?"

Lucas, groaning, dragged Ulrich behind him. Felix almost felt sorry for Ulrich, and he really was starting to question his previous perceptions of Lucas. The chestnut-haired girl shook her head, not a shred of empathy in her eyes. "Surrounded by weirdos."

And assholes. Felix returned his attention to his wand. He had another class right after Ivanov's, and he couldn't afford to be late again. Putting the wand back together proved a challenge, though, as it absolutely refused to cooperate. The pieces wouldn't click together, instead falling onto the workbench. The metal clang reverberated with shame and embarrassment in Felix's ears.

"You having trouble?" the girl asked.

Felix raised his head hesitantly. His first day was already off to a poor start, and there was no way he was going to let it get worse. He didn't fully register the girl's expression, nor whether her voice was laced with sarcasm, or sincerity. Rather, he swept the pieces of his broken wand into his bag in one fell swoop. "Nope."

"You know, I could help if you—"

"I said I'm fine." Without even glancing back at the girl, Felix left. *It was cheap anyway. Probably ready to break right outta the box.* Wanting to put the last hour out of his mind, he focused on getting to his next class: History of Medeian Fashion.

He made his way upstairs. Unlike before, he made sure to be early. *So much for being fashionably late.* This room was just as spacious as the last, but replace the industrial tools with vibrantly colored fabrics hanging everywhere like makeshift drapes. Felix sat at the empty round table in the back, genuinely excited for a course he actually got to choose. Most of the students present were girls sporting designer bags, with a handful of guys here and there. A mixture of preppy and artsy kids, just like his fashion class at Alderwood, which made the room's atmosphere oddly nostalgic.

But as much as Felix wanted to focus on the positive, the lack of anyone to talk to, and the ever-growing fears at the back of his head should he have been unable to spellcast in future classes, compelled him to check on his wand. A crack ran through the cheap core. Somehow, it appeared even duller than before. It hadn't even been used, and it was already nothing more than an ordinary stick. *Scratch that. It's too broken to even be a stick anymore.* Was it even worth the effort of fixing if it was going to break again so easily?

"Hey, Felix!" This surprise was thankfully a breath of fresh air. Zahra, the girl from the other day who'd healed him, walked over. "Mind if I sit with you?"

"Not at all," Felix said. *That's one friendly face so far today.*

She sat. "I didn't expect you to be taking this class."

"I took a fashion class back in high school. Easily the highlight of my days."

"Really?" Zahra's eyes lit up with excitement. "Could I see some of your designs?"

"Uh… sure. Oh, I have some of them on my phone!" At this point, Felix was ready for any opportunity to live up the day, and if there was one thing he took unshakable pride in, it was his designs. He scrolled through his gallery, past old memes and ugly attempted selfies—*Why haven't I deleted those yet?*—to his proudest accomplishment: his fashion illustration final. A pink floral shirt with black sleeves down to the elbows, beneath a black-and-gray vest, completed by a pleated red asymmetrical skirt.

"Wow!" Zahra's eyes sparkled. "You designed that yourself?"

"Yeah." Felix scratched his head, suddenly ready to tilt the spotlight away from himself. "It's not that great, but—"

"A little busy," a female voice said. "The floral print seems an odd choice if you're just gonna cover it with an ugly gray vest. But you've got potential for sure." A young woman wearing the Crest of Sican strutted over. Her platinum blonde hair was abruptly cut, hanging out beneath her orange beret, upon which shimmered blue rhinestones in the shape of a butterfly. "Even if it's buried deep, *deep* down." She threw her black leather Labelle purse onto the table, her teeth glinting more than the bag's encrusted diamonds or her thick sunglasses.

We're indoors, bitch.

Zahra leaned in. "Do you know her?" she whispered. Felix shook his head, hoping he could keep it that way.

The girl took out a vintage Polaroid camera, which—unlike Alec's beat up camera—ironically looked brand new with its glistening polish. "You into photography?" she asked.

"No," Felix and Zahra said, chuckling at their being in sync.

"Figured. Real lost art. No one appreciates good photos anymore, since everyone's got a low-res camera in their pockets they only use for selfies."

She pulled out a flip phone and went through her photos. Felix tried to catch a glimpse of her gallery. Mostly off-angled selfies, among more... sinful content. Felix was ready to shield Zahra's eyes should her curiosity get the better of her, if only he wasn't trying to wipe his own memory. The girl sneered. "Like what you see? I take my selfies ironically. You call by..."

"Is she from the 21st century?" Zahra whispered.

Felix shrugged, wanting only to die in that moment.

"What *do* you know then?" the girl asked, giving Felix a condescending glare. He was tempted to throw down right there, but forced himself to suppress his homicidal rage. Perfect timing, as well, given the professors walked in mere moments later.

"Good morning, my flowering young divas!" An old woman in a floral T-shirt and pink smock stood at the front of the room, her violet eyes more radiant than even the sunlight pouring in. "And welcome to your favorite new class!" This professor's cheery attitude was a welcome change of pace (especially after dealing with hipster girl). "Most of you may know me for my world-renowned fashion line: Dame Labelle. Others might recall my obsession with all things pink. Exhibit A." She pointed to her smock.

"You mean *our* obsession." A man with a matching smock entered. His tall, muscular frame complemented his black beret, which seemed to be all the rage for some godforsaken reason. A small strand of black hair curled out from beneath the cap.

"Yes. *Our.*" She gestured to the man. "This is Videl."

He gestured to her. "And this is Dezirae."

"And we're..." They said in unison, standing back-to-back. "The Labelles!" They looked ready to break into jazz hands, which admittedly would've fit their flair perfectly. Everyone clapped, some cheered, and a couple even gave standing ovations. Even the hipster girl got her Polaroid ready to snag a photo, and the Labelles posed as her camera flashed. They bowed, motioning everyone to sit as the excitement died down.

Videl clasped his hands. "But enough about us."

"This is all about helping *you* unleash your inner designing goddess!" Dezirae said.

"Or god," Videl noted.

"Both are fierce. And don't forget the gender-neutral deity."

"Incredibly vital," Videl said. "But before you can make the art..." He played up his French accent, twirling the tip of his mustache. "You must first *understand* the art."

"So we'll be focusing on how the history of the Medeian Empire has impacted its fashion." The siblings discussed how the empire was closed off from the rest of the world for most of its existence, even from other magical societies that rose and fell in previous centuries. This resulted in some eccentric tastes: giant pointy hats; needlessly long, poofy robes; beards allowed to grow until they touched and dragged along the ground. Truly absurd and hideous concoctions.

But after the Revelation, when the Medeian Empire was forced to catch up with the rest of the world, many sorcerers sought to adapt their old ways to the modern era. Off with the Dragora uniform's large shoulder pads, ugly construction gloves, and inconvenient capes. *NO. CAPES. (Thank you, Alec.)*

Dezirae cracked her knuckles. "And that's about it for the broad intro to the vast world of Medeian fashion."

"Just remember," Videl said. "No matter the time, place, or race, plaid is never acceptable. Ever."

I find that contemptible, but alright. Felix was genuinely surprised it was already time to go. He'd gotten so invested in the history the Labelles had espoused that he'd lost track of time. For sure, this was going to be a routine exorcism of any further bullshit he'd wind up confronting the rest of the semester. But even though the class had ended, a long line of students had formed, begging the professors for autographs and pictures, to which they were more than happy to oblige.

Felix would've happily joined if not for Rosie's barrage of texts. "Argent & I grabbing lunch. Coming?"

"Yes," Felix replied. "FOOD." He was absolutely starving by this point. And with some time to kill before his last class for the day, he might as well make the most of things and put the day's drama further out of sight. Especially if it meant hanging out with Argent. He paused, recalling Zahra's kindness. "Hey, Zahra, wanna grab some food?"

She seemed surprised. "Sure. But I gotta meet up with someone first. Meet you in the cafeteria?"

"Okay. See you in a bit."

Zahra nodded and left.

"Mind if I ask you something?" The hipster girl threw her bag over her shoulder, her camera hanging around her neck.

"Uh… sure?" Felix wanted to say, "No, now please get the fuck away from me," but his mind kept reiterating: *positive vibes; positive vibes; no jail time.* "What's—"

"Are you gay?"

Felix stood there, dumbfounded. "Say what now?"

"You said I could ask." The girl was expressionless.

"I'm bi. Why *are* you asking?"

The girl shrugged. "You don't see a lot of straight guys embracing their feminine side."

He could've argued about how generalizing her statement was, or that preferences of hobby and gender weren't correlated in any imaginable way, or even—if he was desperate enough and willing to assume—pointed to all the guys in the room. But none of those things would've done him any good given this girl's lack of fucks to give. "Better time to be alive?" he said.

The girl snickered, as if dismissing not only Felix's half-hearted response, but every thought he'd had while formulating it. Almost as if she could read them plainly. "But seriously, I *could* help you score a few digits if you'd like."

"No thanks. Single, and no desire to mingle." *Well, mingling with Argent wouldn't be too bad, but I want you involved in no part of that whatsoever.*

"Good one. See you around. Name's Denise, by the way."

Feeling obligated to, he replied, "Felix."

Denise lowered her glasses to reveal shimmering golden eyes. "Super gay name. Ce minet n'est pas mon copine."

The random French caught Felix off guard. She didn't share an accent with the Labelles, so maybe this just came from Denise being an obsessive fan. In any case, ignoring the urge to punch her square in the face and break her pretentiously useless sunglasses, Felix jaunted out to meet up with his friends while she joined the line of students.

Instantly, he relished the aroma of food as he entered the dining hall. The space gave off the vibe of an opulent five-star restaurant, with chandeliers hanging from the ceiling, potted plants dotted between tables and booths, and even staircases and ramps leading to dining areas on higher levels. The clanking of silverware and chattering of students echoed about. A refreshing departure from Alderwood's stuffy café, even despite all the students forced to either jam their way into packed seats, or sit against the walls.

"There you are!" Rosie nearly knocked Felix over as she crashed into him. "'Bout time! We grabbed you some food. The line in the kitchen was a nightmare."

Felix's jaw nearly dropped, his mind going wild with the possibilities of what magi could do applying their spells to cooking. Unfortunately, most of the food being served was American style, or what the Medeians presumed was American: burgers, pizzas, hot dogs, and so on. It all smelled divine, but a slice of Medeian cuisine it was not. The long line of students zigzagging out of the kitchen on the far side of the room, all constantly checking the time on their phones, certainly did not help the atmosphere.

Rosie led Felix to one of the corner tables up top. The thought of finally getting to sit next to Argent alone was a definite improvement to Felix's day. That joy was short-lived, however. Murdered in its crib as his eyes fell on the snarky girl from his tech class seated across from Argent.

Thanks, God. I hate it.

"Hey there, gorgeous." Argent threw his arm around Felix, yet as much as Felix enjoyed it, he was too self-conscious to express that. That, and he genuinely wanted nothing more than to eat before his intestines started digesting themselves.

"May I eat before you touch me without consent?" Felix asked.

"Okay, okay." Argent dug into his food; what seemed to be pizza, albeit topped with a layer of thyme and covered in meat. He smacked his lips. "The one good thing about this place: their manakish is to die for."

"Manakish?" Felix asked.

Argent handed him a slice. "Try it."

Hesitantly, Felix took the slice and nibbled on the end. The moment his teeth sunk into the dough, the tangy flavor raced across his taste buds. "Oh my god," he mumbled with full mouth, all the while Rosie simply held her forehead disapprovingly.

"It's a delicacy from where I grew up," Argent said. "Forget haggis. Manakish is where it's at!"

"It's so good," Felix gargled, his eyes nearly tearing up. "Definitely not cardboard like the pizza at my high school." *Though I do miss Long Island pizza.*

"How do you know it's not?" Argent asked.

Felix pouted. "Shut the fuck up." *Expert flirting.*

"You know…" The girl from Ivanov's class cringed, leaning back in her seat. "There's this thing called chewing."

Felix rolled his eyes, taking extra time to chew as he spoke just to spite her. "Who invited you?"

Rosie raised her hand without hesitation. "Guilty. She's Penny, from my business class. She cool."

"Yes." Penny adjusted her glasses, despite them being perfectly in place. "Cool as fuck."

Felix and Argent glanced at each other, looking almost deaf in their disinterest, then laughed together.

"If you spit food on me," Penny said in disgust. "I will break you faster than you broke your wand."

"Wait, what about a wand?" Rosie asked.

Shit, shit, shit.

"His wand." Penny pointed to Felix. "We had to take them apart earlier, and he couldn't put his back together. I think it bro…" She trailed off once she glimpsed Felix's expression. Her face became absent of the teasing from earlier, now rife with pity instead. Felix's face, in turn, drained of color, going from its natural dark olive to that of a skeleton.

Fuck my life.

Rosie shook her head. "Of course. Lemme see."

Wishing he could disappear, Felix nervously clasped his hands. "You see, what had happened was—"

"Gimme."

Yielding to the ever-growing severity of Rosie's glare, Felix relented and poured the remnants of his wand onto the table. Each thud and clank was another slash upon his pride.

"Jesus," Argent said. "Did you use this thing as a dildo?"

Felix groaned. *Kill me.*

"Hey, relax." Argent waved his hand dismissively, eyes closed and turned away. "We can get you a better wand anyway."

"Forget it." Felix, needing to cope with the warm tide of shame washing over him, stuffed more of his own pizza down his throat. *Eat away the pain.*

"Is he… okay?" Penny asked.

Rosie stuttered. "Well…"

At that moment, Felix wanted nothing more than to go back to his dorm and hope that, upon leaping into bed and blacking out, he could restart the day. Bad enough he'd made not so stellar impressions in his first class, then had to endure Denise the Indulgent. But now he'd gone and ruined his primary tool for getting through the year. As much as he wanted to appreciate the help, Felix resented his dependency, even if Argent seemed willing to oblige time and time again.

Thankfully, a familiar voice brightened his mood, if only slightly. "Felix!"

Zahra approached, holding a lunch tray filled with vegetables. A girl wearing an orange-and-yellow hijab and dark-brown long sleeve dress, reaching down to her ankles, traipsed beside her. Her scowl could burn the very air around her.

"Are you okay?" Zahra asked as she looked on Felix with concern.

"Yeah, yeah, I'm fine," Felix said, trying to hide his exhaustion. "C'mon, sit."

Zahra hesitated. "If your friends don't mind."

Penny smiled, her smart-aleck attitude now completely replaced with a surprising and welcoming warmth. "Not at all." Rosie nodded in agreement.

"Sure," Argent grumbled, arms crossed and looking away. "I guess." Felix was tempted to grumble in turn, getting all up in Argent's face on Zahra's behalf, or maybe even throwing a good ol' fashioned "bobo" or "cabrón" his way. But he'd had more than enough of the negative vibes today.

Zahra, giving thanks, sat beside Penny, and the other girl plopped alongside her. After an awkward pause and glance towards the girl, Zahra gestured towards her. "I'd like to introduce my cousin Nasira."

Nasira glanced up, said "Hi" in the most dry, uncaring tone possible, then looked back down at the table. She had no food. No phone. Nothing that would've explained her diverted attention as she tapped her fingers on the table. She grumbled in Arabic, only picking her head up to eye Argent's manakish every now and then.

"She's... not much of a talker," Zahra said.

"Maybe you should follow her example," Argent mumbled, to which Felix slapped his wrist.

Zahra hunched forward. "So..." She stabbed an artichoke with her fork, twirling it about her plate. "How was everyone's first day?"

"Interesting," Felix gargled while eating again.

Argent rubbed his arm. "It happened."

Rosie and Penny glanced at each other. "Eventful," they said unison.

Nasira ceased tapping. "I wish it never happened." She didn't bother looking up.

Penny leaned in a bit, her concern plain. "Aren't you hungry?"

"I'm fine." Nasira's voice grew sterner. "Besides, none of the food here is halal anyway." Zahra gestured to her vegetable platter, only to pout as her cousin ignored her.

Felix's eyes darted about, looking for any way to lift the tension and break the silence. "So Penny… how'd you and Rosie meet again?" *Please be something positive. This stress is killing me more than the shame.*

"Business class," Rosie said. "With Professor Hakim."

"The headmistress?"

"No," Penny said. "Her husband Seisyll. He's quite the intellect." She flared her nose, emphasizing her inflection.

Nasira rolled her eyes. "Yeah. Uncle sure enjoys acting like he knows everything." Her thick Middle Eastern accent became more apparent.

"Uncle?" Felix asked, his eyes drifting to Zahra. "So you're…?"

She shrunk, looking like she wanted to disappear even more than Felix. "Yes. I'm the headmistress' daughter." The silence returned, with everyone glancing at each other, as if passing the burden of being the next person to speak like an invisible, undesirable baton. Felix gasped dramatically, to which everyone either looked off nonchalantly, or raised an eyebrow.

Felix chuckled nervously. "Sorry. Felt that'd lighten the mood." While Felix sympathized with her feeling of awkwardness, he couldn't understand why she would feel that way in the first place. "Why didn't you tell us?"

"Not everyone is fond of my mother," Zahra said, dropping her fork. She hadn't so much as nibbled on her meal. "I didn't want to start waves, or be treated differently."

"Well, you failed." Nasira pushed herself up.

"Hold up," Argent said. He held out a slice of his manakish. "If you quit being an asshole, then it's yours."

"Look who's talking." Giving Zahra one last glare, she stormed out.

"What a bitch." Argent seemed uncharacteristically concerned for Zahra, albeit more out of pity than sincere worry. "Why do you put up with her?"

"We're… all she has left." Zahra folded her arms, looking down at her tray. "I thought if she and I spent some time together, she'd warm up to us. To the idea of being a magus. But…" She shut her watering eyes tight.

Penny held Zahra's shoulder. "She will in time. But your parents are wonderful. Your mum's really changed this school for the better. I may have gotten in on a scholarship, but half the people in here wouldn't be without the headmistress' hard work."

"Some people would like to go back to those 'good ol' days,'" Argent said, pitching up his voice on those last three words. "Gottschalk comes to mind. Or should I say…" He winked at Felix. "Goat Chalk?"

"That woman from the other day?" Felix asked. He would've normally laughed, but even the mere mention of Professor Gottschalk was enough to chill him to the bone. He gulped. "I… think I've got her class next." *Welp, the first-day curse continues.*

"Medeism?" Argent asked. He shrugged. "Same here."

Rosie gestured to Penny, their expressions grim. "So do we."

"We all do." Zahra tensed up, looking on the verge of shivering. "My mom's warned me that she's cold and unforgiving. They respect each other, but aren't what you'd call the best of friends. I've never even met her. I hope she doesn't start anything."

The impending doom weighed down upon them all. Even so, Felix understood Zahra's anxiety well, meaning it was time to double down on the positive approach. No matter how bad Gottschalk's class turned out to be, he'd suffer with his friends. After all, isn't that how the strongest of friendships are forged? Or rather, you usually hope that's the case.

"We got your back," Felix said. "Right, guys?"

The others agreed. All except Argent, of course, who remained silent and simply pouted. It was Felix's puppy dog face that at last broke through Argent's barrier. "Fine, fine," Argent said. "Just don't hit me again."

After Felix gobbled down another slice for good luck, the group headed off. On the one hand, he was thankful they wouldn't have to climb any more stairs since this class was on the same floor. Yet at the same time, that would've given him longer to brace himself for whatever battered tundra he was marching into.

The classroom was filled with first-year students, all with looks of either apathy or dread. The rumors about this course's professors had apparently carried on a rather swift wind, as the room oozed with foreboding and disquiet. No colorful fabrics thrown about to brighten up the space. No industrial equipment to anchor you for a moment in confusion before returning to fear. Nothing but a dark room with the window curtains drawn shut, and a front desk devoid of books, paper, pens, or even a computer.

Felix's group claimed a clear table way in the back. Hopefully it would be enough distance to keep Gottschalk's wrath at bay. Funnily enough, the moment he sat down, another horde of first-years rushed in. It seemed as though this class had been packed with an extra dozen students than usual, if not more. Within moments, the few available tables had been snatched up, leaving the remaining students awkwardly standing between tables or up against the walls.

Lucas sat up in the front with Ulrich and a few other guys, all with gelled, slicked-back hair, some with white eyes, others with gold. They laughed and shouted over some game. Nasira was nowhere to be found. Probably off sulking somewhere, Felix assumed, leaving Zahra worried sick.

Guess it's no one's day.

"Good afternoon, students." Deathly silence veiled the room as Professor Gottschalk, her hair gleaming, entered. Icy white frosted over her eyes, accentuated by faint traces of pink. Felix could feel their cold glare as she paced towards their table.

Please dear God, don't remember my "outburst."

"Good to see you're making new friends..." Her eyes glazed over as they fell on Argent. "Mr. de la Mort."

Argent leaned back, hands folded behind his head, unfazed. "Thanks for the concern."

"I hope you'll actually pass my class this year."

Felix would've sighed, but he dared not make so much as a peep in Gottschalk's presence. Instead, he focused on Argent. *Why am I not shocked?*

Gottschalk turned her gaze to Zahra, towering over her. "And you must be Ms. Hakim, yes? Our headmistress' daughter?"

Zahra bobbed her head, keeping it low and avoiding eye contact.

"I'd expect more confidence from the kin of such a strong-willed woman."

"I-I'm sorry, ma'am." Zahra's voice quickened, ending her sentence as soon as possible.

"Don't apologize." Gottschalk's face filled with scorn. "If you spend your whole life apologizing, you'll barely accomplish a fraction of what your mother has." She walked back towards the front of the room, casting Zahra's very existence into oblivion as she was left shaking and holding back tears. Felix was repulsed by Gottschalk's negative reinforcement. Witnessing the harsh treatment brought back old memories he prayed he'd one day forget.

Gottschalk closed in on Lucas' table, her contempt now directed at him. Felix would've enjoyed Lucas' turn to be humiliated, even slightly, if his anger at their professor wasn't so strong. He wouldn't wish Gottschalk's ire on even his worst enemy. Her wand glowed green, and a swirl of wind pulled the cards into the air and folded them neatly in Gottschalk's hand. "Gambling? In class, no less? You disappoint me, dear nephew."

Lucas sulked.

Felix leaned back. *Nephew?!* But it made sense. Lucas already came from privilege, and the colors of their hair, skin, and even eyes matched, let alone their shared air of superiority. Perhaps snobbery could be inherited?

"Bolt Spark." Gottschalk's wand turned red. The cards went up in flames, leaving nothing in her palm but a small pile of ashes. "I hope I've made a good first impression." She poured the cinders into the garbage can. "Unlike all of you."

Fuck this class.

"As first-years, you're all new to the world of magic. Specifically, if you're one of the recent grant recipients. Who one uses the term... 'magus.'" Her voice grew graver. She had no qualms in parsing out who she believed belonged here, and who had no business in this castle. "Far too many sorcerers have forgotten our long-held Medeian traditions, and many more don't even know them." She grimaced. "Simply thrown into the deep end, or rather, crammed in." She looked upon all the standing students with a look far too condescending to call pity.

She held up her wand. "Illuminate." A white light from the tip of her wand filled the air, along with a strange symbol: two dragons, one black and one white, devouring each other's tails in the shape of an infinity sign. A third silver dragon towered between them. Beside the white dragon were four smaller ones: red; blue; green; and yellow. Another four on the black dragon's side, darker in color, mirrored them.

"Does anyone know what these dragons represent?" Rosie and Penny, among others, raised their hands. Felix didn't know the answer. Naturally, he abstained. But as he suspected, Gottschalk was well aware of just who had the displeasure of being seated in her class. "What about you?" Her eyes narrowing, she stared dead at Felix. "Mr. Fuck?"

The hands went down. Felix gulped, his blood freezing. He could barely form a question, his vocal cords ready to snap from the strain. "M-Me?"

"Yes. *You.*" Gottschalk's eyes filled with pure, unadulterated scorn. "You were proud enough to put your vulgarity on full display during the introductory assembly. Obviously you can handle a simple question."

Felix squinted at the dragons, wishing they were real. Or that one of the dragons from the reserve would break out, crash through the window, and devour him. That seemed infinitely more desirable than dealing with this professor. *Don't sound like a moron.* "The... concept of infinity?"

Gottschalk raised her chin, looking down on Felix. "A novice answer. But I suppose that can be fixed."

Felix sank in his seat.

"These are the Eleven Dragons: entities believed to have given select humans the gift of harnessing the forces of nature. Magic, in laymen's terms." She pointed to the four lighter dragons. "Representing the forces of light are Seraphina, Asherah, Cybele, and Enlil. Fire, Water, Earth, and Wind." She pointed to the opposing four. "And their dark counterparts: Aviur, Tiamat, Ishtar, and Ba'al."

Rosie raised her hand. "Do each of the four dragons correspond to the Dragora houses? Like, is there some sort of connection between Seraphina and House Pyre, or Aviur?"

"First of all..." Gottschalk's bitterness returned, albeit less potent towards Rosie. "Do not speak until I've acknowledged you. And never use the word 'like' in that manner. It makes you come across as incompetent."

Rosie lowered her hand, holding her wrist. She of all people seemed most likely to muster her courage to stand her ground and sass Gottschalk into a corner. Yet here she was, made to hunch over in shame. Now, Felix for sure wanted to kick Gottschalk's ass.

"And no," Gottschalk resumed. "The houses are named for the four noble families who warred for control over the empire prior to the advent of the De Angelis Dynasty. As for the dragons, you all have a connection to them—according to the religion of Medeism. Your prime pact represents a covenant with one of the eight elemental dragons, passed down through your bloodline.

"All sorcerers fall into one of two alignments: light, or dark. Light sorcerers wield orange flames, water, nature, and wind, and are capable of healing injuries and wounds. Dark sorcerers, on the other hand, wield blue flames, ice, earth, and storm. If you are of one alignment, you cannot wield the powers of the other. That's not even to touch on astral magic."

Ulrich, looking disinterested as ever, even in Gottschalk's presence, raised his hand. "Are dark wizards evil? Do they, you know… use the dark side?" Lucas cringed.

"Not necessarily. While older strains of Medeist theology believed sorcerers of dark alignments to be more inclined towards malice, that school of thought has been largely disproven by the acts of… certain light sorcerers. However, there is a clear distinction in that while light sorcerers can heal, dark sorcerers' powers are far more primal and destructive. Almost as if to further balance the scales."

Given Felix's blue flames, he most definitely was of the dark alignment. He certainly wouldn't have minded fully committing himself to the dark side if it meant getting to put Gottschalk in her place. But something else she said caught his attention.

"What about astral magic?" Felix asked. "What is that, exactly?"

Surprisingly, Gottschalk didn't comment on Felix's outburst. Perhaps his steadfast curiosity commanded just a shred of respect from his professor. Or maybe, she saw another opportunity to humiliate him. Felix refused to let his guard down, but either way, he would get his answer.

"If you're expecting to master it any time soon, or even within your own lifetime, don't." Gottschalk's disdain returned in full force. "Astral magic is incredibly rare for either alignment, and one cannot sharpen their abilities to harness it."

Felix glowered. "That doesn't answer my question."

The room went silent yet again. But this time, Felix had no fear. Only distaste in yet another person looking down on him, discounting his potential, and standing in his way.

Relenting, Gottschalk answered. "As the name implies, astral magic refers to any mystical ability or spell that lies outside of an elemental nature, even those of light or darkness. Unlike other kinds of magic, and likely due to its rarity, astral magic has no attachment to any of the Eleven Dragons. Though some scholars believe them to be similar to what humans have historically called psychics or empaths. Studying astral magic has proven near impossible, but some believe it is inherently connected to life force, what we may call mana, aether, or aura—the soul."

Felix held his chin. A strange, unique kind of magic that was ironically present within human culture, where no magus would ever risk showcasing even the remotest amount of magical ability. Now that was something to keep a tab open for.

Gottschalk pointed to the black and white dragons. "These are Nabu and Mot: the Dragons of Life and Death." She then pointed to the silver dragon. "And this is Raanan, the strongest of the three Supreme Dragons. The Dragon of Rebirth. He maintains balance between the opposing forces, acting as a third and neutral party. Some even believe him to be the custodian of the afterlife. The realm between the shores of life and death."

Argent kicked his feet up on the table, his disregard even agitating Felix. "Why do we need to know any of this bullshit?" Argent asked.

Gottschalk frowned. "Believe it or not, Mr. de la Mort, many pay tribute to the dragons and pray to them as gods. I'd expect you to at least have the decency to respect that. The faith many people need to give meaning to their lives."

"Those dusty old books got nothing to do with anything anymore."

"Are you sure? What do you think those dragon statues in each house symbolize? Why do you think so many put their faith in the Book of Medeis, the very cornerstone of not only Medeian culture, but most ancient cultures across the world?"

Argent, unable to whip up a witty comeback, pouted. Again, while Felix wanted on some petty level to side with him against Gottschalk, he felt more annoyed by the distraction towards even the smallest bit of information he could use to grow stronger.

But his dream of becoming strong enough to enter the Ancient Dragons' Tournament by year's end was slowly crushed by the final topic of Gottschalk's lecture: magus eye color.

Her wand glowed again, and the dragon faded into the image of four eyes: white, gold, purple, and gray. "The color of your eyes represents the strength of your pact. Think of it as a signifier of your capacity to 'pool magic.' Pearl-eyed sorcerers are at the top of this chain. Their eyes are white, with faint traces of red or pink in their irises. These sorcerers, like myself and your classmate Lucas…"

Lucas sulked.

"Are the rarest, and possess the strongest magic. Most of these sorcerers remain in the noble Medeian families, and are the only ones capable of forging pacts with all four elemental dragons, be their alignment light or dark. Golden-eyed sorcerers, meanwhile, can only forge up to three pacts. They're still considerably rare, but don't find it quite as easy to wield magic as pearls." Both Penny and Argent had golden eyes, but Penny's seemed richer and brighter, while Argent's were more of a dark amber. Still, Felix did not like where this was going at all.

"Amethyst-eyed sorcerers, once known as lilacs…" Gottschalk let out a brief sigh. "Are much more common, but can only forge up to two pacts. Though their power is considerably weaker, they still find it difficult to blend into human society given their unnatural eye color."

Rosie grimaced. She'd always been terrified of her contacts falling out back home. All that fear of being found out and hated, and not even the raw power to show for it.

But the last bit of Gottschalk's presentation served as the killing blow for Felix's ego.

"And then, the most common, and the weakest: the cobalts." Gottschalk closed her eyes, her voice filled with pity. "They can't forge any extra pacts, meaning whatever prime pact they're born into is all they have to work with. This has occasionally resulted in more creative uses of magic to compensate, but most cobalts don't need this ingenuity, because they've chosen to integrate themselves into human society rather than embrace their magical heritage and identity."

Cobalt.

The word echoed in Felix's mind, with all the force of actual cobalt metal falling down on him. It almost felt like a slur. A dull, uninteresting cobalt among a bright amethyst, a shining gold, and a brilliant, pure pearl. Yet how else could you describe it? Gray didn't sound like much of a compliment either, and it sure wasn't silver. Gottschalk continued the lesson, but the words fell on deaf ears as Felix processed what this meant for him. Suddenly his struggles in summoning even the weakest of fires clicked right into place.

"Medeism," Gottschalk said, "has roots in many religions historically considered pagan by human societies. The term was first coined by an enigmatic sorcerer by the pen name of Medeis, who traveled the world and collected all his findings on ancient magical societies in the Book of Medeis. Such legends include the origin of the covenant between the Eleven Dragons and the first sorcerers, the lost cities of Atlantis, Agartha, and Iram of the Pillars, the Tree of Life, and the Ley Lines, which were said to create mythril from the Earth itself."

Felix only tuned in now and then in hopes of something else Gottschalk mentioned giving him some small sliver of hope. But nothing. She went on and on about various legends and the impacts of Medeism upon Medeian history and culture. Whenever she'd answer other students' questions, she would scoff and give a patronizing answer, sending several other anxious hands down at once.

But through it all, the only thread resonating in Felix's mind was that single, horrible world: *Cobalt. I'm... just a cobalt. Barely even a magus. I might as well be a human.*

So why am I here?

Gottschalk seemed to sense Felix's dissociation, though she gave him no acknowledgement, nor even concern for despair. "From the look on all your faces, it seems you weren't interested anyway. I expect you all to read chapters one through four of your textbooks by next class, as well as write a list of annotations from the first volume of the Book of Medeis. Be prepared for a thorough, proper discussion." She left the room, leaving only anguish and doubt in her wake.

Why am I even here?

"Felix? Earth to Felix!" Argent shook Felix, tearing him from his stupor. "You okay?"

"Y-Yeah." Felix, trying desperately to put this out of his mind, gathered his belongings and raced towards the exit. His friends did the same, trying to keep up as best they could.

"What a nasty old lady," Argent said. "God, I hate her so much."

"Agreed." Rosie had always made an effort to kiss up to all her teachers, even when she despised them, and even more so than Felix the People

Pleaser as she called him. But the fact Rosie was ready to admit her shared hatred truly confirmed Felix's hesitancy towards Gottschalk.

Penny didn't have an expression of hatred, but rather sorrow. She stared at the floor, keeping one foot in front of the other in perfect rhythm. "I can't believe how she treats her students." Her voice was quiet.

"She kinda has to be like that," Zahra said meekly. "I can't fault her."

Rosie raised an eyebrow. "You'd *defend* her? After what she said?"

"Yikes," Argent said. "You really *are* a pushover."

Zahra shrunk in stature. She mumbled, "I am." Her eyes weren't the shimmering amethyst of her mother's, but a light gray-blue, almost like Felix's. She too was a cobalt. In Gottschalk's eyes, a magus, or sorcerer, so weak she might as well not bother and pass herself off as human.

Felix, now fully prepared to call Gottschalk out, huffed. "Don't excuse her. Argent, how hard's her class?"

"Brutal," Argent said. "Especially in chapter outlines."

Everyone groaned.

"Is that why you failed it your first year?" Rosie asked.

"Nah. I just don't give a fuck. That's what happened in all my classes." Everyone glared at Argent, most especially Felix. "Does this surprise any of you? Did you see me not taking notes?"

Rosie shrugged. "I just assumed you had no idea how that worked. Like Felix."

"Huh? Oh… oops." The day had been such an emotional rollercoaster, Felix had completely forgotten to take notes in any of his classes. *Fuck. My. Life.* Still, with the revelation of what his cobalt eyes really meant, that was the least of his concerns. *No wonder I've always sucked at magic. I wasn't meant to have it in the first place.*

Rosie rolled her eyes. "I'll send you photos of my notes."

"It'll be okay." Zahra held Felix's shoulder, her gray eyes looking into his, almost as if to tell him he wasn't alone. As difficult as it might've been, Felix took solace in the solidarity of being stuck at the bottom of the totem pole. But once his newfound hope sparked a tiny flame of confidence, it quickly grew into a foolhardy grin, and a rather pleasant righteous fury.

This won't stop me. I won't let anything stop me.

"Hope your first day was fun."

Again, Felix shot out of bed, sweat beading on his forehead. The room was nearly pitch-black, silent save for the odd creaks of the floorboards and Lucas' snores. Felix rested his head back on the pillow and closed his eyes. But as hard as he tried to return to sleep, a deep, raspy whisper—unintelligible—flowed into his ear, worming its way into his mind until he could no longer ignore it.

There was no chance this would let up any time soon. Slipping on his shoes and coat, clutching his shirt, Felix crept out of the dorm and followed the murmurs. Something would surely emerge from the darkness beyond his phone's flashlight at any moment and whisk him away into the shadows. *What am I even doing? Am I really gonna be that dumb white girl in every horror movie? Yes. Yes I am.*

The halls were empty, bereft of any light or life. There weren't even any security guards on patrol. It wasn't until he reached the outer gardens that the whispers were joined by the cool midnight breeze, and the pale glimmer of the full moon provided Felix with some sort of guide. The whispers led him into an alcove. To the edge of a pool filled with water lilies. There, on the opposite end, stood a statue of an eastern-style dragon. Its long, thin body wound across the dark-blue stones. While it had no wings, its horns could've easily eclipsed the sun mid-flight. Tendrils hung from its lips, revealing glistening pointed fangs. The sculpture was so lifelike, the dragon looked like it was truly snarling at Felix, ready to come to life at any moment.

"Where is he?!"

Felix jumped at the disembodied voice. He climbed behind the statue for cover, slowly peeking out to find Lucas running into the alcove. He must've just hauled himself out of bed as well. His tired eyes darted about, scanning as he approached the pool. *Crap. He must've heard me sneak out. Great.* Felix half-expected Lucas to be hunting him down, looking for any and all reasons to get Felix into trouble so as to have the dorm all to his pearl-eyed self.

How he wished that was the true reason.

Before Felix could reveal himself, he paused as Lucas took out a shining red pendulum pendant. Lucas sat, and the moment he placed the crystal into the water, a crimson glow rippled past the flowers until the whole pool turned blood-red. Similar murmurs danced across the wind. But it wasn't just one voice this time, like earlier. No. A chorus of voices, far raspier, far more sinister, singing their requiem from the shadows, demanding their cries to be heard.

Lucas pulled the crystal out, returning the water to normal. The voices ceased. "Dammit all!" He pushed himself up. "Damned astral magic." He ripped the crystal from his neck, giving it a hateful glare before tossing it into the water. It hopped a couple times before completely plopping into the pool's dark depths. "Shit!" He looked around once more, then, sniffling and wiping his eyes, ran off.

What the hell? Felix wondered about whatever Lucas was trying to do. Perhaps he was attempting an astral spell, only to find he, like most other magi, was incapable of doing so? One of the few things his wealth and privilege could never buy him. But the eerie voices made Felix shiver slightly, and wonder if there was more to this story. Regardless, he elected to head back inside and forget this ever happened.

That was, of course, until the crystal's red glow caught his eye. It seemed to call out to him. Felix had already decided to keep an open mind when it came to astral magic, so silencing his fears, he reached into the water. The pool froze his fingers as he searched for the crystal, the cold threatening to give his whole hand frostbite. But the moment he touched the crystal, warmth enveloped his entire arm. He pulled the necklace out. Perfectly dry, both it and his hand. The black chain shimmered beneath the moonlight. Faint embers flickered around where Lucas had severed the tether, the chain seemingly repairing itself. The crystal still sparkled scarlet, even faintly humming. Almost as if it had a pulse.

Then, more whispers. A younger voice rose above the rest. That of a little girl, crying out for help, as though she were in pain. She wept, begging not to be left behind. Reaching out for her beloved mother and sister.

"What are you doing out here?"

Again Felix jumped, cramming the crystal into his pocket. Ornella, dressed in a burgundy nightgown with her hair hanging free, stood there. Her eyes narrowed not with anger, but frustration. She, too, seemed ready to settle all this nonsense and return to the comforts of sleep. Felix, ready to scream, snapped his back straight. "S-Sorry! Couldn't sleep. Had to get some fresh air, you know?"

"Past curfew? I'm sure. Follow me." She led him back to House Pyre, where she warned him to never let this happen again. Surprisingly, she gave Felix the advice to light the fireplace and relax to the crackling of the logs. She professed that on nights she would feel uneasy and unable to fall asleep, a little white noise went a long way in helping her forget about the rest of the world's problems. It might not've quelled Felix's fear of the initial voice luring him out of bed, but he did genuinely appreciate the advice.

Lucas was already back to snoring, as if he'd never woken in the first place. Dread welled in Felix. And so, against his better judgment, he dropped the crystal into his bottom drawer and shut his eyes. Lucas didn't seem to want the item in the least. Regardless, Felix could always say he happened upon it and return it at a later date. Closing his eyes, he drifted back to sleep.

I'm going to get where I wanna be. He kept repeating the mantras in his mind, trying to reassure himself. *I will be a sorcerer. I will master my powers. Hell, I'll master astral magic. I can do this. I will get there.*

"All in good time."

Chapter Seven

Towards the Light

"A PARTY thrown by the Lightheads?" Argent asked, groaning. "Bad enough I have to give them my money to get around the city. Now you're telling me I'm doing that just so I can drink away my misery on their turf?! Hell no!"

He'd been complaining nonstop since they'd all received the invitation. The Della Luce family was throwing a welcome gala at their manor in honor of the first-year Dragora students, most especially those from the States. And while Felix had little to no interest in attending the party, much less dressing up for it, he conceded to Rosie's insistence that it'd be a chance to take his mind off things. Argent didn't even want to go. He only bothered because Felix was going, and he had a plus-one rule to take advantage of.

Not to mention, Felix had been genuinely worried about Lucas since that night he'd attempted astral magic. He couldn't shake the image of the pool turning red; the raspy voices carrying on the winds. Perhaps now was the time to give back Lucas' crystal. After all, he wasn't getting any use out of it, too self-conscious to dare attempt any kind of magic with it. And there was also the fact the masked man continued to linger at the back of his mind. He hadn't been directly contacted in weeks, yet even so, Felix knew he'd be hearing from the rogue soon enough.

So here they were. Felix, Rosie, Argent, and Penny, all headed for the Della Luce estate. Argent had, as usual, helped them buy formalwear for the occasion, though he only seemed to care about what Felix was wearing. Too much so, in Felix's honest opinion. Argent was quick to scrutinize many of the brighter colors Felix had veered towards, to the point he was now back to the darker shades he'd tried making efforts to move away from.

Black dress pants, a white buttoned-up shirt, and a navy blazer. The only pop of color he could manage to implement was a fire-red handkerchief, which admittedly even he wasn't too keen on initially. And after the last comment Argent had made about it, Felix had decided against wearing his grandmother's necklace, leaving it back in his dorm. Argent's old suit seemed close to matching Felix's. Nearly identical save for his jet black blazer with no pops of color, along with his outfit being clearly unironed with wrinkles.

Penny seemed comfortable, wearing an oversized peach blazer over her orange dress. She wasn't too excited about this either, but again, Rosie's persuasion took no prisoners.

Rosie was the only person truly radiating confidence. White doves flew across her black wrap dress, accentuated by purple flower petals dotted between their wings. Her cornrows were now tied up into a bun. Heart-shaped black hoops hung from her purple rose earrings, adorned with silver thorns.

Felix envied how comfortable Rosie seemed in her own skin. Perhaps he would feel better once he ran into Zahra, who was heading to the party with her family. Then again, that would also mean dragging Nasira around, and her negative vibes might've been enough to ruin the night for everyone.

At the very least, Felix enjoyed the ocean breeze onboard the ferry bound for Pyre Isle. They'd passed Archangel Island, home of the Elysian Keep from which the empress ruled. Parliament also met within the castle's walls, but whoever cared for the humdrum lives of old, rich, out-of-touch legislators? The castle gleamed gold beneath the light of the gibbous moon, the crimson domes and towers sparkling brighter than the ripples of the tides.

Unlike the capital of Cendrillion, every building here in the bustling port town of Brastius seemed to give off the impression of a fantastical wizard town. Walls of shops and restaurants were curved, with dark-red rooftops so big and overhanging they might as well have been witch hats. The city was completely free of litter. Though while the clean streets were pleasing to the eye, the methods with which this was attained didn't seem to be out of the residents' goodwill. Argent had finished his soda from the ferry ride and missed the waste bin at an attempted toss. Everyone walking by gave him either a death glare or rushed away quickly. One of the patrolling officers even stopped the group, made Argent pick up and throw away his garbage, then gave them all a "kind warning" while brandishing what seemed to be a fusion of a wand and a baton.

The road wound up a hill through the trees. The estate had to be massive, as it was walled off on all sides with gray stone enclosures, torches with bright-orange flames lining the top. Two armed guards, not only wielding wands, but also white uniforms lined with thin plates of silver armor and hats obscuring their eyes, stood at the large gate as the guests formed a line.

"Wow." Penny's eyes sunk behind her glasses. "This security is insane."

Argent scoffed. "Someone wanna tell the Lightheads no one's clamoring to interact with them anywhere, least of all their own house?"

Felix held his chin. It was only natural for a family as affluent and influential as the Della Luces to keep up extra security. Even so, this entire island thus far felt like it was under the watchful eye of not just law enforcement, but the citizenry itself. If you were too scared to even litter, why bother trying to rob the Della Luces of all people? The malevolent facade was enough to inspire a rising sickness in Felix's stomach. This most certainly was not helped by the guards seeming extra skeptical on letting Rosie and Felix in, even with their invitations and student IDs.

Past the gate was a small courtyard before the manor's entrance. A spiral stone driveway where coaches (complete with inbred kelpies) dropped off guests, at whose center stood an impressive fountain surrounded by grass and sylph statues.

Guests were directed through the front doors, down long corridors fully furnished with crimson marble floors so glossy they threatened to blind visitors. The lengthy beige carpets, decorated with black, red, and gold vines resembling dragons, along with snow-white flowers, seemed immaculate, as though they'd never been walked upon. Until tonight as the urchins now dragged their feet along its fibers. Gods help the staff having to clean it afterwards while enduring the wrath of Lucas' family. And even then, they ensured you'd always felt them watching you. Along the walls hung dozens of portraits, presumably of all the Della Luces of every generation. And unsurprisingly, all of them bore pearl or golden eyes. Not an amethyst or cobalt to be seen.

Out the back doors lay a brick patio, whose stairs extended down into lantern-lit cobblestone paths stretching all the way across the gardens and ponds to a massive pool. While the party was marketed as a welcoming to new students, they only seemed to make up half the attendees. Most of them stuck to their Dragora uniforms, waddling around aimlessly and exploiting the Medeian Empire's relatively lower drinking age.

The other half, disguising their graying hair and sagging skin with opulent suits, gowns, and jewelry, had to be nobles. Their snooty laughter grated like sandpaper. And unsurprisingly, most of them were pearl-eyed, with a few golds sprinkled here and there. Servants went around asking for donations to the Dragon Party, and the wealthy guests were more than happy to, muttering about the "cobalt foreign rabble being sent back home."

The only positives of the higher tier guest list were two celebrities Felix had fawned over (and yearned for) since his youth: Eunice Karahalios and Darius Ambrosia. Both were magical athletes renowned in the world of sorcerers for their prowess in the Ancient Dragons' Tournament, along with their various other exploits even the human world seemed interested in.

Eunice was the current Dragon Skinner, the reigning champion of the last tournament six years ago, while Darius was her rival, vowing to take back the gold come next summer. This would also mark the first time she'd be participating since her transition. Felix was utterly obsessed with Erasmus, but Eunice's courage was what truly made her his number one idol.

Darius, though? Well, let's just say he made waves of his own with his side work of "explicit performances" with all manner of folk. A "true switch," if you will. And suffice to say, both of them nearly gave Felix—bisexual disaster he was—a massive nosebleed, and awakened a most ancient conflict within him.

That excitement vanished, unfortunately, as his eyes drifted towards the party's illustrious hosts. A portly man of average height, with slicked-back hair looking more bleached than his alabaster skin, which already appeared unnaturally whiter than even his pearl eyes or the moon high above. He'd locked arms with a much taller woman, rail thin and frail looking. Martino della Luce and his wife Elyse. The affluent businessman who'd had more than his fair share of meats, cheeses, and wines from the buffet table, and his wife who seemed completely disinterested in whatever her husband was spouting on about.

The oddest part was to whom they were speaking: Headmistress Hakim. But then again, perhaps it wasn't so strange. The Della Luces no doubt had provided hefty donations to the institute. Yet even so, neither the headmistress nor her husband appeared too happy to converse with Martino. Ramidha clung to her husband Seisyll's arm for dear life. He was just a bit taller than Ramidha, dressed prim and proper in a beige suit, his graying brown hair tied back into a short ponytail. His golden eyes illuminated his profile. No sign of Zahra or Nasira around them, though.

Lucas, to absolutely no one's surprise, stood beside his parents, miserable. A taller girl, sharing Lucas' skin, hair, and eye colors stood nearby, though her exuberant smile was more than enough to set her and Lucas apart. Funnily enough, she looked more like a younger, happier version of Gottschalk than the daughter of Elyse, especially with her white sleeved dress and flowing hair.

She didn't stay for long, either. The moment Ornella walked over, looking uncharacteristically joyous and carefree in her scintillating scarlet dress and black shawl, Lucas' sister whisked her away, much to the chagrin of her parents. Not that she seemed to care. Felix pitied how isolated Lucas seemed, looking ready to back off into the bushes behind him and hide until the night had ended, even if it meant dirtying his white suit.

"Hey, you okay?"

Felix rubbed his eyes, finding Rosie tilting her head back in confusion at him. Felix stuttered. "Just a little nervous, I suppose." He looked back at Lucas again, then reached into his pocket. The red crystal resumed its heartbeat. The thuds pulsed in rhythm with Felix's conflict on whether to return the item and risk a confrontation, or let it be.

"You're not gonna propose, are you?" Argent gave his trademark smirk. Felix was tempted to fire back a witty response, but elected to simply ignore it, to which Argent grimaced. "We'll, I'm gonna go get a drink. They're rich enough to have a goddamn bar in their own house, so I'm takin' advantage. That, and I need to find the bathroom. Leave the Lightheads a little gift if ya—"

"We get it," Felix and Rosie said in unison.

Waving his hand, Argent walked off. Felix let out a sigh of relief, while Rosie simply raised an eyebrow. "Is it me?" she asked. "Or does he seem way more aggressive?"

"I don't know." Felix looked around. "I wanna see if I can find Zahra. She might need company to lighten the mood if she's stuck with Nasira's misery and nothing else."

"Good call," Rosie said. "Penny and I are gonna scope out the place for cute guys." She nudged Penny, only for her gaze to immediately fixate on one of the older-looking Dragora guys: broad-shouldered, dark-brown mullet, and fair skin. "Welp, I call dibs!" Without another word, Rosie sauntered over to him and struck up a conversation.

"Gotta admit," Felix said. "I envy that confidence." Rosie never had a problem pursuing any guy she fancied, not once allowing herself to feel ashamed. Penny, by stark contrast, sulked, her eyes focused on that same guy. "You okay, Penny?" Felix asked.

"Perfectly fine." Penny's voice was hoarse. "Just a little thirsty. I'm gonna go grab a drink, but you should go ahead and find Zahra." She quickly headed off.

Felix saw right through Penny's charade, but knew full well that when he felt that way, he'd almost always preferred to be left alone, lest one wrong word set off the waterworks. He'd check in on her later. But right now, best not to apply any pressure. Felix chastised himself for misreading Penny so badly upon their first meeting. She was indeed kind and sincere, simply putting up a front of confidence. He knew that approach intimately.

He searched around. No sign of Zahra. He hadn't gotten her number yet, so there was no way to reach her. Just as he was about to give up hope, he noticed Lucas, on his own, slipping away from his family and heading down a poorly lit path through the woods. He shook slightly, constantly glancing over his shoulder. Alas, Felix's curiosity got the better of him.

Thankfully no one at the party seemed interested as Felix went after Lucas. He bumped into one dark-skinned male student with a bad buzz cut along the way, spilling his drink onto his uniform. The Crest of Zephyr, a green tornado with blue bolts of lightning surging around it, was now the deep red of an expensive wine. Felix apologized profusely. But the young man didn't respond. He only gave a vacant stare with his dull cobalt eyes, which slowly warped into a slight sneer, revealing partially yellowed teeth. He warned Felix to be careful where he walked and who he stepped on. But before Felix could say anything further, the stranger slipped back into the crowd. The brief encounter left Felix only a tad unsettled.

Part of Ornella regretted coming here tonight. There'd have been a reckoning should her mother learn she so much as set foot anywhere near the Della Luce estate, but Lucinda insisted there was nothing to fear.

She desperately needed this escape after the disappearance of her pendant. After so long of trying to keep it hidden from her mother, she'd now discovered it had vanished from her belongings. The only thing keeping her from turning the castle upside down looking for it was her fear of rocking the boat. She could've used a divining spell to locate it, but that would've meant reawakening unpleasant memories.

Whenever her anxiety peaked, she would hold onto her shawl—a black shawl with red firebird's kisses; one she'd sewn herself, the scarlet beads modeled after the lost pendant—finding comfort in its protection.

She'd been enjoying the night, certainly, though now her jaunt to the private bar had been made a tad more… interesting.

Perhaps Mother is right about one thing: anyone willing to waste their wealth on an entire bar within their own home doesn't deserve that wealth in the first place. Branching off the west wing, the black-and-white tiled floor reeked of extravagance. The red sofas by the windows were swarmed by drunk students kicking their feet and giggling up bubbles. Over by the bar were even more students, all exploiting the empire's disturbingly low drinking age. Among them, with his signature bad slouch and on what looked to be his fifth drink, sat Argent atop a stool.

"Hey! Refill over here!"

Ornella rolled her eyes and paced over. "Dare I ask what brings you here alone, Mr. de la Mort?" She raised an eyebrow. "And why you're not springing for anything above bottom shelf?"

Argent glanced at her, then waved his glass, spilling some of his drink. "It's what I deserve."

Pity overtaking her, she took the open seat next to him. "What seems to be ailing you? Enough to drive you to ale."

"First of all, terrible pun," he slurred as the ice cubes in his glass clanked. "Second, it's not ale, it's arak. I have a cultured taste. Third…" He burped. "I forget."

"Lovely." Ornella held her forehead. He hadn't changed a bit since last year. Still the same miserable, irreverent loner he was the first day he walked through Dragora's front doors. "I'd expect you to be off with your friends enjoying the night, instead of sitting here alone, numbing."

"Friends?" Argent hiccupped. "Sure, like you know anything abo—"

Ornella swiped the glass. "Don't change the subject."

He was about to make a comeback, but stopped himself and groaned. "If they care, they'll come and find me. Like I need company when I've got… oh wait, I don't have my drink, cuz some asshole took it!"

"What do you think of Mr. Brasher?" Ornella asked.

Argent appeared somehow more confused than usual. "Felix? He's cute."

"And…? Anything else?"

"I don't know," Argent said. "A little too preoccupied with Lighthead Jr.? What exactly are you expecting me to say, Nella'rela? And please don't spout that weird-ass story about the dragon and the phoenix, or the one about the phoenix and the ash tree, or whatever trippy folklore your ma traumatized you with."

"I'm expecting you to note the obvious." Ornella laughed, briefly cursing her astuteness. "Admittedly, I don't know much about Mr. Brasher just yet. From what I've gathered, he seems like he could be a good influence on you. Especially since you've already refused my suggestion to see the school psychologist."

"I don't need some shrink! And I definitely don't wanna offload my crap onto someone I just met. He'll run off soon enough, just like the rest of 'em."

Welp, she tried. She set down the drink, which Argent happily swiped back, much to Ornella's chagrin. She stood, but couldn't bring herself to leave just yet. "But I can tell you do care about Felix. So can I ask you to at least watch over him?"

Argent cracked a grin. "You're really set on this matchmaker shit, aren't ya, Nella're—"

"Argent." Ornella's voice caught Argent off guard, making his eyes go wide, and even attracting the momentary glances of the bartender and other patrons. "I know your home life isn't stellar. Neither is mine. We'd both rather drink ourselves into comas before talking about our mothers. But Felix has his own troubles following him, and if you're not going to try and help yourself, I'd hope you wouldn't add to his list of problems. So...?"

He glanced down. Ornella expected some kind of witty response, or even a simple "Go fuck yourself" before using that damned nickname again. But nothing. Argent didn't order another drink. And even when the bartender gave him a refill, he didn't take a sip. He just sat there, staring at the countertop, eyes locked on his reflection through the fine polish.

There aren't enough prayers I could give that could help Felix with any of this.

Felix ducked between trees to keep out of sight. His pursuit led him out through a small, rusty iron gate, and into the depths of the woods behind the estate. Owls hooted, invisible save for the sharp white glints of their eyes piercing through the faint moonlight. The stone path was shrouded in the dark of night, barely visible thanks to the few sprites, tiny, winged orbs of yellow-green light, wandering between the branches up above. Felix considered this a blessing. Any kind of light from his phone would've been enough to give away his presence to Lucas. He kept a slow pace, not only to keep from being heard, but also to avoid tripping on rocks jutting up from the ground and scraping his knees. To make matters worse, a chilling mist had rolled in. While it didn't completely obscure his vision, it did unnerve him, making his blood run cold.

The path wound wildly through the forest, snaking up a rather steep incline. At this point, any light or noise from the party had long since faded away, lost to the silence. Not even the chirps of crickets or humming of cicadas to accompany the trek. Felix had followed Lucas this far into the darkness, so might as well continue and see what answers lay at the end of this road.

At long last, the path widened out into a small clearing, where stood what appeared to be a long-abandoned greenhouse. Ivy and liana chained around the building, covering dirt-coated windows and crawling through cracks. The entrance was oddly unobstructed, surrounded merely by white flowers gleaming brighter than the moon. With no other path in sight, this was the only place Lucas could've gone. And so, reluctantly, Felix headed inside, wishing he'd taken Argent's offer to get a new wand sooner rather than later.

The windows were so thoroughly caked in soil that the moonlight couldn't even break through, the interior submersed in gloom. *Well, I'd rather give myself away than trip and die.* He switched on his phone's flashlight. Thick vines, growing more of the same blooming white flowers, crisscrossed along the floor, taking over flowerbeds of wilted plants with no effort at all.

One of the flowerbed's labels read "Firebird's Kisses." Inside were the remains of dead blossoms, save for one withering flower. Seven red-orange petals, twirling out into azure tips. The colors, however faded, burned through the shadows like embers. Felix plucked it to inspect it further, only to drop the flower as one of its thorns pricked his finger. He tried to pick it up, but it was nowhere to be found, as if it had disintegrated into ash right under his nose. The blood from his finger glistened crimson, even in the absence of light.

Another light surfaced from the black. Far in the back of the building was a large pool, and though it had turned murky, presumably thanks to the remains of water flowers, a glowing purple film coated its surface. The violet absorbed the light of the moon, and even the radiance of the white flowers, corrupting it and making it its own. And there, at the heart of the decadent film, was another long-dead flower. At least, it looked like it should've been dead. Four sickly petals. Violet, verging on the black of rot. Yet there it was, floating ever so still in the pool, fluorescing just as the strange film all around.

Instinctively, Felix pulled Lucas' pendant from his pocket. It shone far more brilliantly than ever before. The purple flower called to Felix, beckoning him. Without a second thought, he knelt and, holding the pendant by its chain, placed the crystal into the water.

The purple film turned blood-red, and Felix's neck snapped back, forcing his eyes skyward. Crimson spilled across the heavens. Starlight bled from the ether as the moon, a near full circle, cracked. It broke apart, giving way to an eleven-headed serpent tearing itself free, devouring what few stars remained.

The image morphed yet again, the serpents falling back and spinning into tattered angel wings spanning across the sky. The wings beat, their flaps in tune with a deep, masculine laughter, and the roar of a great fire. Felix's body burned, consumed by deep-violet flames. He tried to scream. Yet the inferno drowned out his voice, reducing his vocal cords to cinders.

He fell back, his body reeling from the pain. Biting down on an imaginary bullet, Felix forced himself to sit up, only to find the pool a dull, murky brown. The purple flower, likewise, had vanished. Its petals simply floated atop the water. The pendant had dimmed, sitting near the pool's edge. Despite the excruciating pain and vivid sensations, Felix was unburned, free of any scars. He held his head. Though he now had a massive migraine, he didn't feel any pain that would've come from his skull hitting the ground as it should've.

"What did you see?"

Felix jumped back. Lucas knelt next to him, likely having held Felix's head and kept his skull from cracking like an egg. Though Lucas had no concern in his expression—only frustration. "L-Lucas?!" Felix barely managed to choke out the words, having to press his fingers against his throat just to make sure he could still speak. "What was...?" He glanced at the crystal. Instantly, his fear reignited.

Lucas groaned. "I figured as much." He scooped up the crystal, staring at it dispassionately. "I've trained my whole life to master my magic. But no matter how I've tried, no matter how many books or ancient tomes I get my hands on, somehow the mysteries of astral magic still escape me. Yet you..." He glared at Felix, hate in his eyes. "Cobalt."

Felix gulped.

"You waltz into my school with no business being here, no experience in anything remotely mystical, no *real* power..." Lucas gripped the crystal in his fist, slightly cracking it. A faint, high-pitched whisper reverberated with the crunch. "And you get it all *handed* to you. What did you even see, Cobalt?" His spiteful stare returned to Felix. "Go on. Describe every last detail."

Felix crawled back, trying to get as much distance from Lucas as possible. The anger in his eyes was unwavering. He could've attacked at any moment, and being a pearl-eyed magus, he didn't even need a wand to do it. But he didn't. Lucas stood there, eyes watering, now filling with envy.

Having enough, Lucas tossed the crystal to the ground and moved to stomp on it. No. Felix couldn't allow this. Something in that stone was crying

137

out, begging to be spared. And so, Felix leapt forth, closing his fist as Lucas tried to crush it beneath his heel.

But there was no crunch.

"The end of all things."

The slight whistle of the gravelly voice snapped Felix from fear to shock. There, standing on the water was… him. The masked man. His phoenix sat, perched upon his shoulder. "You really need to work on your anger." He raised his arm, revealing the pendant dangling from his sleeve. "You can't just go around destroying other people's property."

"W-Who…?!" Lucas' eyes shrank with terror. He stepped back, his hands trembling. "Who are you?!" He nearly tripped over himself.

The masked man chuckled. "You could call me a friend. Perhaps a mentor, if all pans out." He turned. "Good to see you again, Felix."

"Y-You… you know him?!" Lucas shouted.

Felix stuttered. He couldn't form a coherent thought, let alone a sentence beyond unintelligible stammering. Every instinct told him to run. That risking getting lost in that forest was better than being here with this man. Even so, he couldn't bring himself to stand and run.

"Now I hate prying eyes," the masked man said. "So to ensure we have no audience tonight…" His hand glowed blue, and arms of water shot up from the pool, grabbing Lucas and Felix. They tried to break free, but the water constricted them. Their skin froze as they were submerged. Felix desperately tried to hold his breath, but the terror of the moment forced him to gasp, water rushing into his mouth. A snap resounded. The water retreated, leaving Felix heaving and gasping for air.

Still, the bitter cold lingered, weighing down on them both as they found themselves sealed in an air bubble at the bottom of the pool. Then, from the murky depths, emerged the masked man. His phoenix was nowhere to be seen. "You're lucky Cinder hates water so much. Poor girl is shivering up there, keeping an eye on things for us."

Lucas was still in shock, looking ready to collapse. Tired of being kept in the dark, Felix assumed the burden of questioning their captor. "What do you want from us?"

"Cutting to the chase." The man laughed. "I like it. Seeing as I have your undivided attention, I might as well introduce myself. My name is Vagus."

He paused, and as he resumed speaking, his voice grew more severe. "And...
I need your help."

Vagus.

Finally, a name to identify the stranger garbed in red. The rogue who'd
haunted Felix's nightmares since that fateful night. No doubt an alias created
to conceal his true identity, but any scrap of information was better than
nothing. "Help?" Felix resisted the urge to laugh. "Sorry to break it to you,
but I'm not in the business of helping people who stalk and terrorize me.
Besides, I've got nothing worth extorting." He looked back at Lucas, still
shivering in fear. "And I don't think you'd wanna mess with such a powerful
family either." Felix's eyes narrowed. "Let. Us. Go."

"Patience, patience," Vagus said. "My my. You really do have his
temper."

Felix scowled. "Get on with it." He could've sworn Vagus was sneering
behind his goddamned mask.

"Your vision showed you the fate of this world and all who inhabit it.
Chaos, followed by destruction, ultimately ending in complete and total
annihilation of all creation." The images flashed in Felix's mind, mingling
with his visions from the Chamber of Kagami. "There are forces at work
conspiring towards the end of life as we know it. Forces you may not be
aware of, but are very much aware of you." Vagus glanced at Lucas. "The
both of you. Though you might know that already, Lucas."

Lucas shriveled up, teeth chattering.

"In any case," Vagus said. "Their first move is rapidly approaching, and
is to be dealt at the beginning of the Ancient Dragons' Tournament at the
end of the school year."

Felix raised an eyebrow. "You're being awfully—"

"Vague?" Vagus laughed. "Sorry. Couldn't resist. Much like you, Felix, I
find comedy helps soothe the old nerves. But I will share more in time.
They've eyes and ears everywhere, meaning the less you know, the less likely
they'll be to suspect you."

"So why drag us down here?" Felix asked. "You still haven't told us what
the hell you're after."

"It's about what we're *both* after." Vagus twirled the azure tips of his
scarlet boutonniere. "The power to protect what matters to us. That same

power I promised you, if you recall. The one that lies deep within Dragora Castle?"

The note.

"It will belong to one of you. Over the next few months, I'm going to be keeping my eye on both of you, closely observing to see which of you will be the right fit to serve as my champion in this war. Who has the strength to do what must be done. Who pursues the truth past all the comfortable lies and delusions. Who possesses the drive to keep fighting."

Felix squinted. "And if we refuse?"

"Oh. Then I'll simply find someone else to fill the role. Someone who will be much more eager to prove themselves and get the job do—"

"I'll do it!"

Felix was taken aback as Lucas, standing upright, outstretched his hand. He didn't even flinch. His eyes narrowed with resolve. A man born into power and privilege, and all the magical abilities he could've dreamt of, and yet he seemed ravenous for more. Felix resented the look on Lucas' face, and everything it stood for.

"Well," Vagus said. "That was easy enough." He turned to Felix. "I suppose if you want no part of it, then Lucas will be more than capable—"

"Fine."

Felix clenched his fists. He wasn't going to let anyone, least of all Lucas, steal what might've been his only opportunity to grow stronger. As far as he knew, he was stuck as a cobalt for life. A permanent limitation on how far he could progress his skills. After all he'd been through, he was ready to do whatever it took to tear those unfair barriers down. "I'll do whatever it takes." Felix glared at Lucas. "I have a reason to want this."

Vagus snickered. "This'll be fun to watch unfold. In any case, you can't tell a soul of this plan unless I explicitly permit it. If one of you is chosen, you must follow through on my instructions. Do I have your words?"

Without a moment's hesitation, Felix and Lucas said, "Yes."

"Excellent!" Vagus clapped, and a sharp sting enveloped the front of Felix's right hand. As though a thousand tiny needles seared into his skin. A white glyph spun over his skin before fading away, along with the pain. "I'll be in touch soon. Enjoy the rest of your night!"

Before Felix could say a word, the water rushed back in, knocking him and Lucas forward. Felix swam for the surface, coughing as he broke through. He pulled himself back onto the ground and spat out what little film and decay he'd nearly swallowed. His hair, shiny and nearly black as it dripped, hung in his face, and his suit was drenched from head to toe. In the absence of warmth, a cold emptiness ran through his body, making him shiver. But this was far more sinister than a mere dip into an icy body of water. No. This emptiness was pervasive, cutting down to the bone. He felt nothing. Nothing save for a deep, insatiable hunger.

Until Lucas spoke, and ignited a rage within him.

"You…!" Lucas, also drenched, grabbed Felix by the shirt collar. "You know him. Vagus. How much *do* you know exactly?! What's a cobalt like you have to do with—"

Felix pushed Lucas back, sending him crashing through a flowerbed. Soot and soil coated Lucas' face, hair, and clothes, and his anger evaporated into fear as Felix towered over him. His fists shook with malice, teeth grinding so hard they might've sparked. "You have no idea what I've been through. The things I had to go through to get this far. So I'm going to make this crystal clear: don't get in my way. Because if you do, I can't promise it'll end well for you."

And with that, Felix left, marching back through the dark forest to the manor. Whether Lucas was following close behind or still lying in shock in the greenhouse was beyond Felix's care.

Rosie and Penny had been looking for Felix for more than a half-hour by the time he got back. Rosie had even run into Zahra, who was worried to death about Felix's disappearance. Rosie had tried blowing up Felix's phone, only to get no reply. Felix couldn't say why, of course, instead telling them he and Lucas went for a stroll to "chat" and "clear the air." Argent seemed skeptical, but didn't bother asking. Felix didn't even check to see if Lucas had returned home. By the time the party ended, he was more than happy to return to his dorm, especially if it meant not having to deal with his roommate.

The trip back to the school was awkwardly silent, with Felix staring off into space, imagining what kind of power Vagus could've referred to, and where in the castle it could've been hidden. Argent appeared sullen. Suddenly, Felix recalled his broken wand. If he was to get any closer to his ultimate goal, he had to start somewhere, even at rock bottom.

Finally, Felix broke the silence. "Too late to take you up on your offer on getting me that new wand?"

Though Zahra wanted to return to Dragora with her new friends much earlier, her parents insisted she stay until they left. A strange request, given they refused to let her be involved in their conversation with the Della Luces, instead tasking her with keeping an eye on Nasira all night. Even the company of Felix and his group of friends she counted on being her saving grace was dampened by his sudden disappearance, followed by his callousness when he returned.

By the time her family was ready to return to the castle, Zahra was ready to head to bed and call it a day. And so, she leaned on her cousin's shoulder, the both of their eyes shut on the carriage ride up to Dragora as Ramidha and Seisyll discussed the night's events.

"I swear on my life," Seisyll said, his voice low yet taut. "If I have to hear Martino refer to your appointment as headmistress as an 'act of charity' one more time…"

"I'm used to this, Sei," Ramidha said. "No matter what the Della Luces or others like them say, we're doing a lot of good for the empire."

"Only because you're fighting tooth and nail with hardly anyone backing you up. Even Isolda is…" Seisyll sighed heavily.

"Sei, you took your medication today, right?"

"Of course." Seisyll shifted away. "I've been stressed with the beginning of the year, is all. Then again, you know me. I'll sleep when I'm—"

"I know you won't like hearing this, but I think it's time to go back to therapy."

"The medicine helps plenty," Seisyll said. "And it's difficult enough sourcing it, having to go all the way to Zephyr Isle for it, let alone how much it costs to import. I simply don't have time to pay someone to listen to my problems for an hour every week."

"That's not the main reason why," Ramidha said. "We both know it."

"You know my family. Traditional in every sense, and that includes 'fighting the demons' all on your own. I mean, if there's any Baisley that needs

142

a psychiatrist, it's Samuel. And he laughed when last I mentioned my diagnosis. 'Depression's something the humans say you have to keep you weak,'" he said in an imitation of Samuel's gruff, hoarse voice.

Zahra wanted to say something. She'd known the struggles her parents had gone through to fight to make Dragora a more inclusive space, and to extend an olive branch to the human world. Her father's family was aghast when he chose to marry an immigrant amethyst, let alone one who threatened all the old ways they held so dear. And to see Seisyll now, afraid of his own family belittling him further, calling him weak while condemning his efforts to help himself... it made her sick. Slowly, she opened her eyes, and looked at her father.

"Uncle is wrong," Zahra said.

Seisyll seemed caught off guard, looking stupefied at his daughter.

"I agree with Mother," Zahra said, focusing on strengthening her cadence. "If they have a problem with you doing what's best for yourself, then that's on them. You shouldn't sacrifice your health for their comfort or backwards beliefs."

He teared up a bit. "Thank you, dear." He locked eyes with Ramidha. "I'll look into going back to therapy. For myself, and for you all." He glanced over at Nasira. "And perhaps... one for Nasira as well. To help her adjust."

"Hell no."

Nasira's eyes shot open as she sat up. "I don't need to be told what else is wrong with me," she said. "Yes, my parents cast me out, but they were right to."

"Nasira..." Zahra reached for Nasira's shoulder, but she swatted it away. "You can't mean—"

"I do! The evil is in my blood. I don't want to learn to be some heretic." She held her necklace—the ta'wiz. A dark-brown necklace with a black pouch. Inside was probably a du'a; some form of prayer, for protection or any other request. She spoke in Arabic. Zahra couldn't follow, but Ramidha followed intently.

"Quran 2:102," Ramidha said. "'And indeed they knew that the buyers of it would have no share in the Hereafter. And how bad indeed was that for which they sold their own selves, if they but knew.' I studied the text as well, Nasira."

Nasira seemed dumbfounded. "But Mama said…" She frowned. "If you believe in Allah, where's your hijab?"

"Not all of us believe it's necessary to show our beliefs," Ramidha said. "Of course, I respect your choice to don one. Personally, I prefer to only wear mine while praying."

"Right. And I'm supposed to believe you follow the Five Pillars?"

"I prayed just before we left for the party," Ramidha said. "And I'll do so again before bed, as I do every night. It gives me comfort that even if today proved difficult, tomorrow may bring some ease. And even before I became headmistress, I was sure to donate as much as I could to charities and community projects helmed by the Kelpie Party. I may not be able to make the journey to Mecca, nor can I astral project myself there, but I cherish the memories of standing before the Kaaba with my family. Including your mother, Nasira."

Nasira simply stared out the window.

"Looks like we're here," Seisyll said. One by one, they filed out of the carriage. Nasira rushed into the school without so much as a goodbye. Zahra simply stood there, looking up at the castle, wondering whether she'd ever one day feel comfortable calling it home. She may have been born here, but would this place ever truly accept her?

"This is your home," Ramidha said, holding Zahra's shoulder. "Our home. Don't let anyone tell you different."

"I can try and talk to her," Zahra said. "See if she might be willing to…"

"Best to leave it be, I'd say. But I'm proud of you." Ramidha kissed her on the cheek. She spoke in Arabic, but Zahra couldn't follow. "I love you," she clarified.

Zahra held her arm. "Would you… mind helping me learn Arabic? So I can talk with Nasira some more?"

"As much as I'd love to," Ramidha said. "I don't quite have the time. But I can give you some pointers from time to time."

Relinquishing, Zahra headed inside. Of course her mother was too busy for her. Still, if anyone could get through to Nasira, Zahra believed it was her.

Chapter Eight

Fountain of Magic

"WAKE UP. Getting u new wand." From Argent. 8:30 a.m.

Normally on his weekend off, Felix would've been ready to sleep in, all comfy in a nice warm bed. He'd have groaned about having to haul himself all the way into Cendrillion with Argent and Rosie. But not today. Today, his heart swelled with excitement. A new wand, packed to the brim with whatever extras Argent wanted to add on, meant he'd be one step closer to his goal. Towards the power he'd sought for so long.

Lucas was still sound asleep. Since the night of the welcome gala, they'd kept their distance from one another. Silence hung over their dorm. The only times they'd speak to each other were over basic things like, "Could you put this book away for me?", or "Could you throw another spell on the fireplace?" Simple roommate stuff.

No mention of the encounter with Vagus, no mention of the strange visions, and no mention of the oath. Almost as if it had never happened.

No, no. We need to get this done today. First and foremost, Felix had to check with Penny about their study group. If he wanted to get into the Ancient Dragons' Tournament, he'd need to survive Gottschalk's class. And to survive that hellscape, a study group was an absolute necessity. And so, pulling himself out of bed and throwing on his clothes, not even bothering to brush his hair properly, and ignoring the grogginess setting in under his eyes, Felix descended a few levels and knocked on the fourth door down.

"Come in!" Inside, Penny sat on the floor, surrounded by cluttered papers, open books, and pens. She was still in her pajamas, her hair hastily tied up into a bun. She didn't even look up as she asked, "Could you shut the door please?"

Felix complied. Another girl, much shorter, sat upside down on the couch, kicking her heavy black boots in the air. A dark-mauve sleeved dress reached all the way down to her ankles and wrists. Random streaks of green and pink clashed against her black hair, offset by her amethyst eyes. She stared at the ceiling, looking either unaware or apathetic of Felix's presence. "Are you guys studying?" Felix asked.

"Oh, yeah." Penny gestured to the girl on the couch. "That's Floria. I met her at the party and asked if she wanted to study."

"Don't rat us out." Floria's voice, high-pitched as it was, was incredibly dry and deadpan.

"Rat you out?" Felix asked. "For what?"

"Floria is from House Ley," Penny said. "I snuck her in so we could study in peace."

"It's against the rules?"

"No. Ornella's just… assertive about house pride."

"She's a bitch," Floria said.

"That's, uh… one way to phrase it." Penny hung her head, focusing again on the papers around her. She'd been quiet since the party, any and all confidence she once exhibited now gone.

"Okay, Penny," Felix said. "I gotta ask… are you gay?"

Penny turned around, raising an eyebrow. "What now?"

"I don't know, it's just…" Felix shrugged. "You kinda gave me those vibes? And it's cool if you are, cuz I'm bi, so…"

"Sorry, Felix, but uh… straight as an arrow, here."

"She wishes I was her date," Floria chimed in. "Not that I date. I'm demi, myself. Waiting for someone decent enough who doesn't make me wanna gouge my eyes out."

Felix shrugged. "That's valid." Not wanting to pry any further, he headed for the door. "I'll leave you guys to your studying. Rosie, Argent, and I are heading into the city."

"Cool." Penny looked back to her papers. "Have fun."

"Don't get mugged," Floria said.

"Thanks?" Felix made sure to shut the door behind him. Thankfully he'd dispelled the awkwardness with Penny. Even so, he wasn't quite sure what was up with her, but he wasn't sure getting involved would do any good, given all the problems they already had to deal with, including Gottschalk's lectures. Which, of course, reminded him… *And I forgot to ask about the study group. Welp, that's failure number one today!*

Suppressing his shame, he made his way down to the lobby, picking up his speed with every ding of his phone as Argent spammed it with texts. Rosie sat reading on one of the benches against the wall while Argent typed furiously on his phone. Felix's phone dinged one last time. Out of curiosity, he opened his texts—five unread messages from Argent. "Save it on the texts, why don't you?"

"Finally!" Argent yelled. "Were you dreamin' of me?"

"Yes," Felix said. "A world where you stopped talking."

Argent rolled his eyes. "Funny."

Rosie closed her book. "Try not to break this new wand. And as a heads up, I'll also need to stop by the bookshop again once we're all done."

"Nerd," Argent said. "Why not use ebooks?"

"Because I prefer the feel of a physical book, even if that makes me hipster trash. Besides, this book in particular has no ebook version. Also, you're illiterate. We both know you're not touching any books, paper or digital."

"Surrounded by smartasses." Argent laughed. "I love it!" He was incredibly excited to lend Felix a hand in getting a new wand. Though at the back of Felix's mind, no matter how much he tried to silence the thought, he questioned whether he was wrongfully taking advantage of Argent. Especially considering they'd just met a little over a week ago. Yet here Argent was, throwing all this money at Felix and Rosie without a care in the world.

The overcast certainly didn't help his mood. It wasn't supposed to rain, but it would've fit Felix's festering apprehension. They rode the coach—pulled by the ever-creepy inbred kelpie—down to the station, where once outside, they were promptly met with a rather large protest. Members of the crowd were all dressed in black, red, orange, and gold, all holding signs with phoenixes. They chanted, "End oligarchy! Save democracy!"

Curious as he was, Felix rushed to catch up with Argent as he darted around the gathering, while Rosie took a few quick photos of the event. They hopped aboard the streetcar just before it left. Felix wheezed from the sudden sprint, trying to play it off as best he could. "What was that exactly?" Felix asked.

Argent shrugged. "God, you look like shit. No offense."

Felix rolled his eyes. "Thanks."

"Did you not sleep?"

"No, I..." Felix could've revealed he was up all night not only studying, but also looking into ancient objects of incredible and accursed power to get an idea of what the mysterious Vagus was after, all the while doing his best to not let the terrible Dragora Wi-Fi and the horridly spotty service drive him to madness. But he decided to keep things simple. "I was... playing video games all night."

"You're a gamer?" Argent asked. "What's your favorite?"

"Must I choose?" Felix stroked his imaginary goatee. "*Kingdom Hearts, Life is Strange, Hollow Knight.*"

Argent raised an eyebrow. "I have literally never heard of those."

Felix huffed. "Not my fault you don't know your gaming roots."

"Roots? Wait..." Argent looked above, pondering, then broke into laughter. "Just how old are these games? And... why?"

"Well over a hundred years old by now?" Felix asked. Alec had gotten him and Rosie into a ton of old movies and video games from across the decades, far before the Revelation. To see pieces of media from a time long gone, where things weren't constantly chaotic (at least relatively), surprisingly made for a nice escape from the horrors of modern life. In particular, anything before 2020 seemed less... macabre. "My friend Alec had an old PlayStation. He was our gateway to nostalgia."

Argent snickered. "Pretty sure nostalgia only works if *you* were the one who experienced—"

"Shush!"

"Mhm." Argent went back to his phone, remaining oddly silent as he scrolled. "Anyway, first we'll get you a custom wand. Durable so it'll last the rest of the year, and outfitted with everything you'll need for the tournament. And then..."

Felix tuned out the rest. With every word, the guilt he'd tried so hard to reason away grew, weighing him down with shame. Slowly, his attention drifted to Rosie. Her nose remained buried in that same book. Once his eyes fell onto the author's name, his curiosity was piqued. "Rosie? What're you reading?"

Rosie looked up. "An autobiography of Ottavio Acerbi. I'm getting a couple more books of his at the Spring of Light."

Argent stopped his list to give Rosie an angry glare. "Really? You're gonna give that asshole your money?"

Felix tensed up. He understood why Rosie read Acerbi's books back home, but given they were now in the heart of the Median Empire, what possible reason was there in running to this virulently anti-magus priest rather than any number of magus nonfiction authors?

Rosie shrugged. "Better to understand where these bigots are coming from so we can meet them where they are and go from there."

"Even if it's one of those Vatican assholes?" Argent asked, scoffing. "The Holy Roman Empire. It's just part of Italy and a bunch of islands smaller than the Pope's—"

"Plus parts of Europe and Africa," Rosie said. "Way more territory, and definitely a higher population than the Medeian Empire, that's for sure."

Felix's will to live quickly slipped away. He partially agreed with Rosie, but he could tell Argent was ready to start a nasty fight. *Need to change the subject. Something positive.* "Um…" He interjected himself loudly, catching both Argent and Rosie off guard as he scoured the recesses of his mind for something to back Rosie up without starting a fight. "I've heard the new pope's way more tolerant of magi! He's even visited Dragora, hasn't he?" He got a few eye rolls and side eyes from the other passengers, making him instantly regret his choice of words.

Argent crossed his arms. "Planning to wipe us all out, I bet." Felix sighed, wishing he'd stayed out of the clash. But his sigh, despite his intentions, replaced Argent's anger with mere frustration. A definite improvement. "Seriously, if you sigh again, I *will* hurt you."

Felix sneered, leaning in and sighing heavily.

Argent cringed as he pushed Felix back. "If you want a kiss, brush your teeth first."

"If you care about my hygiene, don't rush me in the morning." Felix certainly appreciated this more lighthearted interaction.

Rosie looked none too pleased about any of this. She cleared her throat. "If either of you care about my sanity, you'll shut up so we can get off." She hopped off the streetcar, and Felix stumbled to catch up to her. Argent lagged behind, keeping his distance from Felix and especially Rosie. Felix truly loathed being caught in the middle—literally and metaphorically.

Of all the older-looking buildings clashing against Cendrillion's modern architecture, the Fountain of Magic shop looked like it'd be dragged right out of the Dark Ages. The brown stone walls were curved inwards, and above the entrance hung a sign with the shop's name in a harshly contrasted violet and gold. Flowerbeds hung along the display window, filled with four-petal purple flowers so deep with spots of black, they looked on the verge of wilting. The inside was only lit by overhanging, old-fashioned lamps of red crystal. Light from the display window hardly filtered in, obscured past the rows of shelves. The store's coldness chilled Felix's arms.

"If it isn't the rabble-rousers extraordinaire."

Felix held himself together from leaping and knocking over the shelves. Ornella, her hair shining through the store's shadows, wore a scarlet duffle jacket with golden beads, a burgundy pleated skirt, and black boots. Her signature shawl hung from her shoulders, the scarlet beads shimmering like embers. She chuckled at Felix's jumpiness. "Glad to see you know how to wake up before noon."

"Well, well," Argent said. "If it isn't the magnificent Nella'rela herself?"

Ornella grinned. "You ought to mind yourself in someone else's establishment, Mr. de la Mort."

"You own this place?" Felix asked.

"No. My mother does." She looked behind her, yet no one was there. Felix couldn't put his finger about it, but something about Ornella's expression, the very aura about her, gave him second-hand sadness and anxiety. "I'm currently waiting on Lucinda and Lucas before we go out for lunch."

Lucas? Felix's roommate was knocked out cold when he left their dorm. Lucas would've had to have left the room while Felix spoke to Penny and Floria, but that would've entailed Lucas snapping awake and rushing out the door in less than five minutes. Rather than inquire, Felix kept his concerns to Ornella. "Are you… okay, Ornella?" Argent gave an unsettling glare at the question.

"Oh?" Ornella seemed surprised, waiting a bit before responding. "It's nothing. Mother wasn't too happy hearing I'd attended the Della Luces' party. Lucinda was quick to settle things, thankfully."

"And I did a grand job, if I may say so myself!" The blonde girl from the party, about Ornella's height, walked out from the back, her hair up in a ponytail. Her white princess style dress coat looked like it came directly out of the 20th century, complete with coral trims and teal buttons. A black violin case sat on her back, held up by a gold belt slung over her shoulder. She gave a blinding smile. "We're all set." Her eyes fell to Felix's group. "Oh, Lucas, are these friends of yours?"

She didn't even glance back as Lucas traipsed behind her. His normally white eyes now appeared pink from how bloodshot they were. A horrific cowlick leapt from his hair. He wore the same trench coat from when he and Felix had first met, but the blue checkered pants suggested he'd just tossed it over his pajamas. By far the most relatable thing he'd done thus far.

The eeriest thing, however, was the fear in Lucas' expression. His eyes jumped as he frequently looked back towards the back of the shop. And much to Felix's surprise, that fear seemed to fade a bit once Lucas processed Felix's presence. "Y-Yes. The shorter one."

"Oh, so you're Lucas' roommate!" Lucinda examined Felix from head to toe, circling him, throwing Argent into a silent rage while Rosie observed. Felix, meanwhile, had no idea how to react. "You'll have to excuse him," Lucinda said. "Lucas can be a tad… reclusive. I practically had to drag him out of bed."

"Lucinda." Ornella's own fear returned, her expression grave. "You're sure everything is…?"

"You worry too much, Nella!" Lucinda looked back to Felix. "We should be off now. Hope to see you all again!" She whisked past Felix's group out the door, and Lucas rushed after her.

Ornella held Felix's shoulder. "Please," she whispered, making sure even Argent and Rosie couldn't overheard. "Be careful, and watch out for Lucas." Before Felix could process what she'd said, she left. All Felix wanted to do was run after her and ask what she meant, only for Argent to drag him back to reality.

"Thank God Nella'rela didn't prattle on with one of her damned fables," Argent said. "You're not hangin' with that Lucas kid…" He gave Felix a foul grimace. "Are you?"

"N-No." Felix tried to catch a glimpse of Lucas out the storefront window, but he was already gone.

Argent grabbed Felix's shoulder, making him flinch. "Your wand?" Argent chimed.

"R-Right."

Hesitantly, Felix followed Argent to the counter. "Welcome to the Fountain of Magic," the clerk droned. "For all your wand-related needs." It took Felix a few moments to realize this was the boy whose drink he'd spilled at the party. A fellow cobalt: gray eyes, appearing duller thanks to the bags beneath them. His crooked name tag read "Carlos Flores," while his expression read, "Kill me with fire." Before Felix could say anything, Argent cut him off.

"We'd like a customized wand." Argent batted his eyelashes at Felix. "Pretty please." Felix would've given a sarcastic expression, especially given Argent's behavior, but the last few minutes had left him in a stupor.

"I'll show you to the wandsmith." Carlos led them into a small waiting room of tiny metal chairs and outdated magazines. A black spiral staircase led to the higher floors, from which heavy thuds emanated. Beside the staircase was an archway, leading to some kind of workshop. "HEY!" Carlos screamed at the top of his lungs. "MASON."

"WHAT?!" A man's voice, deep and gravelly, called out from the workshop.

"WE GOT CUSTOMERS." Carlos coughed, clearing his throat. "He'll bring you back up once you're done." Without acknowledging Felix, he returned to the front, muttering, "Mal posso esperar que tudo isso acabe."

Before Felix could even process what Carlos had said, an older man with dark-copper hair and olive skin peered through the archway. His eyes darted to the thuds coming from upstairs. "C'mon in." At the end of the workshop was a forge, surrounded by tools Felix only faintly recognized from his war flashbacks to eighth-grade tech class. The man, now perched atop a stool, appeared to be in his mid to late 50s from his dark-red beard fading into copper. The veins in his muscles strained beneath his gray T-shirt. Steel-toed boots, a black leather apron, and a blacksmithing helmet clashed with his soft amethyst eyes. "You're lookin' for a custom wand, huh?"

Argent nudged Felix. "Y-Yes," Felix said. "You're the... 'wandsmith'?"

"I prefer blacksmith. They thought 'wandsmith' was good marketing." Mason leaned forward, staring into Felix's eyes. "Cobalt eyes. Fire type?"

Felix took a step back. "How'd you—"

"You learn to recognize it as you get older. Seraphina or Aviur?"

My fire's blue, so... "Aviur." *I hope I pronounced that right.*

"Father of Flame. Will say, had that wrong. Figured you were a 'child of light.'" Mason grabbed a wooden crate from the storage closet and threw it onto a workbench. The box was full of bright red crystals, all shimmering scarlet. "This right here's mythril. Red mythril, to be exact."

Felix held his chin, nodding aggressively. "I see, I see."

"I like to make sure my customers know exactly what they're gettin'. Their wand, their right. Not many people care for the craft nowadays, but you still can't 3D print these."

The more Felix could learn about the world of magic, the better. Not to mention this blacksmith appeared ecstatic imparting his knowledge. With how somber the day had been thus far, this was a welcome change of pace. Felix gestured to the box. "Can I...?"

"Sure," Mason said. "Just be careful. Red mythril can be... wild."

Slowly, Felix took one of the shards and held it in his hand. It didn't pulse like Lucas' crystal. Still, the scarlet light entranced him. "This is essentially fire mythril, right?"

"Basically, yeah. Bunch of different types for each element."

Argent groaned, but Rosie shut him up with a single glare. "Sorry about all the dumb questions," Felix said. "But I can't help myself. So, can mythril boost your magical abilities?"

"Sadly, no," Mason said. "Mythril makes spellcasting easier, and it does boost your magical endurance, but your raw power's capped at birth."

"Okay." Felix knew that was likely to be the answer, but refused to let it consign him to a life of weakness. He could still use these limitations to his advantage, so long as he kept his head up. "What about familiars? Magical creatures? I've heard you can make those from mythril too."

"Yep. It's no easy task, but with the right expertise and resources, you can shape mythril into the form of a magical creature, then grant it life.

Though usually it takes a gold or a pearl to pull it off on your own." Again, Felix expected things to be much tougher for him, but he was ready for anything. "Anyway, time to smash the shit outta that mythril and make it into a wand! Oh, uh… pardon my language."

Felix appreciated the carefree attitude.. "Swear away!"

Mason laughed. "You *fuckin'* got it, kid!" Felix gave a thumbs up, and Mason got to work. Donning his mask, he heated the mythril in the forge, shaping it into a small orb, then placed it on the bench. "Any add-ons you prefer? Dragon scale grip? Basilisk tail handle? Extra compartment for fairy dust cartridges? You'd be surprised what a round of pixie powder can pack!"

"He'll take all three." Argent jumped up right behind Felix.

No point in arguing. Felix nodded.

"You got it." Mason sculpted the wand, loaded it up, and placed the crimson core into the base slot. "There you go! All done!" He handed the wand to Felix.

The dragon scales made for a solid grip, while the black basilisk tail fit perfectly around Felix's wrist. He didn't know what to make of the fairy dust, but the wand's maroon tip alone looked much sturdier than the cheap wand he'd used before. "Thank you."

"No thanks needed. I love makin' wands and sharing what I've learned. Especially to those willing to li—" Mason cut himself off, his joy vanishing.

"Good to hear, Mason."

A woman in a mulberry tweed jacket and black skirt stood in the archway. Her red-orange hair was pulled back into a neat bun, her cheeks were rosy against her marble-white skin, and her pearl eyes appeared bottomless as they bore into Felix's. Though she was short and dainty, her rigid posture gave a commanding presence.

"Mornin', Priscilla." Mason held his arm, looking down at the floor.

"I see you've made a happy customer. Just remember, cheeriness does wonders!" Her voice grew sweeter and more saccharine as she approached. "I'm Priscilla Fontana, owner of the Fountain of Magic. Pleased to meet you." She extended her hand. Reluctantly, Felix took it. "I take it you're all Dragora students? Glad my dear baby brother could be of help."

Felix wasn't sure what to say, if anything. Part of him wanted to walk past her, pay for the wand, and leave. But part of him was also concerned for Ornella. "Your daughter, Ornella… I don't think you need to worry about her. I haven't known her long, but I think she knows what she's doing. She's got herself together."

Priscilla paused, gently pulling her hand away and wringing it. "I'll… let her know of your compliment. I'll leave you all to look over your wand. Have a pleasant day." She turned to the door. "Oh, and do be careful of those protestors. Those Phoenix Party radicals are causing quite the uproar." And with that, she left.

Letting out a heavy sigh, Mason pushed himself up. "You should all go. Carlos will ring you up front." Felix thanked him, hoping to ease the tension, but Mason didn't even look up as they left. Argent handled the bill—Felix felt sick at the mere thought of looking at it—and Carlos stuffed the wand into a plastic bag. Thankfully it was durable enough to survive the harsh treatment.

The three made their way down to the bookshop. Argent, frowning, folded his hands behind his head. "She was an oddball."

"Priscilla?" Rosie asked. "She did seem a little eager."

Felix held the box tight to his chest. "I feel bad for Ornella. Having to deal with a mom that uptight must be a lot on her."

"Really?" Argent asked. "We're throwin' pity parties for Lighthead Junior *and* Nella'rela?"

Not knowing how to respond, Felix kept quiet from there. Once they got upstairs, and after another brief but petty argument between Rosie and Argent about supporting the Della Luces' business, Rosie left the boys to the small reading area by the windows. She warned them not to "set anything on fire" before getting lost in a reader's paradise. Normally that would've been a harmless joke, but right now, Felix's anxiety did not appreciate it.

Argent lay back in a cozy chair. "I can't believe she's just forking over her money to the worst people possible."

Felix sat in the chair next to him, ready to assume the fetal position and block out everything around him

"You have to agree, right? There's a reason Dragora's never gonna carry anything from that Acerbi douche, but the Lightheads are more than happy to. The board would probably rather burn down the school than carry anything he publishes, and I'd help strike the match."

Felix mulled over Ornella's message. *"Look out for Lucas."* Did it have something to do with Vagus, or something far more mundane? Felix had seemed to scare Lucas out of his wits at the party, and no doubt his family wasn't happy to find him wandering out of the woods soaked from head to toe, unable to explain where he'd been. But moreover, why was Lucas so intent on gaining this power Vagus spoke of? What could someone in his position ever long for that he didn't already possess, or that he couldn't simply buy?

Felix, on the other hand, had been happily leaching off Argent since his flight here touched the ground. As much as he wanted to go along with all this, and told himself Argent had offered to help of his own volition, he wondered, in the midst of his guilt and shame… why? He forced the words past his lips. "Argent? Why are you… paying for all this stuff?"

Argent crossed his legs and stared at the ceiling. "Why not? I got money to spare."

"The streetcar and carriage rides I get. But why my wand? And my suit? And my books?" Felix felt so tense, he needed to resort to comedy. "And lunch after this?"

"Lunch?"

Felix shrugged. "Worth a shot?" Returning to his pout, he sighed. "But I am serious. I just wanna know."

"Act of goodwill?" Argent asked. "Charity's a virtue, ain't it?"

"I didn't mean you were a bad person… but—"

Argent leaned forward, letting out an exasperated groan. "Don't tell me you're on another guilt trip."

"I'm not, but—"

"But?"

"You've gone to Dragora for two years now," Felix said. "Right?"

Argent raised an eyebrow. "Your point?"

"Well… don't you have friends?" Felix asked. "Why stick to two random freshmen you ran into at the airport of all people?"

Argent grimaced, his eyes cast downward. "I don't have many friends, if you haven't noticed."

Felix hunched forward, ready to press his luck. "Maybe if you weren't such a dick—"

"I'm not a dick."

"You kinda are."

Argent switched his legs. "Okay, yeah. I am. But only cuz other people start shit with *me*."

"Like Ornella?" Felix asked.

"What is it with her and Lucas that interests you so much?" Argent waved his hand. "You got a crush or something?"

"No?" Felix tilted his head in confusion. "Lucas can be a handful, but I don't think he deserves the amount of hate you—"

"He's a Luce. A Lighthead. A rich, holier-than-thou snob who's never had to struggle to earn anything he's been given on a silver platter."

To a certain point, Felix was inclined to agree. But while he wasn't sure about Lucas, surely Lucinda and Ornella didn't deserve this kind of treatment.

"I mean," Argent said. "Maybe that's why you two were off in the woods."

Felix cringed. "You're not serious."

Argent shrugged. "I'm just sayin'—"

"¿Che, por qué eres tan cabrón?"

Argent's head jerked around. "What did you just say?"

"Nothing, nothing." Felix waved his hand, mimicking Argent's dismissiveness. *Apparently douchebags have a way of awakening my Spanish. Mami estaría orgullosa.*

"No, no. You tried to be quippy in Spanish! Like that clerk who cursed us."

It took all Felix's strength to resist the urge to slap Argent upside the head. "First of all, he spoke Portuguese. Call it Spanish again and I *will* end you, boludo. Second, I'd rather deepthroat a cactus than hug Lucas, let alone do… *that* with him, in the woods of all places? Just no. And third, this conveniently works for my next point. It isn't just Lucas or Ornella you're like this with. You've been an asshole to everyone but Rosie and I, and even then you're not particularly friendly. Why?"

Argent facepalmed. "Wow. You *are* oblivious."

"You are!" Felix's voice cracked slightly. "You kept trying to exclude Zahra and talk down to her for no reason. You were so—"

"So what?"

Felix paused. "Awful."

"Did Nella'rela rub off on you?" Argent asked.

"Quit calling her that." Felix lowered his pitch to sound stern.

"What's got you so protective?" Argent asked.

"I don't like people who treat others like shit for no reason."

Argent scoffed. "Rosie does it all the time."

Felix deepened his tone. "She isn't malicious."

"Sure seems like a malicious bitch to me."

Felix's blood boiled. "Do. Not. Call her that."

Argent hunched forward, dragging out the words. "She's. A. Bitch."

"Stop."

"A cowardly little bitch who wears contacts to hide who she is, cuz she's too weak to stand up for hers—"

"STOP."

Felix's voice boomed as he glared at Argent. He bolted out of his seat, a vein nearly popping from his neck. "Just stop! Quit talking about shit you don't understand!" Argent sat there, silent, as his eyes drifted away. Felix's fists unclenched as his fury faded, a faint sniffling reaching his ears. Rosie, hugging her books, hung her head, tears dripping down her trembling face. Felix turned his gaze back to Argent, scowling.

"Go."

Breaking from his shock, Argent stormed downstairs. To Felix, good riddance. He hugged Rosie tight, and as a few stray customers stared, he guided her outside. It felt empowering for Felix to pay for Rosie's books himself, even if it meant he'd dealt a decently sized dent to his bank account. They walked down a few blocks, then, once they both had calmed down for the most part, took a seat on a bench and hugged.

"Sorry for the waterworks," Rosie said, trying to laugh away her tears.

"It's okay. You don't have to apologize. It's Argent's fault."

Rosie dabbed her eyes with her sleeves. "It hurt, I admit that. But I don't think he meant it."

Felix raised an eyebrow. "You're kidding, right?"

"From the start, I got the vibe that there's a reason he's so antagonistic. He always had his guard up, kinda like us. It's just he's more willing to press people's buttons to get the truth out of them. Specifically... you."

"To get to *me*?"

"Mess with your head," Rosie said. "Get a reaction outta you besides your usual guilt routine. That doesn't excuse his behavior, not at all. But I think ultimately he's just a dumbass."

Felix had an inkling as to what she meant, but with all he'd been through recently, he had no brain power left to process it.

"He was right about one thing: you *are* oblivious."

"Whatever." Felix elected to put this out of mind. If Argent was going to act this way, better to have it out in the open and learn to avoid him like the plague sooner rather than later. But having to mourn the ideal Argent he'd quickly taken a liking to killed him. Thankfully, that sorrow was quickly overpowered by the fierce growls of his hunger. "Still wanna grab food?" Felix asked.

"Nah," Rosie said. "I'd rather go back to the dorm and read. But I can buy you some lunch if you'd like."

"I think I'll be fi…" Felix stopped himself. "Alright. Thanks." They hugged again. "The love. It hurts."

"Shut the fuck up," Rosie said. They both burst into laughter.

Felix insisted on some cheap fast-food. Rosie, in turn, bought him a couple chicken sandwiches, a large fry and coke, and a chocolate-vanilla shake. Yes, it was bewildering to see a McDonald's in the middle of a kingdom of wizards—and even mildly frightening, in the existential sense— but quite frankly, Felix couldn't have cared less so long as it meant devouring those sweet, sweet calories.

He and Rosie dashed for the coach station through the pouring rain, laughing all the way there as they tried to shield their books and food. The protest had dispersed. By the time their carriage pulled up to Dragora, it was already past noon. Felix brought Rosie over to House Ley before returning to Pyre, and all he wanted to do was rest in bed and forget everything to do with Argent. *Keeping the wand, though, thank you very much.*

Once in the dorm, Felix kicked off his shoes and changed into nice, warm pajamas. He climbed into bed, grabbed his phone, and let the hours fly by consuming his food like a human garbage can, and wandering the internet. He knew he should've done his homework or read the assigned chapters for Gottschalk's class. But in his mind, who needed responsibility when you had shows to catch up on? Especially when it also provided the sweet bonus of spiting Goat Chalk?

"Shoes here? Really?"

The door slammed shut. Felix jumped, some of his crumpled wrappers falling to the floor. Lucas settled down in the living area below. "Mind where you toss your belongings, Mr. Brasher?"

"Sorry." Felix stared at the ceiling, recalling Ornella's message. He climbed down and found Lucas studying at his desk. "Um... hey."

"What is it?" Lucas didn't even bother looking up. His voice reverberated with annoyance as he skimmed through the Book of Medeis. "Can't you see I'm busy?"

"I just... wanted to make sure you were alright."

"Perfectly fine. Why do you ask?"

"Cuz..." Felix debated whether to bring up the oath they'd sworn to Vagus, but opted to keep the conversation light. "You... looked really tired today."

"Lack of sleep and stress. You understand."

"Y-Yeah..." Felix scratched his head. "Do you need any help with your homework? Or... anything else?"

"And what do you mean by 'anything else'?"

Felix stuttered, tripping over both his words and thoughts. "I-I... I—"

"Finish your sentence."

"Your sister seems nice." Felix cursed himself for beating around the bush, but he'd hoped to avoid setting Lucas off.

Lucas kept reading. "Lucinda's a good sister to me, the perfect daughter to our parents, and a role model to the whole student body of Dragora." Disdain dripped from his words like an ichor as he annotated the page in neon yellow ink. "What's she to do with this interrogation?"

"N-Nothing. Just... she and Ornella seem really close. And Ornella asked me to... to look out for you."

Lucas' head jerked up. "What?"

"O-Ornella. She asked me to—"

"What did she say?"

"Huh?"

Lucas slammed the tome shut. "Must I repeat myself? What did Ornella say about me?"

"Just that she..." Felix stepped back. "She wanted me to watch out for you."

Lucas scoffed as he rounded the desk. "I don't need a guardian. Least of all one of the likes of you."

"The... 'likes of me'?"

"A cobalt." Lucas scowled. "A weak little cobalt the acting guardian of a noble pearl-eyed sorcerer? The thought alone is daft."

"I just want to—"

"I don't care what you want," Lucas said. "I don't care what you've been through. I am a Della Luce. A descendant of some of the most pivotal figures in this country's history. And as such, I have certain expectations set upon me that you could never hope to comprehend. Don't assume things about what you don't understand, and especially what's not your business." Lucas grabbed his bag from the couch, threw on his coat, and marched towards the door.

"Lucas, wait!" Felix rushed to hold Lucas back, but Lucas swiped his hand away. "Where are you—"

"None of your concern." Lucas turned away. "What would a runt like you ever need that kind of power for?"

The words stung Felix, paralyzing him as Lucas slammed the door shut behind him. Felix had simply assumed Lucas had no real motivation to pursue Vagus' promise. Yet Lucas didn't seem content with his position, his own status, whatsoever. That look of desperation in his eyes... Felix knew it all too well, no matter their color.

He opted to simply write the day off as a series of mishaps and bad tempers. But before he could attempt to sleep away the strife, the Book of Medeis, still sitting open on Lucas' desk, caught his eye. Perhaps inside, somewhere in this mess of notes and annotations, was a clue to Lucas' true plans, or to what this object of power could possibly be.

And the pendant. That scarlet pendant Vagus had taken now sat beside the open book. Perhaps Lucas had gotten it back somehow and left it in his hurry. But then again, knowing Vagus' ability to do whatever the hell he pleased at any given moment, Felix took it as a sign to continue his search. And perhaps the pendant would come in handy at some point.

Lucas had mentioned his noble lineage. A line of sorcerers leading all the way back to the noble heroes and noblemen whose exploits every Dragora student learned about in their history classes, which would soon include Felix. While Felix came from nothing, Lucas came from greatness, and his family had the affluence to prove it. No doubt they had their own trove of magical items.

And that's when it clicked.

Felix scoured the internet for anything on the Della Luces he could find, and when that failed, he got right to work with Lucas' notes. Most of the scribbles were illegible chicken scratches, but one page stood out: an illustration of the "Organ of Judgment."

"An organ crafted from expert metal work with mythril additions from an unknown land. Acquired by the Medeian Empire's last emperor of the Ó Riagáin Dynasty. When played, the organ's pipes would create torrents of fire to burn prisoners alive as its ominous music filled the hall, along with its victim's dying screams."

This item, no doubt, could very well have been the artifact Vagus had spoken of. Unconventional, sure, but definitely possible. The descriptions alone chilled Felix's blood. A musical instrument whose purpose doubled as an execution device. What kind of sadist would even conceive of the idea, let alone construct it, then choose to use it?

Felix read Lucas' last line of notes: "Currently kept in the Ardor Mausoleum on Pyre Isle."

Oh boy. This one's gonna be fun.

Why must the days meant for relaxing always turn out to be the most hectic?

Ornella had hoped she could convince her mother she hadn't attended the Della Luce's gala, then be on her merry way. But instead, Lucinda insisted on playing mediator, and though she meant well, this only exacerbated Ornella's terror.

Oddly, she hadn't heard from Priscilla since. She enjoyed a lengthy meal with Lucinda and Lucas, then resumed her training alongside her fellow prefects. Sharpening her spellcasting abilities always soothed her nerves. You wouldn't think having to master the flute to create a fiery plume to incinerate your enemies would make for a relaxing evening, but life works in mysterious ways. And that couldn't have been further proven as Ornella returned to her single dorm, opened the door, and dropped her bag. A silhouette looked out the far window.

"Are you ever home, darling?"

Composing herself, Ornella slowly picked up her bag, closed the door, and approached. "Mother? How did you...?" She glanced over to see the fireplace was lit. Her bed was made. Everything was nice and tidy... the exact opposite of how she'd often left it. "Why are you here?"

Priscilla turned, giving her infamously cheery smile. "Why Nelly, I was worried about you! You're always so busy, I hardly hear from you, and your dorm is such a pigsty. It took so long to clean everything up!"

Ornella was at a loss for words. *Don't tell me she found...*

"My little firebird, why are you so nervous?" Priscilla approached. Ornella wanted to step back, but knew it'd only provoke her. Priscilla cupped Ornella's cheek. "You don't have anything to hide from me. And I hope next time, you'll talk to me directly instead of letting your friends do it for you."

Ornella looked down. "I understand, Mo—"

"Look me in the eyes when you promise."

Ornella complied. "I promise, Mother."

Priscilla simpered, then walked back to look out at the night sky. The moon hung low just above the horizon. "Do you remember the tale of 'The Dragon and the Phoenix'?"

"Y-Yes..." Ornella held her arm. "One of my favorite fables you read to me before bed."

"There was once a reclusive sorcerer who lived in the mountains, who feared the end was nigh. As such, they sought to create a familiar who could survive the devastation and carry on all of their knowledge, preserving and hopefully sharing it with whoever it could find.

"Of all the familiars he'd spent hours crafting and breathing life into, the two who showed the most promise were the Dragon and the Phoenix. The Dragon was a mighty beast, able to spout infernal plumes, and carve through the earth like clay. The Phoenix was a far more docile, graceful creature. It shared that coveted gift of fire, but channeled it into forging art of any material that could burn.

"The sorcerer then put both familiars to the ultimate test. They traveled far until they reached a volatile volcano, where they ordered both creatures to descend into the magma to see which could survive, if either. Surely this would tell them which could carry on his knowledge. As the volcano erupted, only the Dragon returned, shattering the mountain in two as it escaped. Surely, this was their messenger.

"But as the sorcerer grew old and weary, the Dragon found itself unable to help its master recover. And when that cold, rainy day finally came to pass, the Dragon could only grieve, shooting its fire into the clouds as it wailed in pain. As other wizards wandered here, to the old recluse's abode, they sought the story of the sorcerer who'd dwelled here, but the Dragon could not tell them. It could not share the words of its beloved departed master.

"Eventually, unable to stand living in this sad, lonely place atop the mountain, the Dragon returned to where its sibling had fallen, only to find a miracle. The Phoenix had lived. Or rather, it had risen from the ashes. And here, many more wizards paid homage to not only it, but many more phoenixes who'd taken refuge where the volcano once stood, looking to their sculptures of molten rock and black glass as sites of worship."

Ornella teared up a bit. "A happy ending."

Priscilla turned. "Yes. But the Phoenix was the only creature capable of sharing its master's knowledge. The Dragon was unneeded." She approached Ornella again. "I know you miss her... but in this story, she was the Dragon. Do you understand?"

Hesitantly, Ornella nodded.

"Do try to be more in touch, my little firebird." Priscilla kissed Ornella on the cheek. "You mean too much to me to lose." With that, she left. After a few moments of standing in the silence, Ornella locked the door. She approached the window and stared at the stars.

I prefer the tale of "The Firebird and the Ash Tree."

Chapter Nine

Angel of Flames

THE ORGAN OF JUDGMENT.

An ancient instrument used by the Ó Riagáin Dynasty not to pass away the hours with music, nor the halls of their castles with distinguished melodies. No. Its primary purpose was to ensure the people of the Medeian Empire would only hear the screams of dissenters. A few strokes of the organ's keys, and the mythril pipes would unleash a hellish blaze which would engulf the players' targets with its haunting refrains. This had to have been the item of power Vagus had mentioned. According to Felix's research, it sat in the deepest, innermost ring of the Ardor Mausoleum, unused since the sixth century.

But marching right into the dark depths searching for this organ would've been reckless. And so, knowing his history class would be covering the death of the organ's last owner, Emperor Concobhar, Felix resisted his impulse and waited.

He hadn't mentioned any of this to Rosie. Not that he'd have gotten the chance with her burying herself under stacks of books to study for all her classes. She took a liking to Seisyll's business class, and who was Felix to interfere? Argent was still a no-show, and while Lucas still attended classes, he never returned to their dorm. Not that Felix minded either of their absences.

As he made his way to class, apprehension slowed his steps. He'd hoped Professor Renascentia-Montanari would prove to be more approachable than the dreaded Goat Chalk. But more so than that, he hoped this class could help him get one step closer to learning about that organ.

"Felix!" Zahra sat in the front row, smiling brightly as usual. Felix took comfort in her boundless positivity, even if it meant having to tolerate Nasira's signature death glare. "Um… are you okay?" Zahra asked as Felix took his seat.

Felix raised an eyebrow. "Yeah? What's up?"

"Rosie…" Zahra twiddled her thumbs. "She mentioned what happened the other day. Between you and Argent."

Of course she did. "I'm fine."

Zahra shrunk. "Sorry. I didn't mean to pry."

"But you did," Nasira mumbled.

Before he knew it, Felix was jumping in to shut Nasira down. "At least she gives a shit."

Nasira glared at him, though rather than firing back, she simply turned away, crossing her arms and muttering obscenities. When Felix first got here, he was ready for a fresh start. And now, just a few days in, everything seemed to be falling apart, his optimism usurped by constant fluxes of anxiety and frustration. *This isn't how it was supposed to be.*

"Settle down, everyone." Professor Montanari, a woman in her late 40s with silver hair—dyed rather than grayed naturally, with a few pink streaks— entered the room. Thick dark-blue glasses sat over her golden eyes, complementing her beige sweatshirt and black sweatpants as she sat atop her desk. "Could someone tell me why you're all here today?"

"Because we're forced to," Nasira said, her eyes cast down at her desk.

Montanari laughed. "Partly true, seeing as you need this to graduate. Though I was hoping for a more optimistic answer."

Nasira leaned back. "That's not what I meant," she grumbled.

Zahra hesitantly raised her hand. "To better understand our history, as not to repeat it?"

"Interesting, albeit a tad cliché. Then again, things are cliché for a reason." Despite her admittance, Montanari still didn't seem pleased with Zahra's answer, looking about the room for any other raised hands. Zahra, as usual, sank in her seat hanging her head. Many other students gave similar answers, some of which were clearly the same idea but reworded, oftentimes rather poorly.

Felix paused, mulling everything over. *They're all repeating phrases we've all heard a thousand times, but none of them sound like they really mean what they say. So if it's something you truly believe...* Not giving himself time to doubt himself, Felix threw up his hand.

"Yes, Mister...?"

"Brasher." Felix sat up straight. "Felix Brasher."

"Mr. Brasher!" Montanari asked. "Would you like to share your answer?"

He nodded. "Obviously we should try to learn from the past, but... it's more than just about repeating our mistakes. It's about understanding why things are the way they are. To understand how history shapes us, and how we can shape history going forward."

He paused.

God I'm a fucking nerd.

Montanari hopped off the desk. "And that, right there, is the response of a leader in the making."

Felix wasn't entirely sure how he'd come up with his answer to begin with, but he'd made the effort to say what was on his heart. If the world's path up until this point had been paved by flawed humans, all with their own beliefs, insecurities, virtues, and vices, then it only made sense that history proved cyclical. Still, Felix desperately wished he'd worded his answer better, or more palatably. He followed Zahra's lead and shrunk as everyone's eyes fell on him.

"Maybe the confidence part still needs some work," Montanari said. "Still, Mr. Brasher's answer might not've been perfect. But you could feel the thought and sincerity he put into it. That he came to that answer on his own, rather than regurgitating someone else's. And *that* is why it resonates. Ironically, Ms. Kader here was the only one besides him who had a true resolve behind her words."

Nasira seemed catatonic. Not angry at being mentioned, nor pleasantly surprised by the praise. Simply empty of emotion.

Montanari looked to Zahra. "Ms. Hakim? Where did your response come from?"

Zahra's hands trembled. "I-I thought it sounded wise. It's something my parents always say, along with a lot of people I respect. So I thought…" She slouched.

"And that's why you faltered. It wasn't something you discovered yourself. As these maxims are echoed, they lose much of their original meaning, sometimes even being altered to contradict themselves. I want you all to think independently and critically. To question everything you think you know about how the world works. That's not to say you should fabricate a reality to your liking, but keep in mind that no one has ever truly changed the world through solely following the words and visions of another. Not for the better."

Felix held his cheeks. *I've never understood something so deeply, yet also been so fucking confused by it at the same time.*

Montanari laughed. "Though I suppose we should move on, considering this isn't a philosophy class. Save that for Professor Gottschalk, right?" She winked as some of the students snickered and even booed at Gottschalk's name.

New favorite professor!

"Now, since I know most of you aren't going to care much about your reading, perhaps we should emphasize the idea of history as the story of humanity. Or sorcerers, in this case. Oh, magi for you American kids. But first, some setup!"

Montanari gave a brief overview of the other ancient magical societies across the world that had risen and fallen. Only the Medeian Empire, a collection of small islands off the coast of Great Britain, had managed to survive to the present day. They'd welcomed sorcerers from all across the world seeking refuge. But over time, the reigning Ó Riagáin Dynasty became obsessed with hoarding the country's resources, leading to famine, instability, and discontent.

She held up her wand, ready to start the "actual story" as she put it. "Any volunteers?"

Felix's hand shot up.

"Yes, Mr. della Luce!"

Dammit! Wow, I really am a nerd.

Lucas, flaunting his scarlet wand with its shimmering white unicorn horn at its tip, marched to the front. He ignored Felix's existence as expected, yet threw in a scowl at Zahra, which really wound Felix up. *Do anything to her and I'll do more than push you into a flowerbed, you comemierda.*

Montanari gave a brief warning about what the lesson would show. Graphic violence, murder, all the things that make history fun. "Repeat after me," Montanari said. She closed her eyes and held out her wand. "Tether Mind." Lucas repeated her words, and their wands glowed white. A faint trail of light flowed between them. "History Unfold!"

Light burst forth, flooding the room. Montanari flicked her wrist. Orange sparks leapt from her wand, falling into a red blaze. The fire spread across the void, taking the shape of boulders, rocks, and trees. Crackling embers gave way to the ringing of crashing tides against a rocky shore far below. A storm gathered over the horizon, turning the sky a dark gray, and a dense fog rolled in from the water. The mist brought with it a sharp chill, along with the scent of sea salt. A butterfly, crimson wings fluttering, perched itself on Montanari's finger.

"After the fall of the Roman Empire," Montanari said. "Many records of human history were lost." A cold breeze blew in, stinging Felix's skin. "And in that chaos, many sorcerers who'd previously lived in hiding desperately flocked to their nearest haven: Ardor Isle, the heart of the Medeian Empire."

A town rose from the ground through the forest. Wooden buildings, all three to four stories leaning to the point their highest floors were mere inches from touching, crowded the narrow cobblestone streets. Villagers, all with amethyst and cobalt eyes, walked through the roads in serf attire. Bruises and dirt coated their tattered clothes. Children waddled behind their parents, bone-thin.

A woman, wrapped in a flowing red cloak, walked through town. Her hood obscured her eyes, and her lips quivered as she looked upon the suffering. One child, a young girl, lay beside her father, crying in pain as she held her stomach. The woman dropped silver coins on a merchant's table in exchange for a loaf of bread, which caught the eyes of several passersby. She knelt, handing the bread to the crying girl.

"Thank you," the father said, his voice hoarse and weak.

"I wish I could do more," the woman said. "For all of you." She looked around, pity in her eyes.

"You did more than Concobhar," the father said. "I miss the days our biggest problem was him gallivanting around the world. I'm doing the best I

169

can for the little one, but…" He hung his head. With nothing left to say, the woman continued down the path up the steep hill.

Dragora Castle erupted in the distance. A crowd of townspeople gathered in the courtyard. Guards lined the palace entrance, armed with bayonet-like weapons: blades attached to staffs, whose tips were those of large wands.

The door to the balcony far above opened, and the crowd's shouts died down as a pale old man with gray hair, bordering on ghostly white, walked out. A deep-crimson cape flowed back from his beige tunic. On his chest was the Dragora Coat of Arms: the three Supreme Dragons. The prongs of his golden crown glimmered, as did its rubies, the red faintly sparkling in their dark centers. The dragon atop his golden scepter snarled, looking ready to come to life and burn the crowd to a crisp.

A short, pudgy man holding a piece of parchment hurried to the older man's side. He cleared his throat. "Citizens of the Medeian Empire! Your emperor Concobhar Ó Riagáin presiding!"

"It is hereby decreed…" Concobhar's voice boomed, cutting off the announcer and silencing all below him. "Entrance to the Medeian Empire shall be barred. Any resources, be they food or mythril, shall be seized by the Crown for the benefit of the commonwealth. Any who are found to possess excess rations or any amount of mythril shall be faced with exile."

"Bloody tyrant!"

"You're leaving us to die!"

"Bastard!"

The crowd tossed their threats and insults, along with rocks and excrement. Guards contained the protestors as they chanted. "Down with the Crown! Down with tyrants!" One woman stood on a wagon and led the chant. Guards surrounded her and prepared to strike, but before they could move in for the kill, she caught ablaze, screaming at the top of her lungs. The crowd backed away as the burning woman fell over. She ceased flailing as the blue-violet fire died out. Her body lay in the dirt, reeking of charred flesh.

A spine-chilling thunder rumbled through the air. Concobhar raised his scepter. "Let this be a lesson to you all. Know your place, lest you wish to be tossed to the wolves." He returned into the castle. The guards chased off what few protestors remained. From her nook behind the tree line, the hooded woman shivered at sight of the castle. She lowered her hood to reveal short, burnt-golden hair, dark-olive skin, and pearl eyes.

"A horrible sight."

A man, slightly taller with a green cloak, walked out from the bushes, though the woman wasn't startled in the least. He lowered his hood to reveal alabaster skin, pearl eyes, and black hair, slicked back and matching his goatee. "Are you alright, Elisa?"

"Does it matter?" she asked. "You've seen what Concobhar's been like. Ever since he returned from his last journey to the east, he's gotten worse. There's… a darkness in his eyes."

"I concur." He glared at the castle. "Are you sure about this? If we're found out, we'll be tried for treason. And not just us. Concobhar would go after our entire families to set an example."

"All the more reason to fight back. If we don't take a stand, no one will, and many more will die." Elisa let out a defeated sigh. "We should make our way inside. The Court will be meeting shortly."

After introducing themselves to the guards as Lady Elisa Pyre and Lord Acacius Zephyr, they made their way inside the castle. Tapestries of past emperors barely hung along the corridors' walls. The cloth was torn and tattered, while those same despots' statues boasted broken arms and chipped faces. The round wooden table in the council room, likewise, shook with the slightest touch as Elisa and Acacius seated themselves.

Around the table sat three other members of the Royal Court. Lord Arnold Ley, beaming with rosy dimples contrasting against his fair skin, pressed both elbows down on the table. Beside him, holding up the table as discreetly as possible, was Lord Santiago Sican. His dark-brown hair hung down in a braided ponytail, and a nervous sweat seeped from his tanned skin. His wife, Lady Ileana, simply stared out the window. The faint sunlight breaking through the clouds rendered her olive skin and wavy black hair lustrous, while the reflective glint of her pearl eyes made them appear completely glazed over.

Elisa looked around. "No sign of His Majesty?"

"You can say Concobhar." Arnold snickered, covering his mouth slightly as he whispered. "Or perhaps… Conco?" He broke into a full-on laughter as he held his chest and tried not to fall over in his chair.

"Arnold, please." Santiago let go of the table and wiped the sweat from his forehead. "We haven't heard nor seen anything from his Majesty, nor have any of the guards."

Arnold tucked his hands behind his back. "Good riddance. Maybe he's in his little lab, torturing all those who've mysteriously vanished after committing petty crimes." He waved his arms about, attempting to give off an ominous vibe. "Or maybe he's in the forbidden chamber. You know, where he keeps that damned mirror he stole from the east?"

Santiago looked like he was about to pop a vein. "Arnold!"

Arnold looked ready to kick up his feet, delivering the final death blow to the table. Santiago, by contrast, rocked back and forth as his eyes darted about. And all the while, Ileana remained ever solemn in her own little world. "Oh relax!" Arnold said. "We're all thinking the same thing. What do you expect to happen when you let a dark sorcerer with goddamn blue flames into power?"

Elisa clutched her cloak.

"Where is Lady Helga?" Acacius asked.

"Back on Ley Isle. She and the boys are leading an effort to maximize food production. Doing all they can to keep the hungry masses from rioting. And yours?"

"Ligeia is doing the same," Acacius said. "Distributing rations with Drakon and Hilarion."

"If you care so much for your families," Santiago muttered. "Perhaps you should show kindness towards His Majesty. If he heard your doubts, you'd quickly wish you hadn't rocked the boat."

Elisa grimaced. "Easy for all of us to say, but you'd change your tune in a heartbeat if it was your children starving in the streets. How can you allow this? This empire was founded on welcoming sorcerers from every corner of the globe. My parents and I were strangers to this land, as were your ancestors." Frustrated with Santiago's fear, Elisa turned her focus to his wife. "Ileana, surely you agree with me. This must change. No one person should ever hold that much power."

Hours must've passed as they awaited the emperor to begin their meeting. Most of that time was spent listening to Arnold and Santiago arguing over whether Concobhar was fit to rule, while Acacius fought off a migraine.

All the while, Ileana stared out the window ceaselessly. Her fingers tightened on her blue dress. "It's so... cloudy out." Her gaze remained fixed upon the gray sky. "Do you all remember the story of Aedan the Sunborn? The founder of the Medeian Empire?"

"More fairy tales?" Arnold groaned. "What good'll those do us?"

"Soothe your gall perhaps?" Acacius snickered, then turned to Santiago, who looked ready to bite his nails. "And *your* nerves." Elisa shushed them all as Ileana walked over, her shadow blocking what little sunlight there already was.

"Long ago, the skies above these isles were black as ink, as were the shadowy mists which obscured them. The 'Otherworld,' as humans used to call it. The cursed isle of Tír na nÓg. Those ancient sorcerers who ruled here, the druids, held dominion over these lands, and they weren't kind to anyone who stepped foot here. The poor sorcerers who would try to settle here, along with the human explorers ready to chart their courses, saw no difference in their fates at the hands of the druids. Some say they'd offer sacrifices to their old gods with the blood of the living. Others believe they might've been kept alive, barely, for... 'research purposes.'"

Thunder rumbled in the distance, as did a great dragon's roar. Elisa stood, but Acacius held her shoulder and eased her back down. "Probably just a dragon in the emperor's hunting grounds upset by the weather."

"Or upset by this dreary story," Arnold grumbled. He nearly fell over as Ileana hushed him. He tipped his bronze hat over his eyes, grumbling further.

"But this land was unoccupied by humans," Ileana continued. "And thus, could prove a safe place for sorcerers wanting to remain isolated from human societies. And so one pearl-eyed sorcerer from Scotia, Aedan Ó Riagáin, Medeis' most faithful disciple, descended on his golden firebird through the clouds, bringing with him the first rays of sunlight these isles had seen in centuries. With his phoenix's flames, as well as a sword so bright it's said to have been forged from light itself, he ran the druids out and claimed this land as the Medeian Empire, for his teacher."

"And then the power went to his head," Arnold said, picking his teeth. "And he went mad, and so did all his crazy descendants, and so here we are now. What a wonderful time to be alive."

"Quite the contrary," Ileana said. "Aedan loved his people, and did whatever he could to help those most in need. Without him, sorcerers might not have anywhere to call home at present." She clasped her hands. "Power does not always corrupt, I believe. It may overwhelm those who aren't ready to bear its burden. But if their virtue is true, they can still rise to the challenge. What power in fact does is reveal."

The words rung true for Elisa. She envisioned all she would've done if she had Concobhar's power. Returning joy to her people's lives, their families safe and secure once more. A happier, more just world, with Acacius and Ligeia by her side. No more need to cower under the harsh rule of tyrants like Concobhar, or power-hungry brutes like…

A thunderclap sounded off. As a flash of lightning filled the room, the doors swung open, slamming into the wall. The table crashed, wood splintering and falling to pieces. Elisa and the others leapt back, their eyes wide with terror at the horror before them: a severed dragon's head. Veins and fresh blood spilled out from its neck. Its slimy blue-black scales glistened as its coal-black eyes, empty, glared. Its mouth hung wide open, revealing a serpentine tongue and cracked fangs.

"Our catch of the day!"

Ettore marched into the room. Sweat beaded on his pale white face, which was now almost as red as his crimson tunic, whose gold buttons and tasseled shoulder pads shimmered. Shimmering nearly as much as his corn-yellow hair. The black crystals of his obsidian cape flashed at the slightest movement, flowing from his shoulders down to his black boots. He set his sights on his latest trophy. His smugness faded as his pearl eyes drifted, warped with contempt.

"What are you doing here, Elisa?"

Elisa forced a slight, albeit painful smile. "A-Antonio was ecstatic to keep watch over Pyre Isle. And I thought that you might like some help with—"

"I specifically told you I wanted Antonio here to see a royal advisor in action. Not to waste his time sitting around the manor with his sisters." Ettore looked back into the corridor. "Speaking of which…"

Santiago rushed to bow, and Arnold, Ileana, and Acacius followed suit. Elisa stood there, still and rife with mixed emotions. Fear. Anger. Sorrow. The thuds grew louder, in tandem with the beats of her heart. Acacius nudged her into bowing.

His Majesty, Emperor Concobhar, staff in hand, towered over the Royal Court. His ring glowed violet. As he raised his hand, a black smoke slithered forth from its jewel and covered the windows. The room turned pitch-black. On instinct, Elisa reached for her wand, but stopped as a blinding purple light engulfed the space. A violet fireball hung in the air, illuminating Concobhar's ghastly profile as his hateful eyes reflected the cracking, unnatural flame.

"Ettore." Concobhar's croaky voice echoed, ringing in Elisa's ears. "I would like to know why you insisted on distracting me from my session."

Ettore rose. He gave a meek laugh, pupils dilating, looking ready to bolt at a moment's notice. "Your Grace, I only called for this assembly…" His eyes narrowed at his wife, chilling Elisa's blood. "At the request of my dear Elisa." He waved his hand and gave a condescending chortle. "You know how she can be."

It took Elisa all of her strength not to chastise him. But as Concobhar's focus shifted to her, the terror set in. She gulped, daring not so much as glimpse towards Acacius for support, lest her hesitation stoke Concobhar's wrath. "Y-Yes," she forced herself to say, her voice cracking. "I believe it is in all of our best interests if we… address the matter at hand."

"Which would be…?"

"The riots here on Ardor Isle. They've gotten far too out of hand to ignore. People on the other isles are desperate for food and shelter. And we have a constant inflow of people desperate to find the isles, but die from the storms and mist keeping them out." She took only one step forward, forcing herself to stop. "We need to end this. Before…"

"Go on, Elisa." Concobhar approached, casting Ettore aside. His figure fell into shadow and completely eclipsed the light behind him, trapping Elisa in the darkness before his silhouette. "Before what?"

"Before…" Elisa's mind rushed through every word, running through every scenario what felt to be excruciating hours. "Before they turn against you."

Silence fell over the room as all eyes fell squarely on her. Acacius' face grew deathly pale. The crimson ring blinked as Concobhar slowly raised his hand. Elisa tensed up, trying so hard not to tremble even slightly, as the emperor grasped her shoulder. He squeezed.

"If they do, they will die."

He released her shoulder, and Elisa fell to the ground. "Forgive me, Your Majesty." She cursed herself for relenting. But as she'd told herself her whole life whenever she felt cornered, or when the odds were stacked against her, she mentally repeated: "Live to fight another day." Still, she wished she'd bitten off her tongue. Especially if the last words she would ever choke out were empty ones to appease such an odious excuse for a living thing.

"I'll hear no more of this."

Concobhar turned, as if dismissing Elisa and her concerns effortlessly. He cast his eyes down upon the dragon's head, frowning, before directing his gaze back to Ettore. "If you waste my time again…" He snapped his fingers. The fireball fell, devouring the dragon's head in mere seconds. A foul stench, along with a heavy dark smoke, filled the chamber. Elisa held her mouth as she fought the urge to gag. The purple flames lit the shock in Ettore's face before dying out, leaving a pile of ashes in the center of the floor. Without another word, Concobhar carried himself back through the corridor, leaving the Royal Court in a stupor.

Elisa held her wrist, composing herself, yet unable to tear her eyes away from the incinerated remains of Ettore's prized "trophy." She and Acacius exchanged glances, while Ettore balled his hands into fists and growled.

Once they'd returned to the Pyre family's estate, Ettore dragged Elisa into their bedroom to give her the usual riot acts. Sunlight poured through the windows' thick curtains, barely illuminating the black room with red carpets and a king-sized bed. There, Elisa sat, staring at the floor, while Ettore towered over her, fuming. "Are you trying to have us branded as dissenters?!"

"You agreed to call the assembly beforehand," Elisa said.

"To stop your incessant whining. We lead perfectly fine lives, and here you are, ready to throw it all away! You may not have a family history at risk here, but I do." He stared into the vanity mirror, and scoffed. "Pyre. Because my great grandfather could conjure fire, those bastards butchered the great Palladino name into Pyre." He turned back to Elisa. "Though I suppose it's better than yours."

Elisa had longed to stand against Ettore for years. Ever since her parents, abandoning their home in Sicilia with their measly fortune, engaged her to the esteemed Lord of House Pyre against her wishes. The only blessing of their marriage was her three children, one of whom had already been turned into a monstrous recreation of his father. And so, calling forth her courage, Elisa met Ettore's condescension with her own righteous glare.

"I'm sure all the starving families weep for you. You and your trophy."

Ettore let out a groan before leaving, slamming the bedroom door shut behind him. As the thuds of his footsteps faded in the distance, Elisa let out a sigh of relief and lay back down, covering her face. The door creaked as it opened slightly.

"Mother?"

Elisa sat up. Before her stood her second-eldest daughter Alonza. Her dark skin and wavy, long black hair, usually rich, now appeared dull in the bedroom's dim light. She wrung her hands, clasping them tightly. Her pearl eyes were fraught with worry. "Are you...?" She sat beside her mother. "Did you have any luck at the meeting?"

"No..." Elisa couldn't bring herself to look at her daughter. "What was I thinking? Of course Concobhar would never listen. Addressing him the way I did, knowing full well how spiteful and cruel he is. It wasn't worth the risk." She held her face, holding back tears. "For all I know, I've endangered you, Gianna, and Antonio."

"As Concobhar endangers all our lives. How many have died before they could feed their children? How many died in the riots over what little food we have left? I'll gladly take a quick death at the humans' hands rather than a slow death in this cage."

Elisa grabbed Alonza's hand. "Don't say that," she whispered. "Never say that."

"You taught me to stand proudly for what I believe in." Alonza pulled her hand free. "I can't stop when it matters most. And neither should you."

"You're as stubborn as I was at your age."

Alonza shrugged. "Runs in the Pyre bloodline, I suppose."

"No, dear. The Pyre legacy is not too different from that of the Ó Riagáin line. Your courage is from your grandmother. My mother." Elisa clutched her knees. "Thought it may have faded in her later years, when she and your grandfather married me to your father, I know she never could have imagined this..." She cupped her hands, imagining her mother holding them and watching over her. "How I wish I could've kept my maiden name, or taken both names like everyone outside the noble houses."

"Perhaps…" Alonza stared at the ceiling. "I think you'd make a wonderful leader."

"You realize your father would take the throne, not I?"

Alonza shivered. "Don't give me that image. I'd sooner die than marry any man, let alone one who was monstrous enough to win his approval. And I certainly loathe the idea of his vicious little lapdog succeeding him. I'd actually like to sleep tonight."

"As much as I love Antonio…" Elisa curled up. "I fear you have a point."

"You still have Gianna and I. Perhaps—"

"No," Elisa said. "You mustn't get involved."

"Mother—"

"You're still children. I couldn't bear to lose any of you so young. Not before you've fully lived."

"What life could I lead?" Alonza held out her hand, and a small blue flame appeared in her palm. "What if Father is right? That I'm another Concobhar in the making?"

Elisa wanted to tell Alonza she was wrong. That her dark alignment didn't mean she was evil or bound to bring destruction, and affirm she was nothing like the mad emperor. But… she couldn't. She couldn't find the words.

Alonza stood. "I… have to help Gianna with dinner tonight. Otherwise those two devourers will never shut their mouths."

She left. Elisa lay back down on the bed, holding her head. "What am I supposed to do?" she muttered. "Mother… please give me a sign."

She slowly turned to stare out the window.

Outside stood a ranch surrounded by a wide, grassy field. The orange-and-pink sunset approached. As the bedroom dissolved in embers, Elisa found herself wandering into the small farmstead, staring off into the plains. The cool breeze gliding across the rustling blades of glass was thankfully enough to silence her fears.

"Are you nervous?"

Acacius approached. His wife Ligeia—flowing gray-black hair, wrinkled tanned skin, and kind pearly eyes—locked arms with him as they strolled over. "Is it obvious?" Elisa asked, unable to keep herself from giving a giddy grin.

"A tad," Acacius said. "Fretting about the future won't do you any good."

"If you're too concerned about disaster," Ligeia said. "It will inevitably come to pass. But if you keep your mind in the present..." She held Elisa's hands tight, looking deep into her eyes. "You can tackle whatever the next moment throws at you."

Elisa looked away. "Are we really doing the right thing?"

Acacius held Elisa's shoulder. "It's for the good of all. Once Concobhar has fallen—"

"Who will stop the realm from falling to madness? Or worse, into Ettore's hands?"

"We will," Acacius said.

Elisa sulked. "If we make it back."

"Don't say that."

"You know it's possible."

Acacius pouted. "And you know I'm entirely against that possibility!" Ligeia chuckled at her husband's quip, and Elisa burst into laughter along with her. "Hey!" Acacius yelled. "Don't laugh at me!"

"I can't help it!" Elisa rested her head on Acacius' shoulder as she held Ligeia's hand. "Acacius, we love you, but you can be so..."

"She's right." Ligeia kissed Elisa's hand. "I don't know what I'm going to do with either of you."

"I don't know what I'd do *without* you both." Acacius brushed Ligeia's hair. "My free Wind Spirit." He gave her a smile, and they both looked to Elisa. "And my Angel of Flames."

Elisa looked up. "And you our naïve fool."

"Tame yourself, children." Arnold smirked as he entered, holding a near-empty glass of beer.

"Arnold!" Acacius yelled. "No drinking before the final battle!"

Elisa laughed. "Always there to lighten the mood."

"Of course!" Arnold beat his chest. "If I were as melodramatic as the lot of you, we'd be too busy sulking to get anything done."

"Where's Ileana?" Ligeia asked.

"Out horseback riding." Arnold nearly spilled the rest of his drink as he used the glass to point towards the plains. "To 'clear her mind,' she said. Really, I think she'd rather not witness you three—"

"We get the picture," Acacius said.

"I will admit…" Right on time, Ileana entered, her horse trotting behind her. "I do think it's rather off-putting. Especially for poor Seamus here."

"Well," Ligeia said. "Tell Seamus the three of us are equals in this. Besides, Acacius is far too timid to pull off an affair."

"Or perhaps… too *airheaded?*" Elisa laughed along with Ligeia, while Acacius covered his face as he blushed.

"I simply meant the displays of public affection," Ileana said. "But I understand."

"Hell yeah." Arnold gulped his drink, letting out a ferocious belch. "Why if I was married off to that Hector bastard—"

"Ettore," Ileana corrected, playing off her inflections.

"Yeah, yeah!" Arnold waved his glass. "A real prick, that one."

"We'll have to face him either way," Elisa said. "He's practically Concobhar's highest-ranking bodyguard."

"You know," Ligeia said. "Once this is all over, whatever happens, we could all live together. Us, along with all of our children." She looked to Acacius. "Your brother Epaphras can keep the crumbling manor for all I care." She grasped both Acacius and Elisa's hands. "Please… come home safe. Both of you. I love you."

Being here, among friends and confidants, Elisa's fears faded. This was what she was fighting for: her true family. She couldn't fail. The people of the empire, and most importantly, her children, were counting on her.

"I promise," Acacius said. Though he and Elisa spoke at once, she did not echo his words. Instead, she said…

"We promise."

The four of them—Elisa, Acacius, Ileana, and Arnold—stood united, their weapons at the ready before the entrance to the throne room. Arnold wielded a war hammer whose bronze head was fashioned with yellow mythril studs.

He held it tight in his hands, ready to slam it either into the ground, or straight into Concobhar's face. Ileana, conversely, bore an azure staff, taller than even herself, with blue mythril adorned at either end. And Acacius brandished his rapier, its green mythril blade shimmering against its black hilt.

Elisa kept her weapon sheathed on her back, preferring not to use it unless absolutely necessary. She had to actively keep herself from reaching for it as she stared down Ettore. In his hand, held across his back, was his flame-bladed sword. The blade, forged from red mythril, extended forth from the golden hilt, undulating towards its tip in waves.

"Can't say I'm surprised." Ettore swung his sword through the air. In a flash of orange light, the blade caught fire. The flickering flames lit his smolder. "I oughta thank you all. I haven't used this bad boy in years!"

Elisa breathed through her nose, trying to keep her composure. She dared not even flinch. "Ettore, we're not here to fight."

"Sure." Ettore scoffed. "That's why you're all brandishing weapons in the castle." He simpered. "Or why your weapons are made from mythril. Mythril that, if I recall correctly, His Majesty strictly forbade anyone besides himself and his guards from possessing."

"Ettore, please." Elisa took a step. "If this continues, things will only get worse. For all of us. If you stand with us, we can end this nightmare. But if you stand against us..."

"You'll kill me." Ettore rolled his eyes. "Trust me, I've had my fill of Concobhar's madness myself. So what if..." He raised his sword. As the others braced for battle, Elisa forced herself to stay still. Ettore pierced his blade through the floor. It stood upright before the great doors, the flames extinguishing. "I sit this one out?"

Elisa stepped back. "What are you—"

"Consider it me being curious." He walked towards the window. "I'll just hang here, and whoever emerges victorious will have proven their strength to me."

Acacius held Elisa's shoulder. "Can we trust him?" he whispered.

"I don't know," she whispered back. "But I'm sure he's up to something."

"I understand," Ettore said, giving Elisa a sick sneer. "If you want, you can cut me down right here. But I can't say I won't put up a fight."

Elisa looked to her comrades, who all gave an affirming nod. "We're here for Concobhar," she said. "Not you. We've no time to forge an oath, but may I have your word you won't interfere?"

"You can have more than my word, if you'd like." Ettore laughed at Elisa's repulsion. "That's to say, go ahead and take my sword. Plunge it right through Concobhar's chest, if you can. But if he winds up killing you all, my story is I was ambushed."

"Understood." Elisa gripped the hilt of Ettore's sword. She pulled, nearly stumbling backward as she drew it forth. She closed her eyes. The blade sparked, creating a black sheath around itself, obsidian crystallizing around the blade. Under no circumstances would she use it, not even if she were on the verge of death. She wouldn't give this monster the satisfaction of blood staining his precious sword. "Let's go."

Once Ettore left the room, Elisa threw open the doors. Before them stood a grand hall with a tall, vaulted ceiling. A long red carpet rolled down the center. At the other end stood a platoon of guards, all at the ready. The golden throne was empty. Rather, Concobhar sat at a large black organ, striking the keys and filling the room with the booms of its golden pipes.

Elisa stepped up. "Concobhar!"

He stopped playing. As the echoes of his infernal melody ceased, silence filled the hall.

"It's time to answer for your crimes."

Concobhar didn't even look back. "You mean sheltering our people from the humans who would burn us alive as heretics?" Not a trace of anger escaped his tone. "A sin among sins."

"Blackmailing them into a life of slavery?" Acacius asked. "I appreciate the effort, but I'd sooner take death's sweet release in a heartbeat."

"And what is your alternative?" Concobhar asked. "In an age of chaos, sacrifices must be made, and a leader must do whatever it takes to maintain the order he has fought so hard to establish. We do not have the luxury of an alternative."

"What order?" Arnold laughed. "Just last week I must've seen a dozen fights over a damn loaf of bread. All while you sit here, skinning dragons, staring into a dusty old mirror, and playing that god-awful piano."

"Organ," Ileana whispered.

"Who fucking cares?!" Arnold yelled.

The guards raised their weapons. "If it's a battle of ideals you seek," Concobhar said. "Then let us have no interference." He struck a sharp note. Fire erupted from the pipes, engulfing the guards. Their bloodcurdling screams were cut short as their bodies fell, shriveling beneath the flames.

Ileana held her staff tight, her eyes wide with fear as her hands trembled. "He's insane."

"We knew that already." Arnold swung his hammer a few times, planting his feet. "Oh, how long I've wanted to break his arrogant face."

"Enough chatter." Acacius raised his sword. "Let's get this over with."

At last, knowing there was no other option, Elisa reached for her weapon: a silver longbow with a scarlet string. She had no quiver, nor any arrows, but she held her fingers firmly on the string nonetheless. She readied herself as Concobhar, standing from his organ, raised his scepter.

"Devil's Flare."

A deep-purple fireball gathered towards the ceiling, plunging the entire room into a violet darkness. The fireball fell, and Elisa's party dodged in all different directions. The flames burst on impact. Black smoke flew into the air as the carpet caught fire.

Acacius rushed at Concobhar, each swing of his rapier blocked by the emperor's staff. The rapier's green mythril glowed. With a burst of wind, Acacius flew into the air. "Howling Gale!" With another swing, he sent a gust of wind forth, pushing the flames below towards Concobhar.

"Golem's Might!" Joining the attack, Arnold smashed the ground with his hammer, releasing a shockwave of debris.

Concobhar waved his staff. "Gates of Hell." A wall of purple fire shot up, blocking both attacks. "Ifrit's Wrath." The flames condensed into an orb, then spiraling into a dark vortex, rocketed forth.

Ileana jumped in. "Ocean's Grace!" A wall of water surged before her, holding off the attack. A thick mist rose from the mingling of smoke and steam. Ileana staggered as the light of her staff's mythril blinked rapidly.

"Ileana!" Elisa yelled, drawing her bow. "Move!"

Ileana leapt out of the way. The purple vortex, evaporating the water instantly, rushed forward.

"Firebird Strike!" She released the string. A burst of red orange flames flew from the bow. The blazes clashed, dispersing as the sparks fell. "Rise!" The sparks recollected themselves, arranging into the shape of two enormous wings. A firebird made entirely of white flames dove at Concobhar, consuming him. He screamed. Seconds later, the fire ruptured. Concobhar's skin, though mostly shielded, was coated in soot and burn marks. His clothes were seared, and what little of his gray hair that remained has been singed black. Staggering, he pushed himself up, his eyes filled with sheer hatred. He slammed his scepter into the ground.

"Infernal Advent."

Concobhar wrapped himself in a violet flame. The fire grew brighter, reaching out to swallow the entire room.

"Everyone!" Acacius shouted. "Stay close to me! Cardinal Winds!" Wind swirled around them, holding back the blaze. The gust lifted them into the air. The blaze followed. On instinct, Acacius sent them all flying through the window, abruptly dropping them onto a nearby castle tower overlooking the whole of Ardor Isle. Elisa held her shoulder, writhing in pain. Acacius did the same. Ileana and Arnold lay unconscious.

Elisa reached for her longbow, only to find it missing. All of their weapons had fallen, no doubt broken having been dropped from this height. All except Ettore's sword. It teetered over the tower's edge. Panic set in as she debated her options, only for her focus to shift to her allies. "Get up!" she shouted, her voice now sore. "Now!"

Acacius grabbed Elisa, jumping to another tower below. Again, pain rocked her body upon impact. But the pain of watching the accursed purple flames erupt from the high tower's walls, burning Ileana and Arnold to a crisp... that pain left her numb. Acacius lay beside her. He held his ribs, blood dripping down his lips. "Acacius!" She held his hand tight. "Acacius, stay with me!"

Acacius rested his palm on Elisa's face as she wept. He coughed, then muttered in a raspy voice... "Kick his ass."

He pushed her aside. Those same damned flames enveloped his body. He screamed in agony, all the while, Elisa found herself unable to take her eyes away from the atrocity. The flames died out, and Acacius' smoldering corpse lay before her. She dropped to her knees, holding his charred hand even tighter, coating her palms in black ash. Her lungs ached with every gasp, each one a single wish: *If only it had been me.*

"Such is the fate of those who would forsake their savor." Concobhar's voice carried all across the castle from above. He stood on the edge of the high tower, looking down upon Elisa and her fallen ally in sickening sympathy. His voice, detached and contemptuous, resounded in Elisa's ears. "I offer protection, yet you attack me. I offer refuge, yet you spite me."

Tears rolled down Elisa's face. All her life, she'd spent cowering to the whims of people with power over her. People who had no right to wield such control over the lives of others. She glimpsed Acacius' corpse, wanting so badly to apologize for dragging him into this. But she knew he wouldn't see it that way. Her eyes drifted to Ettore's sword, which had fallen next to them, yet she hadn't initially noticed. She held the sword and stood. A vision of her being hallowed as the savior of the Medeian Empire flowed into her mind, piercing the blade right through the cavity where the Mad Emperor's heart ought to have been. Finally slaying the monster. She enjoyed the thought, but stopped herself as she recalled Ettore's revolting smile.

"No," she said. "Not like this."

She hung the sword on her belt. All around her were the people she'd been fighting for. She imagined as if all of them were watching her on this tower right now as she stood her ground. Remembering her mother's most powerful spell, Elisa looked towards the night sky. Moonlight began to break through the clouds, falling squarely upon her.

"O, Mother of Light…" She closed her eyes, holding out her open hands. "Grant upon me the heavenly fires of your wrath." She paused, worried Concobhar might attack at any moment, yet she forced herself to carry on. "So I might, in your great name, pass judgment upon these wicked foes before me, and set the mortal skies ablaze with justice."

She opened her eyes, and as she feared, Concobhar launched a purple fireball towards her. Elisa crossed her arms in a guard, and white flames in the shape of wings flung forth, shielding her from the blast. The light poured forth, glowing brighter than the moon. Power coursed through her body. But even so, the spell remained incomplete. Closing her eyes again, she thought back to all the times she'd laughed with friends. All of Ileana's strange mannerisms and jokes. All of Arnold's most embarrassingly drunken moments. To her mother's warm embrace.

Acacius was counting on her. Ligeia was still alive, counting on her. Her children were home, waiting for her to return home a hero.

Elisa's eyes shot open. She now floated in the air, on the same level as Concobhar.

"Angel of Flames!"

Fire burst outwards from her back, taking the shape of angel wings. In a flash, she took to the sky, the white flames turning the sky red as they stretched out. Fireballs rained down upon the castle. Concobhar held back the barrage with a violet shield, and once enough smoke had risen to obscure her, Elisa charged. She broke through Concobhar's barrier, knocking him back through the castle walls. The force of the impact had impaled Concobhar on the armrest of his smoldering throne.

Elisa stepped back as her anger subsided. The entire ceiling of the throne room was now gone, the new moon high above them as the clouds returned to a deep blue. The fire vanished, leaving Elisa exhausted, physically, mentally, and emotionally. As much as she despised what she'd just done, the triumph in her enemy's defeat tasted so sweet. But when she recalled Ettore's words, guilt welled within her, bittersweet.

"Take my sword. Plunge it right through Concobhar's chest, if you can."

Her eyes drifted, almost looking for some kind of sign she'd done the right thing. A small ding caught her attention. Concobhar's black ring, with its shining red jewel, fell to the floor. Unable to contain her curiosity, Elisa picked it up.

Concobhar coughed as blood dripped from his lips. Yet even so, as he lay there, he simply simpered. "What now then? You take this broken throne, and guide these broken people?" He laughed. "And so the cycle continues, until another with no business ruling takes my place. And all repeats until the end of days."

"No." Elisa held her chest. "I won't—"

"Oh damn!" another voice yelled. "Look what we've got here."

The throne room doors slammed shut. Elisa jumped, jamming the ring into her pocket. Ettore, unfazed by the devastation, passed the soldiers' bodies. Those soldiers, killed by the man they so faithfully served. "Looks like there was a riot in here." Ettore snickered. "Nice job, sweetheart. If only you cleaned the manor this well."

"I-I..." Elisa's words faded as reality sank in. "You... you—"

"You were never the brightest, though. In any case, things are about to get a lot more fun for me." Ettore stared at the throne, unable to help himself from cackling. "I just wish I got to be the one to take the old coot out." He held his hand out to Elisa. "My sword then?"

Elisa held the weapon. The obsidian sheath had cracked during the battle, revealing the spindly, waving blade. If she gave this back to Ettore, it would be relinquishing her one chance at escape. It would be admitting defeat. She couldn't give in to anyone. Not Ettore. Not the people. Then she'd be losing ground once again. And then, it wouldn't be long until she was someone else's plaything yet again. No. No more. Any ounce of goodwill or mercy in her had vanished with Ettore's last two words, replaced by a deeply impatient fury.

"My. Sword."

"Of course." Elisa stood slowly, holding the sword with both heads and hanging her head. As she always did, she told herself to submit. To remain passive and docile. Ettore reached for the blade. But as his hand nearly gripped the handle, Elisa drew back the sword and plunged the blade through Ettore's heart. He gasped in pain, and she relished in it, twisting the blade within his chest as it jutted out from his back.

"Burn."

The blade caught fire. Flames spread across Ettore's entire body. He let out a horrific scream, yet Elisa took pure satisfaction from his agony. Once Ettore's body went limp, the fire faded. Elisa let go, and the corpse collapsed, the sword still firmly planted in its chest.

At last, she was free.

She took out Concobhar's ring and beheld its beauty. The light gleaming off the red gemstone caught Felix's eyes, calling out to him. Before he knew it, the throne room had transformed back into the classroom. Students huddled, in shock of what they'd just seen, while Professor Montanari and Lucas broke a sweat. "That's enough for today," Montanari said. She held Lucas' shoulder. "The speech was a little modern for the time period, but a nice touch for the battle. You're quite the cinephile, it would seem."

Lucas appeared flustered, his face reddening. "I uh… well…"

"In any case…" Montanari returned her attention to the class. "Considering how fundamental these events were, we're going to be covering them every now and then. Just remember to read up on the history beforehand so you're not all crying over deaths you should've seen coming."

"That is one hell of a way to get people to give a shit about history!" Felix said. Zahra, wiping her tears, nodded in agreement. "Hey, where's Nasira?" Felix asked.

"Probably back in our dorm," Zahra said.

"Maybe so we wouldn't see her crying?" Felix laughed, as did Zahra. "Welp, I feel like I just sat through a two-hour movie. I need some sleep."

"I may do the same, once I make sure Nasira's alright." Zahra bid Felix goodbye as they made their way to their dorms. Of course, Felix found himself alone, as Lucas hadn't bothered coming back after class. The fireplace was unlit, helping the room harbor a bitter cold. And so, not even bothering, Felix threw on his pajamas and took to bed, not a care in the world for where his roommate or Argent were.

Instead, his mind fixated on Concobhar's final words, and Elisa's dark turn after his demise. He wondered if one day, possibly even without Vagus' help, he could wield such a power himself. He would've qualified for the Ancient Dragons' Tournament no problem.

Yet even so, what Elisa did to Ettore... he was cruel, and might even have proven a worse tyrant than Concobhar. But the evil look on Elisa's face as she took his life stuck with Felix. Under the right circumstances, he absolutely would've empathized with her desire for revenge... and that unnerved him. He'd gotten a good look at the Organ of Judgment, but that was the last thing on his mind. Deep in his gut, Felix knew there'd be no happy ending.

Not for Elisa, and not for him.

Nasira had passed out, and so, Zahra seized the opportunity with abandon. She marched down to House Ley, and after asking around, knocked on the door of perhaps Dragora's most infamously pompous student. Through the door blasted a chorus of discordant violins, along with a man's dying screams in tune with a roaring flame. She pressed her ear to the door, but without warning, it swung open.

"Does your mother send you to do her spying for you?" Lucas asked. "Or does no one in your family know how to mind their business?"

"Lucas, I-I..." Zahra paused. "I wanted to talk to you."

Only now did it register to her that Lucas wasn't in his uniform, nor his signature trench coat. No. He was instead garbed in a heavy blue robe over his pajamas. He groaned, waving her in. "If the alternative is you eavesdropping all night, then come in."

She abided. The dorm was an unlit mess of tossed books, clothes, and empty cans. Ulrich, along with another of he and Lucas' friends—a dark-skinned young man with buzzed black hair and the Crest of Zephyr on his uniform, with his arm around Ulrich—were passed out on the couch, snoring heavily. Their utterances overpowered the movie, which played on the flatscreen TV mounted above the fireplace. A TV which had seemingly been hooked up to mythril power bars to keep it going. "You guys are having a movie night?" Zahra asked. "That's cute."

Lucas rolled his eyes. "Don't patronize me."

"Oh, I didn't mean…" She stopped herself. "What're you watching?"

"An older movie. Horror. So you might want to—"

They both jumped as the TV's sound spiked. A woman emerged from a dark corner, chasing after what seemed to be her son through their home. Zahra couldn't look away. "I love horror movies, but I don't think I've seen this one."

Lucas snapped his fingers. "Can we get through this conversation please? What is it that you want?"

"I just…" Zahra held her arm. "I wanted to ask why you're not dorming with Felix anymore."

Lucas raised an eyebrow. "I suppose no Hakim can mind their own business after all."

"I'm just worried is all. And I just—"

"You use the word 'just' like it's a linguistic crutch." Lucas frowned so thoroughly, he looked ready to jump out the window. "Please, stop beating around the bush and cut to the chase."

Zahra huffed. "Do you know what's going on with Felix?"

She expected Lucas to seem puzzled. But he didn't. He crossed his arms, one hand on his chin, pondering. "How has he been acting?"

"In class earlier today. That ring that Concobhar had, I think I've heard of it before. The way that Felix was focusing on it… I'm worried about him. And I think you know why."

Lucas scoffed. "What? As if I would know? Why not go to your parents about this?"

Zahra hung her head.

"Why so sad? Oh… ooohhhh!" Lucas chortled. "They… they never told you?"

"Told me what?"

"About anything." Lucas laughed. "Oh, this is a twist! Here I am, feeling like a burden to my family, and all the while yours can't even be bothered to trust you with the bare minimum. It shouldn't make me feel any better about myself, but… here we are!"

Zahra took a step back. "Why are you acting like this? I just wanted help."

"Help yourself," Lucas said. "Your mother should've taught you how to do that."

She wanted to fight back. To argue that her parents did trust her, but… deep down, she knew he was right. On some level, she knew there was something her parents had always kept from her. Something they'd talk about behind closed doors, never bothering to invite her in, even after all these years. Yet somehow, Lucas was in the loop. Even if he held only a couple of the cards in his hand, it was still a couple more than she'd ever drawn.

The boy with the buzzcut stirred, yawning and stretching his back. "Is it morning yet?" He turned to Ulrich, jumping back and retracting his arm in disgust. "Oh deuses, por quê?! I have standards, thank you!"

Before Zahra could even process, Lucas pushed her out the door. "Have a good night, Ms. Hakim," he said. "And next time, please knock." With that, he slammed it shut. One phrase carried through. A chant praising what sounded to be the name of some demon or dark lord.

Zahra simply stood on the walkway, unable to move, her hands trembling.

Why can't they trust me?

Chapter Ten

Watery Graves

TODAY was the day. At long last, Felix would find the object of power Vagus had mentioned. The object with the power to make Felix stronger beyond his wildest dreams. The Organ of Judgment, kept somewhere deep within the Ardor Mausoleum.

Going into the mausoleum, at least the public atrium above ground, was the easy part. No new bodies had been preserved within the underground tombs since shortly after the Revelation. This upper portion of the building was meant to honor the memory and exploits of influential sorcerers who'd passed in the last half-century, rather than entomb their bodies. Though he didn't have much cash left to spare, Felix relented and used it for a roundtrip ferry ticket to Pyre Isle, and then to join one of the tours to get a feel for part of the mausoleum. And it also made for a good way to scope out the passages leading to the lower levels.

A table had been set up outside the mausoleum, as Phoenix Party activists tried to get people registered to vote for the December primaries. Alas, most passersby ignored them, some even scoffing at them. Felix was intrigued, but given he couldn't vote due to not being a Medeian citizen, he elected to head inside.

Though the building was built from lifeless gray stone, the atrium's skylight allowed the sunlight to pour through. Perfect for the gardens around the stone pathways crisscrossing through the chamber's center. A tall white monument, gleaming, stood where the paths met. Upon it was engraved a message from the founder of the De Angelis Dynasty: Empress Alonza. The words, however faded, rung of forever remembering those who came before us, and cherishing life before it returns to the void.

The tour group, though, was filled with pearls and golds, all muttering while glaring at the monument. The guide, a golden-eyed magus himself, explained how most citizens of the empire had always used natural burial. It was an effort not only to preserve as much land as possible, but also because a core tenet of Medeism spoke to the importance of returning one's body to the Earth. To preserve the dead was more than a fool's errand. It deprived the world of its own life force, preventing the flow of the eternal cycle of death and rebirth.

Clearly, the nobles didn't see it that way. The rest of the mausoleum beneath their feet was home to countless Medeian aristocrats who'd been embalmed and entombed. There were even whispers of attempts amongst the nobility, using excess amounts of mythril and complex gauntlets of glyphs, to stave off death entirely. All this not merely to preserve their bodies in the hopes of one day being revived, but also to perform experiments in a vain bid for immortality. Even with magic at their disposal, sorcerers, not unlike humans, desperately sought an escape from death, to no avail.

Sick of the tour guide's stories, Felix raised his hand. "Is the Organ of Judgment really kept here?" Everyone gave him an odd look, not that he cared much.

"Yes, yes." The guide gave as fake a smile as Felix had ever seen. "But if you're hoping to catch a glimpse of it, don't. It's kept in the sublevels. Too dangerous for anyone to go near." He droned on, but having heard enough, Felix quietly slipped out.

With the amount of security present at the mausoleum, there was no way he'd be able to sneak in. Not to mention, as desperate as he was to find this organ, it certainly didn't warrant risking expulsion… or worse. And so, Felix turned to something he'd been intrigued by since Gottschalk's first class: astral magic.

He checked out every book on the subject he could find from the library. Something about it called to him. And if this was all to sharpen his magical abilities, he might as well start sooner rather than later. Some of his research proved rather inspiring. Records of ancient amethyst and even cobalt-eyed sorcerers achieving unprecedented feats of innovations. It even turned out the one who'd come up with the idea of using glyphs to mimic modern human technology was a cobalt-eyed woman who'd emigrated from South America. Odds are this all would've been very inconvenient for Gottschalk's lectures, and how Felix oh so enjoyed that irony.

Continuing his research, he discovered one practice that could easily help him slip into the mausoleum undetected: astral projection. With the use of an item called an "anchor," a sorcerer could tether their mind—or as some believed, their soul—to the anchor to keep themselves from dissipating as they left their bodies for a time. This had to have been how he was able to witness the protests in Manhattan all those months ago. How he managed that on his own was a mystery to him, but Felix would've easily wagered it involved more of Vagus' usual meddling.

If Felix focused hard enough and made it quick, he could use one of those anchors himself to astral project directly into the mausoleum. Biting the bullet, he sacrificed the last of this month's money to shell out for a decently priced idol in a local "astro-shop." The Starry Emporium. At the very least, this "astral anchor" was marketed as being on sale. A statuette of the Grim Reaper brandishing his scythe.

Fitting, I guess. Felix could've chosen the angel anchor on display, but he figured that given his dark alignment, the reaper would suit him better. That, and something else beckoned him to use it. Something he couldn't quite explain.

Lucas was still a no-show, but honestly, Felix was relieved. This meant less of a chance of being interrupted and having some horrifying complications occur while he projected. The last thing he needed was for his soul to be trapped in limbo. That would've been a massive pain. He could've also tried integrating the scarlet pendant, but it was probably a smarter idea to save that when he had full mastery over astral magic.

Following the guide to setting up the spell, Felix had to set the right atmosphere so he could relax and meditate. No dramatic moonlight was required—though the crescent moon served the mood well enough—but Felix lit some ocean-scented candles (borrowed from Rosie, of course) around his bed, set the anchor on his bedside table, and lay back. The pillow cushioned his head as he stared at the ceiling. He closed his eyes and counted to ten.

Can I really do this? I'm a cobalt. What are the odds I can pull off the rarest form of magic?

No. He couldn't let himself fall into that train of thought.

I can do this. I can do this.

He focused on the soothing scent of sea salt from the candles. His parents loved the sea. Lydia... and Frank. God, that man loved seafood, as did Aeris, but the smell alone made Felix nauseous. "We live on an island!" his father would always say, but... no, no.

Dig a little deeper, Felix. C'mon.

Frank had gone fishing that afternoon on an old boat he'd rented for dirt cheap, wandering just far enough towards the edges of the barrier systems around Long Island so he wasn't technically doing anything wrong. And then, as his excitement grew as his lure caught what he believed to be a huge striped bass, he instead pulled out a diving flipper. Lydia's diving flipper, to be exact. She never quite let him live that story down.

When he was young, Frank took Felix out on a boat to learn how to swim. Lydia protested, but Frank insisted Felix could handle himself. He wound up swallowing sea water, gagging and even dry heaving afterwards. Frank tried to get him to try again, but Felix refused, much to his father's annoyance.

"Your father is... complicated," Lydia often said whenever Frank lost his temper. *"But he does love you. I guarantee that."*

No. No, don't remember that. Felix imagined he was listening to the rolling tides. No one else beside him. The grains of sand shifting between his fingers and toes. The waves beating against the shore, washing over him, cleansing him of all his worries. He envisioned himself swimming through the depths of the sea, without having to worry about coming up for air. His spirit launching forth into the deep blue.

Before Felix could realize it, the scent had faded away, as did the pit in his stomach. He opened his eyes, and the ceiling was now within reach. Except his hand passed right through it. His arm was translucent, as was his entire body. There he floated, high above the loft, looking down on his physical body, fast asleep.

I... I did it!

Felix would've kicked his arms and feet in sheer excitement and joy, but he didn't want to risk any intense emotions giving him whiplash as his soul was crammed back into his body. He found it difficult to move at first. But as he imagined himself floating in water, he was able to wave his arms and propel himself forward. Almost as if he were in the sea. Except instead of swimming through water, he was swimming through... air? Life energy? Close enough, he supposed. Whatever got the job done.

But for right now, Felix wanted to enjoy the experience. If he could do this, perhaps if he practiced further, he'd be able to make up for his poor fire magic with his latent astral abilities. He flew through the wind and, glimpsing back at the magnificent sight of Dragora Castle sitting atop the cliffside, flew out towards the sea. He did consider flying over the magical creature reserve below the school. But if his suspicions about animals being able to perceive the paranormal were correct, he'd prefer not having a dragon chasing after his spirit, even if it was unable to physically devour him. The fear alone could've given him a heart attack.

Whether he was headed northwest towards Pyre Isle wasn't on Felix's mind. To him, this could've been accomplished whenever he liked. So why not stop and smell the roses? Or the sea-salt air, assuming he could even smell. He flew down towards the rolling dark blue, the waves sparkling white, and stopped as his feet hung just over the water. Slowly, he descended, bracing himself for the cold sting of his foot making contact with the bay. He knew he couldn't feel the cold. Yet as his foot broke the water's surface, he laughed at his apprehension.

His laughter stopped as a figure loomed in the distance. At first, it seemed to be like the water itself rose up to resemble a human. But upon closer inspection, the inky-black shadow distinctly emerged from the tides. It hunched forward. The faint grumbling of a young woman grew clearer, quickly growing louder and more hateful. Its eyes, lurid yellow green, fell on Felix.

"Firebird."

Felix wanted to run, but he couldn't. He found himself locked in place. His eyes were fixed on the dark specter as it trudged across the sea towards him.

"You remind me so much of her."

195

He turned to flee, only to find himself surrounded by even more specters, all with glowing eyes boring into his soul.

"That smile. That naïve, foolhardy smile…"

A shadowy dome fell over him, covering the sky and blacking out the moon. Only the light of the burning eyes, lit with a ghastly yellow flame, remained. Coldness stung Felix's shoulder. Hesitantly, he turned to meet the female geist's gaze. Old. Bitter. Spiteful. It got right in his face, so close Felix could've sworn he felt it breathing on him, even despite neither of them truly being of this mortal coil.

"Despicable."

She lunged forth, plunging him beneath the waves. The lost souls gathered, their cries united in a chorus of screams, sinking their decayed gray-black claws into Felix's spirit. Fear gripped him. A deep, primal fear of how far he'd fallen, and how close he grew to the abyss. He couldn't physically drown, but it felt as though his soul was suffocating within the darkness. He choked on the malevolence all around him. The knowledge that one day, no matter how powerful he became, no matter how hard he tried, he would die. How horrible it would've been to have led a life of melancholy and pain. A life of regrets and failures, only to have ended miserably. To have been ushered into not a peaceful afterlife, nor even a hellish sentence of torment, but oblivion. Nothingness.

On some level… the thought was appealing. An end to suffering. An end to pain. No loss. No joy. No tears. No scars.

Eternal rest.

No.

Felix's eyes shot open. The cold sting had faded, and he leapt out of bed, checking his arms and legs to ensure he was back in his body. He held his chest, enjoying the ability to once again draw deep, slow breaths. Once the dread ceased, he fell back onto his pillow. Whatever, or rather whoever that was, Felix hoped he'd never encounter anything like it again. A soul lost at sea perhaps? Regardless, it didn't take much thought to assume they probably weren't the loveliest person to be around while they were alive, much less trapped between this world and whatever the next one was.

Still, his mission wasn't over. If he put this off, he'd never attempt this again, much less have the perfect opportunity given Lucas' erratic behavior. He popped in his earbuds and played a 10-hour video featuring the sound of the sea. Nothing to get the ball rolling faster to relax than white noise. (*Thank you, Ornella!*) Worst case scenario, he would've returned to an ad break about spirits know what.

This time, he had a theory he wanted to test. He envisioned himself back in the mausoleum's atrium, beneath the skylight with the moon hanging above him. The gardens and stone pathways crisscrossing around the monument. Everything glowing brighter in the moonlight. He opened his eyes, and there he was, a translucent body floating in the atrium. A guard yawned and wandered past, glancing about. He looked right through Felix, but rather than raise the alarms, he simply returned to his tired patrol.

Yes!

Felix had no issue in shouting this time, laughing and kicking in celebration. According to everything he'd read, astral projecting over a short distance wouldn't be a problem, so long as he remained close enough so that his tether to his anchor wouldn't snap. Given how small the Medeian Empire was, that didn't appear to be a problem at all.

But after what he'd encountered out over the water, he wondered if something similar awaited in the tombs below.

No, no. I'm not gonna give them power over me. He had the comfort of knowing that in an emergency, he could always snap his soul back into his body, ideally bringing nothing along with him. And so, he descended through the floor, ready to finally begin his search.

The deeper he went, the eerier the lack of life became. Sealed sarcophagi, with the name of the sorcerers whose bodies lay within, sat in neat rows circling a central pillar. The pillar stretched down, through all the sublevels, with an enclosed staircase within. Red mythril crystals hung above the sarcophagi, lighting the tomb, albeit barely. Flakes of dust floated through the air. Felix couldn't help but be amused as they passed through his projection, as it was something to distract him from the unnerving atmosphere. The silence was deafening. But Felix quickly longed for its return once the faint footsteps sounded off.

A shrouded figure, donned in black, raced down the staircase, stopping at each sublevel to look around before continuing. Their face was completely obscured from sight. It couldn't have been Vagus. This presence was far less intimidating, even despite the jumpscare of its appearance. Felix followed the figure, appreciating the comfort of not having to worry about being perceived. The pursuit brought him down to the mausoleum's lowest floor. A small stone pathway rounded the pillar, with branching paths extending past the sarcophagi towards dens within the walls, likely leading to specific memorial sites. Perhaps for the most hallowed of historical figures?

Yet even so, this part of the tomb, in spite of its magnificence, had flooded. A thin layer of water stretched across the floor, enough to submerge one's foot below the ankle. The figure sloshed through the mess, cursing quietly at the Della Luces for neglecting the facility's maintenance for years, and Felix agreed. But there wasn't a single pipe in any of the sublevels. Any plumbing in the building would've had to have been installed within the atrium at ground level, with the pipes moving outward. The mausoleum itself was rather far inland, so... how in the world did this much water seep its way inside?

Directly across from the staircase's exit was a portcullis, the insignia of House Pyre proudly on display; a pride marred by several dents and chips in the gate. The figure approached. From their cloak they extended their pasty hand, whispering, "Emerald Flame." A small blue-green flame flickered in their hand. As they gripped the gate, the metal flashed white before melting. Black smoke rose as the steel disintegrated into a thick ichor, pooling into a clump in the water below.

The figure cursed once more, this time seemingly at themself, before muttering an ice spell to cool the aperture, albeit coating the opening in frost. They fumbled as they climbed through, and the ever-curious Felix followed down the long, narrow hall.

Perhaps this person was looking for the Organ of Judgment, such as he, or something else. In that case, while Felix could only observe, this mysterious entity was free to make off with whatever they could get their hands on. A grave robber? They'd certainly needed enough expertise, skill, and even dumb luck to make their way past the guards. But then again, given the disrepair the place was in, perhaps this wasn't a priority for the folks in charge. A shame, really. But for right now, Felix kept his eyes on the prize, even as he half-expected the figure to turn around and reveal they were able to see him all along.

The hall opened up into a small dark-blue chamber. Completely empty.

"No. No, it can't be!" The figure raced forward. They banged on the walls, then fell to their knees, fists slamming the floor. "It's... it's not here.

It's supposed to be here!" Their voice was faint and brittle. In a moment, Felix wished he was there to console this person on the verge of tears.

Until they pulled back their hood.

Lucas?!

Lucas sniffled, eyes watering. "Maybe... maybe it's somewhere else!" He stormed right through Felix and back out into the main chamber. Every emotion hit Felix at once. Confusion. Anger. Pity. Compassion. Lucas truly was desperate for whatever Vagus was promising, and arguably willing to risk even more than Felix. Part of him wanted to curse Lucas' name, but another wanted, as crazy as it sounded, to hug him and commiserate.

But as Felix entered the main chamber, he, like Lucas, froze in place.

All around stood mangled bodies. Corpses that had tossed off the lids of their resting places like they were nothing, gnashing their remaining gnarled teeth. Their peeled skin, blackish green, clashed against the pale purple-reds of their innards. Water spilled from their broken joints. Whatever preservatives had been used to keep them intact had only slowed death's approach, but the rot inevitably encompassed their entire bodies.

Felix backed away, as did Lucas. He knew he was safe. Yet these creatures could see him. Some stared right at him, their glazed eyes unrelenting and unblinking.

"Emerald Flame!" A blast of blue-green fire flew from Lucas' wand. The zombie at the front burst into flames, the blaze ripping apart its decaying flesh, chunks falling. The others didn't back off. They didn't react at all. They just stood there, unmoving, waving their arms and heaving.

"Dammit!" Lucas gripped the wand tighter, glaring at the horde. "Emerald Flame!" Another spell, another creature gone down. The undead remained unfazed. They began to move in on the cornered Lucas. "No...!" He raised his wand high above his head.

"Inferno!"

A blue flame emerged from his wand, expanding until it consumed all of the zombies. All that remained of the dead were their skeletons. Burned bones clattered as they hit the ground, and much of the flooding had evaporated from the heat. Lucas collapsed as he panted, dropping his wand.

Blue fire. Felix had simply assumed Lucas was born into a light alignment, complete with orange flames, healing powers, and the utmost respect. *You're kidding...*

One body, still burning, refused to fall. It lunged for Lucas. Instinctively, Felix reached out his hand, and fire lashed forth. The blue flashed white, then turned to a radiant pink, sending the creature back. It collapsed with a thud.

But I didn't have my wand? How did I…?

A woman's laughter caught him off guard. From the darkness, a woman who appeared to be in her mid to late 20s emerged. Her black dress sparkled as she sauntered towards Lucas. She gave a condescending sneer, her wavy dark-brown hair flowing down her light-olive skin. The water didn't ripple around her black heels. Her footfalls didn't sound off, even as she sported heels. Most arresting were her aquamarine eyes, lacking any kind of pupil. The irises seemed to glow, shimmering like marble, the wisps entrancing you to fall into their depths. "You've got quite the temper there, kiddo!" Her smoky voice betrayed her amicable facade. "Impressive!"

Lucas reached for his wand, only for the water to pull it away, almost as if a hand had formed and dragged it across the chamber until it was out of sight. He staggered, rushing to stand. "W-Who… who are you?"

The woman sneered. "Vivien Ichitikos, at your service." She curtseyed. "A friend of old man Vagus, you could say. He wanted me to make sure you don't get yourself into too much trouble. Have to say, didn't expect a rich kid's favorite pastime to be attempted grave robbing."

"The organ!" Lucas shouted. "Where is the organ?"

"Well, I could make a joke about you incinerating these geezers' organs, but I'm curious. Were you expecting to haul that heavy thing out of here yourself? A scrawny thing like you? You'll hurt yourself if you're not—"

"Where is it?!" Lucas' voice slightly cracked.

"Whoa, whoa, take it easy, kid!" Vivien laughed. "That glorified piano got lifted out of here ages go."

Felix moved back, his hope now giving way to disappointment, though Lucas seemed in far worse shape as he clutched his chest. "T-They…" Lucas could barely speak. "They said it was here…"

"The higher-ups keep that myth going to keep people from running around like scared headless chickens." Vivien waved her hand, her smile turning to an annoyed frown. "Speaking of which, you'd better scamper on outta here. Don't want you getting into any trouble when we might need you later."

Lucas rubbed his eyes. "My parents… can't even trust me with this."

"Awe, don't worry, kid. With how cunning you are, and how well you take to the shadows, why would you ever need trust?"

All Felix wanted to do was knock this Vivien woman's teeth out. He could feel his blood boiling, even in his ethereal form this far away from his body through the tether.

Along with his blood chilling as Vivien stared dead at him.

"Surprised you didn't astral project your way in here." Vivien's tone, before playful, was now ice cold. Her expression turned to a grimace. "I thought Vagus hand-selected the best of the best."

Lucas held his shaking fist. "I don't need astral magic. I have the raw power that cobalt dreams of."

That cobalt...

"Cobalt? Oh, you mean that Brasher boy!" Vivien returned her focus to Lucas, again donning her teasing attitude. "Wow. Vagus described him as the dark and fiery one, but you..." She groaned. "In any case, you'd better get outta here before you get caught. See you soon, kiddo!" With that, she snapped her fingers, and the water vaporized into a dense mist, obscuring her as she walked away.

"Wait!" Lucas jumped forward, hopping over the bones. "Get back here!" He wafted the mist way, and Felix tried to locate her, but both attempts were in vain. She'd vanished into thin air. Picking up his wand and giving one last look around the chamber—unknowingly right past Felix—Lucas muttered, "That cobalt doesn't know what he's in for," before throwing up his hood and heading back up the stairs.

Even despite his title, status, and wealth, Lucas hid his dark alignment and broke into his own family's mausoleum. He'd been crushed to realize his own family couldn't be bothered to trust him with where they'd been keeping the Organ of Judgment. And here Felix was, able to easily astral project, when Lucas couldn't pull off what he'd assumed to be the most basic of astral spells.

I'm... sorry.

He could've jumped back into his body. Yet somehow, Felix felt something else had to have been there. Something that could've helped him piece together just what Vagus' plans were, or why the Organ of Judgment was so important. As the mist hung in the air, refusing to fully dissipate, Felix floated past several memorials around the chamber's wall. Each site comprised a much larger sarcophagus with ornate designs, names engraved into shining gold slabs.

Some names were familiar. Ileana Sican, Arnold Ley, and Acacius Zephyr. Others, like Oliver and Oscar Ley, and Mateo, Matías, and Calista Sican, were not. But as he rounded the chamber, Felix found on the opposite side a room with three memorials: one on the right for Antonio Pyre; one on the left for Gianna Pyre; and the third and largest memorial in the center for Alonza de Angelis.

Alonza. Elisa's daughter, who had encouraged her to stand against Concobhar, who was told, without any words at all, that her dark alignment made her a threat. Told all of that by her own mother, before Elisa slew both Concobhar and her husband in cold blood. Felix had told himself that any person would've done what Elisa did in her shoes. But… she didn't have to kill Ettore the way she did. She had a weapon. He didn't. She could've simply detained him, had him arrested, something, anything. But she took so much enjoyment from not only killing him, but burning him alive. Watching him suffer in agony as he collapsed onto the ground.

And if Alonza had become empress after Elisa took the throne, Felix could only have imagined the horrors Alonza had to endure to stop her mother.

A small garden lay around the memorials, all filled with scarlet, seven-petal flowers. Felix searched his memory for their name, barely recalling the words written upon the flowerbeds in the abandoned greenhouse: "Firebird's Kisses."

Then something, he couldn't explain what, drew him towards the back of the room. A brick was missing in the wall. Phasing through, Felix stumbled upon a hidden room with its own memorial. There was no sarcophagus, or even a simple casket. But even without a body laid to rest, there sat another garden, filled with what Felix assumed to be firebird's kisses. Except… they were wilted. Their red petals had dried out and were now nearing a blackish purple. The garden was surrounded by a small iron wrought fence, with an engraving reading, "In loving memory of Elisa Pyre" in script.

Off to the side of the room was a pedestal, upon which sat a black-and-red music box. Felix reached out for the metal handle. Yet even though he couldn't turn it to play the instrument, he backed away as the handle moved itself, and the top of the box snapped open. Inside spun a figurine in the shape of a golden phoenix perched tall, its wings outstretched. Beneath the figurine was what appeared to be a set of speakers, activated in tandem with the strings as they played Elisa singing in time with the melody.

Firebird, o Firebird
I know you're scared
Your wing's broken and it's a long way down
But if you trust the absurd
You can trust me, if you dare

Firebird, o sweet Firebird
You're meant for more
Than hiding away up here in your nest
You long to see the world
But the world is cold and unfair

But Firebird, o Firebird
That's why I'm here
To catch you if you fall
And if you're ever plagued by fear
Remember our song and call

Felix would've teared up had he not been astral projecting. He wouldn't have been surprised if his body were somehow crying back in the dorm room. This had to have been a lullaby Elisa sung to her children. It only made the pain of what Alonza must've gone through even more visceral. Felix recalled the lullabies his mother often sang to him before bed. To have that love turned into scorn would be a living nightmare of unimaginable heartbreak.

But... how? How could this possibly have existed? There would've been no way for Elisa to have recorded this, and it was most assuredly her voice. It was identical to her voice from Montanari's lessons. Moreover, why was this memorial closed off from everything else?

"How many times do I have to tell you kids not to go wandering?"

There Vivien stood. She hadn't made a sound before she appeared, nor had any of the bricks from the wall been removed. She'd seemingly manifested from nothing, staring not through Felix, but right into his eyes.

"Yes. I can see you." She gave a nasty scowl, like that of an exasperated and very terrifying teacher. "Don't give me that look, kid."

Felix, collecting himself, glowered. "I don't suppose I'm gonna get any clear answers out of you, either."

"Now you're catching on." Vivien simpered. She looked past him, casting pity onto the grave. "Such a shame, what happened to Elisa. If only she stopped herself before things got out of hand. Something you might wanna take note of, kid." She turned to leave. "Oh, and just a heads up, you'll wanna be careful where you let your soul wander. Not a great idea to leave your body vulnerable for so long."

Instantly, Felix rushed back to his body, the return of his sensations hitting him like a truck. For a moment, he'd feared Vagus or someone else had tried to take or even kill him. But there his body was, perfectly safe and sound in bed, fast asleep. Well, it was most assuredly safe, but definitely not in the best shape. His muscles and head ached from exhaustion. His stomach, likewise, growled so loudly it might as well have been roaring. And immediately, he regretted not going to the bathroom before projecting for so long, because it took the foul stench and sheer shock of embarrassment to realize that of course without your mind there to keep everything in check, your body has no protections or inhibitions. Even from the most... disgusting things.

Just fuck my life.

As he cleaned himself up and bunched up his sheets to put through the wash in the house laundry room, one thought kept coming back. If the tether had broken while he was projecting, would he have died? Would his soul be lost, like the ones out on the bay? Left to wander for all eternity?

And that secret room, the missing organ, Vivien. What did it all mean? Eventually, Felix forced himself to stop, hopped into Lucas' bed, and wrapped himself in the blankets. *Yep. That bastard definitely snagged himself the comfier bed.*

He'd fallen asleep rather quickly, and awakened early in the morning to find Lucas back in the dorm, stretched out on the coach before the fireplace and snoring louder than even Rosie. Felix stretched, planning to immediately go back to sleep and question this later, only to discover a post-it note on the bedside table.

"Enjoy my bed, Cobalt. I'll probably be gone by the time you wake up, so I don't care either way. I don't want to know what happened to your bed. By Seraphina's light, I hope I never learn."

Felix snickered. *Looks like Lighthead's about as clueless as me.*

Chapter Eleven

Of Pearls and Cobalts

FELIX tapped his foot, leaning against the wall outside Rosie's dorm. "If you could hurry. I don't wanna be late for the combat league."

Rosie laughed from inside. "Have to say, didn't expect you to leap at the chance to learn how to roast some bitches."

He'd skimmed through Dragora's list of extracurriculars, looking for something that could help him hone his magical abilities outside the classroom. Any hope he'd had of wanting to join the Aspiring Spell Engineers' Club was killed when he realized what a bitch trying to learn HSCL was. That's when he stumbled on the Magical Combat League, supervised by Professor Ranbir Jhaveri. Felix didn't know how far he'd get as a cobalt, but he had to try, especially if it meant catching up to Lucas' abilities.

"Earth to Felix!" Rosie snapped her fingers, breaking through Felix's daze. "You good?"

He shook his head. "Yeah. But think about it. Maybe this could help us get into the Ancient Dragons' Tournament."

"You mean the tournament I give no fucks about?" Rosie asked. "Huh. Wow."

He rolled his eyes. "Well, I give *many* fucks. Many!"

"You? A fighter?" Rosie chuckled. "Not to discourage you, but you couldn't hurt a fly, you goddamn marshmallow."

Felix brooded. "I'm constantly insulting people!"

"Yes. Inanimate objects. Specifically when you stub your toe into them. Bloodthirsty little bitch you are." Rosie laughed, then stopped herself. "But seriously, promise me you won't go nuts with this. I don't need you getting yourself hurt."

"Oh c'mon!" Felix waved his hand. "I'll be fine. You know—"

"Promise me." Rosie crossed her arms. Somehow, even though she was slightly shorter than Felix, she managed to give the vibe she was towering over him.

"I promise."

Rosie had to rush back inside to grab her phone. (*Same.*) The dorm was empty, though when Felix asked about Rosie's roommate, he didn't get much of an answer. They'd apparently barely spoken, but from what Rosie had gathered, she was one of the "elite students" in the same vein as Lucas. In which case, it was probably best for everyone they knew as little about her as possible.

They headed downstairs into the common area of House Ley. Lucinda, seated by the flower bed surrounding the central dragon statue, played her violin, her song echoing as if she were centerstage in a concert hall. As she played, her violin's strings shimmered with yellow mythril. And from those strings emerged sprite wisps. The wisps danced through the air, releasing flakes of light that, as they touched the flowers, helped them blossom and pop with color. The melody soothed Felix's nerves as he fell into the tune of the strings. "Good morning, Mr. Brasher!"

"M-Morning." Felix wasn't sure what to say, or even if he should say anything. Especially given… recent events.

Lucinda turned to Rosie. "And you as well, Ms.…."

Rosie put her hand on her hip. "Rosie."

"What a lovely name! Is it short for something?"

"Briar Rose." As ridiculous as it sounded, it wasn't far off. Rosie's dads named her after Aurora when they adopted her. And funnily enough, when they introduced her to the movie, Sleeping Beauty became her favorite princess solely because she got to sleep through most of the story and have the plot done for her. And so the nickname came to be.

"Oh!" Lucinda held up her bow, as if its tip dinged like a lightbulb. "Mr. Brasher, I'd like to apologize for Lucas' rash behavior. I've heard of his grumblings, and I wanted to ensure—"

"It's fine." Felix clasped his hands, recalling the disarray Lucas had been thrown into in the mausoleum as he spewed blue fire everywhere—the proof of his shameful dark alignment. Just as he promised in his note, Lucas had left the dorm before Felix had reawakened, and hadn't returned since. "Is he...?"

"He's currently dorming with his friend Ulrich."

Felix hung his head. "I see."

Lucinda, brushing away her frown, forced a smile. "I'm sure whatever happened, you did nothing wrong. Lucas can be... a handful. Please do try to look after yourself."

He nodded.

"We have to go now." Rosie grabbed Felix's arm and pulled him into the hall. As Felix glanced back, he caught Lucinda rushing to put down her violin and text someone. Something about it disturbed him, and suddenly, he understood Rosie's need to get away.

"What now, Nella'rela?" Argent looked away, sulking.

Ornella shook her head. "Right, right. Sorry to distract you from silently planning out your apology to Mr. Brasher, only to chicken out at the last minute." Normally she didn't enjoy being petty, but if it got the job done, so be it. And it seemed to do the trick, as Argent's apathetic facade dissolved.

"What makes you think this has anything to do with Felix?"

She shook her head. "Look, he's going to be here shortly, and I know you still care about him. And you also regret how you treated him."

Argent, crossing his arms, glanced down both ends of the hall. "Get to your point, Nella."

"My point is we both want to look out for him. And I'm afraid he's messing with things... with people, he shouldn't be." Ornella held her shawl. "So if you do want to make up for what you've done, you need to be there for him. Besides, you both could use some happiness. Take my advice that ripping the band-aid off and feeling uncomfortable for a short time is a far brighter path than venturing down the dark, winding road of procrastination."

Argent closed his eyes. He didn't say a word, but deep down, Ornella knew he'd gotten the message. Perfect timing as she received a message from Lucinda. Felix was on his way down here now, and the rest had to be left in Argent's hands. Without another word, Ornella took off down the hall, hoping things would work themselves out for the best.

May the Dragons have mercy upon Felix. He'll most assuredly need it when it comes to Mr. de la Mort.

"So, Lucinda?" Felix asked, waiting until he was sure they were out of earshot from Lucinda. He pulled his arm free from Rosie's grip. "What's your take on her?"

"I just don't like her."

"What? She too preppy for you? Too happy?"

"Happy people *do* disgust me." Rosie snickered. "But seriously, she seemed kinda… intrusive, didn't she? Almost like she was fishing for info."

He raised an eyebrow. "You sound like Argent."

"I'm just saying, maybe Lucas is the way he is for a reason."

"Whatever. Let's just…" He trailed off as they neared the gym entrance, where stood Argent, arms crossed and whistling. He glanced towards Felix and Rosie, then giving a huff, entered the room. *He's here too? Fuck my life.* Felix hadn't seen a trace of Argent since their argument, even in class. But Argent had no real reason to be here. Unless…

Rosie held Felix's shoulder. Giving a nod, Felix gulped, and they headed inside. The gymnasium was massive with a wooden floor. Students sat in the bleachers beneath the windows. Argent tucked himself away in the opposite corner. With no other options, Felix and Rosie took their seats towards the center. Felix, filling with anxiety, examined his wand from the Fountain of Magic—the wand Argent bought for him. A steady flow of guilt mingled with his nervousness. *How much did he pay for this?*

"Listen up, everyone!" An old man entered the room. While his salt-and-pepper hair tied into a ponytail, along with his goatee, suggested he was nearing his sixties, his muscular physique made him look twenty years younger. If his black muscle shirt and sweatpants didn't say he was ready for a fight, nor the trans pride bracelet proudly displayed on his wrist, then his gold championship belt certainly did. Felix's jaw nearly dropped: the proud Dragon Skinner of 2089, champion of the septennial tournament.

"Hello there," Rosie whispered, her eyes fixed on the man's muscles. Felix gave a questioning look, to which Rosie stuck out her tongue and snickered.

You know what? Honestly, same.

Jhaveri gave them all a brief introduction to both himself and the league as he paced about, sulking the whole time through his slight Indian accent. "Now, while I know that most of you are likely planning on becoming beast hunting majors, and thus will be taking combat classes nonetheless, I appreciate all of you coming here today. Here you'll learn how to stay alive. Because where I'm from, I sure as hell would've loved to know."

He rolled up his pant leg, revealing a scar covering the majority of his lower leg. "This one was from emissaries who thought it'd be fun to see if I had a spell to tame rabid dogs." He rolled up the other leg to reveal a prosthetic. "I was thirteen. India was toying with the idea of joining the New Ottoman Empire. Of course we all know now they declined. But back then, when the caliphate's missionaries came knocking… well, I'm a cobalt, but my parents were amethysts. You can guess how that went."

The students fell silent, and Felix felt sick from the sight.

"You may feel safe right now," Jhaveri said. "But whatever the next few years have in store could leave you all in shock. My job's to make sure that no matter what happens, you'll be able to stand your ground. And hopefully, not end up like me."

The professor's words caught Felix off guard, but helped put his own issues into perspective. Carson was a pain to deal with, sure. But he was nothing compared to what religious zealots, even worse than Frank, would've done had they gotten their hands on him. Even a part of the League of United Nations was still a dangerous place for magi to live. The Medeian Empire truly was a haven—the only one of its kind.

On Jhaveri's instructions, the students organized themselves in a shoulder-to-shoulder line. They were to start with the basics by finding a partner with a matching eye color, as best as they could manage. Before Felix could say anything, Rosie went off looking for her own partner. *Meeting new people. Yay.* He'd lost sight of Argent and Lucas in the shuffle. *Welp, looks like there's a benefit to being a cobalt after all. The dynamic douchebags are officially off the list.*

"Hey, you."

A young man, cobalt eyes vacant of any care or expression, approached. It took Felix a moment to piece together his familiarity. "You..." *Curse my memory.* "You work at the wand shop in the city, right? Carlos?"

"Yeah." His voice was deadpan as ever. "Partners?"

Felix shrugged. "Sure. Why not?" They walked over to their own little area as all the pairs arranged themselves. Rosie had paired herself with the guy she'd fawned over during the Della Luces' welcome gala weeks before. He'd clearly been from the States too. Probably from the Midwest or South given his choice of red flannel shirt, blue jeans, and brown boots. *Look, I didn't come up with these stereotypes, okay? It's not my fault when people fit them perfectly. Exhibit me, a constantly tired bisexual disaster.* Argent, meanwhile, had partnered up with Lucas. Felix snickered. *Good. They deserve each other.*

Jhaveri's voice reverberated across the room. "Now who'd like to volunteer for a demonstration?"

A few students raised their hands, including Felix. Carlos might not've seemed pleased as he rolled his eyes, but Felix couldn't have cared less. The sooner he could get any kind of experience, the better. Felix would be attacking while Carlos defended. Felix readied his wand, waiting for a cue. Waiting... and waiting... and still waiting. "So... do I use any spells in particular, or—"

"What spells do you know?" Jhaveri asked.

"Uh—"

"Too late."

A gust of wind from Carlos knocked Felix off his feet. He pushed himself up, his back aching. "A real enemy won't wait for you to get ready," Jhaveri said. "You don't have the luxury of being able to think. You gotta trust your gut and take initiative. Act, then react."

Carlos sneered, and Felix's blood boiled. *Ooh, okay. Now you're in for it. Raging bitch mode activated.* For a moment, he glanced at Lucas, who was also snickering, and Argent seemed to snap his head away from Felix at the last moment, now glaring at Lucas. *Whatever, jerk.*

Channeling his anger, Felix held out his wand. "Firebird Strike!" He tried to mimic Elisa's spell, picturing the pure white light in the shape of a phoenix's wings, only for a few pink sparks to fall from his wand and die out within seconds. *Welp, that didn't—*

"Tornado!" Carlos shot out another vortex of wind.

"Firewall!" Felix created a column of flames. It formed a shield, then launched forth through the vortex. Carlos dodged.

"Enough." Jhaveri stood between them. "Clunky and mediocre, but it's a start. I want all of you to do the same."

"Uh…" Felix, racked with shame, could barely bring himself to speak. "Professor?"

"Yes? Use your words."

"There's kind of a…" Felix pointed to a small fire gathering on the floor.

"And *why* has no one put it out yet?" Jhaveri asked. "Sure, let the fire rage on. It'll definitely put itself out after a good while." Jhaveri's voice cut through Felix's ego, and assumedly everyone else's, like a knife. "Aqua Torrent!" Water rushed from Jhaveri's wand and extinguished the flames. "There's this thing called initiative, kids. Might save you from letting a fire burn you alive." He muttered in Hindi as he rubbed his temples.

Jhaveri touched the far wall. "Glyph: Domes of Light." A bright symbol appeared before him, and clear barriers rose around all the pairs.

Alright. Felix readied his wand again as he focused on his mind. *Time to redeem myself.* He threw a few fireballs, and Carlos retaliated with gusts of wind to dispel them. Not much actual fighting took place. Just mindless attacks and dodges. Then again, neither of them could do much in the first place, since even such little use of power tired them out after only a minute. They slowed, panting, wiping sweat from their foreheads.

Felix glanced over at the other pairs. Rosie was still able to keep up with her partner, looking only slightly tired, while Argent and Lucas were constantly throwing out spells. Felix cursed himself for his weakness. *Damn cobalt eyes.*

"¿Eres tonto, o…?"

Before he could process what he'd heard, Felix dodged another attack. "What… what did you just say?"

"What?" Carlos asked. "¿No hablas español?"

"But at the shop… you spoke—"

"Glyph: Retract." Ranbir lowered the domes, and everyone stopped. "You'll all definitely need a lot of work. A. Lot. Everyone back to the stands."

They all took to their seats, and Felix was relieved to be able to sit. The shame continued its encroachment as he folded his arms over his knees.

"Hey." Rosie sat beside him. "You okay?"

No response. Jhaveri went over techniques of how to choose which spells to use and different strategies to employ, but Felix tuned them all out. The reality of his limitations had sunk in, drowning out his optimism.

"Now, to finish the day off," Jhaveri said. "We'll be doing some one-on-one fights. Would anyone like to volunteer?" Rosie's partner raised his hand and walked down. "And your name is?"

"Shawn," he said. A slight midwestern twang confirmed Felix's earlier guess.

"And who would you like to challenge?" Jhaveri asked.

Shawn crossed his arms. "Rosie, you up for another round?"

"You know it!" Rosie leapt up, winked at Felix, and ran down. While Felix was envious that Rosie's eyes meant she was more apt for spellcasting, he was honestly more envious of how gung-ho she wound up being about the whole thing. Here she was, seemingly uninterested in magic, yet flourishing. All while Felix pouted over in his corner of secrets.

"Now when you're dueling," Jhaveri said. "Don't overdo it. You're not actually trying to kill each other. At least, I hope you aren't."

Encouraging!

"You'll also be using mythril armor, in case one of you is feeling homicidal."

Where the fuck was this armor before? Also, this professor and I share a sense of humor. Is this love, or am I just creepily infatuated?

Rosie and Shawn donned the armor while Jhaveri backed up towards the far wall. He explained that the gym was designed to use illusory magic for specialized arenas. A sort of augmented virtual reality. One that could distort itself to properly accommodate any fight, but one that could also hurt you if you weren't careful enough, and hurt you badly. With that, he activated the glyph, and a much larger barrier rose around Shawn and Rosie. "And now to add a little chaos to the mix," Jhaveri said. "Glyph, Mirage: Woodland Valley!"

A green symbol emerged along the ground. The wooden floors within the barrier became grassy fields and small hills. Tall trees and dense shrubs formed from nothing, and a small creek ran through the meadow. Felix was taken aback. In moments, these glyphs had created a special arena within the room they could all see from the outside, but likely appeared to be its own world from within the dome.

Rosie ditched Shawn, ducking into the tall grass and losing his trail. As he searched, Shawn approached the stone-covered shores of the creek. Rosie, sneering, peeked out from her hiding place. "Ivy Cage!"

Vines raced forth from the trees, entangling Shawn. "River Cut!" He waved his arms, and a torrent of water from the creek slashed through the vines. He raced up the hill, using the same spell over and over, slashing tree after tree to expose his target, eliminating as many places for her to hide as possible.

Felix held his chin to keep himself from shaking his head. Going berserk like this would've only tired Shawn out, which—as Felix surmised—was exactly Rosie's plan. Shawn was worn out within moments, nearly toppling over, holding onto one of the fallen trees for balance.

"Liana Trap!"

Vines reached down from the treetops. Shawn repeated his spell, but they'd grown much weaker with each blow. The vines broke through, grabbing him, carrying him into the air, and finally tossing him into the creak below. Rosie cackled as she revealed herself, while Shawn spat out water as he climbed his way onto dry land.

Jhaveri ended the glyph's command, and the barrier and forest vanished in one fell swoop. Still, Shawn remained drenched, with small chunks of vines hanging from his clothes and tangled in his hair. Jhaveri frowned. "That certainly didn't last as long as I expected," he said. "Shawn, while going in without a strategy is bad enough, using the same spell over and over shows me you lack initiative. Not only did you exhaust yourself quickly, but your repetition helped your enemy get the better of you."

"Yes, sir." Shawn stood at attention. "I'll be sure to study up."

"Er… good." Jhaveri, looking confused, turned his attention to Rosie. "I absolutely commend your strategy, Rosie! Keep up the good work."

"Of course." Rosie helped Shawn remove both his armor and the bits of vine he'd missed before they took to their seats. "Well?" She playfully nudged Felix. "I kicked serious ass if I do say so myself." She leaned in. "He is mine."

"Which one?" Felix snickered, but was cut off by a light punch on the arm from Rosie. Felix rolled his eyes, to which Rosie rolled hers twice.

"I'd like to volunteer!"

Argent's voice returned Felix's dread as he raised his hand. "Who would you like to duel?" Jhaveri asked him.

Oh boy. Let's get this over with.

"Lucas."

Felix, surprised, kept his focus on Argent, but Argent avoided his gaze. Felix was sure Argent showed up here to try and prove something to him in a fight. But why take on Lucas of all people? *Maybe he hates Lucas more than he hates me?*

Argent and Lucas donned their armor, and a barrier surrounded them. Their arena was an underground cavern home to a natural hot spring. A small body of water formed in the cavern's center, while the geysers all around let off steam.

Argent dove into the spring, and a shard of ice shot up from the water. It floated for a moment before exploding, a barrage of jagged blue rays raining all over the cave.

Lucas dodged. "Arcane Inferno!" He tossed a blue spark, light enough to pass as white in the blink of an eye, into the water. Popping bubbles gave way to rising steam. Argent leapt out, coughing up water as a faint trace of steam rose from his skin. "Emerald Flame!" Lucas launched a sickly green flame from his wand.

"Snow's Emblem!" Argent forged a blue shield in the shape of a snowflake, blocking Lucas' attack. "Diamond Arrow!" The shield contracted, then surged forth. A shard of ice struck Lucas square in his chest plate. He stumbled, and Argent sneered. "Frost Gauntlet!" Ice formed on his arm as he balled his hand into a fist. He rushed in for the kill.

"Flame Strike!" A blue-green fire enveloped Lucas' arm. As their punches met, Argent knocked Lucas off balance. Lucas fell back. Seizing the moment, Argent kicked him into the geyser behind him. It erupted, launching Lucas, headfirst, into the spring. Every student burst into laughter. Except Felix. All the conflicting feelings he'd harbored towards Lucas now instead culminated into sympathy.

The barrier fell. As the gym returned to normal, Argent approached the fallen Lucas, wringing the water out of his hair. Argent knelt and held out his hand. "Need some help, princess?"

Lucas snarled, throwing his helmet and armor to the floor, his face red. He tried to storm off, only for Jhaveri to grab him by the wrist. "Lucas, you have to be more aware of your opponent's strategy. You need to adapt."

Seething, Lucas tore his hand free. "I don't need cheap tactics to win!"

Argent smirked, though that confidence faded as he glimpsed Felix's disapproving glare. On the spot, Argent hung his head, sulking.

"In a real battle," Jhaveri said. "You do what you must to survive. Your noble approach may seem appealing now, but it won't guarantee you walk away unharmed."

Lucas scoffed, huffing and puffing as he passed Felix on his way back to his seat. "Hey." Felix stood, and Lucas paused, his back still turned towards Felix. "What Argent did... I'm sorry. That was shitty of—"

"I don't need your pity, Cobalt."

Felix sat back down, wallowing in exhaustion. *I tried, I guess.*

"What's your problem?" Rosie asked. The moment Felix heard the words, he could feel the tension escalating in the room, and he wasn't looking forward to Lucas' breaking point.

"You heard me, mutt!" Lucas wasn't even trying to keep his voice down. Everyone's eyes fell on his angry stare, while he, in return, looked down upon all of them. "You relied on the same dirty tricks. But I suppose that should be expected from lowly filth calling itself a sorcerer."

Now Felix was ready to fight. He'd quickly gotten used to Lucas' arrogance, but him taking out his issues on Felix's friends was crossing the line.

"Watch it, man!" Shawn said. "Rosie did what it took to win." He blushed, smiling at her. "V-Very smart, by the way. You were awesome!"

Rosie blushed in turn. "Awe, shucks."

Felix appreciated the help, but something else caught his attention: Shawn's eyes. Felix had assumed Shawn was an amethyst-eyed magus, or perhaps a cobalt. But... he was both. His left eye's iris was a dull cobalt, and the right a bright amethyst.

Lucas scoffed. "What a surprise. American scum sticking together."

"What century are you from again?" Felix asked. "You sound like you belong in the fucking Dark Ages." It took all his strength not to punch Lucas' teeth out. He could probably replace them all anyway. They'd put a bigger dent in his jawline than his parents' bank account.

"Keep quiet, Cobalt. You shouldn't even be here. It's a waste of valuable resources trying to build up a nothing like you. Why don't you run along home? Back to whatever hole you crawled out of."

Flustered, Felix threw caution to the wind. "Fuck it."

"What was that?"

"It's time someone knocked some sense into you."

Jhaveri held his chin. "Are you saying you'd like to duel him, Felix? Normally I wouldn't let a cobalt to fight a pearl. But if you're sure…"

Everyone's gaze fell on Felix. Normally, when that happened, he'd wish to disappear. But not now. Now, he knew he had to take Lucas down a peg. Not just to prove himself, but to avenge every cobalt and amethyst who'd ever been, or would be, in his shoes. This was bigger than his ego now. Even if he lost—which he definitely would, considering both his weariness and lack of skills—he still had to try.

"I'm sure."

Felix and Lucas donned their armor. Carlos gave a wink, and while Felix was repulsed, he felt a twinge of pity when he'd realized Lucas was its unfortunate recipient. Pity which quickly turned to schadenfreude at Lucas' own disgust. The barrier went up, and Jhaveri raised his wand. "Glyph…"

Please be a meadow of bunnies. Please be a meadow of bunnies.

"Icy Cliffside."

Should've expected that, honestly. Felix had to appreciate the irony, but that attitude vanished as an icy wind grazed his skin. He shivered as snow fell all around him. The tops of mountains extended out towards the horizon. He looked down, and was greeted by a several-hundred-foot drop to certain death. The only sound was the howl of the wind. If anything, him knowing this was an illusion only fueled his cognitive dissonance, leaving him dazed. It didn't help that Lucas was nowhere to be seen. Felix could hardly make out anything past his now numbed nose.

Suddenly, warmth washed over him. He reveled in it, until a faint red light in the distance grew brighter and brighter. *Shit!* He jumped out of the way as the fire rushed past him. The drop again greeted him as he raised his head out of the snow, and he leapt back. *What the fuck happened to the "nobleman's honor," Lighthead?!*

Another fireball barreled towards him, and Felix ducked beneath a nearby slope to conceal himself. A silhouette on a higher ledge threw another burst of flames. Felix ran out before the snow could trap him and stumbled his way up the trail. The steep path up through frost-covered boulders seemed to be his only hope of reaching Lucas. More fire rained down, and Felix did his best not to be roasted alive. He hid behind one of the rocks, trying to get a good look at Lucas through the snow and fire, to no avail.

"Afraid, little Cobalt?" Lucas' muffled voice carried through the squall. "Can't fight back?"

Felix crunched the snow. He jumped out. "Fireball!" A small spark flickered from his wand, only to die out immediately. Again he took cover. There was no way, with his fatigue and the cold, he'd have any luck with his already pathetic fire spells.

But that's when it hit him: the fairy dust cartridges. He hadn't paid them much mind since that day with Argent, but now was the perfect time to see what they could do. He jumped out, holding his thumb on the cartridges and flicking his wrist. Sparkles of light escaped and collected into a brilliant sphere, only to flare up and knock him onto his back.

"Pathetic!" Lucas' laughter grated Felix's ears. "A waste of effort. No. A waste of life."

Felix pulled himself up. His shoulder ached as pain shot through his muscles, begging for him to stop. Every logical thought told him to surrender and give up before he got hurt. But he couldn't. His pride would never have allowed that.

"Screw you," Felix muttered through gritted teeth.

"What was that, Co—"

"SCREW YOU!"

Felix lunged, tackling Lucas and sending them both rolling off the cliff, slamming into the snowy ledge below. Pain festered throughout Felix's whole body. The cold stung him to the core, and he panted. He tried to push himself up, only for a sharp pain at the top of his head to force himself to let out a short, strained scream.

Lucas, pulling Felix by his hair, dragged him towards the cliffside. He released his grip, and Felix fell once more with a resounding thud. Lucas groaned from exhaustion as he coughed up his words. "I wish... this was a real drop. Then both of our miserable existences... would be over."

He kicked Felix into the ravine. On instinct, Felix grabbed the ledge, clinging to the icy rocks. His fingertips burned, feeling like they were bound to freeze and snap at any moment. His arms' nerves reawakened to an agonizing burning sensation. Lucas slammed his foot onto Felix's hand, but Felix refused to let go. He had to fight back. But his wand had fallen, leaving him defenseless.

An idea sparked in his mind, and he held up his hand.

"ANGEL OF FLAMES."

Deep-blue fire surged from Felix's hand, forcing Lucas back. Flames poured all around Felix, but the ice he'd clung to melted. He lost his grip. His vision blurred as he raced through the air. The last thing he heard was a faint boom. Then it all went black.

What did I do?

As the nurses carried Felix out, Lucas stood there, dazed. He took off his helmet, unable to process that the illusion had crumbled around him. Jhaveri gave Lucas the riot acts for his behavior, but it was nothing Lucas wasn't used to. At least this time, he knew he deserved the reprimanding, and he'd soon be receiving more once he made his way to his aunt's office. But before he could move even an inch...

"YOU PIECE OF SHIT."

Argent shoved Lucas against the wall. The vein in his neck nearly popped as his eyes burned into Lucas. "What the hell were you trying to do, huh?!" Jhaveri pulled Argent away, but Rosie took over the reins as Jhaveri was rushed outside by one of the nurses. Rosie whispered to Argent, and after Lucas heard what sounded to be an apology from Argent, Rosie simply waved her hand and left, holding her forehead.

Gathering himself, Lucas reached for Argent's shoulder. Argent spun and slapped away Lucas' hand, and Lucas couldn't blame him. "Mr. de la Mort, I… I'm sorry."

Argent stormed out. Though Lucas knew it was Felix he owed the apology to, he knew he wouldn't be able to face him. What would he even say? What could he have said after what he'd just done?

"If you're looking for a real drop, the cliff's right outside."

There Carlos stood, his arms crossed. "I thought I told you to leave me be," Lucas said. "How did you… you know what, forget it. I have better places to be."

"I'm sure." Carlos laughed. "I will say this though. You and that Felix kid are some of the most fascinating idiots I've seen in a long time. And that's saying something, given all the twats I've got to choose from."

Fed up, Lucas marched past Carlos and out the door. A strange fellow. Lucas had only turned to him for knowledge about the human world, and also for movie recommendations that Ulrich could get his hands on thanks to his family's connections over in France. But the more time went on, the less Lucas felt comfortable in the arrangement. At first, he thought the young Mr. Flores to be another foreigner thrown into the deep end, flailing, hoping anyone might've been merciful enough to throw him a life preserver. But now? Now it felt as though Carlos was the one holding all the cards. The cards for a game Lucas knew all too well, and one he himself was only now just starting to understand.

A game that he and Felix had been selected for long ago, and one they were now far too involved in to escape from.

Chapter Twelve

Limit Breaker

THE DARK MIST faded away, the blurs solidifying into a tiled ceiling and fan. Air entered his nose, smelling of a doctor's office: sterile and rife with suffering. His mouth was dry, and his body ached all over. Felix sat up to find himself in a baby-blue hospital gown. All the other beds were empty, and light filtered through the windows to reveal dust floating by.

"Good. You're awake."

An older man, in his early fifties and wearing a dark-red sweater, approached. He had a bit of a beer belly, along with an English accent, and his dark-green slacks clashed horrifically with his shirt. The style made him look like a walking Christmas clearance sale. His pasty white skin, dark-brown hair beginning to gray, and untamed goatee didn't help that impression. Give him a few more months, and he would've been well on his way to having a full-on beard to go with his obnoxiously jolly demeanor. And to top it all off, he smelled as though he'd bathed himself in an ungodly amount of mint-scented cologne. Ironically, his eyes were mint green. But that would've meant...

"You're not a magus..." Felix squinted, only to cough as his hoarse voice protested against him speaking. He tried to move his right arm, only for it to sting. Only then did he realize it was in a sling. His left leg, likewise, was in a full cast.

"No, I'm not." The man pulled up a chair. "But I don't need to be to know a fractured arm and a broken leg when I see them. How are you feeling?"

Felix laid his head back. "Like hell."

"That's what comes with high-level illusion magic. Or so I'm told. The headmistress is sorting things out with Professor Jhaveri and your Della Luce friend."

"Friend?" Felix was tempted to scoff, but in all honesty, he didn't even have enough energy to care about what happened to his "friend." Lucas was probably in perfect health, while Felix was cooped up here in the infirmary. "I take it I won't be able to walk for a while?"

"A couple of weeks until you'll be able to use your arm freely. Plus a couple more before you can switch from a wheelchair to crutches. If I have to give the nurses here one thing, it's that they sure know their healing magic."

"Why are you here then?" Normally Felix would've cursed himself for his crassness, but his current apathy demanded answers quickly and concisely. "What could a human offer a school full of magi?"

"I've gotten the same interrogation from nearly everyone on staff," the man said. "And every time, I have to resist my urge to flaunt all my degrees." He looked out the window. "I can never put it into words, but it's always fascinated me, the differences we construct between humans and magi."

Felix raised an eyebrow. "They... *are* different, though."

"When it comes to spellcasting and eye color, yes. But not one person has been able to find a significant difference between the two groups' DNA. At the genetic level, we are still the same species."

Felix clutched the side of the bed. *Tell that to...* He sighed, tying to dispel his anger, to no avail. "I'll keep that in mind the next time I deal with an angry crowd. Just show them a blood sample, and they'll apologize."

The man laughed. "I wish. But you're right. The human heart is far more complex and irrational. Sometimes, that's a blessing. But other times..." He stood. "You've probably heard enough sophistry for one day. I promised I'd notify the headmistress once you woke up." He gave a warm smile, even despite Felix's constant frown and bad attitude, before walking towards the exit.

"Wait."

The man turned. "Do you need anything?"

"I…" Felix paused. "Thank you. For making sure I'm okay. I never got your name."

"Dr. Calvin Bloxham. But you can call me Cal."

Felix closed his eyes as Cal left. A human doctor coming to work in the Medeian Empire, where he knew he'd be unwelcome at every turn. Yet even so, here he was, being needlessly kind and insightful.

He took the time to rest up, but his mind kept returning to the fact he had no clue how to feel about any of this. His ire was directed towards himself, pushing himself too hard, rather than Lucas' actions. It took him a few moments before he registered the headmistress, with her signature ponytail and lavender suit, at his bedside. "M-Morning, Headmistress," Felix croaked out. "It is morning, right?"

"It is," she said. "And just Ms. Hakim will do. Professor Jhaveri wanted me to tell you he was sorry for allowing this to happen. I've spoken with him about his… methods around the combat league. Hopefully this will be his wake-up call."

"It's fine. I should've known better." *What the hell was I thinking, challenging a pearl to a fight? Of course I got hurt.*

"Your friend Rosie explained the situation to me. What Mr. della Luce said and did was inexcusable." She helped herself to the seat Calvin had abandoned. "This should never have happened. It's my job to ensure the safety of all my students."

Felix stared at the ceiling. He'd taken on Lucas to try and prove his ability to stand on his own and rise above his limits as a cobalt. As much as he wanted to scold himself for not knowing better, he also knew deep down this was why he was here in the first place. And from everything he'd heard, he owed much of his gratitude for that privilege to Ms. Hakim. "Would you mind if I asked you something?"

"Go on."

"Why… did you create the grant program?" Felix asked. "I've heard how Gottschalk and Lucas feel about magi like me. Or… *sorcerers*. It can't be that popular."

"From what I've seen, it's incredibly popular among the students who were given the opportunity to better themselves." She stared out the window, crossing her legs. "Those who would normally have been left to their own devices are now able to study here at Dragora and better themselves." She looked back at Felix. "Including you."

"A waste of effort. No. A waste of life."

"No matter what your classmates may say, or even some of your professors, you *do* belong here."

Felix turned his head away.

"If you don't mind me sharing a rather fitting story, I once knew a young girl who faced a similar hostility, growing up in the New Ottoman Empire." She gave a poignant sulk, compelling Felix to listen closely.

"Her parents were sorcerers," Hakim continued. "She and her parents shared amethyst eyes, while her sister's eyes were cobalt. This sister even believed herself to be human. Or rather, she wanted to be. And she knew she could pass as one. And so, to save herself… she sold her family out. The first sister barely escaped with her life, forced to watch her parents be arrested as the boat carrying her away left the port."

Felix sat there, unmoving, unsure of how to respond. He'd recalled Gottschalk's comments on cobalts hiding amongst the populace, but he couldn't bring himself to ever imagine a magus turning on their own. He held his chest. "I… I'm so sorry."

"Don't apologize." Ramidha wiped the tears from her eyes. "I'm not ashamed, nor do I hold any grudges. I may wish what I've gone through never happened, but it's helped shape me into the woman I am today: fighting for justice for all, even those who think less of me. That's why I fought tooth and nail to take in my niece when she was disowned by my sister."

"Nasira?" Felix asked. "Oh, s-sorry. I didn't mean to…"

"I'm simply saying that we all know your struggle. Zahra's told me wonderful things about you. You seem to be a trustworthy and gentle-hearted young man."

Normally, Felix would've let out a tsunami of profanities if someone ever called him that. But this felt different. So, he sucked it up and accepted the compliment.

"Nasira's struggling to accept who she is. But I hope in time, she'll learn the parents who rejected her aren't worthy of being her family." She lifted her head. "I suspect you have a similar story."

"I…" Felix returned his gaze towards the ceiling. "I'd rather not discuss it, if that's alright."

"Of course." She stood. "But please know, you're welcome here at Dragora, and you have many people on your side. Never hesitate to reach out for help if you need it. You may have cobalt eyes, but that doesn't make you any less of a sorcerer than Lucas. All you need is to use your limitations to your advantage. Now get some rest, and try to enjoy the day. I'll be sure to tell your friends of your recovery."

"Thank you," Felix said. As Hakim left the room, Felix lay back and watched the ceiling fan spin endlessly. He closed his eyes. The ambiance was rather soothing, and as he let himself relax, he began to drift off.

"You're okay!"

His whole body screamed in pain as Zahra hugged him tight, crushing him and swinging him slightly to and fro. He'd have been happy to see her if he wasn't busy being strangled by friendship. "Oh! S-Sorry!" She jumped back, hiding behind Penny. Shawn and Floria stood beside them, all looking concerned. All except Floria, who seemed to be apathy incarnate.

Felix stretched his good arm and leg, letting out a fierce yawn. *Good lord, how much time's gone by?* He would've checked his phone, but that was currently being held onto by the staff. "Good to see you guys," he said, his voice weak and dry.

"We heard what happened," Penny said. "So—"

"We wanted to see if you died." As usual, Floria's tone was deadpan as fuck. Everyone glared at her. "What? It's true."

"You put up a real good fight against Lucas," Shawn said.

"Thanks." Felix debated whether to joke away Shawn's compliment. He looked around, half-expecting Rosie to backhand him out of nowhere. But no. There was no sign of her. "Where's Rosie?"

Shawn scratched his head. "Uh... she—"

"She's pissed at you." Again, everyone glared at Floria. "I deal in honesty."

Felix rolled his eyes. "Of course."

Zahra peeked out from behind Penny. "You *did* give us all a scare. Please... don't push yourself like that again."

So that's what this is. Instantly, Felix's regret returned, as did his mental self-kicking. "Okay. Promise." *Like that means much of anything.* "Thanks for coming."

"We'll give you our notes for any classes you miss," Penny said.

"So you don't flunk out," Floria said.

"Appreciate it," Felix said. Penny led Floria and Shawn out, but Zahra stayed behind, wringing her hands and avoiding eye contact. "Zahra? What's up?"

"It's… Argent."

Felix furrowed his brow, ready to bolt out of bed had Argent acted again. "What'd he do this time?"

"He… wanted to know how you were."

"Oh?" Felix waved his hand—his left hand, of course. He had to stop himself from instinctively trying to use his right hand, or else there would've been hell to pay, and a lot of screaming. "Tell him I'm fine, I guess."

"O-Okay." And with that, she ran out.

Felix shut his eyes and lay back down, letting out a sigh most beleaguered. *I hope to fucking God he doesn't start more shit.* In all honesty, he held more frustration towards Argent than Lucas. Even Lucas, from what he could gather, had a reason to be as awful as he was. Argent on the other hand? As much as Felix wanted to understand why, he couldn't bring himself to empathize. He was tired enough as it was, and soon, he drifted back to sleep.

Until an obnoxiously loud snoring ended his rest.

Hours must've gone by, as it was now nighttime. Yet Felix felt like he'd just gone to sleep mere moments ago. He had a visitor, fast asleep, sitting backwards in that goddamn rolling chair: Argent. And he was drooling. *What a lovely sight to wake up to.* "Argent?"

No response.

Felix raised his voice as much as he could, not needing to worry about disturbing a room of empty beds. "Argent!"

Argent flailed, nearly falling as the chair rolled away into the center aisle. "Huh, w-what? Oh. Uh…" He scooted his way back over, nervously smiling. "Hey."

Felix was tempted to tell Argent to fuck off, but his curiosity got the better of him. "How long were you—"

"Doesn't matter. I'm just glad you're okay."

That… was not the response Felix expected. He paused. Nothing really came to mind as to what to say. Instead, his bemusement took hold. "How did the nurses not drag you out of here?"

Argent put on a confident shit-eating grin, reverting to his usual attitude. Felix could've sworn his teeth flashed in the moonlight. "As it turns out, a broken heart's in just as much need of treatment as broken limbs."

That quip nearly made Felix give Argent a broken limb or two of his own.

"Okay, okay." Argent hung his head, his eyes cast to the floor. "I begged them to let me stay. It was more out of pity than anything else."

"I'm sure." Felix rolled his eyes. "Come to insult me?"

"No." Argent sulked. "I... I wanted to say I'm—"

"Gay? A murderer?" Felix smirked. "Not a man?"

Argent looked up, as if the answer was up there somewhere. "Yes, no, and no. Though I have considered the second option."

As much as Felix enjoyed going back to their comical dynamic, his patience was wearing thin. "Argent!"

"Alright, I..." Argent took a breath. "I'm sorry. For everything I said, and for how I acted. I let my awful attitude get the better of me. As always..."

"It's not *me* you should be apologizing to," Felix said.

"Rosie said she forgave me before I even started talking. Don't know why. I was such a bastard to her."

Felix scoffed. "Understatement of the year."

"But I hurt *you* too."

Felix was taken aback. Argent wasn't putting up a facade, nor indulging in his usual callous persona. Felix had learned to smell bullshit from a mile away a long time ago, and he could hear the sincerity in Argent's voice—see it in his eyes. Felix sat back. "Not really. I'm used to that kinda shit. Can't hurt someone if they're jaded enough."

Argent laughed. "You always say that, but you're the biggest marshmallow around."

"Excuse me?"

"S-Sorry." Argent immediately shrank, backing up in his chair.

"Relax, I'm kidding," Felix said. "And I appreciate the apology. I mean, at least I got one from somebody."

Argent punched the air. "Trust me, if I could, I'd kick Lucas' ass for what he did to you."

"I did this to myself. I should've known better."

"Horseshit." Argent sat up straight, nearly leaping from the chair. "He was egging you on. He's a pampered piece of shit."

"And I'm a cobalt who didn't know his limits. I—"

"Stop beating yourself up! The dude insulted you and your best friend. Called you the worst things he possibly could. Then he goes and gets you seriously hurt, and you're sitting here blaming yourself for what *he* did?!"

"What's blaming him for what I could've avoided gonna do?"

Argent raised an eyebrow. "You're not angry? How in the hell are you *not* angry?"

"I *am*. At myself, mostly…"

"You're really somethin' else." Argent stared at the moon. "I paid for all your stuff cuz… I liked you."

"Say what now?"

"Yeah, I like you!" Argent averted Felix's gaze as he blushed. "There! I said it!"

Felix tried so hard not to burst out laughing, relishing in perhaps one of the world's rarest sights: Argent's embarrassment. "Again… what?"

"I thought you were really cute. Please don't make me say it again. Emotions aren't my thing."

"I noticed that. But uh…" Felix blushed at Argent's earlier comment. "Thank you…?"

"And… I'm sorry for getting jealous over and over again. Like with Zahra. And Penny. And Rosie."

"Uh…" Now Felix had to actively keep himself from bursting into an uncontrollable laughter. "Rosie and I aren't…"

"You're… not?"

"Nope. Just friends."

"Oh." Argent sat there, dumbfounded. Somehow, this gay young man hadn't realized men and women… could be friends.

"And yes," Felix said. "I do like guys. And girls. And everything in-between."

"So then…" Argent twiddled his thumbs. "Do you…?"

"If you're asking if I like anyone right now, then no."

"Oh…" Argent moped.

"You *were* kind of a dick," Felix said. "And I have a strict anti-dick policy when it comes to dating. And life in general."

Argent looked ready to grow a pair of devil horns. "I thought you swung both ways."

"Don't make me slap you."

Argent crossed his legs. "Sadist?"

Felix was unamused.

"Okay, too far. But… I'm fine with just being your friend. If… *you're* okay with that."

Felix nodded. "So long as you stop acting like a jackass."

"I can try."

"That's good for now." Felix snickered, enjoying this encounter far more than he felt he should've. But perhaps this was the right call. If Argent really was going to put effort into getting himself together, then maybe, just maybe, it could work out. "And if you shape up… I'll consider a date."

Argent's eyes went wide with excitement. "R-Really?!" His voice must've shot up an octave or two.

"Yes. But before I can consider you a candidate, we must first have five post-midnight conversations about the meaning of life, either in person or through text."

"O-Oka—"

"Then you must pass my one-thousand-seven-hundred-and-forty-seven trials to win my approval."

Argent blinked rapidly. "U-Uh… alri—"

"Then!" Felix held up a finger. "You must pass Rosie's eight-hundred-and-seventy-six trials. Only then will you be considered at all."

Argent sat there in shock. Slowly, he leaned forward. "What's my first trial?"

Felix enjoyed that Argent was ready to play along. He leaned as far forward as possible, meeting Argent's gaze. "Let me sleep."

"Oh, yeah. That'd be good." Argent yawned and stretched. "You mind if I visit tomorrow?"

"I'd like that. It'd be nice to have some company." Felix took a long sigh of relief. "And get Rosie down here if you can?"

"Sure!" Argent looked happier than he ever had before, which is to say he actually looked happy. They bid each other goodnight, and after Argent left, Felix prayed to whatever god he decided to believe in at random not to be disturbed this time. Still, seeing Argent shape up and try to make amends made the day go from bearable to great. Probably the best day he'd had since the year started. Once he could sort things out with Rosie, he was sure things would pick up from there.

As he drifted off, he opened his eyes during the night. A shadow stood over him. It lasted about a minute before he blacked out again. He hadn't had an episode of sleep paralysis in years, though this instance felt... sinister. Far more sinister than any of his encounters with Vagus.

He awakened to the sound of birds chirping and the warm light of the morning sun. Felix spent the next week in the infirmary, and the routine of his friends visiting, along with Cal keeping him company, admittedly felt like a nice break from the usual stress and Lucas' bad temper. Argent would pop in between classes, even risking turning up late to some. Conversations ran from apologies of how much of an ass he could be, to complaining about all the coursework he was never gonna do.

Cal's conversations made the days far more engaging, be they about Samuel's weird obsession with trying to feed the squirrels, or Gottschalk's ice-cold heart. Dr. Bloxham reminded Felix of his stepfather Ian, except much more laid back. At one point, Cal even mentioned how Felix reminded him of his daughter: fiery and abrasive, unafraid to make it clear how he felt. Certainly as time went on, Felix had taken that mantle far more readily.

Of course, the fact that Cal would bring Felix his favorite breakfast—an everything bagel smothered in a truck ton of cream chase, along with a glass of chocolate milk—didn't hurt the appeal to his bedridden status. *If only they were Long Island bagels.*

Once Felix had gotten his phone back (and he was able to hold it), he found several voice messages and unanswered texts from his parents. They'd been informed of what happened, though Lucas' name was of course left out of it. *Not like we could do much anyway. The Lightheads probably have the best lawyers money can buy.* He'd assured his mother and stepfather he was alright and healing up quickly, and that he'd try to stay in touch once he was back on his feet. (Ian did not appreciate the wordplay.)

But even through all the happier moments, Felix wondered without end where Rosie could've been, and why she hadn't shown herself. Was she that angry at him? And could Felix have honestly blamed her?

At long last, after this week of rest, Felix finally wheeled himself back to House Pyre. Ornella was rather welcoming, assuring that she'd have a "word" with Lucas on his behalf. While he rejoiced in the idea of Ornella roasting

Lucas alive, and the dorm was kept peaceful by Lucas' continued absence, Felix's luck ran out as the lift for the loft decided to short circuit. Surprisingly, the couch made for a decent substitute with the fireplace going. It even helped Felix get back into reading, given the bookshelf he'd never given the time of day beforehand was still within each. He had to get creative given he only had one good arm, but holding the book with his chin seemed to suffice. Argent paid the occasional visit to further irritate Felix (lovingly), while Zahra and Penny made sure to keep Felix up to date on classwork—and thankfully, keep him sane.

Ivanov gave Felix a literal pat on the back for standing up to Lucas before droning on with his own conspiracy the— I mean, lectures. The Labelles celebrated Felix's return, despite protocol, with chocolate cake for all. Denise tried to grab a slice from Felix, though he was quick to slap her on the wrist with his good hand. Lunch was a blast. Shawn and Floria joined, and everyone partook in cackling at inappropriate jokes galore. Even Nasira giggled before returning to her grimace.

Then came Gottschalk's class.

As Felix entered, he found Rosie on the far side of the room. She made eye contact with him briefly before turning to the window. Instantly, the world froze. Felix had assumed that making things up with Rosie would be easy. But now…

Argent held Felix's shoulder. "C'mon," he whispered. Felix bobbed his head, and the group made their way to the usual back table. "Are you okay?" Argent asked.

Felix slouched. "I guess…" Penny assured him that with time, Rosie would come around. Felix knew they'd be okay. They always were. It was the confrontation he dreaded.

"Everyone quiet." Gottschalk approached Lucas' table. He wasn't there. Just his friends, including Ulrich, gambling. "Where is my nephew?" Ulrich shrugged, and Gottschalk groaned. "What about you?" She looked dead at Felix. "Do you know?"

Oh here we go. Felix had already gone through hell. Nothing Gottschalk could've said or done would've compared. "No, I haven't seen him since the… incident."

Gottschalk, closing her eyes, exhaled. "I would like to apologize fo—"

"It's not *you* who should be apologizing."

She frowned. "Though I'd like to take this opportunity to remind you all of your limitations."

Felix pressed his back against his wheelchair's cushion, ready to watch the shit show commence. *Here we go.*

"As you all know, only pearl-eyed sorcerers are able to wield all four elements. And even with one element, an amethyst, or *especially* a cobalt, would barely be able to keep up. The toll on their body could prove fatal if left unchecked." Her eyes were cold with pity. "So I'd expect you to know better than to go up against someone you've no hope of beating."

Felix envisioned himself crossing his arms. "But it's still possible."

Gottschalk paused. "That does not make it practical."

"If it's possible, it seems plenty practical to me."

The room went dead silent. "While I do respect you for standing your ground, Mr. Brasher, I am quickly losing my patience." Gottschalk marched towards him. "There are limits to what you can do, and your injuries are a direct result of you pushing yourself past them. You could have died."

"But I didn't," Felix said. "And your brat of a nephew should've known to watch his mouth."

Argent shouted as if he'd heard the burn of his life, and he and Felix exchanged smiles. The whole class joined in as they erupted in cheers. All except Rosie.

"Mr. Brasher..." Gottschalk glared. "I think it'd be best if you—"

"Already planned on it, Goat Chalk." Felix wheeled towards the door.

"I'll help him!" Argent leapt from the table. "Wasn't getting much outta this 'lesson' anyway."

"Go," Gottschalk boomed. "Now."

Penny and Zahra gave Felix a thumbs up, and even Nasira gave an approving grin. Yet Rosie stared at her desk, ignoring Felix's very existence, and that stung more than anything else. Argent wheeled Felix out into the hall, and once they were far enough away, shouted, "Dude! That was awesome! You're a real genuine rebel!"

Felix laughed. "Why thank you. It was nothing." It most assuredly felt good to stand up against Gottschalk, and he relished in that pride. Now Calvin's words about saying what was on his heart without fear really rang true.

"You really put that bitch in her place!"

"Um…" Felix half-expected Gottschalk to sneak up behind them and freeze them solid. The last thing he wanted was to be kept as an example of "a cobalt who didn't know his place."

"Relax," Argent said. "She already hates us."

"True." Felix sighed in relief. "This was the first time I've ever done something like that."

"Hmm, so our resident nice guy's finally been corrupted into a badass."

Felix shrugged. "What now? Food?"

"We just ate."

"Technicalities!"

"How do video games sound?" Argent looked around before whispering into Felix's ear, "I may or may not have smuggled in a… PS4."

"That dinosaur?" Felix wasn't sure whether to be impressed or merely surprised. Just weeks ago, Argent had joked about how old Felix's tastes in entertainment were. And that's when it hit him. "Hold on. Did you…?"

"I admit nothing."

"You bought one? Right after I mentioned it?"

Argent gave a nervous laughter. "You said you were a retro gamer, so…"

"You must've done that in ten seconds flat while I hadn't noticed. Which… sounds right, given how oblivious I am." As odd as it seemed, Felix appreciated the thought, and a day of video games with Argent didn't sound too bad right now. "Sure. Sounds like a fun time to me."

"Brace yourself!" Argent rushed the wheelchair down the hall at top speed. Felix laughed triumphantly as the wind whisked past his face. They entered the elevator—causing the woman who'd been waiting for it to give up, looking too terrified to hop inside with them—and headed up to the tower of House Sican. The designs were similar to House Pyre's, but replace the red and gold with blue and silver, along with a dragon fountain in the room's center. (Felix lowkey missed the pyrotechnics.) Argent claimed their elevator was malfunctioning, which didn't surprise Felix one bit. This made getting up to Argent's dorm tricky, and a tad death-defying. It took twenty minutes of carefully pushing the wheelchair up the steps, along with a few close calls, before they reached Argent's floor.

Right in time for a group of students to take the lift past them.

Felix glared at Argent. "You lying bitch."

Argent's jubilation refused to die. "You gotta admit, this was way more fun!"

"Fuck you."

"Buy me dinner first."

Though he fought the impulse, Felix couldn't suppress his laughter. And he was right—it was hilarious in hindsight. They made their way inside. Books and clothes were tossed all over Argent's floor. Felix cringed. Despite Lucas' many, many problems, he kept tidy.

Argent pushed Felix over to the couch. "You wanna…?"

"It'd be preferred."

Argent helped Felix to his seat, though Argent's humor added a tinge of awkwardness. "Is that a wand in your pocket?" he asked. "Or—"

"Yes. It is a wand. Don't make me attack you with it."

"Ah, so you *are* a sadist!"

Felix groaned, then laughed. He couldn't keep up his front of disapproval. Being around Argent, especially now that he was shaping up, just felt right.

A flatscreen TV sat above the fireplace mantel, adorned with cables all strewn about. Dust coated the console, turning it from black to gray. And true enough, it was seated atop a shelf, which sheltered a trove of physical games. Felix tilted his head. "Did you—"

"Look up the games you mentioned and buy them all?" Argent blushed. "Yes. Yes I did. Plus some other gems I stumbled upon in my research. I figured you'd appreciate physical copies, especially since I literally couldn't find the old digital copies anywhere. You don't wanna know what I had to do to get my hands on all of these in mint condition. A man's gotta avoid work somehow. Now…" Argent cracked his knuckles, puffed out his chest, and held both hands on his hips. "Let's fire this baby up! Oh, but first!" He turned on his heel. "Would you like a drink, monsieur?"

"Water will do."

"You sure? I got ginger."

"Ginger?" Felix asked. "Like… ginger ale?"

"No," Argent said, letting out an exasperated sigh. "Like… a fizzy drink."

"Oh, soda!" Felix felt his brain light up as he put two and two together. He did pause for a moment, contemplating whether ingesting artificial caffeinated poison was the best move after nearly evading death. "Eh. I've got nothin' to live for. Bring on the caffeine!"

"Gotcha!" Argent zipped up to the loft, and after the opening and closing of what sounded like a refrigerator, returned with a water bottle and soda can.

"You have a fucking mini-fridge?"

"Is that a crime?"

Felix took the can. "How do you even power this stuff?"

"Mini-generator." Argent gestured as though polishing his invisible medal. "Castle's too old for outlets, and the empire's never needed human electricity. So, improvise! A pain to get fuel for, and a hassle to keep the exhaust funneled out the window, but it beats carbon monoxide poisoning. Except when it comes to Goat Chalk's class, of course."

"I see." Felix struggled to open the can. He could only hold it in his left hand, though he tried to flick his thumb up in a way he could pop the thing open in one go. And then another go. And another.

"You need a… hand?" Argent nearly laughed at his own (awful) joke. "But seriously, you good?"

"It's fine, I'm perfectly capable of—" With another failed flick, Felix dropped the can, and soda spilled all over him and the floor. "Shit."

Argent held back his laughter. "No worries." He fetched a roll of paper towels. "Braced for the apocalypse."

"Why do you…? Nevermind."

"You filthy bastard."

Felix scowled.

"You have a very sexy scowl, you know," Argent said.

"Help me clean, dipshit."

Argent did so (begrudgingly). Afterwards, he got Felix another can, opening this one himself and leaving it on the table. Felix thanked him and took a sip, grateful he'd finally gotten a sweet burst of caffeine and sugar into his system. "So," Argent said. "What do you wanna play? I've got some old classics. Well, I think they're classics?"

Felix observed the pile of games. "Looks like Alec would have a field day with this."

"Oh he would, would he?" Argent popped an eyebrow.

"Ugh, gross." Felix laughed. "Nothing like that. Alec's an old friend from back home, with… very old tastes."

"Old tastes?"

"Don't. Even. Anyways, what've you got?"

Argent sorted through the games. "Some of the old *Tomb Raider* games, *Gravity Rush*, *Overwatch*…"

"*Kingdom Hearts 3*?" Felix cackled, expecting to send Argent on a goose chase through a thousand different side games without ever being able to find…

"Yep." Argent held up the box. "Right here."

It took Felix a few moments to process the game's existence. "Wait, what? Alec said it was never…" He growled. "Dammit, Alec."

Argent continued rummaging, tossing games left and right when they couldn't catch his interest. "You know, I still don't get the appeal of playing games that are practically ancient."

Felix snickered. "You'd have to ask Alec." Whenever Felix asked that same question, Alec the Nostalgic would melodramatically lambast him for not appreciating the art of the past. Though he'd always laugh off the response, on some level, Felix understood why some would cling to these relics when they were born into such a turbulent time period. Numbing yourself to it all and pretending you were in the lost "golden era"? An alluring prospect, even to Felix. He could've only imagined how the average human felt.

They eventually settled on an old horror game; one that Alec swore they'd even made a diaper for. There were no physical copies of this particular game, so Argent booted up a digital copy he'd snagged. He joked about venturing into the dark web for this, but Felix just rolled his eyes and went along with the tall tale. They'd only made it fifteen minutes into the game before their character's genitalia had been violently severed, leaving them screaming and Argent fumbling to turn the system off. They stared at each other in silence, eyes wide with horror… then cackled. There was no way the censors would've ever allowed something like that in a movie, let alone a game.

"Wait, wait!" Felix caught a glimpse of another old digital game on Argent's system. "*Life is Strange*?!"

"Uh…" Argent double-checked. "Yeah. What's it about?"

"Alec only ever mentioned it in passing. Basically it's the story of a sapphic hipster time traveler. The writing is awful, but it adds to the charm."

"Alright then. Let's commence the gay!"

They spent the night breezing through all the chapters, alternating between cackling, crying, and cursing at the characters, all on the main character Max's journey to use her newfound time rewinding powers to save her best friend Chloe from dying. Finally, after hours of making horrifically unethical decisions and taking a shot of soda every time someone uttered the word "Hella" (had they taken actual shots, they'd definitely have died), they arrived at the ultimatum: sacrifice either Chloe, or the entire town of Arcadia Bay.

Argent groaned. His grip on the controller tightened as his knuckles whitened. "I can't believe this. I'm pissed at a game that's over a hundred years old!"

"Huh? Why?"

"We went through all that bullshit to save Chloe, and now we're being told to kill her?"

Felix shrugged. "Technically, we're letting her die like she should have."

"It's bullshit!"

"She does have a habit of getting into trouble, though. Stuck on train tracks. Getting shot by drug mules and ambiguously pedophilic art teachers. Maybe she's meant to die."

"But she's our... Max's best friend!"

"The universe doesn't care. The universe don't give any fucks. The more times we save her, the more fucked up the timeline gets, and the more innocent people die. What's one life compared to the thousands in Arcadia?"

Argent sulked. "You make sense. But..."

Felix grasped Argent's shoulder, whispering... "We must kill the Chloe."

"Fuck it."

And so, Max and Chloe held hands, gazing from the lighthouse as the tornado destroyed the coastal town. Once the tempest faded, Felix and Argent watched in silence as the duo drove off in their beat-up pickup truck, leaving behind the rubbles of Arcadia Bay.

Felix shook his head. "¿Qué carajo?" Argent held up a peace sign, to which Felix playfully punched him as he laughed. "Great. Now Chloe's gonna get shot in some gas station bathroom in the middle of nowhere."

"Did you write a fanfic of that?" Argent asked.

"No!" Felix held his good hand on his hip. "I read one."

Argent laughed again. "What're you gonna do? Hit me with la chancla?"

Felix was taken aback. "Whoa, the fuck did you just say?"

"What?" Argent froze. "Oh no, was that… did I fuck up?"

"Uh… yeah. You get a pass this one time, but that's not a thing to joke about. Besides, I'm not even sure it's a thing anymore. My mom would only beat someone with la chancla if it was another mom who beat her kids with la chancla."

"Got it," Argent said, his head low. "I'm sorry. God, I suck."

"At least you were willing to listen." Felix leaned back. Yep. He was still the same old Argent, but now, he'd hopefully acknowledge when he fucked up. Baby steps.

"You do speak Spanish sometimes though," Argent said. "Does your mom?"

"Oh yeah, all the time." Felix felt himself ease up a bit. "Usually it just kinda comes out in more emotional moments, or when we address each other. I call her Mami all the time."

"Awe!" Argent's eyes twinkled. "That's adorable."

Felix blushed. "Yeah. I wish my Spanish was better, I really need to practice more. But whenever I speak it, I feel a bit closer to her. Like… as though she's there, by my side, calling out assholes with me."

"Like me." Argent snickered. "Sounds like a hell of a woman."

"She's awesome," Felix said. "You'd like her."

Argent looked off, frowning. "Doubt she'd like me."

"No, she'd probably kick your ass." Felix leaned on Argent a bit. "Way more than I already do."

Letting up, Argent laughed, right as Shawn, looking almost as downtrodden, entered the dorm. "Shawn!" Argent jumped from the couch, letting Felix nearly fall over. "Where you been, buddy?"

Shawn didn't even glance over. "Out."

"Ooh! Meet any petty ladies?"

"No."

Argent threw his arm around Shawn. "Hot guys?"

"What?" Shawn seemed confused, pushing himself free. "No. I just went… out."

"Uh-huh. You're hidin' something."

"I... was out with Rosie. We got dinner."

Felix hesitantly poked his head over the couch. "Rosie?"

"Interesting," Argent said, tucking his hands behind his back. He circled Shawn, trying his best to tower over him, despite them literally the same damn height. "By any chance, did she tell you not to bring it up?"

No response.

"Yep. She did."

Shawn raised his head, looking at Felix. "She's not angry or anything."

"Yeah." Felix shut his eyes, ready to let himself sink into the dark depths of the couch cushions. "She is. Don't worry, it's not your fault, Shawn. *I* was the idiot."

"Well... those kinda *were* her words..."

Someone just shoot me already. Please.

"We'll deal with this later," Argent said, heading back over to Felix. "I gotta get Felix here back to his dorm. Unless he'd like a sleepover?" He winked.

Felix did his best to channel Floria's mastery over the "Give me a break" facial expression. *If I had a dollar for the number of times this boy popped his eyebrows or made an innuendo...*

Argent shrugged. "Worth a shot."

Felix bid Shawn goodbye, to no avail as his sulk remained, as did the dark cloud over Felix's head. Argent wheeled Felix into the elevator (*Not taking any more of that shit tonight.*) and towards the exit. Honestly, Felix was ready for a nice, long sleep.

"What do we have here?"

A figure in the Dragora uniform, this one with the Crest of Sican, greeted them. Their soft amethyst eyes complemented their dark skin and flowing burgundy hair, all glowing in the moonlight.

"Evenin', Theresa," Argent said.

They looked to Felix. "I believe I've heard of you. You're Felix, correct?"

Felix hesitated for a moment. "Um... yes?"

"My apologies. I'm Theresa Ricci-Colombo, prefect of House Sican. I wanted to say, I'm sorry for what happened to you. Are you doing alright?"

"Y-Yes. I'm fine."

"Hate to break this up," Argent said. "But we really should be going, before—"

"If you're worried about Ornella," Theresa said. "Don't be. I spoke with her earlier. She's completely understanding. Oh, I've also spoken with your friend Rosie."

Felix raised an eyebrow. "You did? How did you…?"

"Word travels fast," they said, chuckling. "Sorry, I'm a bit of a gossip. But I'm sure she'll come around in time. I just know it."

He had no clue how to respond.

"In any case, I won't keep you. It was nice to meet you. Good night, both of you." Their presence was perhaps one of the most sincere Felix had seen since his arrival at Dragora.

Once they'd left, Felix eased up. "She seems nice."

"*They*, actually," Argent corrected. "Theresa's nonbinary."

"Oh cool," Felix said. "I'm surprised you don't seem to hate them like 'Nella'rela.'"

"They're a hell of a lot less uptight than Ornella," Argent said. "That's for sure."

"Wow! You used her actual name for once!"

Argent paused. "Well… I know it bothered you."

"How considerate," Felix said.

"Doesn't mean I don't still hate her. Even though she did help get me to pull my shit together."

"Hmm." Felix wanted to inquire further, but he didn't have the energy, and he didn't want to risk making the night any drearier following the news of Rosie's avoidance. "One step at a time." Moonlight slithered through the House Pyre skylight as Argent took Felix up to his room. He flipped on the light, revealing, unsurprisingly, no sign of Lucas.

Argent closed the door behind him, pointing at the loft. "What do you do about the bed situation?"

"The little elevator hasn't been working, and I'm too lazy to have it fixed, so I just sleep on the couch. It's weirdly comfy."

"Ah." Argent helped Felix onto the couch. Felix wrapped himself in a blanket, fluffing his pillow and getting as comfortable as possible. "You sure you'll be okay?" Argent asked.

"Yeah." Felix yawned. "Some quiet will be good for me."

"If you need anything," Argent said. "Text me."

"I will. Don't worry. But could you start the fire? It's kinda chilly."

"Alright." Argent had to light the fireplace manually, considering his ice magic. Felix would've offered to do it for him, or lend a hand (*Ba dum tish!*), but he knew Argent would be entirely against Felix lifting a finger while he was recovering. That, and Argent's ego was as fragile as glass. After some tinkering and fumbling, Argent finally managed to start up the fire with the lighter he'd apparently missed until his fourth round of checking. "Anything else?"

"That's it." Felix relished in the pillow's softness. "Thanks. Today was fun."

"So…" Argent looked sound, twiddling his thumbs. "Can we count it as a—"

"Not just yet," Felix said, trying to keep his composure. Argent was adorable whenever his facade of apathy faded. "But you *are* racking up points."

Argent's face lit up, and he pumped his fist like a five-year-old. "Yes!"

Felix snickered. "You might end up with negative points for that, though." Argent pouted, and Felix laughed so hard, he worried he might've risked hurting his arm and leg further. "Oh, just go, you dork."

After they bid each other goodnight, he killed the lights and shut the door on the way out. Felix closed his eyes. The crackling of the fire gave way to a strange hiss, followed by a faint mumbling, and a warmth over his forehead. As though he were ill, and someone were watching over him, comforting him and dispelling his worries. He opened his eyes, spotting a silhouette by the fireplace. He rushed to rub his eyes, expecting Vagus to be looming over him yet again, only to find Ornella seated in the chair beside him. Felix forced himself to sit up. "W-What the…?"

"Sorry to disturb you," Ornella said. "I needed to make sure you were okay."

"I'm… fine. Thanks for—"

"But I also wanted to ask about Lucas." Her voice was grave. She hunched over, shadows cast over her profile by the burning wood. "Have you seen him? Anywhere?"

"… No?" Felix struggled to keep his eyes open, and struggled even more trying to recall the day's events, and where he'd even last seen Lucas aside from the incident. "He wasn't in class. And he hasn't been in the dorm for a few weeks now."

"Why didn't you tell me?" Ornella's face reddened, a vein in her neck ready to pop.

Felix's hair stood on end as he cowered beneath his blanket. "I-I... I figured you knew. I mean, you *are* a prefect. Besides, didn't Lucinda tell you? He's dorming with Ulrich, I think."

Ornella sighed, her face slowly returning to normal. "Of course she didn't," she muttered. "Did Lucas say anything before he left? Or anything worth noting during the...?" She gestured to the wheelchair.

"The last time he was in this dorm, before he stormed out..." Felix sifted through his memories, forcing himself past the mausoleum. Back to the day at the wand shop, when he'd returned home, after he and Argent's fight. "Was back at the end of September. And the last time I saw him was when he nearly killed me." He held his forehead. "Is he missing?"

"No one's seen him for a couple of days. Lucinda's been losing it." Ornella let out a beleaguered sigh. "As are her parents. And as far as I'm aware, Ulrich hasn't seen him either."

Felix tilted his head. "Does Lucinda have any idea?"

"No. She's very much a 'sweep it under the rug' kind of person."

Of course. Felix would've rolled his eyes, but he felt too concerned for Ornella's exasperation and distress. "He might've headed into the city."

"I'm sure he'll turn up soon," Ornella said, holding her forehead. "His parents have taken matters into their own hands from what I'm aware of. But if you hear anything, let me know. And if you do see him, please... tell him I'm worried."

"... Alright." *Doubt that'll go over well, though.*

"And... one more thing: have you seen anything strange in the past week?"

Felix stuttered. "S-strange? Like... what?"

"Anything peculiar. Or any odd dreams, perhaps?"

What in the world could she have been referring to? Rather than fish for information, Felix opted to keep his hand close to his chest. "No. But I wanted to say... thank you. Argent said you talked some sense into him."

"Ah, yes," Ornella said. "I had a few words with Mr. de la Mort. If he gives you any more trouble, I'll be first in line to talk him down again."

Oh, I'll be sure to take you up on that offer. "Can I ask… why does he call you Nella'rela?"

She furrowed her brow. "An odd question."

"Sorry to pry. But…"

"My middle name is Orela. Same as my mother."

"Ornella Orela," Felix repeated. *Weird.*

"I know, it sounds ridiculous. But… it's a family name." Her grimace returned. "By any chance, have you heard the fable of 'The Firebird and the Ash Tree'?"

"No, can't say I have."

Ornella grinned. "Of course. It's an old Medeian one. I won't bother you with it."

"No, no, it's okay." Felix leaned back. "I've got time. I love this kinda stuff. History, folklore. Besides, if it's boring enough, it may help me sleep."

That nearly made Ornella bust a gut. Complying, she walked back towards the fireplace, leaning on the mantel. "Long ago, on an ancient hill, there stood a weeping Ash Tree. This Tree longed to glimpse the sea just over the horizon, but couldn't given its roots kept it from moving.

"Then one day, a Firebird came to sit on one of the branches, and asked why the Tree wept. Hearing its woes, the Firebird offered a solution. The Tree could experience the majesty of the sea up close, but in a different form. A form which required a most painful, even traumatic transformation, but the Tree agreed. And so, the Firebird burned the Tree—"

"Oh god," Felix said on impulse. "S-Sorry, just… wow, the old folk tales are so grim."

"Quite," Ornella said. "That was my reaction too. Anyhow, the Ash Tree was now nothing more than a pile of… well, ashes. But in those ashes lay a single seed. The Firebird scooped up the ash-coated seed and delivered it to the sea, where the seed is said to have floated upon the waves, eventually washing ashore and finding new soil to grow in, becoming a mightier, happier Ash Tree."

"Huh." Felix nearly laughed. "I'm… not sure if the science there checks out."

Ornella smirked. "A story involving a talking phoenix and a crying tree, and your concern is the logistics of how trees reproduce?"

"I'm just saying!" They laughed in unison. "But that's so… sad, though. That the Ash Tree never really got to live its dream."

"Didn't it, though?" Ornella asked. "I always saw it as a tale of rebirth. How you have to endure the trials of life before reaching your destination. Or maybe even how one life can beget a happier one, with the right help. It is meant to be a tragedy though…" She looked into the flames, and drew a deep, battered sigh. "I should probably go now. Rest easy, Felix." She headed for the door, but a certain question weighed on Felix's mind, and if anyone was likely to have an answer and bother sharing it, it very well could've been Ornella.

"Hey, one last thing?" Felix asked. "Have you ever astral projected before?"

Ornella stopped, not so much as turning around. She froze. "I'm sorry?" Her voice tapered.

"Gottschalk mentioned it a ways back, and I was just curious. Like, is it a thing a lot of people can do? Could you do your magic while—"

"I-I'm sorry, I wouldn't know." She paused.

"Oh…" Felix couldn't help but feel guilty. As though somehow he'd opened an old wound of hers, given he knew that feeling so well. "Sorry. I was just wondering." Still, when curiosity beckons… "Especially cuz I've heard of… *pink* fire when someone was projecting?"

Ornella didn't even respond. Without another word, she turned off the light and left.

Felix stared at the ceiling. *That was pretty heavy. But whatever's wrong with Lucas, it's probably his family that fucked him up. Guess we've got something in common after all.* But Ornella's other question… could it have been about Vagus? And just where was the masked man now? Could he have been involved in Lucas' disappearance?

In any case, whenever he got them, Felix knew he probably wouldn't like the answers.

Have to get away. Have to get far, far away.

Lucas panted, sweat pouring down his face as he ran through the woods. He darted behind trees, sure to keep up the black hood of his cloak, blending in with the darkness as much as possible. Still, he couldn't completely silence himself as he desperately gasped for air, nor could he hide his footfalls as he pushed himself through bushes and spiderwebs. In one hand, he held tightly onto his suitcase, packed with only one change of clothes, a passport, and several mythril cartridges and crystals. And in the other, his wand hidden in his pocket, at the ready in case she'd managed to catch up with him.

He hadn't bothered saying goodbye to anyone. Not Ornella. Not Ulrich. Especially not his family. They wouldn't have missed him anyway. He'd always been nothing but a disappointment to them. A scourge and a burden, no matter what Lucinda told him otherwise. That's certainly the impression his aunt gave him when she'd scolded him for his actions at the combat league.

Ironically, on some level, he wished he could've apologized to that Brasher fellow from the States. The cobalt whose name he hadn't bothered committing to memory. He'd left him injured, trapped in the clutches of all the burdens he'd wanted to break free of for most of his life. And in that, he wasn't sure whether or not he was doing the right thing.

Yet even so, all he truly cared for was his escape.

He'd left a small canoe in one of the trees by the shoreline. After pulling it free, he tossed it into the water, throwing his suitcase in haphazardly with a heavy thud. But before he could jump in and begin his voyage, a sudden riptide yanked the boat out of reach. It began sinking, the water itself climbing over the sides and rushing inside of its own volition. Lucas looked on in despair as the wood cracked. Once his vessel was fully split in half, his belongings sank to the bottom of the Sea of Sagramore.

"How far did you think you'd get, kid?"

Vivien emerged from the tree line, arms crossed and shooting Lucas a death glare. He pulled out his wand, firing off a blue-green "Emerald Flame!", only for Vivien to easily block with a wall of water. Desperate, Lucas dove into the sea, swinging his arms as he tried to swim away. Right as believed he might indeed escape, what felt like a hand wrapped around his leg and lifted him into the air. And there he hung as Vivien, her entire arm transformed into a stream of water, stood on the shore, tsk-tsking.

"Don't scare him too badly, Vivien."

The slight whistle of the gravelly voice chilled Lucas' blood. From the shadows between the trees… he appeared—Vagus. His firebird sat atop his shoulder, cooing as he petted her beneath her beak. "Good girl, Cinder. You kept a watchful eye on our young friend here."

A thousand comebacks flooded Lucas' mind, but his anger was quickly quelled by pure terror when reality set in. His face would've grown paler had it not been for the blood rushing to his head. "I-I—"

"I can forgive you for being tempted to flee." Vagus' words cut right through Lucas' soul. "Even despite your oath, I can understand your desire to run. Even sympathize. But what you did to young Felix…" His voice grew more severe. "You crossed a line."

"I… I'm sorry!" Lucas squelched, his voice cracking as he shouted at the top of his lungs. "I didn't mean to—"

"It's not *me* you should be apologizing to."

With a single nod from Vagus, Vivien plunged Lucas into the water, holding him below the surface until he couldn't hold his breath any longer. His nose burned with a searing, unrelenting pain as he gulped down the water. Slowly, his vision faded. As his kicks and punches ceased, he fell back into the water's grip, and it all went black.

But this was only a warning. Vagus never disposed of a tool, however uncooperative or damaged, if it still had a worthwhile use to provide.

Chapter Thirteen

Spooktacular Failure

"NO, no, and no." Felix lay on the couch, nuzzled up with his book. He had no intention of grabbing his crutches and leaving his luxurious nest, especially for a party filled with loud, obnoxious, drunken college students.

"C'mon!" Argent said, his voice rising in pitch as he begged. "It'll be fun!"

"Parties aren't fun. They're stressful and dumb."

Argent groaned, plopping himself onto the armchair. "It's Halloween! We've spent a month getting this thing together. There'll be booze, man! Booze!"

"I don't drink."

"Of course you don't." Argent facepalmed. "You are... still really adorable. So I can't hate you."

"Still not going," Felix said through an obnoxious smile. "But thank you."

Argent had been talking up the costume party ever since he and Felix had started talking again. The prefects had apparently pitched the idea to the staff to help make American students feel more welcomed, but most shot it down immediately. Rumor had it Gottschalk even took it upon herself to become designated party crasher. But of course it was still on, all somehow kept secret amongst the students, because when a bunch of dumb young adults wanna have a good time and get a little tipsy, there is truly no stopping them.

Yet even so, the party exacerbated Felix's loneliness. While he usually enjoyed Halloween, his family also celebrated La Día de los Muertos. Though Lydia didn't mention relatives beyond her parents, and Frank's family line was literally just him, Aeris, and Felix, Lydia introduced the holiday to help Ian venerate his lost family, including his late sister. But the fact no one here at Dragora besides Felix celebrated the Day of the Dead? It didn't exactly help the sense of isolation. Argent did mention getting a costume for it, but given its... questionable use of Felix's culture, a quick roast sent it right into the dumpster. He did suggest getting a "kinkier" costume to make up for it, though that was enough for Felix to dock a full point.

Not to mention parties were never Felix's forte. While everyone else in his Alderwood graduating class enjoyed prom, he had a fun night watching movies and eating all the popcorn his heart desired with Rosie. But Rosie was now out of the picture, and in her place? A bookshelf. Alas, bookshelves can't sass for shit.

"Are you sure?" Argent asked, hands pressed against the top of the couch as he hung over Felix. "It'll help you forget about... you-know-who."

Felix glanced up. "She's not a dark lord. At least, not yet. But you can just say 'Rosie.'"

"But you need to go out and have fun! Even now that you can walk again, you've done nothing but go to class and get tangled up in that book."

While it was true Felix had been reading this same book in particular over and over, he still felt the need for a sassy retort. "You know there's more than one book in existence, right?"

"You'll have a blast! Plus, it can be a real date."

Felix frowned.

Argent mocked the frown. "Really? Haven't I earned enough points to cash in a date?"

"You're losing points now, actually."

"Ugh!" Argent dragged out the groan, pulling at his eyes. "I hate loving you."

"Your problem. Not mine." It took Felix a moment to process what he'd just heard. "Wait, what did you say?"

"Nothing, nothing," Argent waved his hand. "But…" He sat forward, clasping his hands. "Isn't the Rosie thing bugging you? It's gotta be on your mind."

Felix wanted to inquire more about Argent's… well, he wasn't even sure if it was a confession. Whether Argent was serious about the word he'd just dropped, or if he could've tossed it around with the ease of kicking a crumpled can, once containing Felix's hopes and dreams. And so, Felix simply shrugged. "Not really. It's not the first time she's been pissed at me. She'll come back in time. Just gotta let her blow off some steam."

"It's been a month since the Lucas thing."

"If it takes her that long to stop wanting to gut me like a fish, so be it." The mention of Lucas made Felix think. According to Ornella, Lucas had turned back up at the Della Luce's estate the morning after their conversation. He hadn't yet returned to school, since his family wanted to "sort everything out," but in all honesty, Felix wasn't sure what he'd say were they to come face to face.

Argent sulked. "Fine. But I'm gonna go have fun."

"Good," Felix said. "Enjoy yourself. I'll be here, enjoying my book. But if you do decide the party's lame, you're more than welcome to come back here and chill. Maybe some more video games?"

"Tempting offer, but I need a break from the geeky stuff for one night." Argent headed for the door, stopping just before the knob. "But if you decide to come out…" Slowly, he turned and gave an obnoxiously flirty wink. "I'll save you a dance."

"… Did you go through all my old shows to try and impress me?"

Argent held out his hands. "I am not a crook."

"That doesn't even apply to—"

"Away!" Argent zoomed out, only to pop his head back through the door, say "Bye," then slam it shut as he left for real.

Shaking off that eccentric mess, Felix returned to his book, though he couldn't focus on the words within. His mind kept wandering back to Rosie. He'd at last caved in a couple days into her silent treatment, sending a dozen texts to her in one sitting—to no avail. It didn't help that she'd turned off her read receipts. He checked again just to be sure.

Nothing.

A knock on the door jolted his nerves. "Felix?" The soft-spoken female voice was muffled as it carried inside. As tempted as he was to send her away, he couldn't have done that to Zahra. Especially considering his current situation wasn't all that engaging. He called her inside, and she traipsed into the dorm. "Are you going to the House Zephyr party tonight?" she asked.

"No. Why? I never pegged you for a party animal."

"Well…" Zahra held her arm. "It's going to make it a tad difficult to relax in my dorm. And… Rosie is going. With Shawn."

Felix looked down at his book again. "Good for her."

"Don't you… wanna talk to her?"

"Yeah. But I don't think *she* wants to talk to *me*."

Zahra hung her head. "Sorry to bother you."

The night certainly didn't seem to be treating anyone's spirits well. Reluctantly, Felix accepted that for his lot to improve, he couldn't just sulk and wallow in self-pity. Especially if it meant dragging others into his melancholy. "No, wait." He grabbed his crutches and pushed himself onto his feet. "Do… *you* wanna go?"

"Uh…" Slowly, Zahra turned around, brushing her hair to the side and looking towards the fireplace. "A little bit. I've never been to an actual party before. My parents have always been… overprotective. Especially my father."

Felix laughed a bit. "I can relate." *Kinda, in the over-controlling sense, but no more negativity tonight.* "But I mean… do you wanna go? With me?"

Zahra twiddled her thumbs. "It's written all over my face, isn't it?"

"A tad." As oblivious as he was when it came to Argent, it didn't take much for him to realize Zahra had developed feelings for him. But he couldn't bring himself to leave it unaddressed and lead her on. "I'm sorry. I should've said something sooner. I'm… kinda naturally oblivious."

Zahra chuckled. "You don't have to go if you don't…"

"Can we go as friends?"

"Are you sure?"

"I'll be upfront," Felix said. "I'm not sure how I feel. The last month has been a mess. So, maybe I need this one night so I don't completely lose it. And… maybe I *can* clear the air with Rosie."

"I see…"

"And Argent… I'm not even sure what he and I are." Felix said. "But I don't want you to feel like I don't care about you. I do. I just think of you as a friend. I don't want you to feel like I'm just using you."

"Thank you," Zahra said. "I'd… like us to stay friends too."

"Same here. Oh! I'll need a costume. I'm a scary mess, but I don't think that counts." That got a laugh out of Zahra, and Felix's mood brightened just a smidge seeing he'd brought someone some kind of joy. But that still left the costume. Though an idea quickly presented itself in his mind, he didn't have a choice if he wanted to attend. Especially if the costume could help him mask his identity long enough to get close to Rosie. He had an idea, but none of the resources to pull it together, let alone on such short notice. And so, Felix led Zahra to House Sican, and after asking around, they made their way to the fourth level and knocked on one of the doors.

"MERDE! WHO'S THERE!?" a voice from inside yelled. "I'M BUSY."

"Felix."

"THE GAY ONE?"

He sighed. "Just open the door!"

Denise complied. Fabric covered her dorm, far more chaotic than the Labelles' classroom. Denise had presumably followed Argent's example in smuggling in a generator, as a flatscreen TV above her mantel was blaring some trashy reality TV show that Felix kept finding himself getting invested in every now and then. The couch and chairs had all been pushed towards the walls to make space for a mannequin in the center of the room. Denise lowered her sunglasses, examining Zahra from head to toe, much to Zahra's dismay. "This your date?"

Zahra blushed. "A-About that…"

"Denise," Felix said, cutting right through Denise's bullshit. "We need costumes."

"Oh, I already have…"

"Okay. *I* need a costume. For the party tonight."

Denise pondered. "So you're—"

"Will you do it or not?"

She whistled. "Feisty for a bottom!"

"I hate you."

Denise winked, raising Felix's blood pressure. "Anything you got in mind?" she asked. "Unicorn? Fairy? Dominatrix?"

Felix glared. "Unicorn of War."

"Ooh!" Denise clapped. "Feminine *and* deadly! I like it."

As much as Felix wanted to break Denise's sunglasses and put an end to her attitude, he needed a costume. Plus assault was illegal in most countries, so pick your battles. Zahra agreed to meet up with Felix later, but right after she left, Denise once again made Felix long for death's sweet release.

"So who's the lucky guy?" Denise asked.

"I. Am. *Bi.*"

"Wouldn't that mean guys are still an option?"

He couldn't argue there, but gods her arrogance was insufferable. Hours passed as she took Felix's measurements, drew up some sketches, and accidentally stabbed him with sewing needles. If he wasn't already injured, he'd have walked away both physically and mentally scarred. And in her probing hipster fashion, Denise kept asking passive-aggressive questions such as, but not limited to, "Are you really bi, or are you just curious?" "Are you sure you're not gay?" "So you just switch between gay and straight? What's that like?"

It is 2116, for fuck's sake.

Once the infernal torment had ended and the costume was complete, Felix had to admit that, as annoying as she was, Denise was a damn good designer—even if she did sacrifice function for style. The suit was a dark-gray onesie, with hooves at the ends of its sleeves. They'd made it difficult for him to hold his crutches, but not impossible. A rainbow-colored horn jutted out from the hood, while little red lines were strewn about the whole of the costume like battle scars. "Wow!" Felix clapped his hooves. "Thanks, Denise."

"No prob," Denise said. "Us gays gotta stick together. Lucky for you, I had plenty of free time to kill, and boredom to… also kill."

"You of all people aren't going?"

Denise shook her head. "Not really my thing. Though I'd suggest you get going, since it's about to start…" She flipped open her phone. "Almost a half-hour ago."

"¡Mierda!" Felix nearly jumped out of his suit as he vaulted on his crutches towards the door. "Gotta go, see ya!"

"Lo que digas, bi guy with gay-as-hell name!"

Felix struggled to turn the handle. *Damn hooves.* Before he could even process what Denise had said, he stumbled out the door and fell onto Zahra. "Sorry!" He groaned, and seeing as he couldn't quite reach his crutches, Zahra helped him stand.

Her costume certainly fit her personality. A plastic halo was propped above her head, and her white-and-gold gown flowed into exaggeratedly poofy sleeves. Angel wings were tied to her back. Their plastic sheen and lack of feathery details, oddly, screamed more of a cheap costume store than a messenger from the heavens. There was even a small pair of underwings that threatened to make movement even more cumbersome. One wrong move, and you'd be knocking jars, plates, and everything else off of every nearby counter.

She giggled. "Nice costume."

Felix cleared his throat, deepening his voice as much as he could. "This unicorn has seen some shit."

"And also has a cute tail."

Zahra's comment confused him at first. He hadn't noticed until now, but a long, glittery rainbow tail protruded from the costume's derriere. Felix blushed in embarrassment. *Argent is never gonna let me hear the end of this.*

They made their way to House Zephyr. Save for the steps of students pacing outside its great emerald doors, the corridor was completely silent. No sign of a party whatsoever. Upon entering the common area, they found the entire floor packed to the brim with students, all dressed as vampires, werewolves, and other sinful beasts, dancing wildly as if they were at a nightclub. Garish colors flashed in and out as the bass of the music rumbled.

"Kumusta, House Zephyr!"

Up on one of the walkways was a young woman holding a mic. Her braided jet-black ponytail and dark-olive skin were illuminated by the dance lights hanging off the walkways, while her black witch dress and hat sparkled. "Nina Valmorida-Narula, prefect of House Zephyr here! Everybody havin' a good time tonight?" Everyone cheered, deafening Felix's hearing. Just as he started to recover, Nina pulled out a pair of emerald-green tom toms, and with a couple strikes, a boom of thunder shook the whole room in rhythm with the music.

"HOW'RE THEY DOING THIS?!" Felix shouted. He couldn't even hear his own yells over all the noise. Zahra couldn't hear him, and so he escorted her back out into the hall. His ears thanked him as they relished in the silence. Checking for any professors nearby, he whispered, "How does no one hear this? How is none of that music getting into the hall?"

Zahra held her chin. "I think I saw people using spells around the sides of the room. Maybe they're using wind magic to keep the sound from escaping."

"Huh. Clever." Felix was admittedly impressed. He hadn't even thought of using magic in such a roundabout way. But that also had to have meant that without anywhere for the sound to escape the tower, the music in the hall was being even further amplified. Felix had to stop his thoughts in their tracks before his fascination cost him even more valuable time. "Maybe we can try Professor Montanari's spell? You know, the one to connect our thoughts? That way we can keep in touch if we get separated?"

"Maybe," Zahra mumbled. "But wasn't it..."

"I think it was... Open Mind?"

"There you are!"

Nasira burst through the doors with a smile from ear to ear. The strange sight caught Felix off guard, especially given she wasn't dressed up, but the oddity clicked once his sight drifted to the two empty red cups in Nasira's hands.

Oh no.

"Nasira?" Zahra asked, backing up. "W-What're you—"

She muttered in Arabic while grabbing Zahra's wrist, dropping her cup without a care in the world and yanking her cousin back inside.

The one time she isn't frowning... But if this is what it took to kickstart a change for Nasira, so be it. Felix propped himself against the wall and gripped his wand with both hooves. Keeping in touch with Zahra was out, but maybe he could repurpose the spell to hear Rosie's thoughts? Make it easier to locate her. He closed his eyes. "Open Mind." The wand glowed white, and a strange pulse rang all around him. Then... nothing. *And I fucked it up.*

A slight hiss caught his attention. He flicked his wand, ready to see Vagus, or some other creature, watching him. But there was nothing there. For a moment, Felix thought he saw a small shadow, lizard-like with glowing teal eyes, out of the corner of his eye. But nothing. Another of Vagus' familiars, perhaps? A grotesque little spy that had scurried away, back to inform its master all about Felix's mundane misery.

He shoved his wand back inside his costume. In this moment, he'd wanted so badly to just go back to his dorm and sleep the night away. But if he kept pushing this off, and kept waiting for a better moment, he'd never get it done. He needed to find Rosie. He forced himself back through the doors of House Zephyr, but this time, the chattering pierced his ears before he even got inside.

"God, I can't wait to fuck this guy."

"I can't wait to bang her."

"GET IT, GIRL."

Felix shoved himself through the sea of shit-faced students. Parties always overwhelmed him, but magic had taken it to a new, much more mentally taxing level.

"Watch it, asshole!"

"What's with that guy in the pony suit?"

"Is he on crutches?!"

"Found him!" Zahra ran up to him. "There you are! I haven't seen Rosie. Have you?" *"I hope we find her. I just wanna see him smile again."*

Felix held his head as his skull ached. The pain was immense and unabating, as though this was the headache from hell. So bad that he worried in mere moments, he'd be sick from the vertigo, or that he'd even black out.

"I really hope my parents don't find out about this."

"Just one more drink."

"Need to black out and forget all the work I haven't done."

"I shouldn't be here."

"Felix?" Zahra reached out, but Felix swatted her hand away and backed up. "A-Are... are you okay?" *"Oh no..."*

"I... the spell..." He squinted. Zahra's figure became a dizzying array of blurred colors. The sting grew worse, as if someone took a knife to his brain and slowly twisted it.

"Putting himself on the line for another." Even within his mind, the sharp whistle of the gravelly voice persisted. *"He truly is a worthy candidate."*

You...

Zahra became slightly clearer, if only for a moment. *"He must've..."* "Felix? What did you do?"

Felix struggled to form words. "I... can hear..."

"Can he hear my—"

255

"Yeah. I can."

She gasped. *"Crap. Crap, stop thinking!"* "We need to get you out of here."

"No!" Felix yelled, making Zahra back away. "I… I need to find Rosie!" He knew if he hesitated, Zahra would take advantage and haul him out of here, or worse, he'd collapse. In his desperation, he pushed himself through the crowd, leaving Zahra behind.

"Now I know what Rosie meant."

I'm sorry. But I have to find her. Now. As the guilt gripped him, Felix was further bombarded with people swearing and glaring at him. But he couldn't have cared less. All that mattered was finding Rosie, and making things right.

Nasira stood in the center of a crowd, downing her cup as people chanted, "CHUG! CHUG! CHUG!" Her smile, incredibly unnerving, lingered as she wiped the drink from her lips and let out a burst of jovial laughter. Though her thoughts were in Arabic, Felix assumed they weren't too charitable given how she felt about this place, and the people in it.

Felix filtered through so many different thoughts, from drunken gibberish to sex-craved perverts to crippling self-loathing. Most of the attendees' inner voices followed the trend of dripping with fear and lamentation. All the sadness and hopelessness that slowly ate away at most people day by day, that they tried so hard to bottle up and drink away, totally focused on Felix.

"I don't even belong here."

"Does he even want me anymore?"

"How could anyone ever love me?"

"Why am I even trying?"

The despair grew so heavy, adding to his own sorrow and regrets, that he not only began to question whether Rosie would ever forgive him, but… if forgiveness would ever truly mend the rift he'd driven between them.

"Ooh, there he is!"

Argent threw his arm around Felix. "You decided to show up." Each syllable was dreadfully slurred as he sloshed his drink. Red plastic horns nearly slid off his head. His red devil onesie further irritated Felix's eyes, while the pointed purple tail nearly jabbed his arm. "Nice costume, babe."

"A-Argent, now's not the time for—"

"God, he's cute, even in that ridiculous costume. Still, if it were up to me, he'd be wearing a little less..." "Of course it is!" Argent garbled. He closed his eyes, leaned in, and perked his lips.

"STOP!"

Desperate and unblinking, Felix pushed Argent and sprinted away. *"Did... did I say something again?"* The bitterness towards his actions grew more intense, but Felix told himself he had to do whatever was necessary to find his best friend. He was on the verge of passing out at this point.

"The fucking cobalt. Of course."

Lucas' presence at the party was unexpected, but he was the least of anyone's concerns, especially given his thoughts were so thoroughly laced with vitriol and anguish, they alone could've knocked Felix out in an instant. His heart pulsed as his head throbbed, both with pure adrenaline coursing through them, pushing his body beyond its limits to keep him on his feet.

"Maybe I shouldn't have come to Dragora."

That voice!

"Maybe I should just transfer back home."

Keep going.

"Maybe I'm being too harsh."

Keep going.

"But watching him do that to himself..."

Keep fucking going.

"I just wish Felix could get it through his fucking—"

"ROSIE!"

Rosie's image was rendered fuzzy by exhaustion, the rave lights, and her Dracula costume. But this was her. Felix grabbed her shoulders, and his crutches fell by the wayside.

"F-Felix?!" Her voice was muffled by her fangs.

"I-I..." The words slurred together as he tried to speak. It all went black. He could still hear faint echoes of the other students' shouts, but any words—be they his, Rosie's, or someone else's—were hazy.

A bright light filled his eyes as his head shot up. Mirrors surrounded him on all sides, spiraling out into a labyrinth of reflections. It wasn't until he reached for his crutches, though, that he discovered that not only had they vanished, but his leg was perfectly fine, and a strange black tattered cloak took the place of his costume. The other students were nowhere to be found. No sign of Rosie, Argent, nor Zahra. Not a whisper could be heard.

Silence.

"Breaking through that lousy charm was easy enough."

Him again. The deep, gravelly voice reverberated, and a shadow shot across the mirrors, shattering each one as it whisked past. Glass crunched beneath Felix's feet. Once every mirror had broken, Vagus revealed himself. "Just what do you think you were doing?"

Felix scowled. "Like I need to explain myself to you."

"You and Lucas both exhaust me."

"Then maybe you shouldn't bother," Felix said through gritted teeth. He'd had enough of the runarounds and the deception. Right now, all he knew was that Vagus stood between him and his best friend. "Maybe I shouldn't even get you whatever it is you want. Lord knows it's the last thing on my mind right now."

Vagus let out an exasperated sigh. "Need I remind you that an oath is an oath?"

"To hell with your oath."

"Hmph." Vagus raised his hand. "We'll see."

A sharp sting rocked Felix's hand. He fell onto the shards, his entire arm twitching madly as his palm glowed white. The light was blinding and unceasing, encompassing all of Felix's vision as the mirror fragments reflected it back into his cobalt eyes.

"Mr. Brasher?"

Felix was back in his dorm, out of his costume, and under his blanket on the couch. Lucas sat in the armchair, while Ornella stood before the coffee table looking exasperated as ever. "Good to see you're awake," she said. "Hungover, but awake."

"I wasn't..." Felix groaned, gripping his still throbbing forehead. *Nevermind, I guess.*

"I hope that wild party was enough fun for you both, because you'll both be serving detention for your actions."

Detention in college? Is this a thing? I don't even know what normal is anymore. "What do we have to do?" Felix asked. He could feel Lucas' desire to wring his neck without even glimpsing his face, but all Felix cared about in the moment was surviving Ornella's tirade, and finding out what happened to Rosie.

"You," Ornella said. "As well as Mr. della Luce, Mr. de la Mort, and Ms. Giordano-O'Brien…"

Rosie!

"Among others, will assist Groundskeeper Baisley in tending to the magical creature reserve within the next two weeks. I'll let you know beforehand." Ornella bid them goodnight, and an awkward silence fell across the room.

"Go ahead," Felix said, bracing himself for Lucas' riot acts. "Yell at me. Call me an idiot cobalt."

"… No."

This surprised Felix, though he remained cautious. "Change of heart?"

Lucas glowered. Bags formed under his eyes as he threw himself backward. "I decided to go. I'll deal with it…" Without warning, he hunched forward, pushing his hair back and cupping his forehead. "The consequences…" He slurred the last couple syllables. The color had drained from his face, glistening with sweat. So bloodshot were his eyes that, rather than their usual pearly color, they appeared more like a rosy pink.

Felix lay back down. *Should I even bother asking where he's been?* As curious as he was, he opted not to. Not worth risking a fight. Besides, in his intoxicated state, who knew whether Lucas would've even remembered everything correctly?

"Why were you there?" Lucas asked. "You're… hurt."

"To apologize," Felix forced himself to say. "To someone I care about. Someone I really hurt."

"I… see." Lucas stood, swaying a bit. "I'm going to sleep. You should too."

"I will as soon as you stop talking."

Lucas giggled. "I… suppose I deserve that." He stumbled towards the lift. Felix could've warned him about it not working, but even while inebriated, Lucas could figure it out on his own. A sentiment which died in flames as the elevator carried Lucas without a single issue.

Fuck you too, God. "Hey, Lucas?" he called out.

A pause. Felix waited, wondering how to phrase his question, or even what to ask, only for his contemplation to be interrupted with a loud and blaring, "WHAT?! I wanna sleep!"

Felix giggled. "You're a dark alignment, right? Blue fire and all?"

Lucas remained quiet, then chortled uncontrollably. "Guess everyone knows I'm the black sheep of the family? I must be evil, or broken!" He laughed, though Felix could hear the pain in his voice. To have it drilled into you that your existence itself is contemptible… Felix knew what that was like all too well.

"I just mean…" Felix huffed. "Forget I said anything. But—"

"Ugh, more questions?! I WANNA SLEEP?!" Lucas slouched over the loft's railings, one arm dangling. "Okay fine. But only one more, THEN BED."

Wow! Someone's an even bigger diva under the influence. Thank goodness he's a happy drunk? But snark wouldn't get either of them anywhere. They'd been pitted against each other by a man refusing to show his own face, and neither of them had told a soul about what they'd gone through. Only now did Felix process how acutely absurd this all was. Why risk so much for the promise of a power that might not even exist, or that Vagus was likely to swipe right from under their noses at the last minute?

"I'm! Waiting!" Lucas' shrill screech sounded like a pterodactyl.

"Let's forget about Vagus' promise," Felix said.

Lucas' expression grew darker. Sorrowful. "After all this… being his favorite… you say this?"

Felix wasn't sure what Lucas meant by "favorite" (*Who wants to be the favorite of some crazy occultist?*), but that didn't matter. What mattered was ending this nonsense. "I don't think it's worth it. That it's worth us trying to kill each other like this, and driving ourselves crazy. Can we… at least think about it?"

"Fine, fine, whatever!" A spark of joy lit in Lucas' eyes, though he tried—quite poorly—to mask it behind indifference as he flailed his hands all over the place. "Now good night!" And with that, he made his way back to bed, and the snoring commenced.

Felix tried to forget all about his encounter with Vagus that night, and any promises he'd made. He'd chosen to walk away. As far he was concerned, he was done. All that mattered now was catching up with Rosie once he had the time and energy, and getting his best friend back.

"If you're here to make excuses for Felix, don't bother."

Rosie had removed her fangs and hung her vampire cloak on her chair. She sat on her couch, legs crossed, dressed in a black-and-purple suit and dress shoes. Somehow the argument hadn't woken up her roommate, but Ornella feared that might've changed if things escalated any further. "I'm not making any excuses for anyone. I don't fully understand what happened between you two, but I do think you ought to hear him out."

No response.

"Very well. I'll keep you posted on your duties." Ornella headed for the door, just as Theresa entered. "What are you doing here? I thought I'd asked all prefects to meet in my dorm afterwards."

"Trust me," Theresa said. "I've got this."

Hesitantly, Ornella nodded. Theresa sat beside Rosie. If any of the prefects could've been a diplomat, it was Theresa. Ornella, on the other hand, kept imagining herself losing her temper with Rosie as she made her way back to her single dorm. Even more so when she found Nina, once again donning her forest-green turban, lightly tapping her tom toms out of boredom, her feet kicked up on the coffee table, while Lucinda dusted the place. "Why did I even suggest my dorm knowing it'd be left in tatters?"

Nina scoffed. "She cleans, I muddy up the place. Either way, you're never happy!"

Ornella shook her head. Begrudgingly, Nina placed her feet back on the ground. "Lucinda, you're giving me anxiety with your obsessive cleaning. Would you please sit?"

Huffing, Lucinda complied. "I try to help a friend out and this is the thanks I get."

Ornella rolled her eyes. "Did you learn anything, Nina?"

"Why ask me?" Nina whistled, and several books and desk lamps fell as a faint scurrying approached. A faint green mist flashed over the table, and there appeared her familiar: a lizard-sized creature that looked more like a pale-green kangaroo. Its floppy ears fell back, appearing more like wings, while its whip-like tail ended in several pink spines. Its yellow eyes blinked, revealing teal irises. "When you can ask Lilim?"

Lucinda cringed as Lilim hissed with her forked tongue. "Part of me is still tempted to tell my aunt of your little friend."

"Would you prefer a more accurate sigbin?" Nina asked. "Back in the Philippines, those things were the stuff of nightmares. Devouring corpses, horrible bloodlust, I could've made her a lot freakier."

"I'm just saying you could've stood to make it less… frightening."

"Hey, my 'little friend' gets us plenty of buzz around the school! Theresa appreciates some good gossip."

"Nina," Ornella snapped.

Nina rolled her eyes. "More of Felix talking to himself. Though it looks like that little charm of yours didn't work."

"Of course it didn't." Ornella wanted to chastise herself. She'd spent weeks trying to design that charm to protect Felix's dreams, but now that work was up in smoke. *What good am I?*

"You tried, Nella," Lucinda said. "You did all you could."

"And it wasn't enough." Ornella rubbed her temples. "Anything else?"

Nina shrugged. "Lucas still hangs out at the library whenever he's not in class or crashing with his dopey lackey, but he hasn't seemed to experience anything like Felix since he came back."

"Thank goodness," Lucinda said. She held her chest, only for her relief to vanish as she hung her head.

"You're doing all you can, Lucy," Ornella said. "And you can't tell me otherwise, because that's what you just told me."

Lucinda smiled.

"So what now?" Nina asked. "What's our next move?"

"We keep watch over them both." Ornella stood, walking towards the window and staring out at the sea. *I won't let anything happen to either of them.*

"Just what were you thinking?"

Seisyll paced about the office, hands tucked behind his back, while Zahra sat on the couch. This cold office was where Ramidha would don the persona of the upstanding and shrewd Headmistress Hakim of Dragora. A far cry from the nurturing mother Zahra had always known her as. Though tonight, she seemed more frustrated than anything else, sitting at her desk and holding her temples.

And there, Zahra held onto her cousin Nasira, who'd passed out and now leaned on her shoulder, slobbering and snoring heavily. "I... I-I thought—"

"You *didn't* think!" Her father's pale face grew red as he raised his voice. "You know how hard your mother works to maintain her reputation! *Our* reputation! How could you—"

"That's enough, Sei." Ramidha walked around her desk, holding her husband's shoulder to ease him. "This is the first time Zahra has done something like this. If anything, it's our fault for sheltering her for so long."

Zahra agreed, but despite wanting to voice her feelings, she couldn't bring herself to. Her parents had enough to deal with, especially enduring the constant skepticism of the very empire itself. To them, they were nothing more than an amethyst-eyed sorceress pretending to know how to run their renowned academy, a gold who took pity on her and foolishly cast aside his prestige, and their cobalt daughter who ran around getting drunk at parties. "I'm sorry, Mother," Zahra muttered. "Father. It won't happen again."

Seisyll sighed, his color returning to normal. "Now, as for this Brasher boy..."

Zahra gripped her armrest, bracing herself for her father's judgment.

"He's a nice young man," Ramidha said. "His hardships have left him a bit rough around the edges, but who hasn't known that kind of adversity?"

"Ramidha..." Seisyll whispered into her ear, but Zahra could only catch bits and pieces. It was clear they'd had their reservations about Felix for some time now, but there was something much more to it than they let on. It was no surprise. Zahra had grown accustomed to their tendency to keep more secrets than they ought to have. "Zahra," Seisyll said, sighing. "Just... please, take your cousin back to your dorm."

"O-Okay." Zahra hauled Nasira out and made her way back to House Zephyr, only to pause she noticed her cousin dabbing tears from her eyes. "Nasira? Are you okay?"

"I..." Nasira sniffled. "Drinking is haram. And I..." She slammed her fist into the wall. "What does it even matter? Drinking is the least of my problems."

Zahra gave her a few minutes to calm down and let the tears flow. Part of her wanted to cry, imagining how she'd react if her family suddenly rejected her for who she was. Still, faith was a fundamental pillar in her mother's life. Never once did Ramidha wonder whether her god loved her or not, and deep down, Zahra hoped one day Nasira would reach that place.

They passed the cleanup crew on the way back to their dorms. Nina greeted them both, even cracking a joke about Nasira's stupor, but Zahra ignored the comment, far too engulfed in her own shame and guilt. She repeated the same question over and over in her head: *Why can't they just trust me?*

But then… another question entered her mind.

What do they know about Felix that I don't?

Chapter Fourteen

Trial by Fire

"WHY are *we* the only ones carrying this stuff?"

Felix trudged carefully down the steps with his gargantuan bag of animal feed, grateful that he hadn't needed his crutches since the Halloween debacle a couple weeks prior. Samuel led him Argent, Rosie, and the other students down the poorly lit spiral staircase. "You kids went and got drunk," Samuel said, his voice gruff and hoarse like usual. "Now power through your hangovers and help ol' Samuel take care of the animals like responsible adults."

"He knows hangovers don't last that long," Argent whispered. "Right? Or do you think he's just never been invited to a party?"

"Shut it, Argent!" Samuel yelled.

Felix turned back to Rosie, whose bag obscured her face. "Can you believe this?" he whispered. Slowly, his hope crumbled as she refused to respond. She hadn't even so much as leaned to the side to look him in the eye, as though he wasn't even there. Felix's grip on the bag tightened as he berated himself. *What the fuck is wrong with me?*

The creaks of the wooden door down below pierced Felix's ears, reminding him of the torment from his botched telepathic spell from the party. Inside lay Samuel's office, complete with torches along the walls, a small wooden desk over in the corner, and a disturbingly detailed taxidermic unicorn mounted above it. For a moment, Felix wondered if Samuel had sourced the decor from the costume Denise had made for him. Or that's what he told himself, because the idea of someone killing and stuffing a live unicorn? Nope.

Dropping the feed bag, Felix cracked his back. Both his physical and mental fatigue had taken their tolls on him. Add to that Rosie's ongoing silent treatment, and Felix wasn't entirely sure how he'd made it through the last few weeks, especially given he'd start crying the moment he wasn't distracted.

"Are you okay?" Argent asked.

"Yeah. Just..." Felix glanced over. Of course, Rosie hadn't seemed to even register his existence. She handed her bag over to Shawn, giving him a quick peck on the cheek for his help. It seemed she'd started dating him, and she hadn't even told Felix any of it.

Argent held his hip. "Just you're really—"

"Please shut it." The venom slipped off Felix's tongue as he struggled to lift his bag. His arms, drained of all strength, burned. His mind had dulled from lack of sleep, the sharp sting of a migraine, and his self-loathing. A deep sigh escaped his lungs as he yawned. It took all his strength not to fall to the ground and give up. Argent took the bag, holding both Felix's and his own with little trouble. Again, Felix mentally kicked himself. "Sorry. That was—"

"Don't worry. I've said worse. Just don't kill yourself tryin' to do everything, alright?" Argent looked close, examining Felix's eyes. "Did you get any sleep?"

"If I said yes," Felix said. "You wouldn't believe me."

"Cuz I know it's not true." Argent frowned. "Felix—"

"Enough of your squabblin'!" Samuel sorted through his keys for what had to have been the fifth time. Felix could only tell because the never-ending jangling of metal was murder on his eardrums, worsening his headache. Rosie carried on her conversation with Shawn. Zahra and Nasira kept quiet, averting their eyes from everyone, even each other. Lucas stared into space, giving the most "God-kill-me-now" expression Felix had ever seen.

And then you had Denise, taking selfies while posing with her bag, filling the office with the obnoxious and constant flashes of her phone. Felix would've asked why she wasn't using her Polaroid if he wasn't resisting the urge to kill her.

"Listen up, delinquents," Samuel said. "We're headin' into the reserve, makin' sure everythin' in there's taken good care of. You'll split up to cover different animals. It's a big place, so make sure to grab a copy of the maps on my desk. Or don't. I don't care. I'd also tell you not to die, but lucky for me you all signed waivers before you even started school. So…" He shrugged. "Sucks to be the dead one, I guess."

Argent got him and Felix a map, as he promised he wouldn't leave Felix's side the whole day, and insisted it was to keep Felix company. But Felix knew deep down what Argent meant: to make sure he didn't screw anything else up.

Samuel pushed open the doors, and a blinding light poured into the room. Outside, in the small clearing, floated sprites. Felix reached out to the nearest one, but just before he could touch it, it flashed and stung his fingertip. He waved his hand until the pain faded. It was faint, but it was enough to keep his pessimism going. *Even nature enjoys ruining my day. Great!*

"Are you sure you're okay?" Argent asked.

Felix was tempted to snap something back to get Argent to lay off, but he knew that wasn't right, especially since Argent was just trying to help. Felix forced a laugh. "F-Fine. Just didn't know sprites were such little bitches. Kinda like me, I guess?" He had to strike at least one jab at himself to satisfy his frustration.

"Glad to see you're not completely down today," Argent said.

Felix squinted. "Minus ten points."

Argent's grin widened. "Then I'll get twenty." He booped Felix's nose, and Felix blushed. Rosie glanced over, only to turn back to Shawn. Felix's brief moment of joy had fleeted before it even had a chance to stick.

"Alrighty then. You'll be workin' in pairs, to lessen the odds of death." Samuel pointed at Rosie and Shawn. "You two, down by the creeks in the Gaheris Marsh to check on the mermaids, kelpies, and such. No swimmin' with them either. They get rowdy."

"Oh!" Rosie's eyes went wide with excitement. "Because they don't know that we can't breathe underwater?"

"Oh, they know. They just like drownin' people."

Rosie snorted. "Hey," Shawn said to her. "Just like where we first met! Well, not *first* met, but…"

"You mean where I kicked your butt?" Rosie playfully punched Shawn's arm.

She's so happy... without me.

Samuel pointed to Zahra and Nasira. "You two, in the plains of the Pellinore Forest with the unicorns." Zahra's eyes glittered like the night sky, while Nasira just rolled hers. "Luke and Daniella!" He cut them off before they could correct him. "The drylands of the Lot Plateau for the sphinxes and basilisks."

Felix snickered. *Good luck with her, Lucas. Hopefully you won't get eaten as she stops for a selfie.* But Samuel's assignment for him and Argent would immediately kill what little humor he'd taken thus far in today's events.

"And you two." Samuel pointed to Felix and Argent. "Up in the Bors Mountains for the dragons."

The word was bone-chilling for Felix, making him stutter. "D-Dragons?"

"Yep. And manticores, ogres, trolls. All that dangerous shit."

"S-Shouldn't you—"

"Take a well-earned nap? Good idea, young man! Best o' luck with that there mountain of death!" Samuel cackled as he zipped back inside. He popped back out, said, "Seriously, don't get killed like a bunch o' fuckin' idiots," then vanished behind his office door. Heavy snores followed.

Felix had joked about wanting to die so he wouldn't have to deal with any of his problems anymore. But the moment dragons came into mix, he was ready to piss himself. "A-Anybody wanna—" Before he could finish asking whether anyone was willing to trade duties, everyone else had already sprinted off. Dejected and terrified, Felix stared at his feet, knowing full well that they might've been found days later by Samuel, severed and skeletal in a dragon's nest. "We're gonna die," Felix said. "We are going to fucking die."

"Relax!" Argent held him close, and right away, Felix's anxiety eased up. "We don't have to go and feed them right away. We can just... walk around, check out the sights. Then maybe we can get someone to go with us later."

It wasn't the worst idea Felix had ever heard. He'd have joked about wishing one of the dragons would've eaten him alive had it not been for his fear, but even then, Argent was trying to make it a good day for him. For the both of them. He ought to have returned the favor.

"You've checked this place out online, right?" Argent asked. "Anywhere you have in mind?"

"Not really. I must've scrolled through the gallery over a thousand times, but… it's not the same when you're here in person. I don't even know where to start. What about you? Were you ever out here last year?"

"You think I care enough about this place to commit it to memory?"

"You're…" Felix groaned, but quickly sought to focus on something positive before his frustration festered. "How about those unicorn plains? Can't go wrong with unicorns." The image of the taxidermic unicorn flashed in his mind, and he did his best to shake it off.

"Excellent choice." Argent gave a thumbs up, and they made their way up the northern trail towards what the map referred to as the Pellinore Forest. Dancing sprites lit their way onto the beaten path through the trees, occasionally flashing in front of them. The road opened up into a wide field of shining emerald grass stretching into the distance. Unicorns charged across the plains like a pack of untamed wildebeests. Sprites and fairies flew high above, while pegasi rested beside a gushing spring, their wings folded over their backs. How lovely it would've been to spend an entire day relaxing here. Lying back in the grass, fingers digging into the dirt, and listening to the sound of a babbling brook to forget his worries.

"MOVE!"

Argent pushed Felix to the ground as a unicorn, letting out a distressing neigh, zoomed past. They held tightly onto each other. Once the danger had passed, Argent kept holding on, leaving Felix unsure of what to say or how to feel. Argent's eyes met Felix's. "You really gotta work on that whole lost-in-your-thoughts thing."

Felix's cheeks grew hotter as he blushed. He nervously scratched his head, stammering. "T-Thanks for uh… helping me… you know, not get impaled by a unicorn."

"I think *I* nearly got impaled myself."

This time Felix didn't respond with words, but rather a playful pinch. "¡Pervertido!" They laughed as Argent helped Felix up.

Zahra ran over to them "Are you guys okay?"

"Yeah," Felix said. Argent gave a devious smirk, but Felix just ignored him.

Zahra held her chin as she observed the wild unicorn darting into the forest. "The unicorns are usually very peaceful and docile. But today they seem so agitated. They won't even go near their food."

Nasira leaned against a tree, staring up at the sky from her spot in the shade. "We gave them food." She gestured to the open bag of animal feed next to her, looking otherwise untouched. "Whether they eat isn't my problem."

Argent scoffed. "Maybe it's your attitude."

"Maybe *you* should look in a mirror." Nasira crossed her arms, her eyes drifting down. "It's not like I chose to be here," she grumbled.

Zahra pouted, then began speaking in Arabic. Nasira seemed confused at first. But it quickly became clear as Zahra stuttered, she couldn't keep up with Nasira. Nasira scoffed and shooed her away. Felix wasn't sure he fully understood Nasira's frustrations given everything on his own plate. But he felt he owed them both an attempt to ease the tensions. "Hey, Nasira?"

She scowled. "What?"

He couldn't ask about her family—way too intrusive. Maybe something unrelated to help her come down? Something that didn't involve relying on substances. Something they could easily manage with their surroundings. "Do you... know how to ride a horse?"

"No." Nasira seemed ready to blow a fuse, only for her temper to fade into a sulk as she let out a heavy sigh. "Fine, I do. But unicorns are a definite no for me."

Felix raised an eyebrow. "They're horses with horns. That's it." Instinctively, Felix could sense Argent was about to make a joke about him dressing like a horny horse on Halloween, and thus killed his perversion in its crib with a quick disapproving glare.

Nasira smirked. "Then why don't *you* ride?"

This Felix was not expecting. He'd never been the best person with animals, especially when it came to perilous antics like horseback riding. "Because... I have the coordination of a one-legged flamingo?"

Zahra twiddled her thumbs. "But flamingos are known for their balance."

Felix glared at Zahra, but instantly regretted taking his vexation out on her as she hung her head and held her arm. *Way to fucking go, Felix.* "Sorry, Zahra. It's just... been a week." She nodded meekly. Wanting to further make amends, Felix returned his focus to Nasira. "Alright, this'll be fun. But fair warning: I've never ridden before. So..."

Argent snickered, and this time Felix had no problem shooting dagger eyes as Zahra and Nasira chuckled. "Sure," Nasira said. "Why not? I learned most of the basics on my own. I'm no expert, but I can probably help you not get killed."

"You're self-taught? That's awesome!" Felix's interest and enthusiasm had been piqued now, and all the better if it meant melting away the ice around Nasira's heart. Though whether it was rotten beneath the frost had yet to have been discovered. But truly, Felix hoped this might've helped her start to finally warm up to the idea of accepting her magical identity. He knew firsthand that hating yourself all your life was a fate worse than death. Not to mention this could've taken some of the burden off Zahra and her parents' shoulders.

"C'mon then." Nasira slowly approached a solitary unicorn eating grass. Its silvery skin glittered bright, while its flowing platinum-blonde tail and mane glowed a ghostly white. The deep bronze of its horn glinted with a brilliant luster. It was right out of a fairy tale, though whether this unicorn would've been friendly was still yet to be seen. Nasira turned back to Felix and whispered, "You're sure about this?"

Dear fucking gods no. But dammit, if I'm gonna die, I will die trying to be a good person for once. Felix nodded, telling himself the old mantra, *"Fake it 'til you make it."*

Nasira reached out and, as her fingers made contact with the back of the unicorn's head, stroked its mane. It neighed, trotting a bit before settling down. Once it had calmed, it cast its blackened eyes upon Felix, snorting heavily. If Felix had believed in souls, then this thing was surely staring directly into his, along with all the fucked-up shit attached to it.

Felix took one step at a time towards the unicorn, following Nasira's lead in petting its mane. As he grew sure of himself, he climbed onto its back, and Nasira instructed him step by step how to earn its trust. The view from atop the mount was astounding, perfectly capturing the serenity of the pastures. In this moment, the rest of the world, along with all its problems, disappeared.

Until something caught Felix's eye.

A shadow, unnatural as it almost radiated darkness, leapt through the trees. Felix locked his gaze onto the entity, and as if right on cue, it stopped. Nestled between a pair of trees at the pasture's end, the silhouette raised its hand. The unicorn sprung forward, flinging Felix through the air and plunging him headfirst into the spring.

The crash, along with the fierce, piercing cold, stung his skin. Recentering himself, he pulled himself out of his shock and back onto solid ground, coughing up water and collapsing into the grass. His uniform, heavy and drenched, clung to him. His wet hair hung in his face. The breeze, before gentle and soothing, now felt like slowly drowning in an ice bath.

Argent helped Felix up, holding him and trying to warm him up. Zahra trembled and looked ready to bite her nails. "Are you okay?" she asked. "What happened?"

"T-That..." Felix coughed, nearly gagging. "That guy... in the trees." *Vagus...*

"What guy?" Argent asked. "Felix, you're running on stress. We need to get you back inside the castle and—"

"No," Nasira said. Even she appeared shaken up as she clenched her free hand, her other hand again petting the unicorn's mane to calm it down. "He's right. I saw it too. Someone was watching us from the woods, and they set the unicorn's tail on fire." She gestured towards the tail, whose end was singed black and letting off puffs of smoke.

"H-How?" Zahra's face drained of color. "The reserve is sealed off."

Argent shrugged. "Probably Lucas. I mean, he *is* a jackass."

"N-No..." Felix pushed himself forward as he set up. *It's him.* Vagus must not've been pleased about Felix's retaliation. Immediately, panic coursed through him. *The others don't know. Rosie doesn't know!* He swiped the map from Argent's belt, tearing the edges slightly and crumpling the parchment as he unfurled it. *Where they met. A creek.*

According to the map, there was a series of creeks running through the Gaheris Marsh, east of the central meadow in the Pellinore Forest. It was still morning. After rolling up the map, Felix darted into the woods following the sun. The others shouted to him, but he kept running, their yells fading into the white noise of chirping birds and buzzing sprites.

Please be east. Please be fucking east. He raced off the path, leaves and dirt clinging to his uniform. His legs screamed for rest, lest they be injured any further, but that didn't matter. Whatever angry words Rosie had for him hurting himself yet again, he still had to make sure she was safe.

He came across a stream cutting through the trees. Double-checking the map, he ran upstream, hoping this would lead him to the marsh. He most certainly would've known once he'd laid his sights on any aquatic familiars.

The trees opened up into another, smaller clearing with much softer ground. And over by a small waterfall, sitting on a large boulder, were Shawn and…

"ROSIE!"

Rosie tensed up, sadness filling her shocked expression as she looked down on Felix, quickly usurped by anger. "F-Felix?! What are you—"

Felix panted. "There's… someone." He scrambled, trying to decipher his own thoughts. How could he communicate the danger without exposing his knowledge of Vagus? But even then, the temptation to throw caution to the wind and just blurt out the truth was powerful. Especially as a hot breath went down the back of Felix's neck, raising every hair on his body. He spun around and raised his wand. But rather than being met with Vagus' mask, a pair of black eyes bore into his. He jumped back and prepared to attack.

"Stop!"

Rosie jumped in front of Felix, defending the strange equestrian beast. Gray-green tentacles, acting as a mane, draped over its charcoal-black skin, its scales slick and shining. Gills lined its neck, though it seemed to have no problem breathing on land. "It's a kelpie," Rosie said. "A natural one. Harmless." She petted its mane, giving a kind smile to help it relax. But that smile turned into a foul grimace as she turned back to Felix. "Put your wand away."

"Rosie, you don't understand. There's—"

"No. *You* don't understand!" She marched right up to Felix's face. "I gave up an entire year at Roseford back home to come *here*. Hell, I risked getting drafted at that exam just to be there for you! I chose to take the grant here to make sure that you could stand on your own two feet, not to watch you break one of them because you still can't get it through your head that when you do shit like that, it doesn't just hurt *you*."

Felix found himself choked up as he backed away. He'd known Rosie had never cared for magic the way he did, but… Roseford was one of the top universities back home. Rosie had often mentioned wanting to go there, and maybe one day could've found a way to help with human-magus relations within the system. Felix, by comparison, just made dumb jokes about the similarities in names. Never did he regret his callousness quite like he did in this moment. She'd given up her chance at achieving her goals… for him. And here he was, throwing himself into fires of his own making, again and again, forcing her to run in and pull him out.

Until she'd grown fed up with getting burned.

Before he could muster the courage to speak, Shawn pushed them both to the ground as a column of flames rained down upon the creek. The kelpie neighed. As it leapt into the stream, its hind legs fused into a mermaid tail, and it vanished as it splashed into the water.

Felix raised his head, his eyes darting about. *Where is he?!* He pushed himself up. "COME ON!" He shouted at the top of his lungs. "SHOW YOURSELF."

"Damn kids!"

Samuel, his chest heaving, shot out a blast of water and foam from his wand, extinguishing the flames. The other students raced from the trees behind him. "Dammit!" Samuel yelled. "What do you think you're—"

"Protection of Tides!"

Shawn jumped in front of them, forming a barrier of water just before a fireball evaporated it on impact. Shawn fell to his knees. Rosie rushed to his side while Felix wafted away the smoke. The mist cleared. There he stood, up there on top of the waterfall, eyeing them all from above like a hunter: Vagus. Cinder, his accursed phoenix familiar, sat on his shoulder.

Lucas' face grew deathly pale, while Felix's blood ran cold.

"GO! NOW!"

Samuel's yell broke through Felix's shock, though Argent still had to grab him by the wrist and pull him. "We gotta go!" Argent yelled. Felix knew he was right. Yet even so, he couldn't take his eyes off their assailant. Fed up, Argent picked Felix up and ran.

Cinder flew off Vagus' shoulder and wrapped herself in golden flames. The flames grew. From the blaze, she emerged as a full-sized phoenix whose wings eclipsed the sun. Fire poured forth from her beak, cutting off Felix and Argent' escape route through the trees. Argent moved to double back. He tripped as he turned heel, leaving Felix to fall from his arms.

Air whooshed through Felix's ears as a pressure formed around his waist. Cinder had gripped him in her talons and carried him off into the sky, and in the deafening gusts of freezing wind, Felix could make out what sounded like a faint but shrill scream.

At first, Felix tried to break free. But as he reached for his wand, it hit him that it probably wasn't the best idea to make the firebird drop him to his death far, far below. Instead, he worked his wand into his sleeve. He'd hopefully get the upper hand once they landed. And that's when their destination came into view: the highest peak of the Bors Mountains.

The fall sent more pain through Felix's body as Cinder dropped him. He'd been taken to what would've made a decent spot for a dragon's roost. A rocky perch jutting out from the mountain, overlooking the entire reserve, with Dragora Castle in perfect view atop its cliff near the horizon. The only escape that wouldn't result in going splat was a tunnel opening into the mountain, but Cinder had blocked it off. Felix was ready to reveal his wand just when a sudden groan caught him off guard.

"Lucas!"

Felix rushed to help Lucas to his feet. His fists trembled, though this time his glare ignored Felix altogether, now directed instead at Vagus, seated on Cinder's back. "You…! Just leave me alone!" Lucas sweat bullets as his voice cracked. "I want nothing more to do with you people!"

"You people"?

Felix wanted to question what he meant, but he knew he wouldn't get any answers. Not that it would matter if they'd wound up dead, either at Vagus' hands, from the drop just behind them, or within the jaws of a dragon gobbling up intruders in its domain.

Vagus jumped off Cinder's back. At the thud of his boots, Lucas fell back down. Felix laid him back, making sure he didn't hurt his head before attending to more immediate concerns. Here he was once again: face to face with Vagus.

"No one walks away from me."

"Really?" Felix balled his hands into fists, trying to stand tall and keep his eyes narrowed. He couldn't cower now. If he did, it'd only make it that much easier for Vagus to pick them off, and Felix wasn't about to go down without a fight. "Cuz I was thinking of jumping, honestly. Anything to steer clear of you."

"We made a deal." Vagus' voice grew more severe. "You are bound by an oath. The both of you. You'd abandon what you've sought for so long so easily? Over petty squabbles with those nothings?"

"Those 'nothings' are my friends." Now Felix was ready to break Vagus' mask in half. "And sorry to say, I'm not exactly ready to trust the guy who burned down my house and kidnapped a couple of kids. So how about you take that oath and shove it up your—"

Vagus laughed, only infuriating Felix further. "That fury still burns in your eyes, alright," Vagus said. "A righteous fury. Inextinguishable. Just like his…"

"Quit talking in riddles! Who even are you?"

"… You really have no clue, do you?" Vagus held his mask as though it were his actual forehead. "Though I suppose you wouldn't. You were so young. But I've been with you since long before you were even a thought."

I can't let him get in my head. Felix groaned. "Again with the cryptic bullshit. I don't know who you are or what you want, nor do I care. I'm happy with what I've got, thank you."

"No. You're not."

"What do you even know about me? What—"

"I know there's someone you haven't seen for quite a long time." Vagus' voice grew softer. And yet somehow, that frightened Felix even more. "Someone you've wished to see again face to face. The one who has set you on this path towards power. The one who shaped and molded you from the flames of their own hatred, passing that spiteful torch into your unwitting hands." Slowly, Vagus approached. Felix backed up, only to stop as pebbles fell off the cliff and tumbled down the side of the mountain.

"Emerald Flame!"

A lurid teal fire, more blue than green, forced Vagus back as he dodged. Lucas had risen. He clutched his wand tight. Vagus charged, and before Lucas could try another spell, he was kicked to the ground. Vagus rushed Felix. He gripped Felix's arm, moving to twist it, but Felix was ready to play the ace up his sleeve.

"Bolt Spark!"

A point-blank flash of blue fire knocked Vagus onto his back. He wheezed, rushing to push himself up as Felix grabbed Lucas' wrist and dashed for the cave entrance. *Let's try that again!* "Bolt Spark!" Felix threw another fireball at Cinder, but she craned her head out of the way before lunging.

"Firestorm!"

As Lucas' wand glowed red, a swirl of blue flames erupted from the ground, engulfing Cinder completely as she shrieked. The vortex dissolved. With her eyes shut, Cinder toppled over with a massive thud.

For once, Lucas, I'm thankful you're with me. If we survive this, I promise never to call you Lighthead ever again!

Using a small fire spell for illumination, the pair lit their way through the dark passage. Felix didn't bother looking back—that would've gotten them killed for sure. They ran, their steps in perfect sync, not once needing to speak on where to go. At last, they'd entered a large cavern; Felix could only tell because of continuous deep snores reverberating all around them. He couldn't make out where the source of the rumbling was. But a massive, pitch-black chamber like this was the perfect place to hide.

Or, if his fears came to fruition, the perfect place to meet his end in the gnashing teeth of the dragon whose slumber he was about to disturb.

Breaking free of Felix's grip, Lucas rushed into the darkness. Felix was tempted to yell at Lucas to come back or curse his name. However, that'd probably be followed up with death, either by Vagus or dragon. Hesitantly, Felix followed Lucas' footfalls. Dimming their wands, they took cover behind what Felix kept telling himself was nothing more than a large, moving, breathing rock. They couldn't risk making any sound, even if they were masked by the totally ordinary boulder they'd hidden next to.

And then… footsteps.

Out there, somewhere in the cover of the oppressive gloom, was Vagus, hunting them relentlessly. Though the clanks of his boots were distinct enough to recognize, the snores made it far more difficult for Felix to pinpoint where exactly in the cavern they were emanating from. His lungs heaved, making it harder and harder for him to stay quiet. Here he was, with the person who'd injured him, being pursued by a masked man they'd pledged themselves to in secret. And all for what?

And moreover, Felix kept returning to Vagus' comments. Had he truly always been there, lurking in the shadows, observing him since the day he was born? But why? And what was his connection to both he and Lucas? Why them of all people? Why the pearl-eyed bane of his family's existence, and why the lowly cobalt runt?

"Someone you've wished you could see again face to face. The one who shaped and molded you from the flames of their own hatred, passing that spiteful torch into your unwitting hands."

Lucas wheezed, and Felix could feel from here that he was rocking back and forth uncontrollably. The footsteps quickened, growing ever louder, closer and closer. No attempt to calm Lucas at this point would've worked, and it was too late. If Felix wanted any chance at getting away at all, not in one piece but still alive, there was no other choice. He pulled out his wand and aimed right for the source of the snores.

"Bolt Spark!"

Fire surged from Felix's wand, revealing maroon scales, leathery wings, and what seemed to be giant red cat eyes, easily three times the size of either Felix or Lucas' heads. The beast's rumbles quickly became a full-on roar, shaking the cavern violently.

"Why you little…!"

A cold hand grabbed Felix's wrist, and the red light of his wand exposed the golden mask from the darkness. Ivory eyes glared though the slits of the mask. A high-pitched scream stabbed Felix's ears, even causing Vagus to stagger. The dragon roared once more. Felix took the opportunity to, embracing this as a chance to let out his pent-up aggression, test out a new spell. Particularly, that one Lucas used back in combat class. "Flame Strike!" Blue flames gathered in his fist. Channeling his rage, Felix punched Vagus square in the face. The mask cracked as its pieces fell to the ground, and Vagus stumbled back.

This might've been Felix's only chance to glimpse Vagus' face. But at this rate, whatever lay behind the mask might've risked him getting away at all.

"Illuminate!"

Not even looking in Vagus' direction, Felix grabbed Lucas again and dashed for the exit. The dragon breathed fire at them, and they barely avoided the blast as they ran. Blinding light flooded Felix's vision, giving way to blurs of trees, grass, and stones, slowly forming and becoming clearer. Then in an instant, it all vanished in a surge of rushing water from all sides. Felix resurfaced and gasped for air, finding himself and Lucas in a small spring at the base of the mountain. He climbed out and struggled to stand. He reached for Lucas, only to stumble and fall as another roar, the loudest yet, shook the whole mountain. As Lucas began to pull himself out, a great shadow loomed over them both.

The beast stood on all fours, easily the size of a two-story house, its glassy vermillion eyes burning right through Felix's composure. Its yellowish fangs hung out of its jaw, while two bronze horns shot out from its head. The scarlet scales gave Felix pause. Such a deep, bloody red, shining bright in the light of the sun. Almost as bright as the Infernal Dragon Ira—the harbinger of the Scorch.

Another wave of fire poured from the dragon's lips. Felix pushed Lucas back into the spring, then rolled into the water after him. The ends of his nerves had nearly been seared by the blaze, only for an even more agonizing burn to overtake his right arm. He lost himself in the pain. The thought to resurface was drowned out as he screamed, a jet of bubbles streaming from his mouth, along with the air he just couldn't hold onto.

Felix coughed as something pulled him back up. He'd hardly noticed he was above water, the pain was so intense. Lucas held onto him with one hand, and the rock face with the other, desperately trying to shimmy them both closer to solid ground. The dragon readied to kill them. They braced themselves, but another plume of golden flames stopped the monster before it could strike again. Cinder flew down, clawing the dragon's face, pushing it to the ground before flying off.

"Cyclone!"

A gust of wind knocked the dragon into the mountain, kicking up a dust cloud as the earth trembled. Samuel and the others ran out from the trees. Lucas swam to the edge of the spring, still holding onto Felix before the others helped pull them out. Felix's torn up sleeve revealed that his arm had been badly burned, turning his skin a deep pinkish red, verging on purple. Small patches of blisters had already begun to form. Felix cried out as the pain sank deeper into his arm, ringing through his whole body.

Rosie rushed over. "Demeter's Touch!" Her wand's light enveloped Felix's arm. Felix grit his teeth so hard, they might've risked cracking for all he knew. "Zahra, help me!" Zahra ran to assist her. The pain slowly faded away, though the scars of the burn, along with the blisters and discoloration, remained. Once it was clear they'd done all they could, and that Felix had mostly recovered, Rosie helped him up.

"T-Thanks," he said, panting. "I—"

She slapped him, and a sharp sting shut him up immediately. Tears welled in her eyes. "You fucking idiot!" she yelled, her voice brittle and screechy. "What the fuck were you thinking?! You could've died!"

"I-I was kidna—"

"No!" Rosie pointed at Lucas. "You took the hit for him! For the guy who hurt you! Because *you* were trying to prove something for *me*!"

"Is… is that what this is about? Me trying to look out for—"

"It's about you not caring whether you get killed!" Rosie threw her arms around him, sobbing into his shoulder. "Please. Please stop. Stop treating your life like you can just throw it away. Stop being so fucking reckless. Please…"

Felix didn't know what to say. Or rather, he knew he shouldn't have said anything. Rosie had always been there for him, keeping him grounded on his darkest, most terrible nights. She was the one who'd always brought him back from the brink. Who kept him from tossing his soul down the drain. The one who'd convinced him that life was worth fighting for. That *he* was worth fighting for.

"Okay," Felix said. "I promise."

Rosie hugged tighter.

"My arm still kinda hurts… so—"

"So does my heart. This is payback, you fuck."

Felix snickered. "Good to have you back, puta."

"You too, bitch." After all this time, what had felt like an eternity without his best friend, she was finally back. That's all Felix could've asked for. Apparently, the sight was so touching that Zahra had started sniffling and tearing up.

"Alrighty," Samuel said, cracking his knuckles, followed by his back. "The whelp's all taken care of."

"Whelp?" Felix asked.

"Y'know, the whelp. Li'l baby dragon."

"B-Baby?!" The dragon snored by the cave entrance. The horrific beast that had nearly killed them… wasn't even fully grown?!

"I managed to settle it down, thanks to these two." Samuel gestured to Denise and Nasira.

"She did all the work," Denise said as she typed furiously on her phone. "I mainly just took pics." She snapped a photo as she made a peace sign in front of the dragon.

Of fucking course you did.

Nasira shrugged. "Guess I have a way with animals? I just gave it some food and sang it an old lullaby… from my mother." She held her wrist.

Argent rushed over and hugged Felix. "Thank fucking God you're okay! I'm so sorry, I should've—"

"Hey, relax," Felix said. Argent let go. "I'm okay. You know, minus the little tan." He held up his scarred arm.

Argent pouted. "Not funny!" Judging by Rosie's glare, she agreed.

Felix sighed. "Sorry, not cool." He looked around. No sign of Vagus or Cinder. *Good riddance.* "That guy and his phoenix. Where'd they go?"

"No sign of 'em," Samuel said. "But I *am* wondering where—"

"We're here!"

Headmistress Hakim, along with Seisyll, Gottschalk, and a group of security guards, ran towards them. Ramidha hugged Zahra tight. "Thank goodness you're okay!" Nasira tensed up, but Ramidha grabbed her and pulled her into the hug. "Both of you!" She muttered a bit in Arabic.

Seisyll knelt, examining Felix's wounds.

"It's not that bad." Felix outstretched his arm. "My friends healed—"

He held it. "O Holy Guardian of the Heavens, grant me but a fragment of your radiant shine, and heal the innocent before me. Angel's Tear." Wings of light stretched out from his back before breaking apart. The feathers flew, swirling around Felix's arm, and without any pain whatsoever, every scar, blister, and burn mark had vanished. His arm remained slightly pink, but it had otherwise been restored.

"T-Thank you, Professor Hakim," Felix said, but Seisyll didn't even glance his way as he stood and faced Samuel.

"Hey, bro," Samuel said.

Felix's jaw nearly dropped. *Brother?! I need a Who's Who of Dragora with a family tree.*

"It's *your* job to secure the reserve." Seisyll's voice was as stern as his eyes were wrathful. "How could you allow someone to—"

"I just handed them the key and showed them the way," Samuel cracked a grin. "You know that routine, right?" He glanced over at Ramidha.

"Make another comment about my family, and your place here ends."

Samuel's smile vanished. "Sei, I was just joki—"

"We'll discuss this later." Almost as if discarding his brief quarrel with his brother, and Samuel's very existence, Seisyll joined his family. Samuel simply mumbled to himself, shuffling over to speak with security. Gottschalk hugged Lucas tight as both of them cried. As many problems as Felix had with the both of them, he found the sight rather sweet, their cold personas melting in each other's embrace. It was enough to make Felix miss his mother.

Argent helped Felix up. "So... what do you say we call it a day?"

"Sounds good." Felix turned to Rosie. "We've got a *lot* of catching up to do. So... how does a movie night sound?"

"Sure," Rosie said, eyes beaming. "Just us."

"Ooh, ooh!" Argent butted his way between them, holding them both and forcing them into a group hug. "Can I be official third wheel?"

"If it's all the same," Felix said. "I think Rosie and I..."

Argent relented. "Alright. Guess you guys deserve it." He let go.

"Hey, don't feel bad," Rosie said. "We can still be a terrible trio. I think we're all pretty fucking terrible." She laughed, as did Felix and Argent. But she was right. The air had been cleared with both Rosie and Argent. Maybe now, with Vagus on the run, things might improve just yet, if only for a little while. He looked off into the sky, half-expecting to see Cinder's silhouette diving at him.

And thankfully, the sky was crystal clear.

"An oath?!" Martino squeezed Lucas' wrist, turning it over and over again while squinting. He squeezed so tight he ought to have left bruises on Lucas' hand. "You made an oath?!"

Lucas flinched. He'd tried to keep this all hidden from his family for as long as he could, but the attack in the reserve pushed his parents to their boiling point. They hadn't bothered grilling him about running away, but when it became clear that one of the Enlightened was involved, they'd demanded answers. And so he sat in his father's study, with Lucinda, standing in the corner, too afraid to speak. "Yes." It took all of Lucas' strength to speak. "I did."

"Unbelievable," Martino muttered. "I thought we'd taught you better." He dropped Lucas' hand and walked back around to sit back at his desk. He held his forehead, letting out a prolonged groan and grumbling to himself. "And you know nothing else about this... Vagus?"

He could've mentioned that the cobalt had also made the oath. But with all the eyes that were already on Brasher, perhaps that was the last thing either of them needed. Especially if Lucas' parents had learned that their dark sorcerer son not only made an oath with one of the Enlightened's quaesitors, but that he was directly competing with a damned cobalt—and struggling, to put it nicely.

"No... no, Father. That's all I know."

"Then you can go." Martino opened up one of his drawers, revealing a wine glass and an unopened bottle of cider. "I'll notify Hakim in the morning. Not that she'll be able to do much." His face turned red. "You can go," he boomed.

"O-Of course..." Lucas headed for the door. He hung his head, trying not to tremble or show that he was on the verge of tears. He quickened his pace, but stopped as Lucinda gripped his shoulder, looking on in sadness. So badly he wanted to talk to her. To tell her all that as on his mind. As much as he resented her for being their father's favorite—for being *everyone's* favorite—he knew it was never her fault.

"You stay, Lucinda." Martino slammed his glass onto the desk. "We need to talk about that friend of yours. What's her name...?" He waved his hand. "Ah, forget it." He leaned back in his chair, staring at the ceiling. "Go, Lucas."

With one last concerned glance from his sister, Lucas left. Up the long, winding stairs, down the dim, lonely corridors, and past the massive windows overlooking their estate's gardens. Out there in the woods, in the abandoned greenhouse of some obscure ancestor who'd probably spurn his name, he'd pledged himself to Vagus' cause. A decision he'd now regretted more than anything else in his life.

He entered his room, shut the door behind him, and crawled into bed, wishing that he'd never been born.

Chapter Fifteen

Holiday Horrors

"*AH, WINTER. The pure white snow blanketing the streets, the delicate snowflakes flowing in the cold wind, and the frost hiding on the road waiting to cause an accident. Fuck winter.*

The last few weeks had been splendid. No worrying about Vagus lurking in the shadows, and now, no worrying about classes over Dragora's winter break. While the Medeian Empire didn't celebrate Christmas, it basically had its own version on the winter solstice for the Dragons of Ice and Water. In fact, the empire had four of these holidays, all on the solstices and equinoxes of each season, and for each specific element: spring for earth, summer for fire, autumn for wind, and winter for water. Of course, Dragora needed to be in session during the autumnal equinox in order to make sure everyone was settled, but that was beside the point.

Tired of spending his time all alone in his dorm, Felix had decided to move in with Argent (and Shawn by extension). Though as elated Argent was about this choice, he did pout when Felix insisted that he stay on the couch, at least for a little while. Sleeping beside Argent seemed infinitely more comfortable, but Felix's shyness and general awkwardness kept him chained to the sofa cushions.

Felix stretched out on the couch as he woke up, cozy in his pajamas and under the blanket he'd stolen from the still snoozing Argent. The crackling of the fireplace added to the laid-back atmosphere, even if it was muffled under the music from Felix's headphones, or Shawn's bellowing snores. Felix could've played video games to pass the time. But that involved getting up to grab the controller and turn on the TV, and that was far too much effort for a day like this. Or any day.

His parents had texted him "Merry Christmas!", though he didn't reply. Instead, he relished in the fact he wouldn't be attending any holiday parties with family friends this year, and that he could just enjoy the day doing nothing in his little introvert cocoon.

"Greetings, fellow lazy bastards!"

Rosie barged inside, making Felix jump and roll onto the floor, while Argent leapt from bed shouting. Shawn hadn't so much as stirred and kept on snoring. Rosie was in her uniform, but she carried her winter coat with her. A purple jacket with gold fur, plus matching gloves, scarf, and earmuffs. "You guys ready for today?"

Grumbling, Felix hauled himself back into his nest. "If you mean doing nothing for the whole day, then yes. I am very much ready."

"Don't you remember?" Rosie rushed in, plopping herself onto the couch and trapping Felix's legs. A hostage situation of the highest caliber.

Argent, having taken the lift down from the loft, yawned. His hair was a mess, much like himself in general. "What's happening now?"

Rosie groaned. "You two have the attention span of a goldfish."

"Hey!" Felix tried to pull his numbed legs free. "Don't insult the fish!" He yanked them out, only to shout from the dreaded sensation of pins and needles. "So…" He just barely croaked out the words. "What exactly were our plans again?"

Rosie pushed herself up. "We were gonna check out the other isles today, remember? Visit landmarks, see the sights, all that touristy shit?"

"Oh, yeah. That." Felix retreated into his blanket. *Introvert shield activated.*

Rosie pulled the blanket off and threw it to the floor.

It wasn't very effective… "Alright, fine." He shook his legs until his nerves reawakened, then slowly rose. "I'll get dressed."

Argent, scratching his head, pointed back towards Shawn. "Should I bother waking…?"

"Let Sleeping Beauty rest," Rosie said, waving her hand. Felix got his clothes and headed for the dorm bathroom to get changed, but Rosie jumped between him and the door with a devious smirk. "So... have you two—"

"If you'd like me to enter the public sphere," Felix said. "Please step aside so I might make myself socially presentable. You cow." With a snicker, she let him pass. But no, they hadn't... done the deed. Even saying it felt awkward for Felix. He'd never had a proper conversation with anyone on how that stuff worked. That much required a bit of... "research" on his own. So to have Rosie inquiring about it the way she was? Felix did his best to put it out of mind and just enjoy the day. He rushed to get changed, and after donning his new winter wear courtesy of Argent (and once Rosie had finished cackling), they headed out.

It was hard for Felix not to blush at how well Argent rocked his forest-green bomber jacket. He'd been veering towards black, but Felix suggested he add some much-needed color to his wardrobe. Felix, meanwhile, had no problem going for something a bit different. A crimson, buttoned-up jacket, with a goddamn black cape over his shoulders sporting golden firebird designs. The jacket featured a little skirt, not that Felix or Argent minded. And to top the look off, a red beanie with a black broken heart symbol, for maximum "kill me" vibes.

An ocean of snow had filled the courtyard. Yet even so, the carriage paths down the hill were cleared out. Bright red mythril shone atop each carriage, keeping the wheels from freezing over while the kelpies' hooves melted the snow. The usual view of Cendrillion, and especially the reserve in the distance, were rendered more beautiful from the snowfall, even despite the gray sky. The highest peak of the Bors Mountains pierced right through the clouds... the peak where over a month ago, Felix had faced Vagus head-on.

And not a word from him since.

Once they'd caught a ferry to Sican Isle, Rosie's fervor took hold. She leaned over the railing, staring as the island grew over the horizon, even starting to bounce up and down. The cold breeze didn't seem to faze her. Felix, taking full advantage of the weather, huddled with Argent for warmth (and also cuddles). "God," Rosie said. "I cannot wait to see the museum!"

Felix snickered. "Nerd."

"Philistine whore."

"I don't know," Argent said. "I'm shockingly pretty interested too."

"You?" Felix asked. "Of all people? Really?"

"I know, right?" Argent laughed, and Felix took comfort in his embrace, especially now that Rosie's attention was fixated elsewhere. So much had changed in the near four months since Felix had arrived at Dragora. He'd stopped going to the Magus Combat League, now channeling all his energy from qualifying for the Ancient Dragons' Tournament into his studies—even Gottschalk's class. That day in the reserve had proven to be a turning point for Felix. Granted, Calvin was none too pleased when Felix had to visit the infirmary for a check-up and discovered he'd been burned with *dragon* fire. He'd usually joked about needing a swig of his favorite brand of scotch, but this made him start reciting full unironic prayers to Laphroaig.

Though while things were fine here, they most certainly weren't back home. The recent U.S. election had driven Rosie to profuse drinking and crying. Felix was afraid a Schmitt presidency meant he wouldn't be returning to Dragora next year, but that was the least of his worries. Schmitt had already suggested labelling the Truthseers as terrorists federally, and even "joked" about returning the identifying badges for magi that the Truthseers helped abolish decades ago. And voters had turned out for him in full force.

Still, he couldn't do anything about it now. All he could do was focus on enjoying his time at Dragora while it lasted, and maybe hoping to find a way to come back here if the U.S. became too hostile. It'd be a hassle, but it beat dying.

But this was how his year was supposed to go. And with the three of them together, and Vagus out of the picture, things were finally looking up.

The port town of Barenton seemed like a completely different country from Brastius over on Pyre Isle. More laid-back residents, relaxed blues instead of militant reds, and straightened architecture rather than the sloped walls of buildings. They'd passed the central plaza, where stood a gorgeous fountain with the statue of a long-haired woman in a flowing dress. Though the fountain ran dry, people still tossed their coins in, and even recited prayers towards the statue.

Up the steps, near a lake that had frosted over, stood the museum, appearing more like a grand cathedral. The stained-glass windows, depicting traditional sorcerers adorned with robes and pointed hats, as well as knights slaying dragons, scintillated with all their vibrant colors. Dark-blue spires reached up towards the sky.

"Here we are," Argent said. "The Camelot Museum."

Interesting name. Once inside, Argent approached the front desk, while Felix and Rosie hung out over by the wall. The TV on the wall was reporting the results of the Medeian primaries. While Felix still couldn't follow along with their politics, recent events made it impossible for him to ignore. From what he knew, most of Dragora's staff belonged to the Kelpie Party, while Lucas' family were in the Dragon Party. Democrats and Republicans seemed like a simple enough comparison. The Phoenix Party, unfortunately, hadn't received enough support to reach the general elections in June. Did he know what any of that meant, or what this Phoenix Party was analogous to? Nope. But ah well.

Argent walked back over. "Welp, we should be good to go on the tour in just a bit."

"You booked this ahead of time?" Felix asked.

Rosie raised an eyebrow. "Who are you and what have you done with Argent?"

Argent simply chuckled, not uttering a word. He most assuredly wasn't kidding about this trip piquing his interest. Unfortunately, Felix couldn't say the same about their tour guide. "Welcome to the Camelot Museum." Carlos, wearing his usual "I give no fucks" expression, coupled with his voice devoid of any melody or inflections, greeted them. "I'll be your tour guide today. Whoopee."

Damn, he works here too? You know what, I can't judge.

They followed Carlos into the exhibition hall. The building was empty, though Felix was still intimated by the tall ceilings (with snow blocking out the skylight), the enormous portraits on either side of the corridor, and the glass cases down the center of the walkway. Even despite the lack of anyone else present, Felix straightened his back and minded his posture to appear as sophisticated as possible.

"Many humans have enjoyed the stories of King Arthur and the Knights of the Round Table for centuries," Carlos said, gesturing to the towering statue of a knight. "Despite most of it being ancient fanfiction," he grumbled. He cleared his throat. "Many don't realize that the Kingdom of Loegres—*not* Camelot—did in fact exist."

Felix whispered to Argent, "Is he serious?"

"As an STD," Argent whispered back.

Rosie shushed them both.

"Following the Roman Empire's fall," Carlos continued. "Its western territories descended into complete chaos. While the Byzantine Empire controlled the east, a single power rose in Great Britain, then Albion: Uther Pendragon, who founded the Kingdom of Loegres, along with its shining capital: the city of Camelot."

He pointed to a portrait of a great fortress city resting alongside a cliff. The colors of the dark-green fields had washed out, while both the city walls and the sky above were a lifeless gray. No signs of the sunlight whatsoever. "Once Arthur came to power, he made efforts to create a society in which humans and sorcerers could coexist. By his side were three sorcerers: Merlin, Elaine, and Morgaine Le Fey."

Another portrait depicted three robed figures. A pale man with an obnoxiously pointy blue hat and long, dark-gray beard. A young woman with richly tanned skin, flowing brown hair, and sea-green dress. And an older, olive-skinned woman in a black-purple-and-silver gown, whose black hair was tied up into a bun. All three bore eyes of pearl.

"But two of these allies had qualms with Arthur's vision. And thus, Elaine killed her lover Merlin..." Carlos gave a heavy sigh. "And along with Morgaine and others who stood against the kingdom... slew Arthur." He rubbed his temple. "What followed was an attempt by the knight Lancelot to restore order and quash this rebellion. But the damage was too great. And so, Loegres fell, the once great city of Camelot was destroyed, and the Dark Ages continued. Those responsible for the tragedy fled to the Medeian Empire."

Felix's mind was stuck on Arthur's goal. Not only had he actually existed, but he'd tried something that people still thought was impossible after the Revelation: getting humans and magi to coexist peacefully. He wasn't sure what to think, especially hearing that magi were responsible for the destruction of this dream. Argent still seemed giddy about all the information, though, even ready to spit out random tidbits of trivia.

"You know," Argent whispered. "Elaine was the legendary Lady of the Lake, but people can't keep her name straight. Some say Viviane, some say Nimue or Nyvene. Personally, I like to go with—"

"Her name is Elaine."

Everyone paused, and the echo of Carlos' words hung in the hall, though he still faced away.

"Uh…" Argent stood tall, pretending he was pushing up a pair of invisible glasses. "No one has actual evidence of what her true name was. Some aren't even sure on the spelling, but—"

"No." Carlos turned, his hands balled into fists and his face reddening. "Her name *is* Elaine."

Argent snickered. "Okay, okay. Whatever you say."

Carlos rubbed his temple. "Que porra é essa, filho da mãe?"

Felix raised an eyebrow. "Did you just… speak Portuguese?"

"Yeah." Carlos frowned. "I'm brasileiro. Your point, corno?"

He returned to his silence. "N-Nothing." *Guess he just speaks both Spanish and Portuguese? I mean, if he works at so many places, then I guess it checks out.*

And with that, Carlos resumed the tour. Felix had never seen Carlos so sincere about anything. It felt unnatural to see him sincerely care about something, let alone a subject so trivial. His thoughts returned to the Fall of Loegres. The end of what could've become a utopia of both humans and magi. "But Arthur's plan," Felix whispered to Argent. "Is that true?"

"I don't know," Argent whispered back, shrugging. "But it was bound to fail."

"You're seriously gonna justify this? Imagine what could've been if—"

Again, Rosie shushed them. Carlos cleared his throat and rambled on. But Felix, lost in his own head, tuned out the rest of the tour. What would the world have been like had Arthur not fallen? How different would the life of the average magus be?

"A pipe dream. Never meant to be."

The mental intrusion caught him by surprise, but instantly, he recognized the voice. Felix looked around, but there was no sign of Vagus. Quickly, his fear turned to umbrage. *Should've figured you'd be back by now.* "Keep quiet," Felix whispered, unsure of just how much Vagus could hear. Rosie and Argent glanced at him, though Felix assured them all was well.

After the tour, they took comfort on a bench outside. Rosie tapped her foot. "Okay," she said. "If we wanna get a good look at the mausoleum, we gotta get to Brastius within the next hour. The ferry's a good 15 minutes away, so—"

"Oh relax," Argent said, letting Felix snuggle up next to him. "Who's in a rush to see a bunch of dead bodies?"

"I am!"

"That... is concerning."

"Don't get your hopes up," Felix said. "The mausoleum's lower levels are all closed off, and the atrium only has a bunch of slabs and monuments."

"Oh?" Rosie held her hip. "You sure know quite a bit about that place."

"Well..." Felix averted his gaze, looking for any excuse that wouldn't involve him looking for the Organ of Judgment, or worse, anything about Vagus. "What can I say? History fascinates me. Especially with Montanari's class."

"Oh yeah, Montanari!" Argent's eyes lit up. "She's really chill. Hers was my favorite class."

"Why?" Rosie asked. "She let you sleep?"

"No! I mean, sure, sometimes, but that's besides the point!"

Felix giggled, leaning into Argent and closing his eyes. A puff of mist escaped his mouth. *I did all of that... just for some power I know nothing about. And I kept them out of the loop. How much longer can I keep it from them?* He sat up. "Hey... you guys?"

Argent held Felix's shoulders. "Everything okay?"

"I just... wanted to tell you guys something."

"Excuse me?!"

Felix held his head.

"Felix?" Rosie asked.

"It's... that hooded guy from the reserve. He—"

Before he could finish, Felix shouted in agony and fell from the bench. His right arm burned far worse than it had from the dragon fire. Rosie and Argent tried to ask what was wrong, but their questions rang muffled through Felix's pain. Every single nerve from his fingertips up to his shoulder screamed in agony, as if they were about to be violently pulled apart at any moment. Thankfully, the pain subsided, giving way to numbness. Rosie and Argent brought him back to Dragora. Upon reaching Argent's dorm, all while Felix went through cycles of panic attacks, he curled up on the couch, shaking. Eventually, lulled by the crackling of the fireplace, he lay back.

Argent knelt. "Are you okay?"

"Y-Yeah. I... I'm sorry." Felix held out his hand, searching for something to explain the incident away. "I, uh... guess it was the burn? I don't know. Today was supposed to be fun and I ruined it." Argent held his shoulder.

"What matters is you're okay," Rosie said. "Besides, maybe you had the right idea. Maybe we need a day to ourselves, playing video games or something."

"Sounds good to me," Felix said. "Argent's got some classics."

"Lemme guess…" Argent shook his head. "That friend of Felix's got *you* hooked on this precursor crap too?"

Rosie grinned from ear to ear. "Hipster trash gotta stick together."

They spent the rest of the day jumping between games, all while Shawn remained sound asleep (not that Rosie minded). As day turned to night, Felix jumped at a knock at the door, again shielding himself with his blanket. Argent held onto Felix to help him calm down. Once Felix's nerves had soothed, Argent sang, "Come in!"

Penny waltzed inside. "There you guys are!" Beside her traipsed Floria and Nasira, while Zahra quietly shut the door. "We've been looking for you."

"You have?" Felix checked his phone—five unread messages. "Whoops."

"I figured since we're all stuck here for the holidays," Penny said. "We might as well celebrate together?"

Floria held a bag of candy. "We brought the food coma supplies."

"I've always heard about Christmas," Zahra said. "So I thought maybe we could celebrate it and the winter solstice!"

Rosie shrugged. "I mean Christmas was originally created to tell the winter solstice to go fuck itself, so… yeah, let's tell *that* idea to go fuck itself!"

"I might not celebrate these holidays…" Nasira crossed her arms, looking off towards the wall. "But Zahra convinced me. Why not, right?"

"There you go!" Zahra said.

Nasira giggled. "Anything to get you to shut up."

Though Felix initially wanted to fight her, he could tell from Zahra's laughter and Nasira's warm smile that this was genuine. Nasira had finally mastered the art of sincerity. Maybe things were looking up after all. "C'mon in," Felix said. "The more the crazier!" Everyone settled in, and Felix gave up his spot so Zahra and the other girls could take the couch. Rosie had claimed one of the armchairs, while Argent claimed the other, bidding Felix to sit on his lap. At first, he tried to joke away the offer, but with nowhere else to sit, and a strong desire to cuddle, Felix complied. But not before Rosie had to kill the moment.

"Argent!" Rosie, puffing her chest, pointed at Argent. "Break out the popcorn."

Argent rolled his eyes, gesturing to Felix. "Must I?"

She glared.

"Okay, okay, sheesh!" Apparently, in addition to a vintage gaming console, a portable generator, and a mini-fridge, Argent's dorm also boasted a microwave? A couple high-pitched beeps and the ensuing popping of kernels followed his fetch quest. Truly, he was the man to go to during the midst of a zombie apocalypse. He returned with the bowl, and madness reigned. Nasira unexpectedly proved herself to be a platforming pro, while Floria cried the hardest at *Life is Strange*. (She threatened anyone who handed her a tissue to suffocate them with it.) Before Felix had realized how late it was getting, the clock had struck midnight, and the moment Christmas Eve became Day, the console switched off. "The fuck?" Argent checked the cables, then ran to check the generator, letting out a bellowing groan. "Crap! Generator's fried!"

Everyone groaned along in a chorus of misery and disappointment. Floria blew her nose. "We were just at the good part." She dabbed her eyes. "None of you look at me!"

"I still say we kill Chloe," Penny said. "It's the logical choice."

"Welp…" Rosie, her hands tucked behind her in the armchair, kicked her feet up on the coffee table. "Back to the Dark Ages."

Argent shook his head, tsk-tsking. "No class. Oh! I have an idea!" He ran towards the lift, only to have to wait as Shawn exited, grumbling. "Welcome to the land of the living, Shawn. But not for looooong!" He sang out the last word as he zipped up to the loft, and Felix bashfully enjoyed Argent's antics.

Shawn rubbed his eyes, an ungodly cowlick sticking up from his bedhead. "What time is it?"

"Midnight," Rosie said. "You were literally knocked out all day."

"Oh. Fuck." Shawn dropped onto the couch, forcing Floria and Penny apart. Penny inched away as much as she could, keeping her eyes off Shawn and blushing slightly.

"I'm back!" Argent returned, and in his hands was a mysterious black box.

"What's in here?" Rosie asked. "Drugs?" Argent simply snickered and placed the box on the table. Immediately, Rosie's eyes widened as her feet shot back into her seat. She coiled into a fetal position. "No! No, no, no. Fuck this." She jumped from the chair and raced towards the door. "Nope nope nopity fuck that nope!"

"Rosie?" Shawn asked, again rubbing sand from his eyes. "What's—"

Everyone's eyes drifted towards the golden letters atop the box. "A Ouija board?" Zahra asked. She leaned away, while Nasira, taking Rosie's seat for herself, leaned in. She clasped her hands as an excited grin spread across her face.

Relenting, Rosie walked back over, leaning against the far wall. "Let it be known..." She projected her voice, looking around and moving her hands as if not only addressing the others gathered in front of her, but any other entities lurking in the room just out of sight. "That I am *not* participating in any of this bullshit."

"Yeah, yeah." Nasira opened the box and took out the board. "Let's do this."

"I-I'm with Rosie." Zahra tensed and sat up straight. "This seems—"

"Aren't you the one who's all about keeping your options open?"

"Y-Yes, but—"

"Whatever." Nasira's eyes almost glowed as they bulged. "I'm doing this."

"You seem eager," Penny said.

"What? You think cuz of my religion, I'm scared of summoning some kinda demon?"

"N-No... okay, yeah. But I was wondering the same thing about Shawn." Hesitantly, Penny met Shawn's confused gaze. "You're pretty religious too, right?"

"I mean..." Shawn said. "Yeah. Sorry, I'm out."

Floria scoffed. "If the rest of you wanna mess with shit you don't understand, then leave me out of it." She grabbed a handful of candy, leaving the bag nearly empty. "Go right ahead," she garbled as she chewed.

Nasira rolled her eyes. "Felix, you in?"

As much as he wanted to sit this one out, Felix could tell Nasira was completely absorbed in the board's spell. And on some level, so was he. "I... guess?"

"Good. Argent?"

Argent shrugged, not a shred of fear on his face. "Sure."

"Penny?"

Penny stared at the boar, nudging herself even further away. "I don't believe in ghosts or spirits, so... I mean—"

"Good enough." Nasira's voice was grave. "Fingers. Board. Now."

"Wait, wait!" Argent turned off the mythril lights before rushing back to tackle Felix with hugs. "Now we're good." They leaned forward, as did Nasira and Penny, only to falter and jump back as a bright light blinded them.

"You're all idiots." Rosie had turned on her phone's flashlight.

Felix frowned. "I hope your phone charger breaks."

Rosie gasped. "You blasphemous bitch."

"Are we fucking with the spirit world or not?" Nasira's eyes were filled with an unsettling resolve.

"Okay," Felix said. "So... what do we do exactly?"

"First," Argent said. "We put our fingers on the planchette."

"The what now?"

"The little wood thingy." Winking, Argent put his finger on the heart-shaped wooden piece atop the board, as did Felix, Nasira, and Penny. Though Felix wanted to pull his hand back... he couldn't. Something about the board compelled him. "O, spirits!" Argent donned a strange, indiscernible accent, like that of an old fortune teller holding a crystal ball. As much as it was obviously meant to be funny, it also inspired an eeriness in the air, and the return of the looming dread over Felix. "We mere mortal folk ask this of you: do any of you join us here tonight?"

The planchette remained still. The fireplace's crackles were the only sound in the room.

"I figured," Penny said. "Nothing."

Rosie snickered. "Idiots."

The wind outside howled, and the fireplace whisked out in an instant, making the light from Rosie's phone the only thing keeping the room from plunging into pitch black. The planchette zoomed over to "Yes." Felix stopped. "W Who...?" He could barely form the words. "Who the fuck did that?"

"I-I don't know." Penny's finger shook. "A-Argent?"

"It wasn't me," Argent said.

Felix leaned back. "Argent—"

"It wasn't me!"

For once, Argent's voice was filled with fear. Nasira, meanwhile, was transfixed, her eyes glued to the board. "I-Is…" Her voice was brittle. "Is that you, Teeta?"

"Teeta?" Felix asked.

"Quiet!" Nasira's grimace—looking possessed in the darkness—chilled Felix's blood. "T-Teeta? Is that really you?"

The planchette remained still.

Penny took her hand off the planchette. "N-Nasir—"

"Why would you do that?!"

The planchette zoomed over to "No." Nasira's stare grew vacant, eyes cast blankly to the floor. There was no sadness in her face. No anger. No anything. Felix wanted to ask what was wrong, and whom it was she was trying so desperately to reach.

But that vanished the moment the planchette rushed to "V."

"A-Alright," Penny said. "For real, who's doing this? Argent?"

"I said it wasn't me!" Argent yelled, clutching Felix with his free hand.

"Warned ya," Floria mumbled.

Rosie paced back and forth, her phone's flashlight zipping to and fro in rhythm with her footsteps. "Did you fucking idiots summon a demon? Fuck this. Fuck all of this."

The planchette continued. "A." "G." "U." "S."

No. Not a demon. Worse.

"Vagus?" Penny asked. "What in the world is that?"

You don't want to know.

It resumed. "BLOOD."

"B-Blood?" Penny covered her mouth.

"OATH."

The oath. Felix wanted to pull his hand back, but he couldn't. The planchette moved to spell the last word, and this more than anything else struck terror into his soul.

"L."

No.

"Y."

Stop.

"D."

Please fucking stop.

296

"I."

Fucking stop.

"A."

He'd had enough. Felix grabbed the board and threw it to the floor, splitting it in two. "LEAVE US ALONE!" He tossed the pieces into the fireplace. "BOLT SPARK!" He tried again and again to start the fire back up with his bare hands, to burn the board, but the sparks were instantly extinguished by cold gusts of wind. Bits of soot and ash flew into his eyes, making him tear up more than he already had.

Argent put the lights back on, then carried Felix back to the couch and held him tight. "It's okay. It's okay." Felix cried into Argent's shoulder as he clutched his shirt. He didn't believe Argent. Not for a moment. But slowly, his breaths abated, and he wiped his tears. Everyone gathered around the table, and not a word was spoken.

Felix sniffled. "S-Sorry. I…"

Zahra leaned in. "Are you…?"

He couldn't say a word about Vagus. But in that moment, he was more concerned for Nasira, who was still off in her own little world. Numb. "Nasira?" Felix asked. "If it's okay to ask… who is… 'Teeta'?"

Nasira flinched.

"Like I said, you don't have to—"

"Teeta isn't her name. She was my…" She looked up, meeting Zahra's concerned gaze. "Zahra and I's grandmother. Our Teeta. She died before we were born." Nasira teared up, and Zahra held her shoulder. "I wanted to know… what she would've thought of me." Nasira held her forehead. "If she was… like us. Or… if she would've hated me." Unable to hold back any longer, she wept, and Zahra held her tight and cradled her head.

"So…" Penny held her arm. "What was that, then? What spoke through the board?"

Argent glanced at Felix. Felix wasn't sure what to say, and so, Argent gave a playful smile. "You got me. But you gotta admit, I'm great at the dramatic flair."

"You…" Penny's face turned red. "You terrified us! Terrified Felix!"

"And I'm sorry." Argent held Felix tighter.

"I-It's fine," Felix said. "I overreacted. Guess Rosie's fear is contagious."

Rosie laughed. "Dick."

Felix redirected his focus back to Nasira, who'd started to calm down, though she still aggressively rubbed away the tears from her eyes. "But, Nasira…" Felix kept his voice calm. "Your grandmother probably was a magus. Or your grandfather."

"Y-You… you think so?"

"One of them would have to have been," Felix said. "And for you to be a magus means that… one of your parents…"

Tears rolled down Nasira's face again. "Then why…?"

"That's not the point. I just…" Felix wasn't sure if his wording was right, but Nasira needed to hear it in some form. "Whatever they said, you deserved so much better. Real parents don't just abandon their kids or call them monsters."

Nasira rubbed her eyes. "How would you know?"

"… Because… I went through the same thing."

Everyone went silent. Slowly, Rosie stood. "Felix…?"

"It's okay, Rosie." Felix paused, contemplating what to share. "My dad… my *actual* dad… raised me up on Bible quotes. He controlled every part of my life for as long as I can remember." He closed his eyes, and the images rushed back into his mind's eye with a reckoning. Vagus, shrouded within the darkness, watching. The house going up in flames, and collapsing as Cinder flew off into the storm. His father… holding the handgun to his face.

"And then… he left. I haven't seen him in over six years." Felix fought the urge to cry, leaning into Argent's shoulder. "But Nasira… family is something you build. You're more than whatever your parents called you, or treated you like."

"He's right," Zahra said. She teared up as well. "My father and I may not share you and my mother's faith, but we're all family." She tried to speak in Arabic, but clearly she'd stumbled given Nasira's chuckling.

"Oh, I'm sorry!" Nasira said. "I could try teaching you some Arabic."

"Really?!" Zahra asked. "I'd love that!" They hugged, and everyone grew misty-eyed, even Floria (though she hid her face in her tissues).

Penny looked to Felix. "I'm sorry. I had no idea."

"It's okay," Felix said. "It's… made me who I am. And my family? My mom, stepdad, and sisters? They love me for me." *Well, one sister, but let's not complicate things.* "And I love them." *So much you didn't text them back for Christmas. Good job, Felix.*

Argent kissed Felix on the forehead, further helping to ease his nerves. "If I ever meet the fucker, I promise I'll kick his ass for you."

Felix blushed. "Thanks. Though after getting my ass handed to me several times, I think I'm kind of a pacifist. You know, minus self-defense."

Argent grinned. "Lucky I'm not."

"I know how you feel," Penny said. "I'd like to get something off my chest, too, given this is already one big therapy session. If no one minds?"

Everyone nodded.

"My parents were both magi. We lived in Manchester, but... my mother died when I was little. From mage's blight."

Felix faintly recognized the term. "I think I've heard of that before."

"I've heard it as mageblight," Rosie said.

"No one's sure what causes it," Penny said. "Some say it's the mythril in our wands. Others say it's in all of us, and all it takes is one genetic error. But my parents thought they were in the clear... until one day, my mum woke up in a daze. My dad was rushing cuz they were late for work. They helped to maintain the barrier systems around the U.K. He tried to wake her up, but when he did... she didn't recognize him. She... attacked him." She paused, holding her arms. "Her eyes turned red, and her powers went out of control. She nearly burned down our entire complex. There's no real treatment for it, so when the authorities came..." She dabbed tears from her eyes.

"After that, my dad was... different. Always trapped in his own mind. Distant. And easy to manipulate. He'd tried to move on, but the woman he found... a *human* woman... she was good at fucking with your head. Day in, day out, she asked him why he didn't try to save my mum. Asked if he'd go crazy like that, or if I would. But my dad loved her. Then... one night, they got into a fight. My dad went off the rails... and..." She wept, and everyone fell silent.

Shawn held her shoulder. "I... I'm sorry."

She sniffled, rubbing her nose.

"I, uh... I can kinda relate," Shawn said. "I mean, in being through something tough. Not like that, but..." He paused. "Sorry. I shoulda just kept my mouth shut."

Penny gave a weak smile. "It's okay."

Floria shrugged. "The melodrama's already on a roll, so..."

"Just for that," Felix said, pointing right at her. "You're next."

She scoffed.

"I wasn't born like this," Shawn said. "One cobalt eye, and one amethyst. Originally, I was just a cobalt."

Everyone looked on in confusion, most definitely Felix. He'd wondered in passing why a magus would even have heterochromia, given eye color meant so much more to them than it did to humans. Still, the idea that a magus' eye colors, and presumably their power level, could change—that's what intrigued Felix the most. "H-How?"

"I'm from the Bible Belt," Shawn said. "So magi aren't exactly given the warmest welcome back home. Ironically, my family's Mormon, but you get the gist. In any case, I guess my parents were cobalts and kept it secret. But one day, I was helping out in the church, since my dad was a bishop. He'd help organize community events and was well respected. But no one went into his study."

"But you did?" Floria asked, to which everyone glared.

"I don't remember why," Shawn said. "I think he needed one of his books, and there was one that just sorta... called to me. It had these creepy symbols in it, in a language I didn't understand. I'm still not sure what the hell it was."

"And you read from it," Floria said. "Tonight's full of horror movie tropes."

"Wouldn't you as a kid? But yeah. I read it. And suddenly, my words go from trying to make out this weird language I never saw before... to perfect English."

Floria scoffed. "Now *this* is grade-A horror."

Penny shook her head before nodding to Shawn. "Go on."

"Then it started raining. Inside. It was like all the sprinklers went off at once. I didn't get to finish whatever I was reading since, you know, I was scared shitless. So I ran to my dad in the middle of his sermon, and he looked at me like I'd just set fire to the building. My parents both lost it when I got home and kept me there. It wasn't until I went to the bathroom that I saw I had one dull blue eye, and one bright purple. And the rest..." He hung his head as Rosie sat beside him. "We moved not long after, and they forced me to wear colored contacts."

Shawn's parents had to have been magi. Felix knew that. But they had access to something that could do the impossible. Could it have been similar to what Vagus had promised Felix?

Argent threw a sneer at Floria. "You're up, flower girl."

Floria rolled her eyes. "Not much of a story. Parents left before I could walk. Went from shit foster home to shit foster home. Had both kids and adults treat me like a demon. No idea where I'm even from, or what I am beyond the uncreative Asian slurs tossed my way. Oh, and the random 'l' in my name? The woman who gave me my name thought it'd be a red flag for people that there was something 'off' about me."

"Floria," Penny said. "I—"

"Don't. Last thing I want is pity."

"No pity here," Felix said. All the friends around him had faced some kind of hardship because they were magi, just like him. And in that, he no longer felt alone. "Thanks, you guys. All of you."

Argent yawned. "Anyhow, I'm tired. Everyone get the fuck out."

With that, Penny and Floria bid goodbye and headed out. Zahra gave Felix a quick hug. "I'm sorry," she said. "About…"

"Everyone's got a sob story, I guess," he said.

"Felix?" Nasira held her wrist. "Thanks. For what you said."

Wearing his heart on his sleeve had worked out after all. Zahra and Nasira returned to their dorm. Before Rosie left, she kissed Shawn on the cheek, though when she asked whether he was okay, he simply slurred from exhaustion. "How're you doing, Felix?" Rosie asked. "It's been a long time since I've heard you talk about…"

"It's fine," Felix said. "Honestly, I think it helped."

"Alright. Night all. Terrible dreams."

"Bitch!" Felix yelled as she left. Surprisingly, it had proven to be a decent night, minus the freaky spirit board stuff. But then again, this was Vagus, lord of all that is ominous, cryptic, and melodramatic. Felix tried to laugh it off before breaking into a yawn.

"I feel that," Argent said. "But before we hit the hay…"

Argent, climbing back down from the loft, gave a wide smile as he held out his arms. He'd wrapped a red band around his head, from which hung a mistletoe so obnoxiously green it gave off a plastic sheen. "So what do you think?"

Felix tucked his hands behind his back and stood on his tippy toes. "I think that Christmas is just an excuse for corporations to capitalize on the holiday, so that instead of focusing on the spiritual and familial aspects, everyone instead panics over gifts and money, thus creating an atmosphere of chaos and stress which, ultimately, harms people.

"... I meant about my headba—"

"I know, bitch." Felix cackled. "But good lord, you look ridiculous."

Argent pouted. "I was hoping that, you know..." He took a step forward, pointing to his mistletoe. "We could..."

Felix snickered. "Nope. But nice try."

He removed his headband. "Fine, fine. But seriously, I am drained."

"You two can sleep," Shawn said, lying on the couch. "I'm probably gonna be up all night." He donned some headphones, grabbed the controller, and made himself comfortable. Of course, the generator miraculously started working again once everyone had left. (*Step on broken glass, Vagus.*) Argent changed up in the loft, while Felix insisted he do so in the privacy of the study below. Though as he climbed up and saw Argent resting in bed, he recalled his desire to lie in his arms. Felix joined him. He expected Argent to make a snide comment about Felix taking his time. But he didn't. Argent simply wrapped his arm around Felix, and Felix shut his eyes.

"Hey," Argent whispered. "Was that true? About your...?"

"My dad?" Felix asked. "Yeah."

"I'm—"

"I think we've heard enough of that word tonight. Let's just relax."

"But... I think I get it now," Argent said. "Why you act the way you do." He paused. "Do you... blame yourself?"

Felix searched for the right words. But again, he remembered an old mantra he stole from Alec, who in turn stole it from an old show he got Felix hooked on. One about never fearing the truth. "I'd be lying if I said I don't."

"I'm not the biggest fan of myself, either," Argent said. "Guess we're in the same boat."

Felix recalled everyone's stories from tonight. "I think everyone is, just in different ways. What about you?"

Argent chuckled. "I'd rather keep my demons to myself."

"Alright. I'll admit though, Dragora isn't what I pictured at all."

"How so?"

"It's just… different from how I'd always thought it'd be. I remember as a kid, I thought it'd be something outta those old *Harry Potter* books. I didn't even know about all the stuff about mythril, or the different eye colors." Felix wandered back to Vagus' promise, and his curiosity about what had made Shawn something more than a cobalt. Tying to distract himself, he laughed. "And the inbred kelpies."

"Life ain't no fairytale," Argent said.

"Neither is that world," Felix said before cringing. "Or that author."

"I wouldn't know," Argent said. "I know that Alec friend of yours got you hooked on old games, but damn, that shit's ancient."

Felix gave the brightest smile, imagining what he and Argent could do together once the year was over. "We'll have to change that. But you get my point, right?"

"Kinda. But… once you graduate, what do you think you'll do?"

Felix took a moment to think it over. "I… have no idea. All I've ever wanted was to become a sorcerer. To tame magical creatures, slay dragons, all that stuff. But I guess my eyes won't permit that." He tried his best not to tear up. "Besides, with Schmitt in charge back home… I probably won't be back after this year."

"So then what?" Argent asked.

"I guess… just go day by day. Enjoy the rest of the year while it lasts. But I'll say one thing: meeting you, and Zahra, and Penny, and everyone else. It did kinda make it all worth it."

Argent snickered. "Kinda?"

"Oh, shut up!" Felix laughed. "Thanks, Argent."

"No problem." Argent snuggled in a bit closer.

They drifted to sleep, and for the first time in a long time, Felix woke completely refreshed from a good night's rest. No dreading what the next day would bring as he fell into slumber. Nothing but peace. That was, of course, until he woke up and glanced at his wrist. For a split second, that accused white glyph spun beneath his palm. He sat up, holding his hand, checking it over and over. The mark had disappeared.

"As I said: an oath is an oath. I'll leave you be to think it over for a while. But I expect you to make the right choice."

Felix lay back down. As ready as he was to walk away from Vagus, it was clear Vagus still had business with him. But whatever the masked man had in store, Felix told himself that he could handle it. So long as he had Rosie, Argent, Zahra, and all the others. He reached for his phone and texted his parents and Aeris. "Merry Christmas. Talk soon. Love you," asking Lydia to tell Tracey he said hi. Even sending Aeris a message felt right. He returned to sleep in Argent's arms, ready to quietly rest through the holiday.

After all, peace never lasts as long as you wish.

Chapter Sixteen

A War of Angels

FELIX, excited for Montanari's first class of the new year, leapt into his usual front row seat. His phone was off, and his mind was sharp, the latter in large part thanks to the fact he'd managed to be consistently well rested over the holiday break. Vagus hadn't bothered him since the shit show on Christmas, and in that, Felix rejoiced. He'd even finally gotten himself to proudly wear the necklace his grandfather had given him before he left home. The crack running through the blue crystal, once slightly embarrassing, now caught his eye as it shimmered.

But moreover, today his class would delve back into the story of Elisa and Alonza. They'd summarized the events months before, but Montanari liked to make this particular bit of the curriculum a series of "theatrical events" spread throughout the year, and today they would be covering the beginning of the War of Angels.

"You seem awfully chipper," Nasira said. "It's rare you smile like that."

Felix scoffed. "Look who's talking."

Nasira stuck out her tongue.

"It's a welcome change," Zahra said, chuckling. "For both of you!" She pulled them both into a hug. Instinctively, Nasira protested.

"Morning, everyone." Professor Montanari strode into the room. She dropped her books onto the desk, and after the slam jolted Felix's nerves, her next sentence immediately wrecked his good mood. "Hope you all read the assigned chapters over break. Would anyone like to summarize what they've read and share their thoughts?"

The universe must find me mighty attractive, because it seems to keep fucking me over when I leave my guard down. Sinking in his seat would've made Felix an easy target, but he also refused to raise his hand. He slowed his breath (as though it made him invisible), leaned back against his chair, and fixed his eyes upon the clock.

"Mr. Brasher?"

I give up. "I… uh…"

"You haven't read any of it, have you?" Montanari asked..

"… No."

She laughed. "I admire your honesty. I never understood holiday homework myself. It *is* a break, after all. But seeing how well you've been doing, and the fact most of you probably haven't read anything either…" Most of the students either whistled or snickered. "I'll cut you a break."

Best. Fucking. Professor.

"What about you, Mr. della Luce? I know you've read *A True Reflection* before, and certainly your status has given you a… unique perspective on Veronique's writing."

Lucas, even paler than usual, propped his elbows on the table. His usual friends were gone. Sitting beside him were only two: Ulrich, confused as ever; and a blonde girl with milky-white skin, and an ugly, unrelenting sneer. She nudged Lucas when he wouldn't respond.

"Mr. della Luce?" Montanari asked. "Are you feeling well?"

"Reading this woman's work?" Lucas scowled. "No. Not in the slightest. She was born into nobility, raised in the same 'privileged lifestyle' she criticizes. Yet she acts like it's a curse. Her entitlement stains her prose, and is grossly misused to accuse my family and others like us of crimes we're not guilty of."

Felix tried to follow along. He'd only read summaries of Veronique's memoir, but he'd never sat down to bother reading it. He mentally kicked himself for not touching it during his injury, as then he would've been both killing time and getting ahead on assignments—especially for his favorite class.

From what he recalled, Veronique was a magus born into nobility, but had left in secret and masked her identity when publishing her work. And as far as Felix knew, she wasn't too fond of the royal family for their inaction during the Revelation, nor the Della Luces spearheading the Dragon Party, buying off members of parliament to expand their business and privatize public services.

Though the book also had… stranger accusations. Veronique never said it outright, but she made constant referrals to some dark cabal running the empire since its founding. She'd never been clear as to exactly who they were supposed to be, nor their actual goal, but her claims were hyperbolic enough to sound like they'd come right out of Ivanov's mouth. But then again, the way Lucas has spoken about Vagus, and mentioned "you people," Felix definitely felt it unwise to rule out that possibility.

"Interesting." Montanari held her chin. "What do you think of her claims of abuse and neglect?"

Lucas crossed his arms. "Overblown."

"Her claim of conspiracy?"

"Ridiculous."

Montanari bobbed her head. "What about you, Mr. Deniaud?"

Ulrich's head, which had previously been resting on the desk, shot up. He wiped the drool from his lip, stuttering. "Y-Yeah. Way oversensitive."

Montanari snickered, and she turned to the sneering blonde girl. "Ms. de Palmi?"

She sat upright, her hand over her chest as her nasally voice rang. "Being the niece of Queen Andrea herself, I have to say that the De Palmi family has enough problems beyond the slander of this 'author.' We struggle just like anyone else. As a member of the poorest of the Medeian houses, I can say my life was no different than that of a middle-class cobalt or amethyst. We aren't at all the rich elites she says we are."

"And what about you, Ms. Hakim?" Montanari asked.

Zahra straightened her back, trying not to give attention to the glares Lucas and especially Bianca sent her way. "I think she was very brave for talking about what she went through. A lot of powerful people might prefer bad press not getting out about them."

"Very true," Montanari said. "But there are many other important questions to ask. Who is she, and why did she never disclose her identity? Why say such brazen and charged words only to evade the public eye?"

Lucas and Bianca sneered.

"Then again, Ms. Hakim's point is valid. Many pearl-eyed aristocrats have funded scholars to support their claims on how magic has been slowly slipping from their hands, and that partnering with sorcerers of a lower-level eye color, or even humans, will one day lead to magic totally vanishing." Montanari smirked. "At least, that's a popular 'theory,'" she said with air quotes.

Felix relished in Lucas and Bianca's frustration.

And with that, they began the usual routine of starting up the firsthand history lesson. Light engulfed the room. As it faded, a set of great black doors with golden trims manifested from the void. With a thundering echo, they opened, revealing the throne room still in tatters from the massive battle. Most of the ceiling had been destroyed. The new moon hung high above, thin rays of moonlight shining down through the dark clouds upon Ettore's rotting corpse.

His body had been left here to fill the hall with the foul stench of decay. His mouth—peeled lips, blackened teeth, and shriveled tongue—hung open. The cursed flame-bladed sword remained wedged within his chest. Its red mythril shimmered crimson, just as it had the day he was slew. Concobhar's skeletal body was much the same, remaining pinned onto the great throne.

Alonza stood there before her fallen father, unable to process what lay before her. So many contradictory emotions battled within her. Grief for his death. Relief that he could no longer harm. Anger at herself for her uncertainty. And most of all, a cold, ever-encroaching dread of what could've possessed her mother to become what she was now.

"Horrible. Absolutely atrocious."

The high-pitched, raspy voice belonged to Epaphras, the uncle of her best friend Drakon, and the brother of the now late Acacius Zephyr. His black hair, beginning to gray, had thinned substantially to reveal his glinting scalp. Spindly fingers folded overtop one another, so ghostly white they more resembled bones than flesh. And his eyes. An apathetic white that could pierce through one's soul. He sauntered over, making Alonza take a couple steps back.

"I am so, so sorry, dear." Epaphras appeared sullen, holding his fist. "Losing your father could not have been easy. I still mourn for my poor brother."

"… Y-Yes." Alonza collapsed her hands, looking up at the sky.

"But I suppose this is what revolution is. Power is a sword which requires the strength to wield, and the will to swing. And…" He gave a hoarse laugh. "Well, blades aren't forged for those who flinch at the first drop of blood."

Those words gave Alonza pause. However eloquent, they rung of her father's harsh view of the world. Of his belief that the strong should lead the weak, and a leader's ability to remain decisive and detached ought to have made them judge, jury, and executioner. She looked back down at the mangled body, unable to recognize it as her father.

"It shouldn't have to be that way," Alonza said.

Epaphras snickered. "Young lady, you'll come to accept the way things are one—"

"Where are the others?" Alonza raised both her head and voice, trying to sound stern. "All members of the Royal Court are to be present to hear my mo… Her Majesty's words."

He frowned, though masked his discontent as the doors opened once again. Alonza's sister Gianna led the other three major houses—Zephyr, Sican, and Ley—inside. All were quiet, their faces grim. Though they flinched at the sight of the cadaver, not one dared to even slightly raise their voices or share their disgust. Each family spoke amongst themselves. No sign of Drakon. His younger brother Hilarion whispered with their mother Ligeia, trying to comfort her as she held her mouth and teared up. Alonza wanted to speak with her. But as Gianna approached, Alonza couldn't contain herself, hugging her elder sister tight.

Gianna's auburn hair curled down to her shoulders. She tried to force a smile, though the reddish pink of her freckled dimples contrasting against her pale white skin betrayed her facade. "How are you doing?"

"I've… been better." Alonza pulled herself back. "Though I'd imagine Antonio is even worse, having to serve as Mother's advisor."

"He's…" Gianna sighed. "Not happy." She held her wrist tightly as her eyes fell upon Ettore. Suddenly, her head jerked up, fear in her pearly eyes. "Have you seen Drakon? This assembly is mandatory, and—"

"No." Alonza snickered. "But you know Drakon. He could always make a dramatic late entrance."

"At that point," Gianna muttered. "He'd be better off not showing his face…"

"Gianna?" Alonza didn't want to ask directly about their mother. She hadn't seen her since she witnessed the firestorm atop Tintagel Castle just a week before. Even all the way from Pyre Isle, she knew what this was. What her mother had done. And though Elisa had gone into that fight with noble intentions… she wasn't the same gentle mother who'd raised Alonza anymore. Alas, her concern got the better of her. "How is Mother?"

Before Gianna could respond (not that Alonza expected her to be able to), the doors flung open, far more violently than before. A swift hush fell over the room. Antonio, his skin drained of its naturally olive color, marched inside. He'd long boasted about the day he'd don his father's uniform, complete with the flashy obsidian cape. Instead, he wore a morose uniform of heavy blacks, accented by a deathly purple. His black cap obscured his pearl eyes and buzzed brown hair. On his chest, where once was the Ó Riagáins' crest, now shone a golden insignia of an eleven-headed dragon.

"Members of the Royal Court!" Antonio's cadence was brittle. His face grew redder as he projected himself, his voice hoarse. "Presenting Her Majesty, Empress Elisa Pyre!"

He scurried over to the side of the doors. From the dark corridor emerged a pair of blood-red eyes. An obsidian circlet with bright red mythril jewels hung around Elisa's golden hair, while a golden necklace in the shape of a serpent coiled around her neck. The pure black of her dress was broken up by bits of red and gold, primarily its scarlet hems. From the torso extended bell sleeves, golden cords twirling over her upper arms, while beneath her golden belt jutted a red panel breaking the black of her dress, reaching down to the floor.

"Good evening, all."

Elisa's voice echoed across the throne room, ringing throughout Alonza's entire body. Enough so to make her tremble and kneel. To make them all kneel. Elisa carried herself down the hall, her hands held together, though one was covered with a black glove. She didn't even glance at her daughters. She strutted past them, stepping over Ettore's body without so much as looking down, instead gazing upon Concobhar's body. She turned, not a single emotion in her expression.

"A horrible sight, isn't it?"

Alonza wasn't entirely sure what her mother... no, the empress, was referring to. Certainly not her father's ugly fate, nor that of Concobhar. Slowly, Alonza, along with the rest of the court, gave a hesitant nod. Her blood ran cold as Elisa laughed. Laughed like she hadn't in years. Carefree, jovial and mocking that which Alonza would've been happy to join once, long ago. But now, she didn't dare make a sound.

"Well come now! We've won the day!" Elisa simpered, though quickly returned to her solemn expression. "The tyrants are dead, and now a new era of prosperity will begin. And to commemorate that..." She held out her ungloved hand. From the snap of her fingers, a violet spark grew into a purple fireball cradled in her palm. "We will burn the remnants of the past to nothing more than ash."

The fire twisted upwards into two serpentine tails. One raced over Elisa, engulfing Concobhar's body along with the throne, while the other shot straight down and consumed Ettore. The flames grew brighter and brighter, blinding all the scions as they rushed backwards. Sweat beaded along Alonza's skin. The heat was so intense, tears evaporated as they welled in her eyes. The blaze cleared, leaving nothing behind of either corpse, nor the throne, nor the blade. Nothing but heaps of black ash and sludge.

This is what her mother had become.

She tuned out the rest of the empress' words. Once the assembly had ended, Antonio was quick to push everyone outside. Elisa remained in the throne room, staring up at the nearly invisible moon. As much as Alonza wanted to speak with her, she'd already seen Elisa had become someone else entirely. And so, while the other members of the Royal Court returned to their isles, Alonza rushed to her new bedroom to process what had happened in solitude.

Since Elisa had seized the throne, the Pyres had relocated to Tintagel Castle. Most of Alonza's belongings remained in her childhood bedroom back in the Pyre Estate. This new room, previously unused for dragons knew how long, was cold and dusty. Cobwebs were strewn beside the dresser. The old queen-sized bed rendered the air stale from its musty sheets, and its lack of blankets and pillows provided no comfort for Alonza's tears. She sat on the side of the bed, the mattress creaking beneath her.

Not long ago, she'd spoken with her mother about what a wonderful leader she would've been. That her courage would bring peace to the land. But now? Now she was at a loss for words. What had seemed to be a dream come true had been corrupted into a living nightmare.

A tapping at her window jolted her from the ordeal. Throwing open the tattered curtains, after coughing through the cloud of dust she'd sent flying, she caught a glimpse of a small winged humanoid figure, about the size of her hand, glowing emerald green. She opened the window, and Alonza listened closely to the entity's fast, silvery voice as it repeated its message before fading away into thin air.

"The forest. Drakon and Hilarion. Come soon."

Alonza sighed. "They can never get it clear enough in one sentence." Throwing on her black cloak and grabbing her wand, she snuck out of the castle. There were hardly any guards on patrol, though once she got outside, she did have to hide behind a tree as Antonio led his squadron past. By his side was a tall, slender man wrapped in a dark-green shroud.

She'd no time to humor her curiosity. Her trek led her down the hill towards her friends' usual spot: a small clearing off the beaten path. Here grew a grove of white seven-petal flowers. Alonza plucked one and, leaning against a tree, allowed her nerves to be soothed by its sweet scent of late summer.

"You could really use some beauty sleep."

Drakon entered the grove. His jade-colored cotton shirt appeared first, its baggy sleeves reaching down to his pale hands. A silver belt with ornate wind designs held up black pants and silver boots. His raven-black hair, like his father's, was slicked back into a short ponytail, though he only had a bit of stubble compared to Acacius' goatee.

Alonza snickered. "You're one to talk." Seeing no one was up for Alonza's usual banter thus far tonight, she opted for sincerity. "How're you holding up?"

"Better than Mother, or Hilarion." Drakon held his shoulder, looking up at the rolling dark clouds overhead. "You know me. It hurts, but Father would want me to use my grief to do what's right." He took a heavy sigh. "What about you?"

"Tending to the garden helps." Alonza gazed again upon the grove. "In a way, I'm glad I couldn't have this back at the manor. These firebird's wings would kill all of Gianna's firebird's kisses." She lowered the flower from her nose. "This wasn't how things were supposed to be."

"We can fix this. We can talk to your mother, reason with—"

"There's no reasoning with her." Alonza frowned, cursing whatever could've possessed her mother—whatever took her away. "Perhaps that's just the curse of the throne. Whoever sits upon it becomes a tyrant, no matter who they are."

"You know that's not true," Drakon said.

"Isn't it?" Alonza's voice cracked. "You've seen what she's done. The rationing continues, and now, people are being taken from their homes for petty crimes and offenses, and no one knows what happens to them." She'd heard whispers from the townspeople when she'd snuck out of the palace the night before. The hatred in their words, the conflict in their voices, and the fear in their eyes. Those would never leave her.

Drakon held her shoulder. "Whatever you decide, I'll back you up. That's what friends are for." Since their youth, Alonza, Drakon, and Hilarion had been an inseparable trio, and she'd considered them brothers. Far more than Antonio. Drakon most definitely served as a far more trustworthy confidant than Gianna. Alonza learned very quickly that their father, and now their mother, could easily pry the truth from Gianna with the slightest amount of pressure.

"As will I!"

Ready for an ambush, Alonza gripped her wand. "Hold on!" Drakon said, and right away, Alonza complied. Slowly, Drakon's grimace melted he kept himself from laughing. "Come on out, Hilarion."

"Okay, okay, I'm sorry!" A younger boy, stockier and shorter than his brother, and with no facial hair whatsoever, leapt from the bushes. A squirrel comfortably perched itself atop his head.

Drakon raised an eyebrow. "I see you've made a new friend."

The squirrel jumped onto Hilarion's shoulder, and their eyes met. "Oh, yes! This *is* my new friend. I call him… Nutmeg!"

"Wouldn't that be a woman's name?"

"Let Nutmeg have his—no, *their* moment in the sun before you ruin it. We don't know Nutmeg's story." Alonza giggled, then burst into an uncontrollable laughter. Hilarion squinted. "And what exactly is so hilarious?"

"Nothing!" Alonza tried to stop laughing. "Thank you. You both always manage to cheer me up. Even if you don't mean to."

"In any case," Hilarion said. "Couldn't we ask your sister to help—"

"You know Gianna. Ever the appeaser."

"There's House Sican," Drakon said. "Santiago is a coward, but perhaps Mateo and Matías will be willing to help."

"Or… Calista?" Hilarion swooned as his eyes sparkled.

Drakon rolled his eyes. "Calista the Cynical? I'd rather not resort to that. Now can you take this seriously, please?"

"What?" Hilarion asked. "She's a saint!" As his voice raised in pitch, the squirrel clicked and twitched. "See? Nutmeg agrees!" Without warning, the squirrel dove into the bushes and scurried away. "Nutmeg, wait!" He pouted, only for his eyes to widen with terror as he looked past Alonza and Drakon.

"What?" Drakon asked. "Did Nutmeg's betrayal leave you—"

"Look!"

Hilarion pointed, and Alonza and Drakon's eyes fell on a plume of black smoke in the distance, in the direction of the castle. Fear gripped Alonza. This was more than a simple revolt or attack on the new empress. She raced up the hill, and Drakon and Hilarion struggled to keep up. The smoke animated from the castle's towers, and without a moment's hesitation, Alonza rushed inside and ran for the throne room, her wand at the ready.

And as she feared, what she found were the dying remains of an attempted coup d'état.

Soldiers lay across the floor, their charred bodies letting off choking flames and smoke. Epaphras, bleeding from a gash on his forehead with soot coating his face, was still alive, albeit trapped in a slab of obsidian rock. Antonio brandished a flame-bladed sword, much like his father's, though far cruder in its design. The blade itself had been damaged. Chunks of mythril had fallen, leaving the sword flameless.

"Why? Why would you do this to your own mother?"

Elisa looked down upon Antonio, not with any pain in her expression, nor sorrow, nor anger. Nothing but a look of cold, distant pity. Unattached from any kind of love she once held for her son, waddling in his father's bloodstained footsteps.

"You… you were never my mother!" Antonio's voice squelched as he shouted, his hands trembling as he clutched his sword. "Before you were simply a fool in the way of Father's ambitions! Now… you're a monster!" He charged, ready to swing down his sword, but was sent flying back into the far wall with a burst of purple flames. He fell unconscious. His sword fractured against the floor, its scattered pieces clattering.

"Mother! That's enough!"

Alonza's yell carried across the hall, gaining her mother's attention as she drew her wand. Drakon and Hilarion stood behind her. They hadn't drawn their wands, but rather kept them within reach, just out of sight.

"You as well, Alonza?"

She trembled at her mother's cold voice. Still, Alonza held her wand tightly, ready to raise a shield or launch an attack at a moment's notice. The fear morphed into a deep anger, not at her mother, but at the advent of this tragedy. "My mother was a courageous woman." Alonza projected her voice and straightened her back. "She taught me to fight for what I believed in. A kind, compassionate woman who believed in only necessary violence for the greater good, rather than needless, wanton bloodshed. That's not the woman I see before me now."

Her laughter. That was by far the most unsettling thing about Empress Elisa. Hearing her ordinarily so emotionless and soulless, only for her to laugh so heartily. It was unnatural. "These people," Elisa said, gesturing to the fallen soldiers, her echoing voice booming. "They *make* this necessary."

"No!" Alonza forced herself to speak over Elisa. "My mother would never do this to anyone, even her enemies!" She glanced at her unconscious, injured brother. She'd normally held disdain for him, but now, she could only pity how lost he felt after their father's gruesome death. "She wouldn't enforce the excessively inhumane punishments of Concobhar! What have you even done with all the people you've stolen from their families? Executed them in silence? Forced them into labor camps?"

"They have been called to a higher purpose," Elisa said. "To help build a better world."

Alonza had no idea as to what Elisa meant. But honestly, she would come to wish she never did. "It doesn't have to be like this," Alonza said.

"Yes. I'm afraid it does."

Elisa waved her gloved hand. Alonza braced for an attack, but one didn't come. Instead, Drakon and Hilarion choked out for help. Purple flames surrounded their heads, and they held their throats and coughed violently. The flames dissipated. They collapsed, unconscious, faces slightly burned, hair searing.

"No!" Alonza turned back to her mother. "What did you do?!"

"House Zephyr shall answer for its crimes," Elisa said. "All of the snakes in the Royal Court shall. But you…" She raised her hands. "You may have a second chance. You must see the great work I have planned."

Before Alonza could respond, the same purple flames engulfed her sight. The heat blinded all of her senses. She fell, knees buckling and lungs writhing, desperately fighting for air. Slowly, the purple faded to black, and it all went silent.

"I am sorry, Alonza."

As she awakened, Alonza tried to rub her eyes, only to find she couldn't raise her hands. She couldn't move at all. Obsidian rock had seemingly grown all around her, a slab holding her in place in what appeared to be a shadowy catacomb. A dark chamber that went unlit, save for the flickers of dying mythril torches hanging along the walls, giving off an unnatural indigo firelight. There was no sign of Elisa. No sign of her friends. Nothing but an eerie, resounding silence.

And then the breathing started.

It was faint. Barely audible. But out there, somewhere in the darkness, was what sounded to be a man. Like that of a dog, whimpering in pain and asking to be put out of its misery. It didn't take much for Alonza to realize what this place was. She found herself further paralyzed in her makeshift prison, but she knew her friends needed her.

Alonza concentrated all her power into her palms, imagining her azure flames coursing through her. A sharp whistle ensued, followed by the cracking of stone. The fire split the obsidian cage apart. Now freed, Alonza took a moment to orient herself, unsure of where to go to find the exit before it was too late.

She ran down the narrow, winding passages, the torches lighting her way. The outlines of prison cells briefly flashed just outside her line of sight, along with what looked to be humanoid silhouettes sealed within. But she kept her focus on her escape. Each footfall echoing through the passage was another step closer to finding her friends, and finding her way back into the moonlight.

"P-Please... help..."

The voice was hoarse. It croaked, seeming to gargle between syllables. There was a twinge of sadness in its words, calling back to that painful breathing. For a moment, Alonza debated going back to investigate, and even freeing this person if she could manage. It would cost her precious time, but she also couldn't bring herself to leave an innocent, and perhaps many more innocents, being kept as Elisa's prisoners in this forgotten place.

A bloodcurdling scream, and the gnashing of flesh and bone, cut that desire down, capped off by a deep, bellowing growl.

Abandoning all caution, Alonza sprinted forward. A few sharp turns brought her to a spiral staircase, just in time for the growling to grow louder, followed by heavy footsteps. She flew up the steps, heaving as she desperately raced towards what she prayed was her way out. A thunderous crash from below shook the entire chamber, making Alonza nearly trip, throwing out her hands before she was sent face-first into the stone. Cracks formed in the central pillar. The horrid thing was gaining.

She ducked into another room off to the side, this one with vaulted ceilings so tall, they were covered in shadow. A black tiled floor, so polished it reflected everything perfectly, stretched out into the distance. No light save for those accursed violet torches.

A crash sent her flying forward. Dust from the crumbling walls and stairs plunged the room into even further darkness, and a golem stumbled out from the entrance. Or rather, what appeared at first to be a golem. Human-shaped, hunched, and easily twice the height of an ordinary man. Armor covered its skin, crafted from red mythril. Massive crystals jutted out from its back, as though they'd be callously pierced into its spine. The only exposed skin was a pinkish purple, warped in malice, with a foul, animalistic grin spread across its face, exposing mangled, bloodied teeth. Most arresting were its eyes. Bloodshot, with deep-red irises. Just like Elisa's.

It roared, bursting Alonza's eardrums. A plume of flames flew from its tongue. She dodged, barely given any time to think before she evaded its fist slamming into the ground. For a hulking abomination, this thing was too fast to run from, and without a wand or weapon, she wouldn't be able to fully put up a fight. But wherever in the castle they were, there ought to have been some way out—even if she had to make one herself.

Dodging each attack, Alonza raced deeper into the darkness, hoping to reach the opposite side of this room. At last, she'd touched a stone wall. Right on cue, the room shook with the beast's footsteps as it charged. At the last moment, she jumped, and was immediately blinded. Light poured in and completely engulfed the chamber. The monster had easily blown right through the wall, revealing the night sky just outside.

These passages had apparently been far deeper within the castle, dug within the cliffs it rested upon. The imperial hunting grounds stretched into the distance, and Alonza was greeted by a piercing wind, and a massive drop to where the monster had fallen to its apparent death. There was no telling how long it would take to make her way back up to the castle from here, especially with the staircase out of commission. But if she could somehow break her fall and run around the cliffside, then perhaps she could find a way into a town and go from there?

Alonza had never been able to mimic her mother's fiery wings to take flight for short periods of time. Yet even so, there was no telling how much time had already passed, and if she'd waited any longer, there might not've been an empire to save anymore. If there was ever a time she'd needed to believe in herself without question, this was it.

Closing her eyes, she recalled how her mother described the spell. Elisa would think of the people she loved. Focus on the drive to keep them safe at all costs, and from that ember, there sparked a bright and powerful flame. A flame that could carry her off the ground and take to the skies, if only briefly.

I can do this.

Alonza held he fist, repeating the mantra. *I can do this.* Her hand shook as she envisioned Drakon and Hilarion, fighting alongside her, though her morale sank at the prospect of having to battle her mother. *Come on, come on!*

A scream jolted her eyes open. It was quiet, incredibly far away, likely from town. She didn't recognize the cry. But for a moment, she feared it was someone she held dear, and knew she had to act. Without a moment's hesitation, she jumped.

The wind rushed past her as she fell from the great height. In moments, the ground grew within reach, and her heart nearly burst. She closed her eyes and emptied her mind. Her fear abated as she shouted:

"Angel of Flames!"

Two waves of fire, roughly in the shape of angel wings, sprouted from her back. Her fall slowed, though she could hardly control her direction. She imagined as if the wings were physically connected to her body through muscles. They beat once, twice, again and again, slightly pushing her up as she descended. She crashed into a small grove, this one filled with firebird's wings as well. Her scraped knees dug into the soil, crushing the flowers beneath them. Pain panged through her hands as she pushed herself up. The wings fell around her, scorching the ground, then dissipated, leaving her sweating and coughing in a black-burned grove. It was as though she'd just ran around the entire island without rest.

But rest wasn't an option now.

Alonza's body ached, but she forced herself to her feet and raced towards town. Branches scraped her arms and legs while she trampled over bushes. At long last, the town came into view, and she nestled herself behind one of the trees. A crowd had gathered, all silent, all casting their eyes upon the black crosses erected before them. Each cross gleamed beneath the faint moonlight. Four arms reached out from each cross on either side, with three arms reaching out from the top. Upon each had been strung Epaphras, Antonio, Hilarion, and Drakon.

And there, high above the ground, hovered Elisa herself. Dark-violet wings of fire, letting off immense amounts of black smoke, jutted out from her back. Before her knelt Lady Ligeia, hands clasped and eyes welling with tears.

"Elisa, please!" Ligeia's brittle voice cracked. "This isn't you! This isn't who Acacius and I loved so dearly!"

"You're right."

Elisa's voice struck a terrifying chord with Alonza. The empress outstretched her gloved hand, and in her palm gathered purple flames. The flames shot all around Ligeia, and as Elisa raised her hand, from the fire grew black crystals wrapping themselves around Ligeia's arms and hands. The rocks rose, carrying her high up into the air. Another obsidian cross displayed her alongside her sons. Without a hint of regret in her eyes, Elisa turned to the townspeople, who backed away and murmured in fear.

"There is no place for those who would hold back the realm of magic." Elisa's voice carried all around. "Very soon, my siblings, we will change this world. We will march into the ruins of the human lands, and we sorcerers will lead them into an era of prosperity—as our underlings."

Once she'd finished speaking, Elisa's soldiers, armed with black armor, bayonet-style wands, and mythril crystals plunged into their backs, circled the crowd. A few people tried to run, only to be either impaled by the soldiers' weapons or killed by their spells. Elisa trapped them in a wall of purple flames.

In an effort to keep herself hidden, Alonza made her way around the town through the forest towards Ligeia's cross. She applied a small fire spell hoping it would be enough to slowly erode the cross' base.

"Who said you could leave the castle, Alonza?"

Elisa set her sights on Alonza. Channeling her fury, Alonza strengthened her spell, snapping the base in two. Elisa dodged as the cross toppled over. It crashed into the ground, shattering, sending chunks of glass flying, while Alonza caught Ligeia as she fell. It bought her enough time to throw up a barrier before Elisa rained down a barrage of purple fire.

Alonza's muscles were racked with pain as she held up her defenses. This shield wouldn't hold for much longer, and with how far the blaze had spread in such a short amount of time, there was nowhere to run. If she didn't act now, they'd all be dead. Then, the dark presence impersonating her mother would've been left free to wreak all the havoc it wished upon the world.

There was only one choice.

Alonza focused on the image of herself, Drakon, and Hilarion all together. She didn't know what awaited them after their escape. What would happen if they were able to defeat Elisa, if they even could. But Alonza knew that whatever her life looked like, however disarrayed and chaotic, she wanted them to be part of it.

"Angel of Flames!"

The shield dropped, and white flames reached out from Alonza's back and blocked Elisa's attack. The purple blaze had ceased. The white fire knocked Elisa out of the air, rushed to break each cross, and smothered the flames entrapping the townspeople. Alonza nearly fell over as her vision blurred. Ligeia caught her just in time, and though Alonza's hearing dulled, she could hear the painful cries of an older man.

And so, as she raised her head, Alonza was met with the sight of Epaphras, holding one of the fallen soldiers' bayonet-styled wands, being engulfed in Elisa's flames. He collapsed, nothing more than another would-be tyrant whose obsession led him to his own demise.

Antonio trembled, holding another of the soldiers' weapons close to his chest. He rushed her, only for Elisa to knock him back with a burst of fire. The weapon clattered to the ground. Without hesitation, Elisa grabbed the blade and swung. Alonza's vision had fully cleared as her younger brother's severed head, glassy eyes wide open and unmoving, rolled towards her.

"This ends."

As Elisa's sights fell on Alonza, Ligeia was quick to carry her out of town, along with the crowd rushing with them. But Drakon remained. Alonza cried out for him to run, but Drakon stood there, shielding them as Elisa let out her devastating attacks. Just as the town had fallen out of sight, so too had Drakon's barrier fallen, and him with it. Thunder rumbled as the downpour began.

In a flash of lightning, the forest returned to the classroom. Zahra sobbed, dabbing away her tears, while Felix was taken aback altogether by what he'd just witnessed.

Montanari rubbed her eyes, checking her phone as it buzzed incessantly. "It seems we've gone over our allotted time. But we technically started the war, so…" She shrugged. "You can all go, I suppose." She gathered her belongings and, without a word, left, a look of terror on her face. Felix was concerned, though this wasn't his business. Besides, after that vision, he could understand even Zahra's usual waterworks.

"You know," Felix said. "You really should start bringing—"

Zahra blew her nose into a tissue.

"Ahead of the game," he said. Zahra blew her nose again.

Nasira held Zahra's shoulder. "You okay?"

"Y-Yes. Bit of a cold, I think."

This was undeniably difficult to witness, but perhaps it had reminded Nasira of what truly mattered. That's certainly what it reinforced for Felix. Still, to see someone like Elisa, once so passionate about justice, become such a cold, inhuman creature, more than willing to kill her own children without remorse. It was enough to unsettle him.

Lucas had slipped away immediately after Professor Montanari. As exhausted as he was from helping create the illusions, especially experiencing Alonza's grief and trauma (and even projecting a bit of his own feelings onto her), he needed to clear as much distance between himself and... her, as possible. Holding tightly onto his belongings, his wand at the ready, Lucas rushed down to the main floor, out the entrance, and into one of the carriages. Surely he'd be safe one he reached the estate.

Once the coach reached Cendrillion, Lucas tripped as he rushed out. Others offered to help him gather his things, but he hissed and insulted them until they left him alone. The less eyes on him, the better. After what felt like an eternity, he'd finally made it to the port, boarding a ferry bound for Pyre. Thankfully it wasn't too busy. He found himself a small nook overlooking the water, taking in the scent of sea-salt air.

"You sure seem to be in a hurry!"

The mere sound of her nasally voice was enough to stop Lucas dead in his tracks. Bianca, wearing her signature sneer with pride, hands tucked behind her back, had him cornered. Lucas' blood ran cold. If she'd managed to keep up with him this far, there was no shaking her now. He gulped. "I-I haven't done anything! I—"

"You know how we feel about liars, Lucas. You told them about Vagus." Bianca snickered as Vivien revealed herself. "You know," Bianca continued. "Della Luces have always been so easy to read. You show all your cards right away, and your egos burn so bright, we can see your insecurities from a mile away."

Slowly, Lucas backed away, only to drop his belongings as he hit the railing. He reached for his wand, but it was gone.

"Looking for this?" Vivien revealed the wand. "Impressive." She flicked her wrist, tossing it into the water. "Impressively predictable."

Nowhere to go. Bianca and Vivien surrounded him on both sides. "You look paler than usual, Lucas," Bianca said. "Maybe you need something to help you relax. A refreshing swim, perhaps?"

Lucas' mind flashed back to Vivien nearly drowning him. "I-I... I don't—"

"Don't worry," Vivien said, drawing ever closer. "I'll teach you."

Chapter Seventeen

When Tomorrow Comes

LUCAS had been here, tied down to his bed at Lighthaven Hospital, for nearly a week. Somehow after Montanari's last class, Lucas had arrived at the Della Luce estate drenched and freezing half to death. He'd been spouting about having been attacked. But his parents, if you believed the rumors, were fed up with his behavior in recent months. And so here he was, locked away in a hospital his family owned and funded, kept out of the public eye. Anything to ensure he wouldn't smear the good family name any further.

But Felix knew this was Vagus' doing.

There he sat, gripping the sides of the metal chair just outside Lucas' room, steeling himself as doctors and nurses rushed past, tending to different patients. Noise filled the hall, but Lucas' cries were the only sound ringing in Felix's ears. The doctor said Felix could come in once they'd managed to calm Lucas down. That was nearly a half-hour ago, and at some point, Felix had to check back in with Ornella for his next duty.

All Dragora students were required to do some kind of community service work once a year. And the fact Lucas was here? That sealed the deal. Rosie, Zahra, Penny, and Shawn were more than happy to lend a hand, though it took some puppy dog eyes to drag Argent along, while Nasira was encouraged solely through Zahra's pestering. And Floria? Well, it was Floria. Whatever she was up to today, Felix assumed she was doing with as wide a frown as possible.

Argent, leaning against the wall, tapped his foot. "How much longer do you plan on waiting, exactly?"

"As long as it takes." Felix said. "I wanna make sure he's okay."

"What is it with you and this fixation on being nice to assholes?"

Felix smirked. "I forgave *you*, didn't I?"

Argent was about to snap back, but stopped himself. "Fair." He groaned. "I'm just saying, you dragged me here to do more than keep an eye on Lighthead Junior, right?" Before Felix could respond, another voice froze him in place.

"As strange as it might sound, I concur with Mr. de la Mort."

Gottschalk, holding a bouquet of white flowers, approached. Bags rested beneath her eyes, though she gave a tired smile. "But I do appreciate the concern for Lucas."

Argent sighed. "On that note, I should go see if Theresa needs me to do anything." After giving Felix a quick kiss on the cheek, Argent headed off, averting Gottschalk's gaze.

"Have you heard anything about him?" Gottschalk asked. "Has anything changed?"

"… No," Felix forced himself to say. "From everything the doctors told me, he's exactly the same as when they brought him in."

She sulked. "I see." She clutched the bouquet against her chest. Seeing this side of his worst professor was… not unnerving, not at all. If anything, seeing a more human side of the ice queen felt reassuring. Felix had seen it that day in the reserve, after all, when she held the distraught Lucas tight, as if he were her own child rather than just a nephew.

"Are you okay?" he asked.

Gottschalk looked surprised. "If I'm being honest, not quite. Lucas hasn't been feeling well for a while now. He's always so… distant." She gave a smile again. "But thank you, Mr. Brasher. Lucinda told me you've tried to help him from time to time. I know you might not be the biggest fan of either of us, but I appreciate your kindness."

"No problem," Felix said. "But uh… on that note, sorry I can be such a pain in class."

"Trust me, you're nowhere near as bad as Mr. de la Mort. And I do admire your willingness to stand your ground. Even if I perhaps wish you went about it in a less crass manner."

Unsure of how to respond, and most assuredly lamenting his outburst from back when he was stuck in the wheelchair, Felix nervously laughed while scratching his head.

The mood was darkened when the doctor allowed them inside. Lucas had been given a room all to himself. Though while it might've appeared to be from him being spoiled to someone like Argent, Felix knew the likely truth. Lucas' family couldn't tolerate him embarrassing them to any wandering eyes. There he lay, in the corner bed beside the window, with curtains drawn all around. Straps around his wrists, arms, chest, and legs kept him in place as he flailed in vain attempts at breaking free. The red veins of his eyes, overtaking the pearl color of his irises, bulged as his pupils dilated and darted wildly. The ghostly white of his hair glinted with sweat.

Lucas had been locked away here by his own family, with no sign as to when he'd be set free. Gottschalk spoke with the doctor, but all the while, Felix didn't register a word they said. He tried so hard to listen to Lucas. To parse any kind of clue or message from the shouts. But as Lucas alternated between shouts and mumblings, his words slurred together into gibberish.

"Who attacked you in the reserve?"

The question ignited a spark of dread in Felix. He hadn't noticed that the doctor had slipped out, leaving him alone with an unstable Lucas, and Professor Gottschalk, looking dead at him with a grimace most severe. He wanted to tell her the truth. She deserved that much. But the last time he'd attempted doing that, Vagus had interfered with the sharp pain of the glyph he'd inscribed upon Felix's hand.

"I-I... don't know." Felix nearly choked on the words, afraid even the vaguest description might anger him and Lucas' tormentor. Vagus might very well have been watching now. "He... wore a mask and a cloak, but he never said his name. And he didn't say his phoenix's name either. I just know after she carried us off to the mountains—"

"You called his familiar 'she.'"

Felix paused.

She held his shoulder. "Mr. Brasher, I am not upset." The shakiness of her cadence suggested otherwise. "But you need to tell me the truth. Who attacked you that day in the reserve?" Her grip tightened. "Who did this to my nephew?"

He gulped.

"Is everything alright?"

Immediately, Gottschalk released her grip. Felix took a couple steps to the side as Calvin, his red-and-black laptop tucked beneath his arm, rushed inside. "Calvin?" Felix asked. "What're you doing here?"

"When I heard about Lucas," Calvin said. "I knew I had to help in any way I could. So I spoke with his parents and told them of my qualifications in the psychiatric field, and... they granted me permission to come in." Calvin turned to Gottschalk, extending his hand. "And you must be Isolda, correct? Mrs. della Luce's sister? I'm Dr. Bloxham from the U.K. A pleasure to finally meet you!"

Gottschalk didn't take his hand. Rather, she simply scowled at his mint-green eyes. In a cold, dubious voice, she said, "You can help my nephew?"

"Well..." Cal nervously chuckled. "We can try." He pulled up a chair on Lucas' bedside. Though he pulled open the far side of the curtain to let in some of the admittedly dim sunlight, he blocked it as he sat, casting a shadow over Lucas. He opened his laptop, but paused. "Uh... it would be best if Lucas and I had some privacy. That way he won't be as likely to hide or embellish details of what happened to—"

"I'm staying." Gottschalk placed the flowers in the vase on Lucas' bedside table. "I want to keep an eye on my nephew."

Flustered, Calvin rapidly bobbed his head. "Of course, of course!"

Though Felix wanted to stay, he knew he couldn't keep Ornella waiting much longer. Otherwise, he might end up in a hospital bed of his own. "I should get going. Good to see you, Cal." Calvin, not responding or even looking at Felix, simply kept furiously typing. Gottschalk stared Felix down as he shuffled out. She didn't give a look of anger, nor sorrow, but rather one of suspicion and curiosity.

Ornella, on the other hand, was most definitely frustrated as she held her forehead. "And what exactly took you so long, Mr. Brasher?" she asked. "Ms. Oswald and Mr. Johnson have been needing a third hand in the psychiatric ward for ages now."

"S-Sorry!" At least now while Felix was dealing with Ornella, he didn't feel like he needed to worry about her killing him on the spot (only some light mangling). "I wanted to check on Lucas."

Lucinda, who'd been typing furiously on her phone until that point, glanced up. Her expression was sullen, incredibly unlike her usual self. "How is he?"

"He's... still the same," Felix said. "They're talking to him now, so it'd probably be best to leave him be for a while."

"I see..." Lucinda returned to her phone.

Ornella sighed. "Please get to the psychiatric ward. I highly doubt your friends have finished all their duties on their own." Felix agreed, though he kept his attention on Lucinda. How did she feel about all of this? "Mr. Brasher," Ornella boomed. "Please focus on your own tasks."

Felix relented, apologized yet again, then took off to find Penny and Shawn. He wasn't at all looking forward to this. The psych ward here was said to be filled with patients suffering from severe cases of mageblight, kept under close observation where they couldn't harm the public. Beneath the oppressively bright hospital lights, the dark anguish all around had set in and rattled his bones. For a moment, Felix felt as though he too was trapped within the crushing walls of Lighthaven.

"About time!"

Shawn had been given janitorial duties in the psych ward, and had now moved onto mopping the grimy floors. Felix ran up to greet him, only to skid along the wet floor, forcing Shawn to drop the mop and catch him. "Whoa, whoa!" Shawn laughed. "Careful! I don't wanna clean up your scatterbrained... brain."

Ha. Clever. But Felix held back his snarky retort. Instead, he looked around, finding the corridor empty, the lights flickering. "Where's Penny?"

"She's checking on each of the patients," Shawn said. "Taking notes on their behavior." He stared at his reflection in the water, grimacing before he resumed cleaning. "She... insisted on doing it alone."

"I'm gonna go find her," Felix said. "She could use some help."

Shawn shrugged, and he whistled faintly as he mopped, scrubbing away at the same tiles he'd already thoroughly cleaned, albeit more aggressively. It would've been easier to help Shawn. But with Penny being around patients with mageblight, just like her mother? She was likely more in need of help right now.

Though by that point, it was too late. Penny had been cooped up in a dark observation room clutching a tablet. Through the glass window, inside a padded room, sat a pale-skinned, middle-aged woman with dirty-blonde hair and blood-red irises. A straight jacket bound her arms. Her unblinking gaze upon the floor chilled Felix's blood, as though her head might snap up at any moment.

"Penny, I'm so sorry I'm late!"

Penny nearly dropped the tablet as she jumped. "F-Felix? It's okay." She looked back at the woman. "I've been watching her for a while now. I'm supposed to keep an eye out for any strange behavior, and make sure she doesn't…" She paused. "Doesn't try to hurt herself."

Felix held his arm. He wanted to ask if she was okay, but he already knew the answer. "Do you want me to take over from here? Or, to leave you be?"

"No, it's okay." Penny gave a weak smile. "I could use the company."

"Of course!" Felix's attention shifted to the woman. As far as he knew, people with mageblight were incredibly dangerous, with immense, uncontrollable power. Yet here this woman was, unmoving. "Is she…?"

"Don't worry," Penny said. "The doctors said it's safe so long as we don't go inside." She gestured to the heavy door on the far side of the room, sealed off from the woman's side by a hard light barrier. "The glass is reinforced with glyphs. It won't break, so even if she tried, her spells wouldn't do any good."

"But would someone with that power even need mythril? What's keeping her from—"

"I don't know. They said they had a way to negate the patients' powers, but they couldn't say anything else." Penny checked her tablet. "They also said we can see her, but she can't see us. But… at one point, I thought I caught her staring right at me."

Felix shivered. "What's her name?"

"Eris Galatas. She used to be a magical athlete and got pretty close to being Dragon Skinner. But then…" She hung her head as she trailed off.

"Huh. Eris…" The familiar-sounding name bemused Felix.

"I did some digging," Penny said. "And apparently her family branches off from House Baisley. She's actually Seisyll's cousin, if the family tree is right."

Felix's jaw dropped. "Wait, so this is Zahra's…" He racked his brain. "Would it be aunt, or second cousin?"

"*First* cousin," Penny corrected. "Once removed."

"That's… forget it."

But this woman was once part of someone's family—Zahra's family. And here she was now, locked away, unmentioned and forgotten. Almost as if she no longer existed outside of this place. The red of her eyes pulled him in with their dark allure. A cursed affliction of great power at the cost of one's mind, and even soul. An affliction that, in that moment, he realized had gripped Concobhar and later Elisa as well.

And that's when Eris' piercing gaze made him leap back in terror.

Felix tried to compose himself as he backed away. "I-I thought you said she couldn't see us!"

"S-She shouldn't!" Penny yelled.

Eris gave a disturbingly wicked grin as her head shot up, tossing her long hair back. Her mouth fell open wide as she cackled. Though her laughter was muffled through the glass, it still sent a shiver up Felix's spine. Eris stood, pressing herself up against the glass and beating against it, screaming between bursts of laughter. She had no luck in cracking open her cell. Staggering backwards, she kept trying to break her arms free and recited what sounded like incantations. But no magic appeared. Penny trembled, eyes welling with tears. Finally, the doctor returned, escorting them out and taking the matter into his own hands. What exactly he meant by that, Felix preferred not to know.

Penny kept wheezing, rocking back and forth in one of the chairs down the hall, while Felix kept his distance. He wanted to hug her, but he knew that likely would've only made her anxiety attack worse. Penny needed as much space as she could get until she was able to calm down. Which is precisely why when Shawn dropped his mop and ran over to them (nearly slipping), Felix stood to keep him from crowding Penny.

"What happened?" Shawn asked.

Felix wasn't sure what to say, especially given he wasn't entirely sure how much Penny was willing to share. "Right now she needs some space," Felix said.

"I-It's okay…" Penny still shook, but much less than before. "It was just… a lot more than I could handle." She forced a smile. "But I'll be okay. I think I just need some fresh air."

"Whatever you need," Shawn said.

"You guys head outside then," Felix said. "I'll take the heat from Ornella. Just text me later to let me know how you are, okay?"

Penny nodded. Shawn helped her up, and they made their way to the exit while Felix headed back into the main part of the hospital. Penny would be okay. But the question on Felix's mind was… what even was mageblight? What caused it? What made the inflicted's eyes turn that ominous shade of red? Was it truly just a disease, or was there something more to it?

"You seem to be in a hurry."

This must've been the dozenth time today Felix nearly leapt out of his skin. A blonde girl with sickly pale skin had emerged from the shadows as he rounded the corner, her sneer the only thing making her instantly recognizable. "You…" Felix squinted, slowly backing away. "You were that girl with Lucas in our history class."

"Bianca." Her nasally voice grated Felix's ears like sandpaper. "Good to see I've made an impression."

A shitty one, that's for sure. Felix hadn't seen her in any of his classes until very recently, and now here she was, popping up all over the place. "You're volunteering?"

"When I wouldn't be paid for all that backbreaking work?" Bianca giggled. "Leave that to the people whose job it actually is." Now Felix definitely wanted to push past her. But there was something else about her presence that unnerved him. Something sinister. "I came here to pay Lucas a visit, but they shooed me away. And after I found him and brought him in?" She tsk-tsked. "But you? You went to check on him earlier, didn't you?"

Felix raised an eyebrow. "How did you…? Wait? *You* found him?"

Bianca giggled. "That is what I just said, isn't it? Couldn't have him running off on us, now could we? Not when there's so much left to do."

Felix highly doubted Bianca had found Lucas washed ashore by pure coincidence. According to the rumors, Lucas had boarded that ship alone,

331

and he was far too cautious to just slip into the sea. Not unless someone threw him in themselves.

Perhaps Bianca was one of the backups Vagus mentioned back when he and Lucas first made that infernal oath. Or perhaps she had some other connection to what happened to Lucas? But Felix couldn't have cared less. "Look, I've got more important stuff to take care of. So if you don't mind…" Before she could respond, he stormed past her down the hall.

"Nice meeting you too!" Bianca's mockingly sweet voice echoed down the hall, but Felix kept up his pace. He just hoped he wouldn't have to endure her gross attitude again anytime soon.

He stopped, though, as Professor Montanari spoke with a doctor far down another corridor. Ornella would've been waiting for him to check back in, but the grief in Montanari's expression caught him off guard. She'd rushed out of her last class after all. Felix's anxiety told him to just carry on with his own business, but he knew he ought to do whatever he could to help, even if it just meant giving her someone to talk to. "Professor?"

Montanari smiled. "Mr. Brasher. Volunteering, I see?"

"Yeah. I wanted to ask… is everything okay?"

"Not exactly. I'm here to visit… someone very close to me. Someone who hasn't been doing very well." Her head flicked up, a faint smile across her face. "Would you mind tagging along? You're one of my favorite students, and I'd very much appreciate the company. If you don't mind, of course."

Felix hesitated. On the one hand, he knew he didn't want to leave Ornella waiting again. Yet while he found Montanari's request a tad odd, he'd also felt the sadness hanging in the air all throughout the wings of Lighthaven, weighing down on everyone in each of its barren corridors. He was already here to lend a hand to those who needed it. So why not now?

With a nod, he followed her into a double occupied room. A curtain had been drawn around the first bed, concealing what sounded to be a female patient with a horrid cough. A heart monitor beeped by the bed closer to the window. Montanari opened the curtain to reveal an old woman with sagging pale skin and brittle, messy dark-brown hair. An oxygen mask sat over her face, while IV drips and a catheter had been hooked into her body. Her closed eyelids hid the color of her irises.

"Hi, Mom."

Felix held his wrist. Montanari's mother hadn't so much as stirred, and he couldn't tell whether she looked to be in peace... or pain. A vase of bright-red-orange flowers lay on her bedside table, along with framed photos of herself a few decades younger. Beside her were what seemed to be her fair-skinned, auburn-haired husband, and two children: a pale boy of about eight or nine, with buzzed brown hair and a distinct frown along his face; and a twelve-year-old girl with long blonde locks tied into pigtails, along with a smile that more than made up for her brother's bad mood. The glare across the frame, coupled with discoloration from age and slight tears, made it impossible to see any of their true eye colors. The whiteboard above the bed read: "Sophia Renascentia."

"I'm... sorry for dragging you along." Montanari's gaze remained on her mother's eyes, as if she were waiting for them to open. "I just... it's hard seeing her like this, you know?"

"... It's okay," Felix said, taking a moment to process the sight. "How long has she...?"

Montanari held her shoulder. "A little over six years at this point." Her voice was brittle and low. "Modern medicine is a miracle, isn't it?" She dabbed away her tears. "My father and brother had been gone for a long time, so she was all I had left."

"I'm... so sorry." Felix looked back at the portrait. He had no idea what to say, or what was even appropriate to ask. But to be kept alive for so long when your mind had already gone. Would he want to be kept like this, even if it meant waking up after months, possibly years of being trapped in sleep? Would the people he loved still be waiting for him? Still, if this was Sophia's choice, and her only remaining family was onboard, who in the world was he to judge?

"Mom always had a fear of death." Montanari chuckled. "I'd constantly pester her about what she'd like done with her body. Told her over and over, 'You can't put this off another year, you gotta write that damn will before it's too late!' But she always insisted she was fine, and she could always do it tomorrow. And then... tomorrow came, alright."

"So... you think this is what she would've wanted?" Felix asked.

Montanari hung her head. "I know *she* wanted this. But I don't know how I feel at this point. The doctors said it was a massive stroke caused by a hole in her heart. They said they could patch it up, but it was risky. I wound up insisting that we wait 'til there was no other option. But really… I was just scared. I… I'm still scared. But seeing her like this, stuck in this bed and hooked into these machines…" She reached into her bag, blowing her nose into a tissue. "I'm sorry. You probably didn't need to see your teacher crying like a little kid today."

"It's… okay," Felix said. "I'd probably be the same if it was my mom. The thought of ever losing her…" He remembered the Ouija board spelling out Lydia's name, then pushed the thought as far back into the recesses of his mind as he could manage.

"What would we do without our mothers, right?" Montanari laughed. "I remember when I first brought my sons to visit her, they said, 'Wow! I wish I could sleep as well as Grandma!'" She raised her pitch a bit to mimic a curious child. "My husband wasn't too fond, but… I don't think they really understood. At the very least, I got a strange sort of validation out of it." Her smile weakened, remaining bittersweet. "I wish she could meet them. I met Dominic not long after Mom…"

A sobering moment indeed. Even with modern technology, in a kingdom home to sorcerers, death was still inevitable. You could pretend it wouldn't happen. But one day, it would knock on your door, regardless of whether you were ready. A welcome reminder for Felix to enjoy his time on this miserable rock while he had it. Especially knowing no matter how much he wished, no matter the powers he may have gained, he wouldn't be able to be with the people he loved forever.

It certainly made Felix want to call home, and most definitely apologize for not keeping in touch as much as he ought to. What he wouldn't give to catch up with his mother now. Or perhaps ask questions he hadn't bothered with in years, like about her experiences as a magus, or even where he and Aeris' names came from.

Felix was used to people asking about he and Aeris' unusual names. He'd only dared ask his mother once, back when Frank was still in their lives, to which she answered: "Aeris' name was mostly my idea. Convinced your father she was a saint, but I'll tell you both about the weird 'A' when you're older. He only went for it because of a girl he knew. An old flame of his. But your name, Felix? It's… complicated. You're named for someone who was very important to your father."

"Hey! Could you keep it down over there?! Some of us are trying to rest!"

This was the other patient in the room. Her voice was incredibly hoarse, like that of a chronic smoker, and she quickly flew into a fit of coughs and heaves. The curtain flung open. She sat up in bed with a nasty slouch, face red and gaunt against her light-olive skin, red hair greasy and unbrushed. And to top it all off, an even nastier glower had been plastered across her face to match her harsh voice. Felix wanted to tell her to screw off. But as his eyes drifted towards her name smudged upon the whiteboard, the last name inspired terror.

"D-De Angelis?!" Felix stuttered, rushing to bow. "F-Forgive us, Your Highness!" *I hope it's highness. Please don't throw me in jail. I don't know if that's a thing royalty can do here, but please don't.*

Montanari cackled. "Relax. She's no one, trust me."

"H-How dare you?!" the woman's voice croaked as she yelled. "I am Camilla de Angelis! I am—"

"The empress' frumpy little sister. The princess with no real power." Montanari leaned towards Felix, whispering, "And thank goodness for that."

"I can hear you! And I'm her *twin* sister, thank you very much!"

"Of course, her little *twin* sister!" Montanari laughed again.

Felix was unsure of what to think. This woman hadn't made the best impression, that was for sure. But despite that, one would assume it wasn't wise to go around mocking members of the royal family so brazenly.

"Come along, Mr. Brasher," Montanari said. "We wouldn't want to disturb the 'noblewoman's' rest, now would we?" Giving her mother a kiss goodbye, she shut the curtains. As she and Felix left, Felix's eyes remained locked with Camilla's, her golden eyes wide with scorn.

Once they were far enough away, Felix finally felt comfortable talking again. "Why exactly did you do that?"

Montanari waved her hand. "Trust me, she's nothing like the empress. Stuck up, embezzling funds from the crown for her collection of expensive wines and jewels, and a general nightmare to be around. Not to mention, she kicks puppies!"

Felix raised an eyebrow.

"Okay, that last one was a joke," Montanari said. "But she really is the worst. I even heard a rumor she greased a few palms in parliament to slash the national healthcare budget just a bit. Would not be surprised."

He wasn't surprised. No matter where you went, whether human or magus, sometimes the worst people imaginable just so happened to be born into unfathomable wealth and privilege. In fact, one could argue it was those things that shaped them into such tacky hobgoblins and gremlins to begin with. And if what Montanari said was true, Felix wouldn't be shocked if her title and status were her shield against any real consequences. Even if her own sister, the empress, also despised her.

But his earlier concerns about Ornella's frustrations thankfully never came to pass, both thanks to Lucinda's insistence and Montanari's testimony to Felix being of great help. His last assignment for the day was to help Rosie, Argent, Zahra, and Nasira in taking all of the garbage out to the hospital's dumpsters. Though they had to hold their noses and breathe through their mouths to avoid puking—though Felix could've sworn he could *taste* the foul stench—while also swatting away flies and wasps, Felix didn't mind.

Before he'd gotten there, Rosie and Zahra had done all the heavy lifting and hustling, while Nasira and Argent had slacked. Felix managed to get them both to step up their game. Argent by a little flirting and the potential promise of an eventual date. Nasira was easier to turn around than expected. A quick mention of what he'd seen of Montanari's situation with her mother, and Nasira was more than happy to lend Zahra a hand.

Once their work was done, they all agreed to treat themselves to a celebratory dinner. Argent insisted on only paying for himself and Felix, Felix insisted they all split the check five ways, and through the magic of democracy (four against one), Felix won out.

After they all showered, of course.

Lighthaven was disturbing enough during the day. But after the sun went down, the place ironically grew even more devoid of light. The faintest echoes of patients' cries and screams, along with the beeps of hospital equipment, kept Ornella on edge as she looked over her report. Lucinda and the other prefects would be back soon with food for them all to help take the edge off from today. Even so, Ornella felt as though something wasn't quite right as she sat alone in the break room. The vending machine's occasional creaking and merciless hum preoccupied her mind more than the papers on Felix's volunteer work.

"Vermillion Bar?"

She skidded back in her chair, metal legs scraping against the tiled floor. Bianca stood there, an open snack in hand, waving it around like a wand. Just moments ago, Ornella had been all alone. She knew how to remain aware of her surroundings with all she'd been through, which made this encounter all the more unnerving. "No thank you," she said. "My friends will be back soon, so—"

"Yes, your 'friends.'" Bianca scoffed as she bit a chunk out of the bar. "They seem to know how to have fun. You should really follow their lead, unless you wanna end up like... well..."

Ornella frowned. "Either learn to finish your sentences, or don't speak at all."

Bianca shrugged. "That's unexpectedly cold. I'm only saying, it'd be a shame if you were to forget where your loyalties lie. One ingrate is enough of a headache." She took another bite. "So much better than those garbage human-world candies, wouldn't you agree? I'll give the Della Luces one thing: their money can't buy charm, but it *can* buy taste!"

"Shouldn't you be spending time with your mother?" Ornella asked.

Bianca shrugged. "She shooed me away. Ah well. She'll recover. She's the princess, after all, however disdained. A shame I may not be able to say the same about all of us."

Ornella dropped her pen, pushing herself up so she might tower over Bianca. "Let me make myself clear, Ms. de Palmi. Your empty threats don't scare me. If you, or anyone else you're colluding with, so much as lays a finger on a single hair on either of those boys' heads, damn what my mother would say. I will find you and incinerate you myself."

Bianca backed away, struggling to keep up her facade. "If only you could channel that energy into fighting our actual enemies" She tossed the rest of the bar into the garbage as she walked out, storming past Lucinda and the other prefects.

"Hey!" Nina growled. "I know McDonald's is an acquired taste here, but damn."

Lucinda placed the food on the table, looking into Ornella's eyes as she sat down and held her forehead. "What's wrong?" Lucinda asked.

"Nothing, nothing." Ornella waved her hand.

"You sure you don't want to talk about it?" Though Theresa meant well, the fact they were talking as they chewed through their sandwich was hilarious enough to make Ornella snicker. "What?"

Lucinda handed Ornella her meal, and Ornella took a sip, relishing the sweet taste of ice-cold caffeine. "It's just…" Ornella gave a faint smile. "It's nice to be reminded I have true friends. But in any case…" She gestured to Nina.

Begrudgingly, Nina held off on her salad to whistle to Lilim. On cue, and after some rapid clawed footfalls and a near-spillage of Theresa's drink, the ever-faithful sigbin made herself visible. She tried to snag one of Ornella's fries, but Nina was quick to reign Lilim in. "Not much to report on. Our sneering little friend was apparently wandering the place all day, visiting every goddamn nook and cranny, but didn't technically do anything."

"That concerns me more, honestly," Ornella said. "Whatever they have planned, we need to be ready. And we absolutely need to keep them away from Felix and Lucas."

Chapter Eighteen

A Familiar Wisp

"I CAN SEE IT NOW!" Rosie shouted, waving her arm as if painting a picture in the air. "A penguin wearing a fabulous red scarf and matching beret, able to speak fluent Spanish, fly gracefully through the air, and slaying its enemies with its fiery breath!"

"I'm not teaching it Spanish, for the record," Felix said, chuckling at the over-the-top weirdness of Rosie's mental concoction. They, along with Argent, were on their way to their next class, all about familiars and wisps, and how to create them. Or rather, theories about crafting familiars. Given how complex the process of creating a magical creature out of mythril was, not to mention dangerous if handled without proper oversight, the first-years were kept strictly to summoning wisps. Less lawsuits that way. "You might wanna tone down your expectations."

"That is… creepily specific, though," Argent said.

Rosie pouted. "You know what? Forget you two! Poor little Pablo didn't do anything wrong."

Felix and Argent tilted their heads. "Pablo?" they asked in unison.

"I can't have a minion and not name him. What kinda monster do you take me for?"

Felix rolled his eyes. "¡Qué puta loca, todo por un pingüino!"

Rosie simply huffed, while Argent purred at how "sexy" he found Felix's Spanish (all the while only knowing what "pingüino" meant). They seated themselves at their usual table at the back of the classroom, where Shawn, Zahra, and Floria awaited. "Hello, fellow people!" Rosie yelled. "Have you heard the good news about Pablo the Proficiently Personable Penguin?"

Shawn raised an eyebrow. "What?"

"Nevermind." Rosie rolled her eyes.

As Felix sat, he could feel Lucas' glare, however brief, coupled with Bianca's sneer. Lucas had been discharged from Lighthaven a few days before, if the rumors were true. Felix loathed what people were saying. That the crazy Lighthead kid had finally been tossed out by his family like a stray cat. As far as Felix was concerned, Lucas had every right to be angry at the world, however unbearable it made him. But as to why Lucas chose to let Bianca sit at his table, Felix would rather not know. Thankfully Ulrich was there to lighten the mood with his dragonlike snores.

"Afternoon, everyone." Seisyll, or rather Professor Hakim, stood at his desk. Instantly, Felix's mind shot back to Eris' sick grin as she tried to escape from her Lighthaven cell. "I hope you've all done your reading," Seisyll said. "Because today, you'll be learning all about familiars, and how to create one of your very own."

Felix ignored Seisyll's subsequent disclaimer about not really creating familiars. He'd just killed his slim hopes on his own, after all.

"Dragons, phoenixes, trolls, and all the like are familiars: magical creatures crafted from mythril and given life, with the purpose of either enhancing spells, acting as servants or protectors, or just being cuddly, fire-breathing pets."

Rosie's hand shot up. "If familiars are created from mythril, how can they be made of flesh and blood? And how exactly do they reproduce in the wild?"

Ulrich snickered, but Lucas smacked him upside the head. That's where he lost some sympathy points with Felix.

"All familiars have what Medeian scholars refer to as a nucleus," Seisyll said. "Think of it as their heart, and that heart is forged from crystallized mythril. From there, the glyphs inscribed within the mythril arrange the material into what's needed to bring forth life, which is why the process is so exasperating and complicated. But because of this, they are biological in nature, and thus are fully capable of reproduction. With creatures similar enough in structure, at least."

Felix, having studied thoroughly for class, raised his hand the moment Seisyll finished speaking, before anyone else could ask their own question. "Familiars by default are supposed to return to their crystallized forms when their creator or master dies, right? Unless they're meant to act as a guardian for their grave or belongings?"

"Generally, yes." Seisyll's face remained devoid of expression. "That's how it used to be, in the ages before the Revelation."

"That brings me to my next question. Why did so many familiars awaken by themselves and go rogue during the Revelation? Are there any theories on what caused that? And why do familiars live beyond their master's death now?"

The room fell quiet. Felix's question definitely melted the minds of most of the other students, even garnering some snickers here and there. Argent coughed, "Nerd!", though Felix shushed him promptly. Even so, he'd always wondered what triggered the Revelation to begin with. From all he'd read, something caused hibernating familiars all across the globe to awaken and fully form all at once, going on rampages and destroying everything in their path. That, along with the harsh weather across the world, was what threw the human world into mass hysteria, and what forced the Medeian Empire to come out of hiding to prevent any further damage.

And that's what made humans so afraid and spiteful towards magi. The idea that somehow, the magi had secretly orchestrated this plot to wipe out mankind in one fell swoop, and had only stepped in when it got out of control. Or perhaps, according to some, they'd done so hoping they'd be celebrated as heroes and allowed to control the world.

What a crock of bullshit, Felix had always thought.

Seisyll held his chin, pondering. "No one is still sure. Even the most brilliant scholars can only form disarrayed theories with such little information there is to go off of. But while the Dragora Institute does house many of the rogue familiars here in our reserve, most still roam free about the world, primarily concentrated in the Middle East, Amazonia, and large swaths of Africa, Asia, and Greenland—now Dragonsland," he coughed, trying to stir up some laughter, to no avail. "And the North and South Poles.

But thankfully, that's what we have the barrier systems and beast hunters for."

Felix knew he wouldn't get a concrete answer, but any new information or perspective was absolutely fascinating. Even if he had to keep shushing Argent and shooting him dagger eyes to get it.

Seisyll went on about the different types of familiars. Most peculiarly, he had the oddest fixation on the minutiae of the different types of dragons: wyverns, wyrms, lindwyrms, amphipteres, drakes, and so on. (*If I have to suffer through the whole list, so do you.*) Though his lectures were denser than Ulrich, Felix had no issues in keeping up, even when Seisyll joked about familiars' excrement being made of mythril shards. But the best part was Seisyll's mention of wisps, for which he brought them outside, and along the way, Felix could barely contain his excitement.

"I don't mean to rain on your parade," Argent said. "But you realize most freshmen fail at their first attempt of making wisps, right? Let alone familiars. Most students don't even have basic familiars of their own 'til they're grad students."

"Don't kill it for me," Felix said.

"Seconded." Rosie stood on her tippy toes, nearly tripping.

Argent snickered. "You and what penguin?"

She glared. "Blasphemy!"

Still, Felix hung on Argent's warning. He was just a cobalt, after all, with no magical experience before he'd come to Dragora. But he stopped his thoughts in their tracks. If he was going to be able to do this, he had to believe that he could without question. There couldn't be any room for failure. His mood brightened as their class strolled out into the small field past the castle gardens, basking in the golden sunlight and the clear blue skies.

"Today," Seisyll said, projecting his voice over the cool, gentle breeze. "We'll be trying to create wisps. Allow me to demonstrate." From his pocket, he took out a small fragment of yellow mythril, then knelt as he placed it on the ground. He held his hands over the crystal and closed his eyes. "Awaken, my ally."

A golden glyph spun beneath the mythril. The crystal glowed bright, then transformed into the shape of a small bird, its wings outstretched. The light faded, and a small dove took the place of the mythril. Radiant flames sparkled along its yellow "skin," almost like small stars. Seisyll held out his hand, and eagerly, the dove hopped into his palm and chirped.

"This," Seisyll said. "Is a wisp. They're good to use in a pinch, since they're so easy to create. Though they'll only last for a certain amount of time before…"

The dove flew into the air, then burst in a shower of light.

Floria scoffed. "Tacky."

Zahra's eyes widened. "So beautiful. But so…"

"Fucked up?" Felix asked.

"… Yeah."

Samuel, trudging over with his forehead glistening with sweat, hauled a massive brown bag. Felix would've assumed it was filled with severed limbs given this was Samuel, but as he tossed it onto the ground, out spilled two dozen or so mythril fragments. Seisyll groaned "Sam, could you be more careful please?"

"No." Samuel scratched his back. "I need a nap."

"Three-fourths of your life is spent sleeping."

Samuel scoffed. "You're one to talk," he mumbled. "Whether or not you're on those damn worthless meds." Everyone froze. As Seisyll collected himself, Samuel clearly regretted his jab as he backed up a bit. "I-I'll go now." Seisyll didn't bother responding, and without another word, Samuel returned to the castle.

Once the discomfort had passed (albeit, like a kidney stone), the students all grabbed a piece of mythril and spread themselves out. "When you try to make your wisp," Seisyll said. "Hold your hands over the mythril and channel the magic through it as best you can. Imagine the mythril taking the shape of the creature you wish to create. And if you can't manage it, don't worry. This will change with time, practice, and experience."

Felix put down the mythril, closed his eyes, and focused. Slowly, he placed his fingertips onto the crystal.

"Don't touch the mythril. Your body will prevent the magic from activating."

Felix pulled his hands back, quickly shooting himself an insult out of habit. He envisioned a small dove, just like the one Professor Hakim had created. "Awaken, my ally," he whispered. He opened his eyes. No glyph, no light, and no wisp. He tried again, then again, resisting the urge to grind the crystal into dust. *C'mon! If I can't do this simple thing, then…*

He distanced the thought and stopped. Shutting his eyes again, he sat up straight, holding out his hands again. *I can do this.* "Awaken, my ally." A strange hum entered his ears. He held his breath, trying to remain calm. A soothing energy coursed through his body. Unlike his other spell, all born of his dark alignment, this felt… light. The clear image of a dove entered his mind.

Felix grinned as his thoughts wandered to what he'd be able to do in the years to come: a much larger bird, with bright red, gold, and purple feathers. A bird whose fiery wrath could match Felix's own short temper. A phoenix, and not a simple wisp, but an actual, fully realized familiar.

The humming ceased, and the sense of weightlessness vanished with it. Slowly, Felix opened his eyes, and found the mythril dull and unchanged.

Dammit. I should've known I couldn't. Most of the other students had created their doves, including Zahra, Rosie, and even Floria, while Argent had created a small snake. Lucas had made a dragon about the size of his palm, and his snide grin boiled Felix's blood. *No. I just got too far ahead of myself.*

Felix repeated the process. "Awaken, my ally." The humming returned, and he forced his mind to stay fixed on the image of the dove. After about a minute, he opened his eyes, and in the place of the mythril was a small translucent dove. "I-I… I did it!" He thrust his arms into the air. "Yes!"

The dove flew into Felix's face and vanished instantly. He fell onto his back as his eyes filled with starlight. He reached out towards the sun, imagining himself holding it in the palm of his hand. "I did it," he whispered. Even once class was dismissed, Felix remained there, lying in the grass, triumphant.

Argent towered over him, eclipsing the sun. "You, uh… wanna get out of the dirt now?" Felix laughed as Argent helped him up. Suddenly, out here beneath the crystal-clear skies, something compelled Felix to ask something. Something he'd normally spend hours contemplating before chickening out of his decision. But given recent events, reminding him that he didn't have eternity on this Earth to keep procrastinating, especially if this was indeed going to be his first, last, and only year at Dragora, he couldn't wait a day more. And so, smiling uncontrollably and letting his heart take the wheel, Felix asked…

"You wanna go on a date?"

He bumped into Argent as he stopped in his tracks. Slowly, Argent turned back, a smile wide across his face. "Knew you were worth the wait."

With the light of the waning crescent moon as his guide, Lucas entered the greenhouse. The doors were wide open, no vines crawling about the place, and no broken windows. Every single firebird's kiss bloomed, their red-orange petals gleaming against the teal moonlight, even filling up the pool at the far end.

"So much better, isn't it?"

Lucas looked up, and there Vagus stood across from him, on the opposite side of the pool. "You did this?"

Vagus shrugged. "Technically." He revealed a dreamcatcher from his cloak. "Astral magic makes for good visualizations before carrying out plans in real life. Feel free to use this as a subtle suggestion for your family, if they can be bothered to clean up their messes. If you can remember this all in detail, of course."

"If you're here to scare me into submitting," Lucas said. "You already did that. I don't even have much of a choice but to go through with your nonsense."

"I'm not here to threaten you, dear boy," Vagus said. "Just to let you know I'm... well, to say I'm pleased with your progress would be a lie. On the one hand because you did nothing more than regress, but also, I'm always exhausted. Especially when it comes to you two."

Lucas rolled his eyes. "The cobalt runt still catches your eye?"

"The only runt I see is the one before me, who kept trying to run away or bully another who's put far more work into growing than I've ever seen from you."

Even in a dream, Lucas could feel his blood boiling.

"In any case, the final test will be coming soon. I will finally have my champion."

Lucas scoffed. "And what makes you so sure the cobalt will go along with—"

"His name is Felix." Vagus' voice boomed through the greenhouse. "And I'm sure he will. He's needed some time on his own to figure things out, but

I'm sure a quick reminder of what awaits him will be enough to get him back onboard. Either way, I'll get what I want."

Before Lucas could respond, Vagus snapped his hands. Every window shattered on command, and all the firebird's kisses turned a sickly shade of violet. The purple light filled Lucas' eyes, and before he knew it, he shot up in bed back at his manor. The clouds obscured the moon, thunder quietly rumbling in the distance.

He won't take this from me. This is my destiny.

Chapter Nineteen

What Makes a First Date?

" **F**UCKING EVIL NECK TRAP OF DEATH!"

Rosie shook her head as she finished knotting Felix's tie. "Maybe if you'd stop wriggling," she said. "You wouldn't choke to death. Though you could be choking on… other things." She winked as obnoxiously as possible.

"And *I'm* the filthy one?" Felix asked.

"Filthy in the gross way." Rosie sneered. "I'm tastefully trashy."

"Whatever." Felix had been so busy with coursework in recent weeks that he had to keep postponing he and Argent's date. In all honesty, it relieved him, as not once in his near 19 years of existence had he ever gone on a date. So suffice to say, this date winding up being on Valentine's Day of all days on some level comforted him. Yet simultaneously, it raised his fear that something was bound to go wrong. Felix's black buttoned-up shirt, coupled with his red tie, already brought back war flashbacks to his miserable time at the Sandwich Shack. *I probably look ridiculous. And a virgin at 19, nonetheless. So sophisticated. So alone.*

Rosie simpered. "You're the one who made it a formal dinner."

"I don't know how this shit works."

"Clearly." Rosie examined Felix from head to toe. "Judging by the fact that you've already managed to uncuff your sleeves."

"... Fuck." It took Felix a long, agonizing minute to fix them.

"Relax," Rosie said. "Argent doesn't exactly seem like the formal type."

Felix teared up. "I just wanna have a good night."

"You will." Rosie held his shoulder, smiling. "You deserve some fun."

Grateful for his friend's comfort, Felix hugged her tightly, only to jump at the sound of three heavy knocks on the door. "Hello!" a deep voice sang.

Felix rolled his eyes. "I swear..."

"Coming!" Rosie bolted for the door, but stopped just short of the knob, turning back to Felix. "Do you look good enough?"

He squinted. "Are you being anxious... *for* me?"

She opened the door. In walked Argent, decked out in a full gray suit with his hair slicked back. A red bouquet rested in one hand, and in the other, a heart-shaped box, presumably (and hopefully) filled with chocolates.

"So am I fashionably late?" Argent asked. "Or responsibly early?"

Rosie checked her phone. "Right on time. Aren't you boring?"

His smug facade instantly melted away as his eyes fell upon Felix. Taking the place of his signature devious grin was a warm, genuine smile. "You look..."

Felix shrunk a bit in embarrassment. "Decent?"

"Good." Argent chuckled. "You clean up nice."

Felix blushed. "I was disgusting before?"

"Sass is on-point. As is your—"

Rosie jumped between them. "If you two are going *there* tonight, you'll need to stay safe!"

Argent raised an eyebrow. "Is she serious?"

"As serious as an STD, my dear fuckboy."

"... What did you—"

"Now remember, consent is above all else." Rosie leveled with Argent's eyes, staring right through his soul. She had to stand on her tippy toes to do so, but honestly, it didn't seem Argent had noticed given his fear. "If you do anything to him that he doesn't want or like, I *will* end you."

Argent tried to back away, to no avail as he bumped into the door. "O-Okay."

"I appreciate it, Rosie," Felix said. "But you can get off your tippy toes now."

Rosie wagged her finger in Argent's face. "I'm watchin' you, pal. You break him, *I* break *you.*" Slowly, Argent nodded, and Rosie backed off. "And remember," she said. "Condoms!"

"Condoms," Felix said.

"Condoms," Argent repeated.

Rosie crossed her arms. "Now together."

"Condoms," the boys said in unison.

"Good. And again."

"Condoms."

"And—"

"Is there a reason for this?" Felix asked.

"Nope," Rosie said. "I just like fucking with you morons."

Felix and Argent seethed, then together said, "You little—"

Her grin widened.

"Dammit!" they both muttered.

"Alright, off you go." Rosie pushed them outside. "Have fun, stay safe, and don't get murdered and/or sold into sex trades." She slammed the door, leaving them dazed.

"Uh…" Argent snickered. "She's… protective."

"Yeah," Felix said. "She's the best." But now, it had begun: the date. He'd suggested they go eat somewhere, then a place to relax afterwards. While Argent kept his idea for later a mystery—much to both Felix's excitement and anxiety—he did reserve them seats at a local restaurant that he had sworn by. Felix only hoped it wasn't too fancy, nor too expensive.

Argent handed the box over to Felix. "Chocolates?"

"T-Thanks." Felix took it, hoping that as he clutched it against his chest, his hands weren't already sweating from stress. "I do like food. A lot. More than people. B-But uh, not all people! Yeah…" *Dammit, self.*

"Oh! And uh, flowers!" Argent handed over the bouquet.

"How sweet!" Felix was lost in the bright red of the petals, only to be snapped out of the moment as he noticed the absence of a scent. "Are these—"

"Plastic, yeah. I wanted to get some real flowers from the reserve, but Samuel would've used my corpse as fertilizer. So I just went and, uh… printed 'em."

"Oh…" Felix wasn't disappointed whatsoever. He was happy to get any kind of gift, but moreover, he was happy Argent was willing to give this a try. But he could see the sadness and regret in Argent's expression. "They're… lovely," Felix said.

Argent, casting his eyes to the ground, frowned.

"Are you nervous?" Felix asked.

"… Yeah."

The thought of Argent being more nervous about this whole thing was hilariously ironic. But at the same time, it was incredibly comforting, and definitely endearing. "Haven't you been on dates before?" Felix asked. "I mean, obviously I haven't. But I thought—"

"What'd you take me for?" Argent asked. "A slut?"

Felix cracked a grin. "Maybe a less shameful word, but… kinda?"

"How dare." Argent gave an exaggerated frown, raising his chin and flaring his nose. "I find that offensive! Undeniably true, but mostly offensive."

"So they weren't so much dates as… booty calls?"

"Like to think of myself as sexually liberated."

Felix's smugness got the better of him. "You've got Grindr on your phone, don't you?"

"No," Argent said. "Not anymore."

"Mhm." But Felix didn't mind. He honestly didn't care about who Argent had been with, nor how many. Those were none of his business. So long as they'd both been tested, which Argent was more than happy to agree on, and remained safe, all Felix needed to know was that tonight, he and Argent would only think of each other.

"Can we stop bitching like an old married couple and be all romantical?" Argent asked. "Like dumb college kids in gay love?"

Felix snickered. "Romantical?"

"Shut up." Argent held out his hand.

Felix's blush grew even more intense. *Fuck, fuck, fuck.*

"What's wrong?" Argent asked. "Did I…?"

"N-Nothing. I suck at this."

"So do I," Argent said. "We can suck together."

You wonderfully filthy piece of shit. By this point, Felix's face felt like it was about to combust. He locked arms with Argent, and they strutted out to the courtyard to flag a coach. Despite this, Felix sat across from Argent on their way down the hill, unsure of what to say. All he could do was twiddle his thumbs and avoid eye contact. Normally he would've had little to no problems holding a conversation, but for some reason he was now unable to think up even a basic topic. The closest one he could come up with... wasn't great. Felix raised his head slowly. "S-So... those kelpies."

Argent looked up. "Hmm?"

"The kelpie. Pulling the coach."

"What about it?"

"You said, uh..." Felix kept stuttering, dying a bit each time he tried to string together a coherent sentence. "The rich people... inbreed them. Right?"

Argent raised an eyebrow. "... Where is this going?"

Felix stuttered. "I, uh... ran into a non-inbred one in the reserve. Back in November. Before, you know... shit hit the fan?"

"And...?"

"It looked demonic."

"Oh..." Argent looked back down at his phone. Felix simply sank back in his seat, cursing himself for his awkwardness. Maybe once they were having dinner he would feel better.

Once they'd reached Cendrillion, they made their way to the restaurant. Argent, the master of obnoxious enigmas, insisted on keeping the place's name, and even the type of food they served, a secret. If they wandered into a fast-food joint all dressed up, Felix would've been able to laugh away his nerves, but he didn't count on that opportunity unveiling itself tonight. The city streets glittered beneath the purple evening sky, the faint blue stars gleaming through the clouds. And all the while, Felix walked a couple paces behind Argent, debating a thousand questions in his head.

Do I hold his hand, or will he hold my hand? Is there a minimum number of dates we need to go on before we can hold hands? Are we together, like officially? What is "together" anyway? Was Rosie not too far off on whatever Argent has planned for us after dinner? Is he gonna expect me to be able to...? Why the fuck is this so complicated? Am I making this complicated? God fucking dammit, I hate myself sometimes.

All the time...

His thoughts were abruptly cut off as he bumped into Argent. "Careful, now." He winked, and Felix's fear of intimacy resurfaced with a reckoning.

Argent pointed up. "This is it." Before them was a massive white building. The words carved just above the double glass door entrance read, "Le Spire et Folie Mortelle."

"Wow…" Felix was at a loss for words. "So… sophisticated." *Fuck. It IS a fancy restaurant! I can't fancy! Dear gods, help me.*

"Uh… you okay?" Argent asked.

"Y-Yeah, totally!" Felix bobbed his head aggressively. "Looks nice!" *That's to say you probably spent a fortune in reservations just for me. Wait, do you have to pay for fancy restaurant reservations?! In any case, I'm not gonna disappoint you, when in reality, I'm screaming inside because I am the most uncultured piece of shit you will ever encounter.* Gripping the folds of his jacket, Felix followed Argent inside, only for his panic to worsen as his finger slipped through his empty pockets. *I left the chocolate and flowers back on the damn coach. Fuck.*

The lobby's black-and-white tiled floor dazzled Felix. Dark wood pillars stretched to the vaulted ceiling, and a white chandelier with red-and-blue jewels hung down, candles flickering upon each arm. Once Argent checked in, the receptionist led them up the marble stairs and out onto the overlook at the back of the building. Unicorn topiaries were turned towards the Sea of Sagramore in the distance, while Felix couldn't take his eyes off the peak of the Bors Mountains, even further off, piercing through the gibbous moon.

They took their seats at a white cloth table. Surrounding them on all sides were young couples, all lavishly dressed and enjoying the most expensive food and drink, and of course, all with either gold or pearl eyes. And here Felix was. Some middle-class trash from the States, sticking out like a sore thumb. He read through the menu over and over to try and appear busy. He'd never been one for fine dining (nor breathing, at times), so virtually all the appetizers and entrees read like Ancient Greek—for all he knew, they could've *been* Ancient Greek.

"So…" Felix tried to calm his nerves as he spoke, his voice brittle. "What're you getting?"

"Le Cockatris Irrité." Surprisingly, Argent was able to pronounce the term perfectly.

He said "cock," yet he hasn't made a joke. Perhaps the savage can be tamed?

"Figures. Since… you know… gay. I like men."

Take what you can get. But holy shit, that pronunciation was hot. With Argent, Felix didn't feel out of place. After a few minutes had passed, and still gripped by a crippling indecisiveness born of not knowing what the fuck anything on the menu even was, he was ready to choose his meal by eenie-meenie-miney-moe. *Desperate times call for childish measures.* "I think I'll go with the…" Felix squinted, silently praying he hadn't picked anything disgusting. "La Sirène dans les Profondeurs." He jumbled through his pronunciation, wondering why this place was even using goddamn French of all things for its obscenely pretentious aesthetic.

"Ooh!" Argent popped his eyebrows. "Sexy accent."

Felix scowled.

"You gonna do that every time I compliment you?" Argent asked.

"Good evening, gentlemen."

Felix didn't need to read his name tag. He recognized not only the waiter's face and voice, but also his very aura of "dear God I wanna go home and sleep." Apparently, Carlos worked not only at the Fountain of Magic, nor the Camelot Museum, but also here. No wonder he gave off the impression that he was constantly fed up with everything that breathed.

"If you're done staring," Carlos said, his voice stone cold as his expression. "Drinks?"

"Cola," Argent said.

Felix, shaking himself from his curiosity, rushed to force an answer. "Same here. No ice, please?" Scribbling their orders down with only one or two strokes of the pen, Carlos left before either Felix or Argent could thank him.

Argent propped his elbow on the table and held his cheek. "He sure was cute, wasn't he?"

Flustered, and nervous Argent might've gotten the wrong idea, Felix scrambled to think of a response. "N-No, I—"

"You're blushing, you realize?"

Felix felt his cheeks. *Dammit.*

Argent laughed. "You're pretty cute yourself when you're embarrassed."

Felix, wanting to diffuse the situation, somehow thought it was a great idea to grab the nearest piece of silverware and point it at Argent's throat. "Don't make me cut you."

"… That's a spoon."

Double fucking dammit. Argent laughed again, and this time, Felix felt comfortable laughing along with him. "Guess I'm a marshmallow after all."

353

"You couldn't be threatening if you tried," Argent said.

"Are you suggesting I wasn't trying?" Felix asked, to which Argent smirked once more.

Carlos brought back their drinks (of course, Felix's was iced). He asked what they wanted for their main course, still not a single fuck in his tone to be given. At least Carlos wouldn't have the energy to judge Felix's horrific pronunciations. *God, why isn't there a pronunciation guide?* (There was, but he would've preferred a key he could've understood with his one solitary brain cell) "I-I'll have the… Sirène dans les Profondeurs."

After Argent gave his order, Carlos was off, saying he'd be right back. Argent snickered. "Damn right he better." He gave a dirty smile, though when Felix groaned, Argent simply waved dismissively. "Hey, I appreciate some good booty when I see it. Don't act like you aren't the same."

Felix huffed, crossing his arms. "I admit nothing."

"Mhm." Argent sipped his drink, popping his eyebrows over and over.

"So… do you know what I ordered?"

"Mermaid tail."

Felix nearly gagged. "W-What?!"

"You ordered a mermaid tail," Argent said. "It's considered a delicacy on Sican Isle."

"That's… lovely." The idea of someone chopping off, cooking, and then eating a poor mermaid's tail? Well, there were always familiars meant solely to provide sustainable food sources. Still, the thought left him ill, and not only because of his ingrained hatred of all kinds of seafood. "What about you?" Felix asked.

"Giant demon chicken meat," Argent said, his voice nonchalant.

"… What in the actual fu—"

"Language, young man!" Argent sloshed his drink. "Learn some decency."

As strange as eating a mermaid's tail initially seemed, it tasted like chicken, just like literally every type of strange meat. (*Thank God Argent's not in the narrative to crack another gay joke.*) Argent assured him it was better than any of the food he'd been forced to scarf down back in Scotland. But as far as Argent was concerned, even literal dog shit was more appetizing than Scottish food. At the very least, the meal was made perfectly acceptable once it had been bathed in a truckload of salt. "God, I'm stuffed."

"Same." Argent moaned. "I'd get dessert, but… I think I'd explode."

"So would I."

Carlos walked back over, groaning in annoyance. "But you're both gonna order yourselves dessert anyway, aren't you?"

Of course they did. What they lacked in self-control, they more than made up for in their shared ability to devour a platter of chocolate ice cream and fruit. Again, Felix held his stomach, ready to burst at the mere thought of eating another morsel. "*Now* I'm stuffed," he said.

"As am I," Argent said. "For real this time." Felix was about to laugh along, but his cheeriness disappeared as Carlos tossed the bill onto the table, walking off and muttering profanities in what sounded to be… French? The confusion vanished as Felix peaked at the tab: 3,500 drakons. Immediately, he was ready to throw up (hoping it might allow a refund) as he hesitantly passed the bill over to Argent. Argent, though, seemed totally unfazed. "That's about $400 U.S. Pretty much what I expected."

Felix nearly fainted from the shock. "That's… a lot."

"I mean, when you eat high-class delicacies…" Argent shrugged.

"My parents give me money every couple of weeks on my card." Felix tried to steady himself. "I can—"

"No, no. I'll handle it." Even though Argent insisted on footing the bill, Felix cursed at himself, feeling like a leech. He followed Argent into the lobby. This was Argent's choice, and Felix respected that. Yet even so, the guilt drowned him, and he wallowed in self-loathing. He could've gone for any kind of distraction—a wish he would quickly regret.

A distinct chill ran down his spine as he turned to look out the window. There, atop an edifice across the street, was Vagus' silhouette.

No…

"What's up?"

Felix jumped as Argent held his shoulder, and in the time he glanced away then looked back, Vagus had vanished. *Shit! We need to get outta here.* "Let's just… let's get back to the school."

"Oh. You sure?" Argent asked.

"I can't explain here," Felix said. "But we really should go."

Argent frowned, hanging his head. "No, it's fine. I get it."

Felix's guilt mingled with his dread. He'd forgotten all about Argent wanting to do something after dinner. Felix opted to hear him out, unsure of what their plan at this point should've been. "What is it? What'd you have in mind?"

Argent pulled out a couple of tickets. "I was thinking we could go to Sican Isle. To check out the park by Lake Chalan."

"Oh. I…" That's when an idea hit Felix. "How busy is the park?"

"Wow, you've got a terrible memory," Argent said. "It's the plaza we passed through when we visited the museum during holiday break. Around then it was fine, but it's supposed to be especially crowded on weekends. Barenton is one of the top tourist traps."

"Perfect!" Felix hoped that a crowd would be just the thing to keep Vagus at bay. And this way, he could still keep Argent happy and blissfully unaware. "To the ferry, then?"

"To the ferry!"

Once again, they locked arms and strolled down to the port. Argent's eyes were filled with joy, but all Felix could think of was where Vagus was now, and why he'd taken so long to show himself again. Just what was he planning? When would he strike, and where? For so long, Felix had kept the oath secret from everyone, unable to tell anyone even if he wanted to. Not even his own mother. Even if it meant she'd have dragged him back home, he wished he could've reached out then and there so she might console him.

And all the while, Felix's eyes darted, scanning the area for any red flags. Even if they'd headed back towards Dragora, they'd still need to take a carriage by themselves to get there. The school's walls might've been secure for the most part, but the coaches most definitely weren't.

They boarded the ferry. Despite his earlier comments about being stuffed, Argent grabbed a couple bags of junk food and sodas for them both. He, of course, helped himself to half his bottle in a single gulp. But Felix didn't break into any of his snacks. They stood on the deck, out in the clear night air as stray clouds drifted overhead. The tides rolled against the ship far below. But the tranquil atmosphere couldn't set in, nor could the gentle breeze assuage Felix's fears. He raced through scenario after scenario of what Vagus could've done.

Is he on the boat now? What if he finds a way to get me and Argent alone, or just me? Or what if he goes after Argent? What if he doesn't care about the crowd at all? What if he tries to sink the ferry and kill us quietly to tie up loose ends? Did I just… did I just kill everyone here?

Argent pressed his hand onto Felix's. In that moment, the look of concern on Argent's face brought ease to Felix's nerves. "What's wrong?"

"N-Nothing." Felix stared out at the sea. Given Vagus seemed to have eyes and ears everywhere, he wasn't sure if voicing his concerns was the best idea. He could've attempted a Tether Mind to telepathically inform Argent, and perhaps that might've even circumvented his oath, but supposing he even performed the spell correctly this time, there was no telling whether Vagus had the means to eavesdrop on them anyway. And that's when a terrifying thought crossed Felix's mind: could Vagus hear his thoughts right this very moment?

"I'm... sorry." Argent drew back his hand, leaning over the railing.

"No," Felix said. "It's not you... it's—"

"Don't use that old card. I know I'm not the upstanding, well-mannered gentleman you were hopin' for. The guy that you deserve."

Felix grabbed Argent's hand. "I think we're being followed," he whispered.

"What? You—"

"The masked guy from the reserve. The one who attacked me and Lucas. I... I saw him, back at the restaurant."

A grimace slowly spread across Argent's face. "So did I."

Felix stepped back. "You...? Then why—"

"Coaches are easier targets than ferries. Figured the creep would've left us alone if we were out in public. Though I was hopin' to keep up the act."

"I stared straight at him." Felix gave himself a mental kicking. Of course Vagus would've already been aware of Felix's... awareness (fumbling is contagious). In a desperate attempt to diffuse the tension for longer than a few seconds, Felix, as always, elected for a terrible joke. "He knows that *we* know. You know?"

Argent raised an eyebrow.

"Humor keeps me from puking."

"I won't let anything happen to you." Argent's voice further comforted Felix. "We can text Rosie and the others to meet up with us. If we head back in large enough numbers, then maybe—"

"He attacked us on school property," Felix said. "When we had a huge group with us, including the groundskeeper. That creep's not gonna be afraid of a few half-baked magi all alone at night. Besides, he's probably listening to us right now. He'll find a workaround." Felix hung over the railing, the cold metal nearly freezing his arms through his jacket. The cold, thankfully, was beaten back as Argent wrapped his arm around Felix, the warmth comforting and cradling him.

"It'll be okay," Argent said.

Though the fear of what Vagus could've done to catch and hurt them was still present, Felix leaned into Argent's shoulder, counting to ten over and over in his head to ground himself. "But for the record," Felix said. "I am enjoying this date."

"Me too."

As the ferry docked, Felix checked his phone. "9:25. Rosie and the others should still be up." He texted Rosie, Penny, and Shawn, telling them to meet up near the Barenton plaza as soon as possible. Even if he had Lucas' number, Felix didn't feel right putting him into potential danger like that, especially after all he'd gone through.

Zahra immediately fired back that she'd be there ASAP, and Rosie did the same. Shawn simply left Felix on read. And Penny? Nothing. *Penny, I know you're being a responsible young adult getting her recommended eight hours of sleep. But for the love of all that is holy and most of what is not, please stop having your shit together!*

"They might be a while if the ferry's busy," Argent said. "We should wait at the plaza, and if we need to go anywhere, we stay in the busier parts of town, and we stay together."

"What about Theresa?" Felix asked. "Or Ornella? Don't you have their numbers?"

"You expect me of all people to be friends with prefects?" Argent asked.

"I was just thinking that we could use their help. You know, in case—"

"True." Argent stroked his goatee, and this sight was admittedly enough to pleasantly distract Felix, if only for a moment. "Samuel's probably out cold. Text Rosie and Zahra to bring the prefects if they can."

Felix amended his texts. No replies or reads. *Please see this before leaving. Please.*

Argent grabbed Felix's wrist, and they barged through the crowd, bobbing and weaving in whatever way they could to get lost amongst the rabble. They seated themselves on a bench in the plaza. "This should work," Argent said. "Lots of people coming in and out, but easy to find. Now, we sit and wait."

Felix leaned on Argent again, as this by far had proven the best method for soothing his anxiety. He took this moment to simply admire the sights. The last time they'd been here, the winter weather had coated everything in a layer of frost. But now, Barenton gleamed in its full glory. The cobblestone roads were free of litter. Great trees stood tall and proud, alongside gardens of blue-and-purple flowers. Doves flew around the square, and people stopped to feed them, while others flicked coins into the now running fountain of the supposed Lady of the Lake. The deep blue of the distant lake rolled off into the distance, reflecting the silver moonlight.

"That's Lake Chalan," Argent said. "Legend says it was home to the Lady of the Lake. The rivers that flow into it are named after all the different aliases she'd had through the ages: Nimue, Nyvene, Viviane…" He glared at the Camelot Museum, likely imagining Carlos was there, giving him a death glare. "And Elaine."

"You seem to know a lot about local legends," Felix said.

"Beats the shit we 'learn' in Gottschalk's class. I kinda have a soft spot for the Lady of the Lake. How she tried to help humanity in the Dark Ages, but then gave up and went on to marry into House Sican. You know, this whole city was built for her by the Sicans to remind her of home."

Felix recalled Carlos' story about how Elaine (or whatever her name was) turned against this potential utopia. But bringing it up now for a debate was likely among the worst choices he could've made for a multitude of reasons— not the least of which being that he'd miss out on Argent's snuggling. "That's… really sweet," Felix said. "But… so tragic, too."

Argent cast his look of pity towards the statue. "Humans suck, no matter the era. She learned that the hard way."

"Do you really hate them that much?"

Argent shrugged. "Not *all* of them. About… two, maybe three are fine. Fuck the rest of them, though."

Felix gave a faint smile. "My family's fine. Great, even."

"I thought your mom was a magus?"

"Yeah, but my stepdad and sisters aren't. And they're the best." *Aeris is questionable, but given my life hangs in the balance, imma be nice.*

"Good for you, I guess. You hit the lottery." Argent's apathy suddenly turned into a look of regret. "I-I'm sorry, I didn't…"

Felix took Argent's hand again. "I'm sure they'd like you."

"No one likes me."

Felix held tighter. "You never talk about your family. What about them? If that's okay with you—"

"My sister's a magus. She never talks." A look of disdain filled Argent's expression. "My... my 'mother' is human, and she's a real piece of work." His sulk briefly gave way to a faint smile. "I *do* have a pet basilisk named Fang, though." His face instantly brightened up.

"A basilisk?" Felix asked. "You mean like the snake that turns shit to stone?"

"Yeah. He's a greedy little bastard, but I love him."

"But aren't familiar pets banned in the L.U.N.?"

"No one needs to know," Argent said while winking. "But... I don't have anyone. Not at home, and not here."

Felix's mind returned to the day Frank disappeared. To that crowd gathered the day of his exam for the grant program. His grip on Argent's hand loosened, and he searched for an honest reason as to why he'd wanted to leave Vagus' promise behind him. "I just... wanna live," Felix said. "I don't wanna worry about what other people think of me. I mean, I'll never really be able to do that. No one can."

"What're you going on about?" Argent asked.

"I mean," Felix said. "Even if I was human, I'd still have to deal with people hating me for who or what I am. Like every time I deal with Denise, I get fifty questions about my sexuality that I did not invite, and I have to be careful at home where and when I speak Spanish. I'm grateful I have it pretty easy compared to most people." He recalled the stories Ramidha and Nasira had shared of their own hardships. "But I wish I could just tune out the rest of the world, and be happy in my own little bubble."

"Wow," Argent said. "Didn't expect such an irresponsible answer from such a respectable young man."

"Shut the fuck up." Felix fell into the sound of the fountain's trickling water, along with the footsteps of the people bustling about. He'd forgotten all about Vagus. Right now, Felix would've been more than happy to spend the rest of his existence here, right beside Argent, at peace in his embrace. Time slowed to a still, and the world around him faded into obscurity. It felt as though a massive weight had been lifted from his shoulders. "Hey, Argent?"

No response.

Felix opened his eyes. He leapt from the bench once he'd seen Argent had vanished. Everyone in the plaza had disappeared. The fountain ran dry, and the trees decayed, their blackened leaves fallen and rotting as the garden flowers withered. Doves lay motionless along the ground, and a cold wind bit Felix's skin. The city was silent as death. The most unsettling change, though, was that accursed black sun hanging in the blood-red sky.

"You can never make things easy for me, can you?"

Vagus, without Cinder anywhere in sight, appeared. As though he himself were a wisp manifesting from a dark-red mist. His mask had been fully repaired, and while his eyes were covered, the ire in his stare struck a guttural fear.

"W-What…?" Felix stuttered. "What did you—"

"Don't fret. Your friend is fine. He's of no importance to me." Vagus' voice resounded all around, omnipresent. Slowly, he drifted towards Felix.

"S-Stay back!" Felix couldn't run. His feet were petrified. Gritting his teeth, he threw out his hand, ready to throw a fireball. "Bolt Spark!" Nothing. Vagus grabbed his arm. Felix fought to pull away, but couldn't break free.

"I came with a warning."

Felix stopped.

"Good. You're a better listener than Lucas." Vagus let go. "Like it or not, you and he are still both oathbound to help me. Which is why I've come to tell you that the time to decide between you two is drawing near."

"I told you, I'm not—"

"Even if I told you that I knew where Frank is right now?"

Within moments, Felix's trepidation turned to fury. He'd often wondered where Frank might've been if he was still alive, and just what he would do to him once he was able to wield his magic at full strength. All the anger he'd left behind flooded back all at once. Vagus seemed to know everything, and even if he was lying, this was still a chance at revenge. And if he *was* lying, Felix would've been more than happy to kill Vagus himself. He'd already put both him and Lucas through hell.

"Fine."

Vagus chuckled. "Good to see you still have that drive."

Felix growled. "Don't think I'm happy about any of this. I'm in this for myself, and no one else. But one request."

"What?"

"I have your word that I can tell my friends as much about this as I want. Rosie, Argent, and Zahra, at the least."

Vagus snickered. "I prefer to keep my circles small, so—"

"Don't care." Felix deepened his pitch. "This is *my* circle."

Vagus paused, then laughed. "Now *that's* the fire I've always liked about you. Very well. But only those three. You, nor they, may tell anyone else without my express permission." He raised his hand. "You certainly have his temper, alright," he mumbled.

"W-What?"

Before Felix could inquire further, his right arm burned. He fell as he writhed in searing pain. The nauseating sounds of flesh cracking and bubbling nearly made him sick, fully taking hold as his eyes fell upon his arm. His skin turned a sickly deep purple as black-and-dark-red crust formed over the burns. Agony jolted through his entire body as he released an excruciating, bloodcurdling scream.

"FELIX?!"

He opened his eyes, finding himself being held tight by Argent. Rosie and Zahra knelt before him. They were back on the ferry, and the sky had returned to its usual dark purple, the black sun replaced by the moon. Felix held his aching head. "When did you guys...?" His voice was hoarse, his tongue and the back of his throat dry. Outstretching his arm and checking it over, he found that it was perfectly fine. Not one burn mark or scar to be seen.

Zahra held Felix's forehead. The coldness of her palm was a shock to the system, so much so Felix instinctively backed away a bit. "You're running a fever," Zahra said.

"You need rest," Rosie said, holding Felix's hand. "Argent said you blacked out near the fountain. I'm so happy you're okay."

"So am I." Argent held Felix close. "Rosie nearly clocked me thinking I drugged you."

Zahra nervously chuckled. "I stopped her."

"Hey!" Rosie glared. "Best friend first, logic second."

Felix's eyes were heavy. He was incredibly groggy, though he feared going back to sleep, or even shutting his eyes for more than a few seconds. "That guy. H-He—"

"He didn't show," Argent said. "Not yet, at least."

"We didn't see him." Rosie stood. "Theresa's meeting us at the port to take us back."

"Still impressed Theresa replied to you immediately," Argent said. "I wouldn't be able to get their attention even if I froze House Sican solid." He grinned. "Do I sense a… crush?"

Rosie raised an eyebrow. "What now?"

"I'm just sayin'." Argent nudged Felix. "Gays tend to travel in packs. By which I mean, the L's, G's, B's, and T's. Oh, and also the Q's. The filthy, *filthy* Q's."

"Hate to disappoint you," Felix said. "But Rosie's our token straight. Besides Zahra of course. No offense, Zahra."

Zahra smiled. "None taken!"

Rosie held her hand on her hip, rubbing her temple. "In any case, once we get back to the castle, you are headed to bed." She pointed to Felix.

"No," Felix said. "I—"

"Relax," Argent said. "Don't push yourself. It's—"

"No." Felix raised his voice, coughing. He'd spent far too long keeping his friends in the dark. He didn't feel comfortable telling them everything, but they needed to know what they were in for. The others agreed to head for Felix's dorm once they got back, where they believed they'd be safe. Or rather, *safer.* Thankfully, Rosie knew Felix well enough to offer him soda, which he swiped and sipped. Caffeine surged through his system. He sighed, feeling unbelievably refreshed. "This is why we're friends," he said.

"A dream catcher?" Felix asked.

"Yep." Rosie, seated beside Felix on the couch, pointed at her laptop on the coffee table. The screen showed a sepia-toned picture of a spider woman with slender arms, thin spindly black hair, and pitch-black eyes. "They started with the Ojibwe people in pre-colonial North America. The mythology goes that children were protected by Asibikaashi, a sort of spider woman. Some of her alternate names actually include Spider Woman, or Spider Grandmother. The dreamcatchers were meant to keep away bad dreams for the children she couldn't reach. They're thought to be woven from magical webs similar to a spider's."

Argent leaned against the fireplace mantel. "A legend that acknowledges spiders actually get rid of pests. Refreshing."

But it made sense. Vagus had used a dreamcatcher to enter Felix's daydreams all those years ago. Those spiders, their bodies shining with wildly garish colors as they surrounded him. He shivered at the thought. "Was she a magus?" Felix asked.

Rosie shrugged. "No idea, but according to the Book of Medeis, it was common amongst Ojibwe sorcerers to imbue their dreamcatchers with astral glyphs. I'd make one to keep him out, but astral magic's almost impossible to pull off. I don't know how this 'Vagus' guy even managed that."

"He'd find another way." Felix lay back on the couch.

Zahra, seated in one of the armchairs, sat with her hands clasped, hanging her head. "So, this Vagus. He forced you and Lucas into this?"

Felix hadn't told them that he'd agreed to the oath, nor that he'd taken Vagus' offer earlier that night at the promise of going after Frank. He hunched forward, sighing. "Yeah. We were forced into an oath. He said some sort of 'trial' was coming to see which of us he'd choose to go through with… whatever he wants. Some ancient artifact he refused to name. I couldn't tell anyone."

"I'm… so sorry." Zahra appeared sullen, while Rosie kept furiously typing on her laptop. Argent, meanwhile, averted Felix's gaze, alone off in the corner. Felix wished he could've told Argent sooner. The pain in his eyes killed Felix. "But… if it's an artifact he wants—"

"There are legends about a secret crypt hidden under the castle," Argent said, catching Felix off guard. "If it's real, it's bound to be down there."

"It's a *legend*," Rosie said. "Nothing more."

"You sure about that?" Argent asked. "I'm sure the royals have plenty of secrets they'd prefer not be shared with the public."

"You sound like Ivanov," Felix said. Still, he knew Argent was right. That had been exactly the case with the Organ of Judgment having vanished from the Ardor Mausoleum, while the public was told otherwise and expected to believe at face value. But even then, he dared not bring that up. Not his astral projection. Not Vivien. And most definitely not the terrifying specter that had attacked his spirit out on the sea. "I think I saw something like that in the visions from Montanari's class."

"Oh?" Argent tilted his head. "I don't remember that from last year."

Rosie coughed. "You probably slept through it."

"Fair, but rude." Argent waved his hand, walking over. "I'm just saying, it's worth some..." He stopped mid-sentence, remaining still. His glare drifted towards a tense Zahra.

"Zahra?" Felix asked. "What is it?"

"N-Nothing," she said.

"Nothing is something," Argent said. "You know about this crypt, don't you?"

Rosie scowled at him. "Watch it, Argent." He simply rolled his eyes, while Zahra grew tenser, shrinking as she pulled in her feet.

"Zahra," Felix said. "I won't force you to tell us, but we need to know. To keep whatever this guy wants out of his hands." He hated himself for lying, but he knew the truth might've made things worse. For everyone.

"I've overheard my parents talking about some kind of 'crypt' before," Zahra said. "One that's here, somewhere in the castle. Probably the same one Argent mentioned."

"You're sure they weren't just talking about a myth?" Rosie asked.

"No. Any time I tried asking them about it, they shut me down or changed the subject immediately. Eventually I gave up asking."

Argent crossed his arms. "Pretty bad liars." Again, Rosie glared, but Argent threw up his arms. "What? Means they're decent folks is all."

"This is ridiculous." Rosie shut her laptop. "Beyond far-fetched!"

Argent scoffed. "We're wizards who train at a magic school with an entire field of dragons and unicorns in our backyard. We're already a ten on the crazy scale."

"We won't get anywhere," Felix said. "Unless we get concrete info. Maybe something in the legends will give us a clue?"

"All I know," Zahra said. "Is that Concobhar and his predecessors were supposed to have kept all their relics from journeying across the world in a hidden crypt somewhere in the castle."

"Then we look into those journeys," Argent said. "Maybe good ol' Samuel knows a thing or two." He looked to Felix. "Assuming your masked friend doesn't mind that?"

Felix held his arm, somehow knowing the answer instinctively, though it gave him no reassurance. Quite the opposite, in fact. "It's fine. But if we told the professors, or refused to go through with this... he'd..."

Rosie held his shoulder. "We'll get through this."

Felix forced a smile. *I'm sorry. But... I can't afford to pass on this.* "But Argent, what makes you think Samuel of all people is gonna budge?"

"Cuz we're besties!" Argent said.

Everyone stared at him.

"We commiserate."

Silence.

Argent frowned. "We both hate everything."

Zahra tensed up a bit.

"Are you in, Rosie?" Felix asked.

"Do you even need to ask?" Rosie asked. "Of course! I'm always ready to kick some ass, especially when it's someone messing with my best friend. But for the record, I'm going to be as passive aggressive as possible about all of this."

Felix turned to Zahra, who still looked nervous. "Zahra?"

Zahra hunched forward. "My whole life, I've wanted to follow in my mother's footsteps. To be as strong as her. But I was never able to; too scared of my own shadow to risk anything, or come out of my shell. I've hated myself for that, and for having been born a cobalt. As if my mother didn't have enough to deal with. But..." She paused, taking a moment to collect herself. "I know this is the right thing to do. To stop Vagus and protect my home. And my friends."

Though Felix was thankful for her help, and admired her noble desire, he also envied that nobility. After all, he'd been fueled on nothing but anger, hatred, and spite this entire time. That's why he relented to Vagus. Would he indeed try to protect whatever artifact Vagus was after... or take it for himself? As much as he hated to admit it, Felix's pride had once again longed for the latter.

"Welp," Argent said. "Looks like our terrible trio's now a fearsome foursome!" He outstretched his arms, looking ready to burst into jazz hands. Felix was just grateful it hadn't come out as a sex joke.

Felix leaned towards Zahra. "Withstanding his jokes is part of initiation."

Zahra laughed. "Rosie and I can go to the library tomorrow to find as much as we can."

"Yeah, Rosie!" Argent smirked. "Way to be a team player!"

"It should be educational," Rosie said.

Felix yawned. By now, midnight was fast approaching, and he was ready to forget about this day entirely. "Anyway, I'd say we all need some shut-eye. By which I mean me." And with that, Rosie and Zahra bid Felix goodbye and left for their dorms. Argent had returned to his station, leaning against the wall. "Uh... what?" Felix asked.

"Oh." Argent confusedly pointed to himself. "Me too?"

"Yes," Felix said. "You too. *My* dorm."

"I just... well..." Argent pushed himself off the wall, scratching his head. "You know..."

Felix blushed. "R-Really?! One date and you're already—"

"I-I didn't, I just..."

"Door. There. Now."

Argent sulked. "Yes, sir." He traipsed towards the door.

But Felix knew he was just taking out his insecurities and fears on the easiest target. They'd already spent nights cuddled together in bed, and though he was worried he might fumble trying to take the next step, he also felt deep down, he was ready (even if Vagus had nearly killed the romantic mood). He wanted Argent there, by his side, and for them to grow even more intimate with each other. And so, Felix forced himself to speak.

"Wait!"

Argent stopped.

"I-I just... I've never—"

"Yeah, I get it." Argent turned around. "I'd be your first, right?"

"... Yeah, I know." Felix sank into the couch. "Virgin at 18. What a loser I am."

Argent, sauntering over, pinched Felix's cheek. "An adorable loser. But you don't have to if you don't want to. I want you to be comfortable with it."

"It's myself I'm not comfortable with. If you get what I mean..."

Argent squinted. "Get what you...?" Slowly, his mouth fell agape. "Ahh, I gotcha."

Felix blushed yet again. "Please don't make it a big deal. And don't make that into a pun."

"I won't. I had a good time tonight." Argent ruffled Felix's hair. With that, he bid Felix good night again and headed for the door, albeit far more happily. Yet despite the air having been cleared, Felix knew that wasn't enough.

"One more thing!"

Argent, turning again, groaned. "What is it this—"

Rushing up, Felix kissed Argent right on the lips. Felix had joked about how the idea of two pairs of lips smashing together seemed gross or awkward. But in the heat of the moment, he was elated. Even though he pulled himself back, realizing what a mess it was. "S-Sorry!" Felix said. "I, uh… I've never kissed before, so like… I have no idea what we're doing."

"You're good," Argent said. "I'll show you how."

One of Argent's hands ran through Felix's hair, while the other held his waist. Felix threw his arms around Argent's back. Goosebumps ran along his arms, and just like before, Felix felt completely safe in Argent's embrace. And through it all, they each took turns guiding the other on how best to pleasure them, the curiosity of their questions strengthening their bond rather than coming across as awkward or fumbling.

Argent carried Felix up to bed. As the night passed, Felix eased up as Argent spooned him, both of them bare beneath the blankets. Argent fell asleep rather quickly. He snored as usual, but Felix found it unbelievably cute. Just being aware of Argent's presence, right there, lying peacefully beside him, helped lull Felix to sleep. It didn't matter what life had in store. Whatever Vagus could've done to hurt him, it was inconsequential. So long as Felix had his friends, so long as he had Argent, he believed he would be okay.

Chapter Twenty

But A Sip

A SHRILL SCREECH ended his rest.

Felix shot up from bed, panting and scanning the shadows of his childhood bedroom. He held his hands and squinted. His fingers were smaller, about the size of a 12-year-old's. Throwing back the blanket, he found himself dressed in his favorite fiery-red pajamas that he hadn't worn in years. As the memories flowed back, he shivered, staring into the pitch black.

And there, unblinking in the darkness, glared a pair of amber eyes. Vibrant red, white, and azure feathers, along with a gleaming golden beak twisted into a smile, surfaced from the black. The bird sat atop the desk, as if waiting for him to awaken.

Felix scowled. "Cinder…"

Almost as if laughing through her squawks, Cinder took off and flew 'round the ceiling, the beating of her wings in rhythm with the thunder. In a flash of lightning, the window threw itself open. Felix was more than ready to hop out the window, right into the ire of the storm, and chase Vagus' infernal bird down…

Until he noticed another bird perched where Cinder had been moments before.

This phoenix, however, was blue, with pink-and-purple feathers on the tips of its wings. Its silvery beak wasn't twisted into a nefarious grin, but rather cast towards the floor, looking sullen. Felix reached out, ready to pull back his hand in case this bird tried to bite him. But it didn't. Instead, she simply flew off through the door to the hall, which creaked as it was left slightly ajar. He stood there, unsure of what to make of any of this.

"Felix?"

Lydia's voice carried from his parents' bedroom. But none of this could've been real. This had to have been another of Vagus' tricks—his "trial." If Felix wanted answers, and moreover, if he wanted a shot at finding his father out in the real world, he had no other choice. His mother called for him as he dove through the window, but he ignored it. His skin froze, numbed by the downpour and howling gusts. He opened his eyes, expecting to have to brace himself for something far worse, only for the tempest not to die out slowly, but to vanish in an instant, sunlight blinding him.

"I can't believe I'm finally here…"

Beside him stood a girl whose muted-blonde hair draped over her milky pale face. Her cobalt eyes, looking on the verge of tears, reflected the gleaming golden castle before her. She smiled warmly at the school, as though she'd returned home after a long, arduous journey. Felix squinted, recalling her features from the day of the grant program exams.

Tilda?

Felix's blood chilled as she threw dagger eyes at him, before marching right through the entrance without once glancing back. He stood there, stupefied. It was the last thing he wanted to do, but without anything else to lead him on, he followed Tilda inside.

The school was completely empty. No professors. No students. Not even the faintest echoes of whispers or footsteps across the corridors. Yet even without a real guide, Felix followed his instincts up towards his dorm in House Pyre. He threw open the door.

There, sitting on the couch and playing video games, were Rosie, Argent… and Tilda.

"Yeah!" Tilda jumped up from the couch, shooting her arms into the air as she yelled with joy. She pointed at Rosie. "In your face!"

Rosie rolled her eyes. "Whatever. So you beat us at a hundred-year-old game." She kicked her feet up on the coffee table. "Like I care."

Tilda snickered. "On that note, I'm off to dinner." She eyed Argent. "Care to join?"

"You know it." Argent stood up, cracked his back, and kissed Tilda on the cheek before holding her hand. Felix couldn't move as they strolled out. He didn't know how to react. His eyes simply remained fixed on Argent as he approached, then passed right through him, as though he were a ghost— as if he simply didn't exist. Rosie sat inside the dorm, absorbed in her phone and not even glancing up as Felix stared at her, silently begging to be seen. He choked up, his hope continuing to slowly and painfully crumble piece by piece.

"Argent!"

Felix whipped around, yelling at the top of his lungs as Tilda and Argent headed towards the exit of the common room. Nothing. He screamed again, and again, his vocal cords stinging at his voice grew raspier. Tears welled in his eyes.

"ARGENT!"

Argent didn't turn back towards Felix.

But Tilda did, and she sneered.

The great doors slammed behind her. The echoes crashed in Felix's eardrums as his knees buckled. He held onto the railing with one hand, clutching his chest with the other. Had Tilda gotten her rightful place here, would Rosie have left Felix behind for Dragora? Was Felix simply a fun distraction for Argent that could be easily replaced on a whim? Here he'd been completely forgotten. Tossed to the winds, and trapped in oblivion. The only solace he could take in this moment was that, in this hell, no one could see him cry.

No one except Tilda.

He held the rail tighter, pulling himself up. It hurt to fight against the despair. His body had grown numb, his morale steeped in apathy, but as always, spite was what brought him back onto his feet. The promise of the sweet satisfaction of taking back what had been stolen from him. That familiar craving for vengeance.

As his anger spiked, the railing cracked, and the walkway fell apart, giving way and sending Felix into a free fall. Pain slammed through his body as he hit the ground. His ribs ached as he tried and failed to push himself back up, though as his eyes fell upon the central dragon statue, he'd found that it had changed into a black fountain. Its crystal-clear waters sparkled, as though the water itself radiated light. The font called to him. Promising him that if he drank from it, or even threw himself in entirely, all of his grief and pain would be washed away.

It was only then that he'd registered that he was no longer in House Pyre. He wasn't even in Dragora Castle anymore. Overhead swam fish, and the sun appeared no larger than a murky dot through the deep blue. The only thing keeping out the sea was a clear glass dome.

El mundo es realmente una pecera inmunda.

There were no exits of any kind, though odd columns of coral surrounded the dome on the outside. A sharp chill hung in the air. Felix's arm froze against the tiled floor, further motivating him to reach out towards the alluring warmth of the reservoir. Slowly, digging his nails into the spaces between the tiles, he dragged himself across the floor, longing to have but a sip of water.

Grabbing the sides of the basin, Felix hauled himself up. His face was now mere inches from touching the water's surface. But despite how the depths beckoned him, he remained still. The dance of the ripples transfixed him. He stared deep into the eyes of his reflection, only to find his irises depicted not as their usual cobalt color, but as pearl. Just like Lucas' eyes. He leaned in closer. His nose and hair nearly touched the water…

Until his eyes turned red.

Felix pulled himself back. His eyes remained fixed upon his reflection. The ripples multiplied, blurring the mirage and transforming into a gray silhouette. Whispers, raspy and unrelenting, emanated from all around, clawing at his ears and vying for his attention. They demanded he drink from the fountain. And though he refused, he couldn't shift his gaze from the shadow in the water growing ever darker. Ever larger. The darkness turned the water into a thick, tar-like substance, and a foul miasma poured forth into the air.

Rushing to his feet, Felix stepped back, his nose burning. He hit the dome as the basin overflowed. The water distributor, a once golden chalice, was now black from grime and rot. His skin crawled. The heads of eight serpents, their glassy black eyes vacant and sharp frills jutting out from their scales, coiled about the lower tier. Jets of ichor poured from each mouth, past countless rows of tiny, glistening fangs. But what towered over them all was a sight far more insidious. Surrounding the goblet were the heads of three great dragons, all staring at Felix.

The sludge covered the entire floor. It raced up around Felix's ankles, then his knees, his waist. It tried to pull him under. As the ichor advanced, so did a storm of dark emotions batter his soul. His heartache in seeing his friends forget and abandon him. His self-loathing from lying to them. That his very existence served as nothing more than a poison to bring pain and misery to the ones he loved.

And his hatred of Frank.

Fully submerged in the tar, Felix snapped his finger. A blue spark set off a wild azure flame. The fire burned away the ichor, freeing Felix, but the entire dome caught flame. The serpentine statues of the fountain burned bright blue. Without warning, they twitched and screamed with an ear-piercing screech. The shrieks sent cracks through the glass dome, which spread 'til what lay beyond the fractures had been rendered unseen. And then, with the resounding crash of a thousand glasses breaking at once, the glass fell. The ocean rushed in, extinguishing the flames as it engulfed him. The current enwrapped Felix, spinning him violently, carrying him off with the undertow.

Felix forced his eyes open, only to be greeted by the darkness of the deep sea. A void extending forth without end. But as he squinted, he gasped with fear, swallowing a bit of water as he pushed himself back. A black outline grew larger in the distance, coming closer, and closer. This wasn't the sea. This was some sort of creature, amorphous and rapidly approaching. Its existence alone filled Felix not with any of the terror, anger, or sorrow the ichor had before, but rather a pervasive emptiness. A cold, existential dread reinforcing that he was alone, and that one day, there wouldn't be even one remnant of himself, nor anyone he loved. That his love was inconsequential. Something short-sighted and trivial, and ultimately meaningless.

Then the creature's eyes opened.

Hundreds of glaring, yellow-green eyes shot open, devoid of any and all emotion. They cut through the murkiness of the water. Right through Felix. He floated, trapped in a nauseating paralysis. The whispers returned, ever louder, ever crueler, telling him to remain and accept his fate. To return himself to the depths. He closed his eyes and drifted backward. Nothing left to fight for. No one to remember him.

No one.

Yet despite that, something within him told him to fight back. To hell with whatever this thing was and what it was telling him. To hell with this idea that nothing mattered. Even if they didn't remember him, Felix still loved his friends and family more than anything, and knew he had to do whatever it took to get back to them. Out of whatever nightmare Vagus had trapped him in.

Opening his eyes, Felix focused as much as he could through the mental fog of this demented dream. The water around him turned into air. Though the creature remained, he ignored it and rushed towards the orb of light high above him. He reached out as the light grew stronger, totally consuming his vision.

In an instant, the light vanished, and Felix found himself dry and able to breathe perfectly fine. The black limestone floor extended down a massive dark-brown corridor. High ceilings faded into the darkness, while black torches burned with purple fire. Was this the crypt? Or rather, some warped recreation? He got his answer as his eyes fixed on a white staircase leading to a massive pedestal at the very end of the hall. There, sitting atop it, gleamed a deep-crimson light, calling out to Felix from afar.

The ring.

He sprinted, only to be cut off by a wall of blue-green fire. The flames surrounded him on all sides. Footsteps raced past him, and though this figure was completely obscured and didn't speak, it didn't need to refer to Felix as "Cobalt" for it to be clear who this was. This wasn't another part of the dream, nor an illusion. This was Lucas.

Bracing himself, Felix dashed through the fire. He kept telling himself he wouldn't feel the pain so long as he didn't let his fear take hold. He didn't even pay attention to the slight stinging sensation along his arms and legs. Instead, he threw out his arm.

"Bolt Spark!"

A blue fireball shot forth. As Lucas turned, he fell backward from the blast. Felix ran past him, heading for the ring, only for Lucas to grab his ankle and trip him. Lucas leapt forth and wrapped his hands around Felix's throat. He couldn't strangle him here, but the look in Lucas' eyes disturbed Felix. His face was red, his expression thick with desperation, like a cornered animal in its last moments. Felix tried to speak. To say anything to get through to

Lucas. But when it became clear Lucas wouldn't listen, Felix pushed him off, throwing him into the wall.

"Lucas, you need to stop! This isn't right. You don't need—"

"What the hell do you know?!" Lucas' shout echoed across the corridor. "Don't act like you're above me, Cobalt! All you want is power!"

"And you don't?"

Lucas slammed his fist against the wall. "This is my only chance." His voice grew brittle, tears welling as he shut his eyes tight. "My only chance to prove I'm not a mistake. That I can do the right thing."

Listening to Lucas' words, Felix heard himself in his darkest moments. Slowly, he approached. "Lucas," he said, keeping his voice soft. "Listen to me. You aren't well. Let's talk this out, and maybe we can still—"

Lucas lunged, yelling with his hand engulfed in blue-green fire. Felix dodged. Without any other option, he kicked Lucas to the ground. If he stalled any longer, Lucas would get the ring, and there was no telling how dangerous he would become. At least, that's what Felix told himself. Still, in this moment, Felix believed if anyone was going to beat Vagus at his own game, it was going to be him.

He raced up the steps. A two-headed snake coiled around itself, forming the ring's band, while the roaring face of a lion, crafted in silver, glinted in the head. Tattered black angel wings stretched out from either side. In the center shone a blood-red gemstone. For a moment, within a narrow golden halo, flashed a deep-purple cat's eye. It called out to Felix again. He swiped the ring, and as he gripped his hand in pain, Lucas' muffled scream was drowned out in the bellowing of erupting flames.

He gasped for air as he shot out of bed.

Felix was awake now, panting and wiping sweat from his forehead. He pinched his arm just to double check this wasn't another part of this nightmare. Letting out a sigh of relief, he lay back down, and Argent threw his arms back over Felix. "Everything okay?" Argent's voice was soft and groggy, though he still nudged in closer to hold Felix tight.

"Yeah. Just a bad dream." Felix stared at the ceiling. Once Argent closed his eyes again, Felix held up his hand. No glyph. No sign of the oath. But deep down, he knew it was still in effect. There was no going back now. He was Vagus' champion. Felix lowered his hand, processing what this meant. "Hey, today's the first day of spring, right?"

"Mhm," Argent mumbled.

"In that case…" Felix kissed Argent on the lips. "Happy birthday."

Argent slowly opened his eyes, smiling back. "Huh. Someone bothered remembering. Truth be told, I didn't even wanna remember."

"Well, too bad." Felix held onto Argent, closing his eyes. "If you're nice about me celebrating you turning 20, I'll let you tease me about my birthday next month."

Argent chuckled. "Deal."

So that's how it was.

Lucas put in all that time, all that effort, into gaining the power he needed to put an end to the Enlightened and their schemes. And it was all stolen overnight by some halfwitted cobalt runt.

He didn't bother leaving his bed. Instead, he shut his eyes, and through his tears, drifted back to sleep. There was no point in trying anymore. No point in anything.

He was indeed the worthless burden everyone condemned him to be.

Chapter Twenty-One

O Firebird

"PLEASE keep your sweat to yourself."

Nasira nearly gagged as she held her nose. Felix had plopped himself into his chair, gasping between chugs of his water bottle, all while wiping sweat from his forehead. His skin burned, though not as badly as his muscles. He coughed into his arm.

"Don't... tell me... what... to do." Felix wheezed between fragments.

Zahra twiddled her thumbs. "So... I take it the combat league meetings are going well?"

"Oh no. I got my ass kicked as usual. But damn if I didn't try!" *Two or three fireballs in a row will do that to a cobalt.* Since he'd passed Vagus' trial, Felix had dedicated himself fully to the Magus Combat League once again. Anything to keep him at the top of his game. Though admittedly, he hadn't been feeling well before today's meeting. Lucas hadn't attended any of his classes or been seen around campus since the trial, and Gottschalk seemed more than happy to take out her concerns for her nephew on Felix, as though he were the one tormenting Lucas.

And on a pettier note, Felix was a tad bitter Argent had seemed to completely forget about his birthday. April 26th. Felix never looked forward to this day, but for once, he'd been tepidly excited for Argent to tease him, or acting especially sweet, or... something. But nothing. Argent had even strangely insisted that he needed to be alone in his dorm to focus on his studies, though Felix knew Argent couldn't have cared less for his academics.

"I hope everyone's doing well today."

Montanari threw her belongings onto her desk, then jumped to sit atop a stack of books and kick her feet. Normally, Felix would've been excited for Montanari's class, especially considering today they'd be covering the end of the War of Angels. But instead, dread crept over him and darkened his mood. Lucas was gone. As such, Montanari had to rely on the glyphs inscribed on the classroom's walls. She took out her wand and began the incantation:

"O Watchers of the Past, Guardians of the World, Chroniclers of its Story, and Keepers of its Secrets, open the path to this dead age, and see our journey there is safe. Glyph: History Unfold!"

The illusions took form. The full moon hung in the sky above a vast forest. There, nestled between the shadows of trees, lay a hidden encampment. A red tent stood within the crag of a small hill. Inside the tent, a detailed schematic had been rolled out onto the center table, lit by the flickering lanterns hanging overhead. Gathered around this map and hunched over in observation were Alonza and two others: a slightly older woman in a blue coat, with light-olive skin and black hair curled back into a braided ponytail; and a man younger than Hilarion with messy sandy-blonde hair, freckled white skin, and a dark-orange long-sleeved tunic.

Alonza raised her head, her profile half illuminated, and her voice grave. "Oscar, are you sure this entrance to the mine will be the least guarded?"

Oscar nodded. "Elisa may have stepped up security on the central island, as well as Pyre and Zephyr, but Ley Isle should contain the lowest concentration of her forces."

"I still don't see the point in this." Calista, hand on her hip, stared up at the lanterns, her face devoid of any care or investment. "If we get trapped in those mines, it's all over. What could be down there that's worth all this effort?"

"Resources." Alonza kept her eyes on the schematics. These mines—which ran deep underground, said by some to even connect the isles beneath the Sea of Sagramore—were the empire's primary mythril source, left under the complete control of the Crown for centuries. "Whoever controls these mines controls the tools needed to win this war. If we cut off my mother's supply line for her army, we can further build our resistance. Not to mention our scouts have detected unusual activity around the mines for weeks now. We need to stop her."

"You mean kill her."

Alonza glared, clutching the table and trying to steel herself. The realm needed someone to stop Elisa before she wreaked havoc on the human world. Her friends needed her, especially Hilarion, who was still off in their tent, sleeping the days away and trapped in the shock of having lost his brother in such a horrific way in front of his eyes. And here she was. The daughter of the woman who took Drakon away.

"Alonza?"

Ligeia, dressed in her green nightgown with her black hair flowing down, peeked inside the tent. Her voice was weak. Alonza motioned her inside, and Calista and Oscar let them be, Calista tossing her signature callous smirk on the way out. Ligeia stood on the opposite side of the table. "Please tell me you've been resting," she said.

"I don't have time to rest." Alonza kept her eyes fixed on the layout of the mines, scanning and analyzing for any and all points of access in case they needed a quick escape. "I have to make sure I don't make any oversights."

"You're going to make oversights if you can hardly keep your eyes open."

Alonza held her forehead, giving herself permission to close her eyes for but a moment. And that moment felt infinitely refreshing after days of hardly any sleep. "Perhaps you're right." Her fingers dug into the wood. *Is it inevitable? Is everyone I love doomed to losing themselves or their lives?* A tear rolled down her cheek. She'd kept her mind from idling for too long, because then her thoughts would wander back to why she'd even led this resistance. To the moment she lost her best friend, and it was tragically confirmed that her mother had indeed become a monster.

Ligeia, who'd walked around the table, held Alonza's shoulder. "You've gone over the plan several times. Now, you must rest, so you'll have the strength to lead your forces."

Alonza hung her head.

"None of this is your fault. And I commend your courage." Ligeia's grip tightened as she began to shed tears herself. "Please... help Elisa find peace."

"... I promise."

With that, Ligeia returned to her lodgings, while Alonza rolled up the schematics and made her way back to her tent. She found Hilarion snoring, tossing and turning in his sleep, slightly weeping. Admittedly, Alonza was less tired and more dreading tomorrow. If she'd tried to sleep now, she'd have been fighting her nerves all night. Leaving the plans locked in her desk drawer, and notifying her guards of her stroll, she wandered through the forest until she reached the shoreline. And there, standing before the rolling tides and staring up at the moon was Calista.

"Shouldn't you be asleep?"

Alonza jumped. Calista hadn't turned around, and Alonza didn't think her approach had been that loud, especially given she hadn't even reached the rocky shore of pebbles yet. "Can't," Alonza said. "I have to focus."

"You realize you can't lead an army," Calista said. "If you're about to pass out."

"And what about you?" Alonza asked. "Aren't you tired at all?"

Calista grimaced. "More irritated than tired. The twins wanted to come along and wouldn't take no for an answer." She grumbled. "I swear, I loathe their existences even more than Santiago's."

Normally Alonza would've assumed this was a normal response from any older sibling. When it came to Antonio, even in spite of his actions, Alonza still loved him, and lamented that he'd been dragged down Ettore's dark path towards demise. But Calista? She'd never referred to anyone in her family by "Mother," "Father," or "Brother." Rather, she'd always insisted on using their names—not even nicknames. The scorn in her voice unnerved Alonza.

"If you have something to ask," Calista said, her voice deadpan. "Say it."

"… Why are you helping me?" Alonza asked.

Calista rolled her eyes. "Boredom?"

"I don't mean to sound rude, but… you've always been so apathetic. Even now, after all we'd been through, you still seem unshaken. Ever grim. Ever morose. So… why risk your life for a cause you don't even care for?"

Calista yawned. "Truth be told, Firebird, whether I live or die isn't a big concern for me."

Alonza furrowed her brows. "What?"

"If Elisa wins and we all die, the world is thrown into apocalyptic chaos like humanity has never seen before. Sounds like a fun time to me. But if you win and kill her…"

Alonza gulped.

"Then it'll be business as usual." Calista waved her hand dismissively. "I'd be all for your mother's team if it weren't for… certain obligations." She stared at her hand, her eyes full of contempt. "But I will tell you this: your whole noble approach of wanting to inflict as few casualties as possible? It's pathetic."

Alonza clenched her fists. "I know it's not at all pragmatic. But—"

"Not simply impractical," Calista said. "It's a fundamental misunderstanding of the way our world works." She stared out at the point the horizon met the sea. "People believe in different things, they kill each other over them, and whoever wins shapes the world. Simple. Effective." She sneered. "You know, the humans have their own saying: kill, or be killed." Without another word, Calista winked at Alonza before sauntering back into the woods, though she did mumble under her breath:

"A thousand lifetimes haven't prepared me for this, and neither would a thousand more."

Alonza sat along the shore, shaken as the waves washed over her toes. Perhaps Calista was right. At this point, Alonza had already known there was no saving her mother. But she'd hoped that perhaps she might've been able to convince Gianna to turn back. To take a stand, for once in her life. But soon enough, sunrise would arrive, and along with it, the ultimate choice.

After a good cry, Alonza returned to her lodgings and drifted to sleep. She woke up groggy, the pain still battering her spirit, but she forced herself up and got dressed regardless. Hilarion was already gone, strangely. Donning her red-and-gold armor and cape, and sheathing her red mythril sword, Alonza headed out, meeting Calista and Oscar over by the tent, both dressed in their blue and gold armor respectively.

"Have either of you seen Hilarion?" Alonza asked, to which Oscar shook his head no, while Calista, ever detached, shrugged.

"If you're worried about me, don't be."

Hilarion approached. From head to toe, he'd covered himself in dark-green armor with the Crest of Zephyr proudly displayed on his breastplate. Though his face was pale and his eyes bloodshot, he still possessed a look of resolve.

"Let's rally the troops," Alonza said.

Alonza's forces made their way towards the outskirts of the city of Malory, capital of Ley Isle. Malory had been built within the seaside mountains, and as such, terraces were connected by dozens of staircases. From their position, Alonza's team remained just out of sight in the distance. How distraught were the ordinary people living here? Had they too experienced that deep-seated fear of not knowing what the next day would bring?

Today, Alonza would end their terror herself.

They made their way through the mountain trails, which led them to the bottom of a dark valley. An entrance had been carved into the rock face. Oddly enough, there didn't seem to be anyone on guard. Alonza had expected some kind of patrol to be present, even if underwhelmingly slim, but this wasn't right. "Is it normally this quiet?" she asked Oscar.

Oscar held his chin. "This isn't quiet. It's silent."

"A trap?" Calista shrugged. "Totally a trap."

Alonza wanted to tell Calista off, but she knew she was right. "If we march inside, it'll be easier to take us all out at once. We should send a scout up ahead."

"I'll go."

Hilarion stared down into the dark depths, his eyes narrowed. Alonza didn't want to cause a scene. But at the same time, was Hilarion being brave, or simply reckless? She held his shoulder and whispered, "Are you sure about this?"

He pulled himself free. "If I'm not back in five minutes, assume the worst." Without another word, Hilarion marched on, vanishing into the darkness. Surely he knew what he was doing. He'd report back in no time. But the seconds dragged on, stretching into agonizing minutes. Alonza tapped her foot, trying desperately to suppress any outward sign of her growing fear.

"I'm going in."

Alonza marched towards the entrance, though Oscar rushed to pull her back. "Alonza, we shouldn't just march in when our scout hasn't returned. Maybe we should fall back and—"

She swatted away his hand. "No." Her voice was grave. "My friend is down there and might need help." Whether or not anyone else was willing to follow her, she was ready to dash into the mines, find Hilarion, and stop whatever her mother was scheming single-handedly. But that'd most certainly get her killed, and this fight was bigger than just her and her own issues.

Slowly, Alonza turned back.

"*We're* going in."

With that, she led Oscar, Calista, and the soldiers down the tunnel. The passage wound down through the mountains. Deeper and deeper it went until it opened into a spacious cavern, with several exits into other tunnels. Massive mythril crystals of all colors hung from stalactites, emerged from the cave walls, and sprouted out of the ground. Shining crystals of unimaginable beauty and immeasurable value, all being mined by ordinary people, including even children and the elderly.

Each one of them were in shackles, ceaselessly chipping away at the rocks with pickaxes and tossing the fragments into carts. One older man had seemingly passed out, lying on the ground unmoving as a middle-aged woman cried over him, only to be forced back to work by the guards.

Alonza had to hold herself back from intervening. Still, there was no sign of Hilarion anywhere. They needed some plan of attack, and moreover, to get these people to safety. After informing her forces of her strategy, she led half of her forces around the cavern, keeping cover behind large, untouched crystals, and hiding on the far side of the cavern.

"Quit slacking, kid!"

A pair of soldiers towered a young olive-skinned boy, his brown hair tangled with sweat and dirt as he trembled at the weight of his pickaxe, his cobalt eyes cloudy with tears. He took another swing. The axe hit the red mythril, and a flurry of orange sparks flew as the blade wedged itself into the crystal. The boy covered his face, shouting as some of the sparks singed through his clothing, burning his skin. He fell, clutching his arm and panting.

"What a weakling," one of the guards said while the other laughed. "Can't even handle a little manual labor."

The other guard grabbed the boy by the shirt collar, lifting him off the ground. Alonza's blood boiled at the guard's sick grin. He brandished his bayonet-style wand with his free hand. "What do you say we teach this cobalt runt what real pain is?"

"NO!"

Shooting up, Alonza threw a couple of fireballs, sending the guards flying back into the far wall. She rushed to the boy as he fell. She asked if he was okay, though he couldn't answer. He trembled as Alonza cupped his face and dried his tears. The other miners stared in awe. Some dropped their pickaxes, while the guards whispered and grumbled amongst themselves about the empress' rogue, treasonous daughter.

"You've finally decided to show yourself."

The guards stood at attention as Oliver Ley, the eldest son and heir to his house, marched towards Alonza. He held his chin high. His blonde hair was slicked back, tucked beneath the black cap matching his uniform, upon which was proudly displayed Elisa's crest over his heart. Behind him traipsed Santiago, who'd appeared as though he hadn't slept in weeks from his tired eyes. "Your mother's been worried about you," Oliver said.

"What in the world do you think you're doing?" Alonza returned to her feet, projecting her voice. "How can either of you possibly justify this cruelty?"

"A necessary sacrifice," Santiago said. "If we're to return to the human world and rightfully claim it as our own, then we need as many resources as possible." He averted his gaze as Alonza glared at him.

"You'd do well to know your place," Oliver said.

"I don't believe your father said the same thing when it came to Concobhar," Alonza said.

Oliver gripped his wand tighter. "My father was a fat, drunken fool. It's not our place to question those in power. Concobhar's madness was only stopped by another who had the strength to do what was needed—your mother. If you truly believe that you deserve that power instead..." He pointed his wand at Alonza. "Then prove it."

The guards surrounded her on all sides, their weapons at the ready. Alonza reached for her weapon, but before she could grab it, a torrent of water rushed through and pushed the soldiers back. Those who remained were sent flying back by large rocks shooting up from the ground. Santiago backed away as Oscar and Calista marched to Alonza's side.

"What do you think you're doing, little brother?" Oliver asked.

"What I believe is right." Oscar, slightly shaken, straightened his back as he held his wand. "Can you say the same?"

Oliver simply grimaced.

"I'm honest that I believe you're all horrible and aggravating." Calista glanced at her father. "Especially you, Santiago. You don't even have a spine for me to floss my teeth with." She giggled as her father's eyes widened. "Why don't you go find your mom?" Calista asked Alonza. "We can handle these lowlives."

Alonza raised an eyebrow. "My mother?"

"Just a hunch."

Without time to question Calista, Alonza heeded her advice and ordered her soldiers to escort the civilians to safety. With that, she took down one of the mine shafts, blasting away any guards standing in her way with rapid bursts of fire. She nearly fell as the tunnel violently shook. The deeper she made her way underground, the louder the rumbling became, and the more frequently the tremors occurred. Though she didn't want to believe it, her mother was here. And whatever she was trying to do, it needed to be stopped.

Elisa had to die.

The path opened up, and Alonza stopped as light poured into her eyes. The gray skies stretched far above. Thunder rumbled in the distance, though the sound of a distant storm was easily overpowered with the ear-piercing rumbling growing ever louder, along with what sounded like a jet of flames pouring forth every few seconds. Here, on this slab of earth protected from the sea on all sides by massive rock walls, was a deep pit. A quarry not home to mythril, but ordinary stone used for building materials. Deep-purple sparks, along with a bright-violet light, radiated from the depths in rhythm with the sound of the flames.

"Alonza? What're you doing here?'

Alonza turned to see Gianna, in a black military uniform, running out of the tunnel behind her. She hadn't drawn her wand or any kind of weapon, and so neither had Alonza. Still, Gianna clutched her hands, sullen.

Alonza slowly approached. "Gianna, you can't honestly believe in what Elisa is doing." She paused. "She isn't our mother anymore."

Gianna's face reddened. "Of course she is! How could you even say that?!"

"Our mother wouldn't kill or attack her own children."

"… Alonza…" Gianna cast her eyes to the ground. "Father is gone. Antonio is gone." She began to tear up. "She's… she's all we have left. She's all *I* have left."

As much as Gianna's words hurt, Alonza had never been close with her older sister. Gianna had always been far too servile for Alonza's liking. But right now, it became clear how lost Gianna was, and in a way, Alonza felt the same. But if a new, positive direction was what Gianna needed, then the answer became clear. Alonza stepped forward, smiling. "You have me." She held out her hand.

Gianna looked off towards the pit, wringing her hands. Slowly, she glanced back at her sister, and took her hand. "Okay."

A ghastly scream chilled Alonza's blood, nearly knocking both sisters off their feet as the earth shook once again. They rushed towards the edge of the pit. Far below was Elisa, soot and ash coating her face. Black wings of smoke jutted out from her back as she hovered above the bottom of the quarry, shooting a torrent of deep-violet fire. "W-What...?" Alonza could barely process the moment. "What is she doing?"

"She's been at this for hours," Gianna whispered. "She refuses to explain."

The flames stopped. Slowly, Elisa descended, letting out a hellish wail as she slammed her fists into the rocks relentlessly. Alonza tried to make out her mother had been mumbling to herself. The glimmer of the blood-red ring on Elisa's finger caught Alonza's attention. Elisa's face had grown purple as a corpse, blood vessels pulsing just below the skin, her eyes now a deep crimson with black cat's eye slits.

"R-Run!"

Alonza grabbed Gianna's wrist and pulled, but they both fell as a purple fiery blast shot up from the pit, creating the largest tremor yet. The burning pillar reached into the sky, parting the clouds and eclipsing the sun before it could break through them. The column collapsed. There Elisa hovered, her wings outstretched on either side, staring. She dove. Alonza pushed herself up and pulled Gianna onto her feet, dodging with not a moment to spare.

"Why do you stand against me?" Elisa's cold, raspy voice echoed all around. "Why would you turn against your own mother?"

"I thought you wanted to save this land," Alonza said, trying to project strength. "Yet here you are, enslaving and killing in cold blood. And all for what? To destroy the human world?"

"What I do, I do for the good of all."

"You're doing this for yourself!" Alonza reached for her sword. "You want to lead this coalition of sorcerers who will command the world, even if you have to destroy your own family to get there. But we won't—"

"You misunderstand." Elisa's tender voice cut right through Alonza. "My goal is not for the supremacy of sorcerers over mankind. I seek to end all pain. To destroy this mortal coil and bring about a new era, beyond the short, pointless lives we are born caged within."

Alonza could barely speak. "… You're insane."

Elisa frowned. "I see I'll have to enlighten you both." The deep red on her finger glowed, and a purple-black flame appeared in her palm. She tossed the fireball. As Alonza and Gianna dodged, Gianna's cape fell, as did the firebird's kiss tucked in her hair. Elisa picked it up, twirling the stem. "Such beauty. Such vitality. Shame it must one day wilt and die." The flower burst into flames, its blackened petals scattering as they fell. Without warning, she took flight again, the smoke from her wings spreading to cover the sky.

Absolute terror gripped Alonza. Instinctively, she drew her sword. "Fire Twister!" A fiery cyclone erupted from the blade. Elisa held out both her hands, and the fire stopped just before her. She pulled the fire into her palm, morphing it into a sphere, the flames turning purple.

"Final Tempest!"

A tornado formed around Elisa, pulling the fireball apart and obscuring her from sight. Hilarion, having emerged from the mines, ran to Alonza and Gianna's side. "What the hell is going on?" he asked.

"I don't know," Alonza said. "But we need to go. Now." Alonza grabbed Gianna's shoulder, trying to shake her free from her stupor. "Gianna! Gianna, c'mon!" With no luck whatsoever, Alonza dragged Gianna along.

The tornado turned violet, barreling towards them and quickly closing the gap. Alonza ran as fast as she could. Sweat beaded on her forehead, and her lungs surged, but the entrance back into the mines seemed eternally out of reach. Hilarion flicked his wand, sending Alonza and Gianna forth into the tunnel. Alonza panted as the pain rang through her body. She forced herself up, clinging to the tunnel walls.

But in that moment, she wished she hadn't looked.

The tornado's howls muffled Hilarion's scream. Alonza fell to her knees. As the tornado dissolved, Hilarion's corpse hung in the air for a few agonizing moments before falling into the quarry below. Gianna tried to force Alonza to her feet, but Alonza was steeped in shock.

Elisa landed before the quarry. "The more you fight…" Her voice carried with ease, as though she were speaking directly into Alonza's ears. "The more you will suffer." Alonza's eyes welled with tears. Gianna tried shaking her, but Alonza had lost all will to go on.

> *Firebird, o Firebird*
> *I know you're scared*
> *Your wing's broken and it's a long way down*
> *But if you trust the absurd*
> *You can trust me, if you dare*

Slowly, Alonza raised her head as Elisa approached. Gianna backed away, but Alonza simply sat there, sobbing.

> *Firebird, o sweet Firebird*
> *You're meant for more*
> *Than hiding away up here in your nest*
> *You long to see the world*
> *But the world is cold and unfair*

Elisa knelt, cupping Alonza's cheek and looking right into her daughter's eyes.

> *But Firebird, o Firebird*
> *That's why I'm here*
> *To catch you if you fall*
> *And if you're ever plagued by fear*
> *Remember our song and call*

The tears flowed again. Alonza hadn't heard her mother sing this lullaby in years. She wanted nothing more than to hug her mother tight, and never let go. To give into whatever deranged plan Elisa had concocted, so long as it meant an easy, comfortable life with what little family she had left…

But Drakon and Hilarion were family too.

"I'm sorry, Mother."

With a flick of her wrist, Alonza unleashed a point-blank blast of orange fire, sending both herself and Elisa flying in either direction. Alonza fell back, tumbling through the dirt. Scratches and bruises formed along her arms.

Gianna raced to her side to heal her, but the whole time, Alonza's eyes were locked on Elisa. On her knees, she stared into the pit, clawing at her own arms. After a long, deafening silence, she let out a bloodcurdling shriek.

As if on cue, her wings jutted out again, shooting off purple fireballs at the rock walls. The earth cracked, water seeping through as the fractures spread. Gianna pulled Alonza to her feet and raced back down the mine tunnel, but Alonza's gaze remained fixed. The walls around the enclosure gave way. A thunderous clap sounded off as the ocean rushed in, the tides engulfing the whole quarry, then sending more waves rushing through the tunnel. The water swept the sisters off their feet, numbing their senses as it carried them through the underground passages.

Grabbing Gianna, Alonza dove underwater and, recognizing the main chamber, swam through the passage leading back to the surface of Ley. They reached the valley, and relished in their escape as they coughed and gasped for air. The sun's warmth wrapped around them. A bright smile spread across Alonza's face, only to fade as she fully processed what had befallen her mother.

Tears rolled down her cheeks again. She held her chest, refusing to let herself cry. A glint caught her gaze as she dried them. There, sitting in a nearby puddle, was that accursed black ring with its blood-red jewel. Hatred and anger burned within her. While Gianna was busy looking around for anyone else nearby, Alonza swiped the ring and shoved it into her pocket, determined to never let another soul wear it.

The rest of the lesson was lost on Felix, the ring's glow transfixing him until everything went white, then faded back to the classroom. He rubbed his eyes.

"That went on longer than expected." Montanari cracked her back, checking her phone. "We'll be back to the usual curriculum for the rest of the year, so... go enjoy the day!" She gathered her belongings as she rushed off, but as the other students left, Felix simply stood with his mouth agape.

"Um..." Nasira frowned, shutting Felix's mouth. "Don't do that when your breath smells like death, okay?"

"Felix?" Zahra asked. "Are you...?"

Felix chastised himself for overlooking the ring for so long. The hair on the back of his neck stood on end, as he half expected Vagus to be lurking somewhere just out of sight, observing him. But the one staring at him was

Carlos. He'd tucked himself away in the far back corner, averting his gaze and whistling the moment Felix's sight fell on him. And right away, his blood chilled.

"Felix?"

"I-It's nothing." Felix gathered his belongings and made a break for the door. "I have to check on something."

"Uh, wait!" Zahra rushed to catch up. "Are you going back to your dorm?"

"Yeah? Where else would I go?"

"It's just…" Zahra twiddled her thumbs. "Maybe we could… go somewhere else beforehand? Perhaps in the city?"

Felix raised an eyebrow. "Zahra, are you okay?" He stopped himself, facepalming. "Oh crap, did I forget to tell you?" *Damn my memory.* "Argent and I are…"

"Oh, no, no, you told me!" Zahra said. "I mean, I kinda *was* there on your date. When you uh…"

Nasira tilted her head.

Oh god, I suck.

"Anyway!" Zahra yelled, trying to grab their attention. "Uh… I need you… for—"

Nasira held Zahra's shoulder. "Zahra's been flunking and needs help studying." Nasira smiled, while Zahra nonchalantly scratched her head.

"Really?" Felix asked. "You of all people, Zahra? Well… I guess in that case, we could go to the library. But I need to do some research of my own while we're there."

"Perfect!" Zahra said, while Nasira simply shook her head. They made their way to the library, though not once did Zahra discuss her studies with Felix. Still, Felix didn't mind, and took the opportunity to do a deep dive into Medeian history to learn as much about that ring as he could. At last, he found a hefty, dusty book all about ancient magical artifacts, no doubt cataloging thousands of different objects of power. There was no way this could've helped him pin down what Vagus was after before today. But now…

The moment he hit the right page, he stopped. Even as a drawing, the rendition of the ring's red jewel glowed, capturing Felix's eyes. This was it.

The Ring of Nergal.

According to the book, the ring was believed to bestow its wielder with the power of the Black Flame, which burned darker than even Aviur's fire. Zahra and Nasira insisted they head back to Felix's dorm immediately. Begrudgingly, Felix checked out the book for future reference. He was so obsessed with this newfound knowledge, he hadn't bothered questioning what this was all about. Why they'd insisted on escorting him back to House Pyre without delay.

Until Felix turned the knob, opened the door, and nearly lost his hearing. "HAPPY BIRTHDAY!"

He nearly fell back as the shouts deafened him. Glitter had been thrown into the air, blocking out the ceiling and blinding Felix with how much it shimmered. He staggered as a party horn blared in his ear, nearly rupturing his eardrum. Zahra caught him. Before Felix could recenter himself, he found his back nearly crushed as both Rosie and Argent hugged him tight, lifting him off the ground. "M-My… spiiiiiiine," Felix croaked.

"Oh, sorry!" Rosie and Argent said in unison as they backed off.

Felix fell back to his feet, wheezing and cracking his back. Beside the other members of his fearsome foursome (*Blame Argent*) and Nasira, present were Penny, Shawn, and even Floria, all donning pointy plastic party hats. Floria looked unamused as ever, while Penny and Shawn assisted each other in getting glitter out of their hair and clothes. "So which of you cretins set this up?" Felix glared at Rosie.

Rosie shrugged. "I was just gonna prank and humiliate you. But Argent wanted to throw this instead. So…" She stepped aside and curtseyed, introducing Argent like a king.

Argent, scratching his head, blushed. "Technically you said I could tease you."

"Yeah." Felix kissed Argent on the cheek and held his hand. "I did." His spirits lifted even higher as he saw no less than five boxes of pizza atop the coffee table, along with several soda bottles. "This is all I could ask for! The Lord has shown mercy! For once."

They gathered all around, playing video games on Argent's console that he'd hauled over from his dorm. Surprisingly, Ornella was totally fine with the party, so long as they saved her at least four slices of pizza with pineapple. Felix cringed at the demand. But given Ornella's kindness, it was the least they could do (so long as the rest of the pies were free of that godforsaken fruit). The night went on, and Felix and the others wound up losing their voices from cackling and howling.

By the end of the party, everyone save for Felix, Argent, and Rosie had returned to their own dorms. While the birthday boy relaxed on the couch and groaned from his stomachache—and in defiance of that ache, munching on popcorn as he held the bowl over his chest—Rosie and Argent resumed their duties as cleanup crew. "I told you not to eat so much so fast," Rosie said, tsk-tsking. "And you're still eating! Dumbass."

Felix slurred as he tried to force out the words. "Shut up!" He nearly rolled off the couch as he pointed dramatically at Rosie, though hilariously, he'd missed where she stood. Cheese hangovers apparently made it impossible to turn one's head even slightly. At this point, Felix was ready to fall into a food coma. He held another flake between his fingers, squinting, observing the glistening gold of the butter drenching it. "Last piece of popcorn was that if Eunice becomes Dragon Skinner, we get married. So this one..." He popped it into his mouth, and as he chewed said, "Darius and I get married."

"Uh... you okay?" Rosie asked.

"I'm using false realities filled with my darkest, most sinful fantasies, along with a bucket of unhealthy cope food, to deal with the fact that a psychotic homicidal terrorist and probably cultist is using me as a pawn in his sick game," Felix nonchalantly said. "Now help me decide whether I should go for Eunice and her journeys around the globe, or if I should settle for being a nice house spouse with Darius!"

Argent cleared his throat.

"You need something, babe?" Felix didn't even lift his head.

Argent sighed. "Darius. Darius is hot."

"He *is* very brooding." Felix took a moment to ponder. "Especially with that windswept hair and goatee." He swooned. "But I feel Eunice has a very comforting yet commanding presence."

Rosie snickered. "Commanding?"

"Don't make this weirder than it already is!"

She shrugged. Once she and Argent finished cleaning (Argent insisted on wiping down the table solely because, as he said, "Butter and grease are original sin."), they took their seats. Rosie sat over in the armchair. Argent sat beside Felix, forcing Felix to sit up and lean into his shoulder, holding the bowl in his lap.

"You're not gonna have us go over the plan again, are you?" Felix asked. They'd already agreed they'd head into the crypt with Samuel's help during the dance next month, for some obscure Medeian holiday Felix couldn't be bothered to remember. They'd hoped they'd be able to indirectly raise alarm bells to get the staff involved without directly breaking Felix's oath. But even so, the idea of possessing the ring was so deeply alluring. The idea that the Black Flame would belong to him.

"No," Rosie said. "We're just gonna talk about life."

"Time to greet death," Felix grumbled, pouting in defiance.

"Plans after Dragora!" Rosie pointed at Argent. "You first!"

Argent stroked his goatee for a solid minute, and Felix passed that time playing elevator music in his head. Finally, Argent crossed his legs, and in a deep, confident voice said, "Don't know. Don't give a fuck."

Rosie groaned. "You're the worst!"

"Isn't that everyone our age?" Felix asked. "If you ask me, people just pretend they know what they're doing cuz it's expected of them. On the inside, everybody's just a squishy ball of anxiety and what-the-fuckery."

"You always gotta be so deep and inspirational?"

"Mhm." Felix laughed. "Like you've got your shit together. We're all one big waste of human potential, I say! That's practically our whole brand."

"I resent that a li'l bit," Argent said. "I actually put effort into passing my classes this year."

"Wait, really?" Rosie asked. "Like... *all* your classes?"

"Yep." Argent's teeth nearly sparkled as he grinned. "Even Goat Chalk's. Though I did pass hers by literally one point."

"Good for you," Felix said, nuzzling himself against Argent. "Let's hear it for minimal effort!"

"Here, here!" Argent threw his arm round Felix. "Having two little buddies around to motivate me helps."

Felix blushed. "Well, I... you're welcome? I guess?" To think Argent was so different at the start of the year. Comparing that version of him with who he was now, finally putting effort into his schoolwork, and actively trying to better himself? It assuaged Felix's initial doubts on giving Argent another chance. His concern was now directed at Rosie, who sat quietly in her chair and stared at the empty fireplace. "Rosie?" Felix asked. "What's up?"

She crossed her arms. "I've… been meaning to say this for a long time now. But…"

"You can tell us."

"I… I don't think I'll be coming back to Dragora next year."

"… Okay. Your point?"

Rosie seemed stunned. "That… doesn't upset you?"

"No," Felix said. "Why would it?"

"I only came to Dragora because you were going. I was worried about you. I wanted to make sure you'd be alright here, all on your own."

"Daww," Argent said. "How adorable."

Felix playfully elbowed him. "Don't ruin the moment."

Argent smirked, then turned back to Rosie. "If magic's not your thing, that's fine."

"I never cared much for it," Rosie said. "But I did have a great year with you guys."

"Same here," Argent said. "I didn't wanna actively escape through my window. At least, not as much as I did last year."

"Being here has been a dream of mine for so long," Felix said. "And… yeah, it wasn't what I expected. Specifically the weird cult stuff. But I still loved it. So… where were you thinking of going, Rosie?"

Rosie twiddled her thumbs. "I was planning on transferring to Roseford University back in the States. I miss home. Plus, I wanna get into politics, activism, anything to try and help advance magus rights back home, from the inside."

"Wow… that's fucking awesome!"

"God knows they'll need you with that shit-for-brains president of yours," Argent said. "No offense, of course. Assuming neither of you voted for him."

"Right," Felix said. "I'd definitely vote for the guy who thinks of me as a tool of war and nothing else." Still, he sincerely admired Rosie's devotion. She had a game plan, ready to make the world a better place. But Felix? As far as he knew, because of Schmitt's axing of the grant program, he'd be set adrift, unable to return to Dragora next year despite his wishes. Yet even so, he had to keep telling himself he'd be okay. Part of him wondered that maybe if he could help protect the Ring of Nergal from Vagus, that perhaps Headmistress Hakim might make an exception for Felix.

But no matter what, Felix knew one thing: he couldn't let someone like Vagus get his hands on that ring.

Rosie returned to her dorm not long after her admission. She'd been bottling it up for so long, dreading Felix's reaction. But somehow, the fact he took it so well, and was even encouraging of her goal? That only made her more uneasy.

"Have a good night out?"

The nasally voice caught her off guard. There Bianca was, sitting atop the loft kicking her feet. Her roommate was hardly ever around, but when she was, it made for good gossip. Rosie hopped on the couch. "You could say that. Best friend had a birthday party. Didn't get drunk, sadly, but I *am* stuffed."

Bianca sat up, stretching and pacing about the loft. "Felix? I've heard he's been doing really well in the combat league."

"Wouldn't know. Doesn't usually come up." Rosie paused for a moment, then went to light the fireplace. "What else do you hear, by any chance? And who do you even get this all from?"

"When you hear everyone's stories, you tend to forget whose is whose."

Rosie shrugged. "I guess that makes sense." A sudden chill washed over her. As the flames crackled, splitting apart the logs, Rosie rubbed her palms and held them over the fire. Strangely, there was an absence of warmth.

"You seem worried."

She turned to see Bianca sitting on the couch, legs crossed. Rosie stood. "I, uh… I suppose so, yeah."

"Welp," Bianca said. "If a gossip's good at one thing, it's lending an ear."

Chapter Twenty-Two

Mangling Malevolence

D ARKENSS flooded the sky. No clouds. No stars. Not even a moon.

Just pitch black.

Felix, as usual, had spent the night in Argent's dorm. But there was no sign of him, nor Shawn. Checking the time had also proven impossible. Felix's phone had died, despite him always making a note to use Argent's wireless charger overnight. The same went for the dorm lights. The only source of illumination was that of a wax candle on the coffee table. A piece of parchment had been left out as well, dark brown and worn from use. Climbing down to inspect further, Felix squinted at the faded ink, and the words drifted together…

"Illustratum. Darkness gathers around the Fourteenth Demon: The Infernal Angel. Beware those who reject the path through the night. Question those who scorn the reflection of the dusk, for they in turn forsake the glory of the dawn. Oppose these recusants, their empty promises, and their malicious Old Gods."

The door slammed open, nearly being torn off its hinges. A cold wind howled through the room. The hush snuffed out the candle, making the hairs on Felix's arms stand on end while the parchment dissolved in his hands. Blinding light poured through the doorway. Instinctively, he stepped through. The white void faded into a vibrant cerulean, stretching towards the horizon, wisps of white clouds painted across the sky. His bare feet dug into the rich soil and emerald grass. Laughter resounded all around, though Felix froze at the sight of a small ranch house before him.

His childhood home.

Felix wanted to run. But the gleam of the living room window compelled him. The house he'd once called home, that had been burned down seven years ago. It was fine. In picture-perfect shape, even; as though it had been ripped out of an old photograph and made real. Even the welcome mat on the front porch was brand new, free of any scratches, scuffs, or tears.

Slowly, Felix approached, placing his hand on the glass. Frank sat on the couch with the old family Bible. Lydia, smiling widely, sat beside him. On the floor were a fourteen-year-old Aeris and a twelve-year-old Felix, whose eyes drifted towards the window.

"Who's that outside?"

The young Felix's voice, crystal clear, sent a chill down the older Felix's spine. He stumbled back as his family's gaze turned to him. Pushing himself up, he ran for the road, only to be stopped dead in his tracks as something grabbed his wrist. Try as he might, he couldn't break free. The cold, tight grip felt like it was about to break his skin. Hesitantly, he turned back, and the sun's rays dissipated to reveal Lydia, her face wrinkled and pale, sulking.

"Won't you join us for dinner?"

Fear swirled in Felix. "U-Um…" He wanted to refuse the invitation, but couldn't form the words. Guilt weighed over him. After what felt like an eternity, he yielded, and said, "Yes." In an instant, Lydia whisked him through the front door and into the living room. He was met with a curious stare from his younger self, and the skeptical glares of Aeris and Frank.

"Who's this now?" Frank's voice made Felix's soul shrivel.

"Felix." Lydia cut him off before he could speak. She gripped his shoulder, freezing it on contact. "One of my nephews."

Aeris rolled her eyes. "Two Felixes. Great."

Young Felix stuck his tongue out at Aeris, only to quiver and wring his hands at a single glower from Frank. He jumped as the doorbell rang. "Pizza!" he yelled. Once again, his figure shrank as he cowered away from Frank.

Pushing himself off the couch, Frank trudged past the older Felix. He slammed the front door shut and threw the stack of pizza boxes onto the kitchen table. The sweet aroma of extra cheese, tomato sauce, and stuffed crust compelled Felix, only for his anxiety to return with a vengeance as his younger self tugged on his arm. He gave a wide, unnatural smile. "Trust me, it's really good! You like pizza?"

The older Felix gulped, nodding.

"Me too! Are you my clone or something?" His younger self nervously chuckled.

"I-I should really be go—"

The young Felix gripped tighter. "Please," he whispered, his eyes wide with fear. "Don't leave me alone."

This wasn't right. He knew he was asleep, but he couldn't control any part of this dream. Vagus had to have been up to his usual tricks. But why? Was this another test? As much as Felix wanted to run, he knew it wouldn't do him any good. Besides, seeing his younger self this afraid hit him hard. He forced himself to say, "O-Okay…" He followed his younger self into the kitchen, sitting between him and Lydia, and directly across from Aeris and Frank.

Frank handed him a slice. "Pepperoni?"

"S-Sure." As everyone dug in, Felix simply stared at his uneaten slice. He envisioned himself sprinting out the door to escape whatever was in store for him. Yet at every possible opportunity, he couldn't bring himself to run. He forced himself to take a bite of his food, hoping it might bring some relief, but gagged as the stench of fish filled his nostrils.

The food fell to the floor. A sautéed flounder fillet, and Felix's plate was now packed with shrimp, tuna, and most disgustingly, oysters. The smell was utterly repugnant. But even more sickening, while Aeris happily enjoyed the platter, Frank glared at the young Felix, pressuring him to funnel down his foot as he kept gagging, forcing him to show appreciation for his meal.

Felix cringed. "¡Qué asco!"

Aeris shook her head. "If you're gonna be rude, say it in English."

He sneered. "Whatever you say, ogro." His younger self snickered, only to shut up as Frank shot him a glare. *Oh, now I am really pissed.*

The TV in the other room blared. "This just in! An attack was launched against the Dragora Institute of Magic, and the Medeian Empire has been completely destroyed."

Frank's laughter made Felix tremble. "Good!" he bellowed. "Maybe now those freaks will finally go extinct." Though Felix felt winded, his blood still boiled at Frank's sick grin.

Obtuse as ever.

"You said it, Dad!" the young Felix shouted, his voice brittle. "Death to 'em all!" Hearing this from his younger self killed Felix. How brainwashed he'd been for most of his life, and the scars it had left on him. It disgusted him. Lydia simply kept quiet, holding her hands and hanging her head.

"Devil's forces on Earth," Aeris said. "Demons."

Felix, having enough of this, pushed himself up. "Magi are innocent! They're normal people, the same as you!" He projected his voice, towering over Frank, but in the moments that followed, regret consumed him. The TV went silent as everyone glared. Thunder shook the house, and the lights flickered. Frank stood, looking down upon Felix with that same contemptuous stare.

"They've ruined the world," Frank said, his voice low and grave. "Left it in shambles. Left my life in shambles." He squinted. "You're one of 'em." Reaching into his pocket, Frank pulled out his old handgun, pointing it right at Felix. Felix clutched the table. Even if this wasn't a dream, he knew he couldn't back down. He stared past the gun and right into Frank's eyes.

I'll never back down. Not from you.

"Dad, stop!"

The young Felix ran around the table, only for the deafening blast of gunfire to break the silence. A bullet had been lodged right between the boy's eyes. Aeris didn't even flinch as she kept eating, while Lydia ran for the door, sobbing. The older Felix, horrified, followed. But the moment his mother got outside, the door slammed shut in his face on its own. He threw all his weight into breaking it down, to no avail.

He turned back, and there Frank was, towering over him once again. The only source of light was from the lightning raging outside. His aura was that of an executioner, and Felix was on the guillotine. Frank's eyes turned red as his body twisted and dissolved into a plume of indigo flames.

"You remember that story about the Scorch, don't you?" Frank's voice boomed, echoing all around through the blaze. "That cold winter night, where families, wanting an escape from the destruction of their world, were ready for a white Christmas. But instead…"

A terrifying roar pierced Felix's ears, followed by a deep maniacal laughter. From the red depths, a three-headed dragon, glistening crimson with empty amber eyes, manifested. Its hot breath was rank, wreaking of more than a dozen canisters of gasoline. On the creature's back rode a tall, muscular man. His flowing red hair beamed as brightly as the dragon's scales, while his black trench coat flapped in the wind, releasing sparks. He gave a devilish grin from ear to ear. The only thing more foreboding than that terrible smile were his scarlet eyes.

"Jason Reavey, one of those freak wizards, hopped on his dragon Ira and burned nearly half the country. Cities were razed to cinders. Mothers, fathers, daughters, and sons were roasted like pigs on a spit. And all carrying through Christmas."

Ira let loose his flames, and Felix screamed in agony as his skin flaked and cracked. The violet blaze turned into a deep-red fluid, and the blaze lifted to reveal a cavern of gushing blood and obsidian rock. A sickness rose in Felix, as though his stomach had tried to tear itself to shreds.

The cold, lifeless bodies of Carson and his journalist cousin lay at his feet. Or rather, what appeared to be Carson and his cousin—after having been mutilated. Their bodies were flayed; the skin torn off to reveal the red flesh beneath. Exposed veins and arteries pulsed over twisting sinew wrapped around bone. Carson's hand latched onto Felix's ankle, and his yellow crusted nails dug into the skin. Felix fell, breaking free and crawling away until he hit the wall, panting heavily. Blood soaked his clothes and hands, and the stones cut his palms and legs.

The corpses stood. Their scowls, warped by vitriol and resentment, clawed at Felix's soul. Dried blood, more black than red, stained their peeled lips. They stumbled towards Felix, their bones cracking and snapping as they lunged forth. It took all Felix's strength not to vomit.

"You did this to us." Carson's raspy voice grated Felix's ears. "You killed him."

"N-No!" Felix trembled. He had no idea as to what Carson even meant. But right now, he was too shaken up to process what was going on. Grabbing a rock, he tossed it at Carson's cousin, forcing his shambling body to fall apart into dust. Felix screamed. "I-I didn't... I didn't mean to—"

"He'll bring the next Scorch," Carson said. "He's the next Reavey."

Felix curled up into a ball. "P-Please stop! I don't—"

"You belong here. In the realm of the mangled."

"S-Stop!"

"The place where those you resent most go to suffer and die, over and over and over." Carson pointed to his head. "In here..." He held his chest. "And here."

Felix tried to understand, but as more corpses marched behind Carson, it started to click. Frank, Lucas, and hundreds more. Felix scraped his back against the wall as they closed in. "N-No! No, please! I'm sorry!" They clawed at him. Pain shot through his body as he screamed and wailed, only to fade as the darkness returned. In the pain's absence, that all-too-familiar cold dread resurfaced, this time with a reckoning. A bright light cut through the shadows, and Dragora Castle rose from the mist. The bruises, scrapes, and blood that had covered Felix's body mere moments before had entirely vanished, though the sky was still pitch black.

"Look who came crawling back." Penny stood at the entrance, looking on in pity. Shawn and Floria stood on either side of her.

"We know why you're here," Shawn said.

Felix reached out, trying to get a word out, only to find he couldn't speak.

"You've been to the mangled realm," Penny said. "We know what a sick fuck you are. How you really feel about us." She made Felix step back. "You smile and pretend you care to get on people's good side, when really they're just your tools so you can claw your way up. You're the worst kind of evil."

Floria shrugged. "I've had enough of him." She stomped, and a crevice ripped right through the earth. Felix clung to the rocks as he dangled over the bottomless pit. The rocks slid, about to break off and seal his fate.

"Why don't you let go?"

Above, Nasira stood at the edge of the crevice, looking down with nearly as much contempt in her eyes as Frank. Felix looked down. Holding onto his wrist for dear life and crying... was Zahra. "W-Why?!" she yelled. "Why do you want to hurt me?! What did I do?!"

Felix winced. "I-I... I didn't—"

With a bloodcurdling scream, Zahra fell. Nasira crushed Felix's fingers beneath her foot, sending him plummeting into the chasm before the light completely vanished.

"Your daddy issues make you better than us?" Penny floated around Felix as he fell through the abyss. "At least you *have* a family. Not that you deserve one."

Shawn appeared beside her. "I'll bet you only listened to my story to learn how to get more power. How to make yourself a pearl."

"N-No," Felix said, finally managing to croak out the words. "I—"

"That's why you lied to them," Penny said. "Lied to them about Vagus. You lied to Rosie, to Argent, and to Zahra."

"You were born a cobalt," Shawn said. "You'll die a cobalt. Dull, envious, and worthless."

"A cobalt sorcerer?" Though Gottschalk was nowhere to be seen, Felix could still recognize the disdain in her voice. "Delusional." He covered his ears as she laughed, though her cackles broke through with ease.

"For once, I'm with her." Argent huffed. "You're pathetic."

Felix froze.

Argent held out his hand. A chunk of ice struck right through Felix's chest. The blow knocked him back, ice crawling across his skin until he was totally encapsulated. Cracks raced through the frost, and as the icy tomb shattered, Felix's cold body fell out of the darkness, and into a small blue attic bedroom with a slanted ceiling. Slim rays of light slithered through an ungodly small window. A pale girl, her blonde hair nearly as pale as her milky-white face, cried on her worn bed.

"TILDA?!"

The voice from downstairs was followed by heavy thuds up the steps. Tilda quickly dried her eyes, and the door flung open to reveal an old man with wrinkled white skin, though his face was now bright red. "You went to that exam, didn't you?!"

"G-Grandpa, I didn't—"

"You used my credit card to buy tickets into the city! You told me you were at one of your 'friend's' houses!"

Tilda sniffed. "I-I'm sorry, I just—"

"Well, I hope you got that grant. Cuz otherwise, your ass is outta here."

Tilda kept quiet, simply staring at the floor. In her hand was a letter with Ramidha Hakim's signature at the very bottom. Felix, being invisible to both Tilda and her grandfather, squinted at the letter. It read, "We regret to inform you…"

Her grandfather slammed the door shut, rushing downstairs and yelling along with what sounded to be her grandmother about "that freak sorceress," and how they cursed their daughter for "sleeping with a freak" and leaving them with Tilda. Tilda sobbed. Felix wanted to reach out and apologize, racked with guilt for stealing her only chance at escape.

"You…!"

Tilda's head jerked up as her eyes went from cobalt to red. They filled with red-orange flames, and the fire spread throughout the room, burning Felix's skin as he screamed in pain. The fire faded, and a ruined city emerged from the inferno. Destroyed buildings were toppled over beneath a crimson sky and black sun. An eternal eclipse. All was quiet, silent as death. In the distance, from some sort of temple, a colossal tree had erupted and breached the heavens. It took a minute before the putrid smell of ash and decay hit Felix's nose, making him gag.

"No matter how hard you try, you can't make something from nothing."

Lucas approached. Feathery wings, glowing white, sprouted from his back, and a golden aura surrounded him. He took to the sky like an archangel, and the backdrop of the red sky could've easily passed this moment off as a glimpse of Judgment Day. Arrows of light shot down from Lucas' wings. Felix tried to dodge, but the attacks scraped his skin as they came in fast and relentlessly.

"Spark Shower!" Felix yelled, holding out his hand. Nothing.

Another round of arrows threw Felix from the rooftop. He fell nearly thirty stories, slamming into the concrete below. Covered in bruises, all his bones and muscles screaming in agony, he desperately crawled towards the shrine. And there it was. Inside, atop a lone, gleaming pedestal on the far side, there floated a small black ring with a blood-red jewel.

"O, Mother of Light…"

Not that spell. Lucas' voice echoed all around. Felix had to get to that ring, and so he hauled himself faster, scraping his body against each step leading up towards the pedestal. A trail of blood stained the ground behind him, past obsidian statues of lions. He grit his teeth through the pain. He could've sworn his teeth nearly cracked from his jaw's pressure. His feet sorely ached as he forced himself to stand, his legs wobbling. He nearly fell, but caught the pedestal, desperately leaning on the marble for balance.

"Grant upon me the heavenly fires of your wrath…"

I… I have to… The ring glowed before him. Felix reached for it, his eyes transfixed by the alluring infernal glow.

"Don't."

He turned. A young dark-skinned man with a crude buzz cut had entered the temple, walking through the bloody trail. He grimaced in a mixture of pity and apathy. "You don't know what misery it'll bring you."

"Y-You…?" Felix's eyes narrowed. "What do you—"

"Don't listen to him." This new male voice, deep and disembodied, rang through Felix's head. "Trust me. I will watch over you. I shall be your guardian angel." Felix looked around, trying to pinpoint the source of the promise.

"Whatever that ring is saying," the young man said. "Don't—"

"So I might, in your great now, pass judgment upon these wicked fools before me." Lucas' chant boomed. Dismissing the warning, Felix put the ring on his finger, and black-and-purple flames enveloped him. He flew into the air as a pair of smoky wings jutted out from his back. In one swift motion, he blasted his way through the ceiling, meeting Lucas high up in the air above the ruined city. Rings of white-and-orange fire surrounded Lucas as he prepared his attack. "And set the mortal skies ablaze with justice!"

"Repeat after me," the angel's voice said.

"Angel of Flames!"

In unison, Felix and his guardian shouted, "Infernal Angel!" A vortex of black-and-purple flames barreled towards Lucas' attack. As the fires clashed, the dark overpowered the light, engulfing Lucas. His burned wings collapsed as feathers fell from the sky. Felix flew down to Lucas' charred body. But as the smoke and fire cleared, Frank lay dead in the dirt in Lucas' place.

Rosie slapped Felix. "What kind of monster have you become?!"

Unfeeling and unflinching, Felix outstretched his hand. The last thing he heard before everything returned to black was Rosie's scream.

"Ow!"

Felix jolted up from bed. He checked his arms, turning them over and back to look for any injuries. He was free of any bruises or scars, and as he looked behind him, the morning sky was blue as ever, the sun shining like gold.

"What the hell?" Argent asked, holding his chin. "We really need to do something about these nightmares of yours."

"S-Sorry…"

"It's okay." Argent helped Felix lie back down. He held his hand, giving him a comforting kiss on the cheek. "Was it that Vagus creep again?"

Felix paused. "I don't know."

Argent had to get up for class anyway. While he headed out, Felix opted to sleep in, only to be disturbed by a loud and relentless knock on the door. Hauling himself out of bed and throwing on Argent's spare blue robe, Felix trudged towards the door, only to find Carlos grimacing on the other side.

"So you haven't learned."

"W-What're you…?" Felix's mind raced back to the dream. He stepped back, desperately fighting the urge to wring Carlos' neck. "I'm not gonna get a straight answer out of you, so I won't bother. But tell your boss I'm already going through with it. I don't need any more of these stupid dream tricks. Oh, and also tell him that once he gets what he wants, he can go fuck himself with it."

Carlos shook his head, but Felix slammed the door shut and went back to bed. As far as he was concerned, Carlos could've just been another of Vagus' pawns, like Vivien. It'd certainly explain why he seemed to be everywhere Felix was. Had he been the snitch all along?

Or was he even part of the game to begin with?

Chapter Twenty-Three

Best Night of Our Lives

FELIX, wearing his suit from his date with Argent a few months ago, scowled at Rosie. Her hair was tied back into a bun, though as sophisticated she seemed in her violet suit and black dress shoes, nothing about her style could hide her devious smirk as she held Felix's phone. Though her Devil-may-care attitude should've been evident in her peculiar choice of a zebra-patterned handbag—only a lunatic could've chosen such a garish aesthetic. Part of Felix regretted helping her design it, even if she did rock a suit like it was no one's business.

His eyes narrowed. "Give. Me. The. Phone."

"Not. Gonna. Happen."

Felix tried to snatch his phone back, but missed, stumbling and nearly hitting his chin on the dorm coffee table. "Daww," Rosie said. "Is the little marshmallow embarrassed?" Her grin widened as Felix growled. "Oh, I'm sorry! Little poodle."

Felix plopped onto the couch. "You wound me. Wound my pride."

She sat next to him. "What pride?"

"You're the worst."

"I know." Rosie winked. "So, when's Prince Charming supposed to get here?"

Felix groaned. "A half-hour or so."

"Good. Then we can meet up with Zahra during the dance and go over the plan one last time."

Felix wanted to agree with her. But instead, he rolled over, clutching a pillow against his chest. Tryouts for the Ancient Dragons' Tournament started tomorrow, but despite all his training, he dreaded the fact he likely wouldn't have any energy left for them. It even soured tonight's mood, preemptively ruining what was meant to be a fun, lighthearted dance for the Day of Mages' Reckoning: a day to commemorate the Medeian Empire finally lending aid to the human world during the Revelation. Not the best name perhaps, but accurate enough.

But while everyone else would be enjoying the dance, Felix and his friend would enter the crypt beneath the castle, led by Samuel, to hopefully lure Vagus out into the open and capture him. As for whether the staff would hopefully notice and come to their aid, or they'd be on their own against Vagus, that was all uncertain. And that uncertainty, coupled with the call of the ring, made Felix feel sick.

"So," Rosie said. "How're the folks?"

Though he didn't feel quite up to holding a full-blown conversation, Felix was at least grateful this topic was of a much lighter note. "Sis and I have the odd banter once or twice a week." *By which I mean I haven't heard from Aeris since I texted her "Merry Christmas!", but that's fine.* "Mom's always texting me about how much she loves and misses me, morning and night. And Ian's telling me not to get too wasted."

Rosie snickered. "*Too* wasted?"

"Ian's pretty laid back."

"But you don't even like alcohol!"

Felix shrugged. "Eh."

"Hmm…" Rosie held her chin. "What do they think of Argent?"

Felix, tensing up, pushed himself deeper into the couch cushions, hoping they'd somehow swallow him whole. "Well…"

"You haven't told them, have you?"

He nervously chuckled. "If I said I had, would you believe me?"

"Nope," Rosie said. "Cuz we both know you haven't."

He sighed.

"You two have been going out for, what, three months now?" Rosie asked. "They deserve to know."

Felix knew she was right. His mother and stepfather were more than accepting of his sexuality, and made it clear they'd love whoever he introduced to them: male, female, or otherwise. But on some level, he worried it might've been too soon to take that step with Argent. Gathering the courage just to kiss him took months and only happened on a whim. "What about Shawn?" he asked. "Do your dads know about him?"

Rosie shrugged. "They did while we were still a thing."

He squinted. "You broke up? When? Why?"

"No particular reason. Nothing really happened, and that was kinda the problem. Our chemistry just fizzled out."

"You broke his heart right before the dance?" Felix asked.

"Nope!" Rosie said. "We're still friends. In fact, I may or may not have organized a date for him."

He raised an eyebrow. "With who?"

"*Whom*," Rosie corrected. "And it's a surprise. Plus they made me take a blood oath not to tell you. But *you* have an obligation to let your folks know about Argent, especially given you know they'll be nothing but supportive and loving. No whataboutisms." Felix groaned into the pillow, but Rosie snatched it and tossed it across the room. "C'mon! What reason could you possibly have *not* to tell them?"

Felix sat up. "Argent's nice and all. But…"

"What's up?" She held his shoulder. "You know you can talk to me."

He held his chest. "I don't see it lasting past this year." The words stung, but he hoped the pain would fade once he got it out. "We have chemistry, and I do care about him. But… I don't know."

"Of course he cares about you," Rosie said. "You saw what a jerk he used to be, but he cleaned up his act for you. Wait, you *do* like him, right? You're not forcing yourself to be with him out of obligation, are you?"

"What? No!" Felix cupped his cheek, hoping to hide his blush. "I just… sometimes I wonder if I care about him more than he cares about me."

Rosie raised an eyebrow. "Where is this going?"

"We… we haven't said we… you know… *loved* each other."

"… That's what this is about?"

"I get it," Felix said. "It's not a big deal to you, but… it is to me." Felix scooted over to the far side of the couch. As ridiculous as it might've sounded aloud, and even petty on some level, this concern was all too real to him.

Argent had dropped the L-word jokingly, but never had either of them sincerely admitted it, even in those sweet, vulnerable moments of silently enjoying each other's company.

He hadn't thought much as to whether they'd be together even when Felix couldn't return to Dragora, or whether Argent would simply move on as if Felix had never existed. That thought... it hurt more than he wanted to admit. He pulled up his feet and curled up into a ball.

"I'm sorry," Rosie said. "Look. We have no idea what's going to happen tonight. At all. We could get caught on the way to the crypt and never make it inside, and let the professors take it from there. Or we could make it inside, and then... I don't know. But we *do* have a plan. And it won't just be us. Zahra, Argent, and even Samuel weirdly enough. We're all with you. You're not alone." She knelt, taking Felix's hands. "We might as well enjoy tonight and make the most of it."

"O-Okay," Felix choked out.

She hugged him, letting him cry out his anxiety. The fear didn't fully fade, not even close, but it did help to some extent. "That all said," Rosie said. "I do really think you should talk to your family. Just... in case."

He sniffled. "You're right."

"I hate that I am. But I'm not gonna lie to your face. I'm scared too." Rosie stood. "I talked with my folks earlier. I would've talked to Marcus. You know, if he learned how to fucking answer his phone."

"Yup," Felix said. "Sounds like him."

"Your marshmallow self still found a way to fall for him, though."

He paused. "Y-You knew?"

Rosie sat back down. "Literally everyone knew."

Felix was tempted to lie back down and shove his face into the pillow again, until he realized it was still on the other side of the room, and he was far too lazy to fetch it. "Fuck my life."

"It was cute," Rosie said. "Though seeing you always denying how you felt? Not so much."

He shrugged. "He was—"

"Him being straight's no excuse!" Rosie wagged her finger in Felix's face. "Cuz you do it with the girls you like too."

"Evidence, please?"

"Omitting Zahra, since you've actually addressed it with her…" Rosie leaned in, whispering, "Good job, by the way, very proud." She snapped back to her normal voice as she counted on her fingers. "There was Emily back in middle school. You cried like a bitch when she didn't wanna go to the dance with you."

Felix cringed at the memory. "Even though I never talked to her and knew nothing about her." He laughed. "God, what an idiot I was." *And still am.*

"Then there was Audrey in poetry club," Rosie continued. "You tried so hard to impress her with your 'dark sense of prose and style.'"

"If by 'dark,' you mean cringeworthy and edgy as hell, then yes."

Rosie howled and slapped her knee. "She sure put you in your place. Good thing we had ice cream from Harrison's on standby."

What Felix wouldn't give to head back home, even for a day, to enjoy a nice meal at his and Rosie's favorite diner. He forced a smile. "So the lesson is I'm gonna die alone?"

"Shut the fuck up!" Rosie playfully punched Felix's arm. "No one's fooled by your 'I don't care' attitude and snarky comments." Felix crossed his arms and huffed. "Whether you and Argent last," she said. "That doesn't matter. You like him, and he likes you. So enjoy this for now, and don't be afraid." She leapt from the couch. "I expect to see you two dancing tonight. No ifs, ands, or buts."

"But—"

"And no butt jokes either," Rosie said. "None of that shit."

Felix groaned. "Fine."

Smiling, Rosie headed for the door. She turned back and said, "By the way, I already sent pics of you all dressed up to your family and said you were gonna call them, okay bye!" at lightning speed before rushing outside and shutting the door behind her. As much as Felix knew Rosie had done the right thing getting the ball rolling for him, he still swiped the fallen pillow and screamed into it. Right in time for his phone to start buzzing.

Quickly, he groomed his hair, trying to seem like he had his shit somewhat together. *I can't let them see I was crying. Can't worry them like that.* Seating himself back on the couch, he called upon his courage before answering the call, and his mother appeared on the screen.

"Hi, honey!" Lydia's voice instantly soothed Felix's nerves. "Look at you all dressed up! Rosie said you were headed to a dance tonight?"

"Yeah," Felix said. "Sorry I haven't been in touch lately. Things here have been... hectic. How're things back home?"

"Oh, the usual. But I'm sure things over there are much more exciting for you! Rosie tells me that you have a date!"

Felix silently screamed. "Uh..."

"I knew it! My boy's fallen in love!"

"Love?!" Ian rushed into frame. "You're using protection, right?"

Felix silently begged the couch to devour him whole. "Yes, Ian, don't worry." *God, please have mercy and just smite me now.*

"Good. Guy, gal, or other?"

"Guy."

"Ooh!" Lydia's smile widened. "Is he handsome and rugged?"

"If he hurts you," Ian said. "I will hurt him."

"Yes, yes," Felix said, scratching his head and trying to laugh off the awkwardness. "I know, and I appreciate it."

"I'm sure he's a nice boy," Lydia said. "Just like you, mi corazón."

Ian leaned further into the camera. "Do I detect hesitation? Are you okay, Felix? Do I need to break his legs?"

Lydia laughed. "Oh, you know Felix has always been the shy type! I'm happy for you, honey! I can't wait to meet him!"

Felix smiled. "Thanks, guys. So... school's been good. How're Aeris and Tracey?"

"Tracey's excited for kindergarten next year," Ian said. "But she's really been missing you."

"Awe." Felix let out an earnest laugh. "Let her know I miss her too!"

"Oh!" Lydia raised a finger. "She wants you to bring home a troll club."

"... A troll club?"

"I may or may not have introduced her to *Lord of the Rings*," Ian said.

Of course he did. Alec may have been the king of nostalgia, but Ian specialized in the oldest aspects of geek culture. But at least, unlike his mother, Ian knew that the wizards in the old stories were nothing like the magi of their own world. "And Aeris?" Felix asked. "How's she?"

"We... haven't heard much from her lately," Ian said. "She's been busy with school."

Felix raised an eyebrow. "I thought she commuted. Like last year?"

"No," Lydia said. "She's been dorming this year."

I've never heard this before now. Though Felix hadn't kept in touch with his family as much as he knew he should've, even less so with Aeris, it genuinely surprised him that he hadn't known his own sister had lived away from home the entire time he'd been abroad.

"Are you alright, sweetie?" Lydia asked. "You look pale."

Felix stuttered. "I…"

The door swung open. "Honey, I'm home!" Argent stood in the door, decked out in a salmon suit with his hair pulled back into a ponytail. A bright-blue bow tie popped against the rest of his outfit. Lydia and Ian leaned into the camera, and Felix longed for death's sweet release.

"Felix," Ian said. "Turn the phone towards this young man I'm hearing." Felix complied, and Argent snapped off the wall, standing as straight as possible. "Argent, was it?" Ian asked.

For once in his life, Argent looked intimidated. "Y-Yes, sir."

"Tell me more about yourself."

"I…" Sweat began to bead on Argent's forehead. "I like food?"

If I could kill you with my glare alone, you'd be on the floor crying like the little bitch you're being right now. Now fucking impress my stepdad before he kills you for me.

Ian held his chin. "And what're your intentions with my son?"

Argent nervously grinned. "To… treat him like a prince and punch anyone who might try to hurt him?"

Good God, why?

"That is… acceptable," Ian said. "For now. I've got my eye on you, kid."

Argent gulped. "Y-Yes, sir."

"Nice meeting you, Argent!" Lydia waved.

"Y-You too, ma'am!"

"Oh, relax!" Lydia seemed ready to howl with laughter. "I'm sure you two will have a good time! Let me know how it goes, Felix! ¡Te quiero, Papito!"

"¡Te quiero, Mami!" Felix said. "Love you too, Ian!"

"Argent!" Ian, again, pushed himself to the front. "If you hurt him, I swear I will—"

Felix ended the call. Immediately, a weight had been lifted from his shoulders. He leaned back and took a long, relieving breath. Then, once the anxiety wore off, he donned the giddiest of smiles. "Welp, looks like you've officially met the family."

Argent shut the door behind him. "They're... an interesting bunch."

"Explains a lot about me, doesn't it?"

"How you turned out to be a marshmallow? Yes." Argent kissed Felix, holding his hip as he stood. "But must we go to this dance?" Argent asked, cupping Felix's cheek. "I'd much rather spend the night with you... and your penguin suit."

Felix blushed, only to sigh as he recalled what he'd told Rosie. "Yeah." Slowly, he removed Argent's hand. "Let's get going."

Smiling, Argent held out his hand, and Felix, his mood brightening a bit, took it. They made their way to the castle ballroom. Buffet tables on either side, covered in red cloth, were swarmed with students. Moonlight filtered through the windows, shining across red, white, and gold streamers strung across the rafters. Golden dragon statues lined the rafters as well. Upon the ceiling was painted a vibrant mural of the Eleven Dragons. "Wow!" Felix said. "This is—"

"Overkill." Argent rolled his eyes at the decor.

"Must you always act so jaded?"

"It's my defining trait."

Felix would've rolled his eyes back at Argent had the music not been so soothing. Ornella and the other prefects seemed to be handling the entertainment as a quartet: Lucinda on her violin; Nina on tom toms; Theresa on saxophone (for extra jazzy flair); and Ornella leading them with her flute. Though not all the attendees seemed to enjoy their piece.

Lucas, dressed in white like the rest of his family, looked unhealthily pale. Felix hadn't seen him since Vagus' trial a couple months before. Lucas hadn't attended any of their classes, nor had anyone seen him around school. Moreover, his parents seemed to mirror his misery, forced to carry on a conversation with Ornella's mother over whatever it was rich people talked about.

Unexpectedly, Lucas shot dagger eyes at Felix.

Argent held Felix's shoulder. "You okay?"

"Yeah, yeah," Felix said, looking around. "Let's just find Rosie and Zahra. Do you see them anywhere?"

"Why don't we ask the girl at the buffet table flipping us off?" Argent asked. "You know, before she winds up devouring us all." He pointed at the left-hand table, where Zahra—in a short dark-green dress with pink-and-purple flower patterns and a short ponytail—enjoyed a dish of pasta. Rosie, by stark contrast, unashamedly stuffed her face with veal, staring dead at Felix and Argent, holding up her middle finger.

Classy.

Once Rosie finished her meal ("One does not simply leave perfectly good food uneaten," she said.), they headed outside into the lush gardens. Felix and Argent sat on a bench within one of the gazebos. Zahra leaned against a column on the opposite side, while Rosie jumped onto the railing and leisurely kicked her feet.

The plan was simple enough. Once Samuel was ready, they'd all confirm via text and meet up outside the Chamber of Kagami. They couldn't tell any of the staff what was going on due to Felix's oath, but ideally, they'd notice something was off and come running. Otherwise, it was up to the kids to try and overpower Vagus and capture him. No pressure! At the very least, Vagus hadn't been a mental nuisance since the last "test," which hopefully meant Rosie's makeshift dreamcatcher had done its work in keeping him out of Felix's head, and by extension, keeping him unable to gather the full details of their plan.

Felix thought perhaps donning the ring could've allowed them to take him down no problem. But he'd also sworn to the others he wouldn't so much as look at it, let alone actively seek it out. Still, that temptation burned strong.

Felix leaned into Argent, holding his hand tight. "Thanks, you guys. You're the best."

"I know," Rosie said. "Now, I have some business of my own to attend to."

Argent scoffed, raising an eyebrow. "More important than breaking into an ancient, high-security crypt and luring some crazy, possibly-cultist terrorist into a trap with some object of great and immeasurable power as bait?"

"All issues matter. Equally."

Everyone glared at her. Everyone except Zahra, who just looked confused.

"Oh shush!" Rosie hopped down and headed off. "I'll be in touch, children!"

"Wonder what she's up to," Argent said.

Felix shrugged. "Who knows?" The crescent moon, its pale light waning, was hidden by a few stray clouds. The sight somehow gave him comfort. "So what're you gonna do, Zahra?"

Zahra swayed to and fro on her feet. "For now, I'll keep Nasira company. She's probably off pouting somewhere. Oh! Thanks by the way, Argent. We made sure to get some manakish for the buffet."

Argent shrugged. "No big deal." With that, she bid them adieu. "Such a sweet soul," Argent said, his arm around Felix.

"Did you actually... help Zahra?" Felix asked. "Voluntarily?!"

"I can be nice," Argent said. "She wanted to make sure there'd be plenty of Middle Eastern dishes for Nasira to enjoy." He looked away, mumbling, "And also me." He cleared his throat. "So she asked for my recommendations."

Felix playfully jabbed Argent. "And *I'm* the marshmallow?"

"Guess I'm burnt," Argent said. "So... now what?"

"I don't really mind this." Felix nuzzled closer. "I've never been much of a party person. I much prefer this."

"Me too. You feeling any better?"

"A bit. With you here."

Argent smirked. "Rosie can't do that for you?"

"Best friends don't exactly romantically cuddle," Felix said.

"Friends with benefits?"

"Shut the fuck up!" Felix laughed through his words, and Argent joined. Felix shut his eyes. How wonderful it would be to bring Argent home and introduce him to the beauty of Long Island bagels and pizza—or even pizza bagels. No. The sheer majesty might've killed them both. But moreover (*On an actually important note*), it'd be so much fun to introduce Argent to Felix's family in person. Tracey would probably run up and hug the hell out of him. Argent's attitude would definitely piss Aeris off as they clashed, and nothing seemed more appealing to Felix. Lydia would ask about how they met and what their first date was like (omitting the Vagus part, of course). And Felix's father... *stepfather*, would make sure Argent was good enough for his kid in the most overdramatic fashion imaginable. Felix's "actual" father probably would've had a fit over him dating a guy at all, let alone another magus.

"Hey there, gay boy!"

A flash opened Felix's eyes and made him jump. Denise held her camera in one hand, and a recently-developed photo in the other. Her usual black beret went well with her black-and-pink floral dress, in the sense that both appeared so old, they fit Denise's pretentious hipster aesthetic to the letter. Her simper, accentuated by her eternally-unnecessary sunglasses, was the rotten cherry on top.

Felix forced a smile, trying not to grind his teeth. "Oh! Denise, hi…!" Argent sat there confused, and Felix whispered, "You don't wanna know. Trust me."

Argent bobbed his head in confusion.

"Relax!" Denise said. "I think you two are pretty damn cute. And that cuteness shall be memorialized in the yearbook."

"There's a yearbook?" Felix asked.

Argent shrugged. "I've heard of it, but I've also heard no one reads it."

Denise scoffed. "I'll have you know that yearbooks are a historic staple of every academic institution! To forsake such a vintage treasure would be…" She paused. "Okay, look, I just like flipping through the pages and admiring all the gorgeous women whose beauty utterly destroys me."

I mean I get that. But fuck you and your hipster ways. I'm probably gonna die tonight, bitch, so let me have this. Go on, before I cut you with your Polaroid crap and slap you with your beret.

"Thanks…" Felix said.

"But I mean, it's also nice to look back on nights like these," Denise said. "Before things change. Life's weird. One moment you're having the time of your life, and the next… well…" She shrugged. "Who knows? Maybe you're changing the world. For better or worse." Felix raised an eyebrow, but before he could even process what Denise had said, she cut off his train of thought. "I'll leave you two to your gayness now." She strutted back towards the castle. "Enjoy the night, gaybies!"

"I hate her," Argent said.

"Same here," Felix said. Right as he was ready to growl, his hunger beat him to it. They held hands again as they made their way back for food. The stone path wound past garden topiaries, towards the fountain court just

416

outside the ballroom entrance. "How about we eat out here?" Felix asked. "Maybe next to the fountain, or one of the pools?"

"Ooh, quite scenic!" Argent said, emphasizing all the wrong syllables. "Good aesthetic taste."

"That's... redundant. Did you swallow a thesaurus?"

"Well, I'd like to swallow—"

"Make a dick joke," Felix said. "And I'm breaking up with you."

"Aha! So we *are* dating!"

Felix laughed, holding Argent's hand tighter. Music blasted as students danced inside. Felix and Argent, opting to wait for the slow dance, headed for the buffet table. Felix grabbed some chicken and pasta, while Argent took a full plate of steak. (Felix would've asked if it was raw, but that'd result in more dirty jokes.) Before they could head back outside, Felix's phone buzzed repeatedly.

"Is your dad secretly evaluating me?" Argent asked.

"It's Rosie. She needs us." Felix's stomach twisted, though as Argent held his shoulder, it alleviated some of his anxiety. They entered the hall, looking around for Samuel and the others.

"Hello!"

Leaping back, Felix dropped his platter. Though the plate thankfully hadn't broken, his heart certainly did as his food went flying across the floor. "Shiiiit," he groaned. Channeling his despair, he shot a righteously furious glare. "What the hell? Can't you take anything seriously tonight?"

Rosie waved her hand. "Oh, that's not why I've summoned you all here. Now, I need you two to hold open the doors and clear everyone out."

"Uh... why?" Argent asked.

"Just do it, you numbskulls." Floria, wearing a maroon dress and ponytail, twirled a pink-and-smoky-gray parasol, looking ready to skewer someone with it.

"Alright, alright. C'mon, Felix."

"B-But..." Felix pointed to the floor. "My food!"

Rosie pushed Felix in front of the door. "Make way, make way!" Despite the guys' efforts, the entryway was still crowded. "Floria," Rosie said. "If you would?"

Sighing, Floria pulled out her wand. "O dwellers of the sacred grove, grant us the light of your protection." There wasn't a trace of melody or rhythm in her incantation. "Fairy Waltz." A flurry of golden fairy wisps flew from her wand into the air, leaving faint trails of leaves behind them. The students backed away as they looked in awe. While Felix and Argent held open the doors, a young woman with deep-olive skin and shining auburn hair emerged. Her slim dress was as scarlet as fire, as were her shoes, while her silver raindrop earrings shimmered.

Penny?!

Shawn walked out of the crowd, blushing, his eyes wide. "P-Penny? W-Wow! You look…"

Penny held out her hand. "Care for a dance?" Hesitantly, Shawn accepted, and as the music slowed and the students all around cheered, they waltzed.

Felix tapped Rosie's shoulder. "Is this why you…?"

"Penny liked him way more than I ever did," Rosie said. "So Floria and I decided to help a gal out. Give her a moment in the spotlight."

"Seriously, how am *I* the marshmallow?" Felix asked.

"I don't make the rules."

Floria cleared her throat. "Where's my cut?" Relenting, Rosie handed over a few drakons, and Floria stuffed them into her purse. "About time."

"Why am I not surprised?" Felix asked.

"A girl's gotta survive in this economy somehow."

"You're not gonna stay?" Rosie asked. "Not even to check anybody out?" She popped her eyebrows, tempting Felix to ask if Argent had somehow possessed her.

Floria shook her head. "Dating's never been my thing. Not interested."

Rosie shrugged. "Fair."

Argent snickered. "'Fairy Waltz'?" His confidence vanished as Floria kicked him in the shin, and she simply walked off while he hopped and held his leg, cursing away the pain. Felix was in awe as Penny took control of the dance floor with Shawn, leading him through the motions. She hadn't looked this happy all year.

"All in a day's work," Rosie said. "Now if you'll all excuse me, I gotta scope out the scene for cute boys." She sashayed onto the dance floor, flipping her hair.

Once Argent had endured his seething pain, Felix suggested they finally get food and stick with it this time. (R.I.P. Felix's food platter, 2117–2117.)

"We'll have a funeral for it later," Felix said. "Just pray Samuel doesn't find the remains."

"True enough," Argent said. "Get yourself some grub, since I've already devoured all my food." Felix was surprised, but Argent's plate was indeed already empty, simply stacked on top of Felix's fallen dish. What class. "In any case," Argent continued. "I'll wait outside by the fountain."

A red flag immediately popped up for Felix. "A-Are you—"

"I'll be fine. That creep won't attack where there's lots of people."

"… Just be careful, okay?"

"I will." Argent kissed Felix on the cheek. "That goes for you too."

They hugged, and Argent headed outside, while Felix merely tried to assuage his fears. *Please be safe.* Passing some of his professors—Ivanov dancing with Dezirae, and Videl with Jhaveri (*GAY! And also same.*)—Felix loaded up another plate, ready to eat away his nervousness.

But before he could join Argent outside, Felix caught a glimpse of a small red-and-gold bird watching from top one of the statues along the rafters. As soon as he blinked, it vanished. *Why am I not surprised? Can't even give me a moment to enjoy myself.*

"Cobalt."

As Felix was flung around, his food spilled onto Lucas' chest. Red pasta sauce stained his white shirt. "L-Lucas! I'm so sorry, I—"

"I should've expected as much." Lucas' fury was exacerbated by the red veins in his bloodshot eyes. "You and I need to have a word."

"Is everything—"

"I've been meaning to keep away from you. In hindsight, I don't envy your predicament." Lucas held his forehead. "But tell me, you can't genuinely mean to go along with his demands, do you? Do you even know what you're dealing with?"

Truth be told… Felix didn't. The plan was utterly half-baked, and on some level, he knew it was because deep down, he still wanted the Black Flame for himself. He wanted to believe he could use it to stop Vagus single-handedly, then wield that dark power and keep it under control in a way Elisa never could've. But he also knew this sounded not only ludicrous, but cruel. He hadn't shared the full truth with any of his friends. That he'd gone along with all of this since the welcome gala, or that Vagus had promised information on Frank's whereabouts… or Felix's plans on what he'd do to Frank whenever he found him again.

Lucas' frown twisted into a scornful glare. "Well? Answer me, Cobalt." Felix paused, unsure of what to say, making Lucas' face grow even redder. He grabbed Felix's collar. "Answer me, dammit! You take away my one chance at redemption and you don't even know what you're doing with it?!"

Within moments, Lucas' family swarmed around him, pulling him off Felix and holding him back as he tried to break free. "Get away from me! Get away!" His eyes darted about. Suddenly, they stopped, fixed on something past Felix. A chill ran down Felix's spine. As he turned, a blur faded from one of the windows.

Vagus.

Making matters worse, a crowd had gathered all around them, whispering and muttering about what could've been wrong with Lucas. Eventually, Lucas stopped fidgeting, only to hold his stomach with one hand and his mouth with the other. He threw up all over the floor. Felix leapt back, and students either gasped, laughed, or looked on in silence.

Lucas… what did he do to you?

Samuel barged through the crowd, glancing at Felix before carrying Lucas to the infirmary. Lucas' parents followed, while Lucinda, stepping around the vomit, approached Felix. "I am so sorry for Lucas' behavior," she said. "He must've had too much to drink, or—"

"Just… go be with him," Felix said. "He needs his sister." After a moment of silence, she ran to catch up with her family. Felix's sympathy was abruptly cut off as Ornella spun him around. "W-What the—"

"What did he say?" Ornella's expression was grave.

"W-Well…"

"Ornella, dear!" Priscilla scurried over and took Ornella by the arm. "Poor Lucas needs some help, don't you…?" Her gaze turned to Felix. "Oh, Mr. Brasher! How wonderful it is to see you again! I've heard you've been working hard on qualifying for the tournament."

"Uh…" Felix wasn't sure what to say. "I've been trying."

"Well I wish you the best of luck! If you'd like, I could put in a good word for you with the inspectors. Not to mention that the Fountain of Magic will proudly be sponsoring some of the candidates, so…"

"T-Thank you. I'll… consider it."

Nodding, Priscilla dragged Ornella out of the ballroom. Ornella tried to mouth a message to Felix, but he couldn't tell what it was, and at this point, he was beyond even wanting to try getting food again. He didn't want to tempt the universe to spill it again, even despite his hunger.

The cool night breeze felt refreshing as cicadas buzzed and leaves rustled along the rocky path. Nearly all of the reserve, along with the dragons flying over the peak of the Bors Mountains, were visible from this spot. The burning sensation still pulsed in Felix's arm from that encounter with Vagus all those months ago. He had to actively remind himself of the barrier keeping the creatures contained, holding his hand as it shook. He was safe—from dragons, at least.

There was no sign of Argent by the fountain. A whistle, carried by the wind as it picked up, jolted Felix's nerves. He followed the whistle, readying his concealed wand in case Vagus were to jump out at any turn. The source of the eerie melody came from within an alcove. That same alcove where Lucas had used his crystal to turn the water blood-red at the start of the year. Bracing himself for the worst, Felix peeked inside.

"There you are!"

And there he was: Argent, sitting atop the head of the eastern dragon statue, kicking his feet and whistling his tune.

Felix took a heavy sigh of relief. "Really? Good lord."

"I do what I want." Felix giggled at Argent's nonchalance. After how uneasy he'd felt all night, he envied Argent's ability to shrug anything and everything off and play it cool. Carefully, Felix skirted along the edge of the pool, trying to keep his eyes off the water. "C'mon up," Argent said. "It's weirdly comfy. Plus you get a great view of the stars from this spot."

"You of all people like to stargaze?" Felix asked.

"And find the—"

"Don't even." Felix giggled. "I mean, I doubt Denise has seen or read it, but your track record suggests you actually might have. So… I guess you're the real deal."

"Yeah, yeah, c'mon."

Felix stumbled climbing onto the statue, so Argent helped pull him up. They lay side by side on the stone, gazing up at the stars illuminating the sky's violet backdrop. At first, Felix wondered whether the Medeian Empire had some sort of technique to reduce light pollution. He'd never seen such a clear night before in his entire life. Then he recalled that the barrier systems here were far more efficient than the ones back home. "It's so beautiful," Felix said.

"Eh. I live in a rural part of Scotland," Argent said. "So this kinda thing's lost its charm for me. Though it is nice whenever I come back after a long trip."

"My parents said it's worse than when they were kids," Felix said. "When the barriers first went up when they were little, you couldn't see any of the stars. Even the moon got dimmer."

"Yeah. You guys are real backwards. No offense."

"No, no, I agree. Say, what's it like over in… Britain?"

Argent laughed. "First of all, yeah, the island's called Great Britain, but never use that term when talking to non-English folk, or you'll get murdered, and you'll deserve it." He and Felix snickered. "Not that I care. It's never been home for me."

"Why's that?" Felix asked.

"I moved to Scotland when I was little. Not my choice, but…" Argent groaned. "I've never felt at peace there. Not that my 'mother' ever tried to make me feel more welcome."

An awkward silence followed Felix kept running through scenarios of what Argent was implying, but felt too unsure to ask any further. Especially by how miserable Argent sounded.

"But from what I've heard," Argent said, breaking the silence. "The magi in charge of the L.U.N.'s barriers get treated better than… what do you Americans call it? The 'Magus Black Ops'?"

"*Special* Ops," Felix said. "They're essentially soldiers. Humans where I'm from either treat us like freaks, or useful tools of war. I'm not sure which is worse, honestly."

"For us, they're regular government workers. Not that they're treated much better." Argent went silent and stared up at the sky. Felix, wanting to comfort him, held his hand. "You said your mom's a magus, right?" Argent asked. "What about your dad?"

Felix stuttered. "Um…"

"Shit, I forgot, I'm sorry. You don't have to…"

"No, it's fine." Felix recollected himself. "Like I said at Christmas, my actual dad was human. And a raging bigot. He's been gone for seven years this month. I can't even remember the specific day, weirdly enough. I was so brainwashed in dogma and fear, and the way he disappeared… I just kinda lost all direction for a few months. Maybe even a year. It all kinda blurs together for me. It's… ironic, though. Our house burned down that night… and then I turn out to be a fire type."

Argent held Felix's hand tighter. "I'm sorry."

Felix's eyes remained on the stars. Gradually, his thoughts drifted away from Frank. He felt at peace, isolated from all the world's ugliness for but a moment. If only he could stay this way, up here with Argent, forever. But beneath that desire ran an undercurrent of doubt. Of self-loathing for all the secrets he was still holding onto.

"Also you have vomit on your shoes."

Felix sat up. Chunks of yellow throw-up coated the tips of his shoes, and he nearly gagged at the sight. "Oh, gross!"

"You feelin' alright?" Argent asked.

"It's not mine. A… kid got sick all of a sudden. One too many drinks." *Last thing Lucas needs is Argent going after him on my behalf.* "Fuck, these are leather. You wouldn't happen to have any soap, a sponge, and a towel on you, would you?"

"Nope. But I got lube."

"Not shocked in the slightest." Chuckling, Felix hopped down and took off his shoes, kneeling beside the pool. "Forgive me, shoes. Please don't die." He put the vomit-covered tips into the water. Chunks fell as the leather soaked. He pulled the shoes out, standing and putting one on. The damp coldness froze his toes instantly. Still, Argent could only create ice, not water, and Felix knew that if he tried to use a spell to dry them off, he'd probably set them on fire. (Though admittedly, the prospect did seem alluring for a moment.) Sucking it up, Felix put on the other shoe. *Gotta dry sometime. I hope.*

Argent tapped Felix's shoulder and held out his hand. "Care for a dance?"

"Uh… I—"

"I knew you'd get nervous dancing around other people," Argent said. "Here, we can dance as shitty as we please. So…?"

Hesitantly, Felix took Argent's hands. Felix hobbled about as Argent led, albeit stepping on Argent's toes a couple times. Argent simply laughed while Felix blushed. Eventually, they found the right rhythm, and Argent hummed the same melody he'd whistled earlier. Any concern Felix had melted away as they danced. No keeping an eye out for Vagus or Cinder, nor any sense of eyes constantly peering at him from all angles.

Just Felix and Argent—together.

They slowed, gradually easing into an embrace. Their eyes met, and without a word, they moved in closer, closing their eyes, their lips mere inches from meeting.

"Hey, lovebirds!"

Felix and Argent fell back into the pool. Coldness stung Felix's skin, coursing through his whole body. As he threw his head above the water, his hair hung in his face, and the sound of droplets streaming down from the strands and plopping into the water didn't help quench his temper. He spat out a stem from one of the lilies and brushed his hair out of his eyes. Rosie stood at the alcove's entrance, cackling her ass off. Felix simply huffed. *Way to kill the moment.*

Argent helped Felix out. Their suits had been completely drenched, and so they wrung their hair and jackets, brushing petals and stems off themselves. "Thank God my phone's waterproof," Argent said.

Oh shit! Felix took out his phone. The screen was slightly cracked, and when he tried to turn it on, it remained black. He glared at his reflection. "Fuck." Sighing, he put it away. "What is it this time?" he asked Rosie. His anger dissolved into fear as Rosie's smile faded into what she called her "game face." Felix and Argent glanced at each other, then back at Rosie, and nodded.

That ring is mine.

Chapter Twenty-Four

Into the Crypt

S AMUEL, holding his keys, stood before the doors to the Chamber of Kagami. Slowly, he turned back to Felix's group. "Everybody ready?"

Felix and Argent had finally dried off, though their suits still weighed heavily on them. Zahra asked what happened, though Rosie elected not to brag for the sake of the guys' self-esteem. Still, Felix wished he could've had one last kiss with Argent, if his worst fears became real. Maybe if they hadn't bothered with this plan, it could've become more later on. But now that warmth was gone. And in its place, a cold dread had taken hold. Now, it was time to dive headfirst into the nightmare.

"We have to get through the chamber to reach the crypt," Samuel said. "There's a passage at the back hidden by enchantments. I can't shut off the illusions, but if we all hold hands and focus, we might be able to get through more easily."

"Holding hands?" Argent winked at Felix. "We should be good at that."

Felix forced a smile. He appreciated the gesture, but it wasn't nearly enough to ease his nerves. If this kept up, he'd be joining Lucas in the infirmary from a stress-induced ulcer, long before he'd even had a chance to set foot in the crypt. Ironically, that would've been easier to explain to Calvin.

Holding hands as the doors shut behind them, the group marched into the darkness. Felix couldn't see Argent ahead of him, but he could feel himself being tugged along by some invisible force. "How much further, Samuel?"

Silence.

Felix stopped. Argent's hand—at least, what he believed to be Argent's hand—had slipped away.

"You can't save anyone."

Vagus appeared in the distance, his voice echoing all around. Felix stepped back. Yet no matter how he tried to get away, no matter how fast he ran, he couldn't get any more distance between himself and Vagus. Vagus opened his cloak, and Cinder, full-sized, dove at Felix, raining fire down upon him. As the blaze swallowed Felix, Vagus cackled.

Felix parted his arms to see Lydia, Ian, Aeris, and Tracey huddled together within the flames, screaming and crying in fear and pain. He ran to them, reaching out to grab them, but the inferno completely consumed them as their voices filled his ears. That same cackling returned. The voice was far less raspy, though, and much deeper. The figure of a man emerged from the flames.

Frank.

Felix fell to his knees, closing his eyes and covering his ears, but his father's sick laughter resumed.

"Pathetic!" This new voice caught him off guard. It was... his own voice, but older. Another silhouette, with a flowing tattered cloak and long hair, glared through the flames with piercing blood-red eyes. Holding out its hand, a red light on its finger sparked a deep-purple flame in its palm. The blast engulfed Felix. He cried out in pain as the fire burned his skin, as though his flesh was about to melt down to the bone.

A hand grabbed Felix by the arm and pulled him forward. The doppelgänger laughed one last time, then abruptly ceased as a bright light overtook the flames. Felix opened his eyes, rubbing them as he sat up, and before him stretched forth a vaulted ceiling. Rosie knelt beside him, while the rest of the group stood all around.

"W-What...?" Felix's voice was hoarse. "What happened?"

"We... got separated." Rosie helped Felix up. "I had to haul you outta there." Her voice was soft, and she averted Felix's gaze. Everyone did.

"What's done is done," Samuel said. Reluctantly, they all followed him down the corridor. With the painful echo of each and every step, Felix questioned himself as to why he'd ever agreed to any of this. And moreover, whether his friends might have finally caught on to him.

Tonight thankfully hadn't proven as much of a drag as Ramidha expected. Though she had the distinct displeasure of entertaining the Della Luces earlier, Seisyll managed to keep her from throwing punch in Martino's weaselly face. Now, they found themselves off in the gardens for a leisurely moonlit stroll. Ramidha plucked one of the firebird's wings, admiring its pure-white petals, and placed it in Seisyll's hair, to which he blushed.

"Oh come now, Sei," Ramidha said, barely containing a chuckle. "How long has it been since we've had time to ourselves like this?"

"Far too long," Seisyll said. He adjusted the flower. "I think it was a firebird's kiss you put in my hair the night of our first date, though. You mentioned how it matched my 'fiery temper.' To which I thanked you for appreciating me cursing out Samuel for releasing a horde of ravenous squirrels into my office."

They laughed, nearly howling as Ramidha bust a gut. "How is Samuel anyway? I feel I hardly ever see him anymore."

"You and me both, and I've never been happier for it." Seisyll stopped, staring at his feet.

Ramidha held Seisyll's shoulder. "Sei, you're doing wonderfully. Your new medication is helping, therapy is going great, and our daughter and niece are strong, wonderful young women. Don't let your brother's envy and unwillingness to understand take all that away from you."

Seisyll sighed.

"Ramidha! Sei! We have a problem!"

They turned, greeted by Gottschalk, dressed in a white long-sleeved, frilly gown, face red as she panted. "Isolda?" Ramidha asked. "What's wrong?" She couldn't help but try to lift the mood, given how stressed Gottschalk seemed. "Was there a gorgeous woman out on the dance floor? If you'd like, I can help you ask her—"

"Your niece," Gottschalk said. "Nasira. She said Zahra snuck off with Mr. Brasher and his friends. Apparently Samuel was with them."

"Samuel?" Seisyll asked, fury in his voice. "The hell…?"

"I have no clue, but given the last few months, we have to assume the worst. They must be headed for the crypt."

Deep down, Ramidha knew something like this was inevitable. That Felix was being led down the wrong path, but never did she expect Zahra to go along with him. This had to end. "Let's go."

The black tiled floor of the corridor, along with the pale-green limestone walls, seemed to absorb the already dim light of the turquoise torches hung about. At the very end of the hall stood a circular bronze door. Engraved upon its surface was a rendition of Aedan the Sunborn, his back turned towards those who would set foot into the crypt.

"Wow!" Zahra looked on in awe. "How long have you known about this place, Uncle?"

Samuel didn't respond. Instead, he muttered to himself, to which Zahra shriveled up a bit, and Felix resisted the urge to smack Samuel on the back of the head. Clearing his throat, Samuel took out his wand. "O gates to the depths of this sacred place, hear my command and open the way. Glyph: Halt."

Small glyphs appeared upon the entrance, turning and shifting like gears within a larger glyph. Metal creaks boomed as the door opened. Felix followed Samuel inside, and the others followed him in turn.

Felix instantly recognized the place from Montanari's lesson. His reflection stared back at him, eyes scathing, through the black tiled floor glistening like a salt plane. Even beyond his trivial self-loathing, pain and misery hung in the air here. Perhaps from his knowledge of the mutated prisoners once kept here? Or, if it was anything like that watery specter he'd encountered all those months ago from his astral projection journey, perhaps it was the residual suffering that had left its eternal mark on this place he was picking up on? He could practically hear the screams and cries for help now, clawing at the back of his mind as they demanded to be heard.

Blue-black stones lined the walls, the torches tinting everything with a purplish hue. In the center of the wall was an enclosed staircase winding down. Rows and rows of ceremonial swords, staffs, and scepters filled this whole level, though they appeared to serve more of a decorative purpose rather than being intended for use in battle. The artifacts placed upon the white marble pedestals radiated power, just as the golems sitting between them. Goliaths with no eyes sculpted from black clay, projecting a sense of foreboding and disquiet.

"We're looking for a ring, right?" Rosie asked.

"Y-Yeah," Felix said. "The Ring of Nergal. Uh, Samuel, you wouldn't happen to know where it would be, would you?"

"Nope." Samuel looked around. "Like Sei would ever trust me with that…"

Felix pitied Samuel. Though quickly, he returned to scanning the pedestals, half-expecting Vagus to pop out of hiding in the corner of his eye. He nearly leapt as Argent held his hand. He didn't say a word; neither of them did. Instead, Felix silently loathed himself for making Argent worry for him so badly.

Zahra approached a gold-and-blue bow with a silver quiver. Everyone gathered around her, their curiosity piqued. "I think this is Zeus' Bow," she said.

"Zeus?" Felix asked. "As in Greek god Zeus who sticks his dick in any hole he sees?" Instantly, he cursed himself for his crude joke. He'd attempted to diffuse the tension, only to further cement his own insecurity.

"No." Zahra returned her attention to the bow. "But this did contribute to the legends of his thunderbolt. It's said that this bow belonged to a powerful storm sorcerer who lived atop a great mountain in Ancient Greece. He used the bow to shoot lightning down on any humans trying to climb towards him."

"Wow…" Felix was in awe over the bow's majesty, but the story also stuck out to him. "Is that true, or just a myth?"

"No one knows." Zahra frowned. "But it's such a sad story."

"Kinda rings true, though," Rosie said.. "No pun intended."

Felix held Argent's hand tighter.

"Sorry," Rosie said.

"It's fine." Felix stared at the floor, into the dull-cobalt eyes of his reflection. "You're right."

"Then you children should understand how frustrating it is when you don't take this as gravely as you ought to."

No.

They all turned back. As if from thin air, Vagus had manifested within the crypt by the entrance. Behind him stood Cinder in her full-sized form. "You!" Felix yanked his hand free from Argent's. He marched forth, his yells deafening as they echoed. "So you finally decided to show up!"

"To ensure you hold up your end of the bargain," Vagus said.

"A 'bargain' you forced onto him!" Rosie stood by Felix's side, holding his shoulder firmly. "What's wrong? Too afraid to do your own dirty work?"

Vagus scoffed. "So you're the one who made that charm to interfere with my dreamcatcher. I must admit, it certainly was harder to break through than the last one." He shook his head. "But oh, Felix, you haven't told them the full story, have you?"

Felix's blood chilled.

"What's he talking about?" Argent asked.

"But of course!" Vagus' laughter made it harder for Felix to breathe. "If they knew you'd gone along with all of this willingly, then why would they ever help you get your hands on that ring? The classic pity routine. I knew I was right to choose you. Nothing could stop you from claiming the Black Flame for your own. Nor using it to get revenge upon your father."

Felix stepped back, unable to speak. He gripped his chest. Everyone turned to him, looking on in confusion, except Rosie. She glared, muttering.

"You fucking idiot."

"Though," Vagus said. "I'm afraid I'll have to make one final addendum to our deal: you're coming with me."

"W-What?!" Felix asked.

"You must know what you stand against. As I said, the power you seek is great, but you must learn to wield it properly. And so…" Vagus extended his arm to reveal an obsidian bracelet laced with red mythril. The glass ignited, spinning and crystallizing into a broadsword of burning rock. "You'll be coming along with me, once we get your friends out of the way."

"GO! NOW!"

Samuel drew his wand and, with a flash, teal lines of light appeared across each of the golems. They wound around their bodies like bioluminescent veins. The crypt shook with thunderous roars, booming as the stone shifted, the golems pushing themselves up. With each step, their footfalls released a massive tremor. They towered over Vagus while Cinder stretched her wings. For a moment, Felix felt at ease.

Until he heard Vagus' snickers.

"Suppose we'll have to do this the hard way," he said.

Cinder blasted the golems back with her fire. Once the flames dispersed, Vagus leapt at the nearest golem and plunged his sword into its head. Bright-orange cracks spread throughout the golem's body. With a resounding snap, the rocks crumbled, kicking up dirt as pebbles fell into a pool of molten slag. Another golem barreled towards him. It swung down its fists, but Vagus dodged, slashing the golem to pieces as he rolled. Felix simply stood there, unnerved at the masked man's skill.

"We need to go! Now!"

Rosie grabbed Felix's wrist, but he couldn't move. Instead, he focused on Rosie's scowl. He'd lied to her all this time, and now the only reason he could bring himself to look at her was because of his own shock.

"WHAT DID I TELL YOU KIDS?!"

Samuel heaved as he rushed to create barriers, each one slashed apart by Vagus' sword as Cinder held off the other golems. "Come on, Sammy!" Vagus said, chuckling every few swipes. "Surely you can do better than this."

"Hold on, Uncle!" Zahra yelled, reaching for her wand. "We can—"

"Last thing I need is for your dad to kill me!" Samuel yelled. "Go!"

Pulling her hand back, Zahra led the others down the staircase. As Rosie pulled Felix along, Felix couldn't take his eyes off the battle between Samuel and Vagus. There was no way Samuel could hold his own for much longer. If Samuel were to die because of Felix's desire... if all the others were to die...

The darkness was even more pervasive in the staircase. Every few steps, Felix nearly tripped as Rosie dragged him along. They spiraled further and further into their descent. The torches were practically as effective as dying candles, only the general outlines of Felix's friends visible, along with the eyes of something in the shadows returning every few seconds. Another tremor sent them stumbling. Felix fell into the pillar, his cheek slamming into the stones, and a sting coursing through his jaw.

"Let's try in here! C'mon!"

Argent led them into another chamber from which light poured. Felix grabbed the wall to stop himself, only to stutter as Rosie glared back, while

431

Argent looked on with pity and pain. "W-We're still going after the ring?" Felix asked.

"*We're* looking for cover," Rosie said. "*You* aren't going anywhere near that thing."

Felix couldn't muster a response. His oath bound him to find the Ring of Nergal and deliver it to Vagus. Or rather, that's what he believed. He'd been so caught up in the moment, in that promise of becoming stronger, that he'd never cleared up the specifics of his oath. Whether it would've been fulfilled by simply him holding the ring, or he had to explicitly hand it over to Vagus was unknown. And what would happen to him should he back out? What even constituted the oath being broken? Whatever fate it entailed, Felix genuinely believed that he deserved it. The worse, the more painful, the better.

They entered the chamber. While Argent remained by Felix's side to keep an eye on him—despite not being able to even glance at him—Rosie and Zahra darted about searching for a place to hide, and anything to fight back with. Through it all, the battle upstairs resumed with deafening quakes.

"I-I'm sorry…"

Felix could barely choke out the words, let alone raise his head or keep himself from shaking. He'd braced himself for the worst as footsteps rapidly approached. Though when he forced himself to look up, readying to explain himself to Rosie, Zahra stood there instead, staring him straight in the face. She didn't tear up. Instead, she wore a resentful glare. "You're 'sorry'?"

He gripped his arm tight, casting his gaze to his feet. "Y-Yes. I—"

"Look me in the eyes."

Hesitantly, Felix complied, and the guilt hit him like a bullet yet again. "T-There's no excuse," he forced himself to say, his voice crumbling. "But I wasn't sure… how much I could tell—"

"Stop lying." Zahra grimaced

"I-I'm not—"

"You are!" Zahra's yell silenced him, and the chamber went deathly quiet. "You looked us all in the eyes and lied right through your teeth! About the ring! About your oath! About all of it! I… trusted you. *We* trusted you. And you couldn't bother trusting *us*?" She looked off towards the end of the hall. "I can't believe how wrong I was about you."

Her words stung. But she was right. He'd lied by omission and kept them in the dark for months. He could've easily told them the full context of his deal with Vagus long ago, yet he didn't. And for what? For that ring? For information about a man who'd held a gun to his face and left him for seven years? After all Felix had been through, he'd simply dismissed his friends aside from their use as tools in his pursuit of power.

Perhaps Vagus was right about him.

"MOVE!"

Argent pulled Felix out of the way. Golden flames consumed the staircase, spilling out into the hall. Felix, Argent, and Zahra backed away. As the fiery plume ceased, heavy thuds descending the stairs followed. Vagus, with Cinder now miniaturized on his shoulder, entered, looking unfazed and unscathed, with no sign of Samuel.

No…

Vagus petted Cinder as she cooed. Slowly, he approached Felix, and the others backed away. "Now," Vagus said. "Are we going to have any more problems? Or will I have to—"

"I'll go!"

Everyone stood silent as Felix's shout reverberated. He wasn't sure what he was doing, but he was also desperate to protect his friends—even if it meant throwing himself under the bus. "I'll go with you. No fighting back. On one condition: you let my friends go."

Before Vagus could respond, Rosie tossed seeds from her bag. "Gaia's Protection!" The seeds cracked open with bursts of yellow light. Massive green vines, covered in purple-pink thorns, sprouted up. They enclosed Vagus, only to catch fire not long after. "Zahra, go check on Samuel and get some help!"

Zahra ran up the stairs as the vines collapsed. The fire neatly unfolded to reveal Vagus with his sword raised, glowing like red-hot lava.

"Rosie, move!"

As she ran, a wave of ice rushed at Vagus. He sliced through the attack, and the swing sent flecks of ice flying, creating a thick mist. There Argent stood, holding a double-sided axe with frosty blue blades, a shiny black metal handle, and a silver end knob. The blades' edges sparkled with white diamond dust. "I've got this creep," Argent said.

Gulping, Felix ran, searching for another weapon to help. Rosie grabbed his wrist. "What the hell do you think you're doing?!"

Felix, paralyzed by guilt, paused.

Rosie let go as they dodged one of Vagus' fireballs. Shaking himself from his stupor, Felix kept running. *I'm sorry. But I have to do something.* He passed a small shield with a gorgon's face, a long azure harp, and a giant mirror, all the while glimpsing back to ensure his friends were safe. Vagus knocked the axe from Argent's hand, sending him flying.

"Argent!"

Vagus moved to strike, only to jump out of the way as a bolt of lightning hit the ground where he stood. The floor crackled and smoked. In the entrance stood Zahra, holding up the Bow of Zeus. "Turns out the quiver's a lightning generator," she said, helping Argent to his feet. "Convenient!"

Felix ran over to them. "Is Samuel—"

"He's fine." Zahra didn't even glance at him. "He went to get help."

"In that case," Vagus said as he approached. He reached into his sleeve, revealing his dreamcatcher. "You children leave me with no choice."

Rosie scoffed. "What're you gonna do? Lull us to sleep?"

"May the tangled webs of your mind entrap you in a prison of your own making!"

"Oh no you don't!" Argent, grabbing the axe again, charged.

"Nightmare Web!"

Argent stopped in his tracks, and his eyes glazed over. The axe fell with a heavy thud. He dropped to his knees, blankly staring at the ground, tears rolling down his face. Rosie stepped in front of Felix, only to fall as Vagus uttered the spell once more. Zahra, the last one standing, readied her bow.

"Z-Zahra, no." Felix held her shoulder. "It's not worth—"

"This isn't for you."

She shot another lightning bolt. Vagus dodged. Zahra moved to strike again.

"Nightmare Web!"

Dropping the bow, Zahra, just like Rosie and Argent, fell.

Felix stepped back.

Vagus, walking past each of Felix's friends as they lay twitching on the ground, lowered his sword. Felix pulled out his wand, only for Vagus to knock it from his hand in a swift strike. Felix's hand stung as he backed into the wall. Without the wand, he was useless, but without any other options, he flicked his wrist. "Bolt Spark!" Vagus evaded the measly attack. He grabbed and twisted Felix's wrist, holding the dreamcatcher mere inches from his eyes.

"Nightmare Web!"

The threads incinerated, and Felix lost himself in the roar of the blaze expanding all around him. The cackling of his doppelgänger returned, as did its infernal smoky wings, stretching out across the expanse. Its seething eyes clawed into Felix's soul. With a blast of purple fire, pain shot through his body. He rolled to his side, clutching his arms and convulsing, screaming at the top of his lungs. He caught a glimpse of the figure. The face looking back was his own, albeit older, with deep-blood-red eyes. The Red of Nergal's crimson jewel glowed on its finger. Darkness shrouded him, nulling all sensations until the pain completely faded. The crackling of the fire gave way to a whisper—Felix's voice, but sinister:

"You think you can make something of yourself. But you are nothing. This world will break you, over and over, rending your spirit and tossing it to the wolves. Its flames will reduce you to ash. And once the dust has settled, there will be no one left to remember your name."

A scream followed.

The flames dispersed. Vagus, shouting in agony, leaned against the wall. He gripped his seared arm and further tore at his singed sleeve. Zahra held onto the quiver, smoke and a few stray sparks flying out of it. "You..." Vagus pushed himself off the wall. "YOU BITCH." He charged at her. She swung the quiver, but missed as he knocked it from her hand and lifted her by the throat. She kicked and struggled, gasping for air.

Felix's blood boiled. "BOLT SPARK!"

Vagus blocked the barrier with a barrier.

Felix pushed himself up. *I won't let you hurt them.* "Emerald Flame!" A feeble blue-green fire shot forth from his palm, throwing him back. Again, Vagus blocked with little effort. *Damn cobalt eyes.* His muscles ached. Coughs gave way to painful heaving from exhaustion.

Zahra's eyes closed, her kicks slowing.

"You can't protect anyone," the voice whispered. Felix's mind returned to his family trapped within the flames. To the sound of his father laughing. To his inner demon cackling.

Felix raced towards Vagus, grabbing at his cloak and throat. Weak and bruises as he was, he kept punching over and over, doing whatever he could to free Zahra. Vagus punched Felix with his free hand, knocking him to the ground. Felix picked himself back up. But before he could try anything else, he was met with the edge of Vagus' newly formed blade.

Felix forced a grin. "You can't kill me. You need me."

Vagus scoffed. "No. I don't."

Even if what Vagus said was true, Felix couldn't bear to watch his friends suffer any longer. He'd happily forfeit his life if it meant saving theirs. As Zahra seemed to lose consciousness, Felix steeled himself, ready to lunge again.

"Leave my daughter alone!"

A gust of wind blew through the crypt, throwing Vagus into the wall. Felix caught Zahra as she fell. Headmistress Hakim, her weapon currently on her back, rushed over to them. "Is she okay?"

Felix checked her pulse. "Yeah. She's still breathing."

She directed her focus back to Vagus. She drew her sword: a saw-like blade whose end was split into two prongs; one side crafted from green mythril, and the other red. Vagus tried to stand. "Blazing Gale!" With a single slash, she sent out a powerful gust of fiery wind, forcing Vagus back onto the ground. Seisyll took Zahra from Felix's arms.

Felix forced himself to speak. "I... I'm sorr—"

"Get your friends out of here," Seisyll said as he healed Zahra.

"R-Right." Felix struggled to pick up both Rosie and Argent, throwing his arms under their shoulders and hauling them outside the crypt entrance. Even more drained of energy, and his entire body numb from pain, he sat them against the wall before collapsing. Professor Gottschalk stood on guard, but said nothing. She didn't need to. Felix could feel the judgment in her glare without even meeting her gaze.

Seisyll carried Zahra out and continued healing her, giving Felix only a momentary glower before returning his attention to his daughter.

I am so sorry.

A sharp pain dug into Felix's chest, and he doubled over. But the sounds of the battle deep within the crypt had taken precedence over his own injuries. A battle between the headmistress and the man who'd tormented them all. Who'd hurt Felix's friends and threatened his family. Who'd nearly killed Zahra.

A tug at his arm grabbed his attention. Argent had come around, begging Felix to stay without a word. Still, Felix looked back to the crypt. *I have to end this.* He pushed himself up. *I'm sorry.* He ran for the entrance, past Gottschalk. He'd expected her to try and stop him, and to hear Argent, and perhaps even Rosie, yelling at him to come back.

They did nothing.

Fire and wind clashed, their booms rendering the crypt an echo chamber, nearly making Felix fall as he rushed back down the staircase. Ramidha was busy holding up a barrier, blocking Vagus' attack. No sign of Cinder anywhere.

Without a moment's hesitation, Felix grabbed one of the ceremonial swords from a nearby rack. Hakim and Vagus' attacks clashed again, creating a thick haze across the room, and Felix seized the opportunity. He rushed in. He'd lost sight of Vagus in the swirl of the orange flames and the haze, the flurry singing the tips of his hair, and the rank scent of smoke filling his nose. Then, a motion in the blaze. Felix rammed the blade forward, and the masked man heaved.

The haze cleared. There he was—Vagus, the sword rammed right through his abdomen. He coughed up splatters of blood through the small cracks in his mask onto Felix's face and arms. Felix glared where Vagus' eyes ought to have been. A twist of the blade invoked a groan of pain, much to Felix's delight.

Choke. Bleed.

With a flash of light, Vagus' body crumbled into dust, the ashes scattering across the floor. Felix dropped the sword. He fell to his knees panting as the pain in his chest returned. Ramidha carried him out, setting him beside his friends, who were now awake. He said nothing. No one did. Rosie and Argent stared at Felix: Rosie with fury; Argent with pity.

Felix stared dead ahead at the wall. His hearing, like the rest of his senses, dulled. The muffled arguments of the professors faded as he shut his eyes, replaced by only the sound of his heartbeat. Though for a moment, he chose to listen, and immediately regretted it.

"They got inside." Isolda resumed her argument with Ramidha and Seisyll. *"Children.* And a cobalt, no less!"

"At least they're alive," Ramidha said.

Seisyll shot another glare at Felix, then looked back at Zahra. "Barely…"

"The crypt is an ancient, forbidden sanctum," Isolda said. "And mere children were able to enter it. What kind of groundskeeper would allow this, much less collapse before reaching us? Had your niece not informed us, they'd all be dead, and our treasury ransacked!"

"I'm well aware," Ramidha said.

Isolda frowned. "This can't be overlooked. As headmistress, you can't afford to be so passive."

Felix shut his eyes. *All my fault.*

Chapter Twenty-Five

Consequences

PROFESSOR GOTTSCHALK had been listing off all of her punishments as Felix, Rosie, and Argent sat before her office desk. It had been going on for so long, Felix legitimately felt as though he'd seen the sun rise through the windows behind Isolda and nearly reach the sky's zenith.

"No extracurriculars," Gottschalk said. "No library access. No leaving the castle without express permission. No leaving your dorms after curfew. And most certainly…" She focused specifically on Felix. "No competing in the tournament. And for Mr. Brasher and Ms. Giordano-O'Brien in particular, rest assured that if the grant program is by some miracle reinstated next year, neither of you will be eligible. All three of you are hereby permanently barred from enrollment at Dragora."

Felix sank in his chair, twiddling his thumbs. At this point, the tournament and returning to Dragora, though massive blows to his aspirations, weren't at all his immediate concerns. Especially as his friends seated beside him ignored his existence.

"Your actions put the wellbeing of everyone in this school in danger," Gottschalk said. "I wouldn't expect such reckless behavior from young adults, even you, Mr. de la Mort. You can be sure that your mother will be hearing of this."

Argent tapped his armrest.

"This information should've been brought to our attention immediately, so that we might've contacted the proper authorities. What you all did honestly grounds for far worse than expulsion in the empire's eyes. Count your blessings our empress decided to show mercy." Gottschalk seated herself, rubbing her temples. On her desk were pictures of her family: one of her and her sister Elyse; another of herself with her arms around her niece and nephew in their youth. Felix had never seen Lucas smiling so brightly.

"You know that guy was after Lucas too," Felix said. "Right?"

"Yes. I'm aware."

"Is he getting help?"

"That is none of your business." Gottschalk held her forehead. "Hopefully this will teach you to stay within your limits." With another sigh, she stood and took out her wand. "Hold out your hands." They complied, and she flicked her wand over their palms as it glowed white. "You'll take an oath to never divulge the crypt's existence, nor that of anything you found within it. If you break this oath, we will know, and the full weight of the Medeian Empire will bear down upon you." They all agreed, and in a flash, small white glyphs appeared briefly on each of their palms before vanishing.

"Surprised you didn't burn them right onto our skin." Argent rolled his eyes. "And how long will this 'oath' last?"

Gottschalk frowned. "Of course we don't use branding for oath glyphs. That would be barbaric. Cathartic, but illegal. The glyphs were inscribed onto your souls. They'll only reappear if the oath's terms change, or if the oath is broken, in which case they'll turn red and burn for a moment, and we'll be notified immediately. They won't kill you."

So... I could've just broken mine then?

"As for 'How long?', until the day you die. You don't get to endanger our national security without facing the harshest of consequences. If we find you've broken the oaths, we will negotiate your arrest with your home country and keep you under observation here within the Medeian Empire. We'll have to either use the same oath on whomever you've told, or..."

Felix stuttered. "Or...?"

"Just pray it doesn't come to the alternative," Gottschalk said. "Thankfully, young Ms. Hakim pleaded with us to let you all finish your first year, so you might have time to reflect upon what you've thrown away and plan your future accordingly."

I'm sorry, Zahra.

"You're dismissed."

Felix, Rosie, and Argent all had bags under their tired eyes by the time they left Gottschalk's office. Felix, unsure of what to say, or even if he should say anything, wrung his hands from self-loathing. "So… I, uh… guess we're royally fucked. Huh?"

Argent simply looked upon Felix with exasperation before walking away. Felix couldn't bring himself to follow. Rosie stood there, her eyes shut.

"R-Rosie…?"

She walked away.

Felix rushed after her, grabbing her shoulder. "Rosie, please, I'm sorry, I—"

Turning on her heel, Rosie slapped him, the hit echoing through the entire hall. "You… you think 'sorry' covers what you did?!"

"I know, I… I was wrong to keep you all in the dark." Felix's voice cracked as tears clouded his eyes. "I was stupid and obsessed and—"

"You *agreed* to work with this guy for months, when you know what he might've been capable of. And then, you… you killed him."

"… You're telling me you wouldn't? Out of self-defense?"

"What self-defense? You ran back into the cr—" Rosie stopped. "You ran back inside… specifically to kill him. My best friend wouldn't do that. I don't know what happened to you, but… just leave me alone, okay?" Rosie turned, leaving Felix alone in the corridor.

I'm sorry.

"I want to know the truth."

Zahra, refusing to be seated on the couch where Nasira waited, stood in the middle of her mother's office. Her head still ached, though whether that was from the pent-up stress, using a dark alignment talisman against her light nature, or the near-death experience was beyond her care. Ramidha stood behind her desk simply looking wary, as did Seisyll with his hands tucked behind his back. "You say that," Seisyll said. "After sneaking into the—"

"Maybe I wouldn't have if you'd kept me in the loop!" Zahra never once in her life dared speaking over her parents. But right now, she was past courtesy. She looked into her mother's eyes, unflinching. "If you'd just trust me."

Ramidha glanced at Seisyll, while Zahra tapped her foot. Relenting, Ramidha nodded. "We trust you." She glanced at Nasira. "Nasira, dear, would you mind—"

"She stays," Zahra said.

Seisyll raised an eyebrow, while Ramidha paused.

"If you trust me…" Zahra smiled at Nasira, who simply sat on the couch, holding her wrist tightly. "Then you'll both understand that I trust her. I trust family."

Nasira smiled back.

Zahra looked back at her mother. "So… who is Vagus? What does he want with the Ring of Nergal? And how does Felix tie into all of this?"

"You might want to sit down for this." Ramidha motioned for Zahra to take a seat, and she did beside Nasira. Ramidha pulled her chair over in front of the couch. Seisyll, after using wind glyphs to soundproof the room and locking the door, stood beside her. "Even we don't have all of the answers," Ramidha said. "But… your friend, Felix…"

Seisyll frowned. "He's dangerous."

"Dangerous?" Zahra asked. "He's…" She hung her head. "He's not who I thought he was. And he's certainly reckless and impetuous. But… I wouldn't say he's—"

"He doesn't understand what he's involved with," Ramidha said. "Who the people stringing him along are."

"And those puppeteers would be…?"

Ramidha clutched the sides of her chair. "In passing, we call them the Enlightened."

Vagus stumbled into the disheveled manor.

Reaching the Isle of Ashes and dispelling all the glyphs cloaking it from plain sight was already a pain. Add to that his excruciating pain from using so much of his strength to cauterize his wound, an illusion to keep Felix off his trail, and having to be even more covert than usual to keep both Dragora staff and the Enlightened from intercepting or pursuing him. It was a wonder he hadn't been driven absolutely mad. At least, not yet.

This islet, just off the coast of Pyre, was once home to a lush forest, a gorgeous black sand beach, and an extravagant private estate denoting a noble lineage of "respected" sorcerers. But the years have a way of eroding whatever has been built, no matter how grandiose. Forests burn and turn to fields of ash and dead, fallen trees. Beaches dissolve until every grain of sand is adrift in the sea. And this manor's crumbling halls were empty, its once gleaming golden walls now revealed as the facade they'd always been, burned black as coal, glass shards from shattered windows shimmering in the grass the moment before you stepped on them. A deafening silence hung over this cursed place. As far as anyone knew, even the Enlightened, the Isle of Ashes had been swallowed by the Sea of Sagramore long ago.

And Vagus preferred to keep it that way.

Throwing open the front doors, he shambled up the decrepit stairs and down the lonely corridor, all the while Cinder sadly cooed on his shoulder, her beak hung downward. He passed portraits of late sorcerers and sorceresses—or "magi" as people liked to call them nowadays—all dressed in dark red and gold. One portrait caught Cinder's attention as she flapped her wings: a young woman with flowing strawberry-blonde hair, beaming pearl irises, and a distinctly melancholic frown.

"Now, now, girl," Vagus said, wheezing. He looked with disdain upon the name inscribed beneath the portrait. He dared not utter that cursed last name—the name that would doom poor Cendrilla to a miserable life, and a fate far worse than death.

There hadn't even been a door for what Vagus had long considered his room, but what need would there have been for privacy in this godforsaken place? Setting aside his cloak and mask, he gave Cinder some pellets to enjoy before falling into bed. The mattress coughed up dust. A spring or two jumped, hitting Vagus in the chest, just barely missing where he'd been wounded. But at this point, he was beyond caring.

"I'm sorry, Felix," he muttered. "For what I've pulled you into."

"I told you he was a turncoat!" Rhosyn's voice boomed within the dome as the other council members' images stood atop their pillars. "Vagus has always had his own agenda. And now for all we know, he's still out there!"

Vivien stood in the center of the lodestone pool. She dared not show even the slightest twinge of fear. Even with Their Beatitude absent, the slight glimmer of Her blue-black stone throne, and especially the gleaming orange eyes at the top of the chair, were enough to create a well of despair.

"I hope you're not taking joy in this," the honeyed voice of one of the female council members said. "Vagus was by far our best quaesitor. None of the others even come close. No offense, Vivien."

Vivien didn't respond. Not when she could've been eradicated in an instant.

"It certainly makes things more complicated," the hoarse female voice said. "Can we rely on his choices for calathus at this point?"

"But who else will get that ring?" the middle-aged male voice asked. "We need that talisman, along with—"

"Your impatience never ceases to exhaust me." The older male figure, muttering obscenities in Arabic, rubbed his temple. "The preparations for the attack on Dragora are still underway?"

"Complete, actually," the other old male voice said. "My contact reports that their cover remains hidden. Everything is in order for us to retrieve the Ring of Nergal. We can always secure a proper calathus down the road."

"Wonderful!" the sweet female voice said. "Now, as for who will lead this operation… Vivien!"

Vivien's blood ran cold.

"An undine?!" Rhosyn asked. "You'd have a *familiar* calling the shots?!"

"Relax, Rhosyn," the woman said, silencing him immediately. "Vivien has proven her loyalty. I'm sure she's more upset at Vagus' betrayal than any of us, having been his creation, after all."

In all honesty, Vivien hadn't cared as to whether Vagus had died or turned traitor. He'd never bothered keeping her in the loop as to the details of his half-baked plans. She'd never forged a close bond with her creator, not that he went out of his way to make one himself. With him gone, this was the perfect opportunity she'd craved to become more than just a familiar to be tossed away.

"I'll do it," Vivien said.

"It's settled then!" the woman said.

Rhosyn groaned. "It'll have to do, I suppose." He snickered. "It'll give me an excuse to send one of my chimaeras out for a test run. Terri will be so happy at the chance to play outside the lab."

Chapter Twenty-Six

Rock Bottom

NEARLY A MONTH had passed since the crypt incident.

Every day after class, Felix would return to his dorm and stare at the ceiling. Whenever he'd bothered to go, that is. He'd heard nothing from his friends since, and if he wasn't coming back to Dragora next year, what was the point in trying to pass his classes? And to make matters worse, most of his savings had to be spent repairing his phone from falling into the water during the dance, meaning little to nothing left to pay for food. Not that his appetite was particularly strong after what happened. Calvin thankfully was kind enough to check up on him once or twice, always making sure Felix could take care of himself and bringing him food. Professor Montanari only seemed to glare at him. Word had most definitely spread among the faculty, and his favorite professor most certainly no longer considered him her favorite student.

And Samuel? No sign or word from him since the crypt. Rumor had it Seisyll had grown tired of his brother's laziness and bad attitude, and they'd finally fired Samuel, not even bothering to replace him for the end of the semester. Felix told himself that Samuel would've considered it "funemployment." Yet even so, he spiraled further into self-loathing at the domino effect wrought by his short-sighted arrogance.

So here Felix was. Spending a Friday night, the last night of the Ancient Dragons' Tournament finals, lying in bed, a bowl of popcorn over his chest. Flakes fell as he fumbled for one, butter glistening on his fingertips. He'd been playing his usual game on whether he'd marry Eunice or Darius. These weeks of distraction and constant numbing had left him perfectly content in his misery, and tonight was no different.

Until a heavy, unceasing knock at the door caught his attention.

Pulling himself out of bed, Felix climbed down from the loft and trudged towards the door, ready to clock whomever had broken their knuckles from knocking so aggressively. He flung it open. There stood Nasira, hand on her hip, holding a purple-and-yellow envelope. She grimaced. "You look like shit."

"What is it?" Felix asked.

She handed him the message. "Zahra wants to meet with you at the coliseum tonight."

"Huh. Didn't expect that." Felix had grown so apathetic, he wasn't sure what to feel besides confusion. His expression remained detached. Still, he forced a smile, trying to make it as sincere as possible. "Thanks."

"Just so we're clear," Nasira said. "I don't feel sorry for you, and I'm not sorry for ratting you out that night."

"I know," Felix said. "You did what you thought you had to."

"I *know* I had to." She glared, then walked away.

Suppose I deserve that.

Wanting to forget that interaction, Felix shut the door quietly. He had no idea as to why anyone, Zahra least of all, would've bothered contacting him. But after all he'd put her through, hearing her out was the least he owed her. And so, he tore open the envelope. He'd slightly ripped the letter inside, and the handwriting made him raise an eyebrow. He squinted. "Is that a lowercase 'A' or a '2'?"

Felix held the letter beneath his desk light. After several attempts of reading and rereading, he made out the message:

"Meet me at the coliseum before the finals start tonight. I'll be wearing a bright-purple jacket with a big yellow bunny on the front. It's urgent, so please come. I'll find you."

An odd choice of fashion, but Felix honestly found it endearing. He'd missed his friends' odd antics, though he hated admitting that, namely because he felt he didn't deserve such wonderful people in his life. He lay about until only an hour before the matches began before heading out. He didn't even bother brushing his hair, and despite it nearing the end of June, with the hot sun beating down from a cloudless blue sky, Felix opted for a loose-fitting black hoodie over a baggy brown T-shirt and a pair of black shorts. Whatever was easiest to toss on.

Getting out of the castle was shockingly easy. Even despite Gottschalk's restrictions, he faced no resistance as he boarded the coach bound for Cendrillion, which admittedly did lend to his feeling of being invisible. His apathy dissolved when he caught sight of the Angels' Arena, and was arrested by its awe-inspiring grandeur. Dragon statues lined the top of the coliseum. Locals and tourists alike rushed inside, all while news crews stalked the grounds for anyone to give them a soundbite. The lobby extended all around, with flatscreen TVs everywhere, all blasting replays of previous matchups discussed by commentators.

And of all the people for him to see the moment he entered the lobby, Rosie and Argent stood at the entrance to the elevator with their food. They chatted, laughing amongst themselves, but the moment Rosie caught a glimpse of Felix, she simply glared, while Argent averted his gaze. Felix wanted to run up to them and apologize, but he knew it wouldn't do anyone any good. And so, Rosie and Argent entered the elevator. Felix, taking a heavy sigh, resumed his search for Zahra, pushing through both the crowds and the shame.

"I don't need to take this from you. It's *my* life!"

Penny's voice caught Felix off guard. Over by one of the rest areas, Shawn and Floria sat in black leather chairs, while Penny, her face red, shouted over the phone. Her hair, normally hanging in her face, had been completely pulled back. "Goodbye!" She hung up and sighed, only to nearly jump when she saw Felix.

"S-Sorry." Felix stepped back. "I didn't mean to eavesdrop."

Penny looked at the floor, holding her wrist. "It's fine." Felix didn't know what Penny or any of his other friends thought of him now. He'd cut off contact with anyone and everyone. But as far as he knew, Penny had entered the tournament and made her way to the finals. "It's just—"

"It was her mom," Floria said.

Shawn frowned. "Seriously?!"

Floria simply shrugged, while Penny held her forehead. "A family friend told her I was competing," Penny said. "And she wasn't too happy to hear about that."

Felix had no clue as to why Penny was telling him all of this. Maybe on some level, she still trusted him, though the fact anyone would at this point felt wrong. Still, Penny had worked hard to claw her way to success, and Felix knew firsthand how exhausting and lonely that was—especially when the people who were supposed to be rooting for you did nothing but try to clip your wings.

"Screw her," he said. "Like you said, it's *your* life. You're gonna go out there, and you're gonna kick some ass. I'm sure of it."

Penny didn't respond. She simply stared at her phone.

I tried. Felix turned, ready to continue looking for Zahra.

"Felix?"

He turned back around, and Penny gave a faint smile.

"Thanks."

Normally he'd have smiled back. But instead, Felix gave a slight nod before walking off. He kept up his search, a pit of anxiety forming as he wondered if he'd just missed her. If she'd given up on looking for him.

A hand on his shoulder jolted him as he spun around. The figure was a bit shorter than him, their face obscured by a hood. Purple jacket. Light-yellow bunny stitched onto the front. She removed the hood, revealing not a smile, but a grave expression.

"Z-Zahra…" Felix collected himself, though he instinctively tensed up. "Long time no see." He hung his head. What could he possibly have said to lighten the mood, especially given he had no right to in the first place? "Is everything okay?"

"I can't stay long." Zahra looked all around, scanning the lobby. "It's Lucas."

"Lucas?" No one had seen Lucas since the dance last month. Word was his parents had finally decided to hire a private tutor and homeschool him for the rest of the year.

"I saw him earlier," Zahra said. "Back at Dragora. He was acting strange, hanging around Samuel's office. He kept muttering about Vagus."

Felix's blood chilled. "V-Vagus? That's… but Vagus is dead."

449

"I don't know either, but I already warned my parents to keep an eye out for him."

"... So why tell me this?"

Zahra sighed. "I don't know. Part of me wanted to think maybe you had an idea as to what was up with Lucas. That maybe I could finally get an honest answer out of you."

Felix paused.

"But..." Zahra held her forehead. "I shouldn't have even mentioned this. Just go back to your dorm and forget I said any of this." She grumbled to herself as she disappeared into the crowd. Felix tried to follow, calling out for her to wait. All he wanted was to make sure she was okay, but the moment she turned back towards him, the last Felix saw of her was a scowl before she vanished entirely, leaving him despondent and idle as people pushed past him.

Felix shuffled to the side of the lobby, leaning against the outer wall and hoping the TV overhead would fall and crush him. There was no point in even coming here. Zahra couldn't trust Felix with the truth, and he couldn't blame her. Perhaps he'd be doing everyone a favor if he just quietly returned to his dorm and slept the rest of the year away, all 'til he went home to mull over his failures and drown in his brooding.

But then Lucas walked past, shoving his way through the crowd, slipping into a dark corridor between the elevator and food stalls reserved for staff members.

Almost as if on autopilot, Felix followed, darting across the way and reaching for the door handle. He stopped himself. Was this even worth the time, or the potential fallout? Zahra had just pleaded with him not to cause any trouble. Yet here he was, ready to stick his nose into other people's business.

At least, he wanted to believe it was none of his business.

But there had to have been some reason Vagus had been observing Felix for most of his life. For Vagus to have put so much stock into Felix fulfilling his agenda. For better or worse, Felix had to find the truth himself, no matter to cost. He had nothing left to lose anyway.

Oddly enough, as Felix checked his surroundings, it wasn't the fact that the passersby hadn't cared what he was doing whatsoever that piqued his curiosity. No. Rather, it was the fact the security cameras were all pointed towards the floor. Their lights were all turned off, and once Felix entered the staff corridors, he found the same was true for all the cameras here as well.

And beyond that, there wasn't a living soul walking around here. No employees. No security. Not even a janitor walking down the narrow white passages. The only sounds were the faint echoes of Felix's footfalls, which were drowned out by the buzzing of the overhead lights.

"You heard Vagus! We can't!"

The female voice came from around the corner. Felix, taming his fear, leaned around to see Ornella, flustered, standing before Lucas before he opened the metal door. "You know what they're capable of," Lucas said. "I have to try."

Ornella shushed him. "Keep your voice down." She looked around. "I've tried speaking with him, but the best we can do is wait and—"

"Wait for what? For everyone to die? There must be another way!"

"Lucas, please—"

Lucas threw open the door and rushed inside. Ornella tried to catch him, but stopped and flinched at another voice calling incessantly out for her. Her mother Priscilla, looking exasperated, marched around the corner, the clicking of her heels filling the hall. "There you are! Where in the world have you been?!"

Ornella turned deathly pale. "I-I—"

"I told you not to wander too far from our stall!" Priscilla grabbed Ornella's wrist, pulling her out of sight. But Ornella knew about Vagus? Now there was no turning back.

After ensuring the halls were empty, he pressed his ear against the door Lucas had gone through, then peered inside. Pitch black, with only a faint trace of a downward staircase. With a quick mantra of "I am not crazy," he entered, quietly shutting the door behind him. He'd sorely wished he'd been allowed to bring his wand into the coliseum.

Thankfully he'd managed to get his phone repaired with the last of his allowance. After turning on its flashlight, Felix descended one step at a time into the darkness. Into a deep, disturbing silence. No footsteps. No whispers. No Lucas.

Nothing.

He glanced left and right as he went down the hall, checking for any doors Lucas might've gone through, or for any signs of some unknown assailant waiting to ambush him. A chill in the stale air added to the unsettling ambiance. Even the sounds of a stadium far above, packed with roaring attendees, couldn't breach this place. The occasional clanking of metal and a deep hum slowly drilled away his nerve. There should've been someone down here; perhaps a guard or two. But the fact he'd even managed to get down here at all felt wrong. Something was down here, something insidious, waiting to make its move.

"Vivien? Where the hell are you?!"

Felix nearly shouted and fell on his back. Recollecting himself, he found a set of heavy double doors at the end of the hall, and to either side, eerily hushed corridors. Still, there were no signs of life aside from the unnerving him, and a primal urge to run.

"Understood. We'll be right there, boss."

He ducked behind a trash bin and turned off his flashlight. A faint radio static followed the heavy thuds of boots, and a dim light shone over the doors as two silhouettes appeared. The light emanated from weapons—assault rifles. These were soldiers, and judging from their gear, they were armed to the teeth. What made this even more terrifying was the realization that where these two came from, there had to have been more.

"Let me go!"

A third soldier approached. At the end of the barrel of his gun stood Lucas, his hands raised. "We're taking you to the boss ourselves," the soldier said. "Now quit fidgeting! Or else you might not make it to him at all."

The fuck did you get yourself into, Lucas? The fuck did I get myself into?

Right before the doors slammed shut behind the soldiers, Felix leapt through and hid behind a nearby column. He couldn't just leave Lucas alone. And even if he escaped, no one above ground would ever have believed him. But now, there was no way of going back without giving himself away, and he had no reception to contact Rosie, Argent, or Zahra (assuming they'd bother answering).

Yet even so, actively searching for a quieter way to gather evidence while also finding another way out would've risked Felix getting caught by any other soldiers prowling about. While Lucas managed to avoid being decorated with bullets, Felix took the healthy assumption that he wouldn't be nearly as lucky.

At the very least, this room wasn't nearly as dark as the corridor. Large boxes sat all across the floor. Felix followed the soldiers deeper inside, taking cover wherever he could. His curiosity getting the better of him, he peeked inside one of the boxes, and was greeted by a trove of charges with wires hanging out. Bombs. He gasped, his foot hitting the box as he rushed to hide.

"What was that?" One of the soldiers' lights swung down the aisle as he approached.

"Probably just a rat," another soldier said, giving a sick chuckle. "Maybe one of those freaks keeps it as a pet."

"Whatever. Let's just go. This place gives me the creeps. We'll move the defective charges once we're done with this brat."

The light vanished, and the soldiers marched on. Felix, mustering his strength, forced himself to follow, albeit at a greater distance this time through a downward-sloping hall. Their boss likely set himself up in the lowest sublevel, but that begged the question as to why security in the coliseum of all places was so lacking. What awaited Felix at the bottom of this path?

Straight ahead was total darkness. The soldiers' light became no more useful than a faraway flickering candle. The air, just moments before sickeningly sterile, quickly turned musty as a cold breeze howled through the hall. Felix shivered, making him grateful for his ridiculously oversized hoodie.

The passage led to a metal platform extending into a cavernous space, reverberating with the clanks of steel beneath Felix's feet, alongside the dripping of water far below. Down there, the soldiers muttered until their voices, along with their lights, disappeared into a crevice.

Not wanting to give himself away again, Felix tucked his shoes under his arms. His soles froze upon contact with the platform. Diving straight into a tub of ice in the dead of winter seemed vastly more appealing, as that would've made for a quick hypothermic death. Still, this would help mask his pursuit. He turned his phone's flashlight back on, holding onto the railing as he descended. At the bottom, the coldness of metal became a coldness of stone, pebbles sliding between his toes, jabbing his feet. The rocks' dampness, along with the sudden shift of environment, felt surreal.

More silhouettes entered at the top of the platform, upon which Felix threw his shoes back on and stumbled through the passage Lucas was taken through. Static and low grumbling echoed back to him from up ahead. The tunnel led into another cavern, where Felix hid behind a large rock by the entrance, then dashed to the back corner of a nearby crate.

Construction lights illuminated the chamber, more crates littering the sides of the walls as soldiers sorted through luminous stones, far too iridescent to be mythril. Other soldiers spoke to what had to have been their leader: a tall, stocky man dressed from head to toe in black. Armor clad over his gut, and blood-red stripes ran down his pant legs. A black-and-red demon mask, complete with fangs, horns, and empty eye sockets, covered his entire skull. The crimson hilt of a katana was sheathed on his back, along with two smaller blades.

"Let me go!"

The soldiers, still holding Lucas at gunpoint, brought him in. The boss groaned. "Wonderful," he said. His voice was low and warped, no doubt modulated by some device in his mask. "I was warned you might be a problem. But this is perfect timing."

"I don't know who you are," Lucas said. "But you need to—"

"Can it, kid."

The familiar female voice terrified Felix. A cold hand gripped his arm. Or rather, what Felix assumed to be a hand until that same icy sensation spread across him. Water encased his body from the neck down, pulling him out from his hiding spot and into the air. There stood Vivien. Her entire arm had transformed into pure water. She simpered.

Felix's phone floated out from his pocket, as though it had been intentionally plucked from his person, and flowed down through the water into Vivien's hand. "Didn't anyone tell you it's rude to eavesdrop?" She threw the phone to the ground and crushed it beneath her heel.

Without warning, she threw Felix into the wall. His head rang with pain as rocks scraped him. He struggled to push himself up as the chamber spun, the cold water drenching him, stinging his skin. The soldiers forced him up.

"Cobalt?!" Lucas asked. "What the hell are you—"

"Good to see you again, Felix." Vivien sauntered over and cupped his chin, staring into his eyes. "So glad we're finally meeting face to face."

"Vivien," the boss called.

"Sorry, Bloodworth," she said. "You can't kill this one either."

"You're the one who seems trigger happy," he said.

Vivien scoffed. "Says the one with the melodramatic name and the samurai fixation?"

Bloodworth coughed, then gestured to an unconscious Samuel. He'd been tied up and pressed up against the wall. "We have the groundskeeper for crypt access."

"Please!" Lucas' face reddened as his voice cracked from his shriek. "Don't do this!"

"Oh, honey…" Snickering, Vivien sashayed towards Lucas. "You're a little late." She slapped him across the face. "Tie them up. Leave them somewhere 'til the attack's over."

Bloodworth glanced at Lucas. "Sorry, kid." He gave the approval to his men. Without hesitation, a soldier knocked Lucas out with the back of his gun. Another beside Felix raised his weapon, ready to ram it into the back of his head.

"No, no," Vivien said. "That's far too barbaric." She gave a devilish grin. "Relax, dearie. Just take a nice nap for us." Her arm turned to fluid again. A sphere of water surrounded Felix's head. He tried to hold his breath, but the torrent burned his eyes and nose. Muffled screams broke through as he swallowed the water. Within moments, it all went dark.

"HELL YEAH, PENNY! KICK HIS ASS!"

Argent's yell nearly ruptured Rosie's eardrums, which was saying something compared to the roars of the audience all around. They were towards the end of the lower-bracket finals, and Penny had managed to claw her way through tooth and nail. Just one opponent left, and she'd be named champion. Shawn especially was excited, cheering along with Argent as they howled like wolves, swaying to and fro and dropping popcorn everywhere. At the very least, it beat Argent muttering obscenities when Pope-Emperor Angelov gave his speech earlier that night.

"Could you guys not?" Rosie's question fell on deaf ears (almost literally). She'd wanted to be happy for Penny, and enjoy some time with her friends, but as the sun began to set, she missed her best friend's company. Even after all he'd done, what was she going to do? Ignore him for over a month all over again? He had to learn, but was this the right way to go about it?

A flail of Argent's accidentally hit Rosie's shoulder, making her spill her soda. "Shit!" Argent yelled. "Sorry!"

There was no way he would've heard Rosie chewing him out, so she simply waved her hand. But as she moved to clean her drink, she noticed something odd. At the very end of their row, in the aisle seat, sat a man dressed in a baggy black hoodie and sweatpants. His hoodie obscured his face, not that he would've seen the match without it anyway given his neck was craned so far down. He seemed to be by himself. No food, no drinks, no friends… nothing. He just sat there, muttering to himself. For a moment, she wondered if maybe it was…

"Hey, what's up with— OH, HELLO THERE."

Argent's voice freaked Rosie out so much, she wound up inadvertently rolling her cup down the aisle, through several people's feet, ending at those of the strange man. It tapped his boot, to which he gave Rosie a disquieting leer before returning to his apathy. Her skin crawled. Rosie rushed back into her seat, glaring at Argent. "What's the matter with you?!"

"What?" Argent shrugged. "You're allowed to stare at some guy's package and I'm not? Sure." He sipped his drink, mumbling to himself while looking somber.

Confused, Rosie looked back, trying to glimpse what the hell Argent was talking about. A flicker of light caught her attention, coming from the man's pocket and matching the color of his clothes.

A gun.

She could only see the top of the handle, and it had a peculiar crystalline mold that seemed reminiscent of mythril, but lighter. However elegant, there was no mistaking what it was.

The man leered again.

Quickly, Rosie averted her gaze, her heart thumping against her chest. How did this guy get past security with a gun? The question wasn't what he was aiming to do, but rather, when? How many people could he hurt before someone stopped him? How long would it take, how many people would be hurt or killed, before security could stop him? Could she do something?

She tapped Argent's shoulder. "Hey, I'm gonna go get a new drink."

"COOL," Argent yelled, his eyes still fixed on the sight. She would've found comfort in Argent's blissful ignorance, and in hindsight, telling him would've been the smart idea. But in that moment, it took all of her strength to stand. They were blocked in with a dividing column on one end of their row, meaning the only way out was directly past the gunman. She couldn't raise any further alarms. She marched forth, hoping to get up the stairs and find security as quickly as possible.

"Long time no see, Rosie."

She froze.

He grabbed her wrist.

She couldn't breathe. She couldn't even bring herself to question how he knew her name, let alone look back as the man kept her fixed in place, taking his time as he rose. "Why don't you and I go somewhere private to talk? Catch up?" His voice was low and gruff.

If she went with him, she was dead. There was no way in hell she was about to go out this way. Not to some lone would-be killer who, as far as she assumed, was here explicitly to kill her and anyone like her. If she didn't stop him, how many other magi die at the hand of this lunatic? Slowly, she nodded, feigning acceptance of her fate. Thankfully the asshole was arrogant enough not to bother drawing his weapon.

As he entered the aisle, Rosie waited until he was about to take the next step up before turning on her heel and kneeing him right in the gut. This, along with a push, sent him flying down the staircase, but not before she could snatch the gun from his waist and send it clattering to the ground. His head slammed into the wall once he hit the bottom. The hood fell to reveal a young white man with buzzed blonde hair, sickly lean with a horridly gaunt face. It took Rosie a moment to place it, but once she did, she flashed right back to that day in the Alderwood cafeteria.

Billy opened his eyes, only to give a chilling sneer as he raised what seemed to be a walkie-talkie to his mouth.

"Briggs… Code Crimson."

Just as everyone rushed to see what was happening, or to see whether Billy might need help, a chorus of screams gave Rosie pause. Lights flickered across the other parts of the arena. Before people in her section could trample her, Rosie grabbed the gun and stuffed it into her bag for defense later. Argent rushed to her. "The hell is—"

"No time!" Rosie yelled. "We need to get out of here, before—"

They nearly fell as the entire coliseum violently shook. Fire rushed from the arena, smoke obscuring Penny from view. "PENNY!" Shawn leapt over

457

the stadium seats, stumbling and nearly falling several times, while Floria looked on in horror, paralyzed.

Rosie wanted to stop him, but froze as more rumbling ensued, followed by the roar of what sounded to be a dragon in the distance. She looked to the sky, and immediately regretted it. There, eclipsing the red-orange expanse, was a horde of dragons, griffins, and other familiars, all flying free, some of them flying down into the coliseum and attacking people as they ran.

"DUCK!"

Caught off guard, Rosie heeded Argent, and he shot out a chunk of ice from his hand. A brief scream followed the crunching of ice and tearing of flesh. She looked back, finding another soldier in black, this one masked with a stockier built, falling to the ground from a deep wound in his chest. Thankfully his armor seemed to have been donned incorrectly, as his chest was left exposed. Unable to help herself, Rosie yanked off the mask, revealing a wide-eyed Buck, his blue eyes glazed over as his oily brown hair fell limp.

Oh god... Rosie couldn't take her eyes off of him. But then it hit her. Whatever these Camo Crew rejects had to do with this attack, they were here for petty payback, on both her, and Felix. And she'd seen Felix hours earlier, simply giving him the cold shoulder.

I have to find him.

Chapter Twenty-Seven

Nowhere to Go But...

OBLIVION: an all-encompassing void. An emptiness so pervasive, so deep, no light nor darkness could reach. No dreams. No nightmares. Nothing.

So this was what it was like to die.

"Cobalt?! Cobalt, wake up!"

The murmurs reverberated into thundering yells. Pain split Felix's skull, ringing over and over until it tore his mind from the stupor. A stabbing pain behind his eyes, far worse than any migraine he'd had before, forced them open, and a blinding light blurred his vision. He moved to rub the tears and sand from his eyes, only to find he couldn't raise his arms. A musty old rope had been wrapped around him. Still groggy and disoriented, he dragged his teeth over his dry tongue. How long had he been down here? He tilted his head back, hoping to stretch his neck and survey his surroundings, only to bump into something behind him.

"Ow! Are you awake, Cobalt?" Lucas groaned in pain. "Or are you still asleep?"

If I was asleep, how the fuck could I tell you?

But this wasn't the time for throwing insults. "Yeah," Felix said, his voice hoarse. "I'm up." He and Lucas had been tied with the same rope, thrown into this small cave while Vivien, along with that Bloodworth man, were free to execute their plan. And the people in the coliseum far above were blissfully unaware. Felix tried to squirm free, but his muscles ached. "They didn't tie us to a rock or something? To, I don't know, make sure we couldn't move?"

"I doubt Bloodworth and his men are the sharpest knives in the drawer," Lucas said. "And Vivien couldn't care less. Not that it matters. The city's likely already under fire."

"We have to go," Felix spat out. "Can you get us free?"

"No. My head's pounding. I don't have the focus for a spell that wouldn't immediately incinerate us both. It's pointless."

That truly boiled Felix's blood. As a cobalt, he was practically powerless without his wand, while a pearl-eyed magus like Lucas, to whom magic came with ease, simply chose not to even try. Gritting his teeth and clenching his fists, Felix closed his eyes. "Bolt Spark!" Tiny sparks flickered at the tips of his shaking hand. With a few more flicks of the wrist, an ember jumped from his palm to the rope, burning it from the side. A spray of dust and God knows what else rose from the smoke, stinging his nose. He coughed and leapt to get clear. Brushing the small fires off his clothes somehow felt cathartic, but that didn't last long, as his headache returned with a vengeance. He held his forehead, writhing in pain while his arms throbbed.

"You idiot."

Felix coughed and squinted, rubbing the water from his eyes until Lucas' figure became clear. "We had to do something." His voice croaked as he spoke. He leaned against the wall, waiting out his daze.

Lucas scoffed. "I never thought you would be as dull as you were weak, Co—"

"Would it kill you to use my damn name for once?!" Felix cleared his throat, relishing in the fact he'd finally managed to get Lucas to shut up. "And I didn't see *you* trying to break us free, o noblest of pearls. I didn't see *you* putting up a fight back there. And unless my memory got messed up from getting knocked out, you never bothered letting me in on everything *you* know about Vagus and these other people. So, with all due disrespect... fuck you."

After a heavy sigh, Lucas forced a smile. "Uncouth as ever... Felix."

It's a start. But I still fucking hate you. Felix pushed himself off the wall, stretching his arms, legs, and back. "Bloodworth and Vivien. Who are they?"

"No idea on Bloodworth. He must be one of Vivien's associates. As for Vivien..." Lucas paused, remaining silent.

"Do you know how they're connected to Vagus?"

Silence.

Felix rolled his eyes, but decided to give Lucas the benefit of the doubt that he was being kept quiet by an oath. "We need to get back up there," Felix said. "Up to the coliseum and warn everyone of... whatever they're doing." He wasn't sure what specifics their plot entailed besides stealing the Ring of Nergal, but with all these soldiers and weapons, it couldn't have been good.

"No use." Lucas hung his head. "We're already too late."

Felix seethed. "Unless you've forgotten, my friends... *our* friends, assuming that you have any besides your little minion Ulrich, are up there. Along with *your* family."

"That can't change—"

"So you're fine with them getting butchered?" Felix threw up his hands. "You know what? Fine. If you wanna do nothing, you're welcome to squat here 'til we're all dead. But I'm gonna try. Maybe I'll die. But I won't be a coward who just let this happen."

No response.

Why do I even try?

Felix scanned the area again. They'd been tossed into a small grotto branching off the larger cave system. He pried open one of the nearby crates, and the contents further inspired terror: rifles, grenades, and most oddly, swords. Or rather, katanas, similar to what Bloodworth had been carrying. The blade gleamed. Crimson trims along the black hilt outlined a silvery stone, which seemed to generate light on its own rather than merely reflect it, even despite its cracks.

"Lodestone." Lucas trudged over, his eyes fixed on the blade's gem. "That gem is made from lodestone."

Felix raised an eyebrow. "And that would be...?"

Lucas took the sword. "Lodestone negates magical spells and mythril. It's supposedly rare, and from what I know, a fairly recent creation."

That instilled even more dread in Felix. "So... let's say I threw a fireball at one of the soldiers using this sword?"

"All he'd have to do is cut through it, and the magic would be dispelled."

Felix took back the sword, tracing the stone along the cracks. This crystal had the power to render all of Felix's spells more useless than they already were. And not just him. Even a pearl could be taken down in the shock of their powers no longer working. And there was a coliseum of unexpecting magi right above them. Felix's instinct told him to fling the katana back into the crate and slam it shut, but he needed some kind of weapon. "I'm not gonna ask how you know all this," Felix said. "Cuz I know I won't get any answers. But like I said, I'm not just gonna sit here."

Lucas scoffed. "What good will that do you? I doubt you know how to use it, and it's defective. Everything in that box is. It's likely just a broken weapons cache to make removing the evidence easier for—"

"I. Don't. Care." Felix raised his voice as he held the blade close. "You can sit here, but don't hold *me* back." His head was still ringing, and his entire body screamed for him to rest and sleep off the aches. But there was no time to rest.

He feigned strength and stormed past Lucas, peering through the makeshift wall's curtain. Three tunnels, each lit by torches and overhead lights, extended into the distance. No soldiers in sight. No echoes of their footsteps. As grateful Felix was that this meant his escape would likely be more manageable, it also meant that Lucas was right—their plan was already in motion.

With one last glance back at Lucas, who simply looked away, Felix headed down the center path. Thankfully the floor here was solid rock rather than pebbles, meaning less noise to give away his position. Crystalline fragments, shimmering bright orange, were scattered along the way. Felix picked up one of the shards. Its opaqueness suggested mythril rather than the silver, translucent lodestone. Perhaps these tunnels were part of the mythril mines he'd seen in Montanari's class? But these mines, as far as he knew, had been long abandoned, meaning they should've been dried up. So what was mythril doing here now?

Professor Ivanov mentioned in one of his lectures that mythril was thought to be crystallized mana: the life force of the planet itself; fundamentally, the blood of the earth (not that Felix wanted to legitimize Gennadi's lunacy more than Dragora already had). So if mythril was the planet's "blood" crystallizing near its surface, what was it doing here? The soldiers wouldn't have needed it, and even if the mine still somehow had any mythril left, there was no one present to mine for it. There certainly wasn't enough for some attempt to drain the empire's resources before they struck.

Yells pierced Felix's nerves. Gunfire rang through the tunnels, yet no bullets flew past him. The shots gave way to a bloodcurdling scream, followed by an ungodly, inhuman roar. Felix froze. Forcing himself forward, he kept on his toes, hoping he wouldn't encounter the source of the terrifying sounds.

The passage opened up into a large cavern. Dozens of tunnels branched off from the central chamber, out from which ran rusted iron rails all leading to a heavily damaged turntable. Old mine carts sat along the tracks, and one was knocked on its side. No sign of mythril crystals, or even fragments, anywhere.

"Hey, you!"

A soldier, revealing himself from one of the other passages, rushed over and aimed his gun at Felix. "Drop your weapons! Arms up, hands behind your head!" Felix complied, the cold barrel of the rifle pressed against his back. "Boss said he wanted you alive. Never said you had to be able to walk."

Felix shut his eyes and braced himself. The blast of the gun struck his eardrums as he dodged, grabbing his katana. He felt no pain. He could still move his legs, though his ears ached again with another scream, coupled with the clanging of armor, and the tearing of flesh. Sickness rose in him as a large, hairy creature sat on all fours atop the motionless soldier. Its fangs dug into his neck, viciously lacerating his throat. Blood, more black than red in the darkness, dripped from its mouth. It took all Felix's strength to not heave from the sight.

The monster stepped back from the corpse. Its razor-sharp claws and rich-brown mane were those of a lion, but its body had no actual fur. Black spines protruded from its back. As it roared, leathery wings unfolded from behind, and its tail jerked into the air, revealing a scorpion stinger.

A manticore. It had to be a fucking manticore.

Felix recalled the mythril from earlier. Familiars, like his fluffy new buddy, were themselves created from a mythril core—their nucleus. And so, when familiars needed to "go to the bathroom" (or relieve themselves of used up mythril), mythril was what you got.

Shit. I picked up a piece of manticore shit.

Before he could process how disgusting this was (and honestly, slightly humorous), the beast lunged. Felix rolled out of the way. A sting gripped his arm. The manticore whipped its wings forth, and a barrage of spines flew

Felix's way. He took cover behind the overturned cart as the projectiles lodged themselves into the ground and wall. Running wouldn't help. The manticore could clear the distance between them easily before he could escape, assuming he didn't get lost through the tunnels. Even the soldier's gun couldn't kill this thing.

"Bolt Spark!"

Felix threw a fireball at the beast. Its mane caught fire, and as it howled and staggered, Felix couldn't help but feel sorry for the creature. *Sorry, kitty, but you didn't give me much of a choice.* He dashed at the creature and, keeping as much distance as possible, plunged the katana into its side. Its howls grew louder. Spines shot all about, grazing Felix's upper arm as he dodged the stinger.

He dashed down the nearest tunnel. Stress, a splitting headache, two wandless spells, and to top it all off, a reckless attack followed by a mad dash for freedom, all back-to-back. Not the most fun Friday night. Sweat trickled down Felix's face. He wanted so badly to rest, if only for a moment, but the beast's roars assured him that it would undoubtedly turn into a nice, long rest for all of eternity.

Felix took a hard left down one of the paths, then as he turned on his heel to move right, fell on his side, throwing out his arms to cushion his fall. The tunnels violently shook. Pebbles and stones dropped from above, and Felix covered his head. What would he see when he reached the surface? Or rather, what would be left amongst the rubble? All the people in the coliseum, terrified, without any way to defend themselves against a platoon of soldiers immune to magic.

Rosie. Argent. Zahra. Everyone. I'm so sorry. Please be safe. Please be fucking safe.

The ringing ceased, and yet another roar welcomed his restored hearing. He stumbled across a bank of sediment, which stretched into a vast subterranean lake. Light filtered through an opening in the ceiling far above. Perhaps this was part of the Lamorak Springs running beneath the reserve, in which case, this was where the manticore had found its way underground. And more importantly, this could've been Felix's exit to the surface.

The earth shook again. With no time to lose, Felix somehow had to climb all the way up the rock face to that opening, assuming he had the strength. But if this lake was part of the geyser system, as it had to be given the small bubbles popping up and traces of steam rising from the water, then perhaps…

"You utter fool."

Felix stepped back. *No. It can't be.*

There, standing atop the water and staring him down, was Vagus. Before he could process how he'd seemingly appeared from thin air, he dashed forth. Felix put up his arms to shield himself. With a thud, he fell. Vagus knocked the manticore into the wall with the end of his sword just before it reached Felix. Felix scrambled back, and a sharp pain shot through his arm. Light engulfed it. As Vagus' healing spell faded, the pain dulled, scabs forming over the scratch mark. Felix hadn't noticed his injuries until now. He forced himself up. "Leave me alone."

"I can't have you go and kill yourself," Vagus said. The orange flames running along with his sword flared. There was no escape.

"Emerald Flame!"

Vagus swung his sword and jumped as a green-blue blaze nearly consumed him. Felix found himself reluctantly elated as Lucas rushed over. "Am I so tired I'm hallucinating?" Felix asked as he panted. Or did you actually decide to help?"

Lucas shrugged. "Broken clocks are right twice a day. At least, I think that's what you Americans say?"

Felix raised an eyebrow. "None of you have clo—" He snickered. "Forget it. Thanks for the help." He caught his breath, right in time for Vagus to raise his sword again. "Lucas, would you say your fire could set off a geyser? Enough to launch someone high into the air?"

Lucas cringed. "What the hell kind of question is—"

"Well?"

"I suppose I wouldn't be a 'noble pearl' if I couldn't manage a measly… eruption?" Felix glanced over at the lake, and Lucas caught on surprisingly quickly. "Make it out of here," Lucas whispered. "And I'll never call you 'Cobalt' again."

He's earned a pass on the smartass comment this time.

Vagus lunged, and Felix and Lucas threw up a barrier. As if on cue, Lucas yelled, "Heat Shield!", creating a layer of blue energy over Felix's body. Felix dashed for the lake and dove straight in, his suspicions confirmed not only by his ability to breathe underwater, but by the absence of either heat or cold.

A bright blue fireball shot through the water, racing towards the dark depths below. Within moments, Felix was pushed above water, high into the air by the surge. His body slammed into the rock face, and he clung to the wall for dear life. He gulped as he looked back down. There, on the shore, Lucas did his best to toss out fireballs and dodge Vagus' attacks.

"GO!"

Mentally telling Lucas to stay safe, Felix climbed. His lungs burned as he ascended, the sharp rocks scraping his hands while pebbles slipped, plopping into the water far below. Finally, his fingertips grasped dirt and soil. Despite his muscles aching, and exhaustion panging his entire body, he pulled himself through the opening and rolled out onto the grassy surface. He panted. The sky was still dark, clouds covering the stars. The moon had completely vanished, save for a very slender crescent light hanging over him, slicing through the darkness. For but a moment, he relished in the success of escape—in the peace of this moment.

Until a roar ended his rest.

This was much deeper and stronger than the manticore's, slashing through Felix's nerve. The silhouette of a dragon, three times the whelp's size, flew overhead. Felix forced himself to sit up. The sight of smoke rising over the tree line made his blood run cold. He sprinted up the hill, pushing himself through the bushes and thickets, collecting more bruises and scratches. All mementos of this terrible night.

He came to a clearing.

Both Dragora Castle and the city of Cendrillion shone red orange as pillars of smoke filled the sky. Dragons, griffons, and a horde of other creatures flew above the chaos, all bellowing through the night, with most of them swarming the school up on the cliff. The faintest of screams, the cries of undoubtedly tens of thousands of people, carried from the city.

The storm had finally arrived.

Chapter Twenty-Eight

Into the Line of Fire

FELIX had never been able to get the screams out of his head after that night.

The cries of innocents who just moments before were going about their lives, enjoying a relaxing evening and celebrating life. All of that was now up in flames. The thought of the horrors going on in the city was nearly enough to make Felix sick, and nearly enough to make him give into his terror.

But he didn't have the luxury of breaking down.

Felix raced through the forest, arriving at the doors to Samuel's office by the cliffside. He rammed into it, bruising and nearly breaking his shoulder as he fought the pain, but no matter his efforts, it wouldn't give. And to make matters worse, a far too familiar roar sounded off behind him. *Of all the fucking times...* Felix rolled out of the way as the manticore crashed into the doors. Of course, they still wouldn't open. *What the fuck are these doors even made of?!*

The beast raised its stinger, ready to pierce through Felix's abdomen. The manticore launched a barrage of spines, and Felix dodged, taking cover behind a nearby tree.

A screech jolted his nerves. Bright golden flames consumed the fields as Cinder, in her larger form, flew down. She swiped the manticore with her talons, knocking it back. The manticore lunged, gnawing on Cinder's wing, only to be sent flying into the rock face. The manticore fell, instantly engulfed in another burst of fire. The flames dispersed. At long last, the manticore's charred corpse lay still.

Felix rushed back for cover, crouching and trying to remain undetected. Had Lucas...? No. Vagus was nowhere to be seen, yet the footsteps still approached. He couldn't afford to be captured. Not now. Preparing to make a break for it, he sprinted, ramming his shoulder into the unknown figure's stomach. They both fell. Felix rolled away, only to be gripped by confusion and guilt as he glanced up at his presumed assailant.

"Ornella?!"

She pushed herself up, brushing off grass and dirt. "There are better ways to greet a lady than tackling, you realize."

"What the hell are you..." Felix, recalling Ornella's knowledge of Vagus, stepped back. "Stay the fuck away from me."

Ornella reached out. "I'm not going to hurt—"

He scowled.

She raised her hand. "I didn't want to have to do this." She gestured to Cinder, who readied to pounce on Felix. He rolled the moment he heard the sound of a torch spouting flames, diving behind a tree trunk. Yet he didn't feel a thing.

Cinder squelched in pain, ducking and swinging her wings as Ornella tossed spells. "Sans Oxygen!" A dim red barrier enclosed Cinder. Once she fell, the shield dissolved. Ornella held the phoenix's wing. "I'm sorry." She turned, and Felix hid once again. "Felix, please. I want to help."

Right. Just as much as I'd love to have dinner with Frank.

She sighed. "Further along the cliff, there's a ranch. Through there is a maintenance route up to the woods by the coliseum. That's the fastest way to the city from here."

Ornella had always seemed trustworthy, and even now Felix wasn't sure what to make of her. If she was truly loyal to Vagus, then why would she have attacked his phoenix when they could've easily captured Felix? Praying he was putting his trust in the right person, Felix revealed himself.

"Lead the way," he said.

The reserve was devoid of any magical creatures as the pair made their way to the ranch. Just in case this turned out to be some sort of elaborate trap, Felix kept aware of his surroundings. But this path was his only real chance to get to the city in time. "What exactly happened?" he asked.

"During the final round," Ornella said. "Charges went off all around the coliseum, and soldiers revealed themselves in the city. Their armor and weapons are impervious to magic. They took down the police with almost no effort."

"Lodestone?"

"Yes. Vagus thinks that's how the bombs went off undetected."

Felix's anxiety soared. "And where are all the familiars?"

"The reserve barrier fell from the inside, and all the familiars went violent. They're attacking anything they set their sights on."

Like the manticore. "Are the people in the coliseum okay?"

"I don't know where your friends are," Ornella said. "Vagus said he was going to look for you and Lucas, then told me to flee on Cinder. But I couldn't sit by and do nothing."

"He's probably already got Lucas," Felix said. "Do you know anything about Bloodworth and Vivien?"

"Vagus assumes Bloodworth is some sort of mercenary. He's only here for the paycheck. And Vivien…" Ornella grimaced. "The less said about her, the better."

Felix wanted to pry for more information. He'd learned more about what was going on from a few minutes with Ornella than he'd ever gotten from either Vagus or Lucas, but that thought vanished as the distant screams grew louder, in moments coupled with the firing of assault rifles and the crackling of a great pyre.

The creak of the rusty iron gate at the trail's end was drowned out by the chaos now before them. Fire and smoke poured out from the top of the Angels' Arena. Civilians ran out in panic, while the ones trapped up top cried out for help. Some even jumped, their clothes set aflame. Felix was at a loss for words. He couldn't look away from the horrible sight of so many people, lying motionless, on the ground, their bodies burned and lifeless. He silently prayed to whatever god would answer that he wouldn't find Rosie, Argent, or Zahra among the fallen.

"H-How…?" Felix could hardly choke out the words. "How could this have happened?"

"The headmistress and some other professors helped the royal family retreat to Archangel Island," Ornella said. "I doubt the vanguard will be here anytime soon. Not when their best spells and weapons have been rendered useless."

They... they left their own people. Left them to burn. With or without magic, this is wrong.

A young girl fell, her face slamming into the ground with a nauseating crunch. She lay there, still, her body burning in the dirt. She couldn't have been any older than six or seven—only a couple of years older than Tracey.

Ornella grabbed his wrist. "We need to go. Now."

He wanted to fight against her. To stay here, and to try and save even one person. But she was right. They pressed onwards towards Cendrillion, though there was no sign of any soldiers, neither invading mercenary nor defending police or vanguard. Flames spilled from smashed storefronts, while smoke poured out from overturned streetcars. An arm hung out from beneath the vehicle. Men, women, and children lay about the avenue, gaping bullet wounds across their bodies.

Felix nearly heaved. *Who the fuck could do this?*

A pair of soldiers rounded the corner. Felix and Ornella jumped behind the nearest building, just before the soldiers opened fire. Ornella pulled Felix into the bushes between a pair of trees. Felix, his chest pounding, fought the impulse to run as he and Ornella crouched.

Another round of shots rang off, followed by shouts. Professor Jhaveri hung around the corner, firing at the mercenaries not with a wand, but with a pistol. Both soldiers fell. Once the threat was evaded, he rushed over to the students. "Nella," Jhaveri said. "Get you and your friend to your mom's shop. She's set up a safe zone where you both can ride this out."

Hopefully Felix's friends would be there, safe and sound, waiting for him. But the voices at the back of his mind refused to be ignored.

Professor Videl ran to them. "I'll take them there. You look for the others."

Jhaveri held Videl's shoulder, grimacing. "Please, be careful."

Videl gave a warm smile, holding Jhaveri's hand. That smile vanished as his eyes drifted past him. "MOVE!" Videl leapt in front of Jhaveri. He threw up a barrier, which broke as gunfire poured through, knocking him back.

Ornella and Felix ducked for cover again while Jhaveri took out the mercenary, firing off bullets even after he'd fallen, a vein in his neck nearly popping. Ornella urged him to cease. Hesitantly, Jhaveri lowered his gun.

Videl's throat and torso gushed with blood. Ornella knelt to heal him, while Felix stood there, paralyzed. Jhaveri, on the verge of tears, sniffled. A man who'd seen the worst of humanity, still helpless and small in the face of death. "I-I'm sorry," Felix choked out.

Ornella checked Videl's pulse. "He's still breathing. I've managed to stop most of the bleeding, but he needs a doctor."

"I'll help." While Felix grabbed Videl's feet, Ornella pulled him up by the shoulders. Jhaveri provided cover as they made their way to the Fountain of Magic. Bodies littered the cityscape, either along the pavement or caught in crushed streetcars. Yet there were no signs of magical creatures wreaking havoc. Were they all at the school, or perhaps they'd run loose and left the island altogether? Neither thought was particularly comforting.

Outside the wand shop stood Professors Montanari and Ivanov. Ivanov smiled once he saw Jhaveri, only for that joy to morph into horror once he saw the wounded Videl. "W-What in the...?"

"We'll talk later," Jhaveri said. "Are there any doctors or healers inside?"

"Yes," Montanari said. "Unfortunately our specialist has been missing. The healers inside are rationing care based on ne—"

Jhaveri pushed past, guiding Felix and Ornella inside. For a moment, Montanari glared at Felix, and Felix's wish to disappear briefly resurfaced.

Dezirae ran over, covering her mouth as her eyes teared up. After handing off Videl to a couple of nurses, Jhaveri led Dezirae into the back of the shop. All the shelves have been pushed to barricade the windows. Students either cried or sat silently, deathly pale and shaking. Had Felix been too late? Had Rosie and the others not made it here in time? What if they hadn't even made it out of the coliseum at all? What if—

"FELIX!"

The voice shook him to his core, and as Rosie threw her arms around Felix and squeezed tight, he was left gasping for air. Her face was covered in tears, makeup running down her cheeks. "You fucking idiot!"

He didn't know what to say. An entire month had gone by since they'd last spoken, and part of him wondered if it might've stayed that way even after the school year ended. He mulled over what he could possibly have said to her about what he'd just gone through. All the unspoken apologies over the crypt incident. Felix cried, hugging her back.

"I'm sorry."

Rosie stepped back, wiping her tears on her sleeve. "I'm so fucking relieved you're okay." Her voice cracked. Argent stood behind her, giving a warm, albeit hesitant smile, which instantly soothed Felix's nerves.

"I'll talk to my mother," Ornella said, holding her wrist. "I'll be right back."

Argent approached. "Hey, uh... Ornella?"

"Oh? Not Nella'rela?"

"I-I just... wanted to thank you." Argent glanced at Felix. "F-For—"

"No problem." Ornella held Argent's shoulder. "But if you ever call me Nella'rela again, I will roast you like a pig. Understood?"

"G-Gotcha!"

Smiling, Ornella continued into the back of the shop. The TV over on the wall blared as students huddled around, the headline reading: "Attack on Cendrillion. City burning as magical creatures run rampant."

"The empress has retreated to Archangel Island," the news anchor said. "And has issued a state of emergency. Imperial forces are currently being deployed."

Guess the news is full of shit no matter where you go. Felix steeled himself, trying not to break down again in front of Rosie and Argent. "I... saw the city. And the coliseum. And..." He hugged Rosie again as he sniffled. "I'm sorry. I can't say it enough times. I am so sorry." Slowly, Rosie hugged back. As Argent walked over, Felix pulled him into the hug, making Rosie back up a bit. After going so long without them, just being in their presence melted away every fear that had been weighing him down the last few weeks, their bonds reforging the moment they embraced each other.

Once he managed to calm down, Felix finally managed to build up the strength to ask: "Did the others make it here okay?"

Rosie appeared sullen. "Shawn and Floria came with us. Penny... she was in the arena when the bombs went off, and..."

"She's in the back with the healers," Argent said. "They said she'll pull through. But she... her leg..."

God, no. Felix held his chest. "What about Zahra and Nasira?"

"We have no idea," Rosie said.

Felix, powering through the shock, explained everything he'd been through: Bloodworth and Vivien; Vagus, Lucas, and Ornella; and the soldiers' lodestone weaponry. "Wow," Argent said, stroking his goatee. "Never took Lucas for the self-sacrificing type."

"I just hope he's okay," Felix said. "I just… left him behind." *I had him pegged all wrong. I'm such a piece of shit.*

"So you think this Vagus guy's involved?" Argent asked.

"No. He was trying to stop Bloodworth and Vivien. They're probably after the Ring of Nergal. Why else launch this full-scale attack other than to get inside the crypt?"

"Concentrate all the empire's forces in the city during a crisis," Rosie said. "And they'll never notice a small team sneaking into Dragora."

"You know," Argent said. "We think surprisingly like a bunch of criminal masterminds." Both Felix and Rosie glared at him. "Sorry. Gotta lighten the mood somehow."

"They've got Samuel," Felix said. "Meaning they've got a human key for the crypt."

"Can't we just assume they changed the locks?"

Felix rolled his eyes. "Yeah, sure. Should be no problem switching out a thousand-year-old gauntlet of glyphs and spells within a single month on short notice."

Argent cracked a smile. "I missed that sass."

"No." Rosie stepped up. "We are staying put, where it's safe."

"The entire city's up in flames," Felix said. "Presumably full of armed soldiers and monsters. You really call that safe?"

"It's *safer*."

"So you want that ring, all the power inside of it, to just—"

Rosie slapped Felix clear across the face. "It's *because* of that ring we got roped into all this in the first place! Or did you forget that already?!"

"No. I haven't. This is the one place in the world where magi can feel safe. Until today. If these people get that ring, we can kiss our safe haven goodbye. Then, it'll be open season on us, everywhere, more than ever before."

"I don't know. I mean…"

"I'm not expecting you to come with me," Felix said. "I'm asking you to let me make this choice."

473

"If you're going… you are not going alone."

Argent shrugged. "I got nothin' better to do, so count me in."

Felix didn't want to endanger his friends any more than he already had, but now they knew the full story, and he had the comfort of telling himself this was their choice. So long as he had them, things might turn out alright. And hopefully along the way, they'd find both Zahra and Nasira, safe and sound.

"If we're heading out…" Ornella walked over with her uncle Mason, the "Wandsmith," behind her. "You'll all need wands."

"What about the lodestone?" Felix asked.

"We can't hit the soldiers directly, but we *can* hit what's around them. Besides, it's better than walking out there completely defenseless."

"We never got the chance to fully restock," Mason said. "But I always keep an emergency supply in the back."

Huh. Convenient. They followed Mason through the back. For a moment, Felix glanced upstairs to see rooms filled with nurses and healers rushing about. He couldn't see Penny, but he did glimpse Shawn and Floria briefly, both teary-eyed. Felix forced himself to enter the workshop, silently promising to avenge whatever had happened to Penny.

With a few clinks, Mason opened up a small safe door hidden behind the forge. "Shit!" He slammed the door shut. "The wands are gone!"

Ornella held her chest. "Were those all you had?"

Mason hung his head.

"We'll just have to get our wands from the castle," Felix said. "Ornella, do you have a wand?"

"Better." From her pocket, she revealed a scarlet flute with golden keys. The end shimmered with red mythril. "The other prefects should already be at the school defending the crypt, so hopefully they'll buy us plenty of time."

She led them to the back exit, giving Mason one last hug goodbye. What Felix wouldn't have given to see his parents—to see his mother. Had he stayed in the shop, perhaps he'd be able to go home safely once all this chaos had ended. But he'd come too far to stop now. Especially when Zahra could still be out there, still in danger.

The entire building shook as a great thunder boomed. Everyone fell, and Felix covered his ears as a sharp pain pierced his head. The ringing hung in his eardrums, gradually falling as his thoughts became coherent again, before an all-new terror set in. He'd heard this before. This was no mere thunder, nor an explosion. He traced it all the way back to that day in the reserve.

Felix and the others raced through an alleyway out onto the street. There, off in the distance, perched atop the Enchanted Dawn Airport, sat a colossal dragon. Its slimy pitch-black scales glistened almost as brightly as its deep-violet eyes. Spikes protruded from its bronze club tail, light shimmering across its razor-sharp yellow teeth. Leathery azure wings flapped through the vermillion inferno. It gave an empty stare, then with another bellow, threw the earth into a mighty quake.

Of course this thing shows up now. Fuck you too, universe.

"Uh…" Argent's eyes widened. "I vote we ignore the overgrown lizard."

"Hate to say it," Rosie said. "But I agree. There's no fucking way we can beat that thing."

Ornella stepped forward. "If we leave it free to run rampant, there won't be any city left to save." The urge to press on to the castle anyway was tempting, but Ornella was right. They had an obligation to try and weaken the beast until the professors, or even the vanguard (assuming they were even coming), arrived to finish it off.

The dragon spread its jaws wide, and from its mouth poured a flood of fire. "Shields, now!" Felix led them in creating a barrier, while Ornella used her flute to provide an opposing torrent of flames to help reinforce it. The heat warmed Felix's skin, and he braced himself for the shield to give at any moment and for the flames to melt his bones. Then, as if on cue, the barrier grew stronger.

"Get out of here! Go back to the shop!"

Montanari took the lead, allowing the kids to ease up. As the fire dispersed, a circle of light formed along the ground, and Montanari launched herself forth. As she dashed, the dragon shot another wave of fire. Montanari leapt high into the air with a flash. A dark array of clouds formed around her, and a true thunderclap sounded off. Lightning surged at the dragon. It roared in pain, then snapped its neck and stretched its wings in rage.

Montanari practically levitated in the air with jets of blue fire from her shoes. In her hands hung a chain of blue, red, and green mythril, and with each swing came a lash of ice, fire, and lightning. Felix had no clue Montanari was of a dark alignment, let alone how powerful she was, capable of such astonishing feats of magic. Perhaps one day, Felix would be able to match her power and skill…

"I have an idea," Ornella said. "Felix, Rosie, you two distance yourself from me. Argent, follow me. We're going to form a circle around the airport." They followed her directions and positioned themselves all across the road. On the count of three they all shouted, "Fountain of Light!" White light shot from their hands high into the sky, curving forward and clashing directly above the dragon. Light cascaded down, like a fountain of water surging up, then rushing back down to the earth. A giant barrier encircled the airport.

Felix expected the spell to be impossible without his wand. Certainly as a cobalt, any magic beyond a meager fireball would be impossible, but this felt nearly effortless. Perhaps it came from the others sharing the weight of the spell alongside him, combining their strength into one spell? Whatever the case, they had to do their best to contain the battle and minimize the devastation.

Montanari, now standing on one of the rooftops within the dome, continued her assault. The dragon blocked the bolts with its wings, launching fireballs at the shield. The light flickered. Maintaining the shield may not've tired Felix out, but reinforcing it against the dragon's attacks was what took its toll upon him. No matter how the barrage on the barrier continued, no matter the exhaustion ravaging Felix's body, he remained in place. The dome held steady.

In a last-ditch effort, Montanari released a flurry of ice and fire, only for the dragon to unleash its strongest blaze yet. Montanari created a wall of ice to shield herself. New crystals took the place of melting ones, giving rise to steam, only for the shield to break as the dragon swept its tail, knocking Montanari back.

That's when Ornella jumped inside the dome. She didn't even flinch at the dragon's roar, instead grimacing at its tantrum. The dragon breathed fire once more, and the flames consumed her, spinning into a column. The vortex shot up as Ornella's flute sounded off, then bent down to engulf the dragon. The whole city shook as the airport collapsed into the dirt.

The barrier dissolved, and Felix and the others fell to their knees. His muscles burned from exhaustion. A tall flame and even taller pillar of smoke slithered up from the dragon's smoldering corpse, and from the remains emerged Ornella. Soot covered her face. Her clothes were singed, yet her body was without any burns, her hair flowing in the wind.

Holy fuck.

She held out her hand, helping Felix up. "You alright?"

"Y-Yeah." Felix cracked his back, the pain somehow relieving. His eyes fell to the rubble. There, shimmering in the debris, was a silver tag. He picked it up, brushing off the dirt and ash. A name had been engraved into the metal: "Terri"?

"Oh no…" Ornella crossed her arms as Rosie and Argent rushed over. "This was no ordinary dragon. This had to have been a chimaera."

"Chimaera?" Rosie asked. "You mean like that Greek monster with the lion's head and the goat's body?"

"No," Ornella said. "Chimaeras are amalgamations of different familiars, forced together into a stronger, usually more violent creature. Most often they're forced to fight, and the strongest familiar absorbs the others into its nucleus."

"Oh," Argent said. "That's… lovely!"

"More of Vivien's handiwork?" Felix asked.

Ornella looked away. "Not her specifically, but this was definitely our enemy's work."

"Do you ever give clear answers?" Rosie asked.

Montanari lay on the ground a few blocks away, and was now being tended to by Professor Ivanov. She'd taken the blow to try and protect Felix and his friends. In a way, heading to Dragora seemed a spiteful response. Not to mention he hadn't even fought the dragon himself, yet just trying to hold it back was enough to make his lungs ache from the strain. Still, something told him to press on—a complete failure of the evolutionary process. "If we're still headed to the school," Felix said. "We need to go now, while the professors are busy."

"Are you sure?" Ornella asked. "You look exhausted."

"I have to," Felix said.

"Correction," Rosie said, slightly hunched, all the while smiling like the tank she'd always been. "*We* have to! Dumbass."

"You don't look to… able."

"Able enough to kick your ass!" Rosie playfully punched Felix's arm. He took great joy as she gripped her punching hand, trying to hide the obvious sting in her knuckles.

"Don't touch my man like that," Argent said. Felix twitched as Argent threw his arm around him. His hair was far more unkempt than usual, and a scratch lined his cheek.

They ran for the school, wheezing through their fatigue, not letting up for even a moment. Why Felix wanted to involve himself in another fight in this state never once crossed his mind. Instead, he was consumed by only three thoughts: the injured Penny and Videl, whether he'd ever see his family again, and where Nasira and Zahra could've been now.

Then one thought eclipsed the rest: the Ring of Nergal.

As Cendrillion fell to ruin, Rhosyn delighted in the city of fools burning as he made another cup of coffee. Black, no milk, and absolutely no sugar. It surprisingly served as a decent way to pass the time, given the staff had run out in terror when the bombs went off hours before. Now he had the cozy café all to himself. Not to mention, no need to worry about building up an outrageous tab to send back to his fellow council members.

Admittedly, the ambient noise of the screams, gunfire, and roars of rogue familiars didn't quite capture his interest in the same way as observing the patrons and staff. Human tourists had been mobbing the shores of the Medeian Empire since the tournament's beginning. They were happy to indulge in the spectacle of pearls and golds battling it out in the arena, not once hesitating to chide a poor amethyst or cobalt for being a bit too slow on fetching their orders. If there was one thing that piqued Rhosyn's curiosity more than his chimaera garden, it was the absurdity of human hatred, magical and nonmagical alike.

Fortunately he didn't have to wait too long. Finally, his burner phone rung with the sweet sounds of Swedish pop he'd always shamelessly enjoyed in the depths of his menagerie, and the text read: "All set!"

Welp, suppose it won't hurt to take one last cup for the road.

Grabbing his silver suitcase, Rhosyn made his way to Lighthaven Hospital. The place was on lockdown, unsurprisingly, but what did surprise him was the fact the facility had gone untouched by both the soldiers and familiars. It certainly meant more fun for him.

Getting inside was easy enough. The steel exterior doors were nothing in the face of a simple blue blaze, and once he'd stepped through the makeshift entrance, the Della Luces' security proved ridiculously laughable. A flick of the wrist here, a team of guards incinerated there. At times he shook things up by freezing them, of course, but it proved too much of a hassle having to cut them to pieces. Couldn't leave any witnesses behind, after all.

"Do you need assistance, Your Eminence?"

Of all the damned times to be disturbed, it had to be just before the fun part. The De Palmi girl knelt before Rhosyn. Thankfully her bowed head kept that insidious family sneer from killing the mood. "You've done your part, little one," Rhosyn said, biting his tongue before he could chew the little gremlin out. "You'd best be off now."

"But sir!" And of course, now she'd donned that facade of hollow reverence. "I can do so much more than—"

"Mapping out locations and taking out their security ahead of time? Truth be told, I don't quite care, and if it weren't for your potential for future operations, I'd have swatted you the moment you spoke to me. Now leave."

Prostrating herself, the girl complied and left.

All of this posturing kills me. Why can't people just own their malice? Rhosyn rolled his eyes. At least now with the little brat gone, he could let his newest creations enjoy their first trip out, just as Terri ought to have been now. He threw his briefcase onto the counter, carelessly sweeping off all the junk that'd been left in its way. Rhosyn could barely contain his excitement. One click of the lock, then another, and at last, the sweet humming of kaleidoscopic mythril.

"Time to go to work, my darlings."

With a snap of his fingers, the mythril sparked, light pouring from the crystal, then breaking apart into a thousand little beads. From the briefcase crawled Rhosyn's newest chimeric creation: the orchid weavers (name pending). Tiny white spiders all operating on a single hive mind, in perfect sync with their father. Venomous fangs, all elemental capabilities, and perfectly tethered to Rhosyn's mind to help with surveillance. Not to mention they'd make for an excellent disposal of any evidence. *My finest creation yet. No offense, Terri.*

As he let the weavers get to work, he notified his subordinates to follow suit to help with transport. The mageblight-inflicted patients were to remain untouched for extraction, along with one other patient the Enlightened had kept their sights on for a while now. A poor, comatose woman, trapped in perpetual sleep by her past addictions.

It's such a waste to leave her here. But we'll take good care of her.

Chapter Twenty-Nine

Break the Mirror

DRAGONS AND OTHER BEASTS flew high above the castle, circling the towers and bellowing through the night. The courtyard was devoid of life, the only signs of activity being a pair of black helicopters. "This isn't good," Ornella said. Felix, Rosie, and Argent trailed behind her, all trying not to keel over after running all the way up the hill. "Bloodworth and his men are already here. No doubt Vivien's with them."

Felix examined the copters. "No logos?"

Rosie rolled her eyes. "What? Were you expecting evil corporate artwork?"

"Maybe?" Felix grinned. "Hey, if Argent gets to try to lighten the mood, so do I."

Argent pointed at the sky. "I vote we head inside. You know, before one of those dragons decides it wants supper."

"Let's check out the helicopters. Maybe—"

"No," Ornella said. "We have to stop Bloodworth as soon as possible."

"But there might be something in these things we can use," Felix said.

"I'm with Felix," Rosie said. "They might've left some scrap of their plans, or an identifier."

Ornella waved. "Fine. No dallying." She followed Rosie into one of the copters, while Felix and Argent climbed into the other.

The front console was cramped, with the seats pushed up against the control panel. The buttons were incomprehensible, but the rank smell of spilled coffee, torn leather cushions, and the stabbing scent of spearmint gum sadly were not. Argent had to bend over to avoid slamming his head into the ceiling. (Just this once, Felix rejoiced in his shortness.) Felix checked the front while Argent inspected the back. The helicopter seemed new, but Bloodworth's poor treatment could help it pass for an old dinosaur. Hopefully, this meant he was negligent enough to leave behind a clue.

A box beneath the pilot chair held a collection of spirits, small drops of beer still sloshing within the glass. *Classy.* Admittedly, one lime-green bottle of herbal whiskey (with a nigh unpronounceable brand name) hadn't been opened. Felix may not have enjoyed alcohol, but the gleaming glass alone seemed trophy worthy. Thankfully Bloodworth had left—unshockingly—a red laptop in the passenger seat. Dumb enough to leave it out in the open, but unfortunately smart enough to be password-protected. At the very least, it could be cracked open later, and so Felix happily tucked the device under his arm.

Once they went over their findings, the girls revealed that they'd come across a complete diagram of Dragora Castle, heavily marked with scribbles and notes. "Where'd they get this?" Felix asked.

"Don't know," Rosie said. "But they definitely know where the crypt is. There are notes all about the Chamber of Kagami and the crypt's protections."

Before Felix could quip about the bad guys getting all the conveniences, a strange shimmer on the back of the laminated paper caught his attention. Or rather, a small, faint word breaking through the light stood out:

"Illustratum."

"Hey, Ornella?" Felix asked, tensing up. "Do you know what that says? Is that a language you recognize?"

Hesitantly, she looked it over, mumbling to herself. "No... sorry." She looked off, unnerved. At this point, Felix was begrudgingly used to not getting straight answers. They rushed inside the castle. Fractured moonlight filtered through the broken windows, kaleidoscopic shards littering the lobby floor. Yet for all the destruction, and the chaos outside, the room was empty. No familiars nor soldiers. Silent, save for the crunching of glass.

"LOOK OUT!"

Argent pushed Felix to the ground. A few fractals scraped his arm, giving way to droplets of blood. The laptop, likewise, fell from his hands, smashing apart. A foul hiss cut through the short-lived stillness. Scarlet streaks ran across sickly green scales, around glassy amber eyes, whose yellow pits sank into black slits.

"What the fuck? Felix asked.

"A basilisk," Argent said. "Its venom makes a sea snake's bite feel like a massage." The serpent coiled its tail. Glistening fangs hung out from its jaws, sheathing a forked tongue, while bright-red-and-orange frills popped around its head. Felix moved to stand. "No!" Argent whispered. "No sudden—"

The snake lunged. Argent pushed Felix out of the way again, the both of them now on opposite sides of the basilisk. Ornella rushed over to Felix. "Your arm!"

Felix shook his head, covering the wound. "It's not that—"

"No, your blood. The basilisk is attracted to it."

"Oh. Great. So warm versus cold-blooded?"

"Basilisks tend to target fire sorcerers," Ornella said. "Specifically, ones with a pact with Aviur."

"Fucking wonderful!"

The snake spat a clear liquid. Felix, Rosie, and Ornella threw up a barrier. The venom sizzled as it hit the shield, giving off traces of steam while trickling onto the floor. Argent encased the basilisk's tail in ice. It flailed, shooting venom at him, but he dodged. The basilisk broke free and lunged at Argent. Felix jumped over and shielded him, knocking the snake back.

Ornella threw a fireball, knocking the basilisk against the wall. Rosie raised her arms, and vines from all the plants and foliage wrapped around the beast. Just as she started to wear out her strength, her knees buckling, Argent froze over the squirming basilisk until its body was completely frozen.

"Jesus!" Felix yelled, his voice cracking. "That was fucking horrifying."

"Agreed," Argent stretched. "Thank God Fang's not that bad."

"Fang's your basilisk, right?"

"Yeah." Argent smirked. "You were expecting a dick joke, weren't you?"

Felix blushed. "N-No?" His eyes fell back to the broken laptop, its pieces scattered amongst the glass remains. "Welp, there goes that lead."

"This is no time for self-flagellation," Ornella said. "We need to get your wands. I'll go with Felix to his dorm. Argent, Rosie, you go together for yours."

"What?!" Rosie asked. "We can't split up at a time like this!"

"That's exactly what this calls for." Ornella frowned. "The other prefects have likely been holding Bloodworth and Vivien off since before we arrived, and there's no telling how long they'll be able to fight." She looked to the moon through the broken windows.

"I'm with Ornella," Felix said. "The more time we waste, the worse things will get."

Argent didn't say a word. Instead, he hung his head, then looked to Rosie. They didn't need to speak for Felix to understand what they were thinking, especially as they glanced his way before nodding to each other.

With that, they reluctantly parted ways. As much as Felix knew this was the right call, he still hated himself for it, especially as he caught himself hoping, however briefly, that he and Ornella might be the only ones in the crypt. Two less people to get in his way. No. That couldn't be on his mind at all. Nothing mattered more than keeping the ring out of anyone's hands.

Or rather, out of the hands of the unworthy.

Thankfully, fate decided to show Rosie and Argent mercy as they retrieved their wands. Getting Rosie's was as simple as running inside, swiping it from under her pillow (always for emergencies), and running back out. But now that they found themselves in Argent's dorm, Rosie wished some monster would burst in and halt Argent's attempt at conversation.

"You gonna bother acknowledging me?"

Rosie paused. "Acknowledge you wasting time? Yes, now get your damn wand so we can—"

"I get it," Argent said, refusing to even head for the loft as he made his pointless case. "You never fully forgave me, and you think I'm a douche, but you wanna keep Felix happy. But could you look me in the eye and tell me you have a problem with me?"

"Oh for fuck's…" Fed up, Rosie threw up her arms. "If you won't get it, I'll look for it myself." She stormed past Argent, but as he grabbed her wrist, she pulled it free. "The hell?!"

"You know I was protecting you, right?"

"What're you talking about?" Rosie asked.

"The coliseum," Argent said. "Those guys were gonna kill you if I didn't step in."

"Yeah. I know."

"But you're pissed."

"I'm not…" Rosie held her forehead, wishing she didn't have to do this right now. She'd hoped something might be able to help her forget. But that cold look in Argent's eyes… that hadn't left her for a moment. "You don't just kill someone, even in self-defense, and not break down even a little."

"Excuse me for not being sad about taking out some terrorists."

What a sick full-circle moment, to have the Camo Crew who'd harassed them in their youth now actively trying to kill them. How in the world Billy and Buck managed to get themselves involved in this was beyond her understanding. They couldn't have done this on their own. Was Carson in on this, skulking around somewhere, hoping to get revenge on her and Felix?

"I'm not saying what you did was wrong," Rosie said. "I don't know if I could do the same. If I had to protect myself or Felix, then… yeah. I probably could. But…" She shivered. On impulse, she drew her lodestone gun.

"HEY, WHAT—"

The bullet nearly grazed Argent's ear, giving way to a screech. An awful, hair-raising scratching across the wood floors followed, yet nothing was there. Argent drew his wand, but Rosie held him back. "Wait…" She sighed, chastising herself. "I'm sorry, Lilim. I thought you were a wild familiar."

"Um…" Argent held Rosie's shoulder. "The fuck are you—"

Rosie shushed him. She held the gun up in the air, then slowly, placed it on the coffee table as a show of faith. With a glare, she made Argent do the same with his wand. Some moments passed, but eventually, a flash revealed the little kangaroo-looking familiar. "It's Lilim, Nina's familiar. She's no threat." She petted Lilim's head, to which the sigbin let out a comforting chirp.

"Seriously," Argent said, shaking his head. "What is it with you and being the prefects' pet? Or in this case… their pet's pet."

"Very funny." Rosie listened closely to Lilim's chirps. "I don't understand, but if Lilim's here, something's wrong with Nina."

"Weren't she and the others supposed to be guarding the crypt?"

"Crap! We need to go!"

Felix followed Ornella to House Pyre, but the door to his dorm wouldn't budge. He struggled with the doorknob, and when he tried using his key, a spark flew from the lock and instantly melted it. He flicked his wrist and blew on his burning fingers.

Ornella's wand glowed red. "Glyph Reveal." A red glyph appeared on the door. "It's sealed shut. Vagus must've done this."

Vagus? What was he doing here? "Speaking of Vagus," Felix said. "How do you—"

"Duck!"

Ornella shot fire over the railings as a white horse in mid-air dodged. Its bright-blue mane shone silver, as did its hooves. Felix would've assumed he was hallucinating from the stress until he saw its feathery, angelic wings—a pegasus. It neighed, then galloped away through the air. "Keep it busy while I break the glyph," Ornella said.

Resisting the urge to complain about his terrible luck, Felix ran to the ground level. The pegasus hovered over the dragon statue. *Considering my luck with unicorns, I'm no equestrian.* "Bolt Spark!" Without his wand, the best he could manage were a couple stray fireballs, and weak ones at that. The pegasus evaded effortlessly, looping high above. It charged. As Felix jumped out of the way, the winged horse soared towards the top of the room and broke through the skylight, leaving.

Well, that was anticlimactic.

Ornella had successfully broken the glyph on the door. The room was a mess. The couch and chairs were pushed towards the wall opposite the fireplace, while the coffee table had been overturned. A whimper came from beneath the desks under the loft. Felix ran over to check, and there, crouching in the fetal position and shaking...

"Lucas?!"

Felix and Ornella laid Lucas onto the couch. Felix grabbed the sheets from both their beds, and Ornella wrapped Lucas in them, placing pillows beneath his head and feet. Lucas' face was pale, absent of any pigment. His normally blonde hair was now an icy white. Felix wanted to thank Lucas for saving him, but it likely wouldn't reach him in this state. Guilt tripped him instead, along with a single repeating thought: *It should've been me.*

But why had Vagus been in here? Once it hit him, Felix rushed to check his bedside table. There, buried under all of his socks, was the scarlet pendant. It swung back and forth on its own, the young female voice crying out again.

"What is that?" Ornella asked.

Felix turned back, and the moment he did, the pendulum's light caught Ornella's attention. "What are you doing with my pendant?"

"This is yours?" Felix asked. He climbed down. "Lucas had it back at the start of the year. He was trying to do some kinda astral spell. I thought—"

Ornella swiped it. She glanced at Lucas, but her grimace melted into a somber smile as she held the pendant close, shedding a tear as its soft scarlet light reflected in her eyes.

Finally, Felix had grown fed up with beating around the bush. "Ornella, who is Vagus? Why did he choose us? Does that pendant have anything to do with him?"

No answer.

"And what do *you* have to do with all of this? Whose side are you on?"

She hung her head. "Yours."

"Bullshit." Felix could barely keep himself from shouting. "If you were on my side, then you would tell me what the hell is going on. You wouldn't have left me in the dark for months, with this cloud over my head constantly. You'd tell me what that word on Bloodworth's map of the school means, and what this plan is really all—"

Ornella raised her flute. Felix prepared to make a break for his wand, only to jump as the sound of breaking glass and Lucas' sharp scream met his ears. The pegasus crashed through the loft window. Ornella pushed Felix aside as one of the hooves thumped her in the back of the head, knocking her out cold.

Lucas cowered beneath the couch. Even if Felix had his wand, fire spells in a small, enclosed space probably weren't the best idea. Instead, he tossed one of the couch cushions at the pegasus, then a few books. The pegasus lowered, and silencing what little common sense he had, Felix hopped onto its back. He grabbed its neck as it flew, ducking to avoid smashing his head into the ceiling. Before it could try again, he leapt onto the loft, rummaged through his drawers, and grabbed his wand. He ducked again as the pegasus charged, flying back outside.

"Spark Shower!" From his wand, Felix launched a barrage of blue fireballs. The pegasus dodged until one attack managed to land a hit, followed by another, then another. One more hit would've been enough to finish it off, but of course, his exhaustion arrived right on time. He hunched forward, his shoulder burning. Neighing, the pegasus barreled towards him, going for the kill.

"Felix, move!"

He jumped to the floor and covered his head as a powerful gust of wind blew past him. A small funnel filled with lightning knocked the pegasus clear out of the sky. Zahra and Nasira stood at the door, side by side with their wands.

"Like I said," Nasira said. "I'm fine with normal horses. But flying ones? Out of the question."

"Z-Zahra!" Felix rushed over. "You're…"

Zahra, averting his gaze, moved to heal Ornella, who groaned in pain. Felix held his wrist, chastising himself for not knowing any better.

"Sure," Nasira said, rolling her eyes. "Good to see you care so—"

He hugged Nasira tight. "Thank God you're both alive." Nasira tensed up. She didn't hug back, and Felix couldn't tell if she was smiling. But even after everything that had happened, he was still grateful she was here, alive and well. Taking a hint, Felix backed off. "Have you guys been here the whole night?"

"Yeah…" Nasira glanced at Zahra. "Zahra insisted we stay in case something happened. She filled me in on everything."

Zahra helped Ornella to her feet, and immediately Felix hugged her. Gently, Zahra pushed him back, not once looking him in the eyes. "Where are the others?" she asked.

"Rosie and Argent went to grab their wands." Felix deepened his voice, trying to hide his deflated spirit. "We're heading to the crypt."

"To get the ring?"

Felix paused, unsure of what to say.

"No," Ornella said. "To protect it."

"It's… not Vagus," Felix said. "The masked guy. The people attacking the city have Samuel. They might be in the crypt right now for all we know."

"Then let's go," Zahra said. Felix couldn't blame her for ignoring his presence. But every time it became clearer, and he hated himself just a bit more.

"I'm coming too," Nasira said. "You'll need all the help you can get. But what should we do about…?" She gestured to Lucas, still mumbling and trembling beneath the couch.

"Leave him be," Felix said, his words laced with pity and remorse. "He deserves some rest after all the shit he's been through." They followed Ornella to the Chamber of Kagami. Felix wanted so desperately to demand answers from Ornella, but she'd taken a hit for him. As ominous and infuriatingly vague as her behavior was, Felix never truly felt an imminent threat from her. In a way, she was everything he wished he had in a big sister—everything he wished Aeris was.

Once they'd arrived, they'd found Rosie and Argent tending to an injured Nina and Theresa. A sad familiar, what looked to be a strange hybrid of a lizard and kangaroo, sat beside Nina as she petted its head. A dozen soldiers lay about the hall, presumably either unconscious or dead. Ornella ran to the prefects. "What happened?! Where's Lucinda?"

"We did our best," Nina said. "I took down the whole platoon of soldiers single-handedly."

"She exaggerates," Theresa said. "But it's down to Bloodworth and Vivien. Lucinda healed us both a bit, then rushed in after them."

Ornella nodded. "I'll be back soon to help you both."

"No worries," Nina said. She looked to her familiar. "Lilim, good job on getting help. Go look for some more, would you?" With a nod, Lilim scurried off and went invisible.

"What took you so long?" Argent asked Felix.

"A flying horse with an attitude problem." Felix forced a chuckle, cursing himself silently for impulsively trying to lighten the mood, as always.

Rosie ran over and hugged both Zahra and Nasira. She was ecstatic to see they were both safe, but Nasira squirmed free, insisting they get their mission over with. Zahra pulled Nasira off to the side, whispering with her while occasionally glancing at Felix, and all the while, strengthening Felix's anguish and self-resentment.

"Is Zahra okay?" Rosie asked quietly.

"I honestly don't know," Felix said. "But I'm worried about her."

"Are we sure we wanna bring her along?"

He forced a faint smile. "I don't think she'd take no for an answer."

Ornella took out what seemed to be a full copy of Samuel's keys. With a deafening click, the great doors creaked open. Felix gripped him as his old dream from the dark visions mingled with the dread of whatever lay on the other side. Rosie took Felix's hand, and Argent took his other. Felix held on tight, and together, they marched into the darkness.

The void consumed him, as it had twice before. Yet even so, that same wave of trepidation washing over him felt like an entirely different storm brewing. Rosie and Argent's hands drifted away. Felix stood tall, though his terror refused to be silenced. A high-pitched scream curdled his blood. The wail repeated, this time from right behind him, then again. It stabbed his eardrums like a banshee's cry.

"You let us die."

The cold breath stank of decay, and Felix spasmed from the chill. Red dripped from the bullet wounds in Videl's chest and throat. Chalky-white skin smoldered, a stark contrast to sallow sunken eyes. Videl's body turned to dust, and a cold wind swept the remnants into Felix's face, the sediments stinging his eyes and nose. A blurry figure slowly came into focus.

"Z-Zahra…?"

She smiled, then screamed as flames engulfed her. The fire died out, and Zahra's charred body fell to ashes, revealing the malevolent doppelgänger, his hand outstretched and burning with purple flame. A devilish grin spread across his face. His laugh. That maniacal laughter echoed through the void, ringing ceaselessly, mercilessly tormenting Felix's ears, relishing in his distress.

"Why'd you do it?" Rosie and Argent asked. "Why did you kill her?"

Felix's throat collapsed as he struggled for air. The doppelgänger, cackling like a demon, blood-red eyes scathing, held Felix by his throat. "Look what you did." Frank's scowling image superimposed itself, each expression filled with disdain and twisted enjoyment. The figure dropped

Felix into the dark pit below, and a vortex of smoke and violet flames spiraled around him.

Rosie fell beside him. Felix reached out to grab her, only for his hand to swipe through hers like a ghost. She screamed as she descended further into the blaze. Her screams were joined by Argent's, then Zahra's, and soon, all the voices he'd come to recognize shouted together in a chorus of agony, begging for mercy. The doppelgänger's laughter cut through the screams.

"ENOUGH!"

Felix punched, unsure of what he'd hit, but desperate to end this nightmare. Cracking, crunching glass resounded. His fist had collided with a mirror, striking its pane in the dead center. His mother, reflected in the glass, cried.

A low-bearing hum came through, gradually morphing into a woman's cries. Lydia's image had been replaced with that of an older woman with pale skin, gray eyes, and short black hair, dressed in a black kimono. That same sadness weighed heavily on her. She mouthed a message, but it was too faint make out. The mirror cracked, and in one final crash, thousands of shards flew out, cutting and grazing Felix. A fractal flew towards his right eye, though he didn't flinch. In his reflection, a cobalt eye became crimson, then… amethyst.

"R-Rosie…?"

Felix's head throbbed as Rosie helped him up, carrying him out of what seemed to be a dark chamber. He glanced back, glimpsing a tall broken mirror in the middle of an eight-sided, otherwise empty room. The mirror's glass covered the floor. The doors shut behind them, and Rosie laid Felix against the wall beside Argent, Zahra, and Nasira, their eyes all shut, joined by an unconscious, injured Lucinda. "Glad you're okay," Rosie said. "But now's not the time to go in guns blazing."

Felix's throat was dry. "A-Are they…?"

"They're fine. They just need rest."

But his brief respite ended as the massive Cinder towered over them all. Her wings were outstretched, easily spanning the hall's width, almost as if shielding them. But from what? All the way at the other end of the corridor, outside the crypt's entrance, Bloodworth and Vivien battled Samuel, Ornella, and Vagus.

"W-We…" Felix tried to stand. Just as his headache began to fade, it returned with a reckoning, and he slipped back down against the wall.

"We're staying put," Rosie said. "We'd only get in the way." She glanced away, mumbling. "We never should've come here." Felix's impulse had not only dragged himself, but his closest friends into a hell of his own making yet again. Perhaps they really were safer back in the shop.

"Go back!" Vagus' voice carried from down the corridor.

Videl's corpse flashed in Felix's mind. *"You let us die."*

If only I'd acted sooner. Then maybe… Felix could've turned back for shelter, but what guaranteed that Vagus and the others could handle themselves, or that Vagus himself was suddenly now trustworthy? What if the Ring of Nergal fell into these lunatics' hands? Then no one would be safe, anywhere. Not his friends. Not his family. Not himself. He pushed himself up and rushed down the hall. Rosie yelled, calling him an idiot, but Felix's instincts took hold.

"Spark Shower!" With his wand, he released an onslaught of blue fire.

Vivien leapt and, with her water arms, swiped away the attacks. Felix dodged as she landed, only to accidentally ram into the wall. "Oops!" Vivien laughed. "My bad."

Felix held his aching shoulder.

"I promise I won't go for another cheap shot." Vivien swung, and Felix rolled out of the way.

"Felix, go!" Ornella unleashed a fiery wave, but Vivien held it back with a stream of water, all the while fending off swings from Vagus' sword.

Samuel dodged Bloodworth's attacks. Oddly enough, Bloodworth didn't carry a gun. He instead wielded dual lodestone swords. The massive samurai sword remained tucked away, sheathed on his back. Samuel shot a burst of lightning. Bloodworth blocked with one of his blades, knocking Samuel to the floor with the other.

"Bolt Spark!" Felix's fireball made Bloodworth stumble. "What? Guns not good enough for you?"

"You struck from behind," Bloodworth said. "A coward's move."

"So what's that make you?" Felix asked. "An honorable killer?"

Bloodworth stormed forth. Felix evaded and threw more fireballs, but Bloodworth deflected them all with ease.

"Have to agree with the kid there, Bloody," Vivien said. "You take yourself way too seriously!" All the while, she kept up her battle with Ornella and Vagus.

God, what's worse? Someone who finds killing noble, or someone who just plain gets off on it?

"There is no honor in spilling blood," Bloodworth said. "Only in overcoming your opponent through honest strategy and skill."

Vivien laughed. "How fucking romantic! Be sure to tell your men that next time!"

"Have to agree!"

A barrage of icicles zoomed forth. As Bloodworth smashed them, it gave Nasira enough time to carry Samuel away while Argent joined Felix. "Fighting children?" Bloodworth asked. "Now this I wouldn't consider honorable."

"Oh, give it a rest!" Argent said. "We've had enough of you pricks for one day." He grinned at Felix, and Felix grinned back. "Frost Lance!"

"Firestorm!" Felix and Argent released a plume of swirling fire and ice, the sheer force of which was enough to knock Bloodworth back. "Spark Shower!" Felix threw fireballs at Vivien. She spun, creating a whirlpool shield around her. The whirl expanded, knocking Ornella and Vagus against the wall.

"Frost Lance!" Argent's attack dissipated the water, but Vivien had vanished entirely. Felix and Argent stood back to back, scanning for any signs of her. The pool of water she'd created covered the floor, spreading and creeping around them, until a column of water shot up and entrapped them. It reached around their necks, lifting them into the air. Vivien, with a smug look on her face, revealed herself, almost as if manifesting from nowhere.

Vagus had been knocked out, lying against the wall. Cinder screeched, but as Ornella gestured to her, the phoenix stopped. Ornella raised her flute. "Let them go!"

"I wouldn't try anything, Ms. Fontana," Vivien said. "Unless you'd like me to snap their necks, drop your weapon." Ornella complied without resistance, and Vivien, sneering, froze the flute, then snapped it in two. "Now..." Vivien broke Felix and Argent's wands. "You boys won't be needing these anymore."

"Hey!" Argent yelled. "Those were expensive, you bitch!"

Priorities, Argent.

Vivien giggled. "I'm sure they were. But you can trust I'll do much worse to these boys' spines unless I get into that crypt."

"Let them go!" Rosie's shout boomed down the corridor.

"As soon as your old friend there opens the door. Otherwise…" Vivien clenched her fist. Felix's spine burned, as though a thousand needles were ready to tear it apart. He and Argent screamed so loudly, their voices gave out quickly, turning raspy.

"Stop!" Samuel yelled.

Vivien chuckled, and the pain ceased. Felix panted. "And bring the other kids' wands." Samuel traipsed over and handed her the wands, which she promptly snapped. "Right choice. Now, if you'd be a dear…" Bloodworth whispered to Vivien, and she laughed. "Hey, it worked, didn't it?" The gears wound, and the crypt door opened. "That will be all."

Vivien threw Felix and Argent against the wall. She gestured to Bloodworth. "We won't be needing you anymore, geezer," she said. Mumbling, Bloodworth hit Samuel in the back of the head, knocking him out cold.

No! I can't let them! Felix, resisting the pain in his legs, forced himself up and charged, but Vivien blasted him back with water.

"Felix!" Rosie shouted. "Just stop!"

He held himself up against the wall. His body trembled, but he couldn't just stand by and watch them carry on. "Please forgive me," Bloodworth said as he approached. "But this is for your own good." Felix braced himself to dodge and counter strike, but before Bloodworth reached him, a gunshot ruptured Felix's eardrums. Bloodworth coiled and yelled in pain, holding his upper arm as the wound seeped. There, in the center of the hall, stood Rosie, holding what looked to be a lodestone gun, raised and ready to fire again.

Vivien laughed. "Looks like you hit the wrong one, kid!" She made a mad dash for Rosie. Rosie fired again, but missed as Vivien zigzagged. Turning her arms to water, she knocked the gun to the floor with one swipe, then slashed Rosie's stomach with another.

"NO!"

Everything disappeared except for Rosie. Yelling her name, Felix caught her before she fell. Red stained his hands, blood gushing from Rosie's stomach, making Felix tear off his hoodie and tie it around the wound to try and stop the bleeding.

Argent carried Samuel over. "Is she…?"

Ornella rushed over, healed Rosie, then checked her pulse. "She's alive. I've stopped most of the bleeding, and the wound thankfully isn't too deep, but we need to get her to the nurses." She handed Rosie off to Nasira. "You all get her and Samuel help. I'll handle Bloodworth and Vivien."

"But…" Felix couldn't cry. He had no idea how he felt. All he knew was that he'd caused this. Rosie only stepped in to protect him, as she always had. And now, all Felix wanted was to make Vivien bleed, just like she'd done to Rosie.

Ornella gripped his shoulder, snapping him out of his fury, if only momentarily. "You can't take them, especially without a wand. Go get help." With that, Ornella ran into the crypt.

"C'mon," Argent said. "Rosie needs help."

"R-Right…" Felix glanced at the crypt. Ornella had already vanished from sight. Vagus still lay unconscious, while Cinder, now miniaturized, sat on his shoulder, whimpering. It would've been easy to remove Vagus' mask and finally see who his tormentor was. Vagus kept muttering, "I'm sorry. I'm so sorry. I promised… I'd be home soon…"

"Felix?"

Heeding his instinct, Felix turned heel and dashed into the crypt, ignoring his friends' yells. Was this for revenge? For power? He didn't have the answer, nor did he care. All he wanted to do was end Bloodworth and Vivien. Not to stop them—to kill them.

Chapter Thirty

The Black Flame

I HAVE TO STOP THEM. *I have to stop them.*

Sweat trickled down Felix's forehead as he rushed through the crypt. The Ring of Nergal. It had driven Concobhar mad with power. Even Elisa, who fought for the people, became corrupted and deranged by its dark influence. The sick look in her eyes as she tried to kill her own daughters, right after killing her husband and son, still haunted him. If the Black Flame was wielded by someone who didn't already have the soundest of minds, what horrors would ensue?

The wall had been partially destroyed, revealing the enclosed spiral staircase. Felix raced down the steps, past peering gargoyle statues. If these could attack like the golems, just waiting for some unlucky fool to wander into their hunting ground… no. He had to keep going. He had to stop them. To avenge Rosie.

All that blood, pouring from the wound she'd taken for him.

The staircase shook. Felix clung to the wall, his fingers digging into the central stone column. Once he reached the lowest floor, he'd found the source of the rumbling: a massive lone golem, far larger and more sinister than the others of the high floors, staring straight at Felix as though it were waiting for him. Which could've only meant…

Shrieking, a gargoyle dove at Felix from behind. He rolled out into the hall. The gargoyle wasn't tall, but its razor-sharp claws, jagged teeth, and bat wings more than made up for it. Felix reached for his wand instinctively, forgetting it'd just been broken. Again he was completely powerless. The gargoyle dashed, and Felix dodged, all the while also evading the golem's attempts to stomp him flat, shaking the room violently.

"Bolt Spark!" A blue flame formed in Felix's palm, then poofed out. *Dammit!* He rolled again as the gargoyle barreled towards him. Reaching for the nearest artifact, he grabbed a pair of large, black leather boots that looked like they belonged in an old antique shop. *Oh, fuck all of you.* The golem readied to punch, and the boots beamed blue. They pulled Felix to the ceiling as the golem's fist slammed into the ground. *Nevermind then!*

Screeching again, the gargoyle zoomed at Felix. The boots carried him out of the way across the ceiling, then zigzagged as the golem swiped at him. Felix landed next to a set of old ceremonial swords and staffs. *Oh I like this.* Grabbing one of the swords, he shoved the hilt into one of the boots and held its sole against his chest. The gargoyle leapt, and at the last second, Felix let the boot loose. The sword rocketed forth. The blade smashed through the gargoyle, whose body cracked and turned to dust in mere moments. The sword now rested in the golem's leg, knocking it off balance.

Felix repeated the process, this time with two swords. The golem dashed. Felix readied his arm, and at the last moment, launched the blades through the golem's chest. They remained wedged where its heart ought to have been had it been sculpted from flesh and blood. As cracks formed and pebbles and grit seeped out, the golem fell backwards and turned completely to dust.

He rolled to his back, shutting his eyes and relishing in his brief respite. How he would've loved to go home after such a hellish night. Back to his parents and sisters and hug them as tight as he could. To enjoy banters with Aeris over who snatched the leftover pizza from the fridge, or their debates over whether there was a god or not. To appreciate Tracey's smile and laughter, and helping her dress up for parties. In all the months he'd spent at Dragora, feeling like he'd finally found a home for himself, Felix had never really thought of going back after it was all said and done.

He'd witnessed so many horrors tonight, one after another, with no time to process any of it. The violet flames. His father's hateful glare. His doppelgänger, cackling like a maniac. Videl's presumed death, along with all the corpses lining the streets of Cendrillion. Their bodies burning, leaping from the coliseum. Their screams reverberating endlessly in his mind.

"FELIX!"

The scream broke through like a crash of thunder. Felix sat up. Zahra, holding the Bow of Zeus, faced Vagus and a full-sized Cinder. In Vagus' hand was his accursed dreamcatcher. "Neither of you belong here," Vagus said. "We must go. Now."

Zahra pulled the bow back as the strings crackled with electricity.

"I don't want to fight you." Vagus looked at Felix. "Either of you."

Felix rose, his eyes narrowing. "Who are you? Why did you choose Lucas and I to do your dirty work? What makes us so important?"

"I'm sorry," Vagus mumbled. Felix raised an eyebrow, then leapt back as Vagus lunged at him. Zahra fired off lightning. Vagus dodged. Cinder breathed fire, and Zahra rolled out of the way, quickly pulling out the lodestone gun and popping a shot into one of Cinder's legs. The screech made Vagus drop his dreamcatcher. Not wasting a moment, Felix swiped it.

"Whirlwind!" Zahra swept the hall with a gust of wind, swirling the piles of dust left behind by the golem and gargoyle about the room. They ran, but Vagus, heaving, grabbed Felix's wrist. Right away, Felix held the dreamcatcher in front of Vagus, channeling all of his pent-up resentment and rage.

"Nightmare Web!"

Immediately, Vagus fell. *Whatever hell you're seeing now, you deserve it.* Felix and Zahra continued into a long, narrow hallway at the end of the corridor. Bluish stones shone without the need for torchlight. Halfway through, they stopped as Zahra knelt over, grabbing the wall and panting.

"Are you okay?" Felix moved to help her, but Zahra pushed his hand away.

"I'm fine," she said. "Just... using a storm bow when I'm a wind magus isn't as easy as it looks. My head is pounding, and the lightning bolts just seem to do whatever they like." She grit her teeth as she hit the wall. "Why can't anything ever just do what it's meant to?!"

Perhaps that's part of why she'd changed so much. For a light alignment like Zahra, even so much as dabbling in darker magic was enough to poison her mood. "Why?" Felix asked. "Why did you come down here? Why didn't you make me leave, like the others tried to?"

"Oh. I did consider it." Zahra coughed, cracking her back. She focused on the end of the hall. "But this is more important. Ornella will need backup without her weapon. Now come on." She raced forward.

Felix wanted to go along, but he couldn't wait a moment longer. "Wait!" She stopped.

"I... I'm sorry."

Zahra didn't respond. She held her arm.

"I know now's probably the worst time for this," Felix said. "But you have to understand, I... I've always felt so powerless. I thought this might be my only chance at... I don't even know. But with it being my last and only year at Dragora, even before Gottschalk's punishment—"

"You know," Zahra said. "For someone who used to seem kind and selfless, your apology has nearly as many 'I's as it does excuses."

Felix stood there, dazed.

"The Enlightened."

"What?"

"Our enemy," Zahra repeated. "They call themselves the Enlightened. Admittedly, I don't know much about them yet, but they're a group that's existed for over a thousand years."

"Is Vagus one of them?"

Zahra shook her head. "Not anymore. But you and Lucas were both candidates they'd been keeping their eyes on."

Felix's blood chilled. "C-Candidates? For... for what, exactly?"

"I don't know. Look, I'm only telling you this out of pity. The more time we waste here, the more dangerous things become." Resentment returned to Zahra's expression as she stared Felix down, marching towards him. "But before we go anywhere, I need you to promise me that you won't grab that ring. No matter what."

Felix averted her gaze. "I-I—"

"Look me in the eyes and promise me."

He paused. "I won't." He'd hoped Zahra might smile hearing that. But she didn't. She instead turned, and dashed down the corridor. Hesitantly, Felix followed. He told himself over and over that no power was worth the trust of his friends. They raced through, finding a large empty room save for a pedestal at the very end, just like the one in Felix's dream.

Ornella faced off against Vivien alone. Even without her fire flute, she had no problem keeping up. Fire and water clashed as they leapt about the room. Bloodworth struck his swords against the air above the pedestal, staggering every few seconds as he held his bad arm. With each blow, a blue shimmer revealed an otherwise invisible barrier.

Zahra raised her bow. "Ornella, move!" Ornella jumped back as Zahra fired off a burst of lightning. The bolt struck Vivien's water arms, electrocuting her and knocking her down. Felix and Zahra rushed over to Ornella. "Are you alright?" Zahra asked.

Ornella grimaced, strands of hair hanging in her reddened face. "I told you to run."

"You're exhausted," Felix said. "And we're here to help."

"You should take your own advice," Zahra said. As Felix stepped back, Ornella threw fireballs at Bloodworth, but he blocked with his swords. Zahra raised her bow. "I've got this."

"NO!"

Bloodworth dodged Zahra's attack. The moment the lightning hit the barrier around the pedestal, it shattered like glass, shards falling as their echoes filled the corridor. A sick laughter sent a chill down Felix's spine. Before he could react, a rush of water knocked him and Ornella against the wall. "It's a shame you had to turn traitor, Lady Fontana," Vivien said. "You had such promise!" Ornella shot Vivien a hateful glare, to which Vivien smirked.

Until a gunshot sent her stumbling.

Vivien nearly fell over, cursing under her breath. The wound in her leg didn't release blood, but rather, light. A light which gave way to blue mythril fragments falling from the hole where the bullet had entered. And there, holding up the smoking lodestone gun, was Zahra, panting.

"You little shit."

Turning her arm to water again, Vivien knocked the gun from Zahra's hand. She grabbed Zahra and held her high, holding the Bow of Zeus with her free human hand. "Interesting toy you have here, sweetie." She gave an insidious grin. Vivien tossed Zahra to the ground with a deafening thud. Felix charged, only to be knocked back down with another blast of water. "Wait your turn, young man!"

500

Zahra tried to stand, but before she could escape, Vivien transformed her arm again and trapped Zahra in a sphere of water. Zahra grasped her throat. Vivien tapped her foot, impatiently waiting for her victim to fade away. "Must admit, you're a better shot than that friend of yours." She examined the bow. "Oh I see! This bow conducts electricity, and uses that to fire off arrows of lightning! Such craftsmanship! The ancients were so much more innovative than we give 'em credit for."

Bloodworth approached her. "Vivien, no."

"I said we don't kill those two over there." Vivien gestured to her limp. "This girl's been nothing but a nuisance. Not to mention, I'd bet we'd get a pretty bonus for eliminating the headmistress' heiress. Or at least, I'd get the credit for it."

Bloodworth drew his swords. It was only now it became clear that part of his mask had cracked, revealing a mint-green eye. It took Felix a moment to place it, and once he did, his blood boiled. *You...*

Vivien sighed. "You're no fun." Relenting, she eased up, and the sphere dissipated, releasing a drenched Zahra as she coughed. Bloodworth lowered his weapons and turned towards the pedestal. Vivien scoffed. Turning heel, she blasted him with another torrent, sending him sliding across the floor. His swords clanged as they hit the floor. Pulling back the string and giving a diabolical sneer, Vivien aimed the bow at Zahra.

"A shame I'm not the forgiving type."

Felix forced himself up. His legs stung, and he struggled for air as Zahra coughed up more water. Vivien pulled her arm further back, taking her sweet time and loving every moment. A bolt formed within the bow. Felix punched her in the jaw, but as his fist landed, a thunderclap ruptured his eardrums, followed by a brief but bloodcurdling scream. He fell, his ears ringing. Shock seized his body. Before him lay a motionless carcass, burning with a faint trace of rising smoke. It twitched slightly. A quiet groan of agony croaked from its throat; the cry of a corpse letting out its final plea for life as it fell into death's cold grip.

Zahra.

The entire world froze. This had to have been some awful dream, or some kind of trick. But there Zahra was, right before his eyes, gone. The anxiety that had long been building in his stomach at last erupted, and he threw up. He coughed and gagged, tears streaming down his face as he fell into his own vomit. The floor tiles darkened, shrinking into a blur of self-blame and grief. A faint, raspy, disembodied voice whispered into his ear:

"You let her die."

"My, my. Look at the mess you've made!"

The following moments vanished from Felix's recollection, but the next thing he knew, stone broke as he was thrown into the far wall. He slid to the floor, surrounded by the pedestal's remnants. Right before him was the Ring of Nergal and its shining blood-red jewel. He stretched his arm out for it as far as he could, but it was just out of reach. With a tearing pain in his chest, he nudged himself forward, and in one swipe, held the ring tight in his palm.

A honed pain stabbed his hand. He tightened his fingers around the ring, imagining he was biting down on a bullet. Vivien, standing overhead, crushed Felix's hand beneath her uninjured foot. The heel felt like a knife pressing into his skin, blood seeping from the puncture. "I'm gonna have to ask you to be a good boy," Vivien said. "And hand over that ring."

"N-No…" Felix's vocal cords, like the rest of his body, felt like they were ready to snap.

"You wouldn't wanna end up like your friends, would you?" Vivien asked.

"F-Fuck you."

Vivien pressed her heel deeper into Felix's palm, cutting into sinew like tissue paper. He screamed in pain, but that pain only fueled his hatred, tightening his grip. This woman had been lurking in the shadows all along, tormenting Lucas, nearly killing Rosie, and now killing Zahra. This couldn't be forgiven. No way in hell was Felix about to let this monster get away with all of this. The only way she'd be leaving this room now would be as a pile of ash to be kept in a jar.

The roars of a growing fire ensued. Vivien jumped back as purple flames formed around Felix's hand. He opened his palm, and the ring glowed a deep scarlet as he placed it on his finger. Blood dripped from a small hole in his palm onto the gemstone.

Felix rose into the air. The scarlet light emanated all around him, along with rings of violet flames. Large smoky black wings jutted out from his back. He cracked a grin, held up his hands, and formed a black fireball. Crimson light spilled across the entire hall. Vivien looked on in horror, and Felix took the sweetest delight in her fear.

He swung his arms, and in one fell swoop, the fire completely devoured Vivien. She screamed at the top of her lungs as her hair turned to dust, her skin melting along with the red-and-pink flesh beneath. As the flames cleared, all that was left was a small puddle, a pile of ashes, and a thick cloud of smoke. The shards of blue mythril sparkled atop the remains.

Felix laughed, amused by the fact he'd seen to his enemy's demise before he'd even thought of having avenged his lost friend. He held onto the image of Vivien's widening eyes as the end drew near, and the pain in her screams, both far worse than what she'd inflicted upon Zahra. The catharsis alone was all the justice he needed.

But that pleasure vanished as Felix's gaze fell to Ornella, sitting against the wall, her eyes wide with terror. They were… different. Her left eye lacked a pupil. An endless sea of fiery crimson wisps within the iris, almost like Vivien's eyes.

Then, an applause. A slow clap, gradually growing louder.

"Very good!"

Vagus entered the hall. Before Felix could react, a sharp pain dug into his hand. The ring's light flowed through Felix's arm, his skin glowing red, almost as though his flesh was turning to crystal. His eyes shut, and everything went dark.

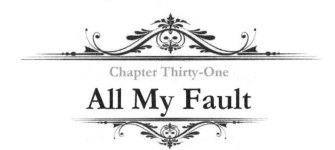

Chapter Thirty-One

All My Fault

ABLURRY ARRAY of colors mixed into brown and beige ceiling tiles. The back of Felix's neck hurt like hell, and his mouth was unbearably dry. He blinked the sand out of his eyes, as his arms were too heavy to do the job, though the hair hanging in his face made it unpleasant to say the least. The memory, the image of Zahra's smoldering corpse, coursed through his mind like venom, taking its sweet time as to crush his soul with every horrible detail.

"You went back for the ring," the raspy, disembodied voice said. *"You broke your promise."*

He shot up, panting. The infirmary was filled with injured students. Nurses rushed between beds, healing patients as they rotated. There lay Nina and Theresa at one end, and at the other, what looked to be Penny, with Shawn fast asleep beside her, and Floria knocked out against the wall. Gauze had been wrapped over the bottom of Penny's right thigh… where her leg should've been. In another bed, Professor Jhaveri sat in a chair next to Dezirae, both of them holding back tears beside a comatose Videl, hooked up to an IV drip and covered in bandages.

An amethyst-eyed nurse scurried over to Felix and gently nudged him back down. "Any pain, dear?"

"N-No…" A sting panged Felix's arm. "Maybe a bit?"

The nurse fluffed his pillow and quickly checked his vitals, during which Felix's eyes fell to the certificate hung up on the wall for the human doctor from the U.K. The image of a mint-green eye behind Bloodworth's mask flashed in his mind, bringing with it the grueling pain of betrayal. "Ma'am," Felix croaked, trying to hide his anger. "Do you know where Dr. Bloxham is?"

"No. Unfortunately he's been missing since just before the attack." The nurse rolled her eyes briefly. "Humans, right?" The bitterness faded as she gave a faint smile. "Get some rest, sweetheart." She rushed to the next bed.

Felix shut his eyes, hoping to get some rest, only for those terrible images seared into his memory to return with a reckoning. Perhaps one of the people he trusted most here, and it'd all been a lie. A lie that had cost him dearly last night.

Rosie…!

Almost as if they'd sensed his fear, one of the nurses rushed to Rosie's side as she lay unconscious. Her stomach was bandaged, and Felix kept seeing flashes of red marking where she'd been wounded. There was nothing there, of course. She was alive. They'd both survived, and soon they could go home and see their families again. Unlike…

"It's all your fault she died."

This was the strange voice from the Chamber of Kagami—perhaps the voice of Kagami the Reflective herself—seemingly confined to Felix's mind. Perhaps this was part of the illusions, having some long-term effect on his sanity. Or maybe he was just losing it.

Felix, choosing chaos, decided to humor the voice within his own head. *Nearly getting killed and watching your friends die would do that to anyone. Right?*

"Cracking jokes already, are we? Good to see she meant nothing to you. So much potential lost in one night, and all because she felt the need to protect a parasite she'd grown oh so attached to. Addicted, you could say."

Kagami, or rather, what Felix elected to call Kagami, was right. The first time he'd met Zahra, she'd healed him after he'd inadvertently walked into a damn pole. She was always so kind and supportive. While Felix benefitted from her friendship, Zahra had only gotten into trouble with her parents and risked her life. And now, she'd paid the ultimate price for standing by his side. For poisoning herself. Had it not been for him, she'd still be here to

505

help Nasira learn not to hate herself, and to eventually succeed her mother and bring even more progress to the Medeian Empire.

But that was all gone now.

Stolen.

If only Felix hadn't gotten lost in his train of thought that day, as maybe then he and Zahra never would've met, she wouldn't have taken a liking to him, and she wouldn't have gotten swept up in any of this. She'd still be alive. If not for him. Hell, if he hadn't come to Dragora at all, then perhaps it wouldn't have been left in ruins.

Felix lay back, his head crashing into the pillow. His thoughts drifted until everything faded away. Silence, wrapping him in its cold, shadowy embrace. He wandered aimlessly through the void—lost.

"How could you…?"

Zahra manifested from the darkness. She lay there, helpless, crying out in excruciating pain. Felix ran to her, only for her body to burst into flames as he touched her. He covered his ears, but the screams, hellish and earsplitting, refused to go unheard. Other screams joined in. Felix's knees buckled, his eardrums now bleeding. The screams surrounded him. The cries of the damned, burning for all eternity. He might not have believed in hell, but if he had, this most certainly was it.

The cackling returned, alternating between the last two voices he'd wanted to hear: his doppelgänger, and Frank. Felix refused to open his eyes. The laughter was ceaseless, and as a column of flames surrounded him, the silhouettes approached.

"They seek to destroy you from within."

This voice, a deep, comforting one emanating from all around, drowned out the tormentors' cackles. The Ring of Nergal appeared on his finger. Its gem sparkled a brilliant crimson, showing his reflection perfectly, his irises red.

"Rise. Rise from the ashes, and burn this darkness away."

Bands of purple flames formed around Felix. He flew, breaking through the smoke to find himself adrift in a sea of clouds beneath an endless, starless purple sky. Orange burned across the horizon, and out from the golden sunset walked a figure made of sunlight. At first, it appeared like an angel, its wings stretching as it reached out its hand. But slowly, it morphed into something else. Its eyes turned a gleaming red as it hunched over, roaring on all fours, ready to eviscerate its prey.

The chattering of nurses returned as Felix was jolted awake. Perhaps he didn't believe in heaven, nor hell, but maybe he could make an exception for his guardian angel. If he could even call it that. Even if it was all nonsensical hallucinations, or simply his imagination, it was ironically something to keep him grounded. To keep him from going completely insane (assuming he hadn't already). But a newfound terror took hold with what he saw, or rather, didn't see—the ring was no longer on his finger.

"This just in on the recent attack on Cendrillion." The news anchor's voice blared from the TV at the far end of the room. Behind them was the image of the burning Angels' Arena. "The imperial army quelled the attack just a few hours ago, and both the city and the Dragora Institute of Magic have been fully secured. More than half of the school's familiars had to be put down, though it has been discovered that an unknown substance was mixed into the reserve's food supplies."

The image of the coliseum changed to a strange white powder, which seemed to glow all on its own. Lodestone.

"Authorities believe this substance to have increased the creatures' aggressive instincts, though it has yet to have been identified. Likewise, the Lighthaven Hospital appears to have been breached, though there are no remains of any victims. According to the vanguard's account everyone inside, staff and patients alike, has vanished without a trace."

So, the school wasn't their only target then.

"Reports suggest there have been around 70 casualties, and over 20 deaths, making this the most lethal night in world history since the Scorch of 2052, and the deadliest terrorist attack in recorded history."

The numbers sounded… small. Felix wasn't sure what to expect, but from the nightmare he'd endured, the amount of suffering seemed incalculable. He wanted to scoff at Bloodworth… Calvin's "honor," if only he didn't feel so sick.

"Unfortunately, one of those deaths was one Zahra Hakim, daughter of Dragora's beloved Headmistress Hakim. Her husband Seisyll confirmed the tragedy was due to their daughter's brave sacrifice in defending her school as it was ravaged by wild familiars. The details are being kept private as per the family's request, and we ask all viewers to show their condolences for their loss."

A "brave sacrifice." Felix closed his eyes. *This place needs her more than ever right now, and she's gone. Because of me.*

But these were no stragglers behind this attack. This went so, so much deeper. The Enlightened. A group that, if Zahra was right, was older than most countries, and had a much bigger scheme in this works than just this operation. They had eyes everywhere. Even back home on Long Island, keeping tabs on Felix since he was born through Vagus. But why? Why would they ever care that much about a cobalt runt with a father who'd left him like he was nothing?

Donning that ring for just a moment granted Felix far more power than he'd ever harnessed before; more than he could ever hope to wield as a cobalt. The power to protect what he loved. The power to prove he was worth something to this cold, uncaring world. If he'd reached his full potential, then perhaps he could've prevented all this devastation. He'd ought to be feared by anyone who'd ever wronged him, beginning with Frank. Yet that promise of everything he'd fought for over the last seven years had been so easily torn away...

Then a more chilling thought occurred to him: they had the ring. Either the Enlightened, or Vagus. Honestly, Felix didn't know which possibility frightened him more.

"Honey, please don't strain yourself!" The nurse ran back over, checking his blood pressure. "Much lower than when you came in. How do you feel?"

"... Fine, I suppose."

"Your hair says it all though."

"Huh?" The nurse handed him a compact. Felix's hair, normally a dark brown, was now a dull gray, perfectly matching the dreariness of his eyes. *Did the ring do this? I know I act like a crotchety old shit sometimes, but damn.* He glanced back over to Rosie. "The girl over there. Is she...?"

The nurse smiled. "Don't worry. We had our best healers treat her the moment she came in last night. She just needs some rest."

"Thanks." *She's okay. But... Zahra...*

"YOU BASTARD!"

Seisyll stormed into the room, his face red and twisted with hatred. He grabbed Felix by the shirt and pulled him up. Pain shot through Felix's body as Seisyll got right in his face, his eyes watery, filled with sorrow and resentment.

"Seisyll, stop!" Gottschalk yelled. The nurses pulled Seisyll back. Gottschalk marched forth, mere inches from Seisyll's face. "SEISYLL." Her voice boomed, sending the infirmary into complete and utter silence.

Slowly, Seisyll headed for the exit, glaring at Felix on the way out. The abhorrence in his eyes burned deep. Gottschalk followed behind, not needing to say a word. Nothing but an ounce of pity and contempt in her gaze. Felix sat back, staring straight ahead as the nurses resumed their duties.

"Hey."

Nasira stood by his bed, crossing her arms. He couldn't find the right words—or any words. Would acknowledging what happened somehow help the situation? Or was it even an insult for him to even speak Zahra's name?

"For the record…" Nasira's voice was cold and brittle. "I don't hate you."

"I…" Felix looked away. "I'm sorry."

"Can't even look me in the eyes when you say it?"

Silence.

"She was a good kid, with a bright future." Nasira clenched her fists. "Brighter than mine," she mumbled. "That's for damn sure. But… I don't hate you."

Felix looked up.

"You're not worth hating."

He was left speechless as Nasira made her way to the door. He could hardly choke out the slightest sound, but he knew he owed it to her to say something. "Wait!" As Nasira turned back, Felix made a conscious effort to look her directly in the eyes with as much concern as possible. "How… how are you holding up?"

"Like you care. Trust me, your fuck-up isn't worth me killing myself over." Nasira had every right to hate Felix for what happened. Her entire family had that right, in Felix's mind. "Oh, and your boyfriend Argent? He's gone."

Felix paused. "W-What… what did you—"

"He's home," Nasira said. "With his mother. Safe from you." And with that, she left.

Unable to fully process what he'd just heard, Felix simply slept both the day and the guilt away as much as he could. The strange visions ceased. A dreamless sleep followed, and when he awoke, the confusion and sorrow returned immediately. Only the faint shine of the new moon lit the room. Déjà vu struck him as he recalled his stay in the infirmary at the very beginning of the year after his fight with Lucas. Vagus' silhouette had seemingly lurked in the shadows, watching. Was he here now? Or was this simply a long-forgotten memory?

"Go back to sleep."

A figure in a long maroon cloak approached, with Cinder perched atop their shoulder. This wasn't Vagus. They were much shorter, with the soft voice of a young woman. Felix reached out, but the figure held his forehead, and a faint red light filled the room. Just before the veil of darkness clouded his sight, Felix made out the face beneath the hood as Ornella.

Her voice echoed: "Find the talismans."

"Felix!"

Arms wrapped around him as the sun broke through the clouds, and chirping birds flew past the open windows. All the other students lay asleep in their beds. There, hugging him so tight she might never let go…

"Mami?"

After all these months, Felix had forgotten how much his mother's embrace comforted him. The homesickness never really hit home, so to speak, until now. To think it took courting death for him to remember how much his mother, the woman who brought him into this world and protected him from his father's wrath, truly meant to him…

"¡Gracias a Dios!" Tears rolled down Lydia's face and onto Felix's shoulders. "¡Gracias a Dios que estás bien!"

Ian stood at the foot of the bed. "How're you feeling?"

"Fine…" Felix sat up. Rosie was still in bed unconscious, while her fathers, Bennie and David, sat next to her and held her hands. Bennie leaned into David's shoulder. Felix wanted so badly to apologize to them for putting Rosie in harm's way. For nearly killing their daughter. If Rosie had died, would her parents hate her the same way Seisyll did? Would Felix and Rosie's friendship have been nothing more than her path to an untimely death? It seemed the common trait among Felix's acquaintances recently.

"¿Mijo? What's wrong?"

Felix met his mother's eyes. "I… I'm sorry. Just tired." After a moment, he caught himself. He'd normally have apologized in Spanish. And beyond an apology, he'd normally enjoy slipping into Spanish as a way to further connect with Lydia. But the harder he thought about it, the more difficult it became to think of the last time he'd even thought in Spanish.

Lydia smiled through her tears. "We'll be going home soon, once you and Rosie are able. The school's offered to cover our flights and hotels. Your stuff's already packed."

"… N-No…"

"What?"

"I… can't. I have to…" Felix held his head as his eyelids grew heavy. "The ring…" His right ring finger twitched as it panged.

"Find the talismans."

"Felix?" Lydia's grip on Felix's hand tightened. "What's wrong?" Her voice grew grave; more panicked.

Ian rested his hand on her shoulder. "Lydia, it's okay. What matters is that Felix and Rosie are okay. They're safe and alive."

Safe and alive. Those words stung more than they ought to. "I need to go." Felix leapt past his parents. They shouted for him to come back, but he kept running. *Ornella? What else does she know?* She was the only person who might've given him a straight answer. The cold floors stung his bare feet, and he ran down the hill to the city, rocks scraping them, nearly tripping countless times. But it didn't matter. A few cuts and bruises could never compare to what the people around him endured. To the price Zahra paid on his behalf.

Most of the buildings in Cendrillion were heavily damaged, having been sealed off by authorities for repairs. Still, people carried on like it was a normal day. Passersby stared at Felix as he whisked past, but the eyes of strangers never once crossed his mind. He burst into the Fountain of Magic.

"Hey there, sexy."

Leaning against the counter, giving a devil-may-care grin, was Carlos. His smirk lit a foul fire in Felix. He'd seemingly been everywhere, always watching, aware of everything. Felix marched up to him, getting right in his face. "What do you know about this?!"

Carlos simpered. "What does anyone know?"

"Don't fucking skirt the question."

"Only skirt I see's—"

511

Felix grabbed Carlos by the shirt collar. "You... you were in that dream! You knew! You knew what was coming! You fucking—"

"What in the world is going on here?!" Priscilla stood in the doorway, her mouth agape, while Mason, sulking, lurked behind her. Felix released Carlos, though Carlos' grin only widened. "Mr. Brasher?" Priscilla asked. "By Seraphina's light, are you alright?"

"I... came to see Ornella. I had to ask—"

Priscilla looked down. Mason gripped his arm.

Felix backed away. "No..."

"Ornella..." Mason could barely speak. "She went missing during the attack."

Priscilla raised her head. "She's been presumed dead."

But... I just saw her. Didn't I?

Carlos snickered. "Anyways, I'm on break now." He strutted around the corner. But before he left, he gripped Felix's shoulder, whispering: "Don't let it get you too worked up. After all, you're just a replaceable pawn in this shitty, shitty game." The bell jingled behind him as he left, Lydia and Ian rushing in right after.

"Don't ever do that again!" Ian yelled. "You had us terrified!"

"I-I—"

Lydia threw her arms around Felix, crying. His parents had no idea what he'd witnessed. It probably would've been the smart thing to explain everything to them. To be brutally honest about the past few months. But if this did go beyond what Felix could've imagined, were they—the Enlightened—still watching? Listening? Was he still their puppet? Would he, or any of his loved ones, ever be truly safe? Felix wept into his mother's shoulder. All of this was too much to bear. Far too much for any one person.

"Lo siento, Mami," he choked out.

"I'm sorry."

Calvin had barely managed to climb back aboard his helicopter and cloak it with his employer's mythril before the authorities arrived at Dragora. He kept to the far corner of the crypt while Felix's power erupted from that ring.

Then, once that Vagus fellow appeared, Cal ran as fast as he could, cursing himself all the while. What he wouldn't give to keep himself from turning his back to Vivien. He should've listened to his gut and cut her down right there. But no. He turned away, and that poor girl paid the price.

As he piloted the copter through the heavy clouds, his eyes tearing up at the rising sun, he tore off his broken mask and tossed it towards the back. It nearly reopened the wound in his bicep, but his pain mattered the absolute least. Once he made it back home, he'd vow to himself to never don that damned mask again.

Home. How could he ever look his family in the eyes after all he'd done? And moreover, could he ever truly feel safe, knowing the "Enlightened," whomever they were, were still out there? He'd only been approached by Vivien for the job months before the start of the school year because of his long career as a mercenary. Venturing across the globe, slaying magical beasts running wild, all to get some kind of thrill out of life that home never could've provided him. He'd thought he could keep this up for a little while longer, not needing to worry about his family discovering the truth.

"It'd be a shame if your wife, or those adorable kids of yours, knew what you were up to."

How Vivien or her employees traced his Bloodworth persona back to him was lost on him, but it was enough to haunt every waking thought. And with what he'd just done, the crimes he'd been an accomplice to, there was no telling what kind of storm was now brewing.

"I'm sorry, Felix."

"You can't just fly off the handle like that!"

Gottschalk rubbed her temples, using all her energy to hold back the nasty combination of exhaustion and a migraine. The dim lighting in Ramidha's office, with all the curtains drawn and the lights kept off, certainly didn't help. Seisyll leaned against the corner wall, seeming like he might slip away into the shadows between the flickers of light. Samuel, meanwhile, sat on the couch with his signature slouch.

They'd been waiting for Ramidha, along with another professor, to arrive, so they might evaluate the damage to the school for their report to the empress. But right now, all Gottschalk wanted to do was find whomever took Seisyll's daughter, and wring their neck.

"Sei," Gottschalk said. "If something like that happened to Lucas or Lucinda…" She cut herself off, too afraid to even acknowledge her niece and nephew had nearly met that same, tragic fate, and that the odds were high they might one day. Instead, she turned to Samuel. "So, the Ring of Nergal is gone?"

Samuel groaned. "Like I said. I looked high and low for that thing, and nothin'."

Gottschalk shook her head. "And there was no trace of it on Mr. Brasher's person, or in his belongings."

"You looked through his room?"

"When it's a matter of life and death, the innocent have nothing to hide."

Samuel rolled his eyes. "Sure. Cuz that's how we do things."

"In any case," Gottschalk said. "The empress will need to be notified. We need to be prepared for anything now. This may very well have been just the beginning."

"Who did it?"

They both looked to Seisyll, the room growing darker as his voice boomed. "I won't ask again," Seisyll said. "Who killed my daughter, Samuel?"

Samuel stuttered. "I-I told you, Sei. I wasn't down there. I didn't see—"

"Of course you didn't. You never see." Seisyll pushed himself off the wall, marching towards Samuel. "Zahra's entire life, you just ignored her. Like she wasn't your niece. Do you know how much that hurt her? How when she was little, she'd ask about her Uncle Sammy? About all the things he must've seen working in this castle? How scared she was to ask if he hated her?"

"S-Sei—"

"No." Seisyll's voice nearly cracked as he shouted. "You don't get to make excuses anymore. You let this happen. You may not have done this, but you let it happen. You showed how little you valued her life." Tears fell through his glower.

Silence filled the office. For once, Gottschalk felt nervous to speak. But as Seisyll began to sniffle, muttering to himself about failing his daughter, she couldn't just watch and do nothing. Slowly, she approached, resting her hand on his shoulder. Not a word was spoken, the only eye contact being when Seisyll glanced over between his fingers before letting out a heavy cry.

After a good while, Ramidha, as well as Professor Montanari, finally arrived. "Apologies," Ramidha said, her voice low and purposefully monotone. Once they were caught up to speed, Ramidha peeked through the blinds, seemingly in deep thought while the others carried on their conversation. Gottschalk wanted to ask how she was holding up, as she hadn't gotten the chance since that terrible discovery.

"My mother's gone."

The words caught Gottschalk off guard. "What?" She leveled with Montanari. "Fae, what in the world are you talking about?"

"Lighthaven," Montanari said. "It looks like it was raided during the attack. Everyone is gone. All the security, all the staff..." She held her arm. "And all the patients."

Another tragedy. Montanari's mother, who'd already been on the verge of passing, was now gone. But why would the Enlightened have struck a hospital of all places? Then it hit, and Gottschalk nearly lost her breath. "The mageblight patients."

"For chimeric experiments, no doubt." Seisyll's voice was brittle.

"This was no random attack," Ramidha said, not even glancing over. "The coordination, the knowledge of how we'd react... I want a thorough investigation of every professor, every member of staff, and every vendor at the tournament. If there were any inside agents keeping tabs on all of us, I want them found and brought to justice."

Everyone paused. Ramidha had never shown this assertiveness before. When it became clear no one else could bring themselves to speak, Gottschalk stepped up. "Of course, ma'am."

"Isolda, I want you specifically to interrogate Mr. Brasher before he heads back to the States."

"I-Interrogate?"

Ramidha clenched her fists. "He knows more than he's letting on. He may not have the ring, but I want every last bit of information he's holding onto in our hands."

Gottschalk had already planned on questioning Mr. Brasher, but Ramidha's choice of words disturbed her. "Yes. It will be done."

"And one more thing," Ramidha said. "This will be a private matter between Isolda and I, so the rest of you can leave." She glanced back. "Even you, Sei…"

Seisyll seemed confused at first. Reluctantly, he escorted Montanari out while letting the door nearly hit Samuel. Once they'd left, Gottschalk clasped her hands. "Ramidha… you know you can talk about—"

"Do you remember when I was appointed as headmistress?" Ramidha asked.

"… Y-Yes, of course!" Gottschalk giggled. "I think that was the first time in years I drank away my anger with gin and tonic… with very little tonic, admittedly. I was about ready to throw my bottle at the empress before Seisyll talked me down." Such simpler times.

"You said I wasn't fit for the job," Ramidha said. "That I was too soft."

Gottschalk paused. "Well… yes. I'd worked hard as head of discipline for years, yearning for that position, so—"

"And you resented an amethyst taking what you'd worked for."

"I-I…" Gottschalk stepped back. At first, she wanted to deny such claims. But the more she thought it over, the more she realized it was plain for all to read, including the students. "When the decision was made, yes. I am ashamed to admit that. But you've shown me through the years how wrong I was. I may have reservations in the way you go about things, but ultimately, I respect all of the good you've done for this school."

Ramidha laughed. "Good? Look around. The castle is in tatters, the city even more so, we've lost the one talisman we've managed to cling onto all this time… and…" She sniffled, then dried her eyes before turning to Gottschalk. "You were right."

"I… I don't understand."

Ramidha faintly smiled. "I'm saying that… maybe it's time we had new leadership."

Gottschalk nearly fainted. Her younger self would've leapt at this opportunity, but now, she was ready to call for Seisyll to talk some sense into Ramidha. "You can't be serious!" Gottschalk's voice cracked. "You're a wonderful headmistress! We need you now more than ever!"

"They don't need me," Ramidha said. "Besides, I… I don't think I could even handle the basic affairs of getting the school back into shape. Not after…" She tried to stop herself, but she couldn't keep it in. The tears flowed forth, and in no time, she was sobbing as she clutched her chest, murmuring in Arabic. Gottschalk couldn't fully gather what she was saying, but she knew enough to understand someone pleading to the gods they loved why their child had been taken too soon. They sat there, in the dark on the office floor, begging to awaken from the nightmare.

But the nightmare was far from over.

After Felix's family had left the shop, Priscilla ordered Mason to close up for the day. Her phone went off with a message: "Illustratum." She rolled her eyes. "It's always while I'm busy, isn't it?" Ensuring her office door was locked behind her, she turned off the lights, drew the blinds, and removed the fourteenth red tome from the top of her bookshelf. The shelf slid over, revealing a narrow downward staircase lit by overhanging red mythril crystals. She stepped inside, the shelf closing behind her with a thunderous boom.

The staircase led to her private "meditation chamber." Ironic, given this room rarely gave her anything but more migraines. Eight-sided, with purple torches casting a violet tint on everything, save for the circular black hatch in the room's center.

"Glyph: Praefectus, Fontana."

The room shook as the hatch opened, and a small fountain rose from the depths: one depicting the Eleven Dragons, all coiling into Her Beatitude's throne, whose projection was strangely absent. The only ones joining Priscilla were the silhouettes of her fellow praefecti: the Synod of the Enlightened.

"Vivien's the perfect one to lead the operation, huh?"

It took all Priscilla's strength not to so much as frown. Rhosyn would never see it, of course, but in order to control the flow of the conversation, one had to maintain an air of calm and superiority at all times. In the sweetest voice she could muster, Priscilla said, "A… slight miscalculation. That Brasher boy is far too much of a wild card." *To think a runt like him would be the one to wield the Ring of Nergal. To become the Fourteenth Demon.*

"At the very least," the hoarse female voice said. "The Medeian Empire will be in disarray for a time. The people are incredibly upset by 'Her

Majesty's' incompetence, and her apparent friendliness with the Holy Roman Empire."

The older male voice scoffed. "It never fails to amuse me how spineless our leaders are."

"And my sweep of Lighthaven was a success," Rhosyn cheered. "Not that anyone will acknowledge it," he muttered, emphasizing his exasperation. "But the ring? At least before we knew where it was. But now…" He groaned.

"It would be safe to assume," the younger male voice said. "That it's in Vagus' possession. One man couldn't possibly evade our reach for too long."

Rhosyn laughed. "Seriously, who invited you, kid?"

"Now, now," Priscilla said. "We have the advantage. This is a perfect time to recement our control over the empire."

"Uh-huh. When we're now short one calathus? A one… Ornella?"

Priscilla stepped back, the words stabbing her pride. "A… temporary setback." She'd created Ornella solely as one of the keys to the Enlightened's success—to her own success. Never had she so strongly resented giving into that accursed lampad's whining about attending Dragora. "We find Vagus, we find our missing calathus. And perhaps even her assigned talisman."

"Priscilla voices a fair point," the hoarse female voice said. "But in that case, we ought to let one of our own handle the extraction. I nominate Rhosyn."

Priscilla's seething rage finally bubbled over. "Him?!" She covered her mouth, cursing herself for her outburst.

Rhosyn snickered. "I'd watch myself, Priscilla. Wouldn't wanna dig yourself an even deeper grave!"

If she could've struck him down right there, she would've without hesitation. She'd risked her cover to help lower security in the coliseum, and even smuggled in the lodestone charges and weaponry. Without her, they wouldn't have even had the chance to strike. But now wasn't the time for a martyr act. And so, she silenced herself.

Rhosyn turned back to the other praefecti. "Consider it done. My chimaeras will be so excited to finally leave the garden. I certainly have some choice words for those brats who helped kill my darling Terri. And thankfully, my little excursion brought me something that Vagus just won't be able to ignore once he catches wind of it."

"You may be Her Beatitude's direct companion," the hoarse voice said. "And the only one of us without a cover to worry about. But rest assured, if you expose us to the world at large—"

"I'll be…" Rhosyn gestured, slitting his own throat before cackling. "I got it, I got it! When I'm done, Vagus will be nothing but an irksome memory."

Chapter Thirty-Two

When it Rains...

"YOU SURE you don't want dinner, honey?" Lydia, arms crossed, stood in the doorway of Felix's bedroom. Felix sat at his desk, unable to bring himself to even glance at her. His back ached from having been hunched over for hours. His eyes burned, staring at his laptop's screen with only it and his flickering lamp to light his room.

"I'm sure, Mami. I'll eat later."

Lydia cleared her throat.

Reluctantly, Felix turned in his desk chair, forcing a smile. "I promise."

"Alright. Please try not to stay up too late. Te quiero, mi cielito." She left, and Felix quietly shut the door behind her before returning to his desk. His stomach growled, but despite his hunger, he had to keep up with the news on Dragora as much as he could, even if it could only come from U.S.-based articles and news sites.

His phone buzzed, startling him. Another text from Rosie. As expected, they hadn't had a full conversation since they'd gotten home two weeks prior. Nothing more than the occasional "Hey" and a few trivial GIFs in passing before going back to the silence.

As for Argent... nothing. Felix tried texting him every once in a while, to no avail, as they hadn't been successfully delivered. He didn't even get to say goodbye. The one time he'd actually felt something genuinely romantic for another person, and had a good chance of those feelings being returned in kind, and now it was gone. Maybe this was karma.

Alec had also tried reaching Felix as well. Cynically, Felix dismissed it as Alec trying to get the scoop on what had happened to him abroad. The fool…

Repairs for the school seemed to be going well, and it would be opening its doors that fall as usual. Gottschalk had even stepped up to become the new headmistress after her predecessor stepped down. Ramidha, so distraught over her daughter's death, left a position she'd absolutely loved. A job where she was able to help so many young aspiring sorcerers find their path. And Felix ripped it away from her.

Arrangements were being made for a massive ceremony in honor of Zahra, but even if he could afford a trip there and back, her family wouldn't want Felix showing his face there. It would be spitting on Zahra's grave. This way, he couldn't cause her parents any more trouble.

President Schmitt announced shortly after the attack that, to no one's surprise, this year would mark the end of the "failed" Dragora grant program. He could've done that himself, but members of the Medeian parliament were more than happy to agree. Most magi in the U.S. who didn't even finish their first year, assuming they'd survived the atrocity, wouldn't be able to complete their academics. Headmistress Gottschalk probably didn't mind.

Before Felix came home, Gottschalk spent about an hour interrogating him about the crypt, but it felt more like an eternity. Over and over, she asked for his detailed account of the story, descriptions of the assailants involved, and where the Ring of Nergal was now. Even when Gottschalk used magic to detect whether Felix was being truthful, she still wasn't satisfied—only about the ring, of course. She never used the truth spell for Bloodworth's identity, and something deep down told Felix not to share. Whether it was out of pity, hope, or a latent wish to make Calvin pay himself, he couldn't say.

A blue shimmer out of the corner of his eye caught his attention. The pendant his grandfather had given him, its blue crystal still cracked, hadn't been worn in months. Back at Dragora it remained buried in in the drawers of his bedside table, with Felix not even quickly checking whether it was still there. He didn't know why exactly. He'd merely… forgotten its existence.

"Felix?" Lydia walked in, phone in hand. "It's Rosie. She needs to talk to you."

Felix took the phone as Lydia left. He half-expected Rosie to start screaming at him the second he spoke. "Hey, sorry I haven't—"

"I need to talk to you. In person. Today."

"… O-Okay."

"Can you get to Harrison's in half an hour?" Rosie asked. "I'll pay for dinner."

"Sure. See you there." Felix hung up and threw himself onto his bed. Harrison's: their favorite diner, with ice cream so absurdly delicious it might as well have been a gift from the gods themselves (whoever the hell the gods were). But now, with Rosie's grave tone, it was impossible to know what to expect. What did Rosie need to talk about so badly it had to be done in person, especially after such a long period of silence?

"You want me to take you?" Lydia asked.

"Sure." Felix watched the ceiling fan spin, not even glancing at his mother.

Lydia sat beside him. "It'll be okay."

She held Felix's knee, but Felix kept his eyes on the gray afternoon sky just out his window. *Fitting.* They'd be leaving in twenty minutes. Lydia left, and Felix let out a beleaguered sigh. If he wasn't obligated to leave so soon, he could've easily fallen asleep, giving himself but a brief respite from his usual crazy making. The sleep served as the only remaining barrier between himself and his self-loathing.

"Felix?"

Tracey had never spoken Felix's name before. He'd have been excited, but her voice, normally joyful, now carried a twinge of sadness and worry. Felix didn't even sit up. That day he first came home, Tracey ran to hug him, but he was too numb from what he'd been through to even feign excitement. As for Aeris, they shared only a brief glare. Nothing more. Felix was anticipating her to bombard him with prayers and lectures about how this was a sign that he should give up magic and be "born again." But she didn't.

"Hey, Tracey," Felix forced himself to say. His tone was dry and lifeless.

A pause.

He groaned, closing his eyes, holding his forehead as his brain stung. "Look, Tracey, I'm not really in the mood right now. Just leave me alone."

His eyes shot open again when he realized what he'd just said. He sat up. "I-I didn't—"

Tracey's face was covered with tears. She sniffled, wiping snot on her pink sweater, running to her room, and slamming the door shut. Felix lay back down. *Good fucking going, Felix.* Eventually he hauled himself out of bed, stepped into his shoes, and threw on his jacket, not bothering to change his wrinkled T-shirt and sweatpants underneath, nor brush his unkempt hair. As his grandfather's necklace shimmered, though, he decided to take it with him. Maybe it'd turn out to be some kind of good luck charm. Lord knew he desperately needed one.

He headed downstairs, but stopped as Lydia and Ian's argument carried from the living room. "Are you sure he's okay?" Ian asked, his voice tense. "Lydia, what he must've seen—"

"I don't know," Lydia said. "I don't... I don't want to press the issue too much."

"I know some good therapists. There's no shame in seeing one."

Lydia paused. "What if he says no?"

"We'll make him go," Ian said. "He needs to confront this, not hide from it."

"Ian..."

"I'm sorry. I care about him too, like he's my own son. I just want him to be okay."

The idea didn't completely shock nor upset Felix. If anything, he agreed it would do him some good. After composing himself, he walked down, reaching the bottom of the staircase. For the first time since he'd come home, he projected his voice.

"Ready."

Ian drank his coffee, looking away while Lydia and Felix headed out. They'd talk about this again later, Felix assured himself. Raindrops fell on the car windshield as they headed down the road. Felix pressed his head against the pane, taking refuge in the soothing sound of the drizzle, as he always did whenever he felt upset or lost. But the distant thunder quickly disturbed that peace.

"She told you not to grab the ring." Kagami's voice resounded in his mind.

The thunder grew louder.

"You broke your promise."

The sky flashed. For a moment, Kagami's image appeared in the window, superimposed over Felix's reflection. He nearly jumped, but he forced himself to remain still, hoping his mother hadn't noticed. The last thing he wanted to do was worry her all over again.

"You know you can talk to me if you need to," Lydia said.

Felix listened as the whirring of the tires slowed his pulse. "I know."

"Would you... want to go to therapy?"

"... Sure." *God knows I need it. Really, everyone does. The strong ones just admit it.*

"Okay," Lydia said. "Ian and I can set up a session for you."

Felix twiddled his thumbs. "You can just call him 'Dad.'"

"Oh believe me, I do."

He cringed, nearly gagging. "Oh God, gross! Mami, that's nasty!" After a moment, Felix laughed, and Lydia laughed along with him.

"La sonrisa de mi angelito ha vuelto."

The sky was still gray. Felix longed for even a single ray of sunshine to break through the clouds. *I could use my guardian angel right about now.*

The car parked along the shopping center's curb. All the way at the other end was the Sandwich Shack, providing Felix with even more awful repressed memories. "Call me when you need a pickup," Lydia said.

"Right." Felix stepped out.

"Te quiero."

Felix shut the door and waved, and Lydia's car drove away. The center was completely dead. He reached for the door to Harrison's, stopping to imagine the worst-case scenario of what Rosie could've said. That she couldn't forgive him for all he'd done. That she no longer wanted to hear from him. With a heavy sigh, he opened the door and headed to the table over in the back corner, where Rosie awaited. A dark-gray hoodie betrayed her usual cheery attitude and bright fashion choices, though Felix assumed it was meant to cover the bandages for her wound.

She smiled. "Hey. Glad you came. Wow, uh... looks like we're matching."

"Yeah, well..." Felix sat down. *What do I even say? "Hey, sorry I nearly got you killed after lying to you for months. Pass the salt, please!"*

"How're you feeling?"

"… Fine, fine. What about you? You're the one who…" He stopped himself, tapping his fingers erratically. "Sorry. I didn't mean to…"

"No, no, it's fine. I don't blame you." Rosie looked down. "It was *my* choice to step in and try to protect you. And… I'm sure it was the same for—"

"Please don't bring her up." Felix cursed himself for cutting Rosie off, but he could already feel the sickness in his stomach rising, just as it had when she… *No, no. Don't think about that.* He coughed, clearing his throat. "S-Sorry. Just… I can't handle…"

Rosie paused. "My bad."

"May I take your orders?" A young woman in a black uniform and red apron stood before them, wearing a bright smile. "Or would you like more time while I get you some drinks?"

"I'll have a diet coke," Rosie said.

"Okay. And you, sir?"

"I-I'm fine…" Felix tilted his head down, clutching his arms.

"Then I'll have a regular soda with the diet," Rosie said. "No ice in the regular, please."

The waitress happily obliged and walked back into the kitchen. Only now did Felix realize that the entire restaurant was empty save for him, Rosie, and some of the employees chatting and laughing in the back. In a way, he found this company refreshing.

Slowly, Felix raised his head, finally mustering the strength to ask. "Why did you—"

"What?" Rosie asked. "You hate ice in your soda. It melts and makes it flat faster, right?"

He cracked a smile. "Thanks."

"No problem." Rosie's carefree demeanor faded. "There's… something I've been wanting to tell you." Immediately, Felix tensed up, waiting for the other shoe to drop. "I got accepted into Roseford University. I start next month."

Felix's jaw nearly broke through the table and hit the floor. "Roseford? *The* Roseford?!"

"Yep." Rosie crossed her arms and straightened her back. "All the way up in Maine, right on the Canadian border."

"Oh, so you can just hop on over in case Schmitt starts a draft."

Rosie chuckled. "To the land of poutine I go!"

"But how?" Felix asked. "It's already July."

"They were one of the schools I applied to before switching to Dragora last minute. After the… incident, they offered me a scholarship for my academics."

"That's… that's awesome!" Felix's joyful laughter took over, and he nearly jumped from his seat to hug Rosie. "Congratulations!"

Rosie wrung her hands. "You're not upset?"

"We talked about this, right?" Felix asked. "You do what's best for you."

"Even though I won't—"

"You realize I can't go back to Dragora, right? Even if the grants weren't axed…"

"R-Right." Rosie hunched over. "Sorry."

Felix shrugged. "Not like it's your fault."

"Yeah, but… I know how much it meant to you. It seemed like a second home for you."

"I suppose…" Felix stared at the napkin dispenser. "So… what're you getting? Food, I mean." For the first time in a long time, he finally felt okay with diffusing the tension with his usual brand of dumb humor. "We are eating, right?"

Rosie picked up the menu. "Honestly, I hadn't thought of that at all. Maybe skip right to dessert? Chocolate swirl sounds good."

"You remember that trick where you eat enough to freeze your tongue, then take a swig of soda and your taste buds go wild?"

"You're still amazed by that?" Rosie asked. "I'd get that from Tracey, but—"

"Hey, you're only as old as you feel. And right now, I feel like a hyperactive five-year-old without a care in the world." *I wish.*

"Sounds like you two are ready to order?" The waitress placed the drinks down. They nodded, and she dashed into the kitchen, returning not long after with the ice creams. Felix and Rosie immediately dug in. Rosie finished hers in just a couple gulps, letting out the belch of a giant.

Felix laughed. "Goddamn, girl!" He forgot how few fucks Rosie gave up how people viewed her. The first glimmer of light followed weeks of darkness.

Rosie stirred her soda, the ice dinging against the glass. "So… what're you gonna do?"

That question hit him like a truck. Felix had always kept his hopes high for Dragora, so when he finally got the chance to go, he felt totally secure. But now with that gone, and with even more pressing concerns weighing down on his mind, nothing else felt real. As though anything else he did would do nothing but further exhaust and distract him. Nothing could fill the emptiness inside. "I doubt I've got the grades to do what you did," Felix said.

"You never know," Rosie said. "I can help."

"It's fine. Besides, I think I need some time to decompress."

Rosie sat back. "Alright…"

"I'll be seeing a therapist," Felix said. "Maybe I can go to Suffolk in spring?"

"That's good. A lot of people start school in spring." Rosie stirred her drink faster. "Do you know what you'd be studying?"

No fucking clue! "Maybe…?" Felix shrugged. "Yeah, I got nothin'."

"Fashion?"

"I'd prefer to pick something I'd get a job in after graduation." Felix hadn't come up with even a sketch in so long, he wasn't sure he still had his sense of style, if he even had one to begin with. Even if he had picked a more "practical" major, there'd be no doubt that him being a magus would lead to not only more advertisements thrown in his face about joining the Magus Special Ops Unit after college, but it'd be his only real option. Who would ever hire someone—or, *something*—that the government considered a weapon of war, and what many people considered a monster, unworthy of human dignity?

"Just make sure you enjoy it," Rosie said.

"What're you majoring in?" Felix asked, hoping to shift the spotlight away from himself.

"Undeclared right now. But I'm thinking political science or law. You know, something that can help me fight for magus civil rights."

"Right, right…" Felix chastised himself for forgetting her mentioning of this just a few months ago. "God knows we'll be needing all the help we can get."

Rosie crumpled her straw. "Yeah…"

Only now did Felix realize that Rosie's eyes weren't their natural amethyst. Instead, they were disguised as brown by her colored contacts. He forced himself to smile. "But… that's great! At least some good came out of all this."

"… I suppose."

Disquiet fell over the restaurant. Carefully, Felix leaned in, held his straw, and blew. Bubbles rose to the soda's surface.

"Oh, gross!" Rosie's laughter broke through.

"Says the one who burps like a mountain troll?" Felix resumed eating his ice cream, then took a large sip of soda. The rush of sugar and caffeine was beyond satisfying. He burped, giving a devious grin.

Rosie facepalmed. "Unbelievable. Unbe-fucking-lievable."

"What? It's only acceptable when you let out an ungodly belch?"

"It is when you're an amateur."

Felix was enjoying the dinner far more than he'd expected to. But as he glanced to his left, he kept imagining how much more fun this would've been if Argent was here. Without him, everything felt incomplete. "Hey, uh… have you heard anything from Argent?"

"Nope." Rosie raised her hand and glanced away. "Though to be honest, he'd probably drive me up the wall even more than you."

"… Fair." Felix stirred his drink for what felt like the thousandth time. Not a single "Are you okay?" or even a "Hey" from Argent. Maybe he'd been injured and was taking a while to fully recover? Or maybe his mother was the overprotective type? Any excuse was better than the fear festering at the back of Felix's mind. What was Felix worth to Argent? Had Felix been fooled? All along, Argent's playfulness, his stride to do better, his love… were they all nothing more than a charade?

"I wouldn't get too worked up." Rosie sipped her drink. "He was kind of a piece of shit."

"Y-Yeah…" Rosie's comment shocked him. The whole time, Felix was under the impression that Rosie had grown fond of Argent and had forgiven him. But now? Unable to fully process what she said, Felix tried to play it off. "I-I've got terrible taste." It killed him to say that, and even more to force a hesitant laugh. "Don't I?"

"No," Rosie said. "It's not… okay, yeah. A little."

He hung his head, his pride stung.

"Turn it up!"

Their attention was redirected to the staff huddled around the TV by the front counter. They were playing CUSN, and the headline read: "Truthseer Protest Turns Violent!"

"I'm Jane Whyte here with breaking news. A Truthseer protest in Queens regarding wages and working conditions for maintenance workers on the coastal barrier systems has exploded into a violent riot. So far there have been two deaths and nine casualties. Residents are urged to take immediate shelter as police forces quell the outbreak."

"Thank you for that, Janet," the other anchor said.

"Jane—"

"And now we go to Raymond with the traffic!"

The staff lowered the volume, muttering to themselves. One paced about, while another jumped onto the counter, kicking their feet. "Unbelievable," one said.

"Do you think a dragon will break through the barrier?" The woman who'd served Felix and Rosie so kindly now looked utterly terrified, shaken to the bone.

"No idea," another girl said. "But it wouldn't surprise me." She shook her head. "They want us humans gone. Wiped off the face of the earth."

Felix wasn't sure how to react. He returned to his drink, which had now gone flat. He glanced up, and was startled to find Rosie angrily staring past him at the TV, her hands balled into fists. "I can't stand them," she said. "They're why so many people are terrified of u—" she paused. "Of magi. All they know how to do is threaten and burn."

"… What makes you say that?" Felix asked.

Rosie raised an eyebrow. "What?"

"We both know most magi don't work on those barriers because it's their passion. It's all they're allowed to do. Either that or join the Ops Unit and become killing machines. What makes you so sure they weren't having a peaceful strike that the police turned violent?"

Rosie frowned. "You're seriously defending this?"

Felix was taken aback. "You wouldn't? Didn't you just say you wanted progress and change for magus rights?"

"Yes," Rosie said. "Peacefully, from within. You can't force people into tolerance by attacking them and destroying their property."

"So we just sit back and let the humans attack us?"

Rosie grimaced. "That's not what I said and you know it."

"I don't know. What *did* you mean?" Felix held his glass tight. He knew what the logical thing to say was. That no real change was made just by sitting around, waiting for your oppressors to hand equality to you on a silver platter. But in that moment, his anger convinced him to go for the quickest way to get under Rosie's skin. "You said it yourself: you've never cared about magic. What's stopping you from just masquerading as a human the rest of your life? You'd never have to deal with any of this."

"... You cannot be fucking serious. You've got a lot of nerve talking like that."

"Do I? You remember what happened to the Rosie who didn't take shit from Carson and his lackeys back that day we met? Cuz I don't."

Rosie facepalmed. "Do you know how dangerous it is for me, a black girl, to even so much as raise her voice to a white boy whose dad is the goddamn sheriff? Marcus told me flat out I was lucky he seemed to forget about that, cuz if Carson wanted..." She held her arm.

Felix paused. "I... I'm sorry. I shouldn't have—"

"Damn right you shouldn't have." Rosie closed her eyes. "Bennie and David..." She stopped herself. "My dads... they love me and Marcus like we were their own. But they don't know what it's like for us... in more ways than one. Sometimes I just feel so lost. Like I don't know where I belong."

He didn't know how to respond. He'd never realized just how much Rosie had on her own plate; she just managed to make it look effortless, all while giving even more of her energy to keeping Felix alive. "Why... why don't you ever talk about this stuff?"

"Because it's uncomfortable," Rosie said. "Because life's hard enough as it is."

That seemed to be the trend. Felix knew he ought to respect that boundary, but in the heat of the moment, he couldn't help but want to lash out to let off some steam, and remembered how Argent liked to dig under people's skin to get the truth out of them. "I mean, ignoring things seems to be what you're best at." Felix's voice grew sterner.

"And what's that supposed to mean?" Rosie asked.

"Oh, you know. When I got hurt back at the start of the year, you couldn't be bothered to tell me how you felt about what I did, so you just shut me out. Oh, or that time when you found out about my deal with Vagus, and instead of asking why, you just shut me out."

Rosie scowled. "I told you why—"

"Yeah," Felix said. "I guess you did. But only after you *slapped* me. And when else did you do that? Oh yeah, after you thought I'd nearly died!"

She sighed. "Look, I'm sorry. That wasn't right. But what you did…" She rubbed her temples. "This is why I didn't tell you—" She covered her mouth immediately.

Felix raised an eyebrow. "Tell me what?"

"N-Nothing."

"Bullshit. What is it? Something about Argent? The ring?" If his gaze could burn, Felix was sure the entire restaurant would've been up in flames right now.

Rosie hesitated before answering. "During the attack in the coliseum, Argent and I… ran into a pair of Bloodworth's soldiers. And… they wound up being…" She trailed off.

"Being…? For fuck's sake, just—"

"Billy and Buck."

Felix paused. "Wait. Billy Brown and Buck Briggs? As in… the Camo Crew?"

Rosie slouched. "… Yes."

For a moment, Felix was in disbelief. There was no way some bigoted lowlives like those two could've wound up part of such a huge operation. But the more he thought about it, the more things started to click into place. If the Enlightened had eyes and ears everywhere, and they'd been keeping tabs on Felix for his entire life, then why wouldn't they have a few people from his younger years keeping him in their sights? And if those two were involved, then no doubt Carson, and maybe even his father, were as well. "Why didn't you tell me?" Felix asked.

"Because I knew how you'd react," Rosie said. "Look, I… I'm tired. I'm gonna go to the bathroom, then pay. Okay?"

Regrudgingly, Felix huffed. "Okay."

Some staff members were now glancing his way. The girl who'd said magi wanted to destroy humanity gave him a cold glare, while the waitress who'd served him merely kept her head down. Felix finished his soda, then dug into his ice cream. He devoured the rest of the platter, but couldn't savor the taste, nor satisfy his hunger. Instead, he clanged the spoon against the metal cup. *Why me? Of all the people to involve in this... why me?*

The downpour outside turned into pellets of hail falling from the sky. Lightning illuminated the restaurant. As Felix looked up, he dropped his spoon with a shrill ring. Outside the window, staring in at him, was a cloaked Ornella. It had to be. It was the same figure he'd seen that night in the Dragora infirmary. She turned and entered the storm. Felix raced outside after her, not even throwing up his hood and ignoring the staff's cries. He ran through the parking lot. Cold wind and ice lashed against his face, and the mist blinded him, but he kept running. He caught up to the figure and forcibly turned her around. The cloak fell, revealing no one inside.

A screech gripped him. Bolts surged through the coal-black clouds, and in a flash of fiery light, another roar shook the earth. Not thunder, but some kind of creature. A silhouette appeared in the sky—Cinder. Her orange fire lit the sky, and in the next moment, she flew out of sight as the tempest resumed.

"Find the talismans. I'm counting on you."

"What the fuck are you talking about?!" The storm drowned out Felix's shouts. He fell, both rain and tears streaming down his cheeks. He slammed the ground over and over. Still without any answers, and still a shadowy threat looming over him. He couldn't go back to Dragora. He couldn't be the sorcerer he'd always dreamt of being. The power he longed for was in the Ring of Nergal, and that was long gone now. Anything else he'd cared for or loved had been ripped away from him.

Nothing else mattered. Nothing mattered. Nothing.

Rosie held him tight, holding her jacket over them both. "It's okay," she said. "I'm here."

But it wasn't okay. Things had never been okay. Now, they were simply being brought into the light, kicking and screaming. Once you glimpse the truth, you can never escape it. It eats at you, day after day, driving you closer and closer to the brink of despair. Perhaps even insanity. Though I? I consider myself remarkably sane. At least, more so than Felix when all was said and done.

The Wanderer and The Oblation

V AGUS had forbidden Ornella from leaving the Isle of Ashes. So she could only imagine his reaction to her traveling all the way to the States to give Felix a cryptic message. She wished she could've said more, but even then, she cursed herself for trying to drag him back into this madness. Her entire life, she'd wanted nothing more than to escape from it all.

But that was never an option for her.

As she made her way into the decrepit manor, her stomach twisted itself, tying into knots within knots. Nothing anywhere near as stressful as finding the courage to deal with her mother, but still far from pleasant. Cinder cooed as she nuzzled up to Ornella's cheek. At the very least, Ornella found a bit of comfort in Cinder's sweetness, which likely was due to Ornella creating a splint for Cinder's wounded leg.

She found Vagus in his study: the remains of a massive library, albeit with most of the books not having been opened in over a decade and a half, all filled with dust and ready to fall apart the moment they were opened. He sat at his table, closely observing that same blue mythril crystal tightly secured in what looked like a cheap glass jar.

"Vagus?"

He stood, giving an incredibly beleaguered sigh. Surprisingly, he didn't say a word. No lectures on leaving for a few days. Nothing. Instead, Ornella simply followed Vagus through the manor, down the corridor. The faint crackling of the red mythril crystals and the clicking of their shoes against the ice-cold tiles were the only sounds echoing through the hall.

"Was this all necessary?" Ornella asked. "All the sudden appearances, attacks, and dream invasions? We don't need to traumatize Felix any further, like you did with Lucas."

"You'd be surprised with how strong a motivator fear can be," Vagus said. "I commend your effort to shield him with those protective dream catchers, though it would seem Felix's little amethyst friend understands the thorns growing in the darker parts of his mind. Much more of a nuisance to break through that charm."

"But what makes you so sure he'll follow through?" Ornella asked. "He could easily go about his own life."

"He won't. It's in his blood. Stupidity is inherited, after all. I know that well." Vagus always had a knack for shaking people's nerves without even trying. "But it's best to let the child rest for now, especially with the Enlightened watching him. Thankfully Vivien is under control, but we'll need to be careful with her nucleus. Keep that crystal away from water at all costs, and that includes the moisture in the air. You can never trust how an undine will behave."

"Speaking of which," Ornella said. "How is it that Lucas got a hold of my pendant?"

Vagus chuckled. "You weren't putting it to good use. And he needed the training. Or, that's what I thought he'd use it for instead of tossing it."

Ornella clutched the pendant, now back around her neck where she could keep it safe. She could've chewed Vagus out, but it wouldn't get them anywhere, as Vagus always did whatever he pleased. She was just thankful her sister's crystal was still intact. "On another note," she said. "Why keep me in hiding?"

No response.

She stopped. "I'm not going anywhere until I get an answer!"

Vagus sighed. "It's too dangerous to have you out in the field right now. Thankfully, I have another ally who's been itching to cut her teeth. Ideally by biting off Rhosyn's arm. That ought to teach him a lesson. Besides, you need to be properly tethered to your talisman."

"W-What...?"

"Your talisman." He turned. "You were kept as Seraphina's calathus, correct? Even though they could never find the talisman you were supposed to be tethered to? Well, I happen to know where it is. Have for a while actually. Come along. I'll show you."

He had to have been lying. Ornella's talisman had been missing since long before she was born, all of her predecessors living and dying without ever fulfilling the great destiny the Enlightened had carved out for them. Yet as Vagus opened the doors to the grand hall, her temptation to run died— there'd be no point. Sitting there at the very end of the hall was a large black organ with golden pipes: the Organ of Judgment.

Ornella wept. There was no escape. Her fate was sealed.

AFTERWORD

Here we are. At long last, after starting this book all the way back in 2016, we're here. *De Cineribus* is published, and I'm an author.

I actually wrote up an afterword a long while back, but wound up losing it when I got my new laptop. Even so, I doubt it needs saying that I'm immensely proud of what I've created, and I hope you've enjoyed my very first novel. If not, then I hope to craft stronger stories as I hone my writing abilities in future projects.

To the people who've helped me get to this point, thank you. Everything I've experienced, and every person I've met, has shaped who I've become. I'm grateful to have such loving friends and family, and I hope I make you all proud going forward.

To the people who've supported me all these years, ever since I started my YouTube channel, thank you as well. Thank you Arnold for helping push me out the gate when I was just starting, and thank you to all my subscribers, viewers, and Patrons who've kept me afloat. I wouldn't be here now had it not been for any of you. Here's to many more creative endeavors that I hope you'll enjoy.

And to any aspiring creators, not just writers, I give you this advice: never give up. Never create solely for the promise of commercial success or material reward. Create because of the story you want to share, and always accept critique so you can hone your craft and enrich those stories. Enjoy life and show gratitude for what you have, and tell the people you love how much they mean to you. Because if you create in the hopes of affecting people, if you're making your art to put a part of your experience out into the world so people feel a little bit less alone, and if you're always true to yourself and your experiences, it will resonate.

I'll cut myself off now before I make this rant any longer, but suffice to say I'm beyond excited to see what life has to offer next.

ABOUT THE AUTHOR

Thomas Vaccaro is an author, content creator, and all-around geek.

His novel writing escapades began towards the end of his senior year of high school. Rather than going to college without a clear goal in mind, he kept his focus specifically on finishing said book and learning as much as he could about how to publish it. All because college is expensive, man.

He is now a YouTuber (Unicorn of War) and has created a loving, supportive community of fellow geeks known across the interwebz as the Asshole Parade (Asshole Brigade in some territories). Even so, writing is his passion, and he couldn't imagine doing anything else… namely because he lacks any other practical skills, but work with the cards you're dealt, kiddos.

His interests include—but are not limited to—writing, profuse swearing, complaining (a.k.a. reviewing), belting Taylor Swift songs, and crying over the deaths of fictional people. Also his favorite food is pizza, so if you ever meet him, be sure to bring a LOT of pizza (Preferably with extra cheese and/or pepperoni–NEVER with pineapple).

For more information, be sure to check out Thomas' YouTube channel. To further support him and his creative endeavors, please consider supporting him on Patreon for extra rewards, including deleted chapters & scenes, writing critiques, early glimpses at future novels, and access to the private Union of War Discord server (It's a real blast).

Please also consider leaving an honest review of this book on the Goodreads page, as well as wherever it's available (Amazon, Apple Books, Kobo, Barnes & Noble, and Google Play). If you enjoyed the ebook version, please consider picking up a physical edition, be it paperback or hardback (complete with fancy dust jacket), to 1. Further support Thomas, and 2. Keep on your shelf for bragging rights.